T0369281

THE GUARDIAN CORPS

Book One—The Argent

Daryl Edwards

Order this book online at www.trafford.com
or email orders@trafford.com

Most Trafford titles are also available at major online book retailers.

Printed in the United States of America.

ISBN: 978-1-4269-4491-8 (sc)

Trafford rev. 11/06/2010

 www.trafford.com

North America & international
toll-free: 1 888 232 4444 (USA & Canada)
phone: 250 383 6864 ♦ fax: 812 355 4082

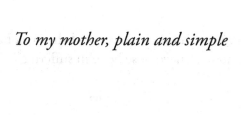

To my mother, plain and simple

"They are daring beyond their power, and they risk beyond reason, and they never lose hope in suffering" –

Thucydides

Twenty-five hundred years ago, the Guardian Corps was founded to rescue the people of Kerguelen from planetary tyranny. Their weapons were the lance, sword and a coat of mail and each Guardian maintained a team of three horses and was assisted by three attendants who saw to their personal needs and aided the Guardians during battle. Each Guardian unit had its own banner that was attached to the lance of the unit commander so all would know which Guardians were in battle.

Today, Guardians no longer travel by horse and their weapons have evolved. The lance and sword have been replaced by kinetic and plasma energy weapons, the coat of mail exchanged for advanced composite body armor and they ride into the fray in high-tech air vehicles. Though the weapons and mode of transportation has changed, their core values have not. A Guardian will protect the rights of the people and the sanctity of just government and law at all costs, even if it means their own life.

Since the unification of Kerguelen, war and conflict between the diverse races and ideologies of the twenty-five provinces is a thing of the past, but the Guardian's role remains the same, for in all cultures, there are those who endeavor to upset the balance with aspirations of their own. In the face of these new threats, the Guardian Corps, now one thousand strong, combat these adversaries based on the Four Rules of Battle:

1. As long as the battle banner flies, Guardians fight;
2. Guardians do not retreat unless the odds are 5:1 or greater;
3. No ransom is paid or deal brokered for the release of a Guardian if captured;
4. Guardians fight to the death.

PROLOGUE

Midnight, Hanover Bay, Southwestern Province, Planet Kerguelen

Commander Jordan panted heavily in the sweltering heat and oppressive humidity of the equatorial region. She wiped away the blood and perspiration that had built up on her face and snorted loudly. As she cleared the mixture of droplets trickling from cuts and scrapes on her cheeks, nostrils and corners of her mouth, she thought of how she had been bested in one-on-one combat. Jordan had never lost such a contest before and had never even contemplated losing one, and even if it did happen, she would not have believed that she would have been so thoroughly devastated.

She had been seriously injured and outnumbered before in battle but had managed to overcome her adversaries and treacherous situations in stellar fashion. Her abilities and exploits were legendary in the Guardian Corps and well chronicled in the news media of every province on the planet of Kerguelen. Her adventures made Jordan a celebrity amongst the citizens and reporters and journalists had dubbed her 'The Invincible Commander Jordan', adding that with her prowess and skill she was without a doubt the greatest warrior of the past hundred years.

Her successes as a Guardian officer made Jordan a mainstay in popular culture and her every move was followed by the paparazzi. The clothes she wore and the men she dated were the most important and vital entertainment news. Women of all ages from every province wanted to be like her. The cult-like phenomena stemmed from her flawless complexion, classic features and flowing golden hair. Young women and teens used the same makeup she did and copied her hairstyling. Called the 'CJ', it was the most requested makeover asked for at beauty salons around the planet.

Whether her opponent was lucky or she had begun to believe her own press or he was just better than she was, the result was the same: The ambush he set for her had worked. She had fought valiantly but was quickly beaten into submission. Her opponent's strength and speed was tremendous and none of the combat skills Jordan had developed and honed to a fine edge over the past eighteen years did anything to stem the tide of his murderous assault. She was now on her hands and knees facing the dark behemoth before her. Her limbs quivered as they struggled to keep her off of the soft ground beneath her. Unarmed, battered and defenseless she waited for the giant to apply the coup-de-grace.

'Stupid, stupid, stupid,' Jordan thought to herself. '*How could I have fallen for such an obvious trap?*'

She raised her head and painfully looked at the giant that loomed menacingly over her through tearing eyes. "I don't know what you're up to or what your plans are, but you won't get away with it. I am one of many," Jordan hissed through swollen lips. She spat a small bit of blood in front of her and smiled at the sight of it as she continued. "Killing a Guardian is not taken lightly. The Corps will avenge my death and when they catch up with you, there won't be a hole deep enough for you to hide in."

"Your faith in your comrades is noble, but unfounded," the giant said in a deep bestial baritone. His voice seemed to reverberate through her. "And I welcome them to try and defeat me. The opportunity to kill more of them will be a pleasure. If *you* could be taken so easily by such a simple ruse, the rest of your Guardians will fall like a house of cards."

"Don't be so sure. We've faced greater odds and more powerful foes and were still victorious. This will be no different," Jordan replied defiantly as she strained her exhausted muscles to their limit and struggled to her feet. She gently brushed sweat and blood soaked locks away from her face adding, "We've done so for two and a half millennia. This is far from over."

"All things end, woman," the giant said condescendingly and shook his head as he stepped towards her. "Your run is over. With their so-called greatest warrior defeated, the spirit of the Guardians will be broken."

He reached out with one of his powerful arms and grabbed Jordan by the throat, jerking her into the air. Her feet dangled above the ground and she kicked in futility as the sound of her windpipe being crushed filled the eerie silence of the night. The giant felt a rush of warmth flow over him as a flock of night birds flew skyward sensing death and the evil presence near them. The huge man continued to hold Jordan aloft after she stopped kicking and examined her closely for the first time. He brought her lifeless form up to his face and inhaled her scent. He let out a dissatisfied grunt and frowned.

"You may be right, woman. This is not over. This will take longer than I expected," he said aloud. "You are not the one I search for. You are but the first of many who will fall."

He effortlessly tossed her body aside as a child would discard a broken toy and stomped off into the darkness. By the time Jordan's body had stopped rolling over the soft earth, the giant was gone.

PART ONE

THREE MONTHS AGO

1

Interstellar space, deep within the Orion's Arm Spur sector of the Milky Way galaxy

Personal In-Flight diary of Omega, commander of Kerguelen Deep Space Survey Ship *San Mariner*:

> *"We have reached our destination and have penetrated the Bow Shock boundary at the southern hemisphere of the uncharted star system before us. Since entering the system we have yet to reacquire the radio signals that led us to this region of the galaxy. If our search fails to bear fruit I am afraid I will never again have the opportunity to venture into this abyss to search for what has been called 'The Unholy Grail'... nor would I want to try. My entire career as a star sailor has been centered on finding proof that life exists on other worlds and if unsuccessful, I don't think I could face the scrutiny of my peers or superiors again. Perhaps this system is the one that I have been looking for."*

Omega closed out his in-flight diary file on his computer and stood up. As he stretched he knew it was time he returned to the flight deck. Tapping out the brief entry in his personal journal had taken longer than he wanted. He could have used the voice recorder system as he did with the ship's official log, but his personal log was private and confidential and it wouldn't do for an eavesdropper to overhear his personal thoughts or ideas... or deepest fears. But a nosey crewmember was the least of his concerns at the moment. The system they had just entered was foremost in his mind. His crew would be busy conning the ship and trying to track down the elusive radio signals that brought *San Mariner* to this faraway star system on the edge of the Milky Way, a system that could possess life... sentient life.

If it weren't for the radio signals, Omega doubted that they would have come to this system to survey it for some time. Though it had similarities to their own system, there was nothing out of the ordinary or special about it. It did possess a large number of celestial bodies, more than Omega had encountered before. Not even their own system had so many components to it, and that alone made this run-of-the-mill system a curiosity. But space was full of mysteries and this system was just another piece of the galactic puzzle. However, the system had the potential to change the course of their history, for Omega came here to search for signs of intelligent life.

Outwardly, to his crew, he was brimming with confidence, positive that this time, they would find proof that life existed beyond the confines of their home world of Kerguelen. On the inside, however, Omega was full of doubt and not an hour passed in which he wished he had never pursued such a foolish endeavor.

As a child growing up in the Northeastern Province, Omega would gaze into the clear night sky and pretend that he was the first to greet visitors from another world. At a time when his friends were fantasizing about becoming Guardians and saving the planet, Omega's eyes were firmly fixed to the stars and dreamt of what lay beyond. Though he too would become a Guardian, Omega wanted nothing more than to become a star sailor and explore space. His studies were concentrated in the sciences and mathematics; disciplines that he hoped would lead to his entrance into the Kerguelen Space Command. He succeeded, but his lifelong pursuit had cost him dearly, both professionally and personally.

Through the years, he had theorized and published papers that life did exist on other worlds. And though many of his peers and revered scientists agreed that there was some validity to his theories, his inflexibility and inability to get in step with popular opinion had forced the Congress of Cardinals to excommunicate him from the Federal Church of Kerguelen. That ruling in turn denied him the right to vote; forced him to forfeit his personal property; and required him to resign his commission as an officer in the Guardian Corps. Only the intervention of the Technology Council and the Planetary Legislature had kept him out of prison and permitted him to retain his flight status as a star sailor.

Despite their severity, the latter edicts were trivial and insignificant to Omega compared with the most devastating blow he received. By Papal decree, his excommunication prevented him from bonding with the woman he loved, for she, like everyone else on Kerguelen, was a member of the Federal Church. And that loss had been almost unbearable. If he could just succeed in this mission, perhaps the Cardinals would rescind their decree and he could be reunited with his love again. But the ship only had the resources for another week before he would be forced to return home. One week would decide his future fate... one week.

His thoughts returned to the present when the call button to his quarters beeped. It would be his second-in-command, Flight Officer Camden. Though not very imaginative or dynamic, he was a proficient command officer and excellent pilot. And though he had once been described by a former superior as having the personality and charisma of a pile of bricks, Camden showed great promise and due to a glowing endorsement from Omega, he would soon command a ship of his own. It was rumored that he was slotted for a captaincy of one of the newest class of deep space survey ships.

It would be a recruiting bonanza for Space Command. Camden was part of the new breed of Guardian officer. He stood over six foot with dark, short-cropped hair and possessed incredible good looks and Space Command was elated to have the Guardian as their new poster-child. What he could do for public relations was incalculable.

But for now, he was flight officer and second-in-command of *San Mariner*, filled with duty and purpose. It was duty, no doubt, that brought him to Omega's quarters. As Omega looked around the cabin he chuckled softly. The disarray and clutter would make Camden cringe. He was so wrapped up in appearances, Omega was surprised he was as proficient as he was. Omega pushed aside a pile of electronic data tablets overtaking his desktop's surface and depressed a button opening the door to his quarters.

As the door slid open, Camden stooped down and entered the small living and office space. He nodded once to Omega, looked around the room and shook his head in disbelief. He frequently wondered how someone could be such a proficient commander of spacecraft but live and work in such a mess. It was amazing to him how much clutter could be had in such a tiny and confined space. Camden had kept his thoughts about his commander's untidiness and slovenly habits to himself, but he felt that Omega knew how revolted he was every time he entered the cabin and took efforts to make it as disarranged as possible. If it had not been for duty, he would never enter the interstellar rubbish can.

Camden quickly recovered and looked at his commander and shot him a quick smile. Omega motioned to the chair in front of the desk and Camden removed a pile of previously worn flight suits occupying the chair to a place of honor on the floor and sat down placing a data stick on the desk as he did. He looked at the three or four days of stubble on Omega's face and the rumpled flight suit haphazardly thrown on and chuckled softly.

"Commander, you look like hell… if you don't mind me saying so," Camden laughed as he shook his head.

"No, I don't mind," said Omega sitting down and flipping the data stick in his palm. He inserted it into a port in his computer and turned to Camden as it downloaded. "Is that your scientific analysis or just a stab in the dark?"

"Just an observation, Commander," Camden replied as his smile faded. "You're over the edge on this mission. Look at yourself. Look at this cabin. Coming in here is like maneuvering through a minefield."

"Does wading through the detritus in this cabin bother you, Camden?" Omega joked. "Maybe we should take a moment and pray about it?"

"I'm serious, Commander," Camden said without smiling back. "We've finished the primary goals of the mission. Let's call it a day and go home. What are the chances that the phantom radio signals are emanating from this system anyway?"

"They are not *phantom* signals, Camden, you know that. And it has to be this system. The signals were strongest in this area. The next closest system is four point two light-years away, where we just came from. Additionally, we've only completed two out of three objectives. And I always complete every one of my mission goals," Omega said wrinkling his brow as he scanned the information on the screen in front of him. He leaned back in his chair and looked at Camden thoughtfully.

The mission of *San Mariner* was divided into three parts. First, they were to deploy a series of space buoys in this area of the Orion's Arm Spur. The buoys would allow future long-range ships venturing into the region the ability to maintain real-time communications with Kerguelen and aid in navigation. Second, they were to find out what happened to a sister vessel, *Seventh Sojourn*. The ship had left on a survey mission similar to *San Mariner's* a year earlier, but had disappeared while investigating a planet of a binary star system in the Libra constellation. *San Mariner* discovered the remains of *Seventh Sojourn* in the system and determined by what was left of the debris pattern, the ship had been a victim of a collision with a meteor or rogue comet. The last phase of the mission was to investigate a series of radio signals emanating from a star system forty light-years from Kerguelen. Space Command, as well as the Congress of Cardinals, believed the signals were nothing more than pulses from stars in the region, but nothing was an absolute in space. The weak signals could be another race's attempt to contact or communicate with others. *San Mariner's* job was to verify what the signals were. And Omega had a few days left to complete the task, and one way or another he would.

"Besides, what do we have to lose?" Omega asked.

"We could lose our reputations for one thing and our minds for another," Camden offered. "Okay, we know the signals are from this system. Great! We go back and tell Space Command and they send another ship out here to verify our findings and…"

"… And someone else gets credit for the find. No, I've been combing space for almost fifteen years and if there's anything to be found out here, I'm going to find it. Even if I have to die to find out the truth," Omega said cryptically.

"And what if the signals are just emissions from a star? Why is it so important? Besides the obvious reasons, why does it have to be *you* that discovers what they are, Commander? You're the reason the Deep Space Program is what it is. It's all because of you, despite the Papal decree. What more of a legacy could you want?" Camden asked trying to convince his commander that he might be just chasing smoke.

"This is not about my ego. I don't want a legacy… not in those terms. You know why I want this," Omega said turning a hard gaze towards Camden.

Camden paused for a second and quickly thought about his next remark. He didn't want to incur the wrath of his commander but he knew he had to say what was on his mind.

"Why does everything you do come back to her? I don't know the whole story, but I do know this: It's over between you and her, Commander. They won't let you bond with her," Camden said firmly. Though he didn't know first hand, he had heard the many stories surrounding Omega and his lost love and Camden didn't want to get caught up in a vainglorious fool's errand. And if he did, his objections would be voiced, regardless of Omega's feelings on the subject. "Give it up. You're what you are and she's what she is. If you think making a scientific discovery will change that, you're gravely mistaken. Maybe it's true what the Clerics say: Too much time exposed to the dark matter of space drives you insane."

Omega sighed. "Maybe I have lost my mind as you say and I may never be with her again, but that doesn't change the fact that the signals *are* here. We can't ignore them and I need you to accept that because we are going in search of them as long as our resources permit," Omega said looking directly into Camden's eyes.

Camden stood and touched his right fist to his left shoulder. It was the Guardian salute. Though Omega was no longer a senior Guardian officer, Camden acknowledged his authority as leader of the expedition. The symbolic gesture also meant that Camden respected him on a personal level. Camden didn't know if he would have had the resolve to give up everything for an unproven belief. It was a strength few in the history of Kerguelen could claim.

"Where you go, I go, Commander," he said.

"I'm grateful for your loyalty, but be careful what you pledge," Omega warned. "Everything could fall apart around us if things go south. It could be too much for you. Unlike me, you have quite a bit to lose."

"The Almighty only burdens us with that which we can handle," Camden responded.

"A Guardian to the end," Omega said with a chuckle.

"Yes, a Guardian to the end," Camden said with a sigh. "How cynical you've become. You were known to be devout beyond that of the Clerics. I was told you were called 'Pious Pete' in the ranks."

"Among other things I'm sure," Omega replied with a smile.

"What happened? Did you lose your faith?" Camden asked.

"Excommunication has a way of doing that to you. When your name is removed from every historical record, when statues that bore your likeness are pulled down and pulverized into dust and when you are prevented from bonding with the only creature in the universe that means anything to you, it tends to shatter your belief system," Omega said sarcastically.

"That was all years ago. You should move on… I'm sure she has," Camden said.

"Does that matter?" Omega said.

Camden turned his gaze to the cluttered deck and considered Omega's words, and then he lifted his head and responded.

"They still allow you to serve in Space Command. There's something in that. You have a lot more to give to other star sailors. Don't let pride blind you to the big picture," Camden said optimistically. "I hate to be one of those 'touchy-feely'-type guys, but a philosopher once said, *'the most painful state of being is remembering the future. Particularly the one you can never have'.*"

"Camden, I want you to know this and believe in it as you believe in the omnipotence of the Almighty. If I fail in this quest, I will never come to deep space again and if I succeed, there are forces on Kerguelen that will kill me," Omega said.

"You came out here knowing this? Why?" Camden asked in disbelief.

"To not come out here when we are so close would have killed me anyway. The only thing I'm concerned about is if we have enough time to get the answers to our questions," Omega said.

"So when do we go back?" Camden queried.

"That depends on whether we find anything or not," Omega answered. Camden cocked his head to one side, causing Omega to sigh. "Okay, seven standard days. Whether we do or do not find anything, we leave in seven days. We do a direct abort, turn around and head for home at best speed."

Camden nodded and turned away but quickly spun around to face Omega. "You know, we may just find something out there," he said.

"Are you saying that you believe in the validity of the signals and my theories?" Omega asked.

"It's not a 50-50 chance, but this mission is worth the gamble we're taking," Camden said confidently. "As you said, what do we have to lose?"

"I'm glad you have such a positive attitude, but there is something that you haven't considered," Omega said.

"What is that?" Camden asked.

"What will happen to me... and all of you if we *do* find something?"

2

Kerguelen Deep Space Survey Ship *San Mariner*

Omega and Camden had joined the rest of the crew in the cramped flight deck compartment of *San Mariner* after a call from the navigator beckoned their presence. As Omega reclined in the commander's couch, he stared absently out of the small forward window into space. The stars of the Milky Way shone brightly and Omega daydreamed about his studies of space and astronomy. In his mind he saw the many different planets – from moons to gas giants – and comets and novae and galaxies and nebulae. How vast and mysterious and scary and wonderful it all was!

Some hours earlier as *San Mariner* approached the system, the crew began the search for the radio signals. Omega had ordered the ship to slow to a crawl as the science specialists aligned their recording and tracking instruments to collect as much data about the star system as possible and locate the signals. It had taken a long time to home in on the radio signals but they did find them again. Once they had contact, the crew notified Omega. When he and Camden arrived, the crew was busy preparing a report. As they worked, Omega considered his crew.

To his left, Camden sat in the pilot's couch, gently touching the attitude controls. On Omega's right was Mission Specialist Delle, the ship's navigator. Delle was an experienced star sailor with two other deep space missions under his belt. He was very good at his job but had only joined Space Command for the tax-free money incentive. After this flight, he would have enough saved to retire quietly on a small tropical island somewhere. In the meantime, he was an indispensable crewmember and provided much needed comic relief during their journey. He and Camden had an ongoing feud spawned by Delle's pacifistic agenda and Camden's militaristic nature. Their heated debates kept everyone's mind off of the tedium and dull routine that permeated an extended deep space mission.

"We're right on course, Commander," Delle said without looking at Omega.

"Very good, steady as she goes," Omega said rubbing his chin. So far so good he thought. "Do we have a lock on the signals?"

"Affirmative," Delle replied. "I have the direction at my station."

"Good," Omega said. It was time to confirm the status of the ship with the crew and push on into the system. "Okay, give me a 'Go-No Go' verification. Pilot?"

"Go," Camden answered.

"Guidance and Navigation?" Omega asked.

"GNC is Go," said Delle.

"Propulsion and Engineering?" queried Omega.

"Go!" Lead Mission Specialist Dela said from the Flight Engineer's station, behind and to the right of Omega.

Dela was the crew's only female and a first-class engineer. She had kept *San Mariner* operating as best as could be done without the support of a space station. As lead mission specialist she made sure that all hands were focused on their tasks and in doing so, was the heart and soul of the crew and Omega's right hand. She was new to Space Command but had accrued extensive orbital and operational time in a short period. This was her first deep space mission.

"Auxiliary systems?" Omega asked Powell, the assistant engineer.

Powell was a field geologist by training and a star sailor out of necessity. With the advent of super-sophisticated artificial intelligence, automation and robotics, field geology was becoming a dead discipline on Kerguelen. Space Command was the only place where a trained field geologist could still practice his art and make a living.

"Auxiliaries are Go," Powell said from the Auxiliary Engineering station located beside Dela's.

"Network?" Omega asked.

"Computer network is Go," the junior science specialist named Jalen answered.

"Telemetry and Tracking Sensors?" Omega asked.

"TNT is Go," said Tallen, the senior science specialist.

Tallen and Jalen were positioned behind Omega to his left at side-by-side consoles. Both were astrophysicists and Delle waxed that everyone needs two geeks in their life to make it complete and if he had his choice in the matter, Tallen and Jalen would be his. He received no argument from the rest of the crew. Tallen was the best scientist in Space Command and self-proclaimed 'King of the Geeks'. And Jalen, under his tutelage, was fast becoming a rival to his throne.

"Right," Omega said. "Do we have any idea how big this system is?"

"About eighteen billion miles in diameter," Tallen offered. "It appears to be an average sized system with a medium sized yellow star producing a moderate cosmic radiation output. Scans imply that it is of normal age for stars in this part of the galaxy. It's remarkably similar to our own sun. It's slightly smaller, but appears to be the same age with nearly identical specs. They could be twins."

The slender scientist from the Southern Province was tapping away at the keypad on his console again before Omega could nod affirmatively to his report.

"The position of the inner planets and the star's make up suggests that if favorable conditions did exist, one or more of them could sustain some type of life," Jalen added with a small tinge of excitement in his voice.

"I concur," said Tallen soberly and nodding his head.

"We've heard that before," Camden interjected. "And all we found was barren planets made of rock and iron."

"True, but all those worlds needed was a chance to form a gravity field and an atmosphere before the creation elements were lost in space," Delle said. "If these planets were lucky in their formation, who knows what we'll find."

"If," Camden scoffed. "If a frog had wings it wouldn't bump its butt every time it hopped."

Though no one argued with Camden or uttered a word, Omega could tell that they were hopeful about the prospects of finding something in the system.

"What's our position relative to the system?" Omega asked.

Tallen tapped on his keypad and a display came to life on a small screen attached to the commander's couch. An animated 3-D model of the solar system appeared and Omega rubbed his chin as he scanned it. The computer model was only a rough outline without exact distances or details, but it gave a color animation depicting *San Mariner's* flight path through the system as it traveled toward the center of the planetary disk.

"As you can see, Commander," Tallen narrated. "We are headed for the heart of the system. We have determined the signals are emanating from either the third or fourth planet. Once we're closer, we can positively confirm which one it is. Once we've verified which one; we'll maneuver towards the planet using as little maneuvering fuel as possible."

"Why don't we use a slingshot maneuver utilizing the fifth planet?" Camden asked. "It's big enough to give us a lot of speed."

"It's the largest planet in the system and its location is ideal for that kind of maneuver," Delle replied, "but Tallen discovered that the planet has a tremendous EM field that is extremely harmful to us. Dela doubts that our shielding would adequately protect us. It extends out a good distance so we should steer clear of it."

"I concur," Omega said. "What else do we know about the planets?"

"The four inner planets are standard iron-ore and rock; the next two are huge gas giants and the two after that are gas giants worlds as well… but not as large as the first two. The seventh planet has a unique characteristic. It appears to be tipped over on its side and rolls around the star like a barrel, whereas other planets spin upright like tops. It was probably knocked off balance when it was hit by something billions of years ago," Tallen said. "The outer planets are interesting, but they don't really concern us. All of our locator sensors are leading us to the third and fourth planets."

"Then that's where we go. We follow the bread crumbs to one of those two and pray we haven't wasted our time," Omega said.

"It will take us two or three days to safely transit that far," Camden offered. "Our unfamiliarity with this system means we can't use maximum speed. Unless of course we want to end up like *Seventh Sojourn*."

"What's your point?" Omega asked.

"That won't leave us much time to do any serious investigating or make contact with the originators of the signals… if they're man made," Camden replied.

"We'll cross that bridge when we come to it," Omega said turning to Camden. "We have to get there first."

"What if it's just severe solar activity or radiation from an exploded planet? We've run into that before. Even at low inter-system speed it could be dangerous," Camden cautioned.

"Dela?" Omega asked looking over his shoulder to his flight engineer.

"If we stay away from the fifth planet, our shielding will protect us from anything that star could put out. And our environmental warning system will alert us of any other hazards long before they become a problem," Dela assured Omega. She turned to Camden and smiled. "But if things get really bad, we have more than enough power to escape any spatial phenomena. I'll keep enough reserve power for breakaway options… as long as Delle and Camden can pilot the ship."

Her words were a friendly poke at the navigator and pilot. Though she was the flight engineer, Dela was also a qualified navigator and back-up pilot for the mission. From the time she joined the crew, the trio had kidded each other about their piloting skills.

"We'll be fine, Commander," Camden said giving Dela a hard look.

"I guess it's settled then," Omega said. "But you may be right, Camden. I see a large gap between the fourth and fifth planets. It seems to be an asteroid belt of some kind, possibly the remnants of an exploded planet, or an unformed planet or moon and a possible source of the radio emissions."

"What are your orders, Commander?" Delle asked flexing his fingers above his navigation console.

"Make preps to throttle up," Omega said leaning back in his couch. "We're going in."

3
Kerguelen Deep Space Survey Ship *San Mariner*

As Omega leaned back in the commander's couch, he was having a hard time concentrating on the moment. As his crew readied the ship for the thrust into the unexplored system, he once again found himself gazing through the flight deck forward window into the emptiness of this desolate and extreme edge of the Milky Way galaxy known as the Orion's Arm Spur. As he did, he thought of the mission statement of the Kerguelen Space Command Deep Space Program:

'The objective of the Deep Space Program is to provide the Technology Council with all knowledge concerning those phenomena beyond the confines of planet Kerguelen and its moon. In addition, the Deep Space Program will positively ascertain if life exists beyond the auspices of planet Kerguelen and make contact with same.'

"Remember, Omega," the scientists and priests had told him when he was theorizing so long ago, "microbes on a frozen moon does not mean life once existed there. That microbe could be a building block of Kerguelen flung into space when it was being formed tens of billions of years ago. We need solid tangible proof."

Only mammalian life or something similar would put an end to the question: Are we alone in the universe? Though the Congress of Cardinals was sure that Kerguelen stood alone in the universe as the sole home of the Almighty's children, many others were not. And the ultimate question was put to Space Command to answer for the past thirty years, though the question was only given serious consideration in the past decade.

The Trans-Light Continuum engine, or TLC, and the Faster-Than-Light communications relay system, known as the FTL, both created ten years ago and in service for the past eight, enabled exploration ships to travel many light years in months and maintain contact with

Kerguelen in real-time. What was once a pinprick of light flickering in the night's sky was now in reach and they could unlock the mysteries associated with them.

And if they were lucky, *San Mariner* would be the ship that might just do that. The mission was finally living up to expectations. Omega had the best crew in Space Command and the finest spacecraft Kerguelen engineers could manufacture, the Type V.

The Type V Deep Space Survey Spacecraft were nicknamed Caravels after the ancient sailing vessels with shallow drafts designed to explore the seas of Kerguelen. The caravel design kept the sailing ships from running aground when sailing in and around unknown and uncharted coasts. *San Mariner* was the second Type V built and was intended to blaze a trail in space as its namesake had done on the oceans of Kerguelen centuries before.

San Mariner was just over three hundred feet long and consisted of four hexagonal shaped detachable modules: Command and Control, where the ship was operated; Habitat, which housed the crew living quarters; Cargo, containing ship's stores, supplies and designed to transport any specimens or material being brought back to Kerguelen; and Propulsion Module, arguably the most vital part of the ship. The Propulsion section contained the control systems for the TLC engines and other engineering systems such as the artificial gravity, life-support and water reclamation systems. Additionally, the Type V spacecraft boasted two ancillary craft that provided the opportunity for landing on a foreign celestial body. Most importantly, the Type V was an extended duration vessel, capable of sustaining a crew of seven comfortably for six months.

The prototype Type V vessel, named *Long Distance Voyager*, had several bugs in its design and never lived up to its name. Because of its numerous problems, it was reclassified as a training vessel and would never leave the solar system. The engineers believed they had worked out the bugs by the time *San Mariner* was finished, but there was always a problem or two when a new vessel went out on its maiden voyage. Every ship had its own unique quirks no matter how much tweaking was done to it. *San Mariner's* was its artificial gravity unit. Luckily redundancy did not make failures in the system critical. However, Omega had his mission and science specialists note every failure and malfunction and make recommendations so engineers at home could make the unit more reliable on the ship's next mission. The sound of Omega's name snapped him out of his reverie and he turned to his flight engineer.

"Commander, we're ready to 'throttle up'," Dela said in the nasal tone that was synonymous with all those hailing from the Upper-Central Province of Kerguelen as she was. "All systems nominal."

"Good," Omega said. He turned a dial on the control panel in front of him and pressed a button beside it. A digital timer began to count down. "T-minus thirty seconds."

"Roger, throttle set at sixty-two percent thrust," Camden said.

A loud rumbling came from the after sections of the ship, drowning out the ever-present sounds of the air recirculating system and the hum of electronics. Even though all hands knew it was the sound of the large solid fuel pumps and valves operating, it was still unsettling every time they heard it. The noise was unnerving to all but Dela. As an engineer she was unfazed by the ship's internal workings and reported calmly.

"Fuel flow positive," she said.

"Fifteen seconds," said Delle. "Course programmed and locked in."

"Star field is clear," Tallen said.

"Roger, 'COMMIT' enabled," said Omega toggling a switch on his console. He exhaled and leaned back in his couch. "Okay, children, here we go!"

When the timer on Omega's console read zero, the solid fuel rockets ignited and *San Mariner* lurched forward from the sudden and violent thrust. The ship rumbled for several seconds and then smoothed out. As the ship increased in speed, each crewmember reported on the status of the vessel. Camden kept a close eye on the ship's orientation, ensuring that they did not tumble or lose attitude stability. Delle's gaze darted between the ship's position indicator and an electronic navigation chart making sure the ship was on course. Dela and Powell appraised Omega on how the ship's systems were functioning, while Tallen and Jalen monitored the space radars and sensors. Everyone was occupied with tasks except Omega. He just sat there feeling like a fifth wheel as he received the reports. It was a feeling that every leader experienced at least once, or hoped that they would. His crew was proficient and didn't really need his presence on the flight deck. They would have done just as well if he had been outside of the ship sending orders in by radio. He realized as he looked about the compartment, his crew was calm and methodical. He had done his job well in preparing them for the mission. The excitement of entering a new star system had ebbed and if it hadn't, they were emotionally detached enough to work through it. *He* was the only one outwardly showing signs of anxiety. Omega was gripping the armrest of his couch tightly, anticipating the wail of the Master Alarm or the shout of a crewman.

But nothing came. The ship quickly stabilized and the control console hardly indicated any fluctuations at all. After the solid fuel rockets automatically shut down as programmed, Camden gave a 'thumbs up' signal to Omega indicating that everything was fine and to his satisfaction. Dela received input on the state of the ship's systems from the flight computer and calmly reported.

"All systems Go," she said.

Omega released the death grip he had on the armrest of his couch and breathed easily again.

"We're on course, Commander. We'll reach our target destination in just over two days once we reach our desired velocity," Delle said.

"Pilot confirms," Camden said.

"TNT confirms," Tallen said tapping on his console and staring intensely into the screen of his radar unit.

"We're in Flight Computer Program 129, the clock is running and navigation is fully automatic. Engineering is in one knob control. Main drive is in one-minute stand-by," Dela said reclining in her chair.

"Commander!" Tallen screamed suddenly from his station. The loudness of his voice caused all hands to turn towards him. "We've got to fire the braking rockets!"

Before Omega could respond, the Master Alarm wailed and the proximity warning alert flashed on every console on the flight deck. When that sensor flashed, it meant that an object in space was close to the ship... too close. The flight computer fired the braking thrusters and the ship began to slow. Dela's hands raced over her console and she spoke to Camden over her shoulder.

"Pilot, the ship is yours!" Dela said as she disengaged the automatic systems and silenced the Master Alarm.

"I've got it!" Camden said as the alarm went silent. He gently took manual control and stabilized the ship's flight.

"Thirty-five seconds until main drive is online!" said Dela.

"I'm ready!" Delle said.

"So am I!" Camden said.

Dela turned to Tallen. "Tallen, talk to me, what do we have?" she said.

"A small object... very close... we're almost on top of it," he replied.

"What is it?" Omega asked impatiently as he craned his neck and looked out of the window for a view of space in front of the ship. "Is it a meteor or a comet?"

"It's metallic," Tallen said.

"What?" Omega said turning to his science specialist. "What do you mean metallic?"

"You're not going to believe it, Commander," Tallen said shaking his head in disbelief. "I'm looking at it myself and I'm not sure if I believe it!"

4

Capitol City, Central Province, Planet Kerguelen

Five staff aides in five different government buildings sped through empty hallways towards their respective offices, the report of their heels on highly polished tiled floors echoed off of the walls as they went. Each had received identical TELCOM calls from Space Command in the middle of the night arousing them from their beds, interrupting much needed slumber. It was rare when the aides to the top figures in the planetary government got an evening of undisturbed sleep and relaxation, and this early morning wake up call would be a prelude to another string of relentless and seemingly endless workdays in which they would sustain themselves with stimulants and catnaps.

When they arrived at Space Command's administrative offices in Capitol City, hardly a half an hour before, they each received a data stick and were instructed to deliver them to their superiors without delay. They had received these instructions from the director of Space Command himself, punctuating the importance and speed at which they were to carry out the assignment. Their superiors would need time to prepare responses to questions regarding the data that would assuredly be planet-wide knowledge via hackers on the Planetary Information Link within the hour. As their colorful gold-trimmed robes flowed, accentuated by the waning light of the single Kerguelen moon, the sprinting aides knew each of the individuals they represented would have a unique perspective on the information they gripped in their tight fists.

* * * * *

Tibor was the first of the aides to reach his destination. He smoothed his deep emerald green robe so it lay straight down his sides and wiped his brow free of the perspiration that had built up there on his way to the office. He rapped twice on the door and entered. Tibor quickly covered the short distance between the door and the desk and handed Bacor, Grand Senator of the Planetary Legislature, a data stick. Bacor, now in the middle of his fifth consecutive six-year term, took the data stick and inserted it into his computer. The room was dark save the computer screen, whose light reflected upon Bacor's face, outlining his craggy features in grim detail. But even if the office had been as black as pitch, its darkness could not have hid the apparent excitement and joy beaming from the senator. He leaned back in his chair and smiled, nodding his head in approval of what he saw.

* * * * *

Reka's blue robe fell to his side as he stopped running and it looked like a dark cobalt waterfall surrounding his body. The former All-Kerguelen university athlete took a second to catch his breath and frowned before he entered the room. Reka cursed himself for the state of his cardiovascular condition. He had allowed his once firm and muscular body to become soft and weak due to overindulgence in food and spirits during his tenure as the aide to Chief Justice Thom, leader of the Planetary Judiciary. He was still breathing heavily but stood rigid in front of Justice Thom awaiting instructions as the judge assessed the data Reka had given him.

Thom's chambers were brightly lit suggesting that he had not yet been to bed and Reka's eyes wandered around the office. Endless volumes of bound legal texts and a variety of other literary works filled the shelves that ringed the office. Reka was mystified as to why Thom still researched using bound books instead of retrieving information from the Planetary Information Link and wrote his briefs in long hand on old sheets of paper instead of on electronic data tablets like everyone else on the planet. Thom said he preferred pen and paper to stylus and screen but that didn't make sense to Reka. Though Thom was nearing retirement age, he was still a child of the Age of Advancements. Bound books and paper had not been produced for nearly 120 years, almost fifty years before Thom was born, and Reka was afraid to ask where the Chief Justice obtained paper. The answer may have compromised all concerned. Since the Age of Advancements began, it was illegal to cut down trees. Nothing was made from wood products any longer.

Synthetics, carbon fiber and metallic hydrogen were now used for virtually everything on the planet.

When the justice finished reviewing the data, he stood and walked slowly from behind his large antique wooden desk, another of Thom's archaic adornments that was at least two centuries old, and paced the floor. As Justice Thom silently walked in the living time capsule he contemplated what kind of era the data he had just viewed would usher in.

* * * * *

All secretaries of consequence had been summoned and were jammed into the waiting room when Ansala swept her white robe aside and strode into the planetary president's workspaces. The main workspace, called the Central Office, was circular and had doors leading to the offices of the president's four principle secretaries. Planetary President Ward waited impatiently as Ansala deposited the data stick on his desk. Ward frowned at her as he picked up the data stick and she raised an eyebrow in response. As Ward placed the data stick in his computer's access port, Ansala remained mute but desperately wanted to respond verbally. However, she remained silent. She had less than a year remaining in her assignment as Ward's aide and would welcome the end of her mandatory three-year civil service obligation required of all of the planet's citizens.

Though the benefits were unprecedented, the hours were brutal and she had to endure the president's slings and arrows as his whipping girl when Ward had a bad day in the media. Additionally, the posting forced her to work for someone she didn't vote for, or particularly like.

Ward was in his second five-year term as Kerguelen's chief executive and had an equal number of supporters as detractors, though it seemed as if the ranks of the detractors grew larger everyday. His supporters chastised any who disagreed with Ward's policies or commented or lampooned the president's lack of oratory skill and seemingly dull wittedness. His detractors on the other hand relished every public speaking engagement he made. Ward provided an inexhaustible source of ammunition for the constant bombardment in the assault against him personally and against his administration. He was from a wealthy and prestigious family and surrounded himself with a cabinet of 'yes men'. Known amongst the lower level staff as the Bobble Heads, they either out of blind loyalty or fear of reprisals, agreed with every one of Ward's policies, no matter how ridiculous or what the populace thought. They seemed to be caricatures of rational people and one reporter had christened them the 'Comic Strip Cabinet'. Ansala was so embarrassed about her position at times she denied that she was his aide.

When he finished reviewing the data, Ward motioned to Ansala indicating that he wanted the Bobble Heads. She retrieved them from the anteroom and as the secretaries listened to Ward, Ansala watched as all of their heads went up and down rapidly and in unison just like the figurines they were named after with each word he uttered. When she saw it, Ansala placed her hand nonchalantly to her lips to stifle a laugh.

* * * * *

Reyes cursed under his breath as he waited for the security doors to open at each checkpoint along the long corridor leading to the office of the chief technologist of Kerguelen. He pushed aside the purple robe he wore as he waited impatiently for the system to recognize his inputs. Though the least political of all the government heads, the chief technologist wielded power and influence greater than the president and was second only to the leader of the Congress of Cardinals. As leader of the Technology Council, the chief technologist controlled and administrated the research, design, development and distribution of all technology and science applications on the planet.

Every scientist, doctor, engineer and technologist on Kerguelen worked for the Technology Council. The council ensured that what they created was put to use to better mankind. Since the end of the last Provincial Wars, the council improved conditions for all and every member of the council strived to make the planet better every day. No longer were the creations of scientists and engineers perverted into implements of death, twisted into cash cows for corporations or regulated for the rich and powerful alone. Morality had finally overcome greed.

Reyes pounded his fist against the final keypad barring his way and swore aloud when it beeped and flashed red indicating that he had failed to input the correct code into it. His voice echoed through the empty hallway and as it faded, he heard another voice replace it.

"That won't get you to me any faster, Reyes," a light voice said through a speaker on the security system. It sounded God-like as it filled the vacant passageway.

Reyes was startled by the voice and looked up at the electronic security strip lining the wall that tracked the progress of persons through the building. He nodded and waved a hand at the strip and a second later, the security door opened granting him access to the inner sanctum of the chief technologist. Reyes hurried to his destination and apologized to the woman seated in front of him. He blinked quickly to adjust his eyes to the brilliant antiseptic whiteness of the office, which was in reality a laboratory.

Chief Technologist Mackenzie uncrossed long and shapely legs that seemed to go on forever and took the data stick from Reyes tossing it carelessly over her shoulder onto a cluttered lab table behind her. Reyes looked at her quizzically and she gave him her infamous disarming smile.

At fifty-two years old, she maintained the figure of a woman half of her age. Only sprinkles of gray hair mixed with thick and wavy dark tresses, which she refused to dye, gave any indication of her true age. She stood over six feet and had a correspondingly shapely figure and Reyes noticed that she was strong for a woman. Another thing that piqued Reyes' curiosity about Mackenzie was that she seldom wore makeup and her youthful look had no hints of cosmetic surgery. Somehow she had found a fountain of youth. Men desired her and women despised her, but all were enamored with her.

"I already know what's on that data stick, Reyes," she said in a voice whose origin was without a doubt from the North Island Province, home of Kerguelen's standard language.

"Then why did I rush here?" Reyes asked confused by his instructions.

"It was a feint, Reyes. You forget Space Command belongs to the Technology Council. There is nothing that happens there that I don't know about," Mackenzie said rising from her seat buttoning her white lab coat as she did.

The action did nothing to cover her attractive lower limbs, nor did the mini skirt she wore. Her attire was an extension of Mackenzie's power over those she encountered on a daily basis, and the effect was not lost on Reyes. His eyes involuntarily tracked Mackenzie from her legs to her slim waist, finally stopping when he made contact with her cool blue eyes. Her smile continued, satisfied that her pose and clothing had created the desired effect.

"I want the other leaders to think we're on equal footing. The reason you were summoned was because I need to begin countering the activities the Cardinals are sure to commence," Mackenzie said. "They will surely try to prevent the data from becoming public knowledge."

"I don't understand. Why would the Cardinals try to prevent the information on the data stick from becoming public knowledge?" Reyes asked completely clueless.

"If I told you everything you believe in and your basis of power was about to be shattered, wouldn't you try everything in your power to stop that from happening?" she asked plainly.

"Yes, I would," Reyes nodded affirmatively.

"Good, I'm glad we agree," she replied. "Let's get to work."

"At what?"

Mackenzie turned to Reyes and smiled. "Isn't it obvious, Reyes? We need to implement a plan to try and keep Omega and the crew of *San Mariner* alive."

* * * * *

"The data stick, Your Eminence," said Venture as he wrapped himself in the scarlet robe that indicated he was the staff aide of Cardinal Gregor XII, President of the Congress of Cardinals. The cardinal motioned for him to be seated as he inserted the data stick into his computer.

As he lowered himself into the chair in front of the cardinal's plastic form desk console, Venture felt a chill and could not be entirely sure whether it was the cool air of the cardinal's office or the information on the data stick that made him shiver. As the cardinal looked at the screen, he looked as though the blood had drained from his face. He pushed himself away from his desk and motioned for Venture to read the screen as he went to the large window behind his desk that overlooked the massive courtyard of Cathedral Prime, the largest place of worship on the planet and the Federal Church's seat of power.

From here, the Congress of Cardinals set religious doctrine and exercised their unlimited power over Kerguelen. Being the only "practiced" religion on the planet had its advantages. Though other very minor religious sects still existed, they were not organized nor did they have a significant following. The cardinals had the only conduit to divinity and spiritual salvation for the populace of the planet. The Almighty could only be reached through them, and as leader of the Congress of Cardinals, Gregor was in many ways, God on Kerguelen.

Venture walked around the desk and lowered his head, quickly reading and consuming the information. He straightened himself and returned to his place in front of the cardinal's desk. If the data was correct, and there was no doubt that it wasn't, the unbridled run of the cardinals might be reined in slightly. Unfortunately, Venture knew that could spell disaster for Kerguelen if not handled properly.

A gentle breeze rustled the leaves on the trees in the courtyard of Cathedral Prime indicating that a pleasant and mild day would grace the eastern coast of the Central Province. Gregor, a farmer in his youth, knew what the weather would be like when the sun rose but he feared the idling tempest that was being stirred by the blasphemy on the data stick. He was truly the master of all he surveyed, but at this moment Gregor felt impotent. This could be disastrous for the Federal Church. Everything that he and his predecessors had created might be lost in one fatal swoop if he was not careful. He placed his hands behind him and gripped them tightly, so tightly that it caused him to wince as he turned to his aide, Commander Venture, senior field officer of the Guardian Corps.

"Is this information accurate?" Gregor asked.

"Absolutely, Your Eminence," Venture said standing at attention as he answered.

Despite the long and distinguished history of the Guardians, Gregor did not hold them in high regard. Though they always displayed great respect to those in positions of power, especially members of the cloth, Gregor, for his own reasons, did not fully trust them. He was impressed by their discipline, dedication, resolve and piety but their failure to integrate themselves into the government was unsettling to the cardinal. He disliked things that could not be fully controlled and Venture was a major source of his unease. The field commander of the one thousand-man Guardian regiment was known for his devotion to preserving life and freedom for all, but he put many people who encountered him on the defensive due to his ever-present acerbic countenance.

"You're sure about the authenticity of the data? There couldn't be an... encryption or decryption error? The ship is over two score light years from us, after all," Gregor queried hoping to create doubt in his aide.

"No errors have occurred, Your Eminence. We were told the data was quadruple verified using every protocol," Venture said calmly as if the statement was rehearsed.

"The survey commander... Omega. His reliability troubles me. Can we fully trust a man who was excommunicated?" asked Gregor.

"Omega is an experienced deep space star sailor," Venture said tactfully.

"Very good answer, Commander. You should have gone into politics with an answer like that," Gregor said smiling. He sat down and continued. "But I know you and Omega once served together... at the famous Battle of the Twin Pillars, in fact. And service together, especially under trying circumstances, can cloud one's judgment... and perceptions." He tapped his temple with his forefinger when he finished but Venture ignored him.

"Eminence, there were many who saw service at the Twin Pillars and due to the importance of the data, I wouldn't let my personal feelings or previous experiences influence my judgment in this matter," Venture replied. "But I will say that Omega is a competent leader. He's a clear-headed thinker and not prone to jump to unfounded conclusions or make rash decisions."

"Really, Commander? I would say that was an untrue statement. Omega *is* known to make rash and foolhardy decisions. Why else would he have been excommunicated?" Gregor said with a sly smile.

"The reasons for his excommunication are between him, the Church and the Almighty. They do not concern me, Your Eminence. I only assume he *is* known to be rational and trustworthy. Why else would the Church have sanctioned him to command a deep space mission? I was unaware that the Church granted impulsive and unworthy persons ex cathedra," Venture responded calmly and without emotion.

Gregor did not reply. There was no winning this fencing match and there was no way for him to make *San Mariner's* data go away easily.

If Venture could make arguments for the survey's find, anyone else could, especially someone who was not on the periphery, like Chief Technologist Mackenzie. He would need to start planning a strategy to combat the data. He sighed and relented for the moment.

Venture saw the cardinal's resolve wan and took a step closer to the desk. As he moved, the early morning rays of the Kerguelen sun beamed through the large window behind the cardinal. Their presence caused the illumination controls to automatically dim the room's lights.

"Your Eminence, this is hard evidence," he said pausing to take a breath. "We must assume Omega's transmission is factual until we can see what he has in person. Until then, we must accept what he has found. It appears he's been right all these years. There is evidence that life exists on another world. Despite our beliefs and feelings on the subject, it appears we are not alone in the universe."

5
Kerguelen Deep Space Survey Ship *San Mariner*

A few hours had passed since *San Mariner* encountered the object in the uncharted star system some forty-plus light years from Kerguelen. Tallen continued to watch it on his radar monitor as Delle and Camden maneuvered the ship to rendezvous with it and come along side. Dela and Powell were aligning extra cameras so that multiple angles could be taken of the object when the ship was close enough. The cameras were slewed to the FTL communications system and every picture taken would be sent to Space Command automatically.

While his crew was working, Omega was busy communicating with Space Command updating them on the find. Included in his messages were the star charts pointing out the exact location of the star system, designated 1-Sol-8, and information about the system itself. So far, there had not been any problems, but Omega was still troubled. He had received no direct communication from Space Command. They sent replies saying that they received *San Mariner's* transmissions, but there were no follow-up queries or instructions, only deadly silence and that silence worried Omega greatly.

In a few moments, the ship would again be in visual range of the object. Since the initial contact, and near collision, the ship had made three fly-bys past the object. Camden and Delle were now maneuvering back to it and each crewman had one eye on their work and the other on the windows of the flight deck. The anticipation of the first interstellar space encounter was overwhelming, but the crew maintained their discipline and the flight deck remained quiet with the exception of required communication between crewmen. The hush was suddenly broken by Tallen.

"Oh, my God," Tallen exclaimed. He adjusted a few dials and then leaned in closer to his console. "Commander... we're coming up on it again! You should have a visual now!"

"Confirmed, Commander," Delle said as he motioned to Camden.

Camden made adjustments to the attitude controls and *San Mariner* slowed down and matched the speed of the object until they were flying side-by-side. Displaying a total lack of discipline, the crew left their stations and leapt to the windows. They were pressed against the windows and gawking like sightseers in a bus on their first visit to a city. Everyone except Camden, who was piloting the ship, and Dela, who was operating the cameras, that is.

The object was small and cylindrical with what appeared to be a large radio antenna atop of it and two booms attached to the sides. The booms seemed to be used to hold deployed equipment and two long aerials extended out from the object's body. The crew spoke amongst themselves and came to the conclusion that the object was a space probe of some kind. It was similar in design to the early versions Space Command had sent out of their solar system during the fledgling days of the unmanned long-range space exploration program. Omega wondered if this craft was an alien version of the same thing. Only a thorough investigation would tell for sure.

"Commander, I've made some calculations and I believe we can grab the craft with our robotic manipulator arm without harming it or damaging us, bring it to a stop and retrieve it," Dela said still engrossed at her station. When there was no response, she turned and spoke again. "Commander?"

"Yes, yes, Dela," Omega said slowly turning from the window. "I heard you. Good work. Write out a procedure and run it through the computer for simulation."

He slipped into his couch as Dela nodded and began tapping on her keypad. She called Powell from the window to operate the cameras and instructed the other crewmembers to go to work as well. A few inarticulate grumbles later, they complied.

Omega took a deep breath and let it out slowly. He had been leading people all his adult life, first as a Guardian officer and now as a star sailor. But none of his training and experience could have prepared him for this. So far, the mission had been textbook. What was not in the textbook was what to do when you enter a previously unexplored star system and encounter a space probe of alien origin. Omega had to make a decision. *San Mariner* and the probe were on a heading out of the solar system. His ship's resources were critical. They had to stay with the probe and give up exploring the system, or give up the probe and go in search of its creators. If they couldn't find the creators, they had to hope they could find the probe again before they had to head home. Both options left part of the third mission goal on the table. Time was the problem that faced Omega. They were just about out of it. Without instructions or guidance from Space Command, Omega was on his own. He sighed and made his decision.

"Okay, let's go to work," Omega said. The crew turned to him and he continued. "Let's get all the data on the craft we can from here and see if we can safely stop it. Once we stop it, we'll do an EVA over to it and make sure there's nothing on it or in it that will kill us before we get home. Jalen, is the containment area large enough to hold that?"

"I believe so," Jalen said considering the question. "If not, it certainly will be if we detach those booms and aerials."

"He's right," Delle said in the smooth cultured tones of professionals hailing from the Hinterlands of the Northeastern Province where he was from.

"Wait," Camden said with concern in his voice. "The containment area is for plants and rocks and water samples."

"The containment area is designed to protect the crew from harm," Jalen said. "It doesn't matter if the material in it is animal, vegetable, mineral... or man-made."

"Just make it work, Jalen," Omega said ending the argument.

"We need to prep the space walk, Commander," Dela said. "How many EVA suits do we need?"

"Four," Omega said.

"Four hard suits, Dela," Camden said. Omega shot him a glance and Camden explained himself. "The hard suits will give the EVA team the greatest protection against radiation and biohazards, Commander. We don't know what we're dealing with. It could be a weapon of some kind."

Omega nodded in agreement and Dela instructed Powell and Jalen to prepare the equipment for the space walk while she finished the procedure for stopping the probe. Omega leaned back in his couch and then turned to Tallen.

"Tallen, based on the craft's trajectory, can we tell where it came from?" Omega asked.

Tallen shook his head. "Doubtful, Commander. Based on what I see, the vessel originated from somewhere in this star system. It doesn't have a main drive unit, only thrusters, so we can surmise that it was launched from a planet using booster rockets or released from a spacecraft. Take your pick. If I were sending this type of craft into space, I would launch it with booster rockets and release it once it achieved maximum velocity. To get it out here, I would use a series of slingshot maneuvers around the outer planets. It would take too long to reach this distance on a straight trajectory," Tallen said.

"Why wouldn't you use a ship?" Camden asked.

"If you had a ship, why use the probe?" Tallen said.

"Which planet do you think could have launched the probe?" Omega asked.

"The third or fourth planet," Tallen said. "Based on our knowledge, none of the others could support life. And if life exists on the others, we wouldn't want to meet it."

"Right. Well, we have two automated probes equipped with our universal greeting. Send one to the third planet and the other to the fourth," Omega said.

"Right away," Tallen said stepping away from his station.

"And Tallen," Omega called. "Add a message that we found their probe and we'll be back. With any luck, the culture that launched that probe will find ours and be able to decipher the message."

"And then?" Camden asked.

"And then," Omega said with a smile. "And then they'll know they're not alone either."

PART TWO

PRESENT DAY

1
Heavy Water Production Plant, Eastern Province, Planet Kerguelen

"My God they move fast," first lieutenant Lindsey thought to himself as he ran through the woods. He trailed the four persons and canine he was with, not by much, but enough to cause him concern. He could hear himself breathe and he calmed himself, remembering to keep his head up so he would have a smooth and even airflow into his lungs and thus control his breathing and limit his respiration. As they continued on, the words of encouragement his commander had given him before they had hit the ground rung in his ears. *"Try not to worry too much, Lindsey,"* she had said patting him on the shoulder and giving him an uncharacteristic smile. *"I know you're apprehensive but your instincts will take over when you need them most."*

And she had been right. All of his limited training had taken over now and he was moving as if he were on autopilot. He couldn't believe he was actually here. He was on a mission. It was surreal... dream-like.

A little over four months ago he had graduated from the Guardian Academy. Fourteen hours ago, he was a lowly second lieutenant in a classroom at the Surveyors School learning the rudiments of combat civil engineering. He was pulled out of class by a captain he had never seen before, shoved into an air ship and given a field combat kit. He was told he was needed for a special op and would not be returning to school. He was told that he had been promoted to first lieutenant and would find an increase of three thousand credits in his bank account. He was told the money was there for him to buy clothes and extra uniforms. He understood the reason for more uniforms but not the civilian clothes. The captain told him that the team he was now part of conducted various types of ops and a good wardrobe was essential. The commander liked her people well dressed. The captain then briefed

Lindsey on the team's protocols and mission parameters so fast, he wasn't sure if he had retained any of the information. And now, at this very moment, he was in the Eastern Province, half a world away from all that he knew to destroy something that was a danger to the population of Kerguelen. That was the purpose of the Guardian Corps. Protect the sanctity of life against any and all threats.

The moonless and starless overcast sky masked the stealthy movements of Lindsey and the other darkly clad figures and canine as they moved silently in the night. Carefully, but swiftly, they wound their way toward the entrance of the large synthetic-concrete building before them. Besides Lindsey, there were two other males and two females. Lindsey and the captain who had whisked him away were the only ones who wore night vision contact lenses to enhance their vision, but they were not in the lead. That task was left to one of the females. She was tall, muscular and had a clear dark complexion and wore her long dark hair in a thick heavily braided ponytail. She held her hand up suddenly stopping the team in their tracks.

Pointing toward the door of the building, she held up two fingers, made a fist and then held up three fingers. The male not wearing night vision contact lenses nodded and aimed the weapon in his hands towards two sentries patrolling the grounds. He was huge. Lindsey estimated he was at least six and half feet tall and well built. He also had a dark complexion and possessed a long braided ponytail. In a few seconds, the two guards barring the quintet's entry into the building would be eliminated.

Though the adaptive camouflage coating on the team's combat suits kept them invisible to the naked eye at a distance, they would be seen if they attempted to move closer. Normally, such a situation was not a dilemma, but this mission had certain parameters that could not be changed. The team had to complete their mission without fighting or being recognized. The operation was also time sensitive. Three other five-person units were conducting nearly identical missions at other locations in the Eastern Province. All of the missions were to reach their climax at the same hour and the team Lindsey was with was running short on time. The watchmen didn't look like they were leaving anytime soon, so they had to be taken out quickly... and quietly.

The big male raised his weapon to his shoulder and clicked the range and then the wind knobs on the Doppler Radar Visual Indicator Scope, or DRAVIS, on the sniper rifle he held. Though projectile weapons were considered obsolete, the DRAVIS sniper rifle was a recent offering in warfare technology development. It was lightweight and its plastic, conical-shaped, .308-caliber ammunition did not use gunpowder. They were fired using a high-pressure air charge. The charge could fire five rounds in rapid succession to an effective range of five hundred meters. The rifle was also recoilless, which gave it unprecedented accuracy. And because it was essentially an air rifle, there was no need for a silencer and thus no loss of muzzle velocity. The big male carefully aimed the weapon and placed his index finger on the trigger.

"Rex, what's your load?" the second female said in a soft but slightly husky North Island Province accent. She was dark like the others but not as tall as the other female, but possessed a more muscular build and her hair was braided similarly. By her posture, there was no doubt she was leader of the team.

"Standard load, Commander," the sniper said with the same accent as the commander.

"I thought I told you to... never mind," the leader said visibly angered. She shook head and handed the sniper a magazine. "Here, reload."

He removed the weapon's magazine and cleared the round that was in the chamber. He placed the new magazine in the weapon, quietly chambered a new round and took aim again.

"What are those?" Lindsey asked. His young eyes were wide and bright and he was trying to take in as much as he could on his first operation.

"Vecuronium rounds, Lieutenant," the female commander said with a heavier accent this time. "We're instructed to blow the facility, not kill anyone... this time."

Lindsey nodded. Vecuronium was a paralytic that cut off the brain from the body's muscles. The sentries would go down, but they would survive being shot and not be able to alert anyone of the team's presence until long after they were gone. The commander knelt and grabbed a handful of soil. She sniffed it and nodded.

"What can you tell me about this soil, Lieutenant?" she asked.

"It is very good soil," Lindsey said with a smile. "Excellent for various uses."

"How can you tell?" she asked.

"It's dark color and rich texture leads me to believe it contains a high content of nitrogen and nutrients," Lindsey answered. "It can retain water but will still drain very well."

"Excellent observations, Lieutenant," the commander said. "I see not all of the lessons you've received at school were regulated solely to drink and picking up women." She dropped the handful of soil and brushed her gloved hands clean. "It is good soil. I wouldn't mind owning a few acres of it."

"If we continue to dally, we'll each own six feet of it," the tall female said in a harsh North Island Province accent.

"Captain," the female commander said to the other male with night vision contacts. "After they go down, you and Lt. Lindsey get them clear. Egress to the extraction point when you finish. We won't be far behind."

The captain nodded his head once and flexed his shoulders. He was from the Eastern Province and had a tight, compact and powerful body. It was toned and hardened from years of martial arts training as a child. The commander said he resembled a coiled spring.

The commander looked at her chronometer. "Take them down, Rex," she whispered to the big male.

Rex took in a breath and slowly exhaled. He pulled the trigger twice, dropping the guards in their tracks. Before he could secure his weapon, the rest of the team was on the move dragging the paralyzed sentries to a spot out of sight, or heading to the building. When she reached the building, the leader peeked inside through a small window in the door. She turned to the taller woman and the big male, who had just joined them.

"Switch to white," she said tapping a button on a bracelet attached to her left wrist. The others did the same and gave her a 'thumbs up' when they were ready. The leader petted the canine that was beside her and the dog sat on his hind legs. "Stay, Lupo. We'll be right back." The dog opened his mouth and let out a soft growl. The commander turned to her team and nodded. "Okay, let's go."

They entered the building unseen by the surveillance cameras that canvassed the interior of the building. The adaptive camouflage setting of their combat suits matched the surrounding background of the facility and the three moved invisibly toward their goals.

"Wow," the tall female said looking around the building. "This is certainly an impressive layout."

"Yes, it is," the commander agreed. "A lot of time and effort and money went into it. It's too bad we're here to destroy it."

They quickly attached micro-explosives to the condensers, storage tanks, pumps and piping, electronic controls and inside the main control booth where all of the equipment was operated and monitored. The commander pressed a button on a wristwatch-like device on her right wrist and a tiny LCD light on the device illuminated in green indicating that the explosives were armed. She jerked her head toward the exit and they left the building. Once outside, they switched back to a camouflage setting for the outside environs. The commander turned her head to the others.

"Let's hit it," she said. "We've got less than eight minutes to extraction. Come, Lupo!"

She slapped her leg and the canine sprang to his feet and followed her. They had to travel a little over a mile to the clearing that served as the extraction point for them. The pilot of their air ship would come into the clearing and remain at hover for forty-five seconds before leaving the area. If they missed the rendezvous, the team would have to find their own way home. And that would be difficult once the high explosives they planted went off. The owners and operators of the facility would not take kindly to its destruction and would actively seek retribution.

The commander sped up to a five-minute mile pace as they dodged and leapt over obstacles in their path along the way. Four minutes later, the taller woman squinted and ducked her head to avoid a low hanging tree limb and then pointed ahead in the darkness.

"Hiroki and Lindsey are just up ahead," she said. "About thirty or forty meters."

"I see them," the commander said. "They're not using camouflage and blazing a trail to the clearing just beyond them."

The commander touched a tiny device in her ear and its signal chirped. Hiroki and Lindsey slowed down. Hiroki reached up and touched a similar device in his own ear.

"Captain Hiroki here," he said.

"Captain, hurry up," the commander said. "The extraction point is only about ten meters ahead of you. Secure the area, we're right behind you."

"Roger," Hiroki said touching the device in his ear again.

"How can she see the extraction point from where she is?" Lindsey asked confused. "We're almost there and I can't see it."

"All three of them can see the extraction point, Lieutenant," Hiroki said. "They're Boroni. Don't be surprised by anything they do."

Though it was pitch black and devoid of moonlight, the Boroni could see as well as the average Kerguelen could during the day. But the captain was well aware that enhanced vision was only one of the many gifts that the inhabitants of the Western Province possessed. Their ancestors were slaves, genetically engineered and bred for extremely strenuous and hazardous work. All of their senses were enhanced and they had great physical endurance and were incredibly strong. Most of a Boroni's early childhood was spent learning about, coping with, and honing the attributes that they had. It took many years to control and use them effectively.

Hiroki and Lindsey stopped when they reached the edge of the clearing and waited for the rest of the team to catch up. They didn't have long to wait. Less than a minute passed before the three Boroni joined them. The canine brought up the rear and Lindsey looked at them curiously, shocked at what he saw. Despite the exertion they had expended, the Boroni were breathing normally. It was like they had walked the distance, not ran it. The commander scanned the clearing and surrounding area and turned to her team.

"Take up defensive positions," she said to her team. "I'll call the ship." She touched the device in her ear again and when it chirped, she spoke. "Gray Wolf 1, this is Gray Wolf Actual. We're in position and ready for extraction."

"Roger, Actual," a voice answered in her ear. "I'm coming over the tree line now."

42

She looked to the sky and saw an air ship skim over the canopy of trees and come to a hover.

"The area is clear, Commander," the tall female said.

"Roger, Sergeant Major," the commander said. "Come on down, Gray Wolf 1."

The air ship came down at a steep angle and pulled up at the last second into a hover again. This time the craft was only a few feet off of the ground. The engines were barely audible and their exhaust gently rolled across the clearing bending the tall blades of grass. The dark blue paint scheme of the air ship and a lack of illuminated running lights made it nearly invisible in the inky night. The pilot slowly turned the craft in a half circle and when it stopped, the left side hatch slid open.

"Go!" the commander said to her team.

They all left the cover of trees and raced across the clearing. The tall female was the first to reach the air ship and she deftly aided the rest of the team inside. The commander took one last look around and tapped the canine on the back. They both sprinted to the air ship and a few steps from the open hatch leapt inside. The tall female grabbed the door handle and slammed the hatch shut and called to the pilot.

"Go, Micah!" she said.

Micah pushed the throttle forward and the craft nosed up and powered skyward away from the clearing. Once they had cleared the trees, Micah looked over his shoulder at the commander.

"We're clear, Commander," Micah said.

"Very well," she said. She sat down in her designated seat and the canine curled up next to her. She petted him and smiled. "Did you have fun, Lupo?" The huge silver and gray half-wolf/half-shepherd barked once loudly in response and then lay his massive head in her lap. As the mixed breed canine rested, the commander turned on a console in front of her and opened up a narrow-band communication circuit.

"How long will those guards be out?" Lindsey asked.

"They'll be down for another hour," Hiroki said. "But they'll have a good seat for the show."

"That they will," the commander said. "Gray Wolf 2, this is Gray Wolf Actual. Status."

"Actual, this Gray Wolf 2. Tasking complete. Awaiting the word," the leader of the second team said. They were just leaving a precision machine component manufacturing plant forty miles away.

"Stand-by, Gray Wolf 2," the commander said. "Gray Wolf 3, this is Gray Wolf Actual... Status."

"This is 3. Tasking complete," the leader of the third team said. Gray Wolf 3 had planted explosives at an intermediate range missile launch facility.

"Stand-by 3," the commander said. "Gray Wolf 4, this is Gray Wolf Actual. Say your status."

"We've obtained the packages, Actual," Gray Wolf 4's female team leader said. She was Major Metis and was the commander's most trusted field operative. Metis was a descendant of an ancient native tribe indigenous to the Central Province. Her ancestors had once roamed the province proud and free but ultimately lost the battle of supremacy against the settlers from other provinces who claimed the land for their own. They had called the war against the native tribes manifest destiny, but everyone knew there was a much simpler term for it... theft.

"Any problems?" the commander asked.

"We received no animosity about our procurement. We're clear and awaiting orders," Metis said.

"Excellent. Stand-by," the commander said.

Gray Wolf 4 had the most vital part of the combined operation. That team was to retrieve ten pounds of plutonium that was to be used in a nuclear device and a dozen vials containing H3 N4 from an underground laboratory operating without Technology Council approval or oversight. H3 N4 was a deadly pandemic virus, and in its weaponized form was capable of killing hundreds of thousands if released into the air.

"Gray Wolf 2, 3, and 4... the word is given," the commander said. She touched a button on the watch device on her wrist and the other team leaders did the same.

Simultaneously, the heavy water production facility, the manufacturing plant, the missile launch complex and the laboratory exploded. The resulting fires and secondary explosions finished the job the initial charges did not. The explosions and destruction would be reported as industrial sabotage or accidents and though the owners of the sites would recoup the majority of their financial losses, they would forever lose the capabilities to make the end products the facilities were intended to provide.

The manufacturing plant made precision parts necessary for high-tech weapons construction. Deuterium oxide, vital for making an atomic weapon, was being produced by the heavy water facility. The launch complex housed the intermediate range missiles designed to deliver atomic or biological weapons. Without the facilities and the loss of the plutonium and the H3 N4 virus, the objectives of the terrorists who operated the sites were no longer achievable.

"Actual, this is Gray Wolf 2, mission accomplished."

"This is Gray Wolf 3, mission accomplished."

"Gray Wolf 4 to Actual, mission accomplished."

"Good work, Gray Wolves. RTB. Gray Wolf 4, see me when you arrive," the commander said. All units responded, acknowledging the order to return to base. "This is Gray Wolf Actual, out."

The commander sighed loudly and switched the frequency on the communications set. She cleared her throat as she waited for the new circuit to be established.

"This is Central Command," a male voice said over the circuit.

"This is Gray Wolf Actual. Request immediate connection with the Chief of Staff," the commander said.

"Stand-by," the voice said.

A minute passed before she heard the familiar voice of the Guardian Corps Chief of Staff. "This is Marshal Pace," he said.

"Marshal, this is Gray Wolf Actual. The cranes have been confined to their nests," she said.

"Excellent," said Pace understanding the code for a successful mission. "Will contact you using the usual encryption procedure for After Action Report. Have your units stand down for seventy-two hours. Pass on a 'Well Done' to them, Gray Wolf."

"Copy that," she said. "Gray Wolf Actual, out."

She secured the communications unit and leaned back in her seat and shut her eyes. She needed sleep but it had not come easy for several weeks. Captain Hiroki quietly moved closer to her and he was startled when she opened her eyes as he attempted to tap her on the shoulder. She raised an eyebrow to him and he straightened.

"Commander Prior, what did Central Command say?" he asked as if he already knew the answer to the question.

"Marshal Pace sends a 'Well Done' to you all. Most importantly, you all get seventy-two hours off. Send that to all of the units," she said closing her eyes again. "Now leave me alone, Captain."

"Yes, Commander, right away," Hiroki said with a smile.

He went to the co-pilot's seat and sent the message to the other units. When he finished, he returned to the commander's seat and cleared his throat and she reopened her eyes.

"Yes?" she asked.

"Permission to dispense rations, Commander?" he asked.

"Granted," she said smiling.

Hiroki nodded and opened an overhead compartment removing a bottle. He opened the bottle and handed it to Prior. She waved a hand and he took a drink from it. He passed it Lindsey and the young first lieutenant and the others drank in succession. It was Guardian tradition to celebrate a successful mission by drinking some kind of alcoholic beverage. Though most units did not practice the old tradition, Prior's teams always did, and the air ships under her command maintained an ample store of whiskey or wine onboard. As per regulations, the second-in-command of a Guardian unit maintained control of it and doled it out to the crew whenever the unit commander approved. When the team had their fill, Hiroki gave the bottle to Prior and she took a healthy swig. She handed the bottle to Hiroki and he placed it back in the overhead compartment.

"Sergeant Major," Lindsey said to the tall woman. "How did you know those guards were there?"

"People from the Eastern Province give off a unique smell, Lieutenant," she said smiling at Captain Hiroki.

"It's so sweet she can't resist it," Hiroki said.

"Yeah, that must be what it is," the commander said.

As the team settled down, the sergeant major turned to Lindsey and looked at him silently. Lindsey noticed and faced her.

"Is there something on your mind, Sergeant Major?" Lindsey asked.

"I was just wondering why you smile every time the commander and I speak?" the sergeant major asked.

"It's your accent," Lindsey answered.

"Our accent? What about our accent?" she queried.

"I just like the way you say lieutenant. You pronounce it *Lef-tenant*," Lindsey said smiling again.

The sergeant major shook her head and waved a hand at Lindsey as Commander Prior closed her eyes once again. The team continued to kid each other and the commander was glad Lindsey seemed to be fitting in. He had much to learn but he was off to a good start. Prior allowed a smile to grace her face as well since it seemed she had made a good choice for a replacement. Most importantly, her teams had completed another successful operation and the planet was safe from terrorist aggression. Though the terrorists would not openly protest the action and Guardian Central Command would deny any knowledge of the event or any involvement in the destruction of the facilities, everyone would know the Guardians were responsible. Such was life in a clandestine atmosphere. It was a never-ending search for plausible deniability.

Commander Prior hoped her teams could take advantage of the break. Some time off would do her people good. According to her intelligence reports, all was quiet on the planet and she had no reason to think otherwise. Kerguelen would not need her teams for a while at least. Besides a little fervor concerning the *San Mariner* expedition, all was relatively peaceful, and Prior could not conceive of the need for the Guardians in the near future, especially not covert special operatives such as themselves.

2
Cathedral Prime, Capitol City,
Central Province, Planet Kerguelen

"The Western Province Grange has announced the opening of its most anticipated new banking institution, World Micro Credit. The bank will give micro-loans to underdeveloped and financially depressed areas around the planet to offset the worsening economic conditions in those areas. A spokesman said that the bank was started by the agro giant in response to the planetary legislature's seeming indifference to the needs of those distressed people. It is their hope that the loans will cause the overall planetary economy to rebound from its present freefall.

"In other news, tensions have risen over the past few weeks concerning the new governmental freedom of information policies and dozens of protests have cropped up in major cities of every province. Not even Capitol City has been immune to the swell of resistance to them. Though severe conflicts have not yet occurred, it seems only a matter of time before the populace voices their outrage. The Judicial Branch has already approved the citizen's call for new elections in the planetary legislature and many political pundits are certain that there will be a huge turnover of senators and representatives.

"Turning to sports, the Southern Province..."

Cardinal Gregor XII turned off the tele-viewer and then removed all of the articles from his desk in a single swipe of his right hand in response to the news report. The problems the planet's ruling body was facing all stemmed from the photos sent by *San Mariner*. While the original photos received three months ago left doubt in even the most optimistic eyes, the most recent pictures were clear and sharp, taken in the soft lighting of the ship's Cargo Module. There was no denying that the tiny vessel shown was of an origin far different from that of Kerguelen. But it was not that revelation which most disturbed the cardinal. It was the fact that the population of Kerguelen was overjoyed, excited and even welcomed the prospect of contacting a species from another world. No one thought there was any danger or potential hazards involved with extra-Kerguelen contact. On the contrary, they believed it could only benefit Kerguelen, despite the fact that if aliens truly existed, they were most likely far more primitive. And to Cardinal Gregor, primitive meant barbaric, hostile and most importantly, impious.

Present day Kerguelen society was predicated on a monotheism theory and that the planet was the only celestial body that could support life and its inhabitants the sole intelligent beings in the universe. This anthropocentric doctrine was preached in the churches and reinforced in the schools. To Church leaders, belief in "little green men" was not only ridiculous it was contrary to the Scriptures.

Gregor initially had tried to restrict access to the photos *San Mariner* sent to the highest levels of the planetary government. He believed that the people had more concerns than debating whether or not aliens existed. When the Judiciary blocked that attempt on the grounds it was unconstitutional, he tried to block the images from being posted on the Planetary Information Link, or PIL. In response, a hacker obtained pictures and posted them on his personal PIL page. Gregor had the hacker arrested, but it was to no avail. Hundreds of other users planet-wide managed to intercept photos from the government's "secure" data links and made them available to anyone with PIL access.

For the first few days the photos were available the planet came to a standstill. Shops and schools throughout Kerguelen closed and provincial and local government offices shut down in order for the people to view pictures of the alien spacecraft and those of the *San Mariner* crew around their prize and hold impromptu celebrations.

Though the work stoppage was troublesome, what truly concerned Gregor most of all was that this was the population's reaction only after *seeing* pictures of the alien spacecraft. As *San Mariner* neared Kerguelen, emotions would be fever pitched. What would happen when the ship did return and they could see the vessel in person? He cringed at the thought. Already several influential and outspoken people had suggested that the Federal Church change their stance on Creation.

Several sullen priests from various parishes around the planet were lined up in front of the cardinal's desk receiving sharp reprimands for not quelling what Gregor considered was impious behavior by the members of their congregations. Though they had many tools at their disposal, the priests had failed to stop the tsunami-like waves of elation over the discovery and open refuting of the Federal Church's ideas of Creation.

Gregor had called them in for a meeting, but it was in fact a one-way conversation. When the cardinal finished berating them, which included questioning their intelligence and devotion to the Church, he dismissed them and then turned his ire on Commander Venture. Venture had patiently stood by in silence as Gregor chastised his subordinate clergymen. When the last priest departed and shut the door to the office, the cardinal lit into Venture.

"And you, Commander," Gregor began accusingly and in a voice that was much louder than it had to be. "What have you and your Guardians done to keep the people in line, hmm? You've done nothing! Absolutely nothing! Not a single thing! No one is working. No one is praying or seeking salvation at any temple. At a time like this, people should be flocking to the churches for guidance and comfort, not avoiding them like they were filled with plague victims! The people are celebrating as if they've been freed from sort of bondage! The Clerics might as well not exist!"

"Eminence," Venture said with a small sigh, "The Guardians are not Papal truant officers. And they're not police or hired thugs. Our job is to protect the rights of the people. Our mission is not to force people into a place of worship; we ensure that they have a place to worship… if they choose to. And to be fair, there are many citizens in the churches and temples."

"Feeble old men and women scared of their own shadows," Gregor said unfazed by Venture's calm interpretation of the situation. "Hardly the demographics I had hoped for. I want the young people in the temples and cathedrals. They're the populace that concerns me, not those who are dead already and don't know it yet." Gregor slammed his right hand down on his desk as a means to ram home his point. Venture was thoroughly unimpressed by the display.

"Eminence, my duty is to…" he began but Gregor cut him off.

"Your duty is to the Church, Commander. As my aide, your loyalty is to me… and I am the Church!" Gregor said. He calmed down realizing that the events were getting the better of him. He took a deep breath, exhaled slowly and continued. "Commander, you will have your forces gather up the young people who are in the streets, at rallies... wherever they are... and take them to the nearest place of worship."

"Eminence, I'm afraid you overestimate your position. My duty is to the people who sustain the Guardians, and that is the general public of Kerguelen. My loyalty is to my fellow Guardians. Beyond that, I have no other mandate," Venture said firmly. He had remained cool and calm throughout Gregor's tirade but even his patience had its limits.

"Are you saying that you will not obey my orders?" Gregor asked.

"If they include inhibiting the rights and free choice of the people, then yes, Eminence, I refuse to comply with your... *request*," Venture said choosing his words carefully. "We... the Guardians... went along with the Church and the Chief Executive when your branches of government decided to monitor PIL activities, public TELCOM calls and the library accounts of every citizen in an effort to combat terrorism several years ago. It was unnecessary, excessive and a total invasion of privacy, however, we reluctantly conceded believing that this breech of trust was for the good of all concerned. But your recent efforts to thwart the population's access to public information that concerns them greatly and your desire to prevent them from seeking individual pursuits of happiness, is something entirely different. It is beyond the scope of governmental power and Church authority. I will not sanction another breech of the people's trust, and no forces under my command will engage in such activities."

Gregor looked at Venture for a few seconds and considered the man. Venture was a long time warrior and genuine hero. He was more than the cardinal's aide; he was also the regimental commander of the Guardian Corps. The four battalions under his command were the vanguard of security on Kerguelen. The Kerguelen government on more than one occasion had asked above and beyond that which would be considered required of the Guardians but under Venture's leadership, no request had ever been denied no matter how dangerous. Guardians were all volunteers and the Corps was independent of government oversight. No one questioned what Guardians did or how they performed their duty. For 2,500 years, they had protected the people with a total disregard of their own safety and without personal or financial gain. But no one, not even Guardians, was greater than the whole. If Venture was asked to put his personal feelings aside for the greater good, then he should do it. Gregor was spiritual leader of all the people, but he needed everyone to do their share and help him in his mission. Gregor hoped that Venture would see that, but he was well aware that the commander had strong convictions and might resist. He had anticipated Venture's almost certain reluctance though, and was prepared for it.

"Is no your final word?" Gregor asked.

"Did you not understand me?" Venture replied.

"So be it," Gregor sighed. "I was hoping we could avoid a dramatic conclusion, but you've forced my hand."

"And you've forced mine, Eminence," Venture said holding up a data stick.

"What is that?" Gregor asked.

"A record of your activities, Eminence," Venture said. "I have been monitoring your TELCOM and PIL activity. You've been very busy, Eminence."

"I have," Gregor agreed. "And I was hoping you would not feel the need to use the information you've collected."

Venture looked at Gregor curiously. "You knew I was tracking your systems?" he asked.

"Yes," Gregor smiled. "Since the first time you did it months ago, my technicians have monitored you. Now tell me, what gives you the right to enter my private accounts?"

"You," Venture said plainly.

"Me?" Gregor said almost laughing. "What do you mean me?"

"The policy you sponsored in the legislature, Eminence. The Government Freedom of Retrieval Act empowers me to do it."

"But I'm the President of the Congress of Cardinals."

"The act covers *all* citizens of Kerguelen. You ensured that the bill covered everyone to prevent the privileged from escaping prosecution. And as a Guardian, it's my responsibility to crush any threat to the people of Kerguelen. A Guardian commander has the latitude to do whatever is necessary in that regard," Venture said flipping the data stick in his hand.

"That was very bold and creative, but it doesn't matter," Gregor said.

"I disagree. I have a record of your orders to Papal security to illegally detain and arrest those protesting your edicts. You're holding them without being charged and have refused them the right to consul or a solicitor. I must say, holding them in detention areas under the control of the Church was a brilliant move. No one would ever think of searching for a loved one in one of those old church dungeons," Venture said. "But your plans to take the free will from the people in order to maintain church supremacy over them are at an end."

Gregor smiled. "You're daring, Commander, and the verve you've displayed is commendable. But you've also been careless. If you had taken the time to look at your own computer database, you would have discovered that what I planned and coordinated was planted in your hard drive. If anyone looks at it, they'll find that it was you who initiated the arrests and detentions."

Venture's face turned stony. It was entirely possible that Gregor could have done that. Venture was not very computer savvy. He had to get help to set up his surveillance of Gregor and it was possible that the technician he used could have been a plant on Gregor's payroll. If what the cardinal said was true, Venture was in a great deal of trouble.

"You know, I may have a few of those detainees killed or severely beaten. Your history would not make that hard for people to believe," Gregor said grinning wide. "My trail is clean and you will take the fall for the situation. Don't worry, Commander, I'll ensure your execution is swift." Gregor leaned forward on his desk and moved his hand nonchalantly across a keypad. His action was unnoticed by Venture.

"It's you who'll be in jail, Eminence," Venture corrected. "You won't be ordering anything but your last meal before you're executed."

Venture removed his TELCOM device from a pocket and placed it in his ear. He gently tapped a button on it and waited for the system to come online.

"Who are you calling?" Gregor asked.

"A friend on the Capitol City police force. It will take him fifteen minutes or so to get here so you have time to gather anything you need before you're taken into custody," Venture said.

"You forget your place, Commander," Gregor said. "I'm the President of the Congress of Cardinals. Only the Chief Executive can order my arrest… if he dared."

"And I'm the Regimental Commander of the Guardian Corps, Cardinal, which means I have carte blanche in this matter. President Ward will defer to the Guardians who will allow the arrest to stand until a formal investigation is concluded. Get your things together, Cardinal, you're under arrest," Venture said.

A heavy rap on the door to Gregor's office interrupted their exchange. Gregor smiled at Venture and shook his head.

"You're gravely mistaken if you think I would allow myself to be arrested," Gregor said. "Come in."

When the door opened, a quartet of Guardians entered. The officer leading the detail was the last man Venture expected to see. It was Centurion Sali. Sali took up a position between Venture and Gregor while the other three Guardians settled in behind Venture. Sali looked at Gregor and the cardinal nodded.

Sali was an imposing figure. At a height of six foot five inches, he was four inches taller than Venture and had a thicker build. He was from the subcontinent region of Kerguelen; an area located between the Middle and Eastern Provinces, and was the commander of the Guardian First Battalion. He stood like a wall between Venture and Cardinal Gregor.

Venture turned to the trio of Guardians behind him. Like Sali, the men wore the standard Guardian day uniform, not combat suits. He knew them. The men were highly trained and combat veterans. Sali had chosen them wisely. They had a record of following and never interpreting orders and did not go off the page. Though it was illegal for anyone except the Papal security force to enter a Federal Church complex armed, these men carried weapons. Not even Guardians were exempt from the rule, unless the sanctity of the Church was in question. It was obvious to Venture the men were told that such a situation was at hand. The detail was small and because they didn't wear combat suits and body armor, suspicions would not be raised by their presence. Since Sali was probably told that they were going to apprehend a single individual he must have assumed the need for combat gear and a large force was unnecessary. The capability of a Guardian compared to the average person was great. Even without combat attire, four Guardians could surely handle any disturbance. Venture smiled at how Gregor had arranged this. It was a hand well played.

He turned his glance to Sali. Venture had seen the officer quickly ascend through the ranks and watched his development with great satisfaction. Though sometimes reckless, Sali had matured into a reliable officer and he had recommended Sali for command of the First Battalion personally. In turn, Sali had made the First Battalion the best in the Corps. Venture turned back to the troopers behind him and tried to size them up. Venture knew they would be ready for a possible action.

"This is your man, Centurion," Gregor said. "Do your duty."

"What goes on here, Centurion?" Venture asked.

"By Papal decree, Commander, I have been asked to detain you for questioning concerning illegal activities," Sali said in a monotone voice.

"What illegal activities?" Venture asked. He could tell Sali was not enthusiastic about his mission, especially when it was Venture standing in front of him.

"You are accused of supporting sedition and unrest in planetary affairs, Commander," Sali answered.

Venture smiled. When citizens began disappearing, Guardian Central Command had ordered an investigation initiated at the request of the families concerned. Sali was in charge of the inquiries but he had uncovered nothing. Gregor obviously shifted the blame of the disappearances onto Venture, planted evidence and leaked it to the police and Sali. With that data in hand, Gregor planned for Sali to come to Cathedral Prime and arrest Venture today. Venture was most vulnerable here. He would not be armed and it would be unlikely that he would be prepared to resist apprehension.

"Please come along quietly, Commander. You'll be treated fairly," Sali said removing the strap securing his sidearm in its holster.

"Centurion, if I gave you an order to stand down, would you?" Venture asked glancing at both Sali and the detail indicating that the question was for all of the Guardians in the room.

"No, Commander. The detention order precludes your commission as regimental commander," Sali said.

Venture could see the cardinal was pleased with the turn of events by the smile on his face.

"This doesn't change anything, Cardinal," Venture said.

"You're an idealistic fool, Venture, just like your misguided excommunicated friend. You'll face the repercussions for your actions just as he will. Your failure to embrace and follow Church doctrine and supporting and inciting sedition during this recent outbreak of impious behavior in the general public has been your undoing. It's a shame too. You've served the planet honorably for many years, but the Almighty *will* have Her revenge against all nonbelievers, as is written in scripture," Gregor said with a feigned sense of sorrow.

"No, Eminence, what you've done is doom yourself... and these men," Venture said moving with lightning speed. The banshee-like scream he let out startled everyone in the room.

In one sidestep, he was in front of Sali and thrust his right fist into the centurion's sternum. Gregor shuddered at the alacrity of Venture's movements and the sound of bone cracking from the powerful blow Venture landed. Venture spun around Sali like a dancer, wrapping his hands around Sali's head and quickly turning it. Sali's head spun three quarters of the way around and his eyes rolled back as he fell to the floor. As his body dropped, Venture pulled Sali's sidearm from its holster, flicked the power select button and pointed at the three-man Guardian detail. He pulled the trigger three times in rapid succession and bright flashes of amplified light reached out to the squad of men who were only just reaching for their weapons.

The crimson colored blasts from the plasma energy weapon found their marks. The force of the weapon's output knocked each man back against the wall and they collapsed in a heap, their weapons never having the chance to be leveled. Venture walked over to them and stared down at the men who were once under his command. He knelt down and gave them a cursory examination. Because the men did not have protective gear on, they did not survive the piercing and lethal high-energy setting of the plasma weapon. Though at such a close range, Venture doubted that even Guardian body armor would have protected them.

Venture had no desire to kill a Guardian trying to do his duty, but his hand had been forced. After a short prayer, he breathed deep, rose and stepped away from the men and turned to Gregor, pointing his weapon at him.

"You won't shoot me, Venture. That would certainly sign your death warrant," Gregor said trying to sound confident but failing miserably. "Besides, you are honor bound not to harm me."

"You're wrong, Eminence, you've made me out to be a criminal. I'm no longer commander of my regiment… and now, I'm your worst enemy," Venture said flicking the power select button on the weapon again.

"I guess I should have asked Sali to bring more men," Gregor said almost chuckling.

"It would only have gotten them killed," Venture said.

"How many people do you plan to kill?"

"As many as necessary to bring you down. And for the record, a Guardian is promoted for his ability as a tactician, his wisdom and his combat skills. Unlike other fields of endeavor, we do not receive rank and status because of political affiliation, favors or whom we know. No four men could ever get the better of a Guardian commander. Four men," Venture scoffed, "That's an insult."

Before Gregor could respond, Venture pulled the trigger of his weapon.

3
Chief Executive's Mansion, Capitol City, Central Province, Planet Kerguelen

Ansala once again found herself hurrying through the Chief Executive's mansion zipping in and out of groups of gathered staff workers lining the hallways. These lower echelon government employees had vacated their tiny cubicles and were having their usual mid-morning coffee clutch discussing how to carry out their instructions for the day and boasting about the adventures they had gotten into, and out of, the previous night. Ansala had never joined in those reindeer games and was glad she was in a position where she could avoid their constant company. Having to deal with them in a limited capacity for work-related issues was more than enough for her. They acted as if they were still in college and Ansala didn't have the patience for them.

She sidestepped an elderly secretary cradling an uneven stack of electronic data tablets in her arms and turned into the communications department aisle. She groaned when she saw Riley, the President's deputy communications director, at the end of the aisle leaning against a wall. His shirtsleeves were rolled up and he was surrounded by a quartet of wide-eyed female interns. He had an easy smile and thought he was far more attractive than he really was. Ever since Ansala had joined the presidential staff as Ward's aide, he had attempted to woo her. She had resisted all his advances from the start, causing her to be a social outcast and the subject of several unfounded rumors. Resisting his charms meant she thought she was better than she was in the eyes of her fellow females. To her male peers, her actions obviously meant she was homosexual. Her exclusion from their cliques pleased her to no end though and in a few weeks, she would be gone. Her mandatory civil service would be over and she could get on with her life.

Ansala hoped she could get by him without being seen but as he held court over the bevy of ingénues, he caught a glimpse of her and called out a greeting. She gave him a cursory wave and continued on to her destination. But he excused himself from his entourage and caught up with her. He tugged at her elbow and Ansala stopped and frowned at him. She had no time for his nonsense.

"Hey," he said looking around. "Is there something going on that I should know about?"

Ansala shook her head. "No," she said. "Why don't you ask your boss, Riley?"

"I can't. He's in a meeting with the deputy chief of staff. All of the department heads are in a meeting of some kind," Riley said.

"Then maybe *you* should get back to work instead of setting up your next conquest," Ansala said tersely. "If something is going on, you'll have to prepare some type of statement for President Ward. Now if you'll excuse me, I have to get to the president."

Before he could say anything, Ansala had spun on her heels and was gone, leaving the confused deputy communications director in her wake.

When Ansala finally reached and entered the Central Office, she found President Ward pacing back and forth impatiently while Norton, his chief of staff, and Chief Technologist Mackenzie sat in two of the four comfortable chairs ringing the president's desk. Norton was tapping away on his PDA with a stylus as Mackenzie lounged, displaying as much of her long legs as was possible. As usual, the chief technologist was dressed to accentuate her lovely attributes.

Ward was visibly upset and that meant he would be more difficult to deal with than usual… if that were possible. Ansala was not entirely truthful to Riley in the hallway. Something huge had occurred less than an hour ago. What it was, Ansala had no clue, but heightened activity by the President's secretaries and the presence of the chief technologist in the Central Office were telltale signs of something cataclysmic. If those things did not ring any bells in Ansala, her instructions to set up a direct line of communication with Guardian Central Command as soon as possible should have led her to believe there was a planetary emergency of some kind.

The chief of staff routinely ran planetary emergency scenarios to test the efficiency of the Disaster Contingency Administration, but the tension Ansala felt in the room suggested that there was no drill. Ansala took a deep breath and stepped across the blue deep pile carpet and stopped in front of Ward's desk. As she stood in the sea of blue, she waited for him to acknowledge her so she could make her report. The president looked at her with a drained and concerned expression and sat down. From the forlorn look on his face, Ansala knew her worst fears were confirmed, this was no drill and it was going to be another long night.

Unknown to her and the rest of the population, a state of emergency had gone into effect shortly following Venture's attack on Cardinal Gregor. As much as Ward hated to admit it, Norton had been right when he said they needed the Guardians to handle the situation. The generations of Kerguelens succeeding those of the last Provincial Wars had become passive and docile, unable to handle and cope with tenacious foes in their midst. Standard departures from normative behavior such as burglary and the like could be handled by provincial or federal law enforcement, but heinous acts of violence like wanton destruction of property, assassinations, genocide and terrorism were beyond their capabilities. When those situations arose, the Guardians stepped in. And they all knew the only way to stop a Guardian on the rampage was with another Guardian.

"The TELCOM link with Guardian Central Command is ready, sir," Ansala said.

Ward nodded to her and she touched a key on her PDA. A large video screen on the far wall came to life with bright illumination. Ansala stepped away from the president's desk and took a seat. The chief technologist looked at Ansala and smiled.

"Good to see you again, Ansala. I hope you're well," Mackenzie said.

"I am. Thank you, Chief Technologist. The days are long, but all is well," Ansala said smiling back.

"I hope you will take me up on my offer when your civil service is over," Mackenzie said with a quick glance at Ward. "This can't be what you expected high-level work would be like when you graduated university."

"I haven't thought about that very much. My work here keeps me quite busy. However, I have been considering your offer carefully," said Ansala cautiously.

"Good. I'll have Reyes contact you. We need to have a meeting about a position... soon," Mackenzie said. She turned to Ward and smiled again. "Forgive me, Mr. President, I don't mean to poach your people."

"No offense taken," Ward said smiling and waving a hand.

He pretended that it didn't bother him but the fact was it did. The Technology Council was an alluring and upwardly mobile organization. It was the workplace of Kerguelen's best and brightest and no one in his or her right mind would decline a position in the Council, especially a job offered by the chief technologist personally. Ansala's days as an underpaid and under appreciated staff member of the chief executive were numbered anyway. Her obligated civil service would be complete within the month. Even if it wasn't, playing gopher to the president was no work for a person who graduated with honors with a degree in structural engineering. Even if he wanted to keep her, he had nothing substantial to offer her.

"Mr. President," Ansala said as figures appeared on the video screen. "Marshal Pace and Marshal Aca, Guardian Central Command, online, sir."

"Thank you, Ansala," Ward said. He spun his chair to face the wall screen and saw the images of a male and female Guardian in the standard day uniform. "Good evening, Marshals. I'm sorry to disturb you so late in the day, but we have a situation here."

There was a six-hour difference between them and it was now after five in the evening in the Northeastern Province where Guardian Central Command was located. However, both Guardians looked as fresh as they would if it were the morning.

"It's our job to be disturbed at inopportune moments, Mr. President," Marshal Pace said recalling in his mind the many times the Central Office had contacted him during his tenure as a member of Central Command. "How can the Guardians help you?"

"I need you to dispatch someone to arrest Cdr. Venture," Ward said.

Pace and Aca smiled simultaneously and gave each other a knowing look. Venture's abrasive nature was known to occasionally chafe the skin and bruise the ego of those in authority. The list of offenses against him was a mile long, and because of this, Central Command had arranged for him to be aide to Cardinal Gregor. It was their hope that the posting would smooth some of his rough edges. Venture would certainly be a member of Central Command in the future and he needed to be able to work with the leaders of the planet peacefully. The marshals wondered what he had done and whom he had pissed off this time.

"I'm sure we can handle this at the lowest levels without going to extremes, Mr. President," Pace said turning back to Ward.

"Obviously this *is* serious," Aca said frowning as she saw the distressing look on Ward's face. "Could you tell us the particulars?"

"This is very serious," Ward said rubbing his forehead. "Did you send the marshals the video, Ansala?"

"Yes, sir, they have it," Ansala said. "But they haven't had time to review it yet."

"What video?" Aca asked as an administrative aide came into view and whispered inaudibly to the Guardians. Aca nodded and waved him away. "Excuse me, President Ward, have you placed the planet in Threat Level 3?"

"Yes, I have and you'll understand the reason for that when you review the video my aide has provided you," Ward said.

The Kerguelen government had three levels of national emergency. Threat Level 3 was the most critical and had only been set once. Just a few years ago, a wayward asteroid was threatening the planet. It had fallen into Kerguelen's gravity field and was due to collide with the planet. Only a lucky gambit, offered by Mackenzie, had averted total disaster. Her foresight, a brilliant plan and decisive action during the crisis had led to Mackenzie being selected as the current chief technologist. With the destruction of their entire civilization as a measuring stick for setting Threat Level 3, it was hard for Aca to believe the actions of a single person, Guardian or not, could cause an equal level of distress.

Pace and Aca asked for the video to be played for them and they watched it intensely four times before they had it shut off. There was no audio, but the video clearly showed Venture killing Centurion Sali, shooting the other Guardians and finally, shooting Cardinal Gregor, severing his right arm from his body with a surgically aimed blast. They were at a loss for words as they faced the president again.

"As you can see, Marshals, this is not just some trivial complaint," Ward said.

"Yes, this is quite serious," Pace said.

"Cdr. Venture is believed to be responsible for sedition and the illegal detention of citizens," Ward said.

"Hmm," Aca said thoughtfully. "And this video is genuine?" She saw the surprise on Ward's face and understood that he was not used to being questioned. "Forgive me, Mr. President, but the question needed to be asked because others will ask us the same question."

"Of course, Marshal Aca, I understand," said Ward as he turned to Norton.

"It has been verified as authentic, though a portion of it was corrupted. The technicians at Cathedral Prime tell me that Venture probably tried to erase or destroy the video and in his haste to flee and avoid apprehension, was not completely successful," Norton explained.

Pace and Aca looked at each other briefly without saying a word and then turned back to Ward. It did not make sense that Venture would commit such crimes, but if the administration had proof, they had to go along with it until they could investigate on their own. One thing was for sure. It was highly unlikely that Venture would take the time to destroy the video if his chances for capture were imminent. And if he had, he would have ensured that the video was completely destroyed before leaving. However, they kept those thoughts unsaid. Ward and the others would not understand that Guardians are conditioned not to panic and did not react to stress the way "normal" people did. This situation would need to be investigated fully and dispassionately. The reputation of the entire Guardian Corps was at stake and they had to be careful of the disposition of the crisis.

"Who else knows about this... event?" Pace asked.

"A few priests at Cathedral Prime, the doctors attending to Cardinal Gregor and my senior staff only. As far as anyone else is concerned, we're going to release a statement that we are holding an emergency training exercise of extended length," Ward said.

"Good, you should take strides to maintain that façade and stand down as soon as practicable," said Aca nodding affirmatively. "We will contact the families of Centurion Sali and the others. Be assured that the First Battalion will not be adversely affected by this."

"Yes, I would think you'd want time to put the appropriate spin on this," Norton said.

"Guardians don't spin the truth. We only have limited information on this incident. We won't give a full account until we do," Pace replied holding his anger in check. The insinuation that Guardians would lie about the true cause of the death of their men nearly caused him to dig into the chief of staff. Aca, however, was not as tactful.

"Unlike the press or politicians, Guardians refuse to act or comment on situations solely based on innuendo, half-truths, rumors and knee jerk reactions. It may give the impression we hide the truth, but it serves to make the first statement we make, the one and only one we have to make," Aca said.

"I'm sorry if I inferred anything else," Norton apologized.

"How is the Cardinal?" Pace asked.

"He is resting comfortably. He will be on his feet in a day or so. The doctors applauded Venture's marksmanship. Despite the pain, the wound was perfectly clean. One of them told me he should have been a laser surgeon," Ward said. "Where is Garath? We need immediate action on this."

"Marshal Garath is attending to other matters away from Central Command at the moment. I'm sure he'll return post haste when we inform him of this," Aca said.

Marshal Garath was supreme commander of the Guardian Corps. As the senior officer, he was leader of Central Command and had a unique rapport with the president. He seldom left the confines of Central Command headquarters and he was conspicuous by his absence.

"We're able to put units into action with all his authority," Pace said reassuringly.

Marshal Pace was the chief of staff and Marshal Aca was operations officer of Central Command and Ward knew they had Garath's full confidence. They had acted decisively in other situations in the past when the supreme commander was absent, and Ward trusted their judgment. However, he had ideas of his own.

"I would like Cdr. Jordan to be assigned to this," Ward said.

"I'm afraid that won't be possible," Pace said. "She is... unavailable."

Pace didn't like to lie, but the truth was, Jordan was missing in action. She had not been heard from since going out on a mission in the Southwestern Province over a week ago and was presumed dead. But without a body, they couldn't confirm it. Garath was coordinating a search for her with Commander Giles, commander of the Second Battalion.

"What about Cdr. Giles? I'm sure he would be suitable," Norton offered. "He's an experienced Guardian with an excellent record."

"Cdr. Giles is with Marshal Garath. I'm afraid it would be impossible for him to break away from his present assignment," Aca said shaking her head.

"What about the officer most recently promoted to commander," Norton said. "His name is Mohab, if I'm not mistaken."

"This does not fall into his area of expertise," Pace said.

"Really? I thought that Guardian commanders were well-versed in all areas," Norton said.

"Cdr. Mohab is a very capable officer, but he is a naval operations, heavy weapons and armor specialist. He could handle this, however, he would not be our first choice. In fact, none of your suggestions would be our first option for something like this," Aca replied.

"Well, with Centurion Sali dead and the other commanders unavailable, who could do this job?" Ward asked.

"All of your suggestions are good, but I believe there is only one Guardian... only one person on Kerguelen... suitably qualified for a mission like this," Mackenzie offered as she stood and walked over to the small bar. She poured herself a glass of water and took a long swallow before she continued. "That would be Cdr. Prior." She took another drink and when she emptied the glass, she sat it down.

"No way, absolutely not," Norton interjected. He turned to Ward and continued. "Mr. President, you can't approve her for this."

"Why? Because she's Boroni?" Mackenzie asked leaning against the bar.

"Cdr. Prior? Ah, yes, the Boroni commander," Ward said. "She's the daughter of former Senator Pitor, isn't she?"

"Yes. She's *that* Cdr. Prior," Norton said sounding almost disgusted.

"She's good, Norton, and you know it," Mackenzie said.

"I can't deny she's been successful… in her own way," Norton reluctantly agreed. "But that doesn't mean she's right for this."

"No matter how far we've come as a culture, the old prejudices still remain," said Mackenzie shaking her head.

Mackenzie knew that Norton was from the Central Province and the Central Province held the people of the Western Province in slavery for nearly a thousand years. A slave revolt, led by Prior's great-grandfather, finally ended their occupation. Though over a century had passed, the Boroni were still considered fourth class by the Central Province and other parts of Kerguelen. No one would ever admit it, but there was still much bitterness in the Central Province over the loss of the slaves and dominance in the Western Province. The bitterness was primarily centered on the loss of great sums of money now in the hands of the Boroni and the power associated with it.

"This has nothing to do with prejudice," Norton said. "They just don't see things the way everyone else does. It's nothing against them, it's just who and what they are."

"The Boroni are an isolated and insular people," Ward agreed.

"This has nothing to do with a person's background. It's about who is best for this situation, and Boroni or not, I believe Cdr. Prior is best suited for the task," Mackenzie said.

Ansala was amazed at the emotion Mackenzie and Norton were displaying. It appeared that Mackenzie was pressing, though she didn't know why.

"We're all aware of your liberal attitude toward the Boroni, Madam Technologist, but we're in a serious crisis. One of our leading planetary citizens has been assaulted, and I don't believe we should leave the apprehension of the assailant in the hands of a person belonging to an isolationist race," Norton strongly averred.

"Then, thank goodness that decision doesn't lie in *your* hands," Mackenzie said.

"No, it lies in mine," Ward said staring at Mackenzie. Though she was powerful and had saved the planet from destruction, the chief technologist sometimes forgot she was not the chief administrator.

"The decision lies with us," Pace corrected as all heads turned to the screen.

They all forgot that the Guardians were not part of the government. They could decline to assist the government or act independently. The Guardians were completely autonomous which gave them the latitude to act against any and all that threatened the people of Kerguelen, whether that threat came from terrorists, disgruntled citizens or elected officials.

Ward cleared his throat in response to the correction. "You seem to know a lot about Cdr. Prior. Why is that, Mackenzie?" he asked.

"She received her doctorate from the Institute of Technology. I was assigned as her thesis advisor," Mackenzie said with a bit of motherly pride in her voice.

"I see," Ward said. "Marshals, is Cdr. Prior your choice for this?"

"She is," Pace said nodding.

"Do you have a dossier on her? I'd like to know what makes her a better choice than the others," Ward said.

"I thought you might," Pace said. He spoke inaudibly to aide briefly and then turned back to Ward. "It's on the way."

Ansala's PDA vibrated in her hand and she tapped on it. Another wall screen came to life and on it was the personal file of Guardian Commander Prior. Ansala shifted in her seat as she and the others intensely read the provided information. Surprisingly to all, the dossier was very detailed.

A 3-D image of Prior rotated in a clockwise pattern on one side of the screen. She was thirty-three years of age but looked much younger. Prior's sparkling brown eyes were full of life and her deeply tanned face was quite attractive. Her chestnut brown hair was long and braided and reached her buttocks. It was obvious that she was in top physical condition. The standard Guardian uniform could not mask the powerful stature and physique her six-foot one inch, 165-pound frame possessed. On the other side of the screen, her Guardian service record and biographical data was listed. It was an interesting read from the start.

Prior was born in the Fertile Valley area of the Western Province to Pitor and Keira. She was the first-born identical twin and eldest of five children. Her twin brother, Poul, was currently the junior senator from their province in the planetary legislature. The third child, Pierce, was a farmer and head of operations for the Western Province Grange. The Grange was the largest privately owned company on Kerguelen and its planetary operations produced over forty percent of Kerguelen's food supplies. The fourth sibling was Pell and he managed the family's mining interests. The youngest was named Pike. A former member of the International Aid Organization, he had died while on assignment, a victim of a horrendous terrorist act.

Prior herself was the first Boroni accepted to the Guardian Academy. Graduating second in her class, she earned dual undergraduate degrees in civil engineering and philosophy, and currently held a doctorate in applied engineering applications. The list of her duty assignments had placed her in all four of the Guardian battalions at one point or another during the early portions of her fifteen-year career. For the past five years, she had served as the Guardian Regimental Officer-In-Charge of Construction, or ROICC, and Chief Surveyor. As such, she oversaw and was responsible for all Guardian field engineering and support services. But the constant transfers of her early years were not normal. A fact overlooked by the others but not lost on Norton.

"It seems as though the commander has been everywhere. I didn't know that was standard Guardian practice, Marshal Pace?" the president's chief of staff said. "I thought Guardians stayed in the battalion they are initially assigned to."

"That's correct, but Cdr. Prior is a combat engineering officer, and there are very few such specialists in the Guardians. Their unique skill sets are vital for the battalions to function effectively. The commander was one of three engineer officers in the service at one point. That's why the commander appears gypsy-like," Pace explained as Norton nodded and continued to scan the record.

There was no doubt that she possessed unique qualifications. Besides being a Guardian, Commander Prior was a registered professional engineer, and a registered professional surveyor and mapper. Her Guardian specialties were numerous including demolitions, underwater construction techniques, strategic and tactical unconventional warfare and psychological operations, and was fluent in the regional dialects of four different provinces. And that made her a vital commodity in the global span of Guardian field operations.

All of her individual work had resulted in an impressive combat record that placed her in twenty-six major and six minor engagements. She was credited with 281 confirmed kills and another 127 probable kills. Prior had been awarded thirty-four decorations, including the Cross of Freedom and the planet's most prestigious award, The Star of Kerguelen. She had also been awarded several non-Guardian awards including the Kerguelen Geographical Society's Gold Medal for her surveying work in the arctic regions of the planet.

"She won the Star of Kerguelen?" Ansala gasped.

"Yes," Aca said.

There had been only fourteen recipients of the Star of Kerguelen, and the gap between Prior and the previous award recipient had been seventy years and she was the last to receive the award. It was obvious to all that she had performed a tremendous act of bravery and self-sacrifice. And the fact that a Boroni had received Kerguelen's highest honor doubly reinforced that she had shown unparalleled courage.

"She's the best the Guardians have hands down. Present company accepted," said Mackenzie nodding to Pace and Aca. They nodded back and she stepped into the center of the room. "She graduated second in her class at the academy despite the fact she was ostracized for the first two years she was there."

"Ostracized?" Ward said. "I wasn't aware that hazing still occurred at the Guardian Academy. I thought it had been completely abolished twenty-five years ago."

"Her time at the academy is a period we're not very proud of," Pace said with a grimace.

"No one spoke to her for two years," Mackenzie continued. "No social interaction of any kind. She was only spoken to for military and academic reasons. For all practical purposes, she was alone in a crowd. We all attended university here. In those first two years, and longer for some, the adjustment of being away from home can be traumatic. Especially for a twelve-year old girl."

With few exceptions, the planet's population started their advanced education at the age of twelve and was completed with their undergraduate studies or technical skills training at eighteen. For professional degrees such as engineering and the sciences, an additional one or two years was required. The fact that Prior had successfully completed engineering studies at the Guardian Academy in six years under stressful conditions was a testament of her character, emotional stability and determination. The significance was not lost on Ward. Acclimating to the rigors of university life had been a hard adjustment for him.

The final pieces of Prior's profile were equally eye catching. She was the author of the infamous book, *'6/10ths – The Biography of Kel and the History of the Western Province Revolution'*. Additionally, she had refused to accept monetary compensation for her duty as a Guardian and had repaid the cost of her education at the academy. The most telling factoid was that she had attained the rank of Commander in ten years, which was faster than anyone in Guardian history.

When he finished, Ward leaned back in his chair and thought for a moment. He was familiar with the exploits of Commanders Jordan, Giles and Venture and knew first hand the level of leadership Garath, Aca and Pace possessed, but somehow Ward felt Commander Prior was something more. She was both thoroughly versed in the ways of a warrior and at the same time possessed advanced education credentials. Through it all, she had maintained her anonymity and had kept herself under the radar. He was ashamed that he didn't know more about her. He still didn't know much, but this two-page document had told volumes. It was certainly the most personal information he had ever seen concerning a Boroni.

"Well, what do you think, sir?" Norton asked noticing that Ward had finished reviewing the dossier.

"She seems to have impressed the Guardians. Truly an amazing resume," Ward said.

"And pedigree," Mackenzie said.

"The woman is amazing. Her book was fantastic," Ansala blurted out.

She bowed her head in silence when she saw Ward and Norton staring at her as if she had two heads. She realized she had overstepped her bounds by talking out of turn and declaring that she had read Prior's book. It definitely would not sit well with the chief of staff.

Prior's book was a fiery assault on the millennium long institution of slavery in the Western Province. It also blasted the entire population of Kerguelen during those times, including the Guardians, who condoned the practice and allowed it to continue. In addition, the book also described, in detail, the trials and tribulations of the slaves and to what lengths they had to go through to obtain their eventual freedom and equality. Though no one ever truly claimed to have read it, the book was internationally acclaimed and was a best seller, with over fifteen million copies downloaded planet wide.

"Yes, she has the makings of a true heroine," Mackenzie said.

"A true heroine or a serious lunatic, take your pick," Norton offered. "Her great-grandfather led the revolt that ultimately ended slavery and drove the masters out of the province. Her paternal great-aunt, Paige, is the present governor general of the Western Province and she led the Boroni when they repelled an attempt by the Central Province to retake the area years after the slave revolt. Her father was the first senator from the province. I believe you served with him in the legislature, didn't you, Mr. President?"

"Yes, I did. His was the lead voice for planetary justice and civil rights. He was a great orator and his death was a greater loss. His assassination was tragic and stunned us all," Ward said recalling his one-time colleague. "And she earned the Star of Kerguelen?"

"Yes. At the Battle of Domtar," Aca said.

"A bad day for all concerned," added Mackenzie.

"The Guardians assigned to that mission were attacked by a force three times their size, if I recall correctly," Norton said. "They suffered sixty percent casualties in that battle."

"Closer to eighty percent," Aca said.

"And still won the day," Ward said. "Well, I must say your dossier is very thorough. Are all Guardian bios this detailed?"

"It's the latest update. We like to… keep track of our officers," Pace said with a smile.

"And she doesn't receive pay?" Ward queried.

"That's correct, but she is not the only officer who does so," Aca said. "Cdr. Mohab and a few others also refuse to accept pay."

"That's not much of a concession for her," said Norton dismissing the act. "Her book earned her millions of credits and the Star of Kerguelen comes with a million credit payment and a lifetime tax-free exemption. To top it off, she is head of her family now that her mother and father are deceased, and is the sole owner of her family's property and holdings. It's estimated at over ten billion credits. She's also inline to take over the holdings of her father's family when Governor General Paige dies. If that occurs, she'll be the richest person on Kerguelen, hands down."

"You have a nice nest egg, Norton, but you still receive government pay," Mackenzie said. "And you don't have people shooting at you."

"That's enough," Ward said. He stood up from his desk and walked in front of the screen and addressed the Guardians. "Marshal Pace, are you sure she is really the one we need for this? Her record is impressive, but I tend to agree with my chief of staff. The Boroni are wild cards."

"That's the problem with non-Guardians," Aca said. "You see Prior as a Boroni, we see her as a Guardian commander. What I think of you has nothing to do with the fact that your ancestors were slaveholders, just as my opinion of Prior has nothing to do with the fact that her ancestors were slaves. A person's character is not come from the womb."

Ward bowed his head. There was no arguing with that. He raised his head and looked at Aca.

"How is she in this kind of crisis?" Ward asked.

"Prior is extremely swift in her... deliberations," Aca offered. "Though we don't like to be involved in this type of work, she is arguably the best suited for it."

"What has she specifically handled?" Norton asked.

"The Northern Province utility workers' strike, the anti-terrorist raid at Emerson Airport, the apprehension of WMD arms dealer Duncan... there are others, but I think that should give you a good idea," Pace said.

"And of course the Domtar situation," Aca added.

"I didn't realize *one* Guardian was responsible for all of those missions," Ward said.

"She's a very special operative and for security reasons the names of Guardians involved in various operations is routinely kept on a need-to-know basis," Aca explained.

"But what do you know about the woman? What more can you tell me?" Ward asked the Guardians.

"We often speak about a person possessing the "intangibles", and they are usually considered exceptional and rare. These persons have the ability to inspire cowards to bravado and the mediocre to greatness. We want all our leaders to aspire to such heights. Some do and some don't and that is the difference between officers who are just in charge of their units and those who truly command. There is a distinct difference between mere posturing and true inspiration. Prior is that difference. She's one-of-a-kind. She's the living intangible," Pace said.

"Obviously you think quite highly of Cdr. Prior," Ward said.

"I do. I've known her since she was a plebe at the academy," Pace said.

"Would you trust her with your life?" Ward said asking the ultimate question.

"Cdr. Prior has saved my life on two separate occasions, so I would say the answer to that is, yes," Pace said.

"I see," Ward nodded. "Marshal Aca, what do you say? Why do we hear so much about Commanders Jordan and Giles and so little about Prior?"

"I believe a phrase from the ancient language describes Prior. Acta non verba," Aca said.

Actions speak louder than words. Everyone in the Central Office nodded in comprehension of the phrase.

"Will she take the assignment?" Norton asked.

"If asked, she'll undertake the assignment. Prior has never failed to accept a mission," Pace said.

"How soon can she begin?" Ward asked.

"Immediately I would think," Aca said. "She just finished a... field training exercise last night. I'm sure we can spirit her away from whatever she's currently doing."

4

The Guardian Academy, The Palisades, Central Province, Planet Kerguelen

The Palisades region of the Central Province had the best weather on Kerguelen during the last few weeks before the season of Harvest began. Though she did not have fond memories of her treatment here, Prior relished the landscape upon which the Guardian Academy was built. The cool lands located just below the low ranging mountains that spanned the northern section of the province, were spectacular, especially now as the sun reached its apex.

She was familiar with every corner of the grounds and her initial isolation afforded her the chance to explore every nook of the campus unhindered. The openness and moderate weather helped her retain a measure of sanity during that tumultuous time in her life. Nature was her true companion during that friendless and lonely era of her early teen years.

In the fifteen years since her graduation, companionship had not been a concern. Compared to her peers, Prior was a throwback to the age of sword and chain mail armor. According to regulations, as an officer, she was entitled to have three personal aides, and she did. Though they were not officially Guardians, her attendants held the appropriate rank for personnel in their positions. All three were Boroni as she was and as part of her combat team, they were ever present, but at this moment, Prior was alone.

Her attendants were close by, enjoying the climate and grounds in ways of their own. They needed a chance to relax as much as she did. Sergeant Major Pana, her senior aide; Master Sergeant Rex, her tactical assistant; and Captain Micah, her pilot, had been going full tilt right by her side for weeks now and even the seemingly inexhaustible endurance of a Boroni had to be recharged every now and then. The other members of her team, Captain Hiroki and First Lieutenant Lindsey, were off as well. No doubt in pursuit of the ever-elusive ideal girl. It was certain that Hiroki was placing the pair in an environment that exaggerated his prowess with the unsuspecting females of Capitol City.

She sat on a hillside overlooking the track and field arena and observed a small cadet detail practicing close order drill on the inner pitch. As she lay back on the soft grass of the knoll, she could see that the cadets were being put through their paces by a upper classman and by his posture, she could tell that the younger cadets were not close to performing at the level he expected. Prior chuckled at the sight. Some things never changed. At her feet, her dog Lupo sniffed the air and she smiled as he snapped at insects that foolishly flew into the range of his large mouth.

Normally, Prior would not have come to the academy during her time off, but she was long overdue for putting in an appearance at the Surveyor's Basic School. The six-month long school taught officers and enlisted personnel in the combat engineering field the art and science of field engineering prior to their assignment to one of the four Guardian battalions.

Thorough knowledge of algebra, basic calculus, geometry, trigonometry, and physics was needed in order to be a proficient surveyor. The ability to use and maintain the delicate instruments of the discipline with accuracy and precision was also required. Surveying, map reading and cartography, celestial navigation, demolitions and battlefield construction equipment and techniques, reconnaissance, tracking, surveillance, small unit and individual tactics, and field medical training was also included in the course of study for the entry-level engineers. In addition, the students were required to learn the laws applicable to surveying and construction in order to earn a rating as a professional surveyor.

Because of it's tremendous mental and physical requirements, the school drop out rate was the highest in the Corps, but in order for the fledgling men and women to properly support the units they would be assigned to, and most importantly survive the rigors of life as a combat engineer, they needed to be the best. And the curriculum standards ensured they were.

Upon completion of the Basic School, the Guardians earned the designation 'Surveyor' and though they were not considered to be regular Guardians, the graduates wore their badge of office with pride. A circular Kelly green patch, superimposed with a theodolite sitting atop of a tripod in black was their insignia. The motto, "Innovate, Adapt and Overcome", was stitched on the bottom in yellow. Worn on the right shoulder, the patch was the only marking permitted on that side of a Guardian's uniform.

Despite the second-class status of their discipline, the placement of the branch's symbol set them apart from other Guardians and gave them an unequalled esprit de corps. When Prior assumed total control of the branch when she was promoted to colonel, engineers that normally would have left the Guardians for lucrative civilian careers, reenlisted for second and third tours of duty. The ranks of the engineers had grown to a level that allowed each battalion to have at least one, and in some cases, two seven-man squads assigned to them. They were no longer transient personnel and highly competent. The Surveyors had proven how vital they were time and time again and though still considered second-class Guardians, every battalion commander respected them and knew his or her success was due in no small measure to the performance of Prior's surveyors.

Occasionally, a student exhibited extraordinary ability and aptitude. Those unique individuals were selected for an additional six months of training and became part of Prior's special operations teams. Currently she had four five-person teams, with a fifth conducting special assignments. A sixth team, the Orbital/Space Operations Team, conducted covert security monitoring in orbit onboard Space Command's largest orbital facility. But she was always on the lookout for new personnel. Special operations inherently lost members due to accidents and the occasional battle casualty. The loss of one of her team members had forced Prior to bring Lindsey onboard early, but she was sure the young lieutenant would make the grade. There were no other outstanding students currently enrolled, but it did the students good to see the legendary surveyor, Commander Prior, in the flesh.

After a brief administration inspection of the school, she had meandered into a classroom to observe instruction. The class she sat in on was discussing the difficulties of field operations and the instructor,

Corporal Elias, had their full attention as she slipped in unnoticed. Any other instructor would have stopped and acknowledged her presence, but Elias was a hard case. He disliked officers and wasn't thrilled over his assignment to the Basic School as an instructor.

Elias was a good surveyor but he was also a drunk. Prior had posted him as an instructor hoping that a few months at the school would dry him out. But she also needed someone like Elias here. He was an experienced field operative and was one her best men. And the young Guardians needed a practical instructor, someone who would give them the blunt facts about the job, not candy coat it. Prior had listened intently to his lecture.

"Remember," Elias had said in his heavily accented Lower-Central Province voice. He almost sounded angry as he spoke. "You've got to maintain your physical prowess as much as you need to stay proficient in the tools of the trade. There are no short cuts around the gym."

A hand shot up and a young officer stood. "But with so many different drugs and supplements we can use to enhance our physiques, why allot so much time to working out?" he asked.

Elias sighed and then smiled. "No," he said shaking his head. "There are no miracle drugs or magic elixirs you can take that aren't illegal for our consumption. The Technology Council creates all of them, and every time a pharmacist creates a drug, another one comes up with a reagent to test for it. It's a game for them. If you want to take enhancement drugs, become a professional athlete. They have no place in the Guardian Corps, and if you're caught using them, you'll be expelled from the Corps and face a possible jail sentence... at the very least."

"But..." the officer began to argue.

"Trust me, Lieutenant," Elias interrupted, "If there was a juice we could drink to mask any drugs we've taken, we wouldn't be wasting our time discussing engineering, we'd be getting high right now!"

The class erupted into a roar of laughter as the embarrassed second lieutenant slowly sank back down into his seat. Elias leaned on the desk behind him and folded his arms. He waited for the laughing and chuckling to subside and then continued.

"Look, even if drugs weren't illegal for us to take, I wouldn't do it," he said turning severe. "We need to be able to operate anywhere and at anytime and free of outside influences. Relying on drugs to maintain your strength is too much of a risk in our line of work. There are enough problems without worrying if your super pill has worn off." He clapped his hands together and walked around his desk. "Okay, since we've been talking about keeping up our strength, tomorrow we'll take a field trip. I think an eighteen-mile excursion with full gear is in order. We'll see what kind of shape you're in."

As groans and frowns replaced laughter and smiles, Prior had slipped out of the classroom, satisfied that she had made the correct choice in placing Elias at the school. She had wandered off alone after that and her aides gave her the space she obviously wanted. As she lay back in the grass, she closed her eyes and basked in the rays of the Kerguelen yellow sun and let her thoughts drift to unimportant matters. It had been a long time since she had really cut loose from her responsibilities and decided that she would have some fun during her time off. There was no sense in having a lot of money and not enjoy it. When they returned to Capitol City, she would wrap up any business quickly and then it was party time.

Her eyes snapped open when her TELCOM sounded. She didn't want to answer it though and planned to let it chirp away until the caller got tired and hung up. But the caller was persistent and the chirping continued. Lupo began to nuzzle at her belt pouch where the device was located and she sighed rolling off of her back and leaning on her left side as she took it out. She looked at the thin caller ID readout and frowned. It was Guardian Central Command calling, and that probably meant her brief vacation was over. Prior placed the device in her ear and tapped a button on it. A thin arm swung out from the device and a monocle fell into place in front of her eye. She tapped another button and answered the call.

"Commander Prior," she said.

"Commander, sorry to disturb you on your leave, but we have a situation," Marshal Pace said.

Wasn't there always a situation? She could see Pace and Aca in the monocle and sat up and crossed her legs.

"What's happened?" she asked.

"The president has issued an arrest warrant for Cdr. Venture," Aca said.

"Surely not," Prior said almost laughing in disbelief. "You can't be serious."

"I'm afraid so, Commander. You've been selected with the task of apprehending him. Anything else you've got going on takes a back seat," Aca said. Though she was getting older, she was far from matronly and Prior was glad someone like her was coordinating Central Command activities. "This has the utmost priority."

"The President and the Congress of Cardinals signed off on my selection for this tasking?" Prior asked. She knew what people thought of the Boroni and was very surprised that the powers of the planet approved her for what was sure to be a high profile assignment. "What's the matter with Jordan? Is she too busy with another photo shoot?"

"We chose you, Commander," Pace said sounding a little agitated. "The whereabouts of your fellow commanders is none of your business."

"I see," Prior said. "I've volunteered... wholeheartedly."

Pace ignored her quip. "As usual, you have full autonomy on this... and if you get in a jam for going off of the play chart..."

"I'm on my own... as usual," Prior said. The activities of her special units were not officially sanctioned by Central Command, and were in actuality illegal. Only Marshals Garath, Pace and Aca knew they even existed. "I'll have a team start a preliminary investigation right away."

"This is intended to be low key, Commander," Pace said. "Minimal exposure."

"I'm going to need at least one other team besides my own for this," Prior said. "If you want me to do it, that is."

"Very well, but no more than that. We've sent all of the intelligence on this to your PIL account. It's embedded in a Spam message with the usual encoding. Your true tasking is to be off of the books," Pace said looking closely at her.

She understood what that meant. The apprehension of Venture was in reality a kill order.

"I understand," Prior said.

"Good," Pace said. "I know this is a hard thing for you, Commander. I know that you two are close."

"Not as close as we once were, but yes, I never thought I'd be asked to do something like this," Prior said. She paused for a moment and

continued in a softer voice. "I have no problems with the assignment, but I do have one concern."

"You're worried about going up against Venture, that's understandable. I would have reservations about that as well," Pace said.

"It's not fear that concerns me, Marshal," Prior said feeling a bit insulted. "I have no fear of any Kerguelen. It's what the man represents that gives me pause. Philosophically, it's a difficult task for me. We Boroni are very devout, as you know."

"Yes, and I know that you two have known each other for a long time, but once you've seen what he's accused of, your concerns will disappear," Pace said empathically.

"Marshal," Prior said staring directly at him. "The mission is not difficult. Venture is a close friend and my regimental commander, but if he's committed a crime against the people, it's my duty to bring him to justice. If I have to kill him, then so be it. He's brought that upon himself. This is beyond that. This has to do with the Boroni regard for the clergy."

"What does that have to do with this?" Pace asked.

"I don't know if you're aware of this or not," Prior said calmly but with a hint of sorrow in her voice, "But Commander Venture is not just a Guardian. He's also a priest."

5

Oceanic Province, Planet Kerguelen

Commander Giles had been contemplating retirement for the past two years, but the idea had reached its zenith a few months ago while he was in the midst of the semi-annual, Ritual Trial of Endurance. Conducted at the Guardian Academy, the Trial's results determined an officer's physical fitness for command, based on their age and gender. Giles often mocked the grading scale because the scores needed for field command at forty years of age were basically the same as was required to receive a commission as an eighteen-year old academy graduate.

As he stomped through the mud drenched Confidence Course, he had no fear of failing the combat endurance exam. He knew he could get through it, but the experience had been trying. It took two days for him to fully recover and walk comfortably, and the ice baths he had to endure in the recuperation process were less than pleasant. While he was immersed in the ice, Giles reflected on his career and knew his time as a Guardian was at an end.

It had been some time since his unit, the Guardian Second Battalion, had been involved in any significant action. He had used his seniority, favors and excuses to avoid front line engagements. He had turned his Guardians into mop up troops and Commander Prior was so annoyed, she pulled her combat engineers out of his battalion for duty elsewhere. Trying to rationalize his decisions, he saw them as a way to keep the Guardians under his command safe. Protecting them was his duty, but underneath it all, he knew that was a lie. The only way to truly keep his troops safe was to put them on the line so they gained experience. Guardians died, that was the nature of their business. They could die just as easily in a rear guard or humanitarian operation as they could in an assault on a gun placement. It was time he stopped lying to himself.

Guardians sometimes dealt in deception, but never in self-deception. He would retire and pass the torch to his second-in-command. After twenty-two years as a Guardian, he might find the idleness of retirement hard to take at first, but he could no longer fool himself. He was done. When a former mentor of his, Colonel Justin, decided to retire, Giles had asked him why. Justin told him his body had made the decision for him. Giles now understood what Justin had meant. His own body had made up his mind for him as well.

Despite ducking out of combat over the past few years, Giles had racked up an impressive record. He had nothing left to prove. He only had one last mission: Find out what happened to Commander Jordan. He would hand the After Action Report to Marshal Garath with one hand, and his retirement request with the other.

Unfortunately, that wouldn't happen, fate had other plans for Commander Giles. He would not go out as he entered. There would be no trumpets or fanfare. No medals awarded for service rendered and no gifts given to make his retirement more enjoyable. He would not make a farewell speech to his battalion and give them his final salute as they passed-in-review for him for the last time and paraded for their new commander.

As the dark giant that had beaten him so mercilessly dragged off his limp body through the underbrush surrounding the beach where they had briefly battled, the tracks Giles' gnarled and twisted limbs made left the only evidence of their presence. As Commander Giles gasped his last breath, his dreams of a long and boring retirement disappeared, along with his life.

6

Commander Prior's apartment, The Spire, Capitol City, Central Province, Planet Kerguelen

Shortly after Prior ended her call with Marshal Pace, she called the team members that were with her and quickly departed the academy and headed for home. Micah got them back quickly and Prior instructed him to have the craft serviced. She wanted it ready to go for possible extended operations. As she exited the craft, Prior felt very much at ease. It was good to be home.

Most of the residences in Capitol City's downtown area lacked space and were not very functional as family units, or even single occupancy, for that matter. That's why most people who worked in the city lived outside of the bustling metropolis. Most Guardians who were stationed in and around Capitol City were not bonded with a mate, and the few who were maintained a permanent home far removed from their duty area and the urban chaos. It created a barrier between the professional and personal parts of their lives. Commander Prior, however, defied all conventions.

Though her command offices were a few miles south of the city, at the Guardian Tri-Rivers Facility, Prior's residence was in the center of the downtown district... and was far more expensive than it was worth. Living where she did cast an unfavorable light on Prior, but that was nothing new for her. It was not Guardian tradition to engage in extravagant displays of wealth and Prior's apartments were a flagrant and deliberate demonstration of how deep her pockets truly were. Her neighbors were some of the most affluent and influential citizens of Kerguelen, and she resided in a 7,000 square foot penthouse. It was the largest and most expensive home in the world-renown residential building called, The Spire.

The famous Kerguelen Spire was the tallest residential structure on the planet. Towering above the city over a quarter of a mile high, friends and enemies alike called her apartment 'The Perch', a place where she could look down upon the world and wonder what the little people were doing. At times, her apartment was above the clouds, giving it the illusion that it was otherworldly and not meant for mere mortals.

Prior did not mind the ribbing she took about it. She relished the resentment of her financial independence, for she was Boroni, born and raised in the Western Province, and a descendent of slaves. Her province was the last area of Kerguelen to receive the benefits of the Age of Advancements, but the one that made the most of them when they finally arrived. She and her family were among the wealthiest of Kerguelen and among the proudest and oldest families of the Western Province.

Her great-grandfather, Kel, led the mass rebellion of slaves who fought for their freedom in a bloody struggle against their Central Province masters. After three years of fighting, they expelled the enslavers from the huge island province. Ten years later, they received a formal emancipation from the planetary president and legislature. In addition, the planetary judiciary amended the Planetary Constitution prohibiting slavery and indentured servitude planet-wide. Though they were successful, securing liberty came at a high cost. Less than fifty thousand Boroni survived to see freedom.

After the rebellion, the former slaves formed communities led by Kel and his lieutenants and began the uphill struggle for equal planetary rights for the newly independent Western Province. The reconstruction was difficult but the transition was eased by the influx of vast sums of money and technological advances. The planet needed the mass quantities of food the fertile lands of the province could produce or the planet's population would slowly starve. The slave uprising ended two years before the end of the last Provincial Wars and the ability to scratch out even the most basic foodstuffs by the other provinces was nearly impossible due to the use of low-yield tactical nuclear weapons and biological agents during the global conflict. Unable to feed their people, the new leaders of the planet called on the Boroni for help and made the small population the most important persons on the planet.

In a single generation, the Western Province became the economic powerhouse of the planet, creating vast new fortunes.

The land given to Kel for his part in the rebellion was a vast tract covering nearly two hundred square miles, and included the tallest peak in the province, Mount Hesse. Though the area was filled with precious ores and minerals, most of it was non-arable land and unsuitable for raising crops of any kind. Due to advancements in land reclamation, the property was transformed into the largest farm on the planet. Years later, Prior's maternal grandfather, Kemper, divided seventy-five percent of the land into twenty-acre tracts, worked by tenant farmers and cattle ranchers. Another ten percent of the acreage was converted into meat processing and canning facilities, and the Western Province Grange was established. The Grange became the largest privately owned company on Kerguelen and gave Prior's family unsurpassed stature and the ancillary wealth that others achieved because of the Grange made Kemper an even larger household name than his father Kel and led to his appointment as the second Western Province Governor General. Prior's mother, Keira, continued the growth of the Grange planet-wide and expanded into mining, fishing and transportation endeavors.

Being the only female sibling, Prior was far different than her brothers. Though she loved the land of her birth, she had always yearned for excitement and adventure and the desire to be a Guardian was a natural extension of those traits. She had wanted to be a Guardian ever since she read about them when she was a young girl. She learned everything she could about them and on her eleventh birthday, the date when Kerguelen children begin to decide what career they wish to pursue, she told her parents she wanted to be a Guardian.

Convincing her family that she should be allowed to become a Guardian was difficult. Though Guardians had always fought for the rights of the people of Kerguelen, they had been prevented from interfering with the institution and affairs of slavery in the Western Province and never had a presence there. In fact, no Boroni had ever seen a Guardian unless they had traveled to another province. The Boroni were suspicious of the Guardians and Prior's family could not understand her fascination with them. Prior couldn't explain it either, but she was adamant and her parents yielded to her desires. However, the Guardians initially had no interest in Prior or any Boroni.

Most Kerguelens knew very little about the Boroni, and their self-imposed isolation did nothing to endear them to the rest of the planet. Though they freely gave the other provinces food in exchange for technology, no non-Boroni was permitted to live in the province. They would never allow themselves to become subjugated again.

What was known was that the Boroni, unlike the rest of the planet, maintained a matriarchal society with the males providing much of the early nurturing and upbringing of their children, a remnant trait of the people the Boroni were spawned from. The early history of those people is all but lost. Only the accounts of mariners and explorers shed any light on their lives before they became slaves.

Living on an island, isolated from the rest of the population of the planet by the largest body of water on Kerguelen, the Peconic Ocean, the original Western Province natives evolved much differently. Despite the huge physical stature of the males, early visitors were shocked by, but admired the kind nature of the fathers and how gently they played with and taught their children. They took note of how the children climbed all over them and how the men held up and effortlessly tossed the children into the air. Men and women shared the workload. Both sexes were hunters and gatherers. It seemed to be an idyllic society... ripe for the picking by an aggressive interloper.

Explorers from the Central Province saw a land rich in wild game, timber and minerals and the surrounding waters were teeming with seafood. They decided early on that if they natives did not give them the land's bounty by choice, they would take it by force.

It didn't take long for the natives to become slaves. They had no weapons outside of the spears and knives they used for hunting, but their strength had prompted the invaders to use excessive force to impart their will on them. Quickly subdued, they began their initial servitude. As time went on, precious minerals and ores were found in the mountains, but they were not easy to extract. The mines proved to be extremely hazardous, and tens of thousands of slaves died every year in the pursuit of the vast deposits of gold, silver, platinum, tin, copper, nickel, galena and bauxite.

After a few centuries, slave manpower was nearly exhausted. To keep the resources of the Western Province continuing to stream into the coffers of the Central Province, a solution had to be found. They could either hire outside hands to help in the mines and crop fields, which would take away from their profit margin, or they could make better slaves. The latter option was chosen.

Doctors and scientists had been experimenting with the genome of Kerguelens for many decades and believed that they could manipulate Kerguelen biology to produce an improved person. The initial experiments went badly and world governments outlawed such research. But Central Province scientists found a loophole: Slaves were not covered by the international law and the scientists continued their work secretly on the slaves, but time was running out. After centuries of physical abuse, unsafe mining practices, and quack medical procedures, the population of slaves had dipped to less than a hundred thousand. Then, a breakthrough happened.

Two hundred and eighty years ago, a Northeastern Province bio-technician named Dr. Boroni, created the XY-Plus quantum chromosome, implanted it into embryos and artificially fertilized them with hybrid sperm. He placed the eggs in a thousand female slaves and waited for the results. At first, Boroni thought he had failed like countless others before him. The women began giving birth in a mere three months to babies much heavier and larger than average. He believed something had gone wrong, but subsequent tests proved that the newborns were more alert and cognizant than normal babies. However, Boroni reserved judgment until they began to mature and grow. And grow they did.

The children were walking unaided in one month, forming complex sentences in six months and at the age of three years old had the manual dexterity of children three times their age. The children reached full maturity between the ages of ten and twelve... and they were strong. Thanks to Boroni's genetic manipulations, these new slaves had greater lung capacity, physical strength and their reflexes and senses were enhanced. Their skin and bones were three times stronger than normal and they had a heightened resistance to disease and infection. An unexpected side effect of his experiment was that both males and females were of equal strength. Boroni had done it! But to ensure he had truly succeeded, a final experiment had to be conducted and a question had to be answered: Could these new slaves reproduce and conceive children identical to them?

Boroni first tried to mate the new female slaves with old male slaves, but for some reason he was never able to ascertain, his creations would only become pregnant by mating with each other. Boroni isolated his one thousand and had them mate. Three months later, the slaves gave birth to children with their dominant traits, but were even more capable. Boroni had indeed created a new race of Kerguelens.

With short pregnancies, the females could produce three children a year. The children could be put to work at an early age and Boroni could replace the losses of slaves in a few decades. Once they went to work, they far out performed their inferior cousins. In a hundred and ten years, the original inhabitants of the Western Province were gone due to overwork and infighting with an invasive new species, the Boroni.

Though the doctor's initial genetic code was designed to limit their intelligence and aggressive nature, the slavers soon found that the succeeding generations of Boroni were quite bright and becoming increasingly unruly to their masters and captivity. But unfortunately, nothing could be done about this. Dr. Boroni was dead and his notes and research had been lost when his lab was destroyed in a mysterious explosion. And no one knew how to recreate his work. The Boroni unrest was culminated in the violent revolt of slaves led by Kel.

Regardless of her people's history, Prior wanted to be part of the world, and she felt that becoming a Guardian was the best way to do that. But many believed the Boroni were not intelligent enough to absorb the academic regimen of the academy, nor did they think the Boroni were able to comprehend the philosophical ideals and the commitment that was demanded of a Guardian. In addition, only fifty new cadets were admitted to the academy each year, and that meant the fifty most intelligent and physically fit twelve-year olds on the planet.

After an extensive battery of physical, mental and psychological exams, Prior received an appointment and was commissioned six years later as a second lieutenant having graduated second in a class of twenty-eight. Twenty-two of the original fifty who had entered with her, failed to make the mark along the way.

Over the past fifteen years, she was both despised and lauded within the Corps, and most of her accomplishments never saw the light of day. It would have been impossible for even the highly moral and enlightened Guardian Corps to admit that one of their best officers was

Boroni. Though highly decorated, Prior served in obscurity, watching her peers receive the planet's adoration. Her only consolation was that those who really mattered knew how great she was and how vital she was to the successes of the Guardian Corps.

The Boroni knew she was a successful Guardian and were proud of her accomplishments, but were most proud of what she had done as head of her family. As the eldest child, she became leader of her family upon the death of her parents. Her father had been assassinated while she was a cadet in the academy and her mother was murdered a few years after she graduated. Under normal circumstances, Prior would have returned home to take full control of her family's holdings, but she had no desire to immediately settle down in the Western Province.

She made arrangements for her brother, Pierce, and his mate, Quinn, to serve as proxy for her. Pierce handled the operations end of the Western Province Grange and Quinn was in charge of the financial and administrative part of the business while she was on assignments. Her brother, Pell, oversaw the mining operations. When she was not on missions, Prior saw to the day-to-day operations via video conferencing. It made for long days, but Prior was the eldest and it was her responsibility to ensure the family's holdings increased. And for the past twelve years, they had.

Under her control, the Western Province Grange catapulted from the thirteenth wealthiest company on Kerguelen to the fourth wealthiest. Prior's family currently owned or controlled over twelve hundred square miles of land planet-wide, including three hundred in the Western Province alone. Her shipping lines transported a large percentage of goods exchanged between provinces over the seas of Kerguelen and the company's ever-increasing mining activities ensured manufacturing continued on steadily.

When Prior arrived at her apartment after leaving the Guardian Academy, Quinn had greeted her with dozens of messages. Prior had told her that she would need to leave in a few hours, but would see anyone who was waiting for her. After she changed, she spent the next seven hours in conferences. It was now almost nine o'clock in the evening, and her current meeting was nearing an end.

As Prior sat in her study, she listened to the man sitting in front of her with feigned interest. His name was Cul and he was one of the two senators representing the Boroni in the planetary legislature; the other was her twin brother Poul. The fervor over denied access to information on the *San Mariner* expedition and the clamp down on personal freedoms had enraged the populace and they had demanded special elections. Prior was besieged by numerous politicians seeking her endorsements and in search of campaign financing. She knew it was only a matter of time before Cul would darken her doorstep and though she disliked the senator, she was looking forward to a meeting with him.

Though the mission she had been given was paramount, the team she had tasked with conducting the preliminary investigation would take a while to come to any conclusions. And she wouldn't start her own work until midnight. In the meantime, she could close out any outstanding business. Cul was the third senator she had met with this evening and Prior was becoming bored with their standard rhetoric.

Cul was once a political ally of her father and though her mother liked Cul, Prior had her own reasons for disliking him. He was not a terribly bad person, but he had a low tolerance for being truthful. This had caused him to lose much of his support base over the years. The Boroni despised lying and deception. They found it a wasteful and unnecessary expenditure of time and energy. They were taught to avoid lying at all costs. In their eyes, words were legal tender and lying was an act counterfeiting reality. Lying to achieve some advantage was a waste of time. Stating what you wanted was far simpler. Maneuvering through words only weakened one's position and eventually, all lies were uncovered. Because the Boroni were tight-lipped and reserved, their reticence often led to them to be characterized as rude. But they believed if you had nothing to say, be silent.

Because of Cul's untruthfulness, only an endorsement from Poul had managed to save his senate seat during the last election. This time he would need Prior to give him a leg up on the competition. An endorsement from the head of the powerful and influential House of Ahrens would be enough to sway the election in his favor. However, he was aware of Prior's animosity towards him. He just didn't know how deep it went or why.

"... And so, you can see how far a donation and statement from you would go in securing my re-election," Cul said ending his sales pitch with a toothy smile.

"I'm sure it would," Prior said smiling back at him and nodding in seeming agreement. "But I'm not going to give you any money or endorse you, Cul. I'm sorry."

"But... why?" Cul said not believing his ears. "Your family has always supported my campaigns. Your father and I were like brothers. Poul has never hesitated in giving his support and your mother was always extremely generous."

"You deceived my father and my mother wanted to sleep with you. And though my brother and I are spawned from the same sperm, he is a fool. In short, Cul, you can't deceive me, I have no desire to have sex with an overweight and over-the-hill philanderer, and I'm no fool. You'll have to find another source of easy income," Prior said still smiling at Cul. "You won't find it as a senator any longer."

"Y-You knew about your mother and me?" stammered Cul. Prior could see he was suddenly feeling uncomfortable.

"I've known from the beginning. I'm not a prude, Cul, and I understand that my mother and father were paired together in an arranged marriage. There was very little love between them. I managed to forgive my mother's infidelity to my father... after all, she gave birth to me... but unfortunately I can't overlook your dealings," Prior said. She stood up from behind her desk and walked over to Cul. "For instance, I know you had nothing to do with my father's assassination, but I also know you knew he was in danger but said nothing."

"Are you accusing me of collusion?" Cul asked.

"If I believed you were responsible in any way for my father's death, Cul, I would have killed you and your entire family years ago," Prior said smiling as she continued. "But I digress. We're here to discuss current events. I'm going to support Tobias in the election. Because I'm a Guardian, I can't vote, nor can I officially endorse any candidate, but as head of my house, I'm obligated to present my people with the best political options available to them, and that's Tobias."

"But..."

"You constantly interfere with bills that would support micro-loans to distressed areas of the planet. Those loans would bridge the gap between the social classes and provide a means for those people to support themselves," Prior said. "That's why I started the World Micro Credit bank. I finally realized that I have enough money and power to make politicians irrelevant."

"The Boroni never needed micro-loans and we've prospered," he argued.

"The Boroni had the benefit of land free of radiation and biological contamination, and that provided the ability for self-sustenance. The rest of the planet wasn't so lucky. The Southern and Eastern Provinces are still reeling from the effects despite our superb technological advancements. Only handouts are keeping those people afloat. And I've found that people don't want a handout, they want a hand up. And that's what micro-loans provide," Prior said as she leaned back against her desk. "But your voting record is only part of your problem, Cul, you've forgotten that politicians should be nonpartisan. Regardless of their ideology, a politician should put the good of all people before their own agendas. You've shifted from being a Centrist to Egalitarian, a far left Egalitarian. And the only thing worse than a staunch Conservative is a Liberal too far to the left."

"This is unbelievable," Cul said shaking his head. "I can't believe you're doing this to me. And you have the gall to lecture *me* on politics?"

"I'm talking about philosophy, Cul, not politics, though many find it difficult to separate the two. If you're looking for someone to blame, take a glance in the mirror. Your own actions have forced me to this end. Don't take it so hard, Cul. This was inevitable. If it wasn't me, it'd be someone else," Prior said with false empathy. "Don't make any plans for redecorating your office, you won't be there long."

"You're going to ruin me," Cul said.

"No, Cul, I'm going to gut you like a fish," Prior said leaning forward. "The mere sight of you makes me retch and want to return to the days when Boroni settled their differences with knives."

"You don't scare me, child. I'm well aware that you've killed nearly three hundred people, or is it more? How many is it anyway?" Cul said standing up.

"I don't know, old man, I only keep track of the ones I've missed," Prior said straightening up. "And that would be three... and I've never missed my mark this close." Her eyes narrowed and the intensity in them caused Cul to blink.

The door of her office opened and Pana stepped inside. She stared at the pair of Boroni looking as if they were about to square off and she cleared her throat and turned to Prior.

"Is there anything I can do for you?" she asked.

"Yes," Prior said continuing to stare at Cul. "You can remove this… person… from my home."

Cul was about to attempt a last effort to save face but thought better of it. Right now Prior was in the mood to kill him and he was sure she could do it and make it look like she was only protecting herself. Despite his bravado, Cul was afraid of Prior. She had proven her ability to fight as a youngster in the Western Province and all of the Boroni were well aware of her abilities. On top of that, he was sixty-seven years old and a lack of physical exertions had turned his body corpulent. Because of his genetic superiority, he was more than a match for any Kerguelen, but he was well past the age when Boroni reach their peak. Prior had seven years to go before she reached her peak and she was no delicate flower. Her youth and harridan-like demeanor made her able to hold her own against any Boroni… male or female. Cul decided wisely that discretion was the better part of valor and bowed slightly and followed Pana out of the apartment.

After showing Cul out, Pana returned to the study. She was surprised to find Prior staring into a full-length mirror in the corner of the room. Despite the frown on her face, her bad attitude seemed to have disappeared. Pana smiled and joined her.

Prior hated the fact that she was slightly shorter than the average Boroni female and always wondered why she had been cursed. Full-grown Boroni women were at least six feet two-inches tall and it was considered a bad omen to be "short". Prior overcompensated for that in the way that she dressed.

She was currently wearing a Boroni-styled silk sarong gown. Made of a single bolt of the finest cloth, it wrapped around her entire body in a way that left her arms, mid-section and most of her back bare, showcasing her highly developed biceps and washboard abs. Though it was form fitting, a small slit at her knees facilitated walking with ease. Prior's chestnut colored hair was combed straight back and reached past her buttocks and the earthen hues of the sarong made her deeply tanned skin appear even darker. Her pampered and well-manicured feet were bare and her topaz colored eyes seemed to flash as she gazed at her reflection.

"If you're done admiring yourself, you've still got things to do," Pana said. She was casually dressed in black leggings and mock turtleneck pullover. Her dark hair was glossy and shimmered in the room's lighting. Like all Boroni, male and female, her hair was long, reaching the small of her back and was intricately braided. She was thirty-two years old and she and Prior had grown up together. Their fathers were brothers and Pana was not only Prior's cousin, she was her best friend.

Prior nodded and returned to her desk and leaned back in her chair as Quinn entered the study. Quinn was Prior's executive assistant, chief financial officer and barrister. Prior teased Quinn by calling her an accountant with a law degree, but was glad Quinn was part of her family.

Quinn was thirty-six and a ruthless business executive and many of the Grange's newest acquisitions were due to her tenacity. She was six years senior to her mate, Prior's brother Pierce, but their relationship was strong and had produced five children, two boys and three girls, thus far. She possessed a solid physique and Quinn's hair and wardrobe was similar to Pana's, though her plaits were made up of simpler weaves. She handed Prior an electronic data tablet and Prior frowned as she read the screen.

"Is this for real?" Prior asked.

"I'm afraid so," Quinn nodded. "It seems that Carlisle's eldest daughter, Colvin, has eloped with St. Pierre."

"Damn," Prior said tossing the tablet to her desk.

Carlisle was head of Hermitage House, one of the oldest Boroni families. Like Prior, Carlisle could trace his lineage back to one of the original one thousand genetically engineered slaves. The Western Province Gold Coast region was run by Carlisle's house and their vineyards, fisheries and underwater mining concerns had provided them a huge fortune. Prior had entered into a joint mining venture with Carlisle and was considering another merger, but this event could very well jeopardize ongoing and any future dealings between the houses.

Colvin was the eldest of Carlisle's three daughters and had run off with St. Pierre, the son of one of Prior's tenant farmers and brother of Major St. Jacques, the second and last Boroni to attend the Guardian Academy. Boroni society was in many ways feudal-like, and the actions of tenants were the responsibility of the landlords. As head of her house, Prior was expected to address complaints lodged against her tenants and employees. And she could tell by the report, Carlisle was not enthused by the union his daughter had recently entered into. Prior could understand why he was so livid.

Arranged marriages were still commonplace but many young Boroni refuted the tradition and sought love matches instead. Such was the case of Colvin and St. Pierre. Obviously, he had impressed Colvin in some way. Boroni females did not run away with males unless they had shown an overt display of strength or bravado. As a female, Prior understood how such a display could evoke strong emotions. As head of a Boroni family, she knew why Carlisle would be upset.

"Carlisle says this is a problem for him," Quinn said.

"Don't all men have problems?" Pana offered.

Prior smiled. "Perpetually," she said.

"Carlisle claims St. Pierre has been known to have a vast array of females in his company and doesn't understand why he's sullied Colvin's reputation. He doesn't know why he's singled her out," Quinn said.

"*All men who avoid female society have gross tastes,*" Prior said quoting a famous poet.

"I don't think reciting the classics will satisfy Carlisle," Quinn said. "He believes the bonding was foolish and potentially damaging to the reputation of his house. He doesn't know what got into Colvin."

"I do," Prior said with a sigh. "Common sense was never a match for Cupid. But Colvin wasn't forced into this. Forcing a Boroni female to do anything she doesn't want to is extremely difficult, as Carlisle well knows."

"Colvin is notoriously stubborn and implacable when she sets her mind to something I'm told," Quinn said.

"What kind of dowry is Carlisle providing?" Prior asked.

Quinn scrolled down the data tablet and laughed. "He says he'll provide a goat for milk," she said.

"That cheap bastard," Pana said. "Such generosity should be carved on the side of Mount Hesse for all the Boroni to see."

"Yes, and children should be sent to Lake Connaught to spread flowers across the waters in his honor," Prior added. "No, that won't do. Tell him to provide them with ten acres of vines and five of trees and a house. I'll provide fifty head of cattle, twenty sheep, ten goats, five carrying milk and fifty thousand credits."

"Do you think he'll go for that?" Quinn asked.

"Yes, especially when he finds out that St. Pierre is one of four boys. Grandsons will be inevitable," Prior said. "Reply to Carlisle immediately and contact Pierce. Have him select the livestock and deliver them personally, with my compliments."

Quinn nodded and consulted her PDA. "There are three other items that we should talk about," she said with a smile. Prior looked up at her and Quinn's expression caused Prior to smile as well.

"Okay, what's up?" Prior asked.

"There are three lawyers in the foyer…" Quinn began.

"Okay," Prior said smiling wider.

"No, this isn't the beginning of a joke. There *are* three lawyers in the foyer and they are armed with court actions accusing you of murder," Quinn said.

"Oh," Prior said leaning back in her chair. "Whom do they represent?"

"The Association of Inalienable Rights and the Coalition for Peaceful Resolution," Quinn answered.

"Deal with them, Quinn," Prior said. "I don't have the patience to listen to another lawsuit."

"Are you sure? They say they have proof of your crimes."

"Every time you shoot someone, it's a crime, Quinn, even if they're evil and deserve it. At the very least, the Almighty is probably upset about it. I'm not above the law… not completely anyway," Prior said with a grin. "You should talk to them. Only lawyers should speak to other lawyers."

"Very well," Quinn said. She turned to Pana. "Could you have them wait for me?" Pana nodded and when she left, Quinn continued. "General Manufacturing doesn't like your plans concerning their bailout. They want to discuss an alternate proposal."

Prior shook her head. "No, tell them if they want the Grange to loan them money to keep them solvent, they'll do what I ask," she said.

"They claim that they're in danger of hostile takeover bids."

"I don't doubt it. The company is run so poorly it would be easy," Prior said. "A child could do it with their weekly allowance."

"What if they go to the government for the money?"

"If the Fed wanted to help them, they would have already," Prior said. "The President knows that it isn't the public's responsibility to keep private corporations alive, and he's not going to destroy what's left of his already weakened public support by pouring billions into failing corporations. They have no choice but to seek aid from other companies."

"They want the money, but they want to maintain control of what types of air ships they manufacture and how they manage their employees," Quinn replied.

"They've got to streamline operations and cut loose their dead weight. And I don't want to hear about the impact of unemployment on society. None of the employees at GM care about others out of work. Those workers will just have to shift to other jobs. There are other fields they can go into," Prior argued.

"But what if they can't maintain their level of comfort?" Quinn countered.

"GM has always bragged about how smart and skilled their workers are, now's the time to prove it," Prior said.

"They're not going to like it."

"GM can't compete with the other air ship companies, Quinn. Not in all areas anyway. They can't stay in business building items of lower quality and no one wants no matter how much money they have. If they concentrate on cargo carriers and mass transit vehicles, they'll recover and we'll get our money back," Prior said. "If they continue to resist, take our offer off of the table. I'm not going to hand a billion credits over to someone and not have a say on how they spend it."

"But they need money," Quinn said.

"Everyone needs money. That's why it was invented," Prior said. "And that's why they will do what I ask. If GM fails it will hurt the Kerguelen global economy but I won't shed a tear over their demise.

Their own practices are the reasons they're in trouble. Tell them they have forty-eight hours to ink the deal. After that, we walk."

Quinn nodded and scribbled on her PDA screen. "The last item concerns the Grange. A consortium has tried to buy huge tracts of your property and companies that support Grange interests. They were unsuccessful, but the actions have caused us to expend large amounts of capital."

"Do you know who heads this consortium, Quinn?" Prior asked.

"Yes," Quinn said handing her PDA to Prior. "I thought you would like to deal with this personally."

Prior looked at the screen and frowned. "Are you positive about this?" she asked.

"If I wasn't, I wouldn't have brought it to your attention," Quinn said.

Prior sighed. "I'll handle him. You take care of the rest of the names on this list. I don't care what it costs. We have to send a message to the business and financial community," Prior said.

"It'll be my pleasure," Quinn smiled as she took back her PDA. "Let me go and take care of those vultures outside."

Prior nodded. As Quinn left, Pana stepped back in.

"Well, what's next?" Pana asked.

"Contact the team," Prior said. "We're going out and they're coming with us. The clubs will be hopping tonight and there's someone I need to talk to."

"Which clubs?" Pana asked excitedly. She wanted to know so she could dress appropriately.

"I was thinking we could start at *First in Line*. Tell the team the dress code is casual attire… but no weapons," Prior said to her cousin. "Unfortunately, our leave is over. We have a mission."

"And that mission is?" Pana asked.

"To kill a friend, Pana," Prior said sadly. "To kill a friend."

7
The Technology Council Building, Capitol City, Central Province, Planet Kerguelen

Chief Technologist Mackenzie pressed a button on her desk and the blinds slowly closed blocking the view into her office from passersby. She reached behind her, retrieving a bottle from a shelf and poured its contents into a five-sided glass. When it was half full, she stopped pouring, set the bottle down and tapped on her keypad, causing the computer screen on her desk to come to life. She tapped a few more times on the keypad, picked up the glass and then leaned back in her chair. Thirty seconds elapsed before the image of an elderly, but still attractive man, appeared before her.

"Hello," the man said in a smooth and cultured voice that was much stronger than his appearance would have suggested. "I'm surprised to get a call from you... especially at this time of day."

Mackenzie looked at the digital chronometer on her wall and smiled. Though it was mid-evening in Capitol City, it was after three in the morning in the Northeastern Province where the elderly man was.

"Forgive me, I wasn't thinking," Mackenzie apologized.

"Hmm, that would be a first for you. What are you still doing at your office?"

"Drinking," Mackenzie said holding up the glass so he could see it.

"Anise whiskey is not conducive for maintaining productive work habits, Mackenzie," he warned. "What's the occasion?"

"We've got a serious problem."

"Something that you can't handle?"

"It's too late for me to do anything about it."

"Hmm. It must be a serious problem indeed. How can I help?"

"That's up to you," she said taking a large gulp of whiskey.

99

"Sounds mysterious. What's up?"

"You'll know about it soon enough, but I wanted you to hear about it first hand and have a confirmation on the report. Cardinal Gregor's been shot."

"Good. When did he die?" the man said cheerfully.

"He's not dead. A shot from a plasma energy pistol at close range cut off his arm... his right arm. Unfortunately, he's making a full and speedy recovery."

"That is unfortunate. Why would someone shoot him and not kill him? If they were as close as you say, they could have... and should have, finished the job."

"I was hoping you'd shed some light on that for me."

"Me? Wait... who shot him?" the man asked leaning forward.

"Venture."

The man blanched for a moment and then regained his composure. He looked at Mackenzie for a moment as she drank more of the strong liquid before he continued.

"I'll get back to you," he said. "Thanks for the heads up."

"I'm just glad I didn't have to wake you. I'm sorry for the late call."

"No worries. You know we never sleep. Good night."

"Good night," Mackenzie said ending the call.

She shut down her computer and opened the blinds. Spinning in her chair, she gazed out of her window and took in the Capitol City skyline. As the airships darted across the darkened city, Mackenzie anxiously awaited optimistic news from her centenarian colleague.

8
The Spire, Capitol City, Central Province, Planet Kerguelen

Prior, Pana and Lupo entered the penthouse elevator after the commander inserted and quickly removed a small keycard from a slot next to the doors. The top six residences in The Spire were each serviced by their own private lifts that ran the entire height of the building. After they entered, the elevator's computer, sensing that the occupants were female, spoke to them in a male voice that was strong yet pleasing to the ear.

"How can I be of service to you?" the voice said.

"Upper landing platform," Prior said tilting her head slightly upwards and speaking in a clear and distinct voice.

"Very well. Would you like any other services?" the voice replied.

"Yes, show this evening's field sports results. Oceania versus the Southern Province only," Prior said. "That's all."

"As you wish," the voice said. "Stand-by."

Prior folded her arms and leaned against the back wall of the elevator car as a small wall screen lit up. The sports score she requested flashed on the screen briefly followed by highlights of the match as the car started upwards. There were only a few clips from the event due to a low score, but Oceania had prevailed, two to nil, and that pleased Prior. Oceania was her favorite team. When the update was done, the screen went blank.

"I hope you're happy," Pana said. "They've won three in a row."

"And that's three that you owe me," Prior said.

Pana nodded in agreement. Her favorite team was the Southern Province club and the loss wasn't good, for many reasons. For one, Pana now owed Prior three nights out on the town. Secondly, the players of the Southern Province team would not get paid... again.

On Kerguelen, professional sports were truly professional and based on performance. If a team or individual athlete lost a match or competition, they would not be compensated. In addition, the winning team took sixty percent of the stadium gate. To the winner, went the spoils, and since that had been implemented into professional athletics, games and events had been of better quality and more competitive. Only the best athletes were employed as professionals. No longer could one continue playing past their prime. It didn't pay for agents to represent them or teams to retain them and they soon retired. Basking in past glory was reserved for bars, nightclubs and book signings. Perennial losers also no longer existed. There was no revenue sharing and owners of also-rans or owners unwilling, or unable, to pay for the top athletes, folded their teams and sold off their players, stadiums and arenas.

Pre-programmed classical music started when the sports update concluded, but ended almost as soon as it started. The elevator quickly came to a stop and the doors opened. As they walked out onto the dark landing platform, the computer voice spoke again.

"Have a pleasant evening, ladies."

"Yeah, thanks," Prior grumbled.

As much as she loved technology, she despised interactive elevators or machinery. She felt communicating with one was perverse in a way.

Despite the late hour, it was still warm and pleasant, even at the top of The Spire. Only the lights for the platform were illuminated, and they pierced the darkness and Prior could see the awaiting air ship's engines were running. Sergeant Rex waved at them and then ducked inside momentarily before reappearing. Prior stopped at the foot of the ladder as Rex saluted and reported.

"Duty report, Commander. We have a two-air ship flight as you requested. The flight consists of your air vehicle and an accompanying gunship, designations Gray Wolf 1 and King 3, respectively. Both craft are fully serviced and armed. We're cleared for operations," he said.

"Very well," Prior said nodding to him. She looked around in all directions and inhaled deeply. "Alright, Master Sergeant, let's go. We're burning daylight."

She told Lupo to go inside and then she entered. Pana and Rex smiled at each other as Pana climbed aboard. No matter what time of day it was, Prior always made that statement before starting out. Pana slammed the hatch shut and then took a seat as the sound of the pressure seal taking hold hissed throughout the cabin. Rex passed a large metal case to Prior and she looked back at him.

"Are they ready?" she asked.

"They're all set," Rex said with a nod.

"Thank you," she said sitting the case on her lap. She shifted in her seat and called to her pilot. "Okay, let's go, Micah."

"Where to?" he asked.

"Cosmopolis, the club district. Take us to *First in Line*," she said.

"The traffic pattern should be good," Micah said. "We should make it in half an hour." He applied power to the craft and they lifted off and disappeared into the night sky.

En route to Cosmopolis, Prior gave her team a rundown on why she called them in off of leave. The team took the news of Venture turning rogue very hard. All of them had varying opinions on the event, but each member kept their thoughts internal. They all knew what the term "arrest" meant.

"I don't understand why he shot the cardinal's arm off," Hiroki wondered aloud.

"It was obviously a religious statement," Prior explained. "The right side is traditionally masculine and the left is feminine."

"That's right," Hiroki said nodding. "Females are forced to be left-handed regardless of whether it's their dominant side or not. But what does it mean?"

"It means the Congress of Cardinals will be on a quest to ensure Venture is severely punished for his actions," Prior replied.

"Is there any chance of taking Commander Venture alive?" Lindsey asked.

"Are you asking will I kill him if I have to?" Prior said without looking at him.

"Yes," he said.

"The answer is yes, Lieutenant. In order to bring him in, I'll have to kill him," Prior said staring out of the window.

"Is that because he killed Sali and the others and maimed the cardinal? Or is this something else?" Hiroki asked.

"It's because I'm a realist. If you were after me, you'd better come prepared to kill me or you'll die. Venture is a Guardian commander and his nature will prevent him from taking to captivity. He's not going to prison willingly and with a smile on his face. Unless we track him down quickly, a lot of people are going to die before this is over. It's unfortunate, but fact. Venture must die," Prior said.

"And what if they order you to arrest Omega when he returns? What then? I believe that alien space ship of his is the root of all this madness," Pana said.

There was truth in what Pana had said. The rumor mill had said the Congress of Cardinals was not pleased at the possibility of a re-structuring of religious stances concerning Creation and the sudden doubt of the Church's teachings by the younger members of the planet's population had caused religious leaders much animosity and concern.

"Omega," she began softly looking down at her dog. She paused for a nearly a minute before she continued. She took a breath and exhaled. "Omega would have to die as well. I won't see him in chains or behind bars again." Her words were icy and without emotion.

"And what would become you?" Hiroki asked already knowing that anything concerning she and Omega was a very touchy subject.

"Me? You would be forced to kill me, Captain," Prior said matter-of-factly.

"Why? In the name of the Almighty, why would it come to that?" he asked standing up.

"Because, Captain," said Prior opening the case on her lap. Inside were her personal weapons. She took out one of the two pistols in the case and inspected it briefly as she continued. "Because I would have to kill the person that ordered his arrest."

9
Interstellar space,
Two parsecs from the Kerguelen Star System

Omega leaned back in the chair of the observation dome and stared out at the stars streaming past his eyes as *San Mariner* sped homeward at low hyper-light speed. Though the ship had a terminal velocity much higher, Omega had ordered a lower speed for the last leg of their journey. The ship would be entering the Kerguelen Star System soon and he wanted to extend his last days in the great void as long as possible.

Before the mission, only Tallen, Jalen and Camden had decided to continue their careers as star sailors. Now, it seemed that all of them were considering signing on again, even the ones that did not find a career in space appealing. Within a year or so they would be back flying through the emptiness of space, for there was now a definitive reason to venture into the great void: A chance for an encounter with beings from another world. The discovery of the alien space probe had changed everything for everyone... including Omega.

The tickets for those space rides would be highly contested and the crew of *San Mariner* would have the inside track. It would be the opportunity of ten thousand lifetimes and Omega would not be part of it. He would not return to deep space.

Space Command had finally responded verbally to his communiqués and the operations director had heartily congratulated him on the find, but informed Omega that they would need his presence on Kerguelen to help break down the alien spacecraft and decipher any messages it may contain. He would also be needed to train future deep space survey ship commanders and crews that would attempt to make planet fall on the alien craft's home of origin. Finding the spacecraft had indeed changed everything and forced Omega to concentrate and focus on things beyond himself, beyond his wants and desires. Though it seemed his flying days were over, he would be allowed to go home again after an exile of more than a decade and that meant he was one step closer to being re-united with his former love.

But as he gazed out into space, he couldn't help shake the feeling that the plans envisioned by Space Command would be derailed and never reach fruition. There would never be a return to star system 1-Sol-8, no search for aliens and no attempts made to contact them. Despite the hard evidence they possessed and the influence of the Technology Council, the rest of the ruling body, led by the Congress of Cardinals, would delay, posture and argue and use whatever means necessary to prevent a follow-up mission and maintain a stranglehold on the populace and stifle the truth.

Cardinal Gregor would make sure the Federal Church's view on Creation and the divinity of the Almighty remained intact. Eventually, all that the survey had discovered would disappear and be forgotten. Wishful thinking they would call it, and anyone who tried to unravel the truth would be branded a heretic, jailed and killed… or worse… starting with Omega.

But knowing this could not help him. He would come out of his exile and finally return home. He could not run and even if he could hide, he had to go back. He had to peel back the layers of deception that he was sure were already forming, no matter what the cost. He had nothing to lose by doing so. He was already dead in the eyes of Kerguelen society. Besides, they couldn't excommunicate him twice. He had an advantage though. His new status as the man who brought the universe to Kerguelen would give him a chance initially to fight the Federal Church, and that may be just the toehold he needed.

But that was a fight for another day. He got up from his seat and maneuvered his way through the ship's small circular passages to the Cargo Module for a look at his prize. The crew would not be around and he wanted a few moments to reflect on what the craft meant alone.

Dela and Tallen had climbed all over the craft when they had successfully stopped it and then renewed their probing once it was retrieved and stowed aboard. Though their study had been brief, they were certain that the craft was a primitive science and reconnaissance probe. Designed to conduct planetary surveys, it sent pictures and recorded data back to its home of origin via old-style radio waves.

Tallen was sure the craft had traveled quite a distance and had been in space for a long time, perhaps decades. After two full days of long and exhaustive work, they closed out their investigations, secured the craft in the containment area and prepared for the departure home.

The only thing that concerned the crew was the craft's power system. Still active, Dela had discovered that it was a radioactive decay, thermo-electric-type power system. Though nuclear power cells were common on Kerguelen, they had struggled to make them safe and reliable. A concentrated effort by the Technology Council had resulted in a stable source of power. But Omega and the others were worried that the culture that created the craft did not have the knowledge their planet had and took extra precautions to ensure their safety.

The shielding on the craft was not very good, probably because the designers of the probe believed the vessel would not be discovered until long after the radioactive material had exhausted itself, becoming inert and harmless. The reasoning was logical. Who would have believed that another race would find it so soon? Besides, shielding would add more weight and that meant the craft would need to be larger and require more fuel. Dela quashed all concerns assuring that the containment area would be more than adequate to protect the crew as they journeyed home.

As they turned for home, the ship's sensors discovered another probe in the system's northern hemisphere at nearly the same location as the first probe. Tallen was not sure if both craft were launched at the same time, but it was obvious that the creators of the ships wanted each to travel into different areas of the galaxy to increase the chances of one of them being found. Omega wondered what the exact mission of the craft was and asked Tallen to speculate.

"If I had to guess, I would say based on how it's equipped, it's a one-way mission craft designed to explore the outer planets and deep space phenomena. Considering the power system they used, the builders didn't think it would last this long. They probably had high hopes, but they certainly would be realistic as well. At the speed it was traveling, if it explored all of the outer planets, it would take upwards of fifteen years to reach this distance after the survey was done. But they were clever and forward thinking. This is the way to study the outer planets close up, relatively close anyway. The probes would do flybys and soak up as much data as they could before they moved on to the next world. Even though the time they spent near the planets was brief, they gathered data that telescopes and observations would never come close to getting. Once the planetary mission is over, then what? If it still has power, send them out of the system. Have them continually transmit data concerning the outer reaches of the solar system until their power is gone," he said.

"Why?" Omega asked.

"The ships will give valuable insight on the edge of the system. Remember, we can go and look if we have a question. They obviously can't. The information they would get about the outer planets, interstellar radiation and the effects of deep space would be invaluable. It would take dozens of years to collect, study and understand the data, but when once they've achieved the ability to come out here, they'd be ready," Tallen said.

"And you're sure you want to wait until we're home to try and decipher the message they included with the ship?" Omega asked looking at the small disc attached to the ship.

"Yes. Who knows how fragile it is? We may only get one shot at it," Tallen said. "And none us is skilled enough in languages to try a translation anyway."

Omega wondered if there were other probes out there and if anyone had found the craft Kerguelen had sent out. Space Command had stopped tracking their progress more than thirty years ago. But what he really wanted to do was find the probe's home world. Now that really would have been something. That mission, however, would fall to another commander and another crew.

"Well," Omega said aloud as he gazed at the craft. "It was fun while it lasted."

"Excuse me, Commander," a voice said from behind him. It echoed in the emptiness of the Cargo Module.

Startled, he turned and saw Dela standing there. He wondered how long she had waited before she made her presence known. He looked at her and smiled. Her already pale skin had grown paler from months without natural sunlight. She had an electronic data tablet in her hands and the ever-present tool belt around her waist. Omega wondered if she had any other interests besides engineering. As he looked at her, he believed that she would have been attractive if she put any effort into it, but her appearance was no different now than it had been during training. She was all business.

"Yes, Dela," he said.

"Ship report, Commander," she said handing Omega the tablet. "All systems are nominal. We're six hours from our next navigational adjustment."

"Excellent. A few more days and we're home," Omega said.

"Yes, another six or seven days, Commander," Dela said.

Omega took out a stylus and initialed the report without really reading it. He knew how thorough Dela was and if she didn't point out any items of interests, there was no reason for him to review the report. He handed it back to her and asked, "What's up with the crew?"

"They've just finished with their allotted time on the PIL. You know, saying hi to their families and making plans for when we get back. Everyone's inboxes are jammed full with messages. I doubt if they finished replying to them all before we were out of transmission range of space buoy 1178. It's just as well though. We're rolling into a sleep period. They're grabbing a bite to eat now before they hit the rack," she said taking the tablet. She looked at Omega closely and put a hand on his shoulder. "You could do with some sleep yourself, Commander. The Flight Officer and I will baby sit for awhile."

"You and Camden together for six hours?" he said amazed at her statement.

"He rotated the watch to accommodate Tallen's extra hours," she explained. "And I replaced him in the slot."

"We're in good hands then. I'll finish up my reports in my In-Flight cabin and then knock off," he said.

"You need it, Commander. Don't stay up too long, sir. All of this will keep for a few hours," Dela said. She moved her hand to his neck and felt the tension there. She squeezed the knot firmly with her strong fingers and the tightness eased a little. He looked at her curiously and she smiled.

"What did you do?" he asked. "That felt great."

"My grandmother was a skilled tension easer. She taught me a few things when I was young," Dela said.

"Why did you do that?" he asked.

"It's been my experience that men under pressure relax a bit when a woman does that... no matter what their relationship. I hope that helps," she said. She released him and started to step away but spun around quickly. "I'll make sure Camden doesn't know you're in your cabin or he'd bother you. I'll tell him you're in the Habitat Module."

"Thanks," he said.

"Oh, there's an addendum to my report you might find interesting," she said with a sly grin.

"Really?" he said.

"Yes," she said handing him the tablet again. "While we were tinkering with the probe, the radio system activated."

"Activated?" he asked as he scanned the screen.

"Yes, Commander," Dela said with an uncharacteristic smile. "It wasn't us, though. Someone was trying to contact the space probe. We tracked the signals and know where they came from. We're confident it came from the third planet."

"The third planet? That's the blue and white one. Are you sure?"

"Yes, Commander," Dela said. "We're positive it wasn't automated. There *is* another intelligent culture in the universe."

10
The Club District, Cosmopolis, Central Province, Planet Kerguelen

As Prior checked the action of her recently repaired pistols, she thought about the situation concerning Venture. She was certain that he had nothing to do with the planetary unrest. She had known him for twelve years and at one point, he was one of her closest friends. They had shared much and she felt she had known him as well as anyone could. He taught her a lot about being an officer and she respected him. She was sure the feeling was reciprocated. Though he was five years senior to her, they had been promoted to commander in the same year group and that's when they began to lose touch with each other.

He took command of the First Battalion and immediately turned it into an elite unit. Two years later, he was made regimental commander, assuming overall command of all four Guardian battalions. Having already been given command of all surveyors when she was a colonel, when Prior was promoted to commander, she was designated Chief Surveyor. No Guardian had held the position in over eighty-five years and Central Command had special plans for the first career combat engineering officer to attain the rank of commander.

Prior was given the task of developing a special duty unit that would, in the words of Marshal Garath, "Carry out undisclosed covert missions of dubious antecedence". The reasons were simple: Global crisis on Kerguelen had changed and the Guardians could no longer perform counter punch operations. They had to strike first to thwart the new enemies of the people.

In the past, the Guardians could wait for an incident to occur and stop the antagonists before there was a major loss of life and property. But the world had shifted into high gear. The huge superior technological advantage the Guardians possessed over the rest of the population had shrunk overnight. High-tech weapons were available to all for the right price and Central Command needed a group that was not bound by the restrictions of planetary law to combat the new threats looming on the horizon. The unit needed to be irregular in their tactics and unconventional in their thinking, but most of all, they needed to be able to absorb the blame if their operations were discovered. In short, Central Command needed Prior and her surveyors. They were the only Guardians accustomed to operating alone and independent of large battalion-sized support.

Prior was intended to be the sacrificial lamb. If she were found out to be leading a black ops unit, it would be expected. She was after all Boroni, a secluded and secretive race. Additionally, the surveyors were not considered to be regular Guardians. The whole situation could be chalked up to a bunch of renegades led by a savage. The Corps would take a few hits but would be clear of scandal and that was the ultimate goal. Only the supreme commander, his chief of staff and operations officer would know of their existence.

After getting the green light, Prior petitioned the Technology Council for special equipment, experimental weapons and one-of-a-kind devices for her troops. The special equipment would go far in making the new group highly efficient. Initially, she selected ten of her best surveyors to comprise two units for covert activity. Five years later, she had a total of thirty operatives working in five-person teams. Three teams were on ready alert, one team would be in reserve, one would conduct individual covert assignments of varying types and one would concentrate specifically on space operations. Two members of the reserve team were currently on undercover missions and the other three were on special leave. Two were doing post-graduate work and the third was recuperating from wounds received on an op.

Prior had tasked two of her special op officers, Major Metis and Lieutenant Addison, to investigate the Venture case. Their investigations would surely reveal much, but they had to work swiftly if what they found was going to help. Prior was sure that they would but they had little time. If they couldn't find any solid intelligence that Venture was being framed quickly, she would have to proceed with his apprehension.

Prior's thoughts drifted back to the present as her air ship descended in altitude and slowly entered into a landing platform area. After the team exited the craft, the ship soared off skyward. Prior and her team walked down a flight of stairs and made their way to the main thoroughfare that spanned the entire length of the club district of Cosmopolis.

The mega-city covered 728 square miles and was the largest urban area of Kerguelen. Home to over twenty-four and a half million people, it was the commercial capitol of the planet. Every major corporation had offices in Cosmopolis, including Prior's own. So many transactions took place here on a daily basis she had nearly taken up residence in Cosmopolis instead of in Capitol City.

But the city was also the cultural capitol of Kerguelen as well. Every trend in music, fashion, art, and philosophy, owed its existence to Cosmopolis. Anything, no matter how radical, could find life and a way to express itself in the city. In every way, Cosmopolis was the unofficial capitol of the planet, and scores of people every year flocked to Cosmopolis to reinvent their life or find out who they truly were.

Though it was a jet-black night, the sky was brilliantly lit by the luminescence of the city. The sounds of the residents and the din of the inanimate echoed and resonated through the air. It truly seemed as if the city was a living and breathing entity. The signs and marquees of the bars and bistros and nightclubs on the boulevard pierced through the darkness like a scythe through grass.

Prior loved the night. She had found that you could see much more at night than you could in the daytime. Most people were very apprehensive about the night, but like most Boroni, Prior had taken the time to embrace the night for what it was. There was nothing really to be frightened of, for darkness was just an absence of light.

To look upon the mega-city, one would believe Kerguelen had an unlimited source of power, and in a sense, that was true. As long as there were people, there was power. Thanks to the Tactile Energy Tiles that covered every walkway and sidewalk in towns and cities, and in every hallway of every structure built, each step taken by the people provided energy to the planet's power reserve. The tiles converted the kinetic energy force of a footstep into direct current electricity and transferred it into the power grid. When combined with fusion power, hydrodynamic, thermal, wind, hydrogen fuel cell and solar energy systems, the planet's energy worries was a thing of the past. And the use of these systems had returned the planet's fragile biosphere to a pristine condition. The resulting planetary atmospheric health had directly resulted in an increase of health in the population. Many of the cancer conditions and respiratory ailments as well as a score of birth defects so prevalent fifty years earlier, disappeared when man-made pollutants were removed from the air.

Prior and her Guardians joined the flotsam of citizens enjoying the fruits of the city's nightlife. The streets were filled with people meandering about carefree. Modern architects had designed or redesigned cities and towns as "walk around" habitats to allow people to freely move without having to worry about vehicles. Mass transit systems got the people where ever they needed to be and air vehicle landing platforms were positioned so walking was a necessity. Walking provided power and helped the Kerguelens in other ways as well. It contributed to the people's health, extended longevity, and increased vitality and most Kerguelens could look forward to long pain-free lives because of it.

As the team neared their destination, the sleek and agile gunship that was supporting them, buzzed overhead. The tandem seat, two-person combat air ship would provide a much-needed punch if and when the time came and it was always nice to know you had extra bullets in your gun. Lindsey looked up and watched the gunship pass overhead and then looked at Prior. She felt his gaze upon her and she slowed her pace and spoke to the young officer.

"Something on your mind, Lieutenant?" she asked moving closer to him.

"No, Commander," he said shaking his head.

"Go ahead and ask," Hiroki said. "You only get one shot at it."

"Does the Lieutenant have questions for me, Captain?" Prior asked with a smile.

"Yes, he does, Commander," Hiroki said.

"What's on your mind, Lieutenant? Don't worry, Lieutenant, I won't bite your head off for asking personal questions. Like the captain said, this is your one shot to ask," Prior said still smiling.

"Is it true you're royalty?" Lindsey asked.

Prior, Pana and Hiroki all laughed at the question. Rex did not laugh. He only stared at Lindsey as if he were the most ignorant person on Kerguelen.

"No, Lindsey, I'm not royalty," Prior said. "The Boroni live what you might call a feudal lifestyle and I am head of my household. It encompasses a lot of people and property, but I am far from royalty."

"I was led to believe that you have a say in what goes on politically in the Western Province," Lindsey continued. "I heard that you are related to every governor general the Western Province has ever had."

"The head of every major and minor Boroni house has a voice in our governing body. Since we are responsible for the actions and welfare of every member of our house, we are their representatives to the governor general, but I have only limited influence politically," Prior said. "As to your other rumor, it is true that I am related to every governor general the Boroni have had. But to be truthful, there have only been three. The first was my great-grandfather Kel, the second was my grandfather Kemper and the present governor general is my great aunt Paige."

"That's an amazing lineage," Lindsey said.

"It's just a lucky coincidence," Prior said. "Governor General Paige is also great aunt to Sgt. Major Pana."

"Yes," Pana said. "The commander's father and mine were brothers."

"Anything else?" Prior asked.

"I know this is probably only rumor, but one of my classmates at the academy said that you were heir to the Boroni house led by Governor General Paige," Lindsey said.

"It's called Cabot House," Prior said. "I'm technically part of that house but I wouldn't consider myself heir to any of it."

"That's not true," Pana offered. "You are in direct line for head of Cabot House."

"So are you, Pana, and your line is more direct," Prior said.

"I'm not so sure," Pana said. "Your father was eldest and you're the eldest child of our generation. I may be the eldest sibling in my family, but succession lines are very clear on the subject. We are equally related to Paige, so the oldest becomes head of the house."

"Cabot House and the House of Ahrens are the richest and most powerful houses in the Western Province," Lindsey said taking in all that he heard. "If you become the head of both, Commander, you'd have more money than God."

"Don't be ridiculous, Lindsey, the Almighty doesn't use money," Prior quipped.

"With all those billions you could find out what the Almighty does use for cash," Hiroki said.

"Before we start making plans for money none of us have, we need to finish this mission," Prior said. "Do you have any other questions, Lindsey?"

"No. Thank you for letting me pry into your life. I know it's none of my business," Lindsey said.

"No problem," Prior said. "I'm glad you're done because we're here."

Prior pointed to a building and her team saw a nightclub named *First in Line*. It had been the premier nightclub in the city for decades and its patrons included the top ten percent of the planet's A-List. It was also a major hub of illegal activity and not a night passed in which some criminal deal was not planned or conducted in the club.

The queue extended around the block and Prior led her team around the mass eagerly awaiting entry into the club. There was no dress code and all manner of attire was represented. Prior had changed out of her sarong and into a blouse, pair of slacks, boots and a leather bolero jacket. Pana still wore her leggings and mock turtleneck; while the rest of the team was clad in stylish club wear. Prior stepped up to the mountain posing as a doorman and flashed a card in front of him. He smiled at her and stepped aside, allowing them to pass, much to the dismay of the crowd that had been waiting hours for admittance.

Inside, the music was louder in some parts of the club than the noise on a battlefield and the aroma of both legal and illegal controlled substances of all types filled their nostrils. The fumes were so heavy, the Boroni members of the team had to consciously dial down their olfactory senses to prevent from being overwhelmed. It also quickly dawned on Prior that the quintet was conspicuous and would draw unwanted attention. She told Pana, Rex and Lindsey to go on one side of the club, while she and Hiroki went on the other. They were in search of one individual who frequented the club and Prior was certain that he would be here. But she didn't want him to spot them and leave before she had the chance to speak with him. After they split up, Hiroki leaned in close and spoke loudly into Prior's ear.

"Are you sure he'll be here?" Hiroki asked.

"Yes. I know he's in the city and if he's in the city, he'll be here," Prior replied.

"How can you be so sure?" Hiroki asked.

"He loves jazz," Prior answered. "And this club has the best jazz musicians in town... on the planet for that matter."

"Is that enough to go on?" he asked.

"Everyone is driven by certain personality quirks. Their loves... desires... and wants. He will be here because he has to come here. A person has "tells" to their personality. And I know his better than he does," Prior said.

"Do I have any quirks?" Hiroki asked.

"Yes, you do," Prior nodded. "You have a penchant for pissing me off to the point where I'd love to kill you. Only my desire to preserve life arrests me from doing what I want." He smiled and she added, "He'll be here because this is also a good place to make friends."

"To make friends?" he asked.

"Yes, it's the perfect place to establish connections. It's easy to make friends in a bar. All you have to do is buy them a few drinks and they're yours," Prior said.

"I didn't know you liked these places! If I did, I would have asked you out sometime!" he said squinting as a set of strobe lights flashed in his eyes.

"You're not supposed to know what I like, Captain," Prior said leaning away from him and looking around the club. "I come here because I'm a rich and morally decadent Boroni female. I'm supposed to come to places like this. I've got VIP status in all of the best clubs on the planet. I'm very popular in some of them."

"I don't doubt it! Maybe I can take you out sometime!" he said still talking very loudly as his eyes zeroed in on a bevy of scantily clad women dancing provocatively together on the dance floor. "This is my type of place! How many drinks would it take for you to be my friend?"

Prior looked at Hiroki and shook her head. "No. No, Hiroki," she said.

"Why not, Prior? Give a guy a chance!" Hiroki said.

"I gave a guy a chance once," Prior said. "That's why the answer is no now. And lower you voice. I know the music is loud, but I have enhanced hearing. I can understand you just fine at a normal level."

"Sorry!" he said in a loud voice again.

Prior shook her head and took Hiroki by the hand. They slowly walked around and scanned the crowd in search of their quarry. If Venture had been secretly undermining the government, even he would need help. The best person to aid in that was the man she was looking for, a Southern Province native named Gabriel, and if Gabriel had declined to help him; he would know who would. It wouldn't take much to drum up support against the government's new policies from the numerous underground activist cells around the planet. With the right numbers and his skills in psychological warfare, Venture could start a revolution. Prior stopped moving through the crowd when the TELCOM device in her ear chirped.

"Yes?" said Prior tapping on the device.

"Commander," Rex' voice sounded. "I've got him."

"Where?" Prior asked as her eyes darted around the club.

"Your two o'clock," he said.

Prior locked in on the direction and she nodded. "I've got him," she said. "Keep the line open."

The DJ lowered the music and introduced the house band. They were well known jazz artists from the Northeastern Province and had several successful and award-winning recordings to their credit. They began playing a funky jazz beat and the crowd began to stir with excitement. The song was one of the group's biggest hits and the dance floor instantly became crowded with couples and singles moving and swaying to the music. The leader of the group was an attractive blonde from the Hinterlands and her slender waif-like build disguised the power of her voice as she belted out the lyrics into the microphone.

Prior led Hiroki onto the dance floor and he looked at her curiously and she smiled at him.

"I love this song. Dance with me," she said.

Hiroki was elated as they moved through the mass of clubbers on the dance floor and he was surprised at Prior's knowledge of the latest dances. Obviously she had not been lying about her spending time in many clubs. As they moved to the music, Prior leaned in close and held Hiroki tightly.

"Who is this band?" Hiroki asked. "I don't listen to jazz much."

"Dulfer," Prior said. "It's the saxophonist's name."

Hiroki looked briefly at the band and saw another attractive and diminutive blonde step forward playing a saxophone solo. "Dulfer. That's a strange name for a woman," he said.

"I don't know, it sounds okay to me," Prior said. "As far as names go, it's better than some and no worse than others."

"Why did your parents name you Prior?" Hiroki asked.

"My mother said they gave me that name because prior to me being born, everything was different," she said.

Hiroki smiled and Prior pulled him to the far side of the dance floor and they closed in on Gabriel. The strobe lights swept through the dance floor and the dark-skinned and slender Gabriel momentarily looked away from the women he was with toward the lights. He nodded in approval when saw a tall and attractive woman swaying to the music and took a moment to gaze at her. When the woman spun, her long and flowing brown hair caught his eye and he gasped when he realized the woman was Prior. Their eyes met and Gabriel pushed away from his table and bolted toward the rear of the club.

"Rabbit!" Prior said as she broke away from the strong hold Hiroki had on her waist and left him standing in her wake.

Hiroki spun around and forced his way through the dancers and drunks as Lindsey caught up with him. Pana and Rex picked up their pace and joined them. Through a hail of vile language protests, Prior fought the crowd and caught a glimpse of Gabriel sliding into a door and ran after him at the best speed she could manage. Her team got held up by the crowd and was losing sight of her as she turned down a hallway.

Prior continued to pursue Gabriel and lowered her shoulder as she approached the door he had gone through. It was no match for her force as she ran into it and it came down loudly. Trying to escape through a window, Gabriel stopped when he heard the sound of the door coming off of its hinges and he climbed down when Prior unceremoniously entered. There were two others in the room as well. Both were dark-skinned like Gabriel and the man and woman gave Prior a stern look.

They were visibly shocked and stunned by her arrival and recognized at once by her complexion, size and long hair that she was Boroni.

The man took out a knife and it surprised Prior. Her attentions were concentrated on Gabriel, but as he thrust the blade at her, she caught sight of his movement with her peripheral vision. She grabbed the man's wrist just before the blade reached her, the tip of it stopping less than an inch from her chest. The man stared in amazement at the speed in which Prior had moved and his eyes grew wider as she slowly, effortlessly, twisted his wrist and gradually increased pressure on it.

The pain forced the man to his knees and the knife fell out of his hand. Prior applied more pressure and then let him go after he yowled in agony. Prior was surprised the man had kept from making a sound for so long. Obviously he wanted to put up the best front he could. It was an admirable but futile attempt at being macho. Prior turned away from him and gave Gabriel the same stern look a parent would give a misbehaving child.

"If you have any other weapons, you'd better put them on the floor before I get angry," Prior said picking up the knife.

"Nobody's got anything, Prior. You know I don't mess with them," Gabriel said.

"Really? What was this?" Prior said gesturing to the knife before she tossed it out of the open window.

"You animal! You broke his wrist," the woman said kneeling beside the man who had tried to stab Prior. He was cradling his hand in her lap and whimpering in pain. She was petite, attractive and like Gabriel had sharp and brilliant blue eyes. "God damned Boros! You're nothing but filthy animals!"

"He tries to stab me and I'm the animal?" Prior scoffed. "Lady, I have the right to kill you right now."

"Adelaide, she's right. Prior is a Guardian," Gabriel said. "And attempted murder of a Guardian is a capital crime, punishable by death." He turned to Prior and continued. "But you aren't in uniform, Prior? What's this all about?"

"I have some questions for you, Gabriel, and I didn't want you to leave the club before I could talk to you," Prior said with a smile.

The woman gasped briefly. "I didn't know they let... those people in the Guardians," she said. "When did they start allowing Helots into the Guardians?"

"Why did you run, Gabriel?" Prior said ignoring the woman as her team finally caught up with her and entered the room. "Running from Guardians? I knew you were crazy, but have you lost your mind?"

"What was *I* thinking? Prior, you shoot people just to stay in practice," he said.

"Don't be ridiculous, Gabriel," Prior objected.

"I've seen you shoot someone just to get the correct time from their chronometer. I ran out of self-preservation," he said.

"Gabriel, we go back a long way. I wouldn't have shot you," Prior said trying to reassure him. He scoffed and she chuckled. "Maybe I would have, but I wouldn't have killed you. I need your help. I don't have much time and I need some info."

"Such as?" Gabriel asked.

"What terrorist activities have you been up to lately?" she asked.

"I'm no terrorist," Gabriel said indignantly.

"Perhaps not, but you've pushed the barrier between harmless activist and wanted terrorist to the limit. I know how far you can go in the name of a cause," Prior said.

"What do you want to know?"

"Where is Venture?"

He chuckled. "He said that a Diablo Negro would come looking for him," Gabriel said. "I just didn't know he meant you."

"So, I'm a black devil, eh?" Prior said with a smile. "What else did he say?"

"That's it," Gabriel said shrugging his shoulders.

"That's all?" Prior asked crossing her arms indicating she didn't believe him.

"That's it, then he took off. Whoosh. I don't know where. He didn't say and I didn't ask. He seemed to be in a hurry though. By now, he could be anywhere. If anyone knows, The Broker would," Gabriel said.

"Great, Gabriel! You're a lot of help. I should bring you all in and have Papal security ask the questions. I wouldn't get the truth, but at least I would get some creative answers," Prior said extremely irritated. "If I knew where The Broker was that might be worth something."

"He's in the south coast of the Northeastern Province," Gabriel quickly offered. "Lago Patria! He's in Lago Patria!"

"Really? I thought he had moved on," Prior said. "Do you have an address?"

"No, I just know he's there," Gabriel said shaking his head.

Prior thought for a moment and then turned to her team. "Sergeant Major, contact the ships. Tell them to prep for a trip to the Northeastern Province. Captain, I want you to contact the Papal police and have them pick up this man and woman."

"Prior! For the Almighty's sake why? They're nobody," Gabriel said as Hiroki and Pana carried out their orders. "If this is about me..."

"This is not about you, Gabriel," Prior said placing an arm around him. "He attacked a Guardian with a deadly weapon. He's a danger to the public."

"But he didn't know you were a Guardian," Adelaide protested. "He just thought you were a Boro coming to hurt us. How was he to know that Boros are now in the Guardians?"

"And that makes it better? If I had been a Kerguelen woman and not a Boroni female, I'd be dead," Prior said scowling at Adelaide. "He's a menace to society regardless of what he does or does not know."

"And why are you having Adelaide arrested?" Gabriel asked. "What did she do?"

"Ah, she's the *real* culprit," Prior said pointing at the woman as a smile reappeared on her face. "The vile epithets she cast toward me and my people are appalling. Casting racial epithets towards another is a felony offense... outlawed for the past seventy-five years. You know, Adelaide, there was a time when you could kill someone for doing that. Luckily for you, we've become a more tolerant civilization."

Shortly after the unification of Kerguelen, the government made it a capital crime for using racial epithets. They were classified as premeditated assaults. Though many people thought the law was excessive, they could not refute that the use of them caused undue stress and animosity between the diverse people of the planet. Even the Congress of Cardinals supported the legislation. Despite preaching universal harmony and brotherhood, they understood that the only thing that turning the other cheek resulted in was getting hit on the other side of one's face.

"They'll send me to a Papal re-education facility," Adelaide said sadly.

"Filled with polar opposites of yourself… for two years," Prior laughed. "You know, most people say the Cardinals are far too stoic and conservative in their thinking. But sometimes we just don't give them enough credit for being creative."

"A unit will meet us at the entrance in less than two minutes, Commander," Hiroki said.

"Good. Let's go, children," Prior said motioning for her team to gather up the prisoners. As they began to walk out, Prior turned to Gabriel who was standing by helplessly as his companions were taken away. "Gabriel, why the long face?"

"Adelaide is my sister, Prior," he said.

"And now," Prior said nodding, "She will know what it feels like to be Boroni."

11
Lago Patria, Northeastern Province, Planet Kerguelen

The city of Lago Patria was one of the most visited places on Kerguelen. The year round warm climate and proximity to three highly populated provinces made it a hub of commerce and international activity. The inhabitants were an eclectic mix of Kerguelen's people and the city served as a crucible for the entire gambit of planetary ideals and philosophies.

But in the wake of planet-wide discourse against the new policies created by the government, Lago Patria had turned into a hotbed of massive protests and the uncontrolled chaos that ensued had forced the provincial leaders in the area to make hard choices. The course of action they took was unfortunately the wrong one and as the unrest grew, the large contingent of police officers called in only infuriated the masses. Peaceful sit-ins turned into scenes of brutality. Police units not used to handling such crisis, turned to the baton, and PIL news links were filled with reports and video of unsavory acts perpetrated by the constables and privately contracted security forces. But both law enforcement and civilians were equally guilty, and without help the situation would not get better any time soon.

Responding to requests for assistance from the governor of the Northeastern Province, Commander Mohab's Fourth Battalion had reported to Lago Patria. Much to Prior's surprise, Mohab had elected to commit the bulk of his 225-man battalion to the enterprise. When she heard about that, Prior had initially questioned his decision, but as she flew over the area, she knew her fellow commander had made the correct choice. It would take a significant force to restore order and maintain peace in the city. She chastised herself for jumping to conclusions, remembering that decisions can only be judged by the situation, not the outcome. From above, Prior observed squads of Guardians successfully and peaceably stopping a series of donnybrooks that had broken out in quick succession.

The two air ships in her party circled the city to give Prior the chance to evaluate the situation from the air before they landed. Since learning that the Fourth Battalion was deployed in the region, she had been in constant contact with Mohab. As a commander, Mohab needed to know she would be operating in his area of responsibility. Despite her seniority to him, this was still his show and he needed to know she and her Guardians would be on the ground there.

Besides the military concerns, she wanted him to know she was in Lago Patria because they were friends. They were classmates at the academy and during her first two years there, he was the only cadet that chose to speak with her and they had remained close ever since. Despite their very different career paths, the two Guardians never went more than a few days without speaking to one another. She had very strong feelings towards him and she was sure he felt the same way. Though they never entered into a serious relationship, Prior knew he would have welcomed something more than the platonic friendship they shared. However, they both knew that was impossible and made the most of what they did have.

"Mohab, we're feet dry over Lago Patria now," Prior said into her TACCOM device. The TACCOM was a multiple frequency communications system used exclusively by the Guardians. Linked by thirty-six orbiting satellites, the Guardians had a constant and uninterrupted telecommunications network. The system was invaluable for Guardian operations. "My team will be on the ground in less than five minutes."

"Copy that," Mohab said. "What's your mission here?"

"I need to reach out to a few people here, Mo," Prior replied. "I'll be exiting within two hours."

"Do you need any support?"

"Negative, but I've sent for additional equipment, just in case you need it," she said.

"Thanks. Lt. McCloud mentioned that he might need some gear," Mohab replied.

McCloud was the surveyor officer-in-charge of the Fourth Battalion's engineering squad and was one of the better junior officers Prior had. All of the reports she had received on him were favorable and Mohab had cited him for outstanding service in the field. Prior was pleased with his performance and planned to assign him to greater responsibilities soon. The final meeting Prior had with McCloud before he left for the Fourth Battalion may have been the reason for his sustained superior performance. Prior had evinced that if he failed Mohab in any way, she would hunt him down and kill him. Though many leaders used similar empty threats to motivate junior officers, McCloud knew Prior had meant every word.

"No problem, Mo," Prior said. "Giles and the Second Battalion don't use any of the troops or equipment I provide anyway. They won't be missed."

"You're too good to me," he replied.

"Anything for you, Mo, you know that," she said. She looked out of the window and continued. "Be careful down there. I don't like what I see."

"You be careful yourself, Pri. There are a lot of irate citizens down here," he cautioned. "They'll lash out at any uniform."

"Don't worry, we'll stay clear. Good luck, Mo. Talk to you soon," she said.

"Fair winds," Mohab said closing the circuit.

She hated to be evasive about her team's intentions, especially to Mohab, but he was not privy to her operations. If he had known why she was in the area, he would have insisted on helping her in some way and she couldn't allow that. He was extremely important to her and if he were injured or killed by Venture she would never forgive herself. Prior settled into her seat in preparation for landing and wondered what Venture was doing and if he was still in Lago Patria.

12
Hampton Shoals, North Island Province, Planet Kerguelen

Archbishop Cornelia stood silently on the terrace of her house and watched the waves of the Dominion Sea roll against the rocky shores of Hampton Shoals. In the distant she could see the faint outline of Reunion Island and she leaned against the railing of the terrace and took in a deep breath. Cornelia loved the sea and had built this cottage as a vacation home. When the pressures of being the Cardinal of Corinth became too much, she escaped to Hampton Shoals to renew her energies.

As the Cardinal of Corinth, Cornelia was senior priest and archbishop of the North Island, Northeastern and Middle Province dioceses, and she did not have much leisure time. She had the largest contingent of parishioners of any archbishop and full autonomy to set policy throughout the three regions without the consent of the Congress of Cardinals. Though not a member of the Congress of Cardinals herself, Cornelia wielded considerable power in the Federal Church. She had been a priest for over two decades and though she was far from one of the first women to ascend to the priesthood, she was undoubtedly the most influential. Though the Congress of Cardinals would not openly admit it, Cornelia was the most powerful clergyman on Kerguelen, male or female. The Federal Church's ruling body often consulted Cornelia when preparing to execute new doctrine, not so much out of respect, but out of fear.

Cornelia had used her position to gain considerable political clout in both the legislature and the judiciary and wouldn't hesitate to use that influence to oust a priest of any rank from their position. If that didn't work, she would use physical force. The ferocity of her security teams was infamous and everyone great and small on the planet knew that Cornelia didn't threaten; she acted.

It was the proficiency of her security that troubled Cornelia at the moment. She had never been plagued with unwelcome or unannounced visitors before, but today had changed that. On the terrace with her was Commander Venture. He had stealthily entered her property and casually strolled to the terrace without the security force even being aware of his presence. After he was gone, she would have stern words for her security chief, but for now she would enjoy her guest.

Cornelia turned away from the water and leaned against the railing and let the cool breeze ever-present on the North Island Province's windward coast blow through her hair. The strands of light brown hair naturally frost by sprinkles of soft white ones brushed across the corners of her oval face. She smiled at Venture and remembered the days when the Guardian commander was a young priest under her charge.

They had been romantically involved for a time and when Venture declined her proposal to bond with her, Cornelia had been extremely hurt and angry. A short time later, Venture returned to the Guardians full-time and Cornelia never again searched for or encountered love. She drowned herself in her work and increased her power base. Freeing herself from emotional ties enabled her to act in her capacity as archbishop without feelings. But as her former lover stood before her, those repressed feelings all resurfaced and it was all she could do to contain them.

"Why are you here, Venture?" Cornelia asked. "Have you come to shoot me too?"

"No, Cornelia," Venture said shaking his head. "I only want to talk."

Venture studied her and was amazed at how little she had changed over the years. She was still beautiful and the scarlet and white vestments she wore were tailored to accentuate her ample curves. She may have been a priest but there was little doubt she was all woman. He remembered she had always been proud of her large bosom and always wore her clothing to remind anyone looking at her that she was well endowed in that respect.

"Why did you shoot him, Venture? Gregor is not a threat that cannot be contained. I, and others, have worked diligently to prevent that from happening. If you had problems or concerns, you should have come to me," Cornelia said.

"Gregor is more dangerous than you suspect," Venture said. "These new church policies are just the tip of the iceberg. There is much more to his plans. I just haven't found out what they are exactly."

"So you sever his right arm and emasculate him without knowing his full intentions? Was that prudent?" Cornelia asked.

"When he tried to arrest and frame me? Yes, I think it was. I needed him to know I was on to him," Venture replied.

"You should have killed him. If you believed he was a threat to the people that was your responsibility... and obligation," Cornelia said almost scolding him. "Isn't that what Guardians do?"

"We don't arbitrarily kill. I was sending him and anyone associated with his plans a message. With him dead, the conspiracy might go unnoticed and remain hidden. It must be brought to light," Venture explained.

"You're still looking at the world through a child's eyes. You can't fight evil by being good. Your Helot friend understands that and acts accordingly," Cornelia said.

"I wish you wouldn't refer to Prior as a Helot, Cornelia. She's not a slave. She's far from it," Venture said.

"My opinion of Prior is not of importance," Cornelia said waving a hand. She took a breath and then pointed at Venture. "What is paramount is what we're going to do about you. I can help you if you can restrain yourself. I can place you under my custody until we can prove your accusations against Gregor, and no one will question my judgment in the matter."

"Even if the president requests my extradition?"

"Ward is nothing that can't be handled. He is a lame duck and with the planetary representatives scrambling to save their senate seats, no one will have the time to worry about a wayward Guardian," Cornelia said. "But the vice president does concern me."

"Shayesteh? Why?" Venture asked.

"Though she is from the Middle Provinces and people believe the Middies are not very smart, she is much more competent and wily than anyone could know. She is the wild card that might be problematic," Cornelia said.

"I'm sorry, but I can't cool my heels at one of your houses while all of this is going on," Venture said shaking his head. "As you said, I have an obligation to the people of Kerguelen."

"Venture," Cornelia said softly as she walked to him. "There is something you should know about Gregor." Venture looked at her curiously and she placed a hand on his arm. "Gregor..."

Before she could say anymore, she slumped forward and Venture cradled her in his arms. He lowered her slowly to the synthetic stone flooring of the terrace and found the reason for her limpness. His palm was drenched in blood and he rolled her over on her back. A powerful plasma energy blast had been the cause and Cornelia coughed blood as she looked up at him through glazed eyes.

He knew there was nothing he could do for her. The blast had raked through her vital organs and death was a certainty. It was only a matter of when. He held her closely and she whispered in his ear.

"Gregor... he is a... Summoner," Cornelia said in a barely audible voice. "You must... stop him. You know... what it means."

"I do," Venture said. "But..."

"I... I am dead, Venture. You must... go," Cornelia said.

She reached up and touched his face and smiled. Her eyes closed and Venture kissed her softly. He gently laid her flat on the floor of the terrace and considered his escape route. She was right. He had to get out of there. Her assassination would be blamed on him. A Guardian caliber weapon had been used to kill her.

The sound of heavy footsteps came from inside the house. It would be a security team and there would be no explaining why he was there standing over the dead archbishop. They would shoot first and ask no questions.

Venture could hear the guards calling for the archbishop and he went to the railing and looked over the side. He shook his head when he saw the cold water and rocks forty feet below him. The security detail entered the terrace and saw Venture. They pointed their weapons at him and the team leader looked to the stone tiles and saw Cornelia lying there. He was about to speak when Venture leapt over the side of the railing.

The guards went to the railing and watched Venture come to the surface and swim away along the coast. The leader of the detail shook his head. Venture was a lucky man indeed to have survived such a jump. They would never catch him now. Even at best speed, by the time he mobilized airships Venture would be gone.

"Call the doctor," the leader of the detail said.

"What about the shooter?" one of the guards asked.

"He's gone. I'll contact Cathedral Prime and inform them of this. Do what you can to secure the perimeter and find out how he gained access to the manse," the leader said.

When his men left, the leader of the detail pulled out a TELCOM device and called a pre-programmed number in its memory. As he waited for the connection to be made, he looked at Cornelia. She looked solemn and content in death and he felt sorry that she gone. He turned away from her when the TELCOM beeped.

"Yes," a female voice said in his ear. The distinctive Middle Province accent was prevalent in its tones.

"It is done," the security chief said. "The archbishop is dead. My team saw Venture flee from the scene and will positively ID him when the time comes."

"Do you foresee any problems on your end?"

"No. It's obvious a Guardian weapon caused the death wound. And everyone that knows about the archbishop's security will testify that only a person with Venture's skill could have infiltrated the house. We're just lucky he showed up himself and we didn't have to use the double. All of the ends are tied off," the security chief said.

"He was actually there? That was kind of Venture to help our plan succeed. Everyone will be pleased. We will contact you when your services are needed again. Good work."

"Thank you, Madame Vice President," the security chief said and ended the call.

The security chief took the encrypted TELCOM device out of his ear and sighed. He was glad he wasn't on the receiving end of the vice president's ire. She was more vicious and deadly than Cornelia.

As the personal physician to the archbishop arrived, the security chief stood silently and knew that the first of the obstacles facing his organization was out of the way. There were many more, but arguably the most dangerous one was gone. A Guardian would be blamed and Corps prestige would be severely tarnished by it. The only thing not in their control was what individual Guardians did and that's what chilled the blood of the security chief.

13

Canton-on-Heath, Upper Northeastern Province, Planet Kerguelen

Seven elderly men sat in the study of a large mansion and contemplated what they had decided a few hours earlier. Never before had they been forced to make such choices and it troubled them greatly. Over the years, the men, and those who presided over the fraternal order before them, had made decisions that affected the outcome of planetary history. But today was different, and never before had such heavy hearts filled the room.

It had been necessary for them to cut ties with one of their own and that had not been done before. A unique precedent had been set and none of them knew what the ultimate outcome would be.

"We must not dwell on what might be," one of the men said. His Van Dyke beard was whiter than newly fallen snow. "What was done had to be done."

"We don't know that for certain," the leader of the fraternal society said. For an older man, he was still handsome and despite his being of advanced age, his caramel-colored skin was unblemished. "We only know that we made a choice, one of many that was open to us."

"Agreed," another of the seven said. "All we can do now is pray that we made the correct choice."

"Prayer is for those who seek forgiveness or strength. We are already powerful and do not desire forgiveness. We act, as we always have, for the best interests of Kerguelen. Let the weak find solace in prayer," the leader said. "We are Celeron."

"Is it weakness to pray?" one of seven standing in the back of room offered.

"No, but the Almighty helps those who help themselves. I don't believe in miracles or angels descending from the heavens. Our brother has made a choice that will disrupt the harmony of the planet and we cannot aid him in that. Our mandate precludes us from pursuing a course of action different from that which we have," the leader said.

"Your confidence is reassuring, but we have not always been so steadfast in our deliberations," the man with the Van Dyke said.

"Over the years we have had to adjust our position based on what is current. The world situation is a fluid substance, and we must be as dynamic to be effective. We have never failed, nor will we as long as we are deliberate in our actions and unwavering in our policies and edicts," the leader said tapping his hand on the arm of his chair.

"But we have strayed from our first tenet," the man from the back of the study said. "Doesn't that infer we should re-evaluate all of them?"

"We have not strayed from our first tenet," the leader corrected. "It still remains intact and relevant, we've only made a necessary adjustment. Nothing has changed. And when you see it first hand, you'll agree."

"When do we see it?" the man with the Van Dyke asked.

"Soon," the leader said resting his hand on the soft cushioning of the high-backed chair. "I've already made arrangements for that to happen."

14
Lago Patria, Northeastern Province, Planet Kerguelen

As Prior's air ship dropped in altitude and speed, she could see Mohab's Guardians calmly breaking up hoards of protestors that had gathered together. The weather was torrid but the mood of the people in Lago Patria was even hotter. It was a difficult job, but they were doing fantastic work. The crowds were dispersing in an orderly and peaceful manner. So far so good, Prior thought. Thank goodness for Mohab. She clicked on the headset she wore and looked at her team sitting in the rear of the craft.

"Listen up people... we'll be putting down in a few minutes. We will egress quickly when we hit the deck. I don't want the ship on the ground any longer than necessary," she said.

Captain Hiroki gave her a 'thumbs up' and looked to the rest of the team who all nodded affirmatively. They were all dressed in their combat suits. The refractive armor exoskeletal uniforms were state-of-the-art. Designed by the Technology Council, the black, form-fitting suits were the pinnacles of Kerguelen garment engineering, custom tailored to the individual wearing it. It had several layers of ballistic nylon covered with an Ablative Armor weave and filaments of mirrored glass threads overtop. It protected against edged weapons, projectile weapons and all calibers of plasma energy weapons, even at close range. It kept the wearer cool in hot climates and warm in cold environments. In appearance, the suit resembled a thin skin-tight scuba suit and left little to the imagination about the wearer's physique. The special gloves and smooth soled boots of the combat suit were high-tech as well and incorporated special tactile adhesive pads in them to facilitate scaling walls and maintaining traction when running or on inclines.

Each team member was armed with two high-caliber plasma energy pistols in quick release holsters strapped to their thighs and they gave their weapons a cursory check as they readied to exit the air ship. Sergeant Major Pana, the air ship crew chief, stood up and hooked a lanyard to an eyebolt above her head and attached the other end to a "D" ring on the back of her flight crew harness. A rush of warm and moist subtropical air entered the craft as Pana slid open the left side hatch. She effortlessly heaved a large laser pulse door gun onto its mounting and secured it in place with a locking pin. The sight of the .50-caliber, rapid-fire weapon would discourage anyone from attacking or approaching the air ship, however, if anyone was bold enough to want to create any animosity, the weapon's powerful discharges would quickly change their minds for them.

Pana powered up the gun and as it purred to life, the air ship banked. She leaned out and looked over the prospective landing area below them. It was empty save a few people milling about and seemed ideal for a quick landing and debarkation.

"The area is clear, Commander," Pana said into the mouthpiece of her headset. "No sign of antagonists."

"Roger that," Prior said nodding.

Prior left her seat and knelt to adjust the body armor on her canine. She slipped an envelope into a hidden pouch in the body armor vest and scratched the top of her dog's head. Lupo lifted his head and turned toward the hatch. His nostrils twitched as he took in the smells coming through the open door.

Prior loved her dog Lupo. Since the day he was born seven years ago, he had been by her side. He loved her back and was the best bodyguard anyone could ask for. In his presence, no one could get within an arm's length of Prior unless Lupo permitted it and had saved her life on more than one occasion. Trained to search for explosives, he was as much a part of her team as the others and arguably more obedient. And that was surprising to all because he was lacking the mandatory surgery that all domesticated animals required.

Since the Age of Advancements, all domesticated animals and animals in captivity were required to have obedience chips. The electronic unit was a behavioral control device inserted in the brain of pets and zoo animals. It prevented them from reverting back to their instinctive behaviors in times of stress, indecision and confusion. Since the inception of the device over ninety years ago, there had been no cases of violent attacks by domesticated animals, either provoked or unprovoked, on the planet.

Prior had refused to have Lupo undergo the procedure. The Boroni were vehemently opposed to it based on their history. They felt none of the Almighty's creatures should live in an unnatural condition. To them, an animal's instincts were part of what made them what they were. The rest of planet disagreed, but the Boroni argued that Kerguelens would not be the same if they were prevented from expressing their emotions. The topic was another in a long list of differences between Kerguelens and the Boroni and helped fuel the distrust they shared of each other and expanded the gulf between them.

Prior kissed the top of his massive head. "Are you ready, Lupo?" she asked talking to him as if he were her child. "We're going in."

Lupo barked in response and she stood up and made her way to the open hatch. As normal, she would be the first on the ground and made one last check of her own equipment. She tapped the long bladed knives strapped to her calves and then made sure the short bladed knives in her weapons harness were in place. On her right thigh, a xiphos was secured in its scabbard. The two-foot long sword was the primary weapon of a Guardian before the introduction of projectile weapons. It had not been standard issue for nearly a thousand years, but Prior found it useful for many tasks. In a shoulder holster, she wore a radio frequency weapon. The device was used for non-lethal force situations. It had two settings: EMD and EMG. The electro-muscular disruption, or EMD, setting was designed to incapacitate a person by taking control of their muscles and forcing them into a ball. The electro-magneto cumulative generator, or EMG, setting was designed to shut down and/or cause electrical and electronic equipment to fail.

Strapped to her left thigh was her main armament, the TKP-7 semi-automatic kinetic energy pistol. It was a unique weapon and only three existed. Prior's mother had them designed and made for her daughter as an academy graduation gift. It was the most powerful handheld weapon on Kerguelen and handcrafted for Prior. The TKP-7 fired special .45-caliber tungsten alloy bullets using a hyper velocity delivery system. Instead of gunpowder, the heavy metal slugs were propelled to their target through a rifled barrel at supersonic speeds by an innovative inverse polarity repulsor unit, and no force on Kerguelen could stand up to its power. At fifty meters, the weapon could penetrate a block of solid steel one meter thick. Its drawback was its weight. The weapon weighed 8.5 kilos empty and twelve kilos fully loaded. Though it was recoilless, it required a steady hand to employ it effectively and safely and only a Boroni had that kind of strength. An errant high-caliber, high velocity tungsten bullet could wreak havoc on an unprepared populace.

Prior slipped her TACCOM device in her ear and called for a communications check. She took a deep breath as all members answered.

"Okay, Captain," said Prior. "Give them the brief."

"Okay, everyone, listen up," Hiroki said clicking on his PDA. He scrolled down and found what he was looking for. He cleared his throat and began. "Deadly Force. Deadly force is that force that when used, a person knows, or should reasonably know, would create a substantial risk of causing death or serious bodily harm. Weapons and firearms are to be used to protect and defend civilians and allies while in the prosecution of duty. If in any case it becomes necessary to use a weapon or firearm, the following precautions shall be observed:

"One, shots shall be aimed to disable. However, if circumstances render it difficult to direct fire with sufficient precision to ensure a person will disabled rather than killed, such circumstances will not preclude the use of a firearm, provided such use is otherwise authorized.

"Two, engage only until the threat is eliminated.

"Three, warning shots shall not be fired.

"Four, only authorized weapons and ammunition may be used.

"Five, a firearm is a defensive weapon, not a tool. It is not to be used as a pry bar, hammer or as any other device except a weapon.

"Six, games, tricks or quick draw are not to be played utilizing a firearm or weapon.

"Seven, never use a weapon to threaten or intimidate."

Hiroki shut off his PDA and nodded to Prior. She nodded back and got ready to exit the craft. The deadly force brief was a necessary evil and part of every briefing of every mission any team or unit in the Guardian Corps undertook. All Guardians needed to be reminded of the proper implementation of weapons. It was also a way to cover a team leader if something went wrong. If an illegal shooting or death took place, the first question an investigator would ask was if the deadly force brief was given. If so, the person firing the shot was at fault. If not, the team leader and the shooter were culpable. The deadly force brief was one of the few mandatory regulations Prior agreed with wholeheartedly.

"Stand-by," Prior said. "We're coming in."

Prior's air ship set down on a public landing platform and as the engines slowly wound down to an idle, the dust they created dissipated revealing a group of police constables gathered to greet them. Prior frowned and stepped down from the air ship with Lupo close behind.

"Keep your distance," Pana said through the ship's loudspeaker.

The rest of the team consisting of Hiroki, Lindsey and Rex quickly joined Prior. The constables stopped short and raised their hands when they saw the laser pulse door gun. It was not pointed at them, but they still froze in their tracks. The leader of the policemen took a small step forward and spoke for the group.

"We're here to coordinate with the Guardians in this area. I'm Deputy Chief Jimenez," he said.

"We're not with the Fourth Battalion, Chief," Prior said. "We're on a different assignment. If you have problems or concerns, you need to contact Commander Mohab."

"We don't have any problems," Jimenez said.

"Then I suggest you get on the street and help the Guardians," Prior said motioning for her team to move out. As they walked away from the constables, she clicked on her TACCOM device. "Gray Wolf 1, Gray Wolf Actual is on the move."

"Roger, Actual," Micah said. When the air ship lifted off he spoke again. "Gray Wolf 1 is airborne."

Prior's transport joined the nearby gunship in orbit in close proximity to the ground team and would maintain their vigil until needed.

Air support had always been a point of concern to many field commanders. In the past, pilots had failed to provide the necessary service required of them when the action heated up. Guardians were aggressive units, but because of their limited size, they did not have a dedicated air service. The much-maligned Kerguelen Air Guard had provided air support previously when needed.

Early air ships were unarmed and lightly armored and the pilots routinely refused to enter hot or heavily contested landing zones and many Guardians paid the ultimate price for their lack of commitment. Due to the nature of her unit's activities, Prior had opted to employ her own pilots to operate air ships used to transport her surveyors. All of her pilots were non-Guardian Boroni and were highly motivated. The vetting system she used was extremely thorough. Her personal pilot, Micah, was commander of her air group and was thrilled to get the chance to fly for her. And thanks to the Technology Council, he had state-of-the-art aircraft with advanced weapons and avionics to fly. The patches that Micah and the other pilots wore on their flight suits described their mission statement. A falcon with spread wings and long talons was depicted on a field of sky blue. The motto: 'There When Needed' was stitched below.

It was a short walk from the landing platform to the building they were going to. Prior's team was headed to the gallery of a rare art dealer named Kinon. Though he was a legitimate dealer, his numerous and varied extracurricular activities were less than above board. If anyone knew where to find The Broker, Kinon would. Prior believed he would still be at his building, despite the fact Gabriel had surely warned him and others that she was coming. And if he wasn't in, there were others in Lago Patria she could ask.

Kinon's showroom was located on the second floor of a new building and entry into it was granted by a special code. Prior looked at the door and motioned to Hiroki. He stepped up and placed a card in the slot on the door and then stepped back. The electronic lock made a low humming noise and then opened. Hiroki pulled out the card and the Guardians walked inside and quickly scaled the granite stairs to the second floor. A female receptionist greeted them with a smile when they entered and looked at their garb curiously. She briefly glanced down to what Prior believed was her appointment PDA and then spoke to them. Her voice was slightly raised to ensure Kinon knew he had unsuspected guests.

"May I help you?" she asked opening her eyes wide when she saw Lupo standing next to Prior.

"Please inform Kinon that he has visitors," Prior said.

"Is he expecting you?" she asked as her eyes followed the other Guardians as they walked around the office.

"We don't have an appointment, but he's expecting us," Prior said with a smile. "Tell him I want to see him right now."

"Whom may I ask wishes to see him?"

"Just describe me," Prior said. "He'll know."

"I'll see if he's free," she said stepping away and towards a set of double doors that led to Kinon's office with tentative steps.

She rapped lightly on the doors, entered the office and quickly walked to his desk and waved a hand at him. Kinon was on his TELCOM and was visibly upset by the interruption.

"Excuse me a moment," he said clicking the mute button on the desk mounted communication device. "What is it, Galena?"

"You have four visitors outside waiting to see you," she said.

"What visitors? I don't have any appointments today. Who is it?"

"Three men and a woman. I believe they're Guardians," Galena said. "The woman said you were expecting them."

"Guardians?" he said curiously. "Who is the woman?"

"She didn't say, but she's Boroni," Galena said sounding a bit frightened.

"Are you sure?" Kinon asked matching her concern.

"I've never met one, but I've seen pictures of them," Galena said shrugging her shoulders. "One of the men is one, I think, but she is definitely a female Boroni. Or is it Borona... what do you call the females?"

"Boroni. They're all called Boroni. Don't ever make the tragic mistake of calling them anything else. They are extremely... sensitive," he said.

"Why?"

"They just are... especially the females," he said. "But never mind about that. What does she look like?"

"Dark tan skin, long braided brown hair... and she's big," Galena said pointing at her biceps. "I don't know. I guess she just looks Boroni. Oh, and she's armed... and there's a dog with them."

"Shit. Why didn't you say that?" Kinon said clicking off the mute on his TELCOM. "I'll have to call you back." He clicked off the TELCOM and looked at Galena.

"What do you want me to do?" she asked.

He was about to tell her he wanted a first-class ticket out of the province when the doors of his office opened and Prior and her team entered. Kinon smiled at Prior and she smiled back briefly.

"Con permiso, senorita," Prior said in Galena's native tongue.

The woman looked quizzically at Prior and the Guardian jerked her head towards the door. Kinon put on his best salesman's face and waved a hand at Galena as the receptionist made a hasty exit.

"Commander Prior!" Kinon said standing and extending a hand. "Good to see you again!" He kept smiling as Galena shut the door and continued. "I wasn't aware you spoke the Lower-Central Provincial language. When did you learn that?"

"Cut the bullshit, Kinon. I don't have time for it," Prior said placing her hands on her hips.

"What do you want?" he asked taking his seat.

"Where is Sebastian?" she asked.

"Sebastian? Why would I know where Sebastian is? I don't delve into anything that would require his type of services," he said innocently.

"No, but you deal with people who do," Prior said with a smile. "I know he's in Lago Patria, and if he's here, you know where he is."

He leaned back in his chair and smiled. "That would probably be true if he were in Lago Patria. I heard he left for greener pastures months ago."

"Why are you lying to me, Kinon? I just want to talk to him. He's not in trouble so there's no reason to shield him."

"Someone like Sebastian is always on the verge of trouble."

"Not from me."

"Whether that's true or not, it doesn't matter. I can't help you, Prior. And you'll find that is the reception you'll get all over town," he said picking up an electronic data tablet.

"Really? Maybe you can help me another way," Prior said looking about the office. She spied an expensive looking vase and walked over to it. She picked it up and examined it closely. "I've been thinking about adorning my apartment with some antiques. Possibly something like this."

Kinon turned white as he looked up and saw Prior holding the vase. He put the tablet down and gulped. "Prior... be careful. That's a very, very expensive piece you're dangling there," he said.

"Yes, I know. It's Southern Provincial, from the Era of the Kings, isn't it? It's fifteen hundred years old," she said looking at it again with great interest.

"Seven... seventeen hundred years old," he said as a bead of sweat ran down his face. "Please put it down. It's the only one of its kind in existence."

"Oh, I'm sure it is, but don't worry. The gloves we wear have a special tactile coating. I couldn't drop this accidentally," Prior said as she threw the vase to the floor. It broke into shards and Prior smiled innocently. "Oops."

"What are you doing!" said Kinon as he made a move towards Prior. He stopped and took a deep breath. "That vase was appraised at three million credits."

"What's it worth now?" Prior asked stepping to another piece. The sculpture she now held was a small figurine that everyone in the room knew was over three thousand years old. "Now this is really something! But it's chipped."

Kinon fell to his knees and held the pieces of the broken figurine in his hands after Prior smashed it on the polished tiled floor of Kinon's office. She picked up another sculpture and Kinon held up his hands and pleaded with Prior through tear filled eyes.

"Please, Prior, no more. Why are you doing this? What in the Netherworld do you want?" Kinon asked.

"Sebastian's address."

"I can't tell you that! He'll know I told you. He can find out anything."

"As you wish," Prior said. She nodded to Rex and he stepped to the other side of the office and took a painting from the wall. The representation was possibly the most famous painting on the planet, *The Smirking Lady*. How Kinon obtained it was a mystery, though Prior was sure his possession of it was undoubtedly the result of an illegal scheme. "You know, I always thought that picture was bigger. It always seemed like it when I saw photos of it."

"That's what everyone says," Kinon said.

"Okay, Kinon, no more games," said Prior picking up another sculpture. "Do you want these men to destroy your gallery or are you going to give me Sebastian? All you have to do is scribble the address on a tablet and no one will be the wiser."

Kinon got to his feet and walked to his desk. He picked up a small tablet and stylus and briefly wrote on it. Prior stepped to the desk and read the tablet.

"Now, was that so hard?" she said tossing the sculpture she held to Kinon.

He cradled it like a newborn and she motioned for the Guardians to leave. Rex replaced the painting and took a few seconds to make sure it was hanging straight before he walked out.

"Is that all you need, Prior?" Kinon asked.

"I hope Sebastian doesn't get a call from you alerting him of my presence in Lago Patria and that I'm coming to see him, Kinon. It would be a shame if I had to return."

Kinon nodded and collapsed in his chair as Prior departed. When she joined her team on the street, Lieutenant Lindsey sported a frown. It was obvious that Prior's actions in the gallery upset him. As they journeyed to Sebastian's apartment, he was sullen.

"Is something bothering you, Lieutenant? It looks like something that's happened doesn't sit well with you," Prior said sensing his displeasure.

"Was all that necessary, Commander?" Lindsey asked.

"Yes," she said bluntly.

"Why?"

"When a Guardian commander asks a question, they expect an answer. Truthful answers. I had to make sure he would give me what I needed," Prior explained.

"But those treasures are lost forever."

"True, but they are only things. And a point had to be made."

"And what about the people in the club? Was it necessary to..."

"It was all necessary, Lieutenant. Everything I do has a purpose. I don't waste time or feel compassion... especially on those who don't deserve it. Gabriel and Kinon, despite their appearance, are not nice people. They have to be dealt with in a harsh way. If my methods are unsettling to you, I'll send you back to school," Prior said stopping on the street. "All you have to do is say the word."

"My apologies, Commander," he said coming to attention.

Prior frowned and turned from him. "Let's go."

The apartment complex that was home to Sebastian was a median income dwelling and would have been the last place Prior would have looked for him. It was filled with working-class families and was the perfect cover for his activities. He was Kerguelen's best information broker, trading anything worth knowing for large amounts of cash. Sebastian knew about, or could find out with a TELCOM call, anything you wanted to know.

As they entered the building, a trio of children ran past them. One of them turned around and gave them a salute and quickly turned to catch up with his friends. Prior looked on the registry and was surprised to find Sebastian's name clearly listed on it. They entered an elevator and Hiroki smiled as he saw Lindsey nervously checking his weapon.

"Relax, Lieutenant," he said. "We're just going to have a sit down."

"I just like to be prepared," said Lindsey placing his weapon back in its holster.

"There's no preparing for Sebastian," Prior said shaking her head. "He's always one step ahead. He probably knows we're on the way. If he wanted to attack us, it would have happened already."

"Who is this guy?" Lindsey asked as the doors to the elevator opened.

"Sebastian is one-of-a-kind," Prior said stepping out. "He has an uncanny knack of knowing everything. And you should be wary of him, Lieutenant, despite the captain's assurances."

"Why is that?" Lindsey asked.

Prior smiled. "He's a former Guardian."

15
Sebastian's apartment, Lago Patria, Northeastern Province, Planet Kerguelen

When Prior's team reached Sebastian's apartment, Rex pushed the buzzer. Prior looked up at the small security camera mounted over the door and smiled. A tall, good-looking man answered the door and invited the Guardians inside with a gracious bow.

"Welcome, Prior," he said with an easy smile. "You're late. I expected you a half hour ago."

"I was helping a friend redecorate," Prior said.

"Helping out a friend has a tendency of slowing your progress, doesn't it? Make yourselves at home," he said.

The apartment was not a large as Prior thought it would be and what made it seem even smaller were the two large, multi-screen high-end computer mainframes occupying the majority of the living room space. With those systems, Sebastian could keep his fingers on the pulse of everything that happened on Kerguelen, from sports to political activities. The units were not currently online, due no doubt to the presence of the Guardians, but Prior could feel their warmth and the high radiant temperature indicated they had just been powered down. Obviously, he didn't want his guests to know what he was currently investigating.

Sebastian padded around the apartment in bare feet offering the Guardians a drink, which they declined. He poured himself a tall glass of amber-colored ale and plopped down on a big synthetic leather couch next to a hard looking female. It was difficult for Prior to tell where she was from. It seemed as though she spent as little time as possible in the sun. Her pale and emaciated appearance was complemented by a tangle of unwashed and unkempt hair and ill-fitting clothes. Her slovenly look was the polar opposite of Sebastian's. He was dressed in dark, pressed slacks and a crisp white shirt and still retained much of his Guardian physique and moved with the lithe grace Prior had remembered. Surprisingly to Prior, he had kept his hair cut short and in Guardian grooming standards. He flashed his brilliant smile at Prior as he put his feet up on the small table in front of him.

"So, Prior, since you didn't come up here for a few drinks and some laughs and reminisce about our old academy days, I'll assume you're here on business," he said in a calm voice that was so nonchalant it was almost unnerving. "Are you sure I can't offer you a cool drink on this sweltering day?"

"No, thank you, Sebastian," Prior said shaking her head. "We're fine."

"That's right," he nodded smiling wider. "Guardians are trained to adapt to any environmental condition. And you Boroni are especially bred to withstand the heat, the cold, high altitude, low concentrations of O2... just about anything, aren't you?"

"More than you realize, Sebastian," Prior said matching his smile. "So, how's business?"

"You know how it is, sometimes you're up and sometimes you're down... but all-in-all, it's good, Prior, very profitable. I'm doing well," Sebastian said taking a drink. "What about you? Still knocking them dead? No pun intended."

"I'm fine, Sebastian," Prior replied. "You know how the game goes."

"Yes, I remember all too well. But the Corps is missing a few pieces now though. With all the activity going on, it's going to be rough maintaining readiness throughout the battalions, won't it?" he said tilting his head to the side.

"What do you mean? Who went down?" Prior asked.

"Jordan and Giles, and from what I understand, it wasn't pretty," he said as the smile disappeared from his face. "And with Sali dead..."

"Jordan and Giles? Are you sure, Sebastian?" Prior said matching his dour countenance.

"Of course he is, that's his business. That's why *he's* the best," the female said to Prior. "Are you surprised we know about that... or all of you? You're the silent and invisible Gray Wolves, the *true* vanguard of the Guardian Corps: Capt. Hiroki, Lt. Lindsey, Sgt. Rex... the incomparable Cdr. Prior... and Lupo. But where is the beauteous Sgt. Major Pana? Don't tell me you've left her behind?"

As she spoke, she pointed at each member of the team. Prior was surprised that she knew their names.

"You did an excellent job in the Eastern Province the other night," the female said. "With those nasty weapons and facilities destroyed, I can sleep soundly again. Thank you so much, Commander."

Prior was a bit troubled. What the unit did was covert and despite Sebastian's vast information network, the fact that anyone, even a former Guardian, knew what they did meant that there was a breech in security. Prior didn't know how he managed to obtain the information but it concerned her. There was no paper trail or computer records, and their missions were completely anonymous. Most of the time, Prior received her orders and assignments from Marshal Pace in person. The knowledge the woman had meant Sebastian was better informed than Prior had been led to believe. She would have to improve her security measures, but that was a task for another day.

"We don't need to be so blatant," Sebastian said tapping his assistant gently on her bony arm. "The commander doesn't need to add a breech of her security to the list of her problems. Especially when she's received such distressing news about her colleagues."

"*What* is that, Sebastian?" Prior said pointing at the woman.

"This is Nicola, one of my... associate brokers. One of her jobs is to keep track of anomalies in Guardian Corps activities. She has become quite fond of you ever since she found out that you were awarded The Star of Kerguelen, and she has made a career out of your exploits in the field," Sebastian said proudly. "That's why she is so familiar with your team. She knows everything about you... everything."

"I'm flattered," Prior quipped.

"You should be. But you came here on business, so let us proceed. I'm glad it's you who came here for information and not that deadbeat Thyssen," Sebastian said nearly spitting as he said the name of Prior's fellow Guardian.

"Why is Col. Thyssen a deadbeat?" Prior asked.

Prior had her own adjective to describe Thyssen, but said nothing. He was their academy classmate and second-in-command of the Second Battalion. To say that she loathed the man was a gross understatement.

Thyssen was an adequate combatant, but was not a very good leader or officer. Prior could have tolerated that if it wasn't for the fact he was a descendent of slaveholders and possibly the most prejudice creature on Kerguelen. He was proud that one of his ancestors had coined the phrase that a Boroni was only 6/10ths of a person.

"Let's just say he has a hard time coming up with... the price of admission. Old friendships and goodwill only go so far in our business. But I know I won't be wasting my time with you, Prior. You still have some credit on your account from the last time we did business. In fact, yours is a very lucrative account. How can I help you?" Sebastian said looking at Prior through steel-gray eyes that had now turned emotionless. He was in his business mode and was no longer jovial.

Prior reached into Lupo's body armor and pulled out the envelope she had concealed in it and tossed it into Sebastian's lap. He handed his glass to Nicola and opened the envelope. He removed two bound stacks of bills and quickly thumbed through the currency. When he was done he looked at Prior.

"Nice bank you have there. This is twenty thousand," he said taking his glass back from Nicola. "Why?"

"Is that enough for something controversial?" Prior asked.

"How controversial?"

"Venture. I need a line on him. I need fresh, I need new... and none of that garbage I could pull from a PIL blog myself. I need something real," Prior said glaring at Sebastian intensely.

"What do you want me to tell you, Prior? He's gone, poof, and I don't know where he disappeared to, it could be anywhere. He's a hard man to keep tabs on," Sebastian said shaking his head. "And I don't want to know where he is."

"I don't believe you, Sebastian. You're too good for that load of bullshit," Prior said looking at him carefully. "If you can find out about my teams, you can find out about Venture. But you won't tell me. Why?"

"It took a long time to discover your secret Guardian life, and I had a little motivation to learn more. You're better looking than he is," he laughed. "If I had a little time I could come up with something."

"I don't have a little time."

"Pity. You know, I did hear that you were selected to bring him in. That's one hell of an assignment," he said taking another drink.

"It's turning out to be. It would be easier if people would help me out. Everyone I talk to is a clam. It's frustrating," Prior said. When she continued, her voice was softer. "Can you help me, Sebastian?"

"I wish I could, Prior, I truly do, but I can't," he said. "It has nothing to do with you or your mission, I just can't. I can tell you that he knows that you're on his trail and he'll be ready for you when you finally catch up with him. I'm sorry, that's the best I can do."

"How does he know I'm coming? Did you tell him?"

"I did," he said bluntly. "And he's upset about it. Old friends pitted against each other. Tsk. It's a sad state-of-affairs. I'm glad I'm through with it."

"Why can't you help me like you helped him, Sebastian?" Prior asked. "I recall you used to think very highly of our comradeship. One might even call it friendship."

"You don't owe her anything, Sebastian. Don't let her play the old friends and comrades card. She's a Helot. They don't understand the concept of friendship. They're just words to her. Don't tell that Boro bitch anything," Nicola said scoffing at Prior's plea with blatant disgust. "Boros aren't even real people, they're a concoction derived from the mind of a mad scientist."

For some reason, Prior was not in a tolerable mood. Perhaps the commander was being affected by the heat and didn't realize it. Maybe she was just tired of Sebastian's playful banter, she didn't know for sure. Normally, she would have let the racial slurs and insults pass and ignored Nicola, just as she had done her entire life and carried on. But this time she could not do it. Before anyone could blink, Prior drew her pistol and shot Nicola twice in the chest. The shots were so closely grouped, they formed a single cavity in Nicola's upper body. The thin woman was dead before she realized she had been shot. The action had been reflex. Prior was still looking at Sebastian when she shot Nicola and didn't realize she had done it herself until she turned to the woman. Nicola's mouth was agape and her dark eyes were still staring at Prior. But she would never utter another word nor would she see another sight.

Sebastian sat there mute and surprisingly sedate. He pulled down the blanket that was folded over the back of the couch and neatly covered his former assistant with it. The Guardians with Prior were a bit more shaken but said nothing. Lindsey had turned away briefly and Lupo barked loudly twice. Prior holstered her weapon and rubbed her forehead before she continued.

"Can you help me, Sebastian?" she asked again as if nothing had happened. Her voice was even softer than it was before.

"You shot her! What in the Netherworld is the matter with you, Prior?" he asked.

"Don't be a child, Sebastian. You were a Guardian and you know how this goes. And don't give me the innocent "boy scout" routine. You know what I do. My hands are tied," Prior said angrily. "Lives are at stake. I don't have time for bullshit."

"I'm not mad at anyone anymore, Prior, I've put that all behind me," Sebastian said standing up and walking away from her.

"I'm not mad either, but you've got to give me something so I don't have to shut you down," Prior implored him.

"Shut me down? You're going to arrest me? For what?" he asked.

"Illegal distribution of electronic information, espionage, aiding and abetting a known felon, compromising the safety of a Guardian, contributing to the delinquency of a minor, and exposing a minor to explicit pornographic material..." Prior rattled off but was interrupted by Sebastian.

"Whoa, whoa, what do mean, 'contributing to the delinquency of a minor and exposing a minor to pornographic material'?" he said with his hands raised. "I've never done that... and you know it, Prior! You can't make it stick anyway."

"My electronic forensic engineers can do wonders... especially with a set-up like that," she said gesturing to the computers. "Do you know that a conviction as a pedophile carries a death sentence? Listen to me rambling. Of course you do, you were a Guardian."

"You wouldn't do that to me. You haven't fallen that far... that deep... to do something like that," Sebastian said hoping he was correct.

"You may have unsurpassed knowledge of planetary events, but you don't know me as well as you think, Sebastian. No one does. Now, the choice is yours, but I'm out of time. You've got to decide what you're going to do," Prior said.

Sebastian could tell that Prior was serious… and she never bluffed. Prior knew that Sebastian would not go down without a fight, a fight that would ultimately end with his death. She was more than capable of killing him alone, and even if he was lucky enough to defeat her, she had help. It was a no-win situation for Sebastian and after some thought he reluctantly relented. Obviously he was not ready to die.

"Okay, okay. But listen, you're playing with fire. All of you are. This is nasty business. You're dealing with the Cardinals, the planet's legislature… the list runs long and deep. What's happening in this city is only the beginning. The government is losing its support base all over the planet, and the powers that be will do anything it takes to keep what's theirs intact. No matter what the cost. We're on the brink of catastrophe, the kind we've never seen before," Sebastian warned.

"How big are you talking about?" Hiroki asked.

"It'll make the last Provincial Wars look like a church outing."

"What have you got?" Prior asked impatiently.

"What I have to tell you needs to be confidential," Sebastian said looking at the Guardians.

Prior turned and nodded to her team and they stepped into the hallway leaving Prior and Lupo alone with Sebastian. When they were alone, he rubbed his neck and poured himself another drink. This time it was a tall glass of whiskey.

"I could get killed for telling you this," he said.

"That's a chance I'm willing to take," Prior said.

"Funny. Have you ever heard of the Celeron?" he asked.

"Of course I have. It's a boogeyman story for plebes at the academy. They're supposed to be a secret order within the Guardian Corps," Prior said. "But no one has ever proved of its existence."

"Or disproved it," Sebastian offered. "It exists, Prior, and Venture is a member. He went to them for help when he left here."

"Will they help him?"

"Yes, he's one of them."

"Why would they get involved?"

"It's what they do. The Celeron involve themselves in various… projects. It's rumored that they aided the Boroni and initiated the slave revolt. But who knows for sure?"

"Where are they?"

"They live up north. A place called Canton-on-Heath. Here's the exact location of their estate," Sebastian said turning on a PDA and pointing to the position. "Naturally, it's fortified and heavily guarded. They don't like visitors or uninvited guests."

"Naturally," Prior said nodding. "Anything else you want to tell me?"

"If I tell you this, am I clear?" Sebastian asked. Prior nodded once and he continued. "The Argent is active again."

"The Argent? What are you talking about? You don't really believe in that stuff, do you?" Prior queried. She studied his face and saw that he was serious. "Never mind. It's not important. Thank you, Sebastian. I'm out of here."

As she was about to leave she turned back to Sebastian and recalled the many times they had shared a drink, fought together, fought each other and watched mutual friends die. He knelt down in front of Nicola's covered body and said a silent prayer. When he was finished, he stood and faced Prior with a crooked grin on his face.

"Does it ever hurt you? Does it ever bother you... inside?" he asked.

"No, not anymore," she replied looking at Nicola.

"When did it stop? After Sierra de Retan or Domtar?"

"They all played a part in it, among other incidents. I learned early on that we had to be harder... more malicious than our foes. I accepted that and moved on," she said.

"Tell me, Prior. Why did you shoot her twice?" he asked motioning to Nicola.

"Multiple insults, multiple shots," Prior said.

"It was *one* insult using *multiple* words, Prior."

"I made a mistake," Prior said shrugging her shoulders. "And so did she. I'll have someone come by and clean up this mess for you. Call it a tip. Come, Lupo."

"Prior," Sebastian called as she reached the door. "I don't need to tell you to be careful. The Celeron are a powerful organization. Don't take them lightly. As far as Venture goes, Venture will kill you if he has to and The Argent, well, let's just say they are less than hospitable. They probably have a sect of Middle Province zealots assisting them, so watch your ass."

"I always do, but thank you, Sebastian," Prior said as she departed.

She and her team quickly exited the apartment building and were surprised to see her air ship waiting with engines running out in front. It was hovering just above the ground and the heat from the engines washed over them as first Lupo and then the rest climbed inside the craft. Prior gave Pana a curious look as she entered.

"You're wanted at 'The Home', Commander, as soon as possible," Pana said. "And the investigators have the data you requested. It's ready for you to download whenever you want."

Prior nodded and called to her pilot. "Micah, drop me off at the closest public transit center. I'm going to follow a lead. I'll rendezvous with you at Strathmore in about six hours. From there, we'll go on to 'The Home'," Prior said. She turned to Hiroki and continued. "Captain, let Central Command know I've been unavoidably detained. Also inform them that I have good reason to believe that Commanders Jordan and Giles are dead. Contact Commander Mohab and tell him that Sebastian needs help. He needs to look in on him personally. Give him the address and send that with my compliments."

"At once, Commander," Hiroki said standing up to carry out his orders.

The air ship lifted off and as Micah flew toward a transit center, Prior reviewed the report filed by Major Metis. The major's results were distressing. Prior frowned as she read the data and tossed the PDA to Pana when she was done.

"Hiroki, I have another message for you," Prior said. Hiroki turned to Prior and nodded. "Contact Major Metis and have her assign one surveyor to each of the persons on the list she gave me. Tell her to keep me informed on any changes in status."

Hiroki nodded and continued on with his messages.

Prior thought quietly as the airship darted across the Lago Patria sky. In less than five minutes, they were orbiting a public air transit center. Once they landed, Prior removed Lupo's body armor and her own weapons harness and handed them to Pana. Pana frowned and stowed the gear in a compartment and handed Prior a medium length leather jacket. Prior winked at her but Pana remained tense. Prior stuffed a wallet into her coat pocket and waved at her team as she and Lupo hopped out of the air ship.

"Why is she going off without us and unarmed?" Lindsey asked as he watched her disappear into the crowd. "What does it mean?"

"She's unarmed because she can't carry a weapon on a public transport, you know that's illegal. And she's going off alone because she's headed for trouble, Lieutenant," Pana said. "Serious trouble." She slammed the hatch shut and called to Micah. "Okay, let's go!"

As the air ship climbed into the darkening sky, Prior made her way amid the mass of travelers trying desperately to find a way out of the powder keg that was Lago Patria. As she searched for a ticket counter that would serve her purposes, she was approached by an attractive man in his earlier thirties and casually dressed in a lightweight suit. The expensive cut and tailoring of his clothes, suggested that he was more than just another traveler. He bowed slightly to her and she nodded as Lupo growled softly.

"My name is Howard," he said. "I can get you to your destination much more comfortably and faster than any public transportation."

"How can you be so sure?" Prior asked raising an eyebrow and casually looking around to see if anyone was with the man.

"Because the transports will be SRO and none of them leave for Canton for at least another two hours. We can leave immediately, and in much greater comfort," he answered.

"You're very accommodating," she said with a smile.

"I try. I realize your time is limited," he said smiling back at her.

"How do you know I'm headed to Canton and I'm on a tight schedule?" she asked.

"Commander Prior," Howard said still smiling. "There isn't much the Celeron don't know."

PART THREE

PART THREE

1
Cathedral Prime, Capitol City,
Central Province, Planet Kerguelen

Cathedral Prime was one of the oldest structures remaining completely intact after the devastation of the last Provincial Wars. Though Capitol City received its fair share of damage during the conflict, the religious facility had somehow avoided destruction and was spared the fate that many other famous and older structures did not. It wasn't because it wasn't targeted, because it was, the building was just lucky enough not to get hit.

Outside of its walls, hundreds of citizens stood silently looking upwards towards the apartments of the pontiff, Cardinal Gregor XII. It was known he was not well, though the people didn't know why. They only knew the Federal Church had asked all of the citizens to pray for his speedy recovery from unknown ailments.

Inside of his bedroom, Gregor's assistants helped him dress in his ceremonial garb much to the dismay of Gregor's physician. As the assistants put the finishing touches on the scarlet and white vestments, Gregor's doctor once again voiced his concerns.

"Eminence, I have to repeat my warning to you," the doctor said. "You have just received a very traumatic injury. I beg you to reconsider this."

"The people... my people... need to see that the leader of the Church is still at the helm. It will soothe their minds and reinforce the power of the Almighty," Gregor said as the assistants adjusted and centered his headdress.

"This spectacle could have waited until tomorrow, Your Eminence. Those people aren't going anywhere," the doctor argued. "I can't guarantee this won't cause you a set back."

Gregor looked at the doctor and smiled. "Have no fears, doctor. I promise you won't be blamed if the Almighty decides to claim me because I failed to heed your instructions," he said. "I must do this. I'm afraid it's out of both of our hands."

Gregor slowly walked away from the doctor and made his way to the window. Gregor's administrative assistant, Monsignor Kellan, placed a crosier in Gregor's left hand and stepped back. Gregor looked at his aides and then stepped through the curtains and out onto the balcony and was immediately bathed in a roar of shouts and applause.

Gregor smiled and raised the crosier in the air and waved the ceremonial staff back and forth. He stayed out on the balcony for a few minutes to receive the adoration of the people and to ensure as many people as possible could view him. When he was positive that enough pictures were taken of him for the breaking news report that would surely follow his appearance, he made the sign of their faith with the crosier and then stepped back inside his apartment. He quickly made his way to his bed and sat down. He appeared weak from his exertions and the doctor immediately began to look him over. Gregor frowned and pushed the doctor away.

"Please don't fret over me like I was an invalid child, doctor," Gregor insisted. "I'm quite alright. I was just hit with a sharp numbing thrust of pain. It has passed."

"I'll prescribe something stronger for you," the doctor said. "We can't have you collapsing in front of the people."

"Thank you, doctor," Gregor nodded. "Now if you will excuse us, I must discuss some private Church matters with my assistants."

The doctor nodded and left the bedroom. When he was gone, Gregor ordered his aides to remove his ceremonial wardrobe and helped him into the cassock he wore everyday. When they were finished he slowly walked to his desk and as he reclined in his chair, he turned to Kellan.

"Are they here?" Gregor asked catching his breath.

"Yes, Eminence, in the library," Kellan said. "Vice President Shayesteh has also recently arrived. I didn't know she was coming."

"Nor did I. I will see her first. After she leaves, bring the others in and then leave us," Gregor ordered.

Kellan nodded and left and when he returned, he had the vice president in tow. Planetary Vice President Shayesteh was petite and extremely beautiful. She was often described as exotic looking. She had clear and sparkling gray eyes that evinced a highly intelligent mind and ample curves that piqued one's imagination. Her dark hair shone like black silk and rested gently upon her shoulders. Many believed it was her presence on the ballot that secured President Ward's re-election. Whether it was true or not, everyone considered her to be aptly named. Shayesteh, in the dialect of the Middle Provinces, meant "Ideal Perfection". She bowed to Gregor and kissed his ring of office and then sat down beside him.

"Cardinal, I am so happy to see you up and about," Shayesteh said in her heavy accent. "The president will be pleased when I tell him the news."

"Thank you, Madam Vice President," Gregor said. "Would you care to stay for lunch?"

"I'm afraid I can't. My schedule is very full, but thank you," Shayesteh said standing up. "I'll make sure *everyone* is aware of your progress."

She bowed to him again and was escorted out by Kellan. This time when Gregor's assistant returned, he led in a group consisting of two male priests and four other men. Kellan bowed to Gregor and left them alone and when he was gone, Gregor asked the group to sit.

The group was a unique mix of individuals. The priests were long-serving clergymen and known to be very conservative in their thinking. Sitting next to the priests, was Grand Senator Bacor. Beside Bacor was a man named Gallegos. Gallegos was an international financier and was rumored to have strong ties with the planet's criminal underworld community. President Ward's Judge Advocate General had never charged him with a crime, but his activities were closely monitored.

Next to Gallegos was a man named Hayward. He was a known terrorist and Kerguelen's public enemy number one. He was not shy about using any device as a means to advance his agenda and goals... or anyone else's if the price was right. He had been responsible for the employment of biological and low-yield nuclear weapons against civilians and the Guardians had a shoot on sight order issued against him.

Sitting behind Hayward was Colonel Thyssen of the Guardian Second Battalion, and the Guardian seemed to exhibit no ill will toward Hayward. Next to Thyssen was the final member of the group. He was tall and well built wearing an expensive suit. His skin was deeply tanned and his long dark hair was tied in an intricate ponytail. At six-foot five, he towered over everyone in the room. He was a Boroni male named Senator Poul. He felt uncomfortable about being involved with the others and he didn't know whether the reason for his unease came from his partners or from what they planned to do.

Gregor leaned forward and spoke. "I'm glad you all could join me," he said.

"We're at your disposal, Eminence," Bacor said. "But are you sure you shouldn't be resting?"

Gregor waved a dismissive hand. "I can rest when this is over. We have to continue to move forward with our plans. Where do we stand? Does anyone have an update?" he asked.

"I have some distressing news," Hayward said with a smile. "I'm afraid Archbishop Cornelia has been assassinated by Cdr. Venture."

"That is a shame, but I'm sure the evening news will have a very respectful tribute in her honor tonight," Gregor said smiling back. "Have you acquired the weapons we need, Hayward?"

"I have, but it was not easy," Hayward said with a sigh. "It cost me several good men."

"What is the loss of a few men compared with what we are about to accomplish?" Gregor said. "What about financing?"

"Adequate, but not good. There are several corporations that have discovered what I was up to. I had to scale back on my dealings. And it looks like we won't be able to acquire General Manufacturing. They received a loan from a private source I'm sorry to say," Gallegos said. "We believe that source was the Western Province Grange."

"I've got to lay low as well," Hayward said. "The Guardians are closing in on me."

"You're lucky," Gallegos said wiping his forehead. "I've got the Grange shadowing me."

"Col. Thyssen can handle the Guardians," Gregor said to Hayward. He turned to Gallegos and added, "And the senators will handle the corporations. Neither of you should worry."

"I don't mean any disrespect, Gregor, but I'll worry as long as there are Guardians determined to catch me," Hayward said. "There's a group of them with their noses to the ground trying to sniff me out. If they catch me, I'm done. Thyssen and the regular Guardians are not the problem. They're nothing. It's Prior and her people that concern me. I believe her operatives destroyed my facilities in the Eastern Province the other night. And without them, we're much weaker."

"Prior is a bigger problem than you think," Gallegos offered. "I can't dodge her people at the Grange indefinitely. Sooner or later I have to surface and when I do, they'll be there. I need assurances… protection… safeguards."

Poul smiled. Though he disliked his sister's meddling, the notion she was causing so much fear, uneasiness and tension amongst these men gave him pleasure.

"Hayward, you will continue to obtain the material we desire," Gregor said sternly. "And you will continue to get the money we need, Gallegos. Bacor and Poul have a plan to handle the Grange and other large corporations. I will not be deterred from the goal by a thousand men and a agricultural company."

"Soon there will be only five hundred Guardians for us to deal with," Thyssen said.

"It only takes one," Hayward countered. "I've been on the receiving end of their operations too many times not to be concerned."

"And the Grange is not just a bunch of farmers," Gallegos said.

"Be assured that the Guardians will have more than you to worry about very soon, Hayward," Gregor said. "And if the Western Province Grange and the other corporations prove problematic, we'll just have to avoid them… or eliminate them completely."

They all nodded in agreement and then said their goodbyes to the cardinal. When they had departed, the door to Gregor's study opened and a large and dark figure emerged, seemingly from nowhere. Though it had the appearance and form of a man, it was both more and much less than a man. Its eyes were red and its skin was scaly and rough like a reptile. The creature opened its mouth, exposing large, yellowish sharp and jagged teeth. It seemed as if someone had placed a set of shark's teeth in the mouth of a man.

Despite its tremendous size, the creature moved with light steps towards Gregor. He looked around the room and then spoke to Gregor using the ancient biblical language.

"<Why did you call me, Summoner>?" the creature asked. In spite of his attempt to keep his voice low, it still echoed like the sound of a rubber ball being thrown against a stonewall. "<Do you have work for me>?"

"<I do>," Gregor said. "<But I also wanted you to see who our allies are>."

"<I saw them, but does it matter who they are>?" the creature asked. "<As long as they serve He who is Dark, who they are is of no consequence>."

"<You are correct>," Gregor said. "<But you must go now. Time is short and you need to be in place when your next target arrives>."

"<I will be in position, Summoner>," the creature said baring his teeth. "<I hope killing this one will be worth my time>."

"<He is>," Gregor nodded. "<He is commander of all the Guardians>."

The creature turned to leave and then spun on his heels and turned back to Gregor. "<The tall, dark skinned one intrigues me, Summoner>," the creature said. "<He looks like he would be a match for my skills. I've never seen you creatures look so formidable. I sense no fear in him, only anger>."

"<Senator Poul and his people are all formidable>," Gregor answered.

"<He is different than the rest of you>," the creature said cocking his head to one side. "<His scent was strange. I've never encountered a scent quite like it before>." The creature thought for a moment and then came to a conclusion. "<He is one of *Man's* creations! He is not a creation of the One of the Light>."

"<That's correct. He is what we call Boroni>," Gregor offered.

"<You Kerguelens once called them Helots>," the creature said. "<But they call themselves Boroni>."

"<Yes, that is true>," Gregor said.

"<I like that one, Summoner>," the creature said. "<The others smell of fear, but that one… that one reeks of anger and hate. He has no fear. Like me, only one being concerns him and I believe he and I are wary

of the same being. Interesting. You are mistaken in calling that one a Helot, Summoner. He is no man's slave. And he is the only one of your allies worthy to be in my presence>."

The creature stared into the air for a second longer and then turned quickly and left the bedroom disappearing through the door leading to the study. When the creature was gone, Gregor sighed and turned to the items on his desk.

As Gregor dove into his work, he reviewed what was written on an electronic data tablet. He knew the group he had allied himself with had a rough road ahead of them and tough hills left to climb. He hated to admit it but Gallegos and Hayward and the creature were all right. The common denominator of the problems of financing and harassment from the Guardians and Senator Poul's fear was the same, the unfeeling and immovable force known as Prior. And she too was without a doubt no man's slave.

2
The Celeron Estate, Canton-on-Heath, Northeastern Province, Planet Kerguelen

If the myths and rumors Prior recalled relating to the Celeron were true, she was not surprised when a representative approached her. What did catch her off guard was the swiftness in which the mysterious group had made contact with her. She assumed that Sebastian would tell them that she was on the way, but even if he did, how did they move in so quickly? Perhaps they had agents in Lago Patria that had shadowed her from Capitol City; or perhaps this was all prearranged. Whatever the case, she was on her way and she wouldn't have to break in to see them. She had been invited into their world.

Lupo was sitting next to her and as she stroked his thick coat, he made soft, throaty noises and placed his head in her lap. The air ship they were in was cruising at just under a thousand feet and Prior gazed out of the window and below to the thick canopy of trees that made up the Ebon Forest, a forest that had been only replanted with saplings less than sixty years before. Once the deadly radiation from weapons used in the last Provincial Wars had subsided, the saplings were planted and their growth was augmented by the use of agro-accelerants. The once pristine forest had been restored to its pre-war grandeur and was once again the signature locale of the region. The forest reminded Prior of the Pine Barons of her own province and she silently thanked the Almighty for saving her home from the same disaster that had befallen this province. As the ship skimmed over the treetops, her thoughts flowed from the forest to those she would be meeting.

According to legend, the Celeron could have been any of the Guardians she knew or had known... a classmate, a superior, a subordinate... anyone. It was rumored that the secret society recruited new members from cadets at the academy and strategically placed them in sensitive posts in the Corps. Whatever they did or whoever they really were didn't matter to Prior. All that concerned her was finding Venture, and if this group of overage fraternity brothers could help, so be it. If they got in her way, she would deal with that too.

She turned to Howard and he smiled at her. She was about to speak and then decided to say nothing. Prior had many questions but doubted Howard would provide her with anything substantial. He must have sensed her curiosity and broke the ice for her.

"You have a question, Commander?" he asked.

"Yes. Several in fact," Prior said. "Why have you come for me?"

"The Celeron wish to speak with you on a matter of great significance. You are considered vital in the future plans of the Celeron," he said.

"Really? What plans are those?" Prior asked.

"I'm afraid the answer to that will have to wait until we arrive," Howard said apologetically. "But I can say like all Celeron operations, the result will be worth the effort."

"I see," Prior nodded.

"I sincerely hope you do, Commander," Howard said.

"Is it true the Celeron are Guardians?"

"Yes. The senior members are vetted from academy stock and groomed for future work that benefits the planet," Howard explained.

"But that's what the Guardian Academy does," Prior said.

"The Celeron are a more proactive organization and not hamstrung by the constraints of the Guardian Corps," Howard said.

"Those constraints are necessary," said Prior. "If they weren't there, Guardians could become vigilantes... or worse."

"You don't understand the purpose of the Celeron, Commander. Guardians act when things go bad. The Celeron try to anticipate the bad and act before it gets out of hand. In a sense the Celeron could be considered... sentinels," Howard said. He looked at his chronometer and back to Prior. "We're about to land, Commander. Please fasten your seat restraint."

The air ship slowed and descended into a lush, well-manicured lawn belonging to a sprawling stone manor. Prior estimated the manor was eight or nine hundred years old, constructed in the era of the land barons. The engines became silent and Howard opened the hatch and gestured for Prior to exit. She and Lupo leapt out and the canine ran around the grounds, sniffing and scratching at the thick grass in front of the great house. As Prior walked across the lawn, she stopped suddenly and knelt down. She pulled out a few blades of grass and examined them. The grass and soil was expensive... and rare. Soil completely free of any remnants of nuclear or biological contamination was a premium and this particular patch had been imported from the Oceanic Province. Difficult to import and hard to maintain in this moderate climate, the fact it was here meant the Celeron had huge financing and possessed considerable international influence. Provincial governments didn't just give good soil away and when they finally did release it, it was only after substantial prodding and pressures were placed on them. As she knelt, Prior watched Lupo as he ran and explored. Howard moved beside her, cleared his throat and she stood up.

"Commander, this way if you please," he said pointing to the entrance of the manor. "If you could call your pet, we can proceed."

"Would it be a problem if he stayed out here?" she asked.

"No, but I wouldn't want him to wander off and get lost on the grounds. The estate is quite extensive. It will be dark soon and there are many wild animals in the surrounding forest. They do not possess obedience chips. He could be injured," Howard said with concern.

"Lupo doesn't have the chip either," Prior replied with a smile. "He's half-gray wolf and very capable of taking care of himself."

"Of that I'm sure," Howard nodded as he looked at the dog. The gray wolf was considered one of the most capable predators of its size on Kerguelen. Considering the animal's mistress and the fact he did not possess an obedience chip, the animal might well enjoy an evening foraging in the forest. "As you wish, Commander."

"Lupo! Come!" Prior called. The canine made a U-turn and sprinted to her. She knelt down and took his head in her hands. "Take a break, Lupo." She kissed the top of his head and he raised his snout and licked her face. She wiped away the wetness he left behind as he ran away to continue playing on the grass. "He'll find me when he's finished. Shall we go?"

"This way, Commander," Howard said.

He led her up the dozen stone steps and into the great house. Prior blinked as her vision adjusted to the interior lighting. They were in a grand foyer covered with old oil paintings. Prior recognized many of them as works of the great masters in art history. Howard pointed and they continued down a long and wide marble hallway. Despite its austere appearance, the manor was bristling with modern conveniences and technology. Besides the obvious improvements, Prior had spotted seismic sensors in the lawn and various security and surveillance monitors inside. It seemed the Celeron were very particular about who visited them.

"How big is this place?" Prior asked.

"This building only has thirty-two rooms," Howard said. "The main house contains sixty-five."

"The main house?"

"Yes. It's about ten miles away. This is the staff quarters."

Prior smiled. Obviously there was a lot more going on here and the Celeron were more than just a boy's club. "What are your duties, Howard?" Prior asked as she admired the various pieces of art that decorated the corridor.

"Presently, I'm your... liaison to the Celeron," he replied carefully choosing his words.

"Liaison? You sound as if I'm going to be here for an extended stay," Prior said turning to him.

"I wouldn't know about that, Commander," he answered without looking at her.

"I don't plan on staying very long, Howard," Prior said.

"The length of your visit is contingent upon many things, Commander, but I don't believe you'll be on the premises any longer than necessary. The Celeron enjoy the solitude they've created and seldom have any guests, especially female guests. However, it is their hope that when you do leave, you'll have a better understanding of many things," he said.

"Is that so?"

"Yes."

"You speak about the Celeron as if you're not one of them."

"I am not Celeron, no. There are many non-Celeron in the organization that serve in various capacities that do not require membership to fulfill," he explained.

"I see. And no women?"

"That's correct."

"Really? Not even to… visit?" Prior asked with a raised eyebrow.

"No, never, but you are considered an exception," he said opening a door. "Right through here, Commander. Go on in, they're expecting you."

"Who's expecting me?"

"The Seven," Howard said stepping in behind her.

They entered a large study that was lavishly furnished and quite inviting. The seven gentlemen occupying the room, by Prior's estimate, were all over eighty years of age. They stood together, dressed in expensive casual attire. One of them waved at Howard and the young man bowed and shut the door behind him as he departed. The same man waved at Prior and she moved closer to the group. Despite their obvious advanced age, they all looked in excellent health and appeared to be in top physical condition.

"May we offer you anything, Commander?" the man that waved at her asked.

"Calvados," she said looking at the collection of bottles on the bar.

"Excellent choice," he said stepping away to pour her a snifter of the apple brandy she had selected.

As he poured, Prior looked at him closely. His face had the tautness and lines of a much younger man. Prior was not sure if his deep tan was natural or artificial, but regardless of how it was achieved, he was handsome in her opinion and she found him strangely attractive. She also believed that she had seen him before as well.

He handed her the glass and raised his. "To Guardians past, present and future," he said.

"To Guardians past, present and future!" every one else in the room including Prior repeated as they raised their glasses high.

"Until the last banner is retired," Prior said finishing the toast.

"Until the last banner is retired!" the seven replied. Several of them nodded in agreement as they downed the contents of their glasses in a single swallow.

The handsome man refilled Prior's glass and motioned to a high backed chair. Prior sat and leaned into the comfortable seat and canvassed the group. The seven men remained standing and her eyes stopped on one sporting a closely cut Van Dyke beard. He smiled at her when their eyes met and Prior would have sworn she knew him as well. The attractive Celeron sat his glass down and took a deep breath.

"I suppose you're wondering why you've been brought here?" the attractive Celeron asked.

"I am," Prior said. "But I was coming anyway."

"Then our intervention serves both of our purposes," the man with the Van Dyke offered.

"Yes," Prior said.

"Well, I was thinking that we could discuss your arrival over a meal," the attractive Celeron said. "I know that your eating schedule is quite different than a Kerguelens, but I was hoping you could join us."

"It's true that Boroni only replenish… eat… every three or four days once we've reached full maturity, but I'm within that window," Prior said. "I would love to join you, but I am on a tight schedule."

"We understand that, but a repast won't disturb your timetable too drastically," he said with a smile.

Prior gazed at the group of men and saw that they were all smiling at her with paternal looks. She knew that she needed whatever information these men had and wasn't going to get it unless she broke bread with them. Having dinner was not going to make or break her operation, she knew it and they knew it. Besides, how often did a woman get to eat with the Celeron? She smiled back and nodded.

"Perhaps a meal is in order," she said. "Lead the way."

"Excellent," the attractive Celeron said. "Bring your glass."

Prior stood and the man with Van Dyke took her coat. She thanked him as they led her to the dining room. The dining room was adjacent to the study and appeared to be the private dining room of the group. Prior sat at a long dining table between the man with the Van Dyke and one with a full beard and was surprised when they held her chair for her. Two male servants handed out hot towels to the Celeron and Prior as another filled the water glasses. After the diners had wiped their hands and faces, the attendants retrieved the towels and began to place down the first course. When they all had a plate in front of them, the attractive Celeron, who sat at the head of the table, led them in prayer.

"Almighty, Bless this food so that it may fuel our bodies and bless this company so that Your wisdom may nourish our souls," he said.

"Amen," they all replied together.

"Dig in, Commander," the attractive Celeron said. "The shrimp was flown in fresh today from the Eastern Province and the bread is made in our own bakery. Naturally, the greens are from the Western Province."

Prior took a bite of her shrimp salad and the flavor leapt onto her taste buds. It was flavorful but not overstated. The greens were fresh and crisp and the whole grain bread was warm and soft. The Celeron with the full beard wiped his mouth with the expensive linen napkin in his lap and leaned back in his chair.

"Commander, you said that Boroni only eat every three or four days once you've reached full maturity. What age is that?" he asked.

"Between the ages of ten and twelve years," Prior said. "More consumption than that is counterproductive. When we do replenish, it's a lot, and designed to last several days. We can go for a week without food and water before we start to degrade in ability. It's part of our... design... and it's ideal for what we were bred for."

"Replenish?" he said curiously. "You make the Boroni sound like they are machines."

"We are in many ways. Like all man-made devices, our design and creation was based on how we could make the lives of people better and more productive," Prior said. "The Boroni have accepted and are comfortable with the fact that we are self-replicating organic machines. Only Kerguelens are uncomfortable with that fact."

The Celeron all looked at her and silently absorbed her words and then looked to the attractive Celeron. He put his fork down and cleared his throat.

"Commander, we brought you here to clear up any questions you may have and help you if we can," he said.

"I appreciate that, it's very gracious of you," Prior said. "My needs are simple: I need to know where Commander Venture is."

"Straight to the point," a dark skinned Celeron from the Southern Province said. "I like that."

"Unfortunately, we don't know where our brother has gone," the Celeron with the full beard said. He leaned back as the servants cleared the first course plates.

"You're not your brother's keeper," Prior sniped.

"In this case, no," the attractive Celeron said. "He has broken some of our tenets and is no longer accepted or welcomed here."

When the plates were cleared, the servants rolled in two carts containing the main courses. Prior was offered four types of vegetables, two starches and two different meats. She selected three of the vegetable choices, a starch and both meats in ample helpings. She passed on the wine when it was offered opting to have her water glass refilled.

"But he did come here and seek you out though," Prior said as she maneuvered her knife and fork around the mass of food on her plate.

"Yes, but we expelled him. Oh, we gave him some logistical support, but he is now cut off from our considerable resources," the attractive Celeron said.

"You gave him one for the road," she said.

"In a matter of speaking, yes," the dark skinned Celeron said amused by her interpretation of events.

"Can you tell me why he shot Cardinal Gregor?"

"He believed he was doing what was best for the planet, and as a member of our order, he followed one of our most basic and fundamental tenets. We Celeron have kept an eye on all that takes place on Kerguelen and act, directly or indirectly, in certain volatile events and confront particular undesirables. It has been our way for almost two thousand years. We attempt to… tip the scales, as it were, for the greater good of Kerguelen. We wanted Venture to cease his obsession with Gregor and take charge of another operation we have set into motion. However, he refused and has chosen another path. He believes his is the best course of action," the attractive Celeron said. He sat back and took a sip of wine.

"I see," Prior said nodding. "You wanted him to stop The Argent and he wanted to continue to undermine Gregor's activities on a grander scale."

"You're quite well informed, Commander," the attractive Celeron said looking at his colleagues and nodding approvingly. "You know much, despite your unenlightened background."

"Thank you, but I really don't know anything. I know that there are those who are planning to do something on a planetary scale to control the people under the guise of a religious banner. But that's all. I'm hoping that Venture stumbled upon this and in his own way, is trying to correct it. But I can't prove any of that until I can get to him. Regardless of why he's doing this, he's got to stop. He's distracting the masses from seeing what is really happening. His plan is not in the best interests of the people. The peripheral damage he's inflicting is hurting his cause. He's an ordained priest as well as a Guardian. The safety of the people has to be in the forefront of his plans," Prior said.

The fact that she knew Venture was a priest surprised the Celeron, and as they glanced at each other, she knew she had thrown them off balance.

"Your ideals and concerns are noble, Commander, but childish," the Celeron with the Van Dyke said. "Only by stopping The Argent can the threat facing Kerguelen be countered. Gregor is only a minor concern."

"How can you be so sure?" Prior asked.

"Commanders Jordan and Giles were murdered by The Argent," the dark skinned Celeron said.

"Murdered?"

"Yes, Jordan was found on a beach in Hanover Bay and Giles was killed in the Oceanic Province while investigating her disappearance," the dark skinned Celeron said. "Both incidents appeared to have been set-ups designed to lure them in and then dispose of them."

"But why were they killed? What could killing them accomplish?" Prior asked.

"The Argent believed that Jordan was the greatest warrior in the Corps. Giles was eliminated because he stumbled upon evidence that would have exposed The Argent," the dark skinned Celeron said.

"I still don't understand," Prior said.

"The Argent follow the scriptures," the dark skinned Celeron explained. "In an old text of scripture, it is written that out of a thousand, one will rise up and lead a thousand in a battle that will decide the fate of Kerguelen. In this battle, The Argent will be defeated and its threat forever removed from the planet. The Argent believed that Jordan was that warrior."

"That myth is from the Sacred Scroll of Katana," Prior scoffed. "The Argent can't actually believe that story. It's clearly superstitious nonsense."

"The Argent is completely devout, Commander. And The Argent that threatens us today is aided by a group of crazed zealots. These fanatics are direct descendents of those defeated by the forces of Katana so long ago. As far as they're concerned, everything is happening as was ordained by the Almighty," the attractive Celeron said. "They hoped to change the prophecy by killing this anointed one before the battle commences. But they were wrong about Jordan being the anointed one. And they know that now."

"And you believe Venture is the… anointed one?" she asked.

"That possibility was debated, but we know he is not the one," the man with the Van Dyke said. "We wanted him to recruit the anointed one for us, but he's as skeptical as you and we were unable to convince him otherwise."

"You believe the anointed one is a Guardian?" Prior asked.

"We know the anointed one is a Guardian," the attractive Celeron said.

Prior turned her head toward the door. She was certain she heard the low but distinctive sounds of her dog. She saw the attractive Celeron smiling at her when she turned back to the men.

"I believe your animal is looking for you, Commander," he said taking a drink.

"You heard him?" she asked looking at him quizzically. Lupo was nearing the dining room but was still distant. There was no way an elderly man could have heard his faint noises.

"This old house amplifies the slightest sound," he said dismissively.

A short rap on the door caused them all to turn to it and as the door swung open, Lupo bounded in, barking in response to finding his mistress. Prior petted him and scratched his head. She fed him the last bit of meat on her plate and gave him a peck on the top of his head as he chewed the morsel. After he had wolfed it down, she patted him on the back and he sat at her side.

"Did you have fun, Lupo?" she asked in maternal voice. He licked her hand and panted. She wiped her hands with her napkin and addressed the men. "Excuse me, sirs."

"Think nothing of it," the man with full beard said.

The entire group looked at the attractive Celeron and he smiled in an, "I told you so" manner. The servants took away the plates again and

Prior saw that the Celeron now all had serious expressions on their faces and seemed to be in deep thought. And Prior was sure that it was she that was on their minds.

The servants came back with the dessert tray and Prior selected an orange. Though the tray was filled with an assortment of luscious desserts, she passed on them. Boroni did not have a sweet tooth. Many believed it was because of their heightened sense of taste. Whatever the reason, an over indulgence in candy or sweets would not be the reason a Boroni would lose their teeth.

"Obviously you want something from me," Prior said as she peeled the orange. "What is it?"

"You're as perceptive as Venture and others said you were," the attractive Celeron said. "We want you to find Venture and convince him that he needs to come back to the fold. You're our last hope. If you fail, The Argent will find him and kill him. Without our protection, he doesn't stand a chance."

"I don't know what I could accomplish when you've failed," she said.

"You're his friend and he holds you in the highest regard," the dark skinned Celeron said. "He'll listen to you."

"He may resent my interference, and if things reach a boiling point, I'm afraid I'll have to defend myself. He's not being rational at the moment," Prior said.

"Are you concerned that he'll attack you?" the attractive Celeron said.

"Yes. He's a wanted man and knows that I've been assigned to his apprehension. I hope you understand my reluctance to approach him with an olive branch instead of a pistol," Prior said. "But for argument's sake, let's say I do convince him to come in, how can you keep him safe from prosecution?"

"That is a minor matter. We are quite adept at swaying the opinions of our planetary leaders," the attractive Celeron said. "The predicament your former fiancé found himself in, for example, was a relatively easy fix."

"My fiancé? You saved Omega?"

"Of course. Why do you think he surrendered without a struggle?" the attractive Celeron said.

"Omega was Celeron?" Prior asked knowing the answer.

"Omega *is* Celeron and we couldn't let him die. He is doing things that will benefit Kerguelen for millennia to come," the man with the Van Dyke said. "You have many colleagues that are Celeron. I know you have many questions concerning our society, but unfortunately, we can't answer them. Just know that we are on your side and as fellow Guardians, we wouldn't place you unwittingly in harm's way."

Too many questions were dashing in and out of her mind. But the answers to them would have to wait. Somehow she would come back and get the closure she needed. Right now, she had to go.

"I will do as you ask, but I will be delayed. Central Command will be upset with me for not reporting promptly," she said standing up. All of the Celeron stood up as well and she waved her hand. "It's unnecessary to stand, gentlemen."

"Forgive us, Commander. We don't get to practice proper social etiquette within these walls very often," the attractive Celeron said. "And don't worry about Central Command. They've been appraised as to why you were delayed. They will wait patiently for your arrival."

"Yes," the dark skinned Celeron said. "They can be quite lucid when given the proper... motivation."

"Who in Central Command is Celeron?" Prior asked.

"To confirm or deny any of them are or are not Celeron is not permitted. As a non-Celeron, you have already been exposed to far more information than is allowed," the man with the Van Dyke said. "But, as we've observed over the years, you are quite exceptional."

"You've been watching me? Why?"

"We keep tabs on all individuals that can possibly aid us in the future," the attractive Celeron said. "I have been pleased with your past endeavors. You've done well."

"Thank you," Prior said a little uneasy. "Do you know where Venture is now?"

"No," the attractive Celeron said. "But we believe he was returning to the Central Province. You have resources of your own in that region to locate him, don't you?"

"I do," Prior nodded. She paused for a moment, unsure of how they would take her next remark. "I'm taking a leap of faith in doing your bidding. If I find that this is a set-up or if you've lied to me, I'm coming back here and kill all of you… Guardians or not."

"I would not expect anything less, Commander," the attractive Celeron said.

One of the servants helped her on with her jacket and after she slipped it on slapped her thigh. Lupo stood up and came to her side. The attractive Celeron motioned to the door and they all left the dining room and walked down the corridor to the entrance. Howard had joined them and was bringing up the rear.

"We will meet again soon, Commander," the attractive Celeron said. "In the meantime, I was hoping you might read up on the prophecy of Katana."

"I doubt I'll have much time for reading," Prior said.

"I was led to believe that you have an appreciation for history," he said.

"I do."

"Then this will be extremely provocative to you," he said as they reached the entrance. He turned to Howard and took the package the Celeron liaison handed him. "This is from the Sacred Scrolls of Katana, Commander. It's an obscure but important portion of the story. Unknown to most Kerguelens, this addendum should erase any doubts you may have… and bring certain revelations to you."

Prior took the package and opened it. It was an original papyrus scroll. She handled it gingerly and felt the rough material. She placed it back in the package and looked curiously at the attractive Celeron.

"It's an original scroll," she said.

"Yes. It may take you some time to translate it I'm afraid. It's written in the original biblical language."

"Ne sollicitus, sis perficiam," Prior said smiling. She stepped through the door and began to walk to the waiting air ship. The pilot brought its engines to life when he saw her approach. She turned and called back to the attractive Celeron. "I don't know your name."

"Yes you do," he said stepping back into the house.

She frowned and jogged to the air ship with Howard and Lupo close behind. Lupo crawled inside and Howard helped Prior onboard and she nodded her thanks to him. He gave her a card and she stared at it. All that was printed on it was a TELCOM number code.

"Call that number code if you need the Celeron... for any reason," he said. He grabbed the handle of the hatch and hesitated for a moment.

"Do you have a question, Howard?" she asked.

"Yes. How do you plan on finding Venture? Not even the Celeron are sure of his whereabouts."

"I'm going to take a page from one of the older races of Kerguelen in order to find him," she answered.

"Oh? What race is that?"

"An aboriginal race that once inhabited the polar regions of Kerguelen. When they went fishing, they didn't look for fish."

"Why?"

"They couldn't see the fish. Usually the ice was too thick."

"What did they do?"

"They looked for the blue heron. Wherever the blue heron was, there were fish," Prior said stepping back into the craft.

Howard slammed the door shut and as the craft disappeared from sight, the attractive Celeron turned to his brothers and smiled. They all nodded and watched the vapor trail of the air ship dissipate.

"Yes," the man with the Van Dyke said. "You were quite right about her, Gideon. She is exceptional and accompanied by a beast of the land. But is that proof enough? There are many who travel in the company of dogs."

"But it's obvious that it is part wolf," the man with full beard said.

"We must be sure," the dark skinned Celeron said. He turned to the Celeron liaison as he returned. "Howard, what can you tell us?"

"I believe in her," he said. "It all fits. The dog is part wolf and does not possess the obedience chip. It's a true untamed beast of the land and she is a formidable warrior. You all know her service... and her pedigree. If it means anything, I'm convinced."

"The death of Venture and others will force her to fulfill her part of the prophecy and join us. It's only a matter of time," Gideon, the attractive Celeron said.

"And if she dies first? What then, Gideon?" the Van Dyke wearing Celeron said.

"She won't, Hamilton," Gideon said looking intensely at his colleague. "She is more than capable of taking care of herself. If she has to kill Venture, it will only strengthen her for the ultimate battle."

"Let's hope Howard's confidence and your unwavering belief in her invincibility is justified, Gideon. We risk everything on this," Hamilton said solemnly. "The fate of the planet is about to be placed in her hands."

"Her last words to me should have been enough to convince you, Hamilton," Gideon replied.

"What did she say?" Howard asked. "I didn't understand her."

"She spoke in the ancient biblical language," Gideon said. "Ne sollicitus, sis perficiam. Don't worry, I'll manage."

3
Northeastern Province, Planet Kerguelen

"Thirty seconds to landing, Commander," Micah said over his shoulder to Prior.

"Thank you," she replied without looking at him.

It was a short hop from the Celeron Estate to Strathmore where Prior's air ship waited. It was an even a quicker flight from there to the next destination, but Prior had lost all track of time. She was engrossed in reviewing the data her investigator, Major Metis, had provided and reports on the deteriorating conditions Commander Mohab's battalion was combating. A small contingent of the Fourth Battalion, consisting of the surveyor squad and ten others, remained in Lago Patria to assist local authorities while the bulk of the unit had moved on to the Middle Provinces to handle a new crisis that had arisen.

Though what was happening in those areas was important, her focus and thoughts were elsewhere. The meeting with the Celeron was overshadowing everything. It was known that the ancient religious order known as The Argent believed in the scriptures verbatim and lived their lives based on them, but what about the Celeron? The Seven never said that they did or did not share the same ideology. And if they did, that meant there were two wild cards in the deck, both unpredictable and potentially dangerous. These thoughts consumed Prior as her craft and its accompanying gunship slowed and descended upon the massive fortress known to the people of Kerguelen as Guardian Central Command and to Guardians as "The Home".

Over 2,500 years old, the castle and surrounding structures that comprised Central Command Headquarters, were built by the notorious planetary warlord Koenig, a despot who conquered and subjugated three quarters of the people and lands of the planet. At that time in the planet's history, it was believed to be the entire world, and Koenig ruled over it with an iron hand. In his eyes, belief in the Almighty and Her Scriptures was false and impious worship. Koenig had forced the clerics and priests of the era to denounce the Almighty and declare him the absolute monarch and living God of Kerguelen. To save the people from Koenig's wrath, and their own lives, the priests ordained him Lord King Koenig I of Kerguelen. Koenig in turn, outlawed the practice of any religion that did not have him as its deity.

To enhance his position, he commissioned a fortress to be built. Construction commenced in the fifth year of his reign and was finally completed in the eighteenth. Still an impressive and imposing citadel, at the time of its construction, it was considered impregnable, a fitting testament to his apparent invincibility. And true to Koenig's form, all persons involved with its construction were killed to prevent any leakage of the facility's weaknesses to potential enemies.

Executions and torture were the mantras of Koenig's forty-eight year rule, and the brutality of his army and governors in the conquered territories prevented him from ever having a moment of rest. The constant savagery of his troops on others, heavy taxes levied by his governors and his belief that he was the true Kerguelen God, led to repetitive swells of rebellion in his kingdom. Every time a faction fought against him and was subsequently defeated, another rose from the ashes to continue the fight for freedom. But to release themselves from the death grip of Koenig's tyranny, the people needed a group that could ultimately force him to capitulate. A group that fought the way Koenig's armies did. A force more fierce and unforgiving than a person could possibly dream of in their worst nightmares. Out of this need the Guardians were formed.

Originally, they were a mixture of men from the era; former soldiers in Koenig's army that had fallen out of favor and wanted payback, noblemen ruined by heavy taxes and the loss of land, gypsies, Bedouins from the desert, farmers, fishermen, shopkeepers, and tradesmen... anyone who could no longer stomach the injustice and oppression. Riddled with shame and the inability to look their wives and children in the eye in the midst of the atrocities had pushed them to the brink. The men decided to look death in the eye instead and took up arms.

Whatever the reasons or motivations, over time they slowly defeated the forces of the dictator, and after thirty years of bloody battles, Koenig's forces were finally vanquished. In the end, his armies decimated and cornered alone in his siege-proof castle, Koenig committed suicide.

With Koenig gone, the planet was now free to govern itself and carve out a destiny based on ethical monotheism. But to ensure new warlords and oppressive feudal systems would not rise up from the carnage and anarchy left by the absence of Koenig's shock troops, the Guardians were retained and officially recognized and commissioned as protectors of free thought and inalienable rights for all. As long as there were Guardians, no one would ever be afraid to voice their displeasure in their leaders or follow their own path.

And so it has been for two and a half millennia. The Guardians continue to safeguard the freedoms of the people, governed only by the Guardian Council of Elders, or Central Command. These seven former commanders reside in semi-retirement at the "The Home". Distinguished in battle and respected for their wisdom, they oversee the employment of the four battalions and advise the planetary government on how they should be used. It was the leader of the council, the Supreme Commander of the Guardian Corps, Marshal Garath, who had summoned Prior to the "The Home" for a private counsel.

Her air ship gently touched down in the courtyard of the castle and the gunship landed ten meters from it. Micah turned to Pana as the engines wound down and became silent.

"All secure, ready to disembark," he said.

"Roger," she replied and as the auxiliary power unit came to life, she opened the hatch and the hiss of the pressure seal released into the air. Pana turned a knob and the access ladder extended to the ground.

Prior stood and ran a hand over her long hair tightly pressed against her scalp in preparation for exiting. She had changed out of her combat suit and into the standard Guardian day uniform. The gray waistcoat had three rows of black buttons down the front and was trimmed with black piping. At the bottom of the left sleeve was a black band one and a half inches wide, indicating she was an officer, and just above it was a gold griffin holding a sword in one of its front paws, denoting she was a commander. At the top of her left sleeve was the Guardian Corps patch. The blue circular patch had two crossed swords superimposed on a shield and the words "The Guardian Corps" and the Corps motto "To Liberate and Oppose Oppression" was written in the outer ring of the patch. A black aiguillette hung from her left shoulder and at the top of her right sleeve, was the Surveyor's patch. Black fitted trousers and knee high black leather boots completed the uniform.

She hated the ostentation of the uniform but was glad she didn't have to wear her full dress garb. She sighed and was about to make an adjustment to her uniform, wishing she had more time to get ready, when she felt her dog's eyes on her. He cocked his head to one side and his pointy ears peaked. She smiled and decided against any alterations. Prior reached for her weapons belt and then decided against it, leaving it on the seat it occupied. It was time to go, Marshal Garath would be waiting, impatiently.

"C'mon, Lupo," she said as the half-wolf arose from the deck of the air ship. The rest of her team, also dressed in the day uniform, made way as the canine took his place of honor on her left side.

Though it was early evening, the Kerguelen moon was nearly full and shining brightly and in spite of the hour and time of year, the air was still warm. As she looked up in the sky, Prior recalled the many nights in her childhood in which she would race along the grassy plains of the Western Province and chase the moon across the sky. Such were the games of children she thought. Now when she chased the moon it was with a weapon in her hand, and the game was the giving and taking of life and not for children.

As Prior, followed by Lupo and then the rest of her team, exited the craft, Hiroki pointed toward the entrance of the castle. A Guardian and a trio of security guards approached.

"It seems your escort has arrived, Commander," Hiroki said as he took up a position in front of Prior. Rex and Pana stood on either side of her and Lindsey filled in directly behind her. It was the standard protection set for a Guardian commander.

"I wonder if I'm under arrest," Prior said.

"We'll find out soon enough," Hiroki said.

The four men stopped a few paces from the formation. The Guardian was an officer and the other three were contracted security guards. Besides the seven elders, there were less than twenty active Guardians at Central Command. A detachment of security guards, numbering around one hundred, patrolled the grounds and saw to the safety of the elders. The apprehension of the guards standing before Prior was as evident as the moon in the sky. They would be cannon fodder if the headquarters were ever attacked. Luckily for them no one in their right mind would ever be that foolish. Thank the Almighty for small favors Prior thought. The men she was looking at would be little more than useless in a pitched battle against a determined foe with a death wish. And that was exactly the type of personality that would dare to storm the edifice. All three of the men were slightly built and small, wearing the signature blue jumpsuits worn by security forces planet-wide. The Guardian leading them, a youthful captain, spoke.

"Commander, welcome to Central Command. We're your escort to Elder Garath," he said. He was surprised when Prior failed to respond. "Commander?"

"Don't junior officers still salute their superiors, Captain?" Hiroki asked.

"Forgive me, Commander," the captain said saluting. Prior saluted back and nodded her readiness to go inside. He motioned to the entrance and as Prior's entourage started toward the building, he raised his hand. "Only your presence is required, Commander."

Prior sighed and spoke to Hiroki. "Captain, I'll be back in an hour or so. Come, Lupo," she said stepping around her team members.

"Sorry, Commander," the captain said pointing at Lupo, "But your, uh, dog, is not permitted inside the facility."

"He goes everywhere I go, Captain. Perhaps you were not advised of that," she said.

"I have no orders granting any animals access. I'm afraid he'll have to wait with the others," he said.

"Captain, I'm late and I don't want to keep Marshal Garath waiting any longer. I'm sure he'll understand."

"I can't let him inside, Commander," the captain said standing firm.

"Captain, what does the aiguillette on my shoulder indicate?" Prior said pointing at her left shoulder.

"It means you're a senior aide to Central Command," he said.

"That's right. Do you know who I am?"

"Commander Prior, ROICC and Chief Surveyor of the Guardian Corps."

"Correct, Captain. And what do I do?"

"You build things?" he said tentatively. He was a regular officer and not really sure what surveyors and combat engineers did. And it was obvious he really didn't care.

"Right again. Now, do you want me to have a building commissioned for you to be buried under?"

"No, Commander," he said shaking his head.

"Then let's get a move on. The Marshal is waiting. Besides, my dog has been looking forward to seeing him again. If he misses the chance, he'll be very upset," Prior said scratching Lupo's head.

Lupo turned his huge silver and gray colored head to the captain and opened his cavernous mouth and growled softly. The canine's blue eyes looked like chips of cold, unfeeling ice as he stared at the Guardian.

"Of course, Commander, this way," the captain said.

The majority of Guardians seldom, if ever, came to Central Command and it had been a while since Prior had last been to "The Home". Most of her dealings with Central Command were conducted via TELCOM or by electronic correspondence or at secret locales and she had not had a private audience with Marshal Garath since her promotion to commander five years earlier. Despite having been here before, the entrance of the complex was still as striking as it was the first time she had visited it.

The captain led her down a hallway with parquet flooring and walls adorned with tapestries of Guardian Elders from antiquity. The soft lighting gave the representations a divine-like quality. Between the tapestries, glass cabinets containing weapons, uniforms and artifacts of Guardians from different eras lined the walls. Prior was awed by the display the first time she came here and each successive visit was no less impressive to her. In the middle of the passage, she stopped suddenly and stared at a wall hanging trimmed in gold. It was Marshal Gideon, one of the greatest Guardians who ever lived.

Prior remembered vividly how the infamous Guardian was described in the military history texts. He was effervescent and at times impudent but had learned that nothing was impossible if you have élan. His ability to manipulate logistics and conditions to produce positive results was uncanny, earning him the nickname "The Magician". Once, with only two usable accesses, he shuttled in troops on a forced march of over twenty miles to augment and re-supply a unit surrounded by the enemy and then without rest, mounted a counteroffensive that ended the battle.

Gideon served in every capacity in the Corps. As the Guardian Academy Superintendent, he modernized the scholastic regimen and changed rules that had been followed for centuries. He updated the military science curriculum, theorizing that the next great battles of Kerguelen would be ones of vast mobility and technology dependent. He stressed to officers expect the unexpected and emphasized flexibility and simplicity in order to deal with the fog of war. He also implemented actual science into warfare. "Simplicity and technical competence," he said, "Will allow combat leaders to visualize war as it actually happens, without actually seeing it. Leaders will be able to position troops using their 'mind's eye'."

Gideon envisioned a new type of warfare, one that did not have troops slugging it out foot-by-foot in sequential fronts and along hardened battle lines, but one in which the Guardians struck anywhere, anytime. And he had been right. Technology had outstripped man's wisdom to properly harness it. And the new Guardian officers, trained by Gideon, used his methods to successfully protect the citizenry of the planet.

When he became supreme commander, he once stated that he had been bequeathed a command staff whose heads had so much wood in them, they'd never have to worry about drowning. He immediately replaced them and trained a new staff. He was most famous for stating, "Don't be in a hurry to screw up. Wait until the last second to make your choice, and when that second comes, act, decisively."

"I wrote my graduation military science thesis on him," Prior said to the captain as she pointed to the tapestry of Gideon.

"So did my roommate," he said. "Do you ever think they'll write about you, Commander?"

"On the bathroom walls for sure, in a graduation thesis, I doubt it, Captain," she said with a chuckle. As they walked away she stopped abruptly and spun around.

She looked up at the tapestry again. Her eyes narrowed and then grew wide with recognition. The attractive Celeron was Gideon! But that was impossible. Gideon would be a hundred years old or more if he were still living and the Celeron man, though well into advanced age, couldn't have been that old. He did say that she did know his name, but they couldn't be the same person. She shook her head and looked at the tapestry once more before walking away.

"Are you okay, Commander?" the captain asked.

"Yes, I'm fine, Captain," she said.

They turned the corner and continued down the hallway called, The Pantheon of Heroes. She had never seen this section before and slowed her pace to take in as much as she could. This collection of tapestries was made up of Guardians who were legendary heroes of all ranks. She recognized many of them from the history texts. Once again she stopped short and stared at one of the tapestries. Prior smiled as she looked upon the face of the Van Dyke wearing Celeron. His name was Colonel Hamilton, a tenacious warrior and infamous lady's man, reputedly breaking the heart of every woman he had ever met. They continued on and as they neared the end of the hall, she saw the tapestries of Commanders Jordan and Venture and Sergeant Darius. Darius was a surveyor who had served with Prior at the Battle of Domtar. He was a great Guardian and had been awarded the Legion of Honor among many other citations before he left the Corps.

"When did they do this?" Prior asked touching Jordan's tapestry.

"A year ago. There were plans for a large unveiling with all the living Guardians attending, but several Elders voted against it," one of the guards said. "I think they were jealous. As you can see, none of them are represented."

They moved on and Prior stopped again when she saw the last tapestry in the pantheon. It was her own tapestry and she gasped as she looked at it. The artist had woven Prior in a battle scene. She was scowling and her braided hair was longer and wilder than it really was. She was brandishing two pistols and Lupo was by her side. He was depicted much larger than he actually was and his fangs were exposed and his fur was standing on end. Saliva was dripping from his open mouth and his muscles were rippling and bulging. Prior smiled at the license taken by the artist. Anyone who had not seen her or Lupo before would think the pair was savage. Perhaps they would be right. This image could be what everyone else actually saw. Maybe it was she that didn't see who or what she really was. Whatever the case, it was striking.

"That's me... and my dog," Prior said.

"Yes, Commander," one of the guards said. "It's my favorite. The others are kind of tame. Yours is more of what people imagine a famous and heroic Guardian commander would be."

"Really?" she asked.

"Yes, and from what I've heard, you truly belong on this wall," the guard said. "A Star of Kerguelen award winner is most deserving."

"Thank you," she said somewhat embarrassed.

She touched her tapestry and they continued on crossing another lobby. Prior was led into a room containing members of the Council of Elders. She entered and the captain nodded to her.

"One moment, Commander," he said. "I'll see if Elder Garath is ready to see you."

Prior nodded as the captain disappeared and she turned to the Guardians in the room. She bowed slightly to the group and they silently acknowledged her presence. Prior knew them all and had served with a few of them as a junior officer. Their reputations were earned not embellished and she had witnessed some of their most daring exploits personally. Most importantly, they knew her and had seen her in combat. Though it had been some time since she had seen most of them, they still were as she remembered but even strong and proud front line warriors fade over time as they passed into and beyond the age of wisdom. Prior always thought that was a favorable way to say one was older than forty-five.

The nearest to her was Commander Antoine and to his left was Commander Rina and on the far side of the room was Commander Demos. Nicknamed "The Lion" in his youth, Demos' once mane-like coif had lost its color, luster and thickness. Thin silver-gray and white hairs had replaced full and thick calico colored ones and were receding from his forehead in an ever-quickening retreat as the years passed.

Prior sniffed the air and realized that there was another female besides she and Rina in the room. She was hidden from view by a high-backed chair. Prior knew the scent of the woman and was not surprised that she remained shielded from view.

"You're probably going to have a lot of work very soon, Commander Prior," Demos said stepping a bit closer to her.

"Why is that, Commander?" she asked.

"Someone relieved a nasty group of Eastern Province terrorists of their heavy water and precision machinery production capability. It was a truly fantastic operation," he said with admiration and a smile. "Your engineers will probably be asked to clean up the mess."

He raised his glass and drank as Prior answered. "You may be right, Commander," she said with a shoulder shrug.

"Oh, don't be so modest, Commander Prior," a voice said from behind the high-backed hair. "It doesn't suit you."

The woman stood up and revealed herself. It was Commander Ceca. As a captain, she was one of Prior's instructors at the academy and the leader of her isolation and hazing during her first two years there. She was from the Central Province and hated everything about Prior and the Boroni. Like Prior's classmate Thyssen, Ceca's family had a long history as slaveholders. Ceca looked at Lupo and her face twisted into a frown.

"I thought I smelled animals in here," Ceca said with a smile. She turned to Demos and continued. "Weren't the guards told that animals were not permitted in this building?"

"Yes, they were," offered Prior. "But we came in anyway when I remembered you were stationed here, Commander."

"Touché, Commander," Ceca said still smiling. "But where are my manners. Can we get you anything? Water, aperitif, raw meat… for your friend, of course."

"Of course," Prior said feigning politeness. "No thank you, Commander, we're both fine."

"I wish you two didn't go through this exercise every time you meet," Antoine said. "It's becoming tiresome."

"I was just trying to be hospitable to our Chief Surveyor. But you know, despite being an aide, she doesn't spend very much time here. One would think she didn't like us," Ceca said smiling wider. "Maybe it's our cuisine. We don't serve many animal dishes."

Among the many differences between the Boroni and Kerguelens, the most glaring was the fact that the majority of the population was vegetarian and Boroni were not. The Boroni physiology could not support a strict vegetarian diet. They would die in a matter of weeks without huge amounts of protein. Denial of meat protein was one of several punishments slave owners had dealt out to the Boroni.

"The fact that I'm a carnivore and you're vegan, pleases me to no end, Ceca," Prior said without smiling.

"Prior, you have so much hostility. You *are* eating too much meat," Ceca said in a goading fashion. "Let me get you a salad."

Prior scoffed. "No thanks," she said.

"Knock it off, Ceca," Rina said.

"Rina, you used to like playful banter," Ceca said coyly. "Since becoming an Elder, you're no longer any fun."

"Some people don't like your idea of fun, Ceca," Prior said.

"Then why don't they say so?" Ceca replied sitting down her glass.

"Maybe they will," Prior said with a flash of teeth.

At forty-three, Ceca was the youngest Elder and very fit and strong. She stood five foot nine and had a solid build. Her posture indicated that she would be more than willing to prove to Prior that she was still fit for full combat duty. Prior wished the opportunity for five minutes of privacy with Ceca could be arranged. Both women knew it eventually would be.

"Enough already!" Antoine said angrily.

"I'm just trying to help," Ceca said raising her hands innocently.

"You? Help me?" Prior scoffed. "Ceca, you're just like the plants that sustain you; you're soft, fleshy and contain very little substance. You're sole purpose is to aid in digestion, nothing more."

"Ahem, Commander?" the captain said clearing his throat as he returned to the anteroom. "Sorry to… interrupt, but Elder Garath is ready to see you."

"Thank you, Captain," Prior said. "Come, Lupo."

As Prior headed out, Ceca called to her. "Perhaps you can make time in your schedule for us to finish our… conversation."

"I look forward to that," Prior said matching Ceca's smile. "Good evening, Commanders." She nodded to them as she left and the Elders returned the gesture.

As the doors shut behind Prior, the Elders turned to Ceca and scowled. They may have had the same sentiments about Prior as Ceca did, but they had the decency to keep their feelings internal. Ceca cared little about what they thought. She believed that there was no place in the Corps for Prior or any Boroni and would continue to try to make her life as miserable as possible. Hopefully soon, they would get the opportunity to end the festering dispute that had been eating away at both women for over twenty years.

4
Guardian Central Command, Northeastern Province, Planet Kerguelen

The captain led Prior to Marshal Garath's chambers and opened twin five-meter tall doors for her. The wooden doors creaked loudly as they parted and she strode to within two steps of his desk and stopped and saluted.

"Commander Prior, reporting as ordered," she said as Lupo sat on her left side.

Garath stood and returned her salute. "That will be all," he said to the captain. "Leave us." The captain stepped backwards and shut the huge doors.

Garath pointed to the chair in front of his desk and Prior adjusted her coat and sat down. Though he was the oldest member of Central Command at the age of sixty, Garath still possessed the stature and build of a younger man. However, the deep creases at the corners of his eyes and graying hair gave away the truth. He stared at Prior in silence with piercing sapphire-colored eyes that seemed more intense because of his dark Southern Provincial brown skin. It was an interesting contrast and when coupled with his snarl and battle cry, he had sent chills through the very souls of his opponents on the battlefield. Marshals Pace and Aca sat on either side of him.

"Welcome, Commander," Garath grumbled in his deep voice. "I'm glad you could join us, we have much to discuss."

"I agree, Supreme Commander, but if you're looking for an update about Venture, I have nothing new to report," Prior said. "I haven't had time to get a definitive line on him as of yet."

"But you have had enough time to disrupt a nightclub in Cosmopolis and have two civilians arrested by the Papal police," he said consulting a PDA. "Breaking one of their wrists in the process."

"Supreme Commander…" Prior said attempting to explain.

"You were able to make time to wreck an exclusive art gallery in Lago Patria, then walk a few blocks to the residence of a former Guardian officer and shoot an unarmed female before you said your good-byes," Garath said ignoring her. "And then, deciding my recall order was unimportant, you had dinner in Canton-on-Heath with a bunch of relics from Guardian Corps history to celebrate and reflect on your accomplishments of the day. Yes, Commander, I can see why you haven't achieved much in the past eighteen hours. I can't wait to see what happens when your full attention is given to your assigned mission."

"Supreme Commander, there were reasons for all that has transpired," Prior said.

"I'm sure of that, Commander, I can't wait to hear the story," Garath said.

"First of all, one of the civilians at the club tried to stab me and the other used racial slurs at me," Prior said. "And the dealer of the gallery had information vital for me to locate Venture."

"And the employee of Sebastian?" Garath asked. "What was her capital crime? Did she fail to guess your favorite color?"

"She also used a racial affront," Prior said.

"And that justified her summary execution?" Garath asked.

Prior nodded. "She also had full knowledge about the activities of my special units… and she had a big mouth. It was only a matter of time before she let those secrets slip. Her death, while unfortunate, keeps me out of trouble," she said. "I know you believe succumbing to an emotional response because of a racial slur shows a lack of self-worth, Supreme Commander, but the law is explicit: 'A citizen has the inalienable right to defend themselves against racial attack, verbal or physical, no matter how small or trivial'. It took the population a long time to realize and accept, at a great loss of life, I might add, that if you don't put an end to assaults on others because of race or creed, the antagonists will eventually get around to everyone."

Garath sighed. "I understand your feelings, Commander, but it's not your job to hunt down racial bigots. Leave that to the Papal police. Your job is to fix special problems," he said tossing the PDA to his desk.

"I assure you, Supreme Commander, those incidents were all part of finding Venture," Prior said. "But I will endeavor in the future not to kill anyone that really doesn't deserve it."

The temptation to smile was impossible for Prior to contain and when she did, it brought stern looks from Garath, Pace and Aca.

"Don't fuck with me, Prior," Garath growled leaning back in his chair. "Not today." He exhaled and calmed down. "Do you know where Venture is now?"

"He is either in or on his way to the Central Province. I have assets in place that can help me locate him," Prior said.

"You have less than six hours to find him," Aca said. "The Congress of Cardinals has given us that long to solve this before they issue a public announcement about Venture's crimes and assign a team of mercenaries to his apprehension."

"Why?" Prior asked.

"While you were having brandy and cigars, Venture broke into the manse of Archbishop Cornelia and killed her," Garath answered.

"It was only a matter of time before someone did," Prior said not entirely broken up about the demise of Cornelia. "It was Cornelia's policies and actions that got her killed, not anyone's gun, if you ask me."

"No one asked you anything, Chief Surveyor," Garath said. "I know you've been snooping around and investigating this case on your own, but be careful. The cardinals are far from thrilled you're on the job. Do your duty and don't screw up. They're waiting for you to slip. We'll be powerless to assist you if you get into trouble following one of your cockeyed schemes."

"How do they know Venture killed Cornelia?" Prior asked.

"A Guardian caliber weapon was used and Venture was observed fleeing the scene," Garath said.

"Hardly conclusive," Prior said.

"In light of recent events, what other reason could Venture have to seek out Cornelia but to kill her?" Aca asked.

"They were once very close… intimate," Prior said. "It's not a stretch to believe he went to see her for personal reasons. I doubt he would kill her. Besides, Cornelia had many enemies in and outside of the Church.

It was no secret that her security force was very brutal. Cornelia had stepped on many important toes through the years."

"Perhaps," Garath said. "Perhaps Venture went to see her for personal reasons, and perhaps he didn't kill her, and perhaps he isn't trying to destroy the Papal power structure. All those things may be true, but his being there when she was killed… and with a Guardian weapon as the implement of death, it's not looking too good for him."

"I have evidence that everything is not what it seems concerning Venture," Prior said. "The Cathedral Prime video has been doctored and I've come into possession of computer files linking Gregor with the detention of the missing civilians. My investigator also found out some interesting facts about the crime scene. In addition, I have a list of Federal Church priests targeted for assassination."

"How did your investigators come into possession of this data, Commander?" Pace asked.

"It's better that you don't know, Marshal," Prior replied.

"If what you have is correct, then we have a bigger problem than just a rogue Guardian," Aca said.

"And if you expect us to go in front of the planet's ruling body and accuse Gregor, I need a picture of him with his hand in the proverbial cookie jar," Garath said. "Not guesses and suppositions."

"But Venture is not the cause of the problems. Not directly. It's Gregor and whomever he's partnered with. I need more time to unravel all of this," Prior said.

"There isn't anymore to give," Garath said. "Find Venture and solve the problem, Commander."

"I only have six hours," Prior said.

"Then you'd better get going, Commander," Garath said. "Find Venture and stop him before any more dignitaries are knocked off. If you fail to meet the dead line, the job will be contracted out to a team of mercenaries."

"And if they get in my way?" Prior asked.

"Make sure they don't," Garath said. "Good luck and good hunting."

Prior stood and saluted and turned to leave but quickly spun around when Pace called to her.

"Commander, how did you enjoy your visit with the old men?" Pace asked with a smile.

"It was interesting," Prior said. "They asked me to do them a few favors."

"Will you?" Aca asked.

"I don't know if I can," Prior said. She nodded to them and quickly departed the office.

She pulled out her TACCOM device and called to Micah as she sped down the hallways of Central Command.

"Micah, wind up the engines and be ready to take off when I get there," she said.

Prior heard the air turbines beginning to turn over as he replied to her. "Where are we going?" he asked.

"The Badlands, Micah," she said. "And we don't have much time."

5
Interstellar Space,
One Parsec from the Kerguelen Star System

Discovering that someone or something was sending the alien space probe radio signals was proof that there was intelligent life beyond Kerguelen. When he heard the news, Omega was elated. It was obvious to Omega that the probe's controllers wanted a data download or position report or conduct a course correction or any of a million other things. What they wanted was not important. What did matter was that the signals verified his theories. Tallen had determined with almost a hundred percent certainty that the signals originated from the third planet. Because of the signal's strength, it was obvious that the culture was decades, if not more, inferior to Kerguelen society.

Dela told Omega that Camden had speculated that they were centuries behind, and though that may have been true, it was possible that they might get lucky and make a quantum leap in science and catapult forward a hundred years, as the Kerguelen society had done. All that was needed was a few lucky breaks and logical guesses and they would be zooming off into space as well.

The transmission was also determined to be the first in a series of signals to the craft. Tallen believed, because of the signal's strength and the billions of miles they had to travel, it took many days or weeks for the craft to receive its orders. Multiple signals would make it easier to control the craft. The controllers had probably become highly proficient in such operations when the craft was nearer to home. When it was closer to home, the signals would only take seconds or minutes to reach the craft and as it traveled further away, formulas could be created to properly handle the craft as time went by and it ventured farther out into the solar system.

Camden doubted Tallen's theory but the science specialist explained it easily to the Guardian. Camden forgot that everything has a time delay; people just don't notice it beçause of proximity. If one could isolate a single photon of light emanating from the Kerguelen sun, you could see that it took that photon 8.5 seconds to travel the ninety-six million miles to their planet.

Omega had other thoughts. Since the builders of the probe wanted to contact it, it was almost certain that the craft had taken a picture of *San Mariner* and sent it home. He wondered what the people on the third planet would think when they saw his ship. The answers to those questions would have to wait until he delivered his precious cargo to Kerguelen and they could return to system 1-Sol-8. And the sooner they got home, the sooner a return mission could be mounted. But at the moment, the TLC engine was carrying *San Mariner* home at hyper velocity, and the crew had settled into the dull routine of a straight passage home… as straight as Delle could plot that is.

Delle's job as navigator was as difficult as it was vital, for one slight error in calculations could send the ship dozens of light years in the wrong direction. He had to find six known locations in space, and use them as reference points, with Kerguelen in the center. Once he loaded the reference points into the light-speed navigational computer, and accounting for celestial drift, its software projected a course for the ship to follow home. It was not as direct as Omega wanted, but the dangers involved with known hazardous space phenomena in their path required a wider arc than normal. As they cruised home, the monotonous routine of general maintenance, performing experiments and writing standard reports took hold.

A star sailor's life was filled with a myriad of ups and downs, and highs and lows. Upon selection, candidates undergo a rigorous battery of physical, academic and psychological examinations, all designed to determine and ensure the candidates can adapt to space and be as comfortable in that environment as they were on the surface of Kerguelen. Once the year long, rudimentary training period is completed, star sailors are designated as pilot/navigators, mission specialists or science specialists depending on the needs of Space Command and desires of the candidates. Each designation has its own unique career path leading to the coveted spacecraft commander qualification or assignment to command one of the space outposts located throughout the Kerguelen star system. But the path is long and only a small percentage of star sailors achieve those distinctions and even fewer still actually have the opportunity to command a spacecraft or outpost of their own.

New star sailors can be assigned to various tasks to support ongoing or upcoming orbital or deep space operations. These tasks are usually repetitive, mundane and far beneath the capabilities of the individuals they are assigned to, but serve to give these entry-level star sailors the chance to work within the Space Command system. They will also continue training on Space Command equipment and simulators, working in teams and alone and are evaluated on their performance. Depending on how well or poorly the junior star sailors do, they are assigned as prime or backup crewmembers for a future manned space mission. The better they perform, the sooner they get a mission.

Being assigned to their first prime crew is the highlight of a star sailor's career. Their focus, from anywhere between six months to a year, is solely concentrated on the mission. Their fellow prime crewmembers become their family and their actual family has to take a backseat to the needs of Space Command and the mission. Months in ship simulators, test flights, reviewing mission objectives and star charts, and training their bodies to the peak of perfection for the two to six month long mission takes its toll. In addition, visits to schools and social and public relations requirements put the star sailor and their families on an emotional roller coaster ride. Their families have to try to continue on with their lives, but for the star sailor, life is the mission. For him or her, there is nothing else, and sometimes the families suffer from the strain.

Such was the life of a star sailor and nothing had changed much in nearly a century of manned space flight. Despite the help of Kerguelen psychiatrists and psychologists, Space Command could not find the perfect balance between mission requirements and family obligations. There was no magical combination or accommodation that allowed for complete dedication to duty and coping with and accepting family separation.

Omega had never put much stock in mental health professionals. He considered them psychological shade tree mechanics. As far as they had come as a species, as enlightened as they believed they were, they still were basically clueless when it came to the workings of the brain and psychosis. The average star sailor was right down the middle of the scientific model. They were intelligent and highly trainable, they could adapt to different conditions and environments with little discomfort, reacted to stimuli in a predictable manner and followed orders without hesitation. They needed to be that way, for an emergency in space, no matter how trivial, could prove fatal. Omega had been through so many simulations he knew them all by heart. The sound of different spacecraft alarms were engrained into his soul and pushed invisible buttons in his mind subliminally and his body reacted automatically when he heard them. This instinctive behavior had saved his life more than once. It was as much a part of him and as important as any of the other involuntary bodily functions he possessed.

Thus it was understandable that Omega was upset and confused that it was the second series of gongs from the ship's general alarm that brought him out of his slumber. He freed himself from the sleep restraint wrapped around his body in case the ship lost artificial gravity, and rolled off of the bed by the end of the fourth series of gongs. It was not until the fifth series ended, however, that he realized he was floating.

It took Omega over a minute to reach the flight deck from his In-Flight cabin. Located directly behind and below the flight deck in the Command and Control Module, it should have only taken ten or fifteen seconds to get there, but Omega had trouble negotiating the sharp turns and narrow passages in the weightlessness of zero-G.

When he finally arrived, only Camden and Dela were present and that troubled him. All hands should have reported when the alarm sounded to take controlling actions, but Camden and Dela were alone and scrambling around the control stations trying to work and correct whatever problem had arisen.

Both crewmembers were hovering just above the deck plating and in between controlling actions they were slipping off their shoes and putting on friction socks, which would allow their feet to adhere to friction pads located on various sections of the deck. That would give them solid footing in the zero gravity environment.

The emergency lighting was illuminated and the master alarm was sounding every two or three seconds. Multiple systems were malfunctioning at once, and that was not supposed to happen. According to the engineers that designed *San Mariner*, such an occurrence could never happen.

A mission normally has a glitch or two and because that is expected, secondary and tertiary backup systems are installed in all spacecraft no matter what its size. If a main component or primary system failed, an installed backup or secondary system kicked in and the mission goes on. But not all systems had redundancy and it was failures in these seldom used or stand alone systems and components that made an occupation in space the most daring, hazardous and exciting way of life known. But at this moment, Omega could do without the hazard or excitement.

San Mariner had dropped well below light speed and was slowing down even further. The automatic control system had shut down the TLC engine and fired the ship's braking thrusters. At least something was working Omega thought. He could make out the basics of what was wrong, but didn't know why it was all happening.

"Status," Omega said as he batted away data tablets and other material floating in the module and settled into the commander's couch and strapped in. "And where is everyone?"

"Commander?" Camden said startled by Omega's presence. He was trying to stabilize the flight of the ship without much success and was fighting with the controls as he spoke. "We've had some kind of explosion."

"What kind of explosion?" Omega said as he looked around the flight deck.

"We *think* it was an explosion. But there has definitely been some type of hull breech," Dela explained as she peeked over her shoulder. She folded herself into a ball and slipped on her friction socks. When she finished, she flipped and secured her feet to a pad by the flight engineer's station. "There's been a violent decompression in the Habitat Module. We… we haven't heard from the crew since we isolated and locked it out. They can't… we don't know what their status is."

"What else?" Omega asked.

"The TLC is offline and the braking thrusters have fired. We are well below sub-light and coming to a stop. Main and auxiliary gravity systems are offline but power systems and life support seem to be holding… barely," Dela said.

"Damn!" Omega cursed. "Where are we? What's our position?"

"A little over one parsec from our star system… I think," Camden offered.

"You think?" Omega asked looking at his pilot.

"I can't be sure, Commander. We're slightly off course from the explosion and almost in a tumble from intermittent RCS thrusting. I can't be positive because the computers aren't cooperating. Every time Dela reboots them, they trip offline again," Camden replied still fighting with the controls. "They aren't online long enough to give us our position and I can't get a manual star fix and pilot this thing at the same time."

"Great," Omega said. "Is there any way to get the crew out?"

"No," Dela said shaking her head. "We can't go in there without suits because of the breech. There's no atmosphere in there. And even if they haven't already been vented into space, the lack of an atmosphere should have finished them by now."

The klaxon of the master alarm sounded again and Omega depressed a few buttons on the armrest of his couch and a heads-up display flipped up in front of him. The display lit up and showed the condition of all of the ship's systems. Some were illuminated in green, which meant they were functioning at better than eighty-five percent efficiency; some were colored amber, indicating they were less perfect but still in operation; some systems were blinking red and others were solid red. Blinking red meant the system was online but failing and solid red meant total failure.

What it told Omega in broad strokes was that the condition of the ship was going south… and in a hurry. More systems were blinking red and solid red than green and amber and the diagnostic program could not shed any light as to why. The most recent alarm was a warning that the main electrical system was failing. As he eyed the display, Omega's eyes grew wide and he shuddered. They had bigger problems than a non-performing electrical system.

"Switching to battery power," Dela said. She hoped it would give the main power system a chance to recover. Her hands danced over her console as she called to Omega. "Commander, do you see the display? We have to act, and quickly! We'll lose the after half of the ship if we don't!"

"And us with it," Camden said as he turned a series of knobs and switches on his console sequencing a chain of automatic functions. "I'm ready here."

"So am I," Dela said completing her own procedure.

"Please don't tell me you two are planning what I think you're planning," Omega said looking at his display.

"No choice, Commander, there's nothing we can do," Camden said. "How much time, Dela?"

"I'd say we have about one minute until we lose it," she replied in a calm and steady voice. She seemed placid, unafraid by the ship's predicament.

"Commander… Omega… if we don't do this, we're finished," Camden said.

Omega stared at his display and knew that Camden was right. There was no alternate proposal.

"Forty-five seconds," said Dela calmly.

"Omega!" Camden implored.

Omega stared at Camden and then gave the order as if he were reading it straight out of the flight operations manual.

"Separate Command and Habitat Modules and prepare for reacquisition and docking," he said.

Camden turned a lever and the trio in the flight deck heard the characteristic sounds of explosive bolts releasing and the Habitat Module's separation rockets firing. Dela held onto her console tightly and shut her eyes as the Command and Control Module's own separation rockets ignited and freed them from the Habitat Module.

"Brace for shockwave!" she said.

Camden steered the Command and Control Module away from the Habitat Module using the reaction control system jets and when the Habitat Module exploded, the Command and Control Module was rocked by the brief shockwave.

They began to tumble and Camden struggled furiously to maintain stability with violent inputs to the RCS controls, but he was losing the battle. If he could not regain stability, the Module would spin out of control into space.

"I could use some help here!" Camden said.

"I've got pitch control," Omega said taking hold of a joystick controller and looking at the ship's orientation display. "Thrust forward, Camden! Thrust forward!"

Slowly, the pair regained control of the module and began maneuvering back to what was left of *San Mariner*. The Cargo and Propulsion Modules were drifting serenely in the darkness of space some distance from them. Dela was sending maneuvering commands to the after modules so they could dock with them, while Omega and Camden were aligning the Command and Control Module using the pitch and yaw thrusters.

"After sections are steady and ready to receive us," Dela said.

"Okay, Dela," Omega said. They all knew that if those sections drifted too far away, they would not have enough maneuvering fuel or inertia to catch up with them and that meant they would die out here. "Keep them that way."

"They're not going anywhere," Dela said as she pointed a handheld camera at the debris field that was once the Habitat Module. She stopped recording and gazed at her console when a low dull beep emanated from it. She shifted over to the Auxiliary Engineering console and cursed inaudibly. She tapped a few buttons and shook her head.

"Dela, while we're lining up, send a message to Space Command and inform them of our situation. See if there's another ship out here that can possibly assist us," Omega said.

"I've got an indication on my board that we've lost the signal on the high-gain and FTL systems," Dela said settling back at her station. Her voice was still calm, devoid of emotion and had no undercurrents of tension, but Omega could tell something was wrong.

"Are they still receiving our telemetry signals? Do we still have the emergency uplink from Space Command?" Omega asked.

"Negative, Commander," Dela said shaking her head. "There's no joy on any circuit. We've completely lost contact with Kerguelen. We're on our own."

6
The outskirts of the Central Province, Planet Kerguelen

A flight from the Northeastern Province to the Central Province normally took about three hours in a high-performance air ship, but to the quartet that made up Prior's combat team, it seemed like an eternity. Each one took pains to do nothing that would set her off and the commander had said nothing since she returned from her conference with Marshal Garath except, "Let's get the hell out of here. Take me to The Edge."

Since then, she sat mute, staring at the headrest in front of her, fuming like a scolded child. Her demeanor changed slightly two hours into the flight when Lupo, tired of sleeping on the deck, curled up on the seat beside her and placed his head in her lap. As she gently stroked the dog's soft coat, all indications leaned toward her returning back to normal.

To avoid heavy turbulence and expedite their journey as they traveled west-northwest across the Great Sea, Micah had decided early into the trip to adjust the flight plan. He increased altitude and speed to escape untoward weather and excess buffeting. The alteration would use more power and lower fuel cell efficiency but Micah would rather have that than have Prior all over him the entire trip. Trying to deal with her when she was in such a funk was akin to wrestling with a bear, and Micah didn't want that while trying to cope with the adverse conditions above the Great Sea that were prevalent this time of year. It would also make the trip smoother for the smaller and lighter gunship escorting them. The modifications made the crossing relatively fast and everyone onboard silently prayed it was time enough for Prior to get rid of whatever monkey it was that was on her back.

As the air ship crossed over the outer banks of the Central Province and into the region known as The Edge, Prior crossed her arms and legs and sighed deeply and continued her silence. The white caps of the swirling and cresting ocean and waves crashing violently against the rocky cliffs below were descriptive of Prior's emotional state.

Micah had set the controls to automatic after reaching high altitude early on in the flight but now prepared for manual piloting. He stretched and rolled his neck and looked over his instruments. Despite the conditions, he would enjoy the last leg of the trip. It wasn't often he had the chance to manually fly at supersonic speed, but this wasn't a normal ocean transit. He slid the door panel of the cockpit shut to prevent any distractions from the passenger compartment and settled in.

Normally he would be communicating with interurban or provincial air traffic controllers once they reached Central Province airspace, updating his position and receiving status on other craft and weather, but there were no such niceties in The Edge. Any air ship venturing into these badlands was on its own and traveled into the region at their own risk. Every pilot knew the hazards of The Edge and avoided it at all costs.

Twenty minutes after crossing into The Edge, Prior snapped out of her silent vigil and called to Micah. When the door opened, she spoke to her pilot.

"We're close aren't we?" she asked.

"Yes, Commander," Micah replied. "We're turning for our final approach now. We should be down in about fifteen minutes."

Micah waved at Lindsey and the young lieutenant entered the cockpit and sat down in the co-pilot's seat to help Micah safely maneuver the craft. Too many things could occur or go wrong in The Edge and an extra set of eyes could mean the difference between a safe transit and a crash landing.

Once the cockpit door was shut again, the craft slowed down and dropped in altitude. The air ship banked and settled into a straight-line course eighty feet above the ground as the engine exhaust rustled the trash on the desolate and empty streets below into the foul and polluted air.

As Micah maneuvered between the ruins of buildings on the outskirts of what was once a modern metropolis and industrial zone before the last Provincial Wars, Prior stared out of the window. It saddened her to see the old paved roads now in disrepair from neglect and strewn with garbage, derelict machinery and the occasional decomposing corpse. She recalled her history lessons on why roads were no longer used as thoroughfares, and the old vehicles that once ruled them called machinas.

Kerguelen society had stopped using the rolling vehicles after the last Provincial Wars but kept roads and streets for pilots to use as visual reference aids. The machina, however, did not survive. They had gone the way of animal driven transportation, a distant memory and the subject of modern planetary folklore.

How special it was to be on the open roads, traveling overland from ocean to ocean the stories would say. How thrilling it was to receive your operator's authorization and "drive" your machina alone for the first time. It was the first taste of freedom for many young people. How great an invention they were! The style and type of machina one owned was a symbol of status and the manufacturers of machinas made tremendous amounts money and influenced not only provincial economies but political parties as well.

But those tales were fodder for fiction writers and daydreamers, for there was no one left alive who had ever seen a machina in operation first hand. A machina could only be found in a first-class museum or in the private collection of the elite class. Not that it mattered much. The fossilized fuel used in the machina's archaic internal combustion engine had been exhausted long ago. The last Provincial Wars had seen to that. The seventeen-year long war had depleted the very commodity that had caused the conflict to begin with. As that and other natural resources dwindled, the first to create and implement viable alternative sources of energy would ultimately win the war and, for better or worse, control the destiny of the planet. And the winners of that race for supremacy, supported by the Guardians, were the Clerics and the Technos.

The Clerics were the forefathers of the Congress of Cardinals and used the bond they had with the Technos and the Guardians to reshape the political and social structure of Kerguelen. Before the Wars, the Technos, a name given to the scientists and engineers of Kerguelen, tried to persuade the business community and provincial governments to convert to renewable energy sources and expand the use of new and exotic materials. Unfortunately, too much money could be had in the manipulation of fossil fuel and speculation into its production and distribution, and their pleas fell on deaf ears.

Many of the provinces based their economies on it. The complete conversion to the use of exotic materials and alternate power sources would handicap many provinces as well and planetary leaders were sure none of the people would want anything made from or powered by them. Of course the leaders knew that fossil fuel would soon be depleted, but to change prematurely would seriously damage the fortunes of many powerful people and corporations. Things were good on the planet as it was and the provincial leaders decided to leave the question of what to do and when to do it to the next generation.

Seeing that the powers of the planet would not change, the Technos banded together and refused to supply governments with any new creations or upgrades to existing technology. They continued their research, but denied governments and corporations access to it. The Guardians protected their right to do so and the Technos rewarded them with advanced defensive and offensive materials powerful enough to defeat any provincial military force.

The Clerics allied themselves with the Technos when the Wars started and as provincial infrastructures failed, the alliance forced the population to concede to their doctrines or perish. The provincial rulers and their military leaders at the time had no choice but to accept the terms proposed by the Clerics and the Technos, for without an energy source to power their war machines and factories and vehicles, they could not maintain their influence and control over their war-torn societies.

They reluctantly agreed to the strict terms set forth by the Clerics and the planet adopted their ideals completely, including the implementation of a new planetary economic and political system. This system gave the Clerics and the Technos major controlling roles. In a short time, the Clerics had removed the old guard and sat nearly unchallenged as the supreme power on Kerguelen, using everything at their disposal to control the populace.

The highly conservative Clerics believed that the Wars had started because basic human values had been forgotten and this was because an overwhelming lack of faith in the Almighty and Her teachings had spread amongst the people. The Clerics changed that overnight.

Mandatory attendance at a religious sanctuary became required of all citizens. In the beginning, the type or sect didn't matter, only that each person on the planet did attend some sort of service. Children studied all religions in school so they had the ability to choose the best religion for them when they became adults. Eventually, the Clerics' sect, due to their vast influence, became the sole religion practiced and encompassed the entire population and was officially declared the Church of Kerguelen, or the Federal Church as it is now called. And for a hundred years now, they've held majority control of the planetary government, barely held in check by the Technos, now known as the Technology Council, and the Guardians.

But the Clerics were now losing that control and the people were beginning to turn their backs on the age-old anthropocentric theory that sustained the Clerics for so long, and the Clerics could not understand why. Why was there a planetary renaissance occurring and massive resistance to their doctrines? Why was the populace turning on the very group that had saved them from the brink of extinction? Was it not the Clerics who restored order and created a world where all could live and prosper? Their planet was a place where hunger, disease, war and prejudice, regardless of provincial origin, had been virtually extinguished. And all the Church wanted in return was blind obedience and for no one to question their decisions. To do so would be treason, would it not? Wasn't the loss of a few insignificant freedoms worth the cost?

Unfortunately, the pious leadership failed to realize that in all their teachings of the Almighty's word to the populace, they forgot the Almighty's greatest gift given to Her children... free will. The Children of the Almighty were exercising it now in protest to what they felt were unjust laws issued by the Church and the President, laws that had been upheld by the Legislature. The Technology Council and the Judiciary were unsuccessful in blocking the new doctrines but had been able to lessen their severity. And so far, that was all that was keeping a lid on a possible planetary revolution. A revolution the government said was being instigated by Venture.

As she looked at the remnants of a civilization lost below, Prior sighed and wondered how Kerguelen could have fallen so deeply in despair. She ended her inner reflections and unbuckled her seat restraint and moved to the rear of the passenger cabin as the air ship made its final maneuvers to land. Lupo watched her walk to the back and crawled to the deck again, lying strategically so he could watch her without moving his body. Prior opened an overhead compartment, removed a canvas bag that was inside and started to strip off her uniform. Pana and Rex went back to assist her as Hiroki spun his swivel seat toward her and broke the deafening silence onboard the air ship.

"You're suiting up?" he asked with a smile.

"How long have we known each other, Hiroki?" asked Prior as she undressed and handed the previously worn items to Rex who neatly hung up and stowed each garment as it was handed to him.

"I've had the privilege of serving with you for five years," he said proudly.

"Then explain to me why *I've* had the privilege of hearing you ask questions that you already have the answers to?" Prior said sounding annoyed.

"My apologies, Commander," Hiroki replied, but instead of letting a sleeping dog lie, he continued. "I deduce that your meeting with Marshal Garath didn't go as planned."

"Save your deductions for your taxes, Captain," Prior said icily. "I have no time for them."

Prior was now completely undressed and stood naked before her team. Pana handed Prior a pair of worn leather pants as she turned to face Hiroki. Her highly developed musculature was superior to any female, and most males, in the Guardian Corps and admired by all who saw her au naturale. Her deeply tanned body was symmetrical all over, with every muscle group well defined as if she were a medical school static display. It was only blemished by a two-inch scar near the second rib on her left side, the remnant of a wound she received when she killed her first wild animal as a child. Prior's tight abdominal muscles flexed as the words she spoke came out of her mouth, verifying that as was believed, she spoke from the diaphragm not the throat.

"Again, my apologies, Commander," Hiroki said as he stood and saluted her.

He held the salute until she nodded and then sat back down as she slipped the leather pants over her trim hips. Prior turned to Pana, who gave her a black sweater, and pulled it over her head and shoulders and slipped her arms into the sleeves. She pulled it down and turned her head to Hiroki and closed her eyes for a moment before she spoke.

"Captain Hiroki, it is I who should apologize to you," she said in a voice that was softer than it had been previously.

"What do you want us to do concerning Commander Venture?" he asked. "What are our mission parameters?"

"You are to do nothing, Captain," she replied as she sat down and slipped on socks and pulled on her boots. "The mission is mine and mine alone. And the parameters are simple: I am to kill Venture and anyone who stands in the way of allowing me to do that."

She stood up and saw Hiroki look at the deck and then back to her as he absorbed the words she had said. He understood that there was nothing in her power she could do to keep from killing Commander Venture. She wrapped a lightweight scarf around her neck and then put on a shoulder holster. She rolled her shoulders once and then slipped on her bolero jacket. She patted Hiroki on the shoulder and smiled at him as he looked up at her.

"Don't look so down, Hiroki, your deductions were right on target," Prior said picking up her TKP-7 pistol. She made sure the chamber was clear and then inserted a magazine in the weapon and chambered a round. "You were quite right. Things did not go as planned."

7
Interstellar space,
One parsec from the Kerguelen Star System

San Mariner had conducted trouble free space operations for nearly half a year and traveled a distance of over seventy-five light-years without incident, but suddenly, everything had gone to hell in a hand basket. An unexplained decompression and resulting explosion of the ship's Habitat Module and multiple systems failures had thrown the crew's so-called, "textbook space flight", out with the trash. Four crewmembers were dead and Omega, Camden and Dela were now attempting a treacherous deep space re-docking procedure. If they were successful, they would begin scrambling to maintain the systems that still functioned and restore those that weren't and continue their journey home... if they could manage to mate-up with the after portions of the ship, that is. Failure to do so meant certain death. They would perish in the void of interstellar space, slowly and miserably as the batteries that sustained them discharged. And in the vastness of the great abyss, it was likely they would never be found.

The after sections of the ship were stationary and awaiting for the Command and Control Module to mate with them. Though the Command and Control Module's systems were far from ideal for a re-docking maneuver, the crew knew the sooner they reconnected, the better it would be. Even in the best of conditions, the maneuver was a risky proposition. Many things could go wrong during the procedure. According to the book, the crew should have stabilized the Module's systems before trying to re-dock to ensure the safest operation possible, but for some reason the Command and Control Module's emergency batteries were discharging at a high rate and wouldn't last long, so immediate docking was imperative. The crew had to go for broke and hope for the best.

Omega took a second and thought about all of the things that could happen and then sighed. He decided not to worry about them. What was happening was out of his control. He looked at what was left of his crew and addressed them.

"Are you two up for this?" he asked looking back and forth at them.

"Yes, sir," Dela said with a shoulder shrug as she completed her preps at the flight engineer's station and then floated into the navigator's couch.

"You're always ready, Dela," Omega said forcing a smile to his face and giving her a reassuring wink. "All set, Camden?"

"I hope so," Camden said touching the maneuvering control console. "Let's give it a go."

"All right then, let's dock the ship," Omega said adjusting in the commander's couch. He scanned the screen in front of him and frowned.

The module was in bad shape and even if they successfully re-docked, there was a chance that they would not be able to return the ship to full operational condition. And that meant no light speed. Without it, it would take them centuries to get back to Kerguelen and he and his crew would be long dead. But the alien spacecraft would still remain. There was some consolation in that. He shrugged off those thoughts and shifted priorities. First, dock the ship, and then worry about getting home.

"The initial damage we sustained must have affected our battery compartment," Dela said looking at her console. "We're down to critical levels of amperage in all cells."

"Do we have enough power for docking?" Omega asked.

"I'll have to do some creative power management," she answered. "I'll have to cut some of the hotel services."

"Which ones?" Camden asked.

"The waste system, the internal sensors and the heating system," she said.

"It's going to get cold in here fast," Camden said.

"It'll be even colder if the batteries die altogether," Dela replied.

"Do whatever is necessary, Dela," Omega said.

Dela slipped out of the navigator's couch and floated to the engineer's station and quickly made the adjustments. After a minute, she returned to the navigator's station.

"Well?" Omega asked.

"That's the best I can do right now," Dela said settling into the couch. "We'll be okay, sir."

"I hope so," Omega said. He looked at his console and continued. "The docking probes are extended and clear and indicating ready. I have a green board. Pilot, you have a Go for reacquisition and docking."

"Roger," Camden said. "Ready to roll the module into position. We're set."

"Confirm program," Omega said.

"We're in flight computer program 418," Dela said. "We're synced and ready."

"Rotating 180 degrees," Camden said gently touching his joystick control.

The module slowly spun and rotated 180 degrees, settling into a position a few hundred feet from the after sections of the ship. Dela looked through the eyepiece of a viewing and range finder and turned a knob on its base. The knob clicked loudly twice and Dela turned briefly to Omega.

"We're aligned. The docking target is clear. Ready to thrust aft," Dela said.

"Distance?" Omega asked.

"Two hundred and fourteen feet," said Dela without looking at him. Her eye was now firmly affixed to the range finder's eyepiece. "Alignment confirmed. Two-one-four feet, plus two degrees."

"Very well," Omega said nodding. "Thrust aft."

"Thrusting aft," Camden said barely nudging his controls.

The ship was two degrees high and Camden would have to adjust their orientation as they backed into position. As they began to move, Dela called out range and orientation to Camden. She was her usual calm and methodical self, but Camden was a little unsteady with the flight controls. Instead of smooth inputs, his movements were jerky causing the module to slide out of alignment. Dela constantly gave him corrections, but his non-precision resulted in him having to thrust away from the after sections twice. Omega became irritated and Camden frustrated, but Dela remained cool. On their third attempt, Camden managed to keep the module steady and docked with the after sections. The indicator on Omega's console showed that the mating surfaces were flush and a positive seal between them had been established and the ship's commander hoped it was. If the surfaces were misaligned, the ship would split apart when they came up to speed.

"Docking probe indicators are green, we're indicating a hard seal," Omega said. "Lock the docking collar."

"Recycling the valves," Dela said flipping two switches. She looked at her panel and nodded. "The seals are holding. Valves indicate shut." Dela pressed a button and the metallic sound of the collar fitting into position rang throughout the module. She scanned her console and reported. "Positive pressure established between the modules. Docking collar in place and locked. Secondary bolts inserted and the shrouding is in place."

"Right," Omega said exhaling in relief. "Let's get ready to get underway."

"I've got to see what the power situation is," Dela said now appearing somewhat agitated and floated over to the flight engineer's station. Her hand danced over the console nimbly and the sound of the main drive system coming online drowned out the air recycling system momentarily. She tapped a few more buttons and red lights on her console turned green. She nodded in approval of the indicators and continued working. In a few minutes, she was finished and made a report. "Commander, propulsion is online and oxygen systems are restored. All hotel services are activated and in operation and the emergency electrical system is stabilized. We're in fifteen minute stand-by and ready to get underway."

"Very well, Dela," Omega said over his shoulder. "What about the artificial gravity?"

"No joy," she said shaking her head. "If it can be fixed, I'll have to go to the Propulsion Module to repair it. The computers are re-booted though, and staying online."

"Good," Omega said looking through the star finder in an attempt to calculate their position.

"I hope they stay that way," Camden said nodding. "Because without communications, we have no telemetry data. And without those computers, we're lost out here."

Camden was right. Normally, telemetry data was received from Space Command via a constant transmission beam. That data provided the ship's navigation system with up-to-date reports on their home planet's position in space in relation to the ship and automatically adjusted the ship's flight to compensate for any drift caused by the gravitational pull from celestial bodies. Even without telemetry data, they would be okay. The navigation computers could verify their position in their default setting.

If telemetry was lost, the navigation computer's default setting automatically sought out pre-programmed reference stars with their sensor arrays to navigate the ship. If the computers failed, the crew could make it to their system via the telemetry data. All they had to do was follow the communications beam. Once in their system, they could be assisted by another Space Command vessel or navigate by the stars and space buoys. Without either source of information in deep space, traveling at light speed was out of the question, and they were doomed to die a cold and brutal death in the void of space.

"Give me Kerguelen's position, Camden. I need to start calculating our home transit course," Omega said.

"One second," Camden said pressing a few buttons. When nothing happened, he tried again. He tried a third time and still had zero results. "Sorry, Commander, there's something wrong here. I can't pull up Kerguelen's position from the computer."

"That's impossible," Omega said floating over to the pilot's station. "If the computer's running, you should be able to pull it up."

Omega tried several times and was unsuccessful in his attempts. He tried another console and again came up empty. Dela slipped away from her station and joined them. She shook her head and floated to the Science console. The main computer console had several red lights illuminated.

"Damn!" Dela said.

"What's wrong now?" Omega asked.

"The computers are working, and the sensors are picking up reference data, but it's inaccessible. There's some kind of damage to the operating system, or the circuitry. I'm not sure which. If it's a core problem, the computer is useless," she said.

"What does that mean?" Camden asked.

"The software is corrupted or the hardware is damaged. I don't know which it is, how it happened or how bad it is, but it's enough to prevent us from accessing navigational data," Dela explained. "It's there, we just can't get to it."

"So what do we do now?" asked Camden slightly panicked.

"We use our only other choice," Dela said. "Dead reckoning."

"From out here?" Camden scoffed. "Are you out of your mind? That's not only crazy, but it's impossible."

"He's right, Dela," Omega said.

"You're damned right, I am," Camden said.

"And so is she," Omega added.

"What?" Camden asked not believing his ears. "Without exact coordinates, we might as well flip a coin on which direction we travel."

"With the right reference points, we can manually maneuver to our star system and then get help from another ship once we get there," Dela offered.

"And how do we contact this help?" Camden asked. "Send up a signal flare?"

"Exactly," Dela said. "Once we get to our system, there are dozens of ways we can call for help. But we've got to get there."

"Why can't you fix the computer?" Camden asked. "I thought fixing things was your job on this mission?"

Dela floated closer to Camden. "Listen closely, you idiot," she began glaring at him through piercing eyes. "This is far from a simple problem. A corrupted software program would require me to re-write the entire program to make it work. Even if I could, I would still need a position on Kerguelen and upload it. We're talking about hundreds of thousands of lines of programming... and I'd have to do it by hand. One keystroke error, a zero where a one should be, and we'd end up in Canopus, or Orion or Virgo... or some other system, if we were lucky. Even software engineers back home use a specialized computer to program the navigational systems of Space Command vessels.

"If the hardware is shot, we're out of luck. I'm not a 2M specialist by any means. It's not like changing a light bulb. There is very little room for error in micro-miniature repair, especially in the navigation system. I could make it worse by trying to repair it. Dead reckoning is our only option." She turned to Omega and added, "And whatever we choose, we've got to do it soon. I have to get main power back online because we're going to need what's left in the batteries when and if we get home. We all need to start working now. The batteries and emergency life support won't sustain us long."

Omega thought for a moment. He knew that whatever they tried would be a crapshoot. But they had little choice in their options. The ship was expiring and they could only delay the inevitable from happening for so long.

"If you have an alternative proposition, Camden, now's the time to say it," Omega said.

"I'm just a pilot, not a tech," Camden said. "I've given you my opinion."

"There is another option," Dela offered.

"Which is?" Omega asked.

"If I can restore communications, we can navigate using only partial dead reckoning," Dela said. "We'll get back the telemetry signal and locate Kerguelen. Then, it's only a matter of locating reference stars manually using the star finder."

Omega nodded and rubbed the coarse hair on his chin. There was another option. Dela had given him an idea. If they could find out what their current position was, they wouldn't need anything. But it would have to be done without navigation aids of any kind.

"Camden, hold the ship perfectly still. I need a steady platform. Once you have it steady, help me with the star plotting. This is going to take two sets of eyes," Omega said.

"What are you planning?" Camden asked as he stabilized the ship.

"A long shot," Omega said. "A very long shot."

Omega and Camden went to work and spent over an hour finding reference stars, while Dela was busy at her consoles. Using the star finder platform, Omega and Camden plotted Canopus, Ursa Minor, Sirius,

Virgo, Vega, and lastly, Kerguelen's Pole Star. Omega crossed his fingers as he input the star positions into the navigational computer.

Omega then grabbed an electronic data tablet that was floating near him and began to scribble on it with a stylus. Camden waited impatiently as Omega made his calculations. When he was done, he consulted the navigational computer.

It seemed fortune was on their side. Not all of the navigation program was corrupted. The computer's calculations matched Omega's exactly. They could find their position and a path to home now. Using the star references as constants, they calculated the Kerguelen sun's position in relation to the reference stars and determined where they were. A few minutes later, they had plotted the course they had to take to make it home.

The problem they now faced was more daunting. Without an uplink, they couldn't just set the controls on automatic and fly away. The ship was slightly less than a parsec from Kerguelen, 3.01 light-years to be exact. However, without course corrections in flight, they could overshoot Kerguelen. Short one light-year traverses at maximum speed was the only solution. At the end of each hop, they would calculate their position and jump again. It was not the ideal way to travel and required precise manual star plotting but it was all they had. It took another forty minutes to manually input the jump position and then they were ready. With any luck, in a few days they would be basking in the light of the Kerguelen sun.

"The course is set and the helm control has accepted the input," Omega said. "Give me a Go-No Go for light speed. Pilot?"

"Pilot is ready," Camden said. "But I'm still lodging a protest to this procedure. We can't fly this way. It goes totally against Space Command operations directives."

"Your protest is noted," Omega said sarcastically. "Dela?"

"GNC is Go," Dela said. She tapped a button on the navigation console and then shifted to the flight engineer's station. "Main and Auxiliary Engineering are a Go." She shifted positions to the Science consoles and made her last report. "TNT and Network are a Go."

Omega pushed a plunger on his console half way down and called to Dela again. "Status on the TLC system?"

She floated back to the flight engineer's station. "Ready," she said looking at the display on the console. "TLC is stabilized and in flux. The ship stabilizers and system compensators are nominal. Because of the computers, I'll have to operate the system manually, but the TLC is ready to answer all bells up to and including flank speed."

"Stand-by to answer a full bell, Dela," Omega said looking at his console.

"Ready," she said opening a clear plastic cover protecting the TLC engine control from being accidentally pushed.

"Three... Two... One... Go to light speed!" Omega said.

Dela depressed the TLC engine control button and the ship vibrated as it moved forward and then the resonance dissipated. A second later a loud thunderous roar came from the rear of the ship and then *San Mariner* leapt through space, leaving a blur from its running lights in its wake. Omega clutched his stomach and Camden swallowed deeply choking back a burning sensation that had built up in his throat. Dela rubbed her temples and shook her head as the ship quickly came up to and passed through the light speed threshold. Omega glanced around the flight deck after the transition and asked for a status.

"Report," Omega ordered.

"All systems nominal," Dela said as the glow from her console surrounded her face. "The ship is steady and a Go at light speed. Ready to come up to ordered speed."

"Answer the bell at your discretion," Omega said.

"Coming up to full speed," Dela said pushing the T-handled throttle control to the Full Speed setting on the Engine Order Telegraph. She turned a small dial next to the throttle control and looked at the speed indicator and reported. "Power Level Actuator at Full Speed, Commander. The ship is answering the command."

The ship shuddered as its speed increased, and Dela made an adjustment on her console. An unfamiliar metallic noise from the rear of the ship got the full attention of Camden and Omega.

"What's going on?" Omega asked turning his head to Dela.

"We're fine," answered Dela still looking at her console. A loud bang sounded again and she turned toward Omega. "Just a little hiccup. We've reached full speed. All systems nominal."

"Excellent," Omega said able to breathe again. He looked at his own console and saw they appeared to be still on track. "Take us to flank speed when she's ready, Dela."

She pushed the T-handle all the way forward to the Flank Speed setting and turned the dial as far as it would go. The ship vibrated slightly again and groaned with the speed increase. It was short-lived and then *San Mariner* smoothed out again. She looked her console over and smiled as the ship's familiar characteristic hum returned.

"Power Level Actuator at Flank Speed. Maximum velocity obtained, Commander," Dela said.

Omega nodded and looked at the navigation plot. "Time to target position... eleven hours and twenty-seven minutes," he said.

All three breathed a collective sigh of relief and Omega slipped from the commander's couch and floated in the center of the flight deck.

"Right," he said. "We're on our way. Each of you needs to log the effects of light speed travel while in zero-G. I'm sure the Space Command physiologists will be interested in the results."

Dela and Camden both nodded and continued to monitor their stations. Though they had adjusted to the weightless condition without any discomfort, there was no data on the effects of weightlessness and light speed travel on the body. It had never been done before and Omega didn't know if there would be any long-term side effects from the condition. He did know they had to return the ship to normal as soon as possible.

"Dela, are your systems stable?" Omega asked. She nodded and he turned to Camden. "Camden, I need you to monitor the flight deck while Dela and I take a look at the communications system," Omega said.

"What do you think you can do with it?" Camden asked.

"I'm not sure," Omega said. "We'll have to go into the crawl space just below the high-gain unit."

"It's a pretty tight area," Camden said. "It's not really meant for a man to crawl around in there."

"Yes, but Dela should fit perfectly," Omega said looking at his flight engineer. He smiled at her and she nodded back.

"I'll get my tools," she said with a sigh.

Omega and Dela left the flight deck and floated through the hatches and passageways to the Cargo Module. As Dela prepped for her work in the crawl space, Omega felt she had something to say to him, but he didn't pursue the matter. If she had something on her mind, she would tell him eventually. They readied their equipment in silence and when they were ready, Dela donned a low-pressure suit and pulled herself upwards and inside the crawl space.

The low-pressure suit was not designed for work in space but would protect her from the cold and if there was a lack of oxygen in the tunnel. When she reached her desired position, she plugged a thick cord into a communications box and Omega could hear her breathing in his own headset.

"What have you got?" he asked.

"Give me a second," she said as she shifted her head back and forth looking at the FTL communications control unit.

She saw instantly what the problem was. The unit had received a high amount of voltage that overloaded it. Resistors and a series of fuses protected against such an event, but a large surge had been constantly applied to it and resulted in the destruction of the circuit board for the unit. It was easy enough to fix, unfortunately a spare circuit board was not in their onboard stores.

"I see what the problem is," Dela said as she removed the fuses and circuit board. "I'm coming out."

When she returned to Omega, she removed her mask revealing a devilish smirk. Omega had seen that look before. It meant she had an idea, usually one that was not altogether practical.

"What's the deal?" he asked.

"Well, the circuit board for the control unit is trashed," she said handing him the circuit board.

He examined it and smiled. "Is that the technical term for it?"

"Yeah," she replied smiling. "And it's a descriptive one as well. It's been overloaded."

"What can we do?" he asked placing the circuit board in a bag so it wouldn't float away.

"I can combine systems," she said running a hand through her hair. The action freed her hair from the hair tie she was using and in the zero gravity, her hair stayed suspended and looked as if invisible fingers were holding up the strands. "The low-gain control board is good. I'll plug the low-gain into the high and that should restore the telemetry signal and I hope give us the ability to communicate at short range."

"It won't work," Omega said shaking his head. "I know a little about that system, Dela. The systems are incompatible. They have different power requirements."

"One of our mini-power converters and a series of fuses will solve that problem. And they'll protect against any further power spikes or reverse power conditions. It won't be one hundred percent, but we'll have the uplink and the capacity to communicate with Space Command using a space buoy if we come near one," she explained.

"How long will it take to do that?"

"About thirty minutes," she said. "After that, I need to get main power back online. Using the TLC system will drain what's left of our batteries before we reach the first position."

"Any way to cut back on usage?" Omega asked hopefully.

"Negative. I could cut everything we've got and it wouldn't make a difference. *San Mariner* has about nine and a half... maybe ten hours on the outside, of life left if we continue on batteries," she said.

"Okay, I'll do what I can to help you," Omega said.

Dela nodded and quickly gathered the materials she needed to repair the FTL unit. Omega watched her work and appreciated how deftly she handled the tools of her trade. When her makeshift device was completed, she entered the crawl space again and placed it into position. Once she powered it up, she came back to Omega and pulled off the low-pressure suit.

"Well?" he asked.

"It's online," she said. "I would give it some time to calibrate itself before you tried it. It's designed to automatically slew towards Kerguelen and receive the uplink data. It's been down for a while, so it's going to go through an extensive re-booting process. Unfortunately it's going to take a few hours to complete."

"Then let's get to the Propulsion Module," Omega said.

He jerked his head toward the after module and pushed himself away from a bulkhead and floated across the Cargo Module. As he reached the Propulsion Module access, Dela tugged at his friction sock. He grabbed onto the hatch leading into the Propulsion section and stopped his forward progress. He spun and looked at Dela puzzled as to why she had stopped him. Before he could ask, she spoke.

"Commander, we don't have much time," she said.

"I know, Dela. We've got to…" he began but was cut off.

"You don't understand, Commander. I have to talk to you. I have reason to suspect Flight Officer Camden rigged the Habitat Module disaster and caused the problems with the FTL and navigation systems," she said. Her eyes had a different kind of intensity to them and Omega noticed that her voice had changed. It was strong and clear and free of the regional accent it once had. It no longer sounded quaint like a country cousin, but sophisticated like a cosmopolitan.

"What do you mean?" he asked becoming curious.

"While you two were working, I had the chance to look over some of the data. The systems, the indications… it's all wrong… and it doesn't feel right," she said shaking her head.

"Mission Specialist Dela, do you know what you're saying? Camden is a high-ranking Guardian officer, a centurion. He's one rank below commander. To accuse him of sabotage without solid proof can be detrimental to your career… not to mention your life," Omega said almost scolding her.

"Regardless, there are things that don't add up," she said indignantly.

Since she appeared adamant, Omega decided to indulge her. "What doesn't add up?" he asked.

"The watch rotation, for one," she began. "He switched my rotation so I could be on with him."

"You told me yourself he did it to accommodate Tallen's extra work with the alien space probe," Omega countered. "Or maybe the reason he did it was because he likes you."

"That causes me more concern than him being a saboteur," she answered. "He's as repulsive as a kiss on the lips from a snake."

"Watch rotations mean nothing, Dela," Omega said dismissively.

"That would be true if he and I were not the only ones in the crew to have successfully separated, reacquired and re-docked space modules in an emergency. Not even Delle or you have done that," she argued crossing her arms in front of her as she floated.

"So? What does that prove?" Omega said. "Coincidence. Pure coincidence."

"Isn't it peculiar that the only two people who have done the maneuver end up on the same watch just when that skill is most needed? After six months in space and after all of the other variables are tallied, it's more than coincidence, it's planned," Dela said. "The odds of it happening are too great."

"Dela..."

"You saw that fried circuit board. That damage was deliberate. A blind man could see that with a cane. And the navigational computer could have only been compromised by sabotage. Only selected line items were corrupted, and enough remained so we could find a way home," she added.

"Dela, you're accusing a Guardian of an illegal act. Even if you're correct, as master of this vessel, I have to stress to you how very serious... and dangerous that is," he said with concern in his voice. "He won't take kindly to it. You've already called him a moron."

"No, I said he was an idiot," Dela corrected. "But I know what you're eluding to, Commander. I shouldn't cast stones at others, I know Scripture. And I also know the law: Only the Church or a Guardian may accuse a Guardian of a treasonous, seditious or subversive act. Only those individuals may accuse a Guardian of a crime. Since you're no longer a Guardian, I'll have to do it." She floated closer to Omega and continued. "You see, Commander Omega, you may be master of *San Mariner*, but I was assigned to this mission to observe the crew, Centurion Camden in particular. My real name is Arcuri... Colonel Arcuri... and I am a Guardian."

8
The Edge, The Northern Frontier, Central Province, Planet Kerguelen

Prior dipped her head slightly, turned up the collar on her bolero jacket and left the main street to avoid the brunt of a windstorm that had stirred up. She tentatively walked through the dark, trash-filled alleys and back streets taking care to avoid drawing any attention. Though the avenues and byways appeared vacant, the walls of the derelict buildings had eyes and the lampposts ears. The former city, once known as Boleen, was dead, but life was far from extinct in The Edge. It was well past sundown and the streets would soon be crawling with predators looking for easy prey. Though she was not afraid, Prior did not want to fight, she didn't have time. She was here only to get information from an acquaintance in her past and he would be found at Rosie's Blue Heron Tavern, the unofficial headquarters of criminal activity on Kerguelen.

The Edge as a whole was a wide-open area. There was no government oversight to control the area's activities and there were no laws or police to enforce them even if there were. The Edge was the last frontier, the last free range on the planet and if someone wanted to disappear from existence, The Edge was the place to do it.

This was not Prior's first time here. She came to the region several times a year in search of those who were out of reach using normal channels and each visit was different than the previous one. It had been about four months since Prior ventured here, but some things didn't change. The stench in the air was as bad as it always was and it felt as dangerous as it had been before, probably more so.

It was a risky proposition coming to The Edge, for not even Guardians were given carte blanche or respected. That was the reason Prior always entered alone. Not even Lupo joined her. The people would kill him on sight, if not out of fear, for food. Rex and Pana would have been fine in the zone because they were Boroni, but Hiroki and Lindsey wouldn't have made it five feet. They would have instantly been identified as Guardians. However, the safety of her team was not the main reason for Prior's lone excursion. Entry into The Edge by Guardians was strictly forbidden and any Guardian violating that order would be ousted from the Corps and face up to a year of confinement.

Safety was the reason for the regulation, but Prior knew the ins and outs of The Edge and knew all would be fine if she limited the duration of her visits. She couldn't stay longer even if she wanted to. Micah had instructions to takeoff one hour after landing, with or without her onboard. And no one wanted to be stranded in The Edge. She always finished her business with plenty of time to spare and so far Central Command had no idea she had ever been in The Edge. As she turned a corner and walked past a group of men rummaging through a pile of refuse looking for anything useful, she saw her destination in front of her, Rosie's Blue Heron Tavern.

Rosie's Blue Heron Tavern occupied a unique building. It was a way station for some and for others it was a seat of power. The most notorious and deadliest characters on Kerguelen held court on the main floor and the many backrooms of the establishment. But all manners of lost souls found refuge and cohabitated in the tavern. Derelicts and undesirables, escaped convicts and thugs, and wise guys with one foot in their graves, all found solace in The Edge and a home at Rosie's Blue Heron Tavern. It was the perfect place to lose oneself, for no one asked questions here, and those who were curious found their stay... and life, short-lived.

Rosie's was completely off of the grid, a criminal/law enforcement DMZ and safe haven where underworld characters could not be extradited. The Federal Police was said to have a secret handshake with the proprietor of Rosie's (whoever that really was), agreeing not to pursue anyone in The Edge for any reason. Not even bounty hunters dare enter. In turn, the police were occasionally tossed a bone. A low to mid-level criminal was often given up to the police every now and then in exchange for autonomy. More than likely it was a person or persons who had outlived their usefulness and had become a liability.

The planetary government overlooked The Edge as well, mostly because the general population knew very little or nothing about the true nature of the region and because it served to keep all the bad eggs in one rotten basket. Sometimes convicted felons would be given the choice of prison or banishment to The Edge. Depending on the individual, imprisonment might be a better option than freedom in The Edge. The area received no support from the government and its inhabitants had to provide their own food, energy, medical supplies and telecommunications. To get these things, the residents had to steal them and this was a high-risk operation. If they were caught and found to be a habitual felon banished to The Edge, they would be put to death, so everything these masters of crime planned was calculated down to the lowest common denominator of risk and hazard. And that meant that a criminal from The Edge was the best in the business and a superstar in the criminal hierarchy.

It was believed that Rosie's Blue Heron Tavern was the first permanent structure built in the region when the first settlers occupied the area after a huge vein of silver was discovered in the neighboring hills over four hundred years ago. Constructed by a former female burlesque entertainer, it was the only respite the early pioneers had. A place to enjoy yourself no matter what your taste. The mines made the region grow and provided economic stability for the area. Some years after the silver rush, a large pool of petroleum was found and The Edge grew to gigantic proportions. Despite the brutal bone chilling winters and harsh drought filled summers, people flocked to The Edge for work. The opportunity to do more for their families in half a year than they could in three years elsewhere was the driving force. Life was tremendous for anyone with a piece of The Edge until the last Provincial Wars turned The Edge into a wasteland and virtually uninhabitable. After the Wars, the criminal element took up residence and through it all, Rosie's remained. After four centuries of existence, it still caters to any individual's taste, no matter how exotic or extreme.

Prior passed an old barfly standing atop of the steps of Rosie's leaning against a post. His body reeked and from his condition, Prior believed the post was the only thing holding him up. She pushed open the doors to the tavern and he followed her in. He stayed four or five steps behind Prior as she worked her way through the smoke filled barroom. The smell of sweat, cheap tobacco and cheaper whiskey assaulted her enhanced senses and she consciously tuned them down.

She blinked her eyes to adjust to the lighting and looked around as she brushed the dust off of her jacket and pants.

The structure was very large and Prior believed that there were as many, if not more, subterranean levels as there were upper floors. She had been as far as the second floor once, but on every other visit she had conducted her business on the main floor. She could only imagine what occurred above the second floor and in the depths of the basement levels.

There was gaiety in the voices of the patrons on the main floor, and the look of satisfaction on those returning from the upper floors. The spring in their gaits as they bounded down the steps could have filled volumes. Prior walked slowly across the room, taking note of the heads that turned in her direction and of those giving her more than a cursory glance. The majority of them paid her no attention. They were too busy hunched over tables conducting whatever illegal enterprise they were into or plotting their next move or just simply drinking.

Some of the patrons had male or female prostitutes on their laps or beside them. Misery loved company, even if you had to pay for it. As Prior passed one table, a female suddenly became angry with her prostitute and pushed him to the floor, kicking and cursing him as he tried to crawl away. The female pulled out a low-power laser pistol and uttered something in a provincial dialect Prior did not understand. Whatever she said convinced the male whore to come back and join her. He stood silently next to her and the female said something else that elicited hearty laughs from the other occupants of the table. The female turned to the prostitute and said another brief statement and he nodded submissively. Prior didn't know what she said, but grasped the gist of it: Behave or be dead.

Prior looked closely at the female and recognized her. She was an Eastern Province native and arms dealer named Anora. She specialized in supplying and more notably, using exotic explosives. The men at the table with her were freelance mercenaries. Prior had crossed paths with one of them before, but didn't know his name. The posture of the group told Prior that they were ironing out last minute details for an upcoming operation, one that would happen soon. High-level players never got together to chat about the good old days, it was too risky and they didn't trust or like each other that much. But who they were and what they were doing didn't interest Prior. She was looking for one person in particular and needed to find him as soon as possible. Prior went to the bar and leaned forward against the rail. The old barfly that followed her inside shimmied up to the bar a few feet away from her. He looked at her through clouded eyes and smiled.

"Whiskey," Prior called to the bartender on the other side of the bar.

He recognized her immediately and quickly grabbed a glass and a bottle, filling it to the rim as he sat it down in front of her. Prior sighed. She knew him all too well. His nickname was Smiley and she neither knew nor cared what his real name was. Smiley was a living example of a pain in the ass and possibly the only truly innocent person in The Edge but he wanted desperately to be a tough guy and a gangster. However, no one liked him so he would never get his wish, and that was fortunate because he was weak and wouldn't have lasted two days as a criminal.

The old barfly cleared his throat and Prior looked at him. He looked much older than he was. The Edge had taken its toll on him and the consumption of large amounts of spirits was probably the only way he coped with his situation. She nodded toward the old man and spoke to Smiley.

"Give him a glass," she said.

"It ain't necessary," Smiley said. He turned and scowled at the old man. "I thought I told you..."

"Just give him a glass," Prior said. "I'll decide what is and what isn't necessary concerning my money." Smiley hesitated for a moment and then caught her eyes. They were soft but her words confirmed her annoyance with the situation. When their eyes met and locked, she continued. "I'm not talking just to hear my own voice." Smiley nodded and sat a glass down in front of the barfly. He filled it and the man picked it up with shaking hands and gulped it down.

"Another," Prior said as she downed her own shot, wincing as she swallowed. It was the possibly the worst liquor she had ever tasted. Smiley filled both glasses and Prior threw it back. She pointed to the glass with a forefinger. "Again." Smiley complied and she drained the glass again, snarling in response to its taste.

Smiley had other customers at the bar but stayed in front of Prior. He knew she was a Guardian but also knew she was not here to cause trouble. She came into Rosie's a few times a year and met with a regular for a few minutes and then left. Most importantly, he knew that if he had mentioned her true identity to anyone, he would be dead before he got to finish his thoughts on the subject. But it didn't matter to him why she came here. She didn't stay long and her money was good, that's all that mattered. Perhaps she was just slumming. Guardians were always considered to be a bit eccentric. She may have just come to The Edge for a quickie. He grinned at her with his picket fence smile loaning credence to his nickname and the old joke: *How do we know the toothbrush was invented in The Edge? If it were invented anywhere else it would have been called a teeth brush.*

"It's been a long time, where have you been?" Smiley asked refilling the glasses.

"Why do you want to know, Smiley? Are you writing a book?" Prior asked looking annoyed. She drank the swill down and shook her head to ward off its harshness.

"I'm just trying to be sociable," he answered still grinning.

"You want to be sociable, go visit your neighbors. If you want to be useful, leave the bottle," Prior said tossing three large platinum coins on the bar.

The grin on his face disappeared as he picked up the money and walked away to serve his other patrons. Prior looked around and finally spotted the party she had been searching for. He slowly worked his way down the stairs and settled in at a table on the far side of the barroom. Prior poured the old man another glass of whiskey and picked up her glass and walked over to the table. She stood over the lopsided table for a moment before she sat down and spoke to the man sitting there.

"Mind if I join you?" she asked.

The man acknowledged her presence by jabbing a stubby finger at the chair opposite of him and she sat. He shuffled a deck of cards as Prior stretched her legs out in front of her and watched him. After a minute, he dealt the cards out to play solitaire and when he was finished, put the remainder of the deck on the table and took out a half smoked cigar butt. Prior tapped his hand and offered him one of hers. He smiled at the open platinum plated case containing small neatly hand rolled cigars and took one. She lit it for him and left the case on the table. The man inhaled deeply and closed his eyes as he exhaled. When he opened his eyes, he poured whiskey into Prior's glass and then his own. He placed the cork back in the bottle, picked up the deck of cards and commenced playing his game. The pair remained silent for a few minutes before the man spoke.

"The word in the Ether is that you've got a contract to do Venture," he said softly and without looking at her.

"Is that a question?" Prior asked looking at him closely.

"More of a speculation," he answered looking up at her as he felt her eyes on him.

It had been four months since she had seen him last but he still looked the same, though his color was a little off. His voice was still the same though, far too cultured and refined to be in a place like this.

"Guardians don't do contract work," she replied.

"That depends on your point of view, doesn't it?" he said with a chuckle. "You know, a lot of people wonder how different things might be if the G-men and the Technos had taken full control so many years ago… like they should have."

"Is that what you do now, sit around and gossip?" she asked.

"Just idle chitchat amongst tradesmen, you know how it is when things get slow," he said turning cards over. He put the deck down again and raised his glass. Prior picked up her glass and leaned forward as he offered a toast. "To days of future past." They touched glasses and drained them together. He refilled the glasses and returned to his game.

"How are you?" Prior asked.

"I think you're looking at it," he replied.

"You look thinner," Prior said. "Any problems?"

"Nothing that a little good whiskey and a lot of a bad woman couldn't take care of," he said laughing. His smiled faded and he continued. "Venture has been busy. He's running with his old mates Marco and Vitana in Capitol City right now."

"Is that the reason I'm here?" Prior asked.

"I didn't know you were here at all," he said gathering up the cards and shuffling the deck several times. When he finished, he fanned the worn cards out in his hands. "Pick a card."

Prior chose a card, looked at it and placed it back in the deck. He shuffled the cards again and then cut the deck twice. He dealt out four cards face down and turned the fifth face up on the table.

"Is that your card?" he asked.

"Yes," she nodded.

"That's where you'll find him," he said shuffling the cards again. "But you'll need to hurry."

She nodded again and stood up. They both drank the brackish brown liquid in the glasses and she smiled at him. He gave her a quick grin and she gave him a hug. She rubbed her cheek against the rough stubble on his face and stuffed a thick envelope inside of his jacket as she broke away.

"I added a bonus in there," she said.

"It's unnecessary, but I thank you just the same. It's always a pleasure doing business with you," he said patting his jacket.

"Buy yourself something nice."

"I'll do that," he said smiling. "Listen, if you don't catch him in Capitol City it's going to be tough to track him down."

"Is he going traveling?" she asked.

The man nodded. "And there are other players on the board. Without his sugar daddy, he can't stay exposed. He needs to find some shade."

"You know about the Celeron?" she asked astonished at his knowledge of Venture's past and colleagues.

"Yes, and they're not very pleased with him."

"I know, I've talked to them," Prior nodded.

"You have? That's surprising," he said impressed. "They must have a high opinion of you. They don't talk to very many women."

"I'm special," she quipped.

"Of that I'm sure," he said. His eyes darted across the room briefly before he continued. "Look, there's a lot of nervous talk in the air about the resurgence of The Argent. They've partnered up with some bad characters and are gunning for Venture as well. I've heard they acquired Guardian weapons and mean business. Veterans of the business like Anora are stockpiling weapons in case there's a big blow."

"I find it hard to believe Anora is running scared because of The Argent," Prior said. "They're supposed to be just a legend."

"If you had been here two days ago, you would have a different outlook," he said. "One of their agents came in here kicking down doors and ripping off heads, literally, to get information."

"Who was it?"

"I don't know, but he's a stone cold killer, Prior. Don't fuck around with him. If you see him, kill him. Don't try any of that Guardian ethics stuff. Just shoot… a lot," he said with wide eyes.

"If the legend is true, The Argent is supposed to work in groups, like a mercenary cell. They don't use one guy to conduct their business," Prior said.

"Maybe, but that was the past," the man said. "This guy was a loner and killed three people before he even asked his first question."

Prior had some questions too, but no time. She had to go. She squeezed the man's hand once and turned to leave. He called to her and she turned her head.

"I know you got to go," he said. "But there's one more thing."

"What is it?"

"Some people have been complaining about a busted deal in the Western Province. A business deal that went really wrong. It's the kind of business deal that's not reported to the government," he said. "You wouldn't know anything about that, would you?"

"Yes, I would," said Prior. "Unfortunately those people found out that the Western Province Grange is more than just a mere international farming collective and philanthropic organization. It also has sharp teeth."

The man smiled. "I'm glad to see you're on top of things," he said.

"Always," Prior smiled. "If you have any friends involved with the deal, advise them to cut ties with it quickly. Take care of yourself. Hopefully I'll see you soon."

Prior spun on her heels and quickly departed the tavern. When she was gone, the man pulled out a small case of anti-radiation medicine and gave himself a dose. He shuddered from the potency of the medicine and breathed heavily. He needed the money Prior gave him for information badly because his stockpile of medicine was just about gone. He had unfortunately become a victim of his own deadly work. Once upon a time, he was a scientist but turned his knowledge toward the lucrative world of arms dealing. He had trafficked in low-yield atomic weapons but received a deadly dose of radiation from one of his dirty isotope weapons and it was only a matter of time before his internal organs failed from the exposure.

He returned to his cards and shuffled the deck. He cut the cards and flipped over the card Prior had chosen. He was glad she understood its meaning. He put it back in the deck and shuffled the cards again. The card was the 'Suicide King'.

9
The Green District, Capitol City, Central Province, Planet Kerguelen

The house Prior was standing in front of was once a fashionable residence and the center of social activity in Capitol City. Located in one of the older sections of the city, it was built during the time when individual governments were status quo on Kerguelen. Its last occupant was the Central Province governor named Marlow. A self-styled martinet, he was nicknamed The King and was considered a half-Robin Hood. He stole from the rich and kept it.

But his enemies and political opponents had discovered his crooked dealings, as well as his peculiar personal habits and appetites. Marlow had committed suicide instead of facing public scrutiny and embarrassment about his business practices, money laundering and sexual proclivities. His house had now come to ruin along with the neighborhood it inhabited. Lush ivy that had once decorated the stately stonewalls had long since decayed and the vacant neighborhood was now ideal for conducting affairs that could be considered illegal or unethical.

As Prior walked around the abandoned grounds, she was saddened by what she saw. It wasn't the rundown house and ruined landscape that caused her melancholy it was the loss of life Prior had come across. It was unnecessary and a waste of great potential.

At first glance, the scene seemed straightforward. A former Guardian officer turned mercenary named Xavier and his crew had caught up with Venture on the mansion property and attacked him in the hopes of catching him unaware and cashing in on the bounty that was on his head. Unfortunately, Xavier was not as stealthy or as clever as he had thought. A quick battle ensued resulting in the death of Xavier, his team of mercenaries, as well as Venture and his crew.

Judging by the amount of residual heat still emanating from the bodies, Prior knew what she was looking at in the courtyard had not even been over for ten minutes. She knelt down over Xavier's plasma energy weapon riddled body and shook her head. Lupo was nearby, sniffing and scratching the ground. With the exception of her canine, Prior was alone. She had sent her team aloft to search for signs of anyone who might have witnessed or been involved with the slaughter. Prior stiffened when her senses registered another presence, it was an obscure scent and one that she was not familiar with.

She called her dog to her and he slowly meandered to his mistress and gave a low growl as he looked around the property. He too sensed another presence on the grounds. Prior seemed to ignore him as she stood and faced the mansion turning away from the source of Lupo's attentions. A slight breeze was blowing against her back and she breathed in deeply. The unfamiliar spoor in the air caused her to ready herself for a possible attack. Prior exhaled and as the scent became more faint and then dissipated she relaxed again. The possible threat had gone.

Prior turned from the mercenaries to Venture and his aides, Captain Marco and Major Vitana. It was obvious that Venture and his aides had killed the mercenaries, but it was not a mutual destruction scenario. Someone else had killed Venture's group.

Two of the mercenaries had been severed in half by a laser pulse rifle at close range, the third, a female named Lani, was decapitated. Her fallen crown had rolled into a pile of dried leaves a few feet away from its host body. Prior knew such an act was Vitana's signature handiwork.

Weapons had been the cause of the demise of Xavier and his crew, but Venture and his team had died in hand-to-hand combat. To be blunt, they had been literally beaten to death. If someone had reported that to Prior, she would have called the person making the statement a liar. All three of the Guardians were in peak physical condition and highly skilled in unarmed combat. A large force would have to have been employed against them, but there were no signs of anyone else except the mercenaries and the Guardians in the courtyard.

"Who did this to you, Venture?" Prior said aloud looking at the crushed sternum of her former regimental commander.

Prior searched for a rational explanation of the deaths and could only come up with an irrational one. It had to be The Argent, or someone claiming to be The Argent.

She pulled out her TELCOM and punched in a code. In a few seconds, a voice rang in her ear.

"Directory assistance," a computerized female voice said.

"Connect me with the residence of Sebastian, Via Ennio Number 15, Lago Patria, Northeastern Province," Prior said.

"Stand by please," the voice said. Five seconds later, the voice said, "Hold for your connection."

"Thank you," Prior said.

"What do you want, Prior?" Sebastian said sounding annoyed.

"I'm surprised you picked up when you realized it was me," Prior said.

"If I didn't, I'm sure I would have a visit by a squad of your Guardians five minutes from now," Sebastian said. "Or worse, a couple of your Boroni leg breakers."

Prior smiled. Sebastian knew her all too well. "I need your help," Prior said.

"What is it now?" he asked.

"Venture is dead. He, Marco and Vitana were killed in a hand-to-hand battle in Capitol City about twenty minutes ago. I want to know who has the capability to pull something like that off," Prior said.

"You mean besides you?" Sebastian said.

"Yes," Prior said ignoring his quip.

"You're not going to like my answer," he said. "It was The Argent. Probably acting under orders from Cardinal Gregor."

"Why do you and Venture have this fixation with Gregor? He is only one of many involved in this mess, Sebastian," Prior said.

"Our interest in him stems from the fact he was once the Archbishop of the Southern Province," Sebastian said.

"So? There are many who have held that title," Prior countered.

"That region is the home of The Argent. He attained his position and power base through their influence and support, and he's still in league with them now. It's their dominance and ideology that's at the root of the madness engulfing the planet," Sebastian said.

"I thought The Argent were from the Middle Provinces?" Prior asked confused by his explanation.

"That's what they want everyone to believe. It's part of the overall deception they've practiced for centuries," Sebastian said.

"There's got to more to it than that, Sebastian," Prior said. "It'll take more than a bunch of zealots to overcome rational people."

"There is more, Prior. Much more," Sebastian said. "You're aware of the many skills that priests can achieve, skills that have been mostly lost due to the passage of time."

"You're referring to things like exorcism, right?" Prior asked.

"Yes. There are others as well. Gregor has expertise in these arcane skills and his abilities have reached the master level. No other priest is even close to him in that regard," Sebastian said. "None except Archbishop Cornelia maybe. And unfortunately, she's dead."

"What skills does Gregor possess? Is his power as an exorcist the reason Venture began his campaign against him?" Prior asked.

"He is an exorcist but that is not the reason he's so dangerous," Sebastian said. "Gregor is, among other things, a Summoner."

Prior was silent for a moment. She was well aware of the occult-like aspects of the Clerics. Many still believed the numerous superstitions surrounding the Church and feared the power some of the religious leaders were said to possess. Prior had never believed in that portion of their religion but the fact Sebastian did troubled her.

"You mean to tell me that Gregor can resurrect spirits and dead people? C'mon, Sebastian, how can you expect me to believe that?" Prior said. "You're claiming that Gregor is a warlock bringing demons from the Netherworld to plague Kerguelen. You've got to give me something better than that."

"I'm sorry, Prior, that's all I've got right now," Sebastian said.

"So where does that leave me?" Prior asked.

"The late but unlamented Archbishop Cornelia was not killed by Venture. He needed her help and I believe she was about to embark on her own mission against Gregor before her light was extinguished. Her powers in the arts were formidable and she may have had a plan to counter Gregor's activities," Sebastian said. "But since she's dead now, we'll never know, will we?"

"Are you telling me Gregor had Cornelia assassinated?" Prior asked.

"Yes," Sebastian said. "Who else has the ability and resources to pull off such a coup?"

"A Guardian Corps regimental commander," Prior answered.

Sebastian sighed. "I guess we're done here. Good luck, Prior. When you're ready to listen with an open mind, give me a call."

"You mean I can call you again if I have more questions?" Prior asked surprised by his willingness to help her.

"Of course," Sebastian said. "I have been instructed to help you any way I can."

"Who instructed you?" Prior asked.

"I'm afraid I can't tell you that. Just know that you have important friends in very high places," Sebastian said.

He broke transmission and Prior took the TELCOM out of her ear and put her TACCOM in its place. She called for her air ship to pick her up and waited for her team to arrive.

On the perimeter of the mansion's property, a dark and large figure watched Prior from the shadows as she waited for her ship with great interest. The woman in the courtyard intrigued him. She was someone he had to find out more about. Somehow she had felt his presence and no mortal had ever been able to do that. The huge man deftly slipped away into the night as a flight of two air ships descended into the courtyard and landed. His red eyes glowed like coal embers and he was delighted that he may finally have found a warrior that was worth his time to fight.

10
Interstellar space, less than three light years from the Kerguelen Star System

With short-range Faster-Than-Light communications established, Omega and Dela went to work on the main electrical and artificial gravity systems. They worked diligently in the Propulsion Module and the hum of the Trans-Light Continuum engine filled the compartment and drowned the silence between them. Though the components and systems of *San Mariner* were designed by the most brilliant and creative minds of Kerguelen, their construction was quite simplistic, and their theory of operation was well within the comprehension level of the star sailors who operated the equipment. Basic pre-deployment training included systems integration and component level repair of all types. A competent crew could manage to repair or modify any system on the ship in an emergency.

The Propulsion Module was a cramped space and not designed to accommodate a repair crew while underway. Luckily for Omega and Dela, zero gravity made it easy for them to maneuver around the numerous components in the module and created idyllic conditions for repair work. What made their jobs even easier was the use of non-torque tools. Normally reserved for EVA duty, in a weightless environment, they were perfect for their current situation.

Dela restored lighting to normal levels, and brought the main electrical system back online within the first few hours of their work. They then dug into the artificial gravity system. The system proved not as easy to tame and Omega hovered in front of the gravity control console cursing inaudibly as the unit failed to respond to his inputs. Dela seemed to be in her element and appeared in no hurry to have gravity restored. She was like a child playing a game as she floated inverted next to the TLC machinery tinkering with another portion of the artificial gravity system. She was replacing logic components in an attempt to coax it back into operation. As she worked, Dela could not help but worry about the ship's overall situation.

Though electrical power had been restored, it was still a major concern. Aside from water and oxygen, electrical power was the most crucial element to ensure the safe return of the ship. Two high capacity hydrogen fuel cells provided main power under normal conditions and were intended to last the duration of the mission. They needed to maintain ship's power without assistance until the ship returned to their solar system. Once there and on final transit to Kerguelen, the electrical load would shift to the batteries. Photovoltaic cells on the hull of the ship converted the powerful rays of the Kerguelen sun into direct current electricity and recharged the batteries until the ship docked with Space Station *Condor*, located 530 miles above Kerguelen in mid-atmospheric orbit.

But due to their emergency, they had to use the batteries early and without a source of solar regeneration, the batteries had been drained to catastrophic levels. Every minute they had been in use put the crew in greater danger. If they had been drained too far, the chance of them being too weak to support the ship when needed was a distinct possibility.

Omega glanced in Dela's direction and stopped his work for a moment. They had not spoken about her revelation that she was a Guardian since they had begun their repair work. In fact, they had said very little to each other. He needed to know more about her mission and tapped her inverted leg.

"So, Dela, who sent you here?" he asked. He paused and added, "Can I call you Dela or would you prefer Arcuri... or colonel?"

"Dela is fine," she said still busy at work. "It was my great-grandmother's name. And to answer your question, I was assigned to my mission by Commander Prior."

"You're a combat engineer... a Surveyor?"

"Yes, I'm the Master Builder," she said. "Consider me a... special operative."

Omega knew that the Master Builder was second-in-command of the combat engineers and that obviously Dela was a proficient Guardian and expert technician. The fact that Prior had tasked her executive officer to this mission meant the Guardians felt it was of vital importance.

"But as a senior Guardian, why doesn't Camden know you?" he asked.

"My own mother wouldn't recognize me," Dela said. "I've undergone eight cosmetic procedures that have completely altered my facial and physical features. My skin tone is even different."

"That must have been painful," Omega said wincing at the thought of the surgeries.

"It was," Dela said. "But I like the work they did on my breasts."

Omega ignored her joke. "But why should you go to all that trouble? And why would Prior get involved? We haven't spoken in years. And when did Prior become interested in space? When did Guardian Central Command for that matter?" Omega asked not really believing her.

"Neither Central Command nor Commander Prior is interested in space… outside of its applications for our needs. I'm here for another reason," Dela said still not looking at him.

What Dela said was true. Guardians had never deeply concerned themselves with space. Their sole interest in it was how it could aid in their operations. The use of satellites for communications, surveillance and weather conditions were paramount in achieving success in missions. Though Prior did have a team in orbit onboard the space station, their job was primarily monitoring systems. Beyond that, the Guardians couldn't care less.

"What's the reason you're here?" Omega asked.

"Through the work of other counter-intelligence operatives, Commander Prior discovered that someone… possibly multiple persons or organizations… was planted in this crew to ensure that the mission would not succeed," Dela said. She paused for a moment and released one of her tools. She exchanged it for another that hovered next to the panel she was working in. The discarded tool floated harmlessly beside her as she continued her explanation and work. "We also know that a similar operation was carried out on *Seventh Sojourn* which led to its demise."

"Why would someone want to see this or any mission fail?" Omega asked.

"I don't know," Dela said as she stopped tinkering. She pushed herself back from the panel and spun around to look at Omega. She was still in an inverted hover as she continued. "There are many reasons, I suppose. I do know that Commander Prior discovered the plan for *Seventh Sojourn* too late to act. Whoever was responsible for the operations discovered the commander's... interest in the missions and she had to cease her external inquiries. But she had learned about the danger to this mission and needed a way to keep tabs on you and the crew. She needed someone on the inside and I was that someone. I was already in Space Command under an assumed name for another assignment. All I needed to do was get assigned to this mission."

"And you did," Omega said.

Omega thought for a moment and quickly realized what had happened. Dela was not an original member of the prime or back-up crew. She was selected as the prime crew flight engineer *after* the rest of the crew selections had been made. In the early training phases of the mission, the prime and back-up flight engineers had been injured and scratched from the rotation. Dela had been recognized as a talented engineer and skilled pilot and impressed the Space Command mission managers and was selected as the replacement. It was all clear to Omega what had happened, and he didn't like his speculation.

"You arranged for Crawford and Hagan to have accidents, didn't you?" he asked.

"A necessary adjustment," she answered.

Omega scoffed. "Some adjustment," he said looking at her intensely. "Guardian counter-intelligence and special operatives, eh? Well, the Corps has certainly changed since I was an officer."

"There has always been an unconventional element in the Corps," Dela said.

"But not on the scale you're suggesting. That type of work is illegal," he said.

"Call it evolution... a necessary adjustment to the norm in order to ensure the survival of the species. We had to evolve or die. Many combat engineers are cross-trained in some type of specialty. We are divided into small covert cells designed to handle... unique situations around the planet. We even have done some work on the moon and on the space stations around the solar system. My mission is one of many clandestine activities being conducted. Combined with the support we give the four battalions, the combat engineering force is very busy," Dela said.

"But why go to such lengths?" Omega asked.

"The Corps is the only thing that stands between a free society and totalitarianism. Several people in power would not shed a tear if we no longer existed. Several Guardians in key leadership positions, Commander Prior and Commander Jordan specifically, have begun to seriously question the motives and intent of the planetary government… and other Guardian senior officers. There are Guardians within our ranks that tamper with and undermine missions. They believe that what they do is unknown, but we know who many of them are and what they're up to. They are not as clever as they think," Dela replied.

"And they don't know about you or the other operatives?"

"Naturally, Commander Prior's special units were furtively created and don't exist officially. Very few know about the units and fewer still know the extent of our activities. Central Command isn't even aware of my mission on *San Mariner*," Dela explained. She pulled herself closer to the panel to continue her work and added, "I'm afraid that's all I can say about the subject."

"Well, that explains a lot, Dela. Maybe you shouldn't have told me anything. I could be one of the bad guys," Omega said.

"I doubt that, sir. I've been observing you very closely for a long time, even before I began training with you," Dela said busy at work again. "If I had any doubts about your sincerity or commitment to the success of the mission, I would have killed you by now."

"You would have killed me?" Omega said in shock. The thought of it made him cold. "Another necessary adjustment?"

"Yes. I would have asked for a kill request if time permitted. If not, I would have acted on my own initiative based on what I had learned. Commander Prior gives me quite a lot of latitude in the prosecution of my duties. It's another of the… new things we do," Dela said.

"What is? Murder?" he asked.

"It's called a sanction," Dela corrected.

"You're an assassin," accused Omega.

"I'm a troubleshooter," she replied.

"Really? Is that what you call it? Well how many troubles have you shot?" Omega quipped.

"That's not your concern, Commander. Just know you wouldn't have been my first," Dela said.

"I'd like to hear more about that."

"I don't think you really would, besides, Commander Prior has instructions forbidding operatives from speaking about past missions. She could have me sanctioned just for talking to you about my assignment," Dela said.

"Regardless, I do have one more question for you, Dela," Omega said.

Dela pushed away again and looked at him. "Yes?" she asked.

"What is your mission exactly?"

Dela sighed. It made no difference now what she told Omega. Revealing a portion or all of her mission were equal violations of her orders.

"Very well, I'll tell you. My mission is as follows: First, to ensure that the mission of *San Mariner* has every opportunity to succeed by preventing sabotage or other subversive activity; second, to identify any operative and/or operatives assigned to the crew of *San Mariner* and third, terminate the activities of said subversives," Dela said obviously verbatim from her orders. "According to my investigations, Centurion Camden is that operative and therefore, my objective."

"I still find it hard to swallow that Camden is guilty," Omega said refuting her statement. "What solid proof do you have?"

"You have the entire ship's database accessible to you there. Look at the systems and ship readouts before and after the Habitat Module accident. You will find no reasonable explanation as to why it occurred. Camden created it and used the accident as a swift and efficient means to get rid of the rest of the crew. If he didn't need me alive for reacquisition and docking, Camden would have waited until we were all in there. Why are you still alive? It was a stroke of luck that you decided to sleep in your In-Flight cabin and told me not to tell Camden where you were. Once our usefulness is outlived, he'll find a convenient way to dispose of us both. Read the data, sir," Dela said imploring Omega to read the information.

Omega studied her for a moment and then turned to the console next to him. He accessed the main database of which she spoke and after a few minutes realized that everything Dela had stated was true.

The emergency egress hatch was programmed to open by an artificial external input from the flight deck. A command level protocol was required for that, and only he and Camden had those protocols. A secondary explosion was picked up on external and internal sensors. It would give the crew the indication that there had been some type of explosion or collision. Omega also saw that the electrical sensors had recorded a large surge sent into the communications and navigational systems. All indications pointed at Camden. But why kill the crew? Was the discovery of life beyond Kerguelen reason enough to kill? Was it that blasphemous? Considering the condition of his ship and the loss of *Seventh Sojourn*, it obviously was. Omega began to see that there would be more deaths attributed to the alien spacecraft. What was happening out here was only the beginning and he wondered what was happening on Kerguelen. They needed to get back in one piece and with the spacecraft intact. He owed that much to Delle, Tallen, Jalen and Powell. They couldn't die in vain. He shut down the terminal and went into deep thought. His heart was heavy. His dream had caused the deaths of his crew and countless others. It was almost unbearable.

"It seems that you were correct, Dela," he said. "But all this seems incredible. A Guardian turning to murder is unthinkable."

"Trans light speed was unthinkable a decade ago," Dela countered. "The unthinkable is just that, something that we haven't or don't want to think about. My branch deals with the unthinkable and exists to provide contingencies against the unthinkable. Camden's information is almost as good as mine. He damaged the navigational computer knowing that I could re-write the program."

"You could have fixed the program?"

"In time, yes. He knows my technical ability, that's why he was so frantic when I said I couldn't fix it. He panicked because he had no contingency for that," she said.

"But you had a contingency for his plan," Omega said.

"Yes, and I have prepared for his other moves," she said.

"What other moves?"

"Camden will try to kill us soon," she said matter-of-factly.

"Are you sure? He still needs us, doesn't he?"

"No, not now. We're too close to Kerguelen now. Our death is his next logical move, and he has to do it before we enter our star system.

He will come up with a plausible excuse for our deaths after he throws us out of an airlock. The wrecked FTL unit is perfect for his plans. It would be a believable and viable excuse that we died trying to fix it during an EVA that went bad. Our histories as risk takers and the bad luck of *San Mariner* in general would make it believable. Camden will destroy all evidence that the probe existed and return home to a hero's welcome on Kerguelen, the sole survivor of the doomed *San Mariner* expedition," Dela said.

There was no doubt in her mind that Camden would do the things she envisioned and events would unfold as predicted. Omega was now also convinced.

"When will he make his move?" Omega asked.

"Soon. Shortly after we finish the last light-speed jump."

"Are you sure he has to kill us?" Omega asked hoping for an answer he knew wouldn't come.

"In order for the Congress of Cardinals or whoever is sponsoring him to refute the discovery, the alien probe must be destroyed… along with any witnesses. And that's us," she said.

"He's an agent of the Cardinals?" Omega asked.

"Possibly, but there are a lot of other players in the game. They're the biggest fish though and they do have a wide spectrum of influence," Dela said. "Who he works for matters little."

"Why is that?"

"I'm only concerned about bringing the space probe to Kerguelen and killing him."

"I'm not sure I can swallow all of this. Secret operatives in the most highly trained paramilitary force ever known are turning to murder," Omega said shaking his head. "What could possibly stop them from succeeding?"

"Secret operatives in the most highly trained paramilitary force ever known determined to stop them," Dela said putting the finishing touches on her work and closing the panel.

She flipped to an upright position and tapped on the electrical control console and the indicators for the gravity system switched from red to green. She briefly allowed herself an uncharacteristic smile and brought a portion of the system online.

Slowly, gravity was restored to the Propulsion Module and various items around the compartment fell gently to the deck plating. Dela glanced at the battery gauge and frowned when she read the percentage of power that remained in them. She would need to do some more creative power management on their final run to Kerguelen orbit to make them last.

"Good work, Dela," Omega smiled. "All that's left is this last section and gravity will be fully restored."

"How's it going back there?" Camden said over the ship's intercom. "When are you two coming back up?"

"We still have some work to do on the gravity system," Omega replied as he clicked on the squawk box. "It's only partially restored."

"Don't take too long. We're just about ready to come out of light speed and take our bearings," Camden warned. "And I'll need to get with Dela to make sure everything is buttoned up in the Cargo Module and finish the checklist for entry into our star system."

"We won't be long," Omega said clicking off the intercom.

"That's when he'll make his move," Dela said calmly as she worked on the artificial gravity unit.

"I'm glad you can read his every move," Omega said with a smile. "It's a good feeling knowing that you're here to keep me alive."

"I was instructed to ensure the mission succeeds and those assigned to its failure are exposed and stopped, that's all," Dela said as she stood next to him. She faced him and with emotionless eyes stared at him adding, "Keeping you alive is not one of my mission parameters."

PART FOUR

1
Trans-Kerguelen Investments Building, Capitol City, Central Province, Planet Kerguelen

Gallegos breathed a huge but silent sigh of relief when his air ship landed at the building that housed his company's offices. His security detail ensured the area was secure and led him inside and into the elevator leading to his private offices. There was word on the street that a representative from the Western Province Grange was looking for him and wanted to speak with him immediately. He knew that could only mean one person… Quinn. Gallegos knew what she wanted and had no desire to talk to her. As the elevator rushed upwards, he repeated his instructions to his head of security.

"Make sure you keep that woman away from me," Gallegos said. "I don't care what you have to do."

The security chief nodded and understood what he needed to do. He was one of the best corporate security specialists on the planet and his men had conducted many other types of similar jobs. He was aware of the financier's uneasiness but was certain Gallegos would be safe. His people had the entire building locked down and no one would get inside that didn't belong. As the doors to the elevator opened, the security chief stepped out and turned to Gallegos. He was about to speak when he was grabbed from behind and snatched into the air and thrown against a wall by a pair of powerful hands. Before Gallegos could speak or react, a long knife entered the chest of each of the two security men still inside of the elevator. As their lifeless bodies slumped to the floor, a woman stepped into the opening. It was Quinn and she smiled at Gallegos and took him by the hand leading him out of the elevator.

She spoke to two huge darkly clad men accompanying her in a language Gallegos had never heard before. Obviously the men were Boroni, but they were the largest he had ever seen and they dragged the dead security guards out of the elevator. They removed the knives from the bodies by the intricately carved handles as Gallegos looked at Quinn and then to his security chief still lying on the floor. He was barely conscious and unable to help his employer. Gallegos could only imagine what had happened to the other men employed to ensure his safety located throughout the building.

"Gallegos, I thought you were a good businessman," said Quinn. "But you don't return any calls."

"I-I've been busy, Quinn," he stammered. "Believe me, I've been wanting to get back to you."

"Then it's a good thing I stopped by and saved you the trouble," she replied. "But why is it so hard to get into this building? I had to argue with about thirty members of your security staff before they agreed to let us in… reluctantly I might add."

"It's all of the unrest in the streets, Quinn," Gallegos said as two drops of sweat ran down his from his forehead. "You know how it is out there."

"Yes, I do," Quinn nodded. "But I didn't come here to discuss the social activities of the people, I came here on business. Grange business."

"Of course," Gallegos said. "How can I help you?"

"Your attempts to weaken the Grange have failed and I'm here to close out the account. Since I've always admired your skill in the financial world, I'm going to allow you to live. But the operations of your dummy corporation Oxford Mutual are over. You will dissolve it tomorrow morning and liquidate its holdings, transferring them to the Federal Reserve Authority. If you don't, I'll have to come back and you'll face the same fate your confederates in the deal suffered," Quinn said.

"You mean…"

"I mean they are all dead," Quinn said. "Don't disappoint me, like they did, Gallegos, my admiration for you only goes so far."

Gallegos nodded and Quinn and the male Boroni with her stepped toward the elevator. As she moved past him, the security chief stirred and sprang to his feet. He moved toward Quinn and she spun and swung her forearm into his chest. He flew into the wall behind him and lie stunned gasping for air on his hands and knees.

Quinn awed Gallegos with her speed and reflexes and strength. Her actions seemed effortless though obviously very powerful. One of the male Boroni spoke to Quinn in the same strange language she had used before and Quinn replied to him in the standard Kerguelen language so Gallegos would understand.

"Kill him," she said.

The Boroni male brought the security chief to his feet and effortlessly broke his neck. He let the man fall to the floor and joined Quinn and the other male in the elevator. Quinn pressed a button and smiled at Gallegos.

"Don't fail me, Gallegos," she said as the doors to the elevator shut.

2

The Situation Room, Chief Executive's Mansion, Capitol City, Central Province, Planet Kerguelen

"In conclusion, by the time I arrived on scene, all of the persons involved were dead and no signs of the antagonists was seen. I called Marshal Garath and he dispatched Cdr. Ceca to take charge. Cdr. Ceca and units of the First Battalion took over the site when they arrived and my units departed after I conferred with her," Prior said as she stood before President Ward and a hastily gathered advisory panel. She was physically present but mentally absent from the proceedings. She should have been elsewhere and felt that talking to President Ward was a waste of time.

"And you have no idea who killed Cdr. Venture and the others?" Ward asked.

Prior shook her head. "I'm afraid not, Mr. President," she said. "There are no traces of who is responsible. A thorough investigation was conducted."

Ward nodded and looked to the other members of the panel. The advisory panel consisted of Grand Senator Bacor, Chief Justice Thom, Chief Technologist Mackenzie, and Cardinal Gregor. The cardinal appeared to have fully recovered from his injuries and seemed energetic thanks to the attentions of the Surgeon General. Mackenzie had ordered the planet's chief physician to see to the needs of the cardinal and ensure that he was returned to perfect health as soon as practicable, despite her personal feelings towards the clergyman. Along with the medicine, the death of Venture undoubtedly aided in Gregor's renewed vigor. Marshal Garath, Commander Ceca and Commander Mohab were also present to provide Ward with the Guardian perspective on recent events.

Prior stood silently in front of the panel clad in her ceremonial dress gray uniform. The gray waistcoat and seamless gray fitted pants were accessorized with a pair of black patent leather corsair boots. A crimson sash draped across her body from her right shoulder to her left hip and wrapped around her waist twice before being pinned into place with a small gold brooch resembling a griffin. The sash was covered with icons of military heroics and humanitarian deeds received during her fifteen years of service. A leather scabbard containing a xiphos was attached to a black leather belt and hung from her right hip. Though not required, the xiphos gave the uniform a traditional look. As she stood waiting for a response, Prior shrugged her shoulders slightly to move the black aiguillette on her left shoulder to a more comfortable position.

The other Guardians present also wore their dress uniforms. Their medals were numerous but the citations on their sashes paled in comparison to Prior's regalia. Prior's sash was wider than normal to accommodate the multitude of awards she had. The Presidential Silver Cross of Freedom occupied the majority of the sash near her right shoulder, but what was most prominent was the highest honor the planet could bestow upon an individual. Around her neck was The Star of Kerguelen.

The platinum eight-pointed star edged in 24-karat gold, had a huge sapphire surrounded by diamonds in the center and hung around her neck attached to a light blue ribbon. The Star's jewels glistened in the light, causing the members of the panel to unconsciously glance at it, distracted by its brilliance. It was not only a tremendous honor for Prior to wear it, but a singular distinction. She was the latest recipient and the only living person holding the award.

After the panel had heard Prior's report and Ceca's addendum, Bacor cleared his throat and addressed the panel.

"We must continue with our current plans," he said as the panel pondered what to do next. He seemed confident that the policies in effect were the best for the people.

"But with Venture eliminated, surely the major threat to planetary stability is gone," Ward said. Though he had signed off on the new policies, he had not been entirely for them but conceded to the wishes of Gregor and Bacor.

"Forgive me, President Ward, but I disagree," Ceca said. "We have no reason to assume that the individuals or groups that assisted Venture won't continue. We must continue to apply our own pressure on them until they are completely destroyed. And I believe the Guardians should assist in that cause."

Prior looked at Ceca in disbelief. Her comments were not characteristic of a Guardian. A Guardian never contemplated aggression against those voicing opposition to the government. The right to protest was something they protected, and there was no solid proof of a planetary conspiracy. Prior looked suspiciously at the panel and felt that there was something terribly amiss.

"The people have lost their faith and are turning their backs on the Church," Gregor said. "Anti-Church activists have sprung up all over the planet and have begun to take advantage of the confusion and despair to undermine the Papal seat. Government's law enforcement needs to be augmented and given the funds to combat this heresy and terrorism wherever it may be and stomp it out. The Guardians should be integrated with the federal police to give them added striking power."

"I believe that His Eminence has voiced what *all* of us think," Bacor said. "Federal law enforcement needs help in the Middle Provinces. And that's where the chief culprits of the dissent reside. An expedition should be immediately dispatched to that province."

Commander Mohab was known to be a thoughtful and subdued individual. But when he heard Bacor's statements, he lost his composure and it was all he could do to prevent a mad outburst. Mohab stared angrily at Bacor and the look evinced pure hatred. As a native of the Middle Provinces, he had endured complaints about his fellow Middies his entire life. There had always been a level of distrust concerning them, but he had never before heard blatant statements threatening the welfare of his people.

"I agree," Ceca said. "The lack of faith is distressing as well as the troubling attendance figures of the cathedrals and temples."

"That can be directly attributed to the Middle Provinces," Bacor said. "I have tabled a resolution for sanctions against the people and corporations of the region with the Senate."

As Prior listened to the committee, she wondered if the whole planetary leadership had gone insane. Only Justice Thom and Chief Technologist Mackenzie seemed unaffected by the fervor to escalate the use of force around the globe. Thom had retained his sedate demeanor throughout the proceedings, hoping perhaps common sense would prevail in the end. Mackenzie was chomping at the bit, ready to pounce on the panel when she got the chance, but Mohab beat her to the punch.

"I have listened patiently and intently to all of your statements and I can't believe what I've heard," Mohab said standing up. "What you intend will lead to destruction. Old provincial prejudices that were buried and forgotten will resurface creating new disputes. It is already happening in many regions and if we don't take measures to ease tempers, war will commence. If war comes, federal law enforcement will have to intervene, and I tell you this: I will not commit Guardians under my command to work with federal officers in such operations."

"You don't have to, Cdr. Mohab," Ceca said. "Col. Thyssen has already volunteered the Second Battalion and I am mobilizing the First to support them."

"Col. Thyssen has volunteered the Second Battalion for this?" Prior asked.

"Yes," Ceca said smiling.

"And you approved such usage?" Prior said pointing at Garath.

"I have, but I have instructed Thyssen to not actively engage in any operations until Central Command authorizes it," Garath said.

"You can't do that," Prior said. "Using Guardians as law enforcement is illegal."

"What do you mean illegal, Commander?" Ward asked fearing the possibility of charges being levied against his administration.

"The Posse Comitatus Act precludes the use of Guardians as law enforcement agents," Prior explained.

"The legislature has temporarily suspended that law," Bacor said.

"How can you do that?" Mohab asked.

"Due to the severity of the situation, that law can no longer apply," Gregor answered.

"You can't just throw away laws when they become inconvenient," Prior protested.

"The Legislature, Chief Executive and the Congress of Cardinals disagrees with you, Commander," Bacor said.

"There's a basic unwritten law of jurisprudence," Mohab offered. "You can't employ a law or decree that goes against the will of the majority. For those who do, there's a name for them, they're called tyrants."

"Your stepping beyond your powers, Cdr. Mohab, and accusing three of the planetary leaders of being despots is bordering on treason and sedition," Gregor said. "Venture was victim of the same folly."

"And who are you going to get to kill Mohab?" Prior asked.

"Be careful, Commander," Garath said. "You're treading on thin ice. Even commanders are not above being reprimanded for insolence."

"Then charge me," Prior said pointing at Garath. "I'll take my chances in a court of law." She took a deep breath and calmed herself. "And this isn't about insolence. You know what they're proposing is illegal, Supreme Commander. Don't close your eyes to those facts just because their plan seems expedient."

"I'd like to know when you and Mohab earned law degrees?" Ceca said. "You seem to be preoccupied with legal interpretations instead of following orders. The decisions of this committee are unquestionable. Your job is to follow whatever orders you're given, nothing more."

"You don't give me orders, Cdr. Ceca," Prior said. "My Guardians are *mine* to command. They do what *I* determine is necessary."

"Are you saying that you have no superiors?" Gregor asked.

"Not at all, but an officer has the right… and the obligation to interpret orders received and determine whether they are in the best interest of the people," Prior said. "If they are not, it's an officer's duty to bring such concerns to the attention of their superiors."

"More legal chatter," Ceca said.

"It's ethics, Commander," Mohab said to Ceca. "A perceived lack of faith in the people by the Church is no reason to commence an armed campaign. Tell me a time when a lack of faith was never a concern for the Church."

"You know," Prior began as she canvassed the panel with her eyes, "I have listened to and heard your fears and concerns of a lack of faith in the populace, and don't understand it. In my experience, I have found that everyone and everything loses faith at one point or another. I have lost faith before in battle and believed that the Almighty had abandoned me, and there were times when I believed the Almighty was right beside me. A lack of faith is a natural condition we all experience. Anyone who claims differently is a liar."

"What makes you believe that, Commander?" Gregor asked.

"The Church is not the beginning or end of Divinity, and a temple is merely a place for us to gather together," Prior answered. "We all worship and believe in our own way. A building is not necessary for worship to take place or belief to exist."

"Are you saying that the temples and cathedrals should be closed?" Gregor asked.

"No, but if there were no churches, would we still believe in the Almighty? Would we still have religion? Those are the questions you must ask yourself," Prior said. "Because you don't attend a service, does that mean you're impious or a non-believer? I think not. Temples and churches were abolished under Koenig's rule for almost half a century, and the people still believed. And that faith was the reason he was ultimately defeated."

Gregor was visibly angry by Prior's statements and let her know how upset he was. "Cdr. Prior, I can't believe I'm hearing such unpatriotic and impious rhetoric... especially from someone like you. A great warrior; a community leader; a learned and honored scholar... it's incredible. How can you say such things?"

"The Scriptures support my statements, Cardinal. *'The Almighty does not dwell in a temple made with hands'*," she said moving closer to the panel. "And as far as patriotism goes, it's hard to quantify. Patriots are often pushed into a corner and have to decide what is more important: The erasure of the enemy or the health of the people of the state. As war increases, dissent becomes impossible and the views of the status quo become the driving force. And the maintenance of the status quo soon becomes the only thing of value.

"The weakest in society suffer and become victims in times of terror, war and military adventurism. And though the status quo may accomplish great things, the fact remains that in the end, all that the status quo does favors the strong and the rich. Women, children and those unable to protect their rights are crushed. And that is the sad part. Conflicts cost us dearly. The government loses its status amongst the people and tremendous amounts of money and irreplaceable resources are poured in to sustain wars. Citizens lose lives and most importantly, the danger that the conflict was supposed to destroy is not necessarily impacted.

"Legitimacy is in question here. You can only distract the people for so long and you can't destroy the individual mindset of the people no matter how many you kill or imprison. Violence only begets violence. A few months ago, we were one people, a planetary community nearly one billion strong. Now you seek to isolate and divide the people. You meet disagreement with force of arms instead of with dialog. That's no way to govern or live. I resist that way of life… and I will fight it with all that I have."

When she finished, she received an approving nod from Mackenzie and Thom slapped his hand on the table in front of him. Bacor was not pleased but didn't show his displeasure openly. Ward looked as though he was in deep thought and Gregor still fumed. But it seemed the proposal to use Guardians as police had lost its steam. Protection against tyranny was the reason the Guardians had been created and part of the reason Prior had become one.

"I see your father's gift for oratory extends to you as well as your brother, Cdr. Prior," Bacor said. "However, I have to agree with the Cardinal, your attitude is not acceptable."

"I will not support the use of Guardians against civilians, Grand Senator. Marshal Garath and the others know it's wrong and contrary to our code," Prior said. She turned to the Guardians on the panel and continued. "And I will attack any Guardians attempting to assault civilians, and will continue to do so… until the last banner is retired."

The Guardians knew she meant every word she said and the thought of it should have caused fear in all of them. If Guardians fought each other the result would not be pleasant, especially a fight involving ones led by Prior. As much as each believed in their own battle prowess, they knew they didn't possess the generalship of Prior nor her élan and ability to inspire. She would fight to the death… hers and that of the others, and in combat against her, the outcome would be simple: They would lose.

A dispute between Guardians only happened once. Eight hundred years ago, two units engaged each other over a trivial misunderstanding and the result was three months of hard fighting and thousands of casualties. After a ceasefire was established, each Guardian unit was given its own area of responsibility and ever since, no Guardians had ever attacked another. But if Ceca and Thyssen decided to pursue their course of action, history would repeat itself.

"Is trying to do good wrong?" Ceca asked.

"In an ancient philosopher's third essay he said, *"We can contend with the evil that men do in the name of evil, but Heaven protect us from what they do in the name of good."* What you decide here today, you'll have to live with for the rest of your lives," Prior said.

"We only want to re-unify the planet. We just want to take care of everybody. What could be wrong with unity?" Bacor asked.

"Calling for unity is a lie, Grand Senator. The person who calls for it is fine with unity as long as everyone is unified under the rules and ideals they want," Prior said. "And taking care of everyone's needs requires a huge government, and a government big enough to take care of all the needs of its entire people is powerful enough to take away their God given rights."

"I'm glad your father is not here to witness your disdain for good order and discipline, Commander," Bacor said.

"I'm a Guardian officer, Grand Senator, a commander. Good order and discipline are my life," Prior said. "My father's views are buried with him, taken away by an assassin's bullet. But he was a centrist and believed in minimal government intervention in people's lives."

"There are many things we can do, Commander, what we propose is just one of many cures for what ails the planet," President Ward said.

"Of that I'm sure," Prior nodded. "I'm sure you have developed many cures, but I learned a very important lesson in politics from my father in that respect."

"And what was that, Commander?" Ward asked.

"He said political problems are like a child's ailment," Prior said. "If there are many cures for it, you can be sure none of them work."

3

Kerguelen Deep Space Survey Ship *San Mariner*, Just beyond the Kerguelen Star System

"You didn't really think you could take me, did you, Dela?" Camden said breathing heavily through his nostrils. His right eye twitched uncontrollably from the repeated blows it had received.

"The thought did cross my mind," Dela replied with a snort. She was also breathing heavily, gulping air through her mouth. And each lungful of air was excruciatingly painful.

Shortly after Omega and Dela had repaired the artificial gravity system, *San Mariner* dropped from hyper-light to space normal speed in order to take position fixes for entry into the Kerguelen star system. With the telemetry signal reacquired, they could now proceed at a faster rate. Though they still had to make jumps instead of a straight transit, their operation was much smoother and safer.

The second jump they made brought them in close proximity to their home star system and spirits were high as they prepped for the final jump that would bring them to the edge of the system. As Omega began plotting, Camden slipped away to assist Dela in prepping the Cargo Module for entry into the system. As Dela was busy stowing loose equipment, Camden put his plan into action.

His scheme was simple. He had hoped to catch Dela off guard and quickly kill her and then eliminate Omega. He would then place them in EVA suits and release them into space. After they were gone, Camden would destroy the alien spacecraft and return home.

Camden's attack on Dela was to be quick and painless... well, relatively painless. His feelings toward Dela had grown from a slight dislike to downright hatred over the past months. Her annoying exactness and always having the right answer to a problem before anyone else had irked him. Normally, he would have felt bad about killing an innocent, as he had with the other crewmembers, but her mere existence had made him look forward to her death. She would not have an answer to the swiftness in which he planned to kill her.

But to his surprise, she seemed ready for him and the fight that ensued was heavily contested. Early on during the pitched struggle, Camden realized quickly that Dela was not merely a competent flight engineer but was also a proficient hand-to-hand combatant... and a Guardian. Her style of fighting was unmistakable and the two warriors inflicted devastating blows upon one another. And even though Dela was more skillful and scored more hits, in the end it was Camden's superior body mass and heavy, bone crushing body shots that allowed him to come out on top.

Omega had realized something was going on when neither Camden nor Dela responded to his calls over the ship's intercom. He left the flight deck to investigate and found that he had been locked out of the Cargo Module. Camden had input some security code into the door control panel and Omega was unable to override it. In time he could eventually break the code, but the fight would be well over by then.

Omega furiously tapped on the door control icons over and over again but it was useless. Omega could only watch helplessly as Dela and Camden fought. He opened the intercom so he could hear the sounds of the fight as he observed the action. For a while it appeared as though Dela might be victorious, but the tides quickly turned against her, and now it was all but over.

"Camden, open this door!" Omega screamed as he pounded a fist in futility on the Cargo Module's access hatch.

Camden looked over his shoulder at Omega and grinned with delight. Dela was finished and Omega would be next. The ex-Guardian would be easy prey and Cardinal Gregor would reward Camden handsomely for his deeds. He hovered over Dela's kneeling body, as the alien spacecraft loomed in the background, securely strapped down in the containment area. He stepped around her and reached for the side of the containment area with his hand and winced in agony. The ring finger and pinky of his right hand were twisted, bent and on fire from pain. Dela had broken them early on in the fight and he could no longer flex them. Dela noticed his discomfort and it pleased her.

"It hurts, doesn't it?" she quipped as she rose to her feet and painfully raised her arms in defiance of his seeming victory.

Her mouth and left side of her face were swollen, so much so she could no longer open her left eye. She believed the bones around her eye were broken as well, but the pain was miniscule compared to the agony her ribs were causing her.

"How are the ribs?" Camden asked.

"Just peachy," Dela said as blood followed the words from her mouth. Her breathing was labored and she prayed she didn't have a punctured lung due to broken ribs. If she did and it was her third lung that was damaged, she was finished.

All air-breathing creatures on Kerguelen evolved with a secondary filtration organ in their respiratory systems. Because of the planet's heavy gravity, many of the heavier gaseous elements remained in the Kerguelen atmosphere instead of escaping into space. The Kerguelens had developed a third lung to filter and process them out. Without that adaptation, air-breathing creatures could not have developed or existed on the planet.

If her third lung were damaged, Dela would not have major problems until the ship neared Kerguelen… if she were still alive, that is. While in mission mode, the ship's atmosphere was a mixture of oxygen and nitrogen, free of the deadly pollutants that fouled their home world's biosphere. But when the ship was in its return mode, the flight computer program instructed the life support system to revert to Kerguelen-normal environment, and the air would take on the planet's atmospheric conditions to make crew transition to Kerguelen easier. If her third lung were non-functional, Dela would feel the effects immediately. Her heart would not be able to pump the heavy gas laden blood of her circulatory system and in minutes, her heart would fail and she would go into cardiac arrest and die. Third lung damage was evident by the color of the blood. If it had a greenish tint that meant the third lung was not functioning. As she wiped her mouth, Dela saw a trace of green and at that moment wished she were Boroni. They were bio-engineered with four lungs and could survive if only two were functional. She wiped the smear of blood on her flight suit and sneered. The sight of the blood pleased Camden. The internal injuries made her vulnerable and all he had to do was wait for the pain to overcome her. All Omega could do was wait for his turn with Camden. Dela, on the other hand, could not wait.

She moved away from Camden towards a console on the bulkhead of the module. When her legs failed and could no longer support her weight, she crawled like an insect to it, barely fighting through the pain. She pulled herself up and leaned against the console moving her gnarled fingers as nimbly as she could across the keypad.

Camden ignored her fumbling. She was already dead to him. He instead eyed his prize, the alien spacecraft. With Dela about to die and Omega soon to follow, he could destroy the craft and set everything right. The people of Kerguelen would no longer have their precious alien vessel and he could expose Omega as the fraud and heretic he was, dispelling any rumors or false hopes about life existing on other worlds. The speculation about the Almighty's "Other Flocks" as was stated in the much disputed and unsanctioned *"Lost Scripture"*, would be at an end. He had successfully carried out his mission, just as his counterpart had done onboard *Seventh Sojourn*. His attentions turned quickly back to Dela when he heard the klaxon of the ship's general alarm sound and saw the overheard warning lights in the Cargo Module illuminate.

The Cargo Module's main access hatch was beginning to open and that was impossible, so Camden thought. He had planned early on to kill Dela in the Cargo Module and re-programmed the system to prevent the hatch from opening until he activated it. Only his command authorization should have allowed the hatch to be opened. How could she have done it? Camden thought for a moment and then it came to him. With all the poking around she had done within the computers and subsystems, she might have come across what he had done. She could have re-programmed the systems to respond to her commands. But how could she have known about him? How could she have known this was going to be his endplay? Obviously Dela was a smart girl... a very smart girl. She was as clever as she was annoying. He had believed he had locked Omega out and isolated them, but what he had actually done was lock himself in with her. She knew he would come after her and if she could not defeat him one way...

"Dela!" Camden yelled as he heard the door interlocks release. "For the Almighty's sake, stop what you're doing!" He looked about the module, frantically searching for a way out of his impending doom.

"This *is* for the Almighty… and all of Her children. Your plans, no matter how dark, can never envelope the Light!" she said as a deformed smile took shape on her face.

"Dela! Don't do it!" Omega pleaded watching from outside.

Dela turned to Omega and winked at him with her good eye and then turned back to Camden. "May you find solace with The Second!" she said.

Dela hooked a strap that was secured to the bulkhead to her belt and then ran one hand across the keypad while the other grasped the console. The air in the module immediately was evacuated when the main hatch quickly slid open. Everything that was not tied down flew out of the hatch with a rush air. Camden began to slide across the module's deck and reached for the nearest thing to him, the door of the containment area, and screamed from the electrical shock he received when he touched it. As he convulsed, Camden's neck craned and he saw the power line Dela had ran to the door. She had rigged the containment area as well. She had made sure that it was not going to be easy to destroy the alien spacecraft. As the electrical pulse repelled him, he was slung out of the module and his screams were lost in the oblivion of interstellar space.

As Camden flew past her, Dela touched the keypad again and the hatch began to close. As the door shut, she tapped the keypad once more and an atmosphere started to reestablish in the module. She fell to her knees in pain and gasped for air. She was hyperventilating and the large expansions and contractions of her diaphragm were causing her overwhelming agony. She lifted her head and looked at an indicator on the console and tapped on the keypad again, barely able to complete her input before she slumped to the deck. The hatch denying Omega access to the module opened and he rushed in and raced to her.

He lifted her up and she collapsed in his arms. He unhooked the strap and gently placed her on her back. He looked her over and shook his head. It looked as though she would live, but Dela was in bad shape. He patted her hand and retrieved a medical kit from the bulkhead and removed a scanner from it. He passed it over her body from her head to her feet. It beeped when he passed her eyes. The device told Omega she had minimal damage to the eye socket. When he reached her chest it beeped again and he read the display. According to the scanner, Dela did not have a punctured lung but did have fractured ribs, a bruised kidney and liver damage. The damage to her kidney and liver was the cause of her greenish blood. He tapped the scanner and the display gave him treatment instructions. Omega noted them and continued his examination. As he ran the scanner over the rest of her body, he found that she had a few hyper-extended joints on her fingers and numerous bumps, bruises and lacerations, but would recover from all of the damage in time.

If they still had the Habitat Module, her recovery would have been complete in two days by placing her in a medical capsule. The device would induce a semi-conscious state in her and provide a painless convalescence. Without it, her recovery would be extremely uncomfortable. He administered a relaxant and painkiller and Dela opened her eyes for a moment and gave Omega an uncharacteristic smile. He smiled back and patted her hand softly.

"Well," she said moistening her lips. "How did I do?"

"Not bad," he answered. "You rigged the module, didn't you? It was you who locked me out, wasn't it?"

"Camden locked you out, I just programmed the module to do certain things once the door was locked," she said. "It was safer for you not to be inside when he made his move."

"I thought you said your mission wasn't to keep me alive?" he said.

"My mission…" she began pausing to let a wave of pain subside. "My mission was to ensure the *San Mariner* expedition was a success. I didn't try to keep you alive. I just kept you out of the way so I could do that. As you saw, I had everything under control." She laughed at her own words causing her to cough and followed with a vile exclamation of pain.

"You could have killed yourself with a hair-brained stunt like that," Omega said pointing to the Cargo Module's hatch. "The odds of surviving it are incalculable. Depressurizing the module was crazy."

"The odds were not as long as you think," she said wincing as she smiled.

"Really? What stupid high-risk trick did you pull?" he asked as he began giving her first-aid.

"I... ouch..." she said as he applied disinfectant to her cuts and scrapes. "I gave myself a tri-ox booster shot when we began to come down in speed. I knew I had enough stored O2 in my system to survive the depressurization. The only thing I had to worry about was not getting sucked out into space."

Tri-ox was a compound used by star sailors before conducting an emergency EVA. If normal pre-breathing requirements could not be performed, the tri-ox was injected as an alternative. But despite the years of testing and refinement and certification of the compound, it was dangerous to the system. The bends could result from its use as well as permanent internal organ damage. There were only two documented cases of tri-ox usage on file with Space Command, and only one of them reached a happy ending.

"You're a fool," Omega said dabbing the disinfectant so it stung. She sucked in air through her teeth and scowled at him. He shrugged his shoulders innocently and smiled. "Sorry."

"I bet," Dela said gritting her teeth.

"Where did you come up with the dumb ass idea to use tri-ox?" he asked.

"From you naturally," Dela said closing her eyes.

Omega nodded. Of course she did. During her investigations, she probably ran across the incident in his personnel file. It was considered one of the bravest acts on record with Space Command, and the most foolhardy thing he had ever done. He was glad she had survived the experience and hoped there would be no lingering after effects. He closed the medical kit and carefully lifted Dela and brought her to his In-Flight cabin. He gingerly placed her in his bunk and finished treating her. When he was done, he closed the kit and as he stepped away from her, she touched his arm.

"Thank you," she said nodding to him.

"It should be me that's thanking you," he replied.

"Did you take our final bearings?"

"Yes, we're just outside our system, right on the numbers. We're still too far away from a space buoy to contact Space Command by voice, but they can receive our telemetry now. They'll know we're close and still en route. I've sent a CQD message stating our situation, so if there are any ships on the outer rim of the system, hopefully they'll pick it up," he said.

"You should also try to reach Cedilla or one of the other outposts," Dela suggested. "Cedilla has a receiver just as large as Kerguelen's. If there are no ships out here, they'll hear us."

"I'll try after we get into the system," he said. "You get some rest, Dela. We're only a few days from home and I'll need you when we dock the ship."

"Yeah, yeah, always work," she said dreamily as she closed her eyes. The painkillers and sedative he gave her finally took effect and she drifted off to sleep.

Omega went to the flight deck and locked in the course to Kerguelen into the automatic flight system. After he increased speed and the ship was arcing its way home, Omega opened the ship's log and entered the day's events. It took him a long time to decide what to put into the ship's diary. He chose to take a page from Camden's book and be creative. He wrote that despite great danger to himself, Flight Officer Camden attempted to repair the defective FTL unit and was lost in space. Flight Engineer Dela sustained massive injuries while conducting repairs to the main electrical and artificial gravity systems but availed herself as a competent star sailor and technician. He was sure Dela would backup the entries he made and a review board would draw their standard conclusions. Accidents happen in space, case closed. The names of the dead crew would be inscribed in The Sacred Hall of Capitol City and life would go on. He closed out the ship's log and opened his personal log. He could be honest in this journal for it would not be read until after his death. He sighed heavily and began tapping away on the keypad. Since there was no crew left to overhear him, he didn't have to worry about eavesdroppers, but force of habit compelled him to type instead of using the voice recorder.

"Camden is dead and the threat to the ship and the mission... and myself... is gone. Dela has shown unbelievable resourcefulness and determination while carrying out her assignment. She not only saved the alien craft, and thus the mission, but she also saved my life. Prior certainly knows how to pick her operatives. If they all are as effective as Dela, the troubles of the planet should soon disappear. I shall remember to tell her so, if we ever meet again. Before Dela vented Camden into space, she cursed

him, hoping he would find solace with The Second. Despite his actions, that is the most vicious curse one can place upon another.

"The entity she was referring to was from scripture and was the second child bore by the first man and woman of Kerguelen. According to the ancient text, the Almighty gave Sol (the first woman) a mate named Terra (the first man), to bond with so she would not be alone. Sol was the giver of light and warmth and life. Terra was the foundation and strength of which our race was built and depended. Together, they flourished in Paradise.

"Sol and Terra bore two offspring, Eden (a woman child) and a man-child we know only as The Second. It is written that Sol and Terra ceded Paradise to Eden to have dominion over and The Second would assist her, for without woman and man united together as one there can be no Paradise. Eden and The Second were promised mates to bond with so Paradise could continue to thrive. In due time, the Almighty gave Eden a mate named Astral and The Second's mate was named Luna.

"Shortly after they bonded, Eden was with child and aglow with happiness. The Second and Luna were not so pleased. Try as they might, Luna remained barren and the closer Eden came to giving birth the more resentful and hateful she and The Second became. The Second was full of jealousy and rage and Luna asked him to make the Almighty provide a child for her as well. When The Second prayed to the Almighty, She said it was not in her power to grant such a gift. The power to conceive resided only in the bonded pair. They had to find the power of creation within each other. Upon hearing this, Luna renounced the Almighty and The Second killed his sister Eden just before she was to give birth.

"Astral prayed for revenge, but the Almighty told him that all who seek vengeance; all whose only desire is avarice, and all who are driven by jealousy shall lose Paradise. Astral told the Almighty that without Eden, Paradise was lost, but the Almighty assured him that Paradise would continue on as long as he had faith. The Almighty then created a Netherworld and banished The Second there for killing Eden and made Astral and Luna forget his name.

"From the Netherworld, The Second could see all that happened on Kerguelen but could not enjoy or share in any of it. It was a place where he could have all the jealousy and envy and greed he wanted. He could desire all he wanted but would never have any happiness, only hatred, for the Netherworld was barren. In the nexus the Almighty created, The Second *would have the dominion he longed for and would rule over all men and beasts like him, those who put themselves and material gain before the welfare of others. It was a place where hate and anger were the norms and love non-existent. The Almighty would banish any future undesirables to live in misery for eternity with The Second.*

"In the Netherworld, The Second saw Astral's goodness turn Luna's heart and soul and her faith was reestablished. She became one with Paradise again and the Almighty soon bonded Astral and Luna together. In this new life, she was resurrected. What was once barren became fruitful, and over time Luna bore twenty-four children. These children, known as 'The Seed of Kerguelen', left Paradise when the youngest child matured and they spread over Kerguelen and established all but one of Kerguelen's provinces.

"It is not known how many years passed before Astral and Luna bore their last children, the twins Kullen and Katana, but it is written that when they matured, the Almighty tasked the man-child, Kullen, with traveling to the provinces and delivering Her laws to his brothers and sisters and his twin sister, Katana, was responsible for the protection and enforcement of the Almighty's laws.

"The fate of Kullen, the Giver of God's Laws and Katana, the Preserver of God's Laws is unknown. It is believed that they established the twenty-fifth and last province on Kerguelen when their tasks were complete, but that is only speculation. It is known that Luna and Astral spent their remaining days in Paradise. Luna became known as the matron saint of motherhood, hearth and home and Astral became the patron saint of fatherhood, strength and integrity.

"Many scoff at the validity of the Scriptures, but as I reflect on those biblical stories and characters they are not a thing of the past for me. And they are not actors or players in a fantastic drama. They have come alive to me. Today, Dela and I are entrusted with delivering the alien spacecraft to Kerguelen and if the Almighty wills it, we will bring our strange cargo home. For I, like Kullen, am delivering the people a message from the Heavens and Dela, like Katana, has protected it."

4
Chief Surveyor's Headquarters, Guardian Tri-Rivers Complex, Central Province, Planet Kerguelen

Commander Prior arrived at her headquarters thirty minutes later than she had planned. Once again, she had a long and disturbing night filled with strange visions causing her to toss and turn in her bed. The visions seemed to be warnings of impending doom and they had followed her in her sleep for several weeks now. She didn't understand them nor did she know what they meant, but they were persistent and ever- present and whenever she slept, they were there… and they upset her immensely. When she finally stirred, she was visibly irritated and Pana had warned Rex and Micah that she was not in the mood to be trifled with.

Though the morning sun was bright and the day was promising to be cool and pleasant Prior felt danger looming in the future. As her air ship came in for landing, she saw something even more ominous than her night visions. On the flag pole of the Tri-Rivers base, just below the tri-colored planetary flag and right above the banner of the base commander, was the distinctive banner of Garath, Supreme Commander of the Guardian Corps. The battle pennant depicted a large falcon with spread wings on a field of purple trimmed in white and it fluttered in the breeze proclaiming to all that Garath was present.

Prior had no doubt where he was and why he was here. The supreme commander would be in her office waiting to chew her out for her outspokenness during the briefing with President Ward the previous day or for some other indiscretion. She shook her head as Micah gently touched down and waited as Pana opened the air ship's door and extended the ladder to the ground. Prior stood and walked to the open hatch and paused for a moment. Pana looked at her curiously and gently touched her cousin on the arm.

"Anything wrong, Prior?" Pana asked.

"Everything... and nothing," Prior said staring out of the open hatch.

"You don't look well," said Pana concerned.

"I don't feel well, Pana. Garath is here and it's not going to be pretty," Prior said looking at Pana. "He's going to ream me for yesterday and I'm not really in the mood for it."

"We could always leave," Pana said with a smile. "You could use a break anyway. What can he really do to you?"

"Not much really," Prior said.

"Exactly," Pana said nodding.

Pana knew that Central Command frequently reprimanded Prior for her attitude, and Prior had always taken it in stride. Why she did, Pana didn't know. Prior could have simply resigned and got down to the business of running her company, like she should have been doing. Prior was a billionaire and didn't need the job... or the headaches accompanying it. Nor did she need the status associated with being a Guardian commander. She was head of the leading Boroni house and already had more social status and respect than she could ever get in the Guardian Corps.

"As appealing as a long vacation would be, I'm afraid I have to put it off for a while," Prior said. "I have much to do. Garath is only a minor inconvenience and a necessary evil I have to put up with."

"As you wish," Pana said.

"Since I'm going to be in conference for a while, I need you and Rex to track down Sgt. Arrix and give him a turnover and instruct him on flight procedures. He needs to come up to speed rapidly," Prior said. "I'm going to give Hiroki operational command of a team. Arrix will be his crew chief, and Elias will be his lead NCO. We'll have to find some others to augment him as well. But he and his new team will be heading out as soon as they locate Elias."

"I'll see to it at once," Pana said. She looked at Prior and added, "If you're going to see Garath, shouldn't change into your day uniform?"

"No," Prior said shaking her head. "I'm dressed appropriately. The combat suit is the proper attire for battle."

Pana smiled. "You're probably right."

"Besides, I don't want to change," Prior said. "Talk to you later. C'mon, Lupo."

She tapped her thigh and her canine slowly followed her down the ladder. She took the long way from the air ship landing area to her command offices, passing by the work areas of her combat engineer company. The Guardians there nodded to her, acknowledging her presence, but quickly returned to their endeavors. Though she was their commander, Prior had always stressed that they shouldn't stand on ceremony when she came through. She was only there to see what was going on and be available to speak to her troops or answer their questions or address any concerns, not to garner salutes. She felt it was the best way to determine the pulse of her unit and their combat readiness. Her personnel and administrative officer, dubbed the action MBWA, or management by walking around, and the Guardians under her command thought it set her apart from her peers in the senior leadership of the Corps. They appreciated her seeming genuine interest in what they were doing. She did not interfere or micro-manage and they were glad they had a true leader, not a martinet, as their commanding officer.

She stopped in front of a large excavating hovercraft. The vehicle was in the reconditioning and maintenance workspace and had obviously just returned from being used on a deployment. Prior saw that the construction vehicle had been used vigorously. Deep scratches on the sides had removed its yellow paint and gray primer coating down to the bare metal in several areas and shovel on the front of the vehicle seemed to be slightly off-center.

The curses of the Guardians working on vehicle caught Prior's attention and she stepped closer to get a better look at what was going on. Two sergeants, one tall and slender and the other short and beefy, were trying to pry the bent portion of the shovel device back to its natural position. As they struggled to force the metal back to its original shape, they failed to notice the arrival of their commanding officer.

"What's up?" Prior asked.

"Good morning, Commander," the beefy sergeant said looking at her. "We're trying to sort out this mess."

"What's the problem?" Prior asked.

"Before we can finish our preventative maintenance, we've got to fix the shovel. It won't move," the beefy sergeant explained. "The idiot who operated this last must have run into a boulder the size of a mountain at full speed. The hinge mechanism is bent and the shovel is misaligned and won't translate up and down."

"It's jammed pretty good," the slender sergeant said as he strained to fix the problem.

Prior eyed the bent metal and frowned. "What kind of metal is that hinge made of? Steel?" Prior asked.

"Reinforced steel," the beefy sergeant said. "It's hardened for work like digging in granite or breaking up concrete."

"And the pivoting pin of the hinge is made of titanium," the slender sergeant offered. "I'm afraid we're going to have to get a portable hydraulic power unit to bend this back into shape."

"If we can make an adapter to fit between the hinge and the shovel," the beefy sergeant said. "It's too tight to use our standard gear."

"How long will it take you to make an adapter?" Prior asked.

"A couple hours, I hope," the beefy sergeant said scratching his head.

"Do you mind if I take a crack at it?" Prior said stepping closer to the vehicle.

The slender sergeant handed Prior the pry bar and wiped his hands on his coveralls as he stepped back. She grabbed the bar with both hands and inserted it between the hinge and the shovel. She rolled her shoulders, exhaled and closed her eyes as she pulled the bar toward her. The hinge slowly gave way to her and the sergeants watched in awe as reinforced steel and titanium bent to her will. The pivoting mechanism moved the three or four inches needed and Prior opened her eyes when she was done. She turned to the mechanics and handed the bar back to the slender sergeant.

"Will that do?" she asked.

"That's perfect, Commander. Thanks a lot," he said.

"No problem," Prior said. "Now you can finish your work and rig up that adapter at your leisure if you need it in the future."

"Will do," the slender sergeant nodded. "If you ever want to give up supervising and get a job as a tech just let us know. We could use you."

"I'll keep that in mind," Prior smiled. "Keep up the good work. I'll try and find out who was responsible for cracking up the excavator and send them out here to help you."

"Thanks, Commander," the beefy sergeant said. "But we got this covered... now."

"Very well. Carry on, then," Prior said continuing on.

When she reached the building that housed her own spaces she sighed loudly and opened the door. Waiting impatiently was Captain Ernst, her personnel and administrative officer. Prior could tell he was glad she had finally arrived.

"Good morning, Commander," Ernst said. He was in his combat suit and the twenty-five year old officer was blatantly tense.

"Morning, Captain," Prior said nonchalantly. "Do you have the daily reports for me?"

"Affirmative," he said handing her an electronic data tablet.

She took it and as she reviewed the screen, Ernst cleared his throat and Prior looked up at him.

"Yes? Is there something else?" Prior asked.

"The Supreme Commander is waiting in your office. I think he's upset," Ernst said.

"He probably is, it's his natural condition. Anyone with him?" Prior asked.

"His aides, Col. Raia and Col. Marcus, are with him," Ernst said.

"Very well, Captain. I'll look at these later," Prior said handing Ernst the data tablet. "Find Major Metis and Lt. Addison and have them come here as soon as possible. We've got a lot to discuss."

"They're on post," Ernst said. "I call for them at once."

"Good," Prior nodded. "I'm going in now. And please, no interruptions until the Supreme Commander departs."

"Understood," Ernst said.

Prior and Lupo entered her office and she immediately was assaulted by the scowl of Garath. He and his aides, Colonel Raia and Colonel Marcus, were dressed in the standard day uniform and Garath's eyes narrowed when he saw her. Prior stopped at the entrance and smiled as she looked at him. She saluted and Garath saluted back. She ordered Lupo to the back of the office and told him to lie down. After he did, Prior stepped closer to Garath.

"Good morning, Supreme Commander," Prior said very pleasantly. "Did Capt. Ernst offer you anything?"

"Yes he did," Garath grumbled. "But this isn't a social call, Commander."

"Oh?" Prior said stepping to her desk. "Can I sit or do you want to give it to me standing up?"

"I think we can sit," Garath said.

Prior gestured to the chairs in front of her desk and Garath and his aides sat down. Prior sat down in a high-backed leather chair and pushed aside electronic data tablets in front of her and looked at Garath.

"What brings you here, Supreme Commander?" Prior asked and then held up her hand. She pressed a button on her desktop TELCOM unit. "Excuse me a moment. Capt. Ernst, could you bring in some coffee?"

"How many?" Ernst asked.

Prior looked at Garath and he frowned. "Just one, Captain. Very large, very black and very strong," Prior said smiling. She clicked off the intercom and leaned back in her chair. "Now, you were saying?"

Garath knew her coffee order was a quip on his looks and an attempt to get under his skin, but Garath refused to play along with her. His aides on the other hand voiced their displeasure with Prior.

"Commander, you may think your antics are amusing, and your glib comments clever, but let me assure you, the Supreme Commander does not," Marcus said.

"Colonel, are you reprimanding me for my demeanor?" Prior asked. "Is a subordinate telling a superior how they should conduct themselves?"

"I'm just relating the Marshal's feelings," Marcus said.

"Let's get one thing straight, Colonel, you don't tell me, or any commander, anything," Prior said as the smile disappeared from her face. "I'm a peaceful individual but I won't be hectored by junior officers and I don't care who your boss is or what position you hold. I've taken about as much nonsense from subordinates as I'm going to." She turned to Garath and smiled again. "What can I do for you, Supreme Commander?"

"First of all, you can stop clowning around, Prior. I'm here on serious business," Garath said. "I'm here to see you end your inquiries concerning Cardinal Gregor. The Venture Affair is over. Concentrate your efforts on other matters. Secondly, I don't relate *my* feelings to junior officers. That's why I have aides."

"Then get one who is a commander," Prior said. "I'm a member of the Central Command advisory, in case they've forgotten, and I'm going to start throwing my weight around if things don't change."

"I hear you, Commander," Garath said nodding. He turned to his aides and added, "The commander has voiced her displeasure with you. I hope you understand what that means."

The aides nodded. They knew that they pushed their influence as assistants to the supreme commander to the limit as far as Prior was concerned and any further disrespect to her rank and status would not be tolerated.

"You have our apologies, Commander," Raia said.

"Fine," Prior said. "Now that we understand each other, let's get back to business. Venture may be dead, but this is far from over."

"Why?" Garath asked.

"The evidence I've collected forces me to continue inquiries," Prior said.

"You keep mentioning evidence. What do you have?" Garath said.

A rap on the door to her office put their conversation on hold. When it opened, Ernst came in with a large mug of coffee. He sat it on Prior's desk and quietly departed. Prior blew on the steaming contents and took a small sip. When the door shut again, she put the mug down and spoke.

"First, the tape from Gregor's office was doctored. The audio portion was purposely deleted. And the only video available showed Venture killing Guardians and shooting Gregor and nothing else," Prior said.

"That's because Venture tried to destroy the tape," Garath said.

"We both know that's a lie," Prior said shaking her head. "He would never try something like that with all of those Papal security guards around."

"You may be correct," Garath said. "I certainly wouldn't."

"My next piece is Venture's computer database," Prior said picking up a data tablet. "It was infiltrated and incriminating data was placed into it by a cyber criminal named Cressida."

"Isn't she the woman who hacked into the Cosmopolis mass transit financial database and stole millions before she was caught?" Raia asked.

"Yes," Prior said. "She was recently released from prison and recruited by Gregor to frame Venture."

"How do you know this?" Garath asked.

"My lead investigator caught up with her trying to catch a shuttle to Space Station *Condor*. She had a one-way ticket for an interstellar transport to Cedilla," Prior said.

"Why there?" Garath asked.

"To escape extradition," Marcus offered. "Cedilla is the only place in the solar system besides The Edge, where planetary law enforcement has no jurisdiction."

"She was apprehended and detained and admitted under oath that the cardinal was the one who hired her to do the deeds," Prior said.

"Was the confession coerced?" Garath asked. "Your personnel are known for their... persuasiveness."

"The information was given freely and without reservation in the presence of *Condor's* safety department supervisor," Prior said. "And third, a list of seven priests was found in Venture's database. Archbishop Cornelia was on that list," Prior said.

"And Venture killed her," Garath said. "A Guardian weapon was used and he was seen fleeing the manse. He dove into the sea to escape apprehension."

"If he intended to kill her why would he get so close? Her security is the best on the planet. Everyone on Kerguelen knows that. The odds of getting out are so high no one would try a point blank assassination. And if you had a Guardian weapon, you don't need to be up close and personal," Prior said.

"Are you saying Venture didn't kill her?" Garath asked.

"I know he didn't," Prior said. "They had a history. He wasn't in love with her, but he had feelings for her. We all have people in our lives that we love and wished were dead, but no one ever kills someone they like. And he liked her. Besides, why would a Guardian who is an ordained priest kill an archbishop? Especially one that would have done anything to help him."

"Are you saying Cornelia would have aided Venture?" Raia asked.

Prior nodded. "It was no secret that she had no love for Gregor and anything Venture could have done to disrupt him would have been to her advantage," Prior said.

"But can you prove someone else did it?" Garath said.

"When the Guardian detail from the First Battalion arrived at Cathedral Prime to secure the scene of Venture's misdeeds, *two* of the weapons were unaccounted for," Prior said.

"Venture took them. He used them to kill the detail accompanying Sali and shoot Gregor," Raia said. "It's right there on the tape."

"Venture took Sali's weapon, but nothing else. The other three Guardians still had their weapons. All three are visible on the tape. And the forensics on Cornelia's death revealed that the weapon used had the signature pattern of the weapon belonging to Corporal Benson of the First Battalion," Prior said. "And Benson was one of the men with Sali."

"Residual plasma energy patterns aren't exact. That's inconclusive and you know it, Commander," Raia said.

"Even if that is true, there is enough doubt in my mind that I feel further investigation is in order. And I plan on following up on what I have," Prior said.

"You have a lot of ingredients, Commander. Ingredients that can turn into a poison pill if things go sideways on you," Garath said. "I won't be able to help you if you run afoul of the Federal Church."

"I can take care of myself in that regard, Marshal Garath," Prior said. "Something is not right about this whole thing and I'm going to find out what it is. With or without your blessing, I'm going forward. If you order me to stop, I'll resign. I have many resources… enough to conduct this investigation on my own if necessary."

Garath grunted. During the entire conversation the frown had remained on his face. Her resignation was out of the question. He needed Prior. And if she were correct, the problems that would arise would require her involvement even more.

"Okay, Commander," Garath said. "Do it your way. Go ahead and play with fire if you want to. I'm not going to stop you. But watch your back. When Cathedral Prime gets wind of what you're doing, and they will, they will be gunning for you."

"I'm aware of the seriousness of the situation, Supreme Commander," Prior said. "And I promise not to embarrass the Corps."

"You'd better not," Garath said standing up. "If you do, you won't have to worry about the cardinals, you'll have to deal with me."

Prior nodded and stood up. She saluted and Garath saluted back. When he and his aides left, Ernst came in with Major Metis and Lieutenant Addison close behind.

Addison was from the Oceanic Province and the junior officer ran a hand through her light brown hair that was naturally highlighted with blonde streaks. The sun bleaching was a common trait for all hailing from the province and the strands pleasantly framed her face.

"Metis, Addison, I'm glad you're here," Prior said. "We've got a lot of work to do."

"We're ready," Metis said.

"Good," Prior said. "Take a seat. I have a mission for Addison that is right up her alley."

Prior detailed a mission that required Addison to infiltrate Cathedral Prime. It was an espionage assignment and Addison would be conducting it alone. She would have no support and if she got into trouble there would be no way for anyone to help her. When the briefing was over, Prior folded her hands in front of her and looked Addison squarely in the face.

"This mission is vital and as I said you'll have no support. We can't even provide extraction capability for you. You understand what that means?" Prior said.

"I do," Addison said. "I'll remove all Guardian material from my possession. If I'm captured or killed, no one will know of our involvement."

"Very well, Good luck, Lieutenant," Prior said. Both women stood and shook hands. As the young woman turned to leave, Prior added, "And Addie, I need you back here as soon as possible."

"I'll be so quick you'd never know I was gone," Addison said with a quick smile.

After Addison was gone, Metis looked at Prior.

"The surveillance ops are going well," she said. "So far, none of the priests left on that list have been killed."

"Are there any working close by?" Prior asked.

"Singh is trailing Father Joubert in Capitol City. He's been reporting regularly and has had no problems thus far," Metis said.

Lieutenant Singh was a young officer from the vast sub-continent region of the Eastern Province. His family was prominent in business concerns there and Prior knew his father. Singh's mission was just as hazardous an undertaking as the one given to Addison, but he could at least call for backup. Despite this, Prior still had reservations about sending her people on missions without adequate support, but it had to be done.

At least Singh would be able to call on his fellow combat engineers if he ran into trouble. Though there would be only two squads available, Prior was sure the sixteen Guardians on hand would be all the aid Singh would need. And they would have to be, for the rest of them would be engaged elsewhere, primarily in the Middle Provinces in case hostilities broke out there.

Singh was not the only one operating on his own but Prior worried about his safety more than the others. He had been bonded to his mate for less than a year and the recent nuptials had resulted in a newborn. And this made Prior even more tentative about him being out in the cold. But she was short on independent operatives and Singh had been willing to take on the job. With any luck, he would be fine.

"If something explodes, he knows to send out a general alert. Col. Thyssen or Cdr. Ceca will send assistance from either the Second or First Battalions," Metis said. "I wish he had more support though."

"I know Col. Thyssen," Ernst said. "He was operations officer of the Second Battalion while I was temporarily assigned there. He's a steady officer but… very cautious."

"The result of having been mentored by Cdr. Giles, no doubt," Prior said a bit tongue-in-cheek. "However, he has the complete confidence of Central Command."

Ernst and Metis nodded noting the undertones in Prior's voice. They knew she didn't really believe in the reliability of Thyssen but there was little she could do about it. Prior hoped Singh could finish his mission with involving Thyssen or Ceca.

"What plans do you have for the rest of the surveyors?" Ernst asked.

"We're going to be stretched thin," Prior said. "And we need to find the connection between the priests on that list we discovered. What can you tell me about it?"

"I gave it to the electronic forensic techs and when they came up empty I gave it Ernst," Metis said.

"Why?" Prior asked.

"As much as I hate to admit it, he's a genius," Metis answered.

"Modesty prevents me from responding," Ernst said. "But I have discovered what they have in common. They are all experts in the arcane arts and occult aspects of the Federal Church."

"What are these arts?" Prior asked.

"Demonology, conjuring, exorcism… you know, the stuff we now consider BS. The priests on the list have all studied the rites intensively and are officially categorized as experts in the field. Archbishop Cornelia was the highest rated of them all," Ernst said.

"What does all that mean?" Metis said.

"I think I know," Prior said with narrowing eyes. "A source of mine mentioned that Gregor was a Summoner with supernatural ability and there is a rumor floating around in many circles that The Argent are back. If both are true, then it all fits together and the use of arcane arts would be essential."

"Why?" Metis asked.

"The Argent believed in those old superstitions and used them to psyche themselves up for battle… at least that's what the legends say. And if Gregor is indeed a Summoner, and if he's in league with this new Argent resurgence, then he can call on the dark spirits to aid them in whatever they are doing. Despite all of our knowledge and enlightenment, many people still believe in the old legends and the power of demonology," Ernst said. "If the Church can convince the people they possess great spiritual power and can conjure evil demons into our dimension… our world, there will be nothing, absolutely nothing anyone could do to stop them from seizing complete control of the planet."

"We are a scientific people," Metis said. "No one believes in that spiritual garbage anymore. Not even my people. And we were arguably the most superstitious of any race."

It was true the tribal people Metis descended from were highly superstitious and now refuted most of their ancient beliefs. But she could not forget many of them still practiced some of the millennia old rites to this day, including the use of natural hallucinogens extracted from cactus to commune with the spirits.

"What you say is true, Metis, but remember there are those who still believe strongly in the spiritual world," Ernst said. "Astrology has never been out of fashion. We all think it's a harmless pastime but what if our horoscopes were proved true consistently?"

"You're crazy, Ernst," Metis said dismissively.

"Oh, really? What's your sign, Metis?" Ernst asked.

"The Fish," she answered quickly. Her response was given without thought and she realized that Ernst might have hit on something.

"Kerguelens know that there are other planets in faraway star systems and believe in science wholeheartedly, but science requires facts, religion and spiritual matters only require faith," Ernst said.

"But they couldn't wrest control from the other branches of government and control the people unless they had the Technology Council in their pocket," Metis said. "And the Council has the Guardians to protect them."

"Yes, that is correct," said Ernst. "But what if they had designs on us?"

"What are you getting at?" Prior asked.

"Maybe nothing," Ernst said shrugging his shoulders. "But the reason Metis and the E-forensic techs came up empty in their queries about the priests was because the list she had was incomplete."

"What are you talking about?" Metis asked.

"You're fortunate to have a person well-versed in the subject of religion," Ernst said with little humility. "My degree is in religious history. Part of my studies included research about the arcane arts."

"Yeah, we're all aware of you graduating magna cum laude, Ernst," Metis said knowing how intelligent he was. "Okay, we know you're a great theologian and a genius. So illuminate me, tell me why you're so brilliant and we're blessed to have you grace us with your presence."

"There are *ten* priests with high ratings in the black arts. Only seven were listed. I think they are targets because they are the only ones that could prevent the other three from successfully doing whatever they are planning," Ernst surmised.

"Why do you think the other three are in on this together?" Metis asked.

"The legends say one priest can perform an exorcism, but it takes a minimum of three priests to do really powerful arcane rites… like conjuring some Netherworld demon or spirit. But it only takes *one* powerful priest to stop them. My guess is the three not listed are planning to do away with the others so they can't be stopped," Ernst explained.

"Are they planning to resurrect a demon?" Prior asked.

"It's possible. It's also possible they have already done so. But, without delving into this deeper, I can only guess what their end game is," Ernst said.

"Who are the other three?" Prior asked.

"Monsignor Hayden, Father Dimitrios… and Cardinal Gregor," Ernst said. "You said your source told you that Gregor is a Summoner. If he is, I would guess the others are helping him bring a demon to Kerguelen."

"Everything seems to always come back to him," Metis said.

"He's the common denominator," Prior said.

"What do you want to do, boss?" Ernst asked.

"I want you two to work out a contingency plan for countering those black arts. If we can't stop them, determine how we can contain it," Prior ordered. "I don't care what resources you have to use to get it done, just make it happen."

"Do you think there's really something in what Ernst has said?" Metis asked.

"It's a reasonable line of thinking," Prior answered. "Many things are happening around the planet. Financial institutions are being taken over by other corporations. My own company was attacked economically. The Grange has lost thousands of acres planet-wide because provinces are claiming eminent domain over the territory. Protestors against the government are disappearing and public information is being suppressed. And the Church is trying to get stronger than it already is and appears to be getting rid of those who possibly could oppose them. If we combine all of the variables together, I'm sure they all tie in."

"I'm sensing you want us to spread out all over the planet," Metis said.

"There's nothing wrong with spreading our wings a bit and I suggest we get a detachment of surveyors to Central Command as well," Prior said.

"Why there?" Ernst asked.

"If the Guardians are at risk of attack, I want extra muscle protecting the Council of Elders. Besides, it's a good place to launch from if they are needed elsewhere," Prior said. "They could reach any trouble spot in a few hours."

"I'll see to it," Ernst said. "We have nine Guardians idling away here without orders. I can have them prepped to go to The Home in less than an hour."

"Excellent," Prior nodded. "Who is the senior NCO?"

"Sergeant First Class Tanith. She just got through with her medical leave," Ernst said. "She's been pestering me for a new assignment for over a week. Warrant Officer Fukuani would be the officer-in-charge."

Prior knew both women well. Tanith had been Prior's dive partner during underwater construction school and had been a member of a special ops team before she had been injured during a recon mission. Prior liked her and wished she could have put her back on a team, but it would be several weeks before she was fit for that kind of duty. Fukuani had served with Prior on numerous occasions and was arguably the tops in the field of special weapons.

"Okay, put the detail under Fukuani's command and make Tanith NCOIC. Have the detail outfitted with the full complement of field gear and assign two air ships for their use," Prior said.

"Full gear? You mean everything?" Ernst asked.

"Yes, everything... including specials," Prior said. "I want them ready for any contingency."

"Tanith is going to love that," Metis said with a smile.

"I'm sure she will," Prior said. "Now you two get busy. I want a plan on my desk before I have to head out."

They both nodded and stepped out of the office. Before he shut the door, Ernst poked his head back inside.

"Excuse me, Commander," Ernst said. "Cdr. Mohab is here and wishes to see you."

"Mohab? Send him in, Captain," Prior said standing and stepping away from her desk. Ernst disappeared and Mohab entered the office. Prior smiled at him and extended a hand. "Assalumu alaikum, Mohab."

"Wa alaikum assalum," Mohab replied shaking her hand. He was always surprised by Prior's language proficiency. "You know speaking Middle Province dialects and using ancient religious greetings could get you into trouble these days."

"Don't worry, Mohab, that's the extent of my knowledge of your provincial dialect," Prior said. "Take a seat, I'll be with you in a moment. Can I get you anything?"

"No, I'm fine," he said.

Prior nodded and stepped out of her office for a moment as Mohab sat down in a chair in front of her desk. He placed his feet on the edge of her desk and pulled out his PDA and began scrolling through his messages. When Prior returned to her office, she walked to her desk and leaned against the front of it by Mohab's feet and looked at him and smiled.

"New shoes?" she asked.

"I'm sorry," Mohab said looking up from his PDA screen.

"I asked you if those were new shoes," she said.

"These? No, I've had them for a while," he said looking at his boots and then back to Prior.

"Then get them off of my desk, Mohab," she said as her smile faded. He lost his own smile and cleared his throat as he swung his feet down to the floor. She folded her arms and continued. "So, what brings you to Tri-Rivers?"

"I just thought I'd pay you a visit while I'm wrapping up some business. I'm heading back to my battalion soon and because it's been a long time since we had a face-to-face I thought I'd drop by," he said. "You bolted out of our meeting yesterday before I could talk to you." He looked down and saw Lupo lying quietly in the corner of the office and smiled. "How's your pooch?"

She looked over at Lupo and then to Mohab. "He's fine. Aching to get into action again, but he's good. Aren't you, Lupo?" Prior said as she glanced at the dog and he raised his head and let his tongue hang out. She smiled at Lupo and turned to Mohab again.

When she faced him, she saw that he was looking at her closely. As she leaned against the desk, Mohab took in all of her lines. Her ample curves were never so apparent as they were in the form-fitting combat suit. With her arms folded, Mohab could see the flex and shape of her biceps and triceps and tautness of her abs and thighs. And the suit's torso armor protection did nothing to mask the fullness of her bosom. Prior raised a questioning eyebrow at Mohab in regard to his firmly fixed gaze.

"What's wrong?" she asked examining herself.

"Nothing. Nothing at all," he said standing up and walking to the other side of the office ashamed that he had allowed her to notice him ogling her. "What are you up to?"

"I have a lot of irons in the fire at the moment," Prior said with a sigh. "Among operational plans, I've been discussing possible changes to the curriculum at the Basic School."

"But why? It's tough enough as it is. I've always wondered why you emphasize civilian qualifications so much," Mohab said. "The military applications are rigorous enough."

"My Guardians need that training. What they do is vital to the Corps, but they're basically special recon scouts. After ten, fifteen or twenty years as a Guardian, what do they do then? Unfortunately, there is little call for middle-aged commandos around the planet. But there will always be a need for competent people in the construction and civil engineering fields," Prior explained.

Mohab nodded and stepped to the map of Capitol City and faced her. "What are your plans now that the Venture problem has been solved?"

"I'm not entirely sure the situation has been resolved," she replied. "Based on my inquiries, I have reasonable doubt about many things. I'm going to continue to scrounge around to see what I can pick up."

"Do you feel like sharing those conclusions?"

"Not until I have something solid," she said shaking her head.

"I wish you had told me about your mission. I disagree with the methods our leaders used, but I could have helped you," he said.

"I know, but doing that kind of business is not something that you share, not even with your closest friends. And if you ever have to kill anyone… out of context… never, ever tell another living soul about it," Prior said icily.

"Why not?"

"Just don't, Mohab, trust me on that," she said with empty soulless eyes. She blinked once and the life returned to her eyes and she stood up. "How is your deployment shaping up?"

Mohab clicked on the map showing Capitol City and it changed to one depicting the Middle Provinces. He picked up a few small tokens that represented platoon-sized units and arranged them on the map.

"My units are here," he said. "That leaves them in a position where they can counter any movement in the region by any force. I've got a satellite tasked to monitor the area for ninety-six hours."

"That must have taken some doing," Prior said impressed. "Space Command doesn't like expending fuel on its satellites for something that may happen."

"I called in a favor," Mohab said. "I went to grad school with one of the project managers."

She nodded. "You're in good shape then. Where do you want my surveyors?"

"I thought you'd deploy them yourself," he said.

"This is your show, Mohab. I'm senior, but you have tactical command in this area. My Guardians are there to support you. Major St. Jacques is in charge of the detail, but he knows it's your show," Prior said.

Mohab nodded and was thankful all parties understood each other. The Middle Province region was his area of responsibility and was glad that they could work together without the uneasiness that often surfaced when who was in charge was in question.

"All I need is for them to scout and protect the left flank of my main body," Mohab said pointing to where he wanted her troops.

Prior nodded and was glad he was not pensive. A paralyzed commander was the cause of more deaths than any weapons had ever been. "Very well," Prior said. "I'll see to it."

Prior stepped into the hallway and called out to Captain Hiroki. When she returned to the office, he was with her. He walked to Mohab and the two Guardians discussed the deployment of the surveyors. When they were finished, Hiroki stepped to Prior.

"I'll send a message to Major St. Jacques at once," he said.

"Very well," Prior said. "By the way, why are you still here, Captain? Weren't you recently given command of a fire team?"

"My team is incomplete," Hiroki answered. "Sgt. Arrix is getting a turnover from Sgt. Major Pana and Sgt. Elias is absent."

"Why?" Prior asked with a smile.

"He was given leave before the transfer order reached the Basic School. I sent Lt. Lindsey to track him down and bring him back here."

"Your fire team is off to an auspicious beginning, Captain," Prior said in a playful tone.

"Begging the Commander's pardon," Hiroki said tilting his head to one side. "But did you know Sgt. Elias would be on leave when you issued the order?"

"Of course, Captain," Prior said. "I approved his leave request."

"You set me up," he said.

"The disposition of the Guardians under your command is *your* responsibility, Captain. A competent leader knows where all of his men are at all times," Prior said.

Before Hiroki could respond, a short rap on the door caused all of them to look to it and revealed the presence of Lieutenant Lindsey and Sergeant Elias. They entered and came to attention, though Elias was having trouble maintaining the position on his own. By the condition of his day uniform and the smell of his breath, he had obviously gotten his leave off to a good start.

"Lt. Lindsey reporting my return," Lindsey said. He elbowed Elias and the recently promoted sergeant straightened his posture as best he could and looked at Prior.

"One moment, Lieutenant," Prior said. "Cdr. Mohab, would you please excuse us. I need a few words with these gentlemen." Prior stared at Elias with a hard gaze as Mohab excused himself. When he was gone, Prior stepped closer to Lindsey and Elias. "Where did you find him, Lieutenant?"

"Getting wasted in a dive bar in Capitol City. He was… reluctant to accompany me, but I managed to persuade him to join me, Commander," Lindsey said.

Prior looked at the bruise beginning to form near Elias' left eye and smiled. "I trust there'll be no permanent damage from your... gentle persuasions, Lieutenant?"

"It'll take more than a love tap from a first lieutenant who doesn't even shave yet to keep me down," Elias said rubbing his eye. "And I'm on leave. I can get drunk if I want to. And I want to."

"You *were* on leave, Sergeant," Prior said in a stern voice ignoring his quip. "You're needed for a strike team and time is short. You'll have to quickly come up to speed on Capt. Hiroki's procedures. You'll be deploying today."

"But I've earned my leave. I've been stuck with those wet nose recruits for a year now," Elias protested. "Including this one." Elias jabbed a thumb in Lindsey's direction and Prior smiled.

"You have my sympathies, Sergeant, but you have work to do," Prior said. "And I'm afraid liberty is a privilege not a right."

"Thank you for your sentiments, Commander," Elias said sarcastically.

"Just be ready to go when Capt. Hiroki makes the call," Prior said.

"Thy will be done... Commander," Elias said staggering a bit. He nearly fell as he tried to stay at attention.

"Be careful, Sergeant," Prior said moving closer to him. "I'm not just a Guardian commander, I'm also a Boroni female. And our least favorite personality is a smart ass. I won't bring you up on charges of insubordination if you get out of line, I'll kick your ass."

"In other words, shut up unless you have something worthwhile to offer," Lindsey scolded.

"Would it be pertinent to ask why I have the pleasure of serving with Capt. Hiroki?" Elias asked.

"That's a good question, Sergeant," Prior said smiling. "The reason is simple, Sergeant. Capt. Hiroki recently assumed command of a fire team and he needs a good field NCO to assist him. And you're the best I have. He'll need you, because he's most assuredly going into harm's way."

Elias was known for hard drinking and harder fighting. Despite his proficiency as a surveyor, he had been passed over for promotions because of his off-duty antics and disrespect to superiors. But he was also requested for when the tough times came. During battle, he was focused and had an innate ability to understand battle conditions. And that was what Hiroki would need. If he could manage to deal with a little insubordination, Elias would make him a great leader. By the change in Elias' demeanor, Prior could tell he was ready to give up books and booze and get back into action. The possibility of a combat action had begun to clear his head from the gin soaked fog it was in.

"Will we see a lot of action?" Elias asked with piqued curiosity.

"That's for sure and against great odds for certain," Prior said.

"I like action," Elias said grinning. "When do I start?"

"You're already late, Sergeant," Prior said. "And you're out of uniform. Get three chevrons on that tunic and get sober before I see you again."

"If I don't get it done, what then?" Elias said refusing to submit to her will.

Prior stepped directly in front of Elias. She was at least two inches taller than he was and he gulped as he stared up at her. "If you don't do as I say, I'll rip your lungs out of your chest and show them to you so you can watch yourself breathe," Prior said.

Lupo stood and slowly walked over to Elias and sniffed his leg. Lupo looked up at him and Elias sneered at the dog. Lupo walked around Elias and Lindsey and then sat down next to Prior. She patted him once and looked at Elias.

"What's up with him?" Elias asked.

"It looks like you passed inspection, Sergeant," Prior said. "You won't get a better recommendation. Now, get out of here. You've got work to do."

Lindsey and Elias stepped out of the room and Mohab returned when they had left. Hiroki looked at Prior and shook his head.

"Why him, Commander?" Hiroki asked.

"Elias is a good trooper. He's a drunk and reprobate but he's the finest field NCO there is. Most importantly, he's a university graduate, geology major. He's smart as a whip," Prior said. "I've worked with him, Hiroki. Listen to him, he'll help you immensely."

Hiroki nodded. He excused himself and when Prior and Mohab were alone, she paced the floor in deep thought.

"What's on your mind?" Mohab asked.

"A lot. Too much, in fact," she replied.

"Well, I just got word that Space Command has picked up the telemetry signal of Omega's ship. They should be home in a few days," Mohab said. He saw that the news didn't cheer her up and frowned. "Isn't that good news?"

"Yes, of course it is. I'm happy for Omega," Prior said half-heartedly.

"Prior, that wasn't very convincing," he said.

"What do you want me to say, Mohab? I'm glad he's accomplished what he set out to do. Everyone should have the opportunity to attain their personal goals, but it is a sore subject with me," Prior said.

"He had a hard decision to make."

"And I supported his decision, but that doesn't mean I'm happy about it. He chose space over me. I could have prevented it, but that would not have helped our relationship. I had to allow him to make his own decision. But how am I supposed to feel about that decision? He gave up a warm body for the cold of space."

"He gave up a lot more than that, Prior. He gave up his property, his fame... he can't even set foot on Kerguelen."

"And I would have given up the chance to have children, Mohab, or did you forget Boroni and Kerguelen can't conceive together. I would have given up being head of the House of Ahrens for him. Choosing to bond with a non-Boroni would have cost me as well. He made his choice, and I wish him luck, but there's no joy in it for me."

"You won't see him when he arrives?"

"No. I'll send him a message of congratulations, but that's it. I won't see him again... ever. We've already had our last words."

"Do you remember what you said to him last?"

"We spoke for eight hours before he left Kerguelen to start his exile. Just before he boarded the spacecraft, he pointed to a star and told me we all were created from stardust. I kissed him and told him to go and find out where we came from."

"That's a sad story," Mohab said. He was going to console her but he could see that there was no need. She was well past any emotional ties to that segment of her life. "What are you so upset about then?"

"I believe that someone is trying to weaken the Guardians by disposing of the field commanders. Venture was forced to kill Sali and he and Jordan and Giles were killed mysteriously. I am under severe scrutiny and close to losing my command. This is all somehow calculated and planned, I'm sure of it. I believe I know who is behind it, but I don't have enough conclusive proof yet. That's why I've sent surveyors out to snoop around," Prior answered.

"I know the situation is tense, but what does it all mean?"

"It means we watch our asses, Mohab," Prior said solemnly. "Because we're the only two commanders left."

5
The Metro District, Capitol City, Central Province, Planet Kerguelen

When Lieutenant Singh was eleven years old, his father told him he was going to the Guardian Academy for his formal education. Singh had never wanted to be a Guardian and didn't understand why his father had pushed for an appointment. Unknown to Singh at the time, his father was infamous for trying to save money at any cost. It was said he could pinch a dime and get eleven cents out of it and would follow a dollar all the way to Hell if there were a chance of him acquiring it. So it was no surprise to anyone that when he found out he could send his son to school at government expense, he would jump at the chance regardless of the child's feelings or desires.

At first, young Singh hated the pomp and ceremony of the academy, but he slowly began to take to the regimen and fellowship the institution had to offer. He participated in varsity sports and numerous cadet clubs and made many friends. He studies improved with his change in attitude and he slowly worked his way up his class standings.

He graduated sixth in a class of thirty-eight and despite warnings against it, he chose to join the combat engineering career field. Singh was assigned to duty with the Second Battalion after completion of the Basic School and thought he had done well in his first three years. He enjoyed his time under Commander Giles and was given many outstanding performance evaluations as a combat engineer and surveyor team leader. And though his time with the Second Battalion was pleasant, the battalion's lack of activity stifled his chances at promotion. When he finally made first lieutenant, three years after graduation, he found that everyone else he graduated the Basic School with were already captains. Singh knew he could make a career for himself in the Corps but he was falling behind and needed to get out of Giles' battalion to make his desires come true.

When Commander Prior approached him with an offer to join her special units, Lieutenant Singh had not even been a veteran of a single major or minor engagement. He was unsure about the offer but Prior had convinced him that she needed his skills in demolitions and reconnaissance and pressed him to at least take a look at it. After all, what did he have to lose?

He did take a good look at it and accepted the challenge she offered. Singh found out in quick order the true nature of what Prior offered and what her special teams actually provided to the Guardian Corps. Besides conducting covert activity, the special units tested newly developed next-generation weapons and special equipment for the Technology Council. But the covert activity missions were what really appealed to the adventurous spirit in his soul. He dove into his training headfirst and after six months, was designated an independent field operative.

As a Guardian, he had witnessed brutality and acts beyond the pale of what was absolutely necessary to make a point in the past, but what he was observing now was different. The men applying the punishment were animals in Singh's eyes… wild and feral animals that needed to be put down. He thought he had learned to adjust to brutality during his tenure as a Guardian, but there were times when seeing acts like these over and over again began to affect him. This was one of those times.

Father Joubert and five Capitol City residents that had been watching a protest against the government's new policies were taken from the crowd earlier in the day and held in seclusion until now. Singh had trailed them and when they came out of the building where they were being held, he followed them and their captors to the Metro Section of the city. In an empty and deserted downtown commerce center, the six people were tied to posts that supported the lights of the air vehicle landing area. The area was empty only because of the late hour. It was just past one in the morning and in less than six hours, the sun would begin to rise and the commerce center would fill with employees soon after. Shoppers would follow and that's when the bodies would be found. Local law enforcement would determine that a radical element had savagely tortured and murdered a priest and five innocent people and thus the tide of dissent would begin to swell and turn against those who were involved with protests, marches and sit-ins.

This was the eighth such incident in less than a week and Commander Prior's suspicions that they were staged seemed to be true. She would now be able to act based on Singh's first-hand account. But he was troubled as to his next course of action. He was tasked with the protection of Father Joubert, but he was also instructed not to engage any forces unless he had backup. Unfortunately, backup was far away. He did have an alternative though. He could call Colonel Thyssen or Commander Ceca and have units from their battalions assist him. If they could get here in time, Singh thought, they could save Father Joubert, the civilians and finally discover who was responsible and end the madness.

Singh checked his surveillance device making sure it was recording the scene from his vantage point and sent out a general alert on the Guardian TACCOM circuit. He waited impatiently for a response and was rewarded when his TACCOM beeped softly in his ear. He answered it quickly.

"Lt. Singh," he said quietly. "Go ahead."

"This is Col. Thyssen. What's happening?"

"I'm at the Metro Section Commerce Center. A priest named Joubert and five civilians are being tortured, Colonel," Singh said. "Capt. Ernst could be here in minutes and I can…"

"Don't do anything!" Thyssen said. His voice was loud and had lost its usual calmness. He took a second to regain his composure and continued. "Don't make any moves until I get there. I'm en route to your location. Stay put. We don't want anyone to get away. I repeat, hold your position. Over?"

"I copy," Singh replied with a sigh.

"I'm less than three minutes out," Thyssen said and ended the transmission.

Singh switched off his TACCOM and continued to observe the landing zone. It appeared as though the torturers were not getting the cooperation from their captives they desired and were stepping up the punishment. Through the long-range infrared monocular device pressed against his eye, Singh could see wires inserted into the victims between spread fingers and they were being zapped with an electrical charge. It seemed as though the amperage was being increased every time the captives gave an inappropriate response to a question and at the rate they were being abused, they wouldn't last long. Singh made a fateful decision and began to make his way down to the landing zone. He knew he could get close to them undetected because of the adaptive camouflage of the combat suit he wore, close enough to take out the six antagonists with his pistol before they could get a clear shot at him. Even if they got him, Colonel Thyssen would arrive and then it would be over. The good guys win.

Singh crept down to the edge of the landing zone and took a deep breath making a mental note of whom he would shoot first and who would be last. By the time he had completely exhaled, his sidearm was drawn and he was sprinting across the tarmac at his best speed. He estimated he was less than fifty yards from them and it would take him two and a half seconds to reach optimal firing position while on the run. Those seconds passed like an eternity as Singh turned his thoughts to his first target. He gave a yell and raised his weapon blasting his first and second target in quick succession. He was amongst the remaining four when he dropped to the tarmac and rolled to his right. The antagonists could not train their weapons on him and held fire long enough to seal their fate.

As he came out of his roll, he aimed his plasma energy pistol and fired on his third and fourth targets and felled them instantly. The remaining two dove away from each other making it impossible for Singh to get them simultaneously, but he didn't need to. He took the short blade from his boot and tossed it at one while firing at the other. The blade found its mark in the throat of the fifth man and his sidearm found the range of the sixth. The sixth man did manage to get off a shot that hit Singh in the shoulder section of his body armor. Though it was a glancing blow, it was fired at close enough range for its power to knock Singh off balance. Singh dropped his weapon as his back hit the blackened surface with a loud smack.

Singh was stunned for a moment and lay motionless, thankful for his protective gear. Though his shoulder felt like it was dislocated, the armor had saved his life. He rolled to his side and surveyed his handiwork. All six antagonists were down and he was still alive… and so it appeared were Father Joubert and the civilians. He had disobeyed orders but he had been successful. Commander Prior would reprimand him but forgive his impropriety. Following orders was secondary to preserving life. Surely Colonel Thyssen would understand that when he arrived. What danced around in his mind was why the shot he took hurt so much. Weapons available to non-Guardians shouldn't have caused so much pain. He looked at one of the fallen weapons and saw that it was a Guardian pistol. Before he could contemplate it further he looked to the sky.

He heard the sound of an air vehicle making a tactical landing and attempted to rise to his feet but failed on his first try. His shoulder was really hurting and he adjusted his body placing his weight on the unaffected side and slowly rose to his feet. By the time he was standing, Colonel Thyssen had exited his air vehicle and was rushing in with his assault team. Singh gingerly walked over to one of the civilians and smiled at her. She was the only one who still was conscious.

"Don't worry, you're safe now. We're Guardians," Singh said as he loosened the restraints that held her.

"Lieutenant!" Thyssen called as he approached and looked at the bodies scattered over the landing zone. "I see you've taken them out."

"Yes, sir," Singh said as he finished releasing the woman. She fell to the ground at his feet and wrapped her arms around his legs for support. She was disheveled and sobbing uncontrollably. Her words of gratitude were unintelligible as Singh stroked her matted blonde hair. He turned to Thyssen and saluted. "I felt I had to, Colonel. The situation was going sideways so I…"

"Disobeyed a direct order," Thyssen finished for him. "That may be the way Cdr. Prior runs an operation, but I don't."

"But this *is* Cdr. Prior's op, Colonel. And she gives me the latitude to act freely and unencumbered," Singh replied as he consoled the woman.

"These… people are witnesses in a terrorist action and should have been taken care of properly. It looks as if I'll have to be more careful who I select for such delicate matters in the future," Thyssen said walking away.

Singh did not understand what Thyssen meant but the woman obviously did. She began to shake and tugged at Singh's legs. Singh was about to ask Thyssen to clarify what he said when two of his Guardians shot the four civilians still tied to the light posts in the chest. Father Joubert received a headshot. Singh screamed and the woman sobbed louder, placing her hands over her ears to shield them from the noise of the weapons. Singh looked at the slumped bodies and frowned from the smell of seared skin and internal organs. He was shocked into silence. He could not believe what he had just witnessed.

"What the hell is going on here, Colonel?" Singh asked still in shock. He took a step back as Thyssen's men aimed their weapons at him.

"You will become part of Cardinal Gregor's plans to right the wrongs of the protestors in this city and of those all over the planet. The men you killed were Guardians. They were new recruits, but Guardians nonetheless... my Guardians. They were trying to find out why the people are resisting the new planetary laws and where certain colleagues of Father Joubert were located. But now, that mission has changed," Thyssen said as he faced Singh.

"I don't understand," Singh said.

"It will appear as though a group of heavily armed dissidents attacked you and these brave young recruits. However, as you and the recruits attempted to save the civilians, they overpowered you with their stolen high-powered weapons. Your efforts will be applauded and will be remembered as one of the great deeds in Guardian history. We'll lay you out for everyone to see... I'll even leave the young lady by your side... a casualty of the brave and noble fight you and those green troops put up," Thyssen orated as he looked to air as if it were inspirational. "It will be glorious. Lt. Singh and a handful of boys killed while trying desperately to protect innocent civilians and a cleric from evil and impious dissidents. It will make for good copy in the news and on the PIL."

"This was all part of a plan?" the woman asked not believing what she had heard. "You're sick! You're sick and twisted! What kind of men are you that plan something like this?"

"I'm a true believer, and this was not part of any plan I came up with, my dear," Thyssen said bending down to pick up Singh's weapon. "What I have to do now is improvise to cover up the obvious. You were a good man, Singh. We could have used you for so much more than this, but that potential is wasted. If you had only followed my orders, you might have survived this night. You were taught at the Academy failure to follow orders and overt compassion will get you killed. You should have remembered those lessons."

Thyssen nodded to his men as he walked towards his air vehicle. They clicked the safeties of their weapons to the OFF position and aimed at Singh and the woman. Singh reached behind him and removed a four by one-inch dowel shaped object and threw it at Thyssen's team members. They managed to get their shots off but the tiny black cylinder exploded less than two feet from them, causing instant death and littered the landing zone with their body parts. The woman was cut in half by a plasma rifle beam, killing her instantly, but Singh was not so lucky. His body armor absorbed some but not all of the blast that hit him and it prolonged his inevitable death. His demise would be agonizing instead instantaneous.

Thyssen and his senior NCO had been knocked to the tarmac from the concussion of the mini-grenade and they picked themselves up off of the ground and quickly dashed to the carnage. A woman severed in half, four of his men blown to bits and Singh, a broken and bloody mess. Thyssen looked around quickly and calculated what he needed to do. If the noise from the previous exchange of gunfire didn't alert local law enforcement in the area and bring bystanders out of the woodwork, the detonation of high explosives would. He needed to do damage control and fast. Singh opened one eye and cackled at Thyssen as the colonel waded through the bodies.

"I-I suppose... you'll have to... do some more... improvising..." Singh said as blood trickled from his mouth.

"Yes, I will," said Thyssen as he dropped Singh's weapon to the tarmac. He removed his own weapon and shot Singh once in the chest and once in the head. He turned to his NCO and pointed to the air vehicle and they jogged to the craft. It took off quickly after they were inside and Thyssen sat fuming as he opened a TACCOM circuit and waited for a reply. He was so hot you could see the steam rising off of him. When a voice answered his call, he spoke. "I need you to clean up a mess at the Metro Section commerce center immediately. Police and other Guardians will be there within fifteen minutes. Do what you can."

Thyssen ended the call and punched his seat. He looked out the window to his right and thought about his next moves. His confederates would not be happy with tonight's results. It was most definitely not a step forward.

"Damn you, Prior," he said barely able to contain his rage. "Your people can't even die right."

6
Cardinal Gregor's Office, Cathedral Prime, Capitol City, Central Province, Planet Kerguelen

Cardinal Gregor looked out of the large window in his office and watched the nuns and priests in the courtyard pass below him on their way to mid-morning prayers in silent reverie. He seemed distant and distracted, but was listening intently to the reports of his secretary, Monsignor Kellan, was delivering. Gregor rubbed the stump that was once his right arm and closed his eyes. He was pleased that the operation his secret group had undertaken earlier in the morning had been carried out, but the loss of Lieutenant Singh was disturbing. Despite the efforts of Colonel Thyssen, someone would want additional inquiries to be made. Singh's family was influential and a full accounting would be necessary to close the book on the incident for good. The cardinal made a mental note to have the archbishop of the Eastern Province visit Singh's parents personally.

In spite of the unforeseen death of Singh, the core of the plan seemed to have worked well. The media was fiercely attacking the activities of dissidents in editorials in the news and in blogs on the PIL and a poll taken this morning reported that the people had given President Ward and Cardinal Gregor a 61% approval rating, up from the 38% they had just a few days before. Public opinion was turning sharply toward a position fully supporting the government, but Gregor was far from feeling confident. More work needed to be done to totally secure their hold on the people.

But what was most prominent on Gregor's mind was Commander Prior. The death of Singh would bring her from the Middle Provinces back to Capitol City and she would start asking questions. She had the instincts of a bloodhound on the trail of a fox and he knew it was only a matter of time before she arrived on his doorstep and her arrival would have nothing to do with the death of her lieutenant. By the time she arrived, she will have found proof of Gregor's dealings and would be there for a reckoning. Gregor hoped that she would take too long to discover the truth, for in a few days, it wouldn't matter what she knew or could prove, for he would have control of the entire planet. And for that control to pass to him, he needed to be ready. Gregor turned to Kellan and waited for his secretary to finish his report.

"… And the Church has sent representatives to console the families of those citizens and Guardians slain last night," the thin and myopic Kellan said looking up from his PDA and over his spectacles.

The secretary wore spectacles because he hated using vision correction eye medicine. The drops stung and irritated the optic nerves for several hours after being administered, but the treatment lasted at least three months. To most people, the pain was worth the result but Kellan avoided discomfort whenever he could and opted for eyeglasses. Most people were surprised that Kellan evinced a low tolerance for pain, especially since he was Gregor's personal secretary, a post he had volunteered for. It seemed obvious to all that he was a glutton for punishment.

"Very well, Monsignor Kellan," Gregor said sitting down at his desk. "That will be all for now."

"Eminence, we have yet to discuss the afternoon agenda," Kellan said. "And you are expected at this evening's vespers."

"Later, Kellan, we'll discuss it later," Gregor said waving his left hand dismissively.

"As you wish, Your Eminence," Kellan said gathering his things and leaving the office.

As Kellan departed, he passed Colonel Thyssen who was just entering the cardinal's chambers. Obviously he had an appointment and priority over the secretary. They nodded to each other as they passed and Kellan shut the door as Thyssen entered the inner office. Cardinal Gregor looked up as Thyssen came in and the Guardian looked around the office to ensure they were alone before he spoke.

"Good morning, Eminence," Thyssen said throwing his overcoat on the back of the nearest chair and walked to the cardinal. He kissed the cardinal's ring and flopped down in a chair and continued. "I trust you slept well last night?"

"Yes, quite well, thank you," Gregor said nodding.

"At least one of us did," Thyssen said sounding exhausted. "Do you realize how much covering up I did and still need to do to clean up our trail?"

"Colonel, calm yourself. This will all work out. Our plans are coming together very nicely. Soon nothing and no one will stand in our way. Trust in the power of the Almighty," Gregor said confidently.

"I only trust in the power of a gun," Thyssen said slapping his holster. "And the only thing that stands in our way is Cdr. Prior... and her cohorts." Gregor could see the very thought of Prior annoyed Thyssen. "She and her... *surveyors*... can foul up our plans by just waking up in the morning. That's why everything went off of the page at the commerce center. I knew we should have used more seasoned Guardians for the operation."

"Don't be ridiculous, Colonel," Gregor said almost laughing. "We got the results we wanted. The people are fearful of the dissidents and no one knows we were behind it. The loss of Singh is tragic, but there was no way for us to know Prior or her Guardians would be so proactive."

"I should have," said Thyssen incensed. He knew he should have prepared for every contingency and was upset about his failure. "Prior's people don't even have to do anything. All they have to do is show up."

"There's no way to bottle them up? This will be over in a few days and then they won't matter. Why don't we buy some of them off?" Gregor asked.

"The numbers in Prior's bank account are longer than train smoke and I doubt any of her surveyors would take a taste anyway. They have a strong sense of comradeship because they are not fully embraced within the Guardian Corps, and don't really trust Guardians outside of their ranks. I'm afraid they're unapproachable," Thyssen said shaking his head. "And Prior makes sure she keeps her ranks free of Central Province natives and anyone vulnerable to bribery."

"I can't say I blame her for excluding Central Province natives from her ranks, can you?" Gregor said raising an eyebrow.

"The slavery issue again," Thyssen scoffed. "How long does the planet have to apologize for it? It's been over for a century."

"A few generations are nothing when you stack it against a millennium of bondage," Gregor said.

"The Boroni only had to endure just over two hundred and eighty years of it, but they seem to have jumped onto the coattails of all of it," Thyssen said.

"Come now, Colonel," Gregor said with a smile. "Your view on the matter is a bit off center. You forget that the first one thousand Boroni were harvested from embryos of the original Western Province female slaves. The resulting children were the last guinea pigs in a long line of ghastly genetic experiments. But whether it was one year or a thousand, the fact remains that slavery is wrong. And we have to live with it as long as there are strong feelings... on both sides of the equation. Derogatory words are still dropped, and don't forget, the entire planet was free... everyone... except them. The whole lot of them were subjugated, beaten, chained and tortured in an effort to see how much they could take. The females were raped, the children were victimized and the males... they were helpless to stop it. They were without hope.

"Yes, I believe we have a lot to apologize for, but they don't need an apology. They just want everyone to allow them to live and prosper in whatever they chose to do, just as we allow everyone else to. We open our arms and embrace the members of every other province, except them. If we embraced them in the same way, there would be a lot less animosity and all of the strong feelings, angst and problems would slowly dissipate."

Gregor spoke as if he was testifying and Thyssen nodded when he finished. But the Boroni did not concern him. The threat of Prior's surveyors did.

"Putting the Boroni aside for a moment, the surveyors are our concern, not former slaves. The surveyors are a proud group, but predictable. Their egos will never allow them to be put in a situation where there would be a question of integrity," Thyssen said with a sigh. "Regardless of what has or what may happen, bribery is out of the question. Prior's vetting system is too rigorous. She handpicked every member herself and they're beyond reproach."

"You make it sound as if they have a disease," Gregor chuckled.

"They do, they have the Prior Strain. It's a highly contagious and virulent disease and everywhere she goes, she spreads it and if it's not contained it will burn a hole through the center of us," Thyssen warned.

"We'll take care of Prior, Colonel," Gregor assured.

"We who? There's no one in the Corps who can take her one-on-one. It was speculation before but after witnessing fifteen years of her exploits it's now a certainty. And Singh's death will only make her more cautious and doubly suspicious of deception. She'll accept my report on Singh for Corps continuity, but she won't believe it for a nanosecond," Thyssen said warily. It was clear to Gregor that he feared Prior.

"We can always attack her with our forces," Gregor said.

Thyssen shook his head. "Her troops are significantly better than other Guardians. A head on assault against them would be unwise. No, suicide is not the way," Thyssen said.

"Then we eliminate them piecemeal," Gregor offered. "Single them out and then kill them off one-by-one. Then we can deal with Prior. Certainly without her vaunted surveyors, any troops she commanded couldn't stand up to you."

Thyssen shook his head. "I don't think so," he said.

"Can't she be defeated using analytical thought or clever schemes?" Gregor asked.

"No," Thyssen said.

"Why not?"

"She can see right through it. She's got more degrees than a thermometer and a lifetime of actual experience. Prior can think you right off of your feet... just before she kills you," Thyssen offered.

"But you are all highly trained," Gregor said.

Thyssen saw that Gregor did not grasp the situation. "Cardinal, did you know that there is a section in the Guardian Advanced Warfare Analysis Course titled, '*Commander Prior*'?" Thyssen asked.

"No, I didn't know the study of Prior's tactics was required by senior Guardian officers," Gregor said.

"There's a section with the same title in the Intermediate Warfare Analysis Course as well," Thyssen added. "When I took the course I was surprised myself."

"Then you know her tactics," Gregor said.

"Not exactly," Thyssen said. "Those sections discuss ideas more than tactics. She has no set tactics, or rules of conducting battle. She never fights the same way twice."

"But your knowledge of her should give you an advantage," Gregor reasoned. "You've read all about her style."

"We're not talking about a game, Cardinal," Thyssen said. "We are talking about combat. Combat is like a hangover. You can read about it for years, but until you've experienced it, you have no conception what it's really like. The same goes for Prior."

"She's unpredictable, you mean?" Gregor asked.

"Yes. That's the only thing about her that is constant and unvarying. After I completed those courses, I found myself in fear of Prior," Thyssen said. "And that realization was unsettling."

"I think I understand," Gregor said.

"I don't believe you do," Thyssen said. "The reason I was fearful was something my instructor Col. Justin said."

"Col. Justin? The hero of the Battle of the Twin Pillars?" Gregor queried.

"Yes," Thyssen nodded. "He said he was glad he never had to face Prior in combat."

"Why?"

"He said she was a pure battlefield commander. She is capable of taking her best troops and beating yours, or taking your best troops and beating hers," Thyssen said solemnly. "The Guardian acronym for COMBAT is: Confidence, Orders, Morale, Battle lines And Training. Prior's version is: Coordination, Observations, Mobility, Blood, And Tactics. You can see the difference and her results speak for themselves. She has been entirely successful every time out."

Gregor stood up and looked out of the window. As he gazed out, he spoke to Thyssen. "The desert nomads of the Middle Provinces have a saying, Colonel: *A lion can be killed by the jackal if the jackal knows where to bite*," Gregor said.

"Where do we bite Prior?" Thyssen asked.

"In the heart," the cardinal said with confidence.

"I hope you're right," Thyssen said with some doubt.

Gregor turned and faced him. "Absolutely. The Prior Strain will become a terminal disease... for her," Gregor said with a smile. "I'm confident that Prior will not be a problem for much longer."

"When it comes to Prior, the only thing I'm confident in is that there will be chaos," Thyssen said.

"I am confident. Very confident," Gregor said turning back to the window and watched a pair of nuns scurrying across the courtyard. "I'm confident in the outcome because I don't trust her any more than she trusts me."

7
Coastland, The Middle Provinces, Planet Kerguelen

Commander Prior stood on the highlands looking down on the remains of what was once the jewel of the Middle Provinces, the city of Coastland. Lupo lay beside her, his pointed ears twitched as he listened to the sounds of air vehicles above and people in the valley below. The half-wolf's olfactory was working overtime processing the scents of stray animals nearby causing him to occasionally turn his massive head in one direction or another. The cloudless sky and warm breeze gave the region an air of tranquility but hid the true and current demeanor of the Middle Provinces.

Just a few days ago, Coastland was a picturesque city bustling with vitality. The modern shops and stores, five-star restaurants and hotels, and nightclubs and casinos had brought all of the elite class to the city. The beauty and cleanliness of the seaside resort had always impressed visitors and vacationers and at times the city was overrun with outsiders. Colorful tropical birds roosted and sang in the neatly landscaped gardens of the red tiled stucco houses. It was the signature stamp of the province, along with the pastel colors the residents painted their homes. The tidy inhabitants had prospered through centuries of commerce and trade and were in sharp contrast to the less cultured environs found a few miles away across the Auric Straights in the Southern Province.

Recent government policies and a touch of good old fashion psychological manipulation had caused many in the Southern Province to readdress the disparity between the two cultures and a border clash had ensued. It was this trouble that brought Prior to Coastland, but she was no stranger to the city.

Prior was always delighted to visit Coastland and relieve the tensions of her occupation. Even Lupo seemed rejuvenated as he splashed in the cool waters of the Tri-Province Sea. She stayed at the Starlight Resort Beach Club and Hotel and fondly remembered the maitre d'hotel, Tuco, who had the uncanny ability to speak any regional dialect required, making his guests feel at home and their stay more comfortable. Tuco always provided first-class service and had made special accommodations for Lupo. When she had vacationed here with Omega many years ago, Tuco made the couple feel as though they were the only persons in the world and Prior and Omega were in turn polite, cordial and friendly to him. They were a refreshing change to the regular clientele of the hotel and the love that flourished between them was in full bloom in Coastland.

But everything changes and not always for the better. She and Omega were no more and according to her Guardians, Tuco had either been killed or taken captive by the invading forces. She had sent a few men out to find out for sure, but right now all she wanted was to feel the sun and remember those glorious times she spent at the Starlight Club.

The Starlight Club was a delightful place. It was spacious, with verandas and snow-white tables with cool pseudo-wicker chairs around them. Plus, there was plenty of the safflower oil brandy that she favored. Omega had even begun to acquire a taste for it, but she knew he only drank it because she did.

Prior had been amazed at how much the natives of Coastland ate. They would devour plate after plate of klisterand, a prickly skinned but surprisingly tender and delicious edible root indigenous to the region and a local delicacy. It would take an eighteen member wait staff to serve all of the courses and meals made with the tasty tubers. Dinner would last at least three hours and Prior was not at all shocked that most of the people weighed over three hundred pounds.

The beautiful and benevolent dark skinned and blonde haired people were now suffering for all of their sumptuous and extravagant living. Their free-spirited way of life had allowed a haven for large groups of anti-Federalists and anti-Federal Church sects to develop in and around Coastland, many of whom were supported by well meaning, but politically naïve entrepreneurs. For the most part, Coastland and the rest of the Middle Provinces were loyal to the established system but felt it was a person's right to express displeasure if they believed the government's policies were wrong. It was these factors that had prompted Cardinal Gregor and Senator Bacor to insist federal law enforcement officers, supported by provincial police of the Southern Province, storm into Coastland and surrounding areas and take control of the city. It didn't take much pressure on President Ward for him to fold and sign the order authorizing the action.

Local officials were arrested and the people were stripped of all that they owned and the city was placed under martial law. It was claimed that the citizens of Coastland were abetting treason and sedition. The envious Southern Province wasted no time in looting Coastland and returning the booty to their coffers. Though the Judiciary and Technology Council voiced dissent and officially denounced the action, it was only words. The Middle Provinces were unsupported and left to the mercy of the occupying force. The only hope for them was the Guardians.

Against instructions to the contrary, Commander Mohab moved his battalion into the area and attacked the federal and Southern Province units. Supported by Prior's Guardians, they quickly stabilized the area and forced the invaders to retreat to the Southern Province border. Prior recruited five thousand Middle Province natives and planned a lightning counterstrike, executed by her operations officer, Major St. Jacques. It crushed a potential counter-offensive and stalled the federal law enforcement officers in their tracks. The campaign was so successful and swift President Ward ordered all federal forces out of the Southern Province. He hoped the gesture would save him any more embarrassment and allow some type of closure to the hostilities. Guardian Central Command ordered Prior to assume overall command of the stabilization force and negotiate a ceasefire agreement before Mohab and St. Jacques crossed deeper into the Southern Province and continued their campaigns.

It took Prior a mere ninety minutes to prepare and have the principles sign an agreement ending hostilities between the two provinces. The governor of the Southern Province had been reluctant to accept the terms in the document at first but quickly changed his mind. Something about the fact Prior was willing to allow Mohab and St. Jacques to continue the campaign starting in Champlain, the capitol of the Southern Province, convinced the governor to sign the treaty.

The majority of the money stolen was recovered and the Southern Province also paid for the damages sustained in Coastland. The monetary fine would hurt the province but the political leaders had little choice but to concede to Prior. The terms of the treaty went into effect immediately, but Prior would not be in the region to see them carried through. She had to return to Capitol City and follow up on the death of Singh and discover what had become of Addison. Thyssen's report was sketchy and full of holes and she wanted to look into it herself. The loss of Singh was unacceptable and she was sure there was more to his death than was written in the report. Additionally, she needed to contact her brother Poul. She had put off meeting with him and there many things she had to clear up with her twin. She took a deep breath and brought her thoughts back to the heights above Coastland.

Major St. Jacques stood next to her on the hill staring off toward the east. A few hundred miles away was the Holy city of Shiloh, the birthplace of religion on Kerguelen and the most sacred region on the planet. With the exception of the Western Province, Shiloh was the sole area spared during the last Provincial Wars, and had been protected by the Guardians during the entire conflict. Every religion ever conceived on Kerguelen believed its roots spawned from Shiloh, including the Federal Church. The great prophet, Virgil, believed to be the son of the Almighty, and his disciples taught the lessons of love, benevolence, kindness and forgiveness in Shiloh. Though they were all persecuted and eventually arrested and killed, their message found expression in those that followed. Every year, millions visited Shiloh on pilgrimages to pray and pay homage to Virgil and the disciples and give thanks for their sacrifices.

St. Jacques was as quiet as ever and seemed as though he were a statue. Like all Boroni males, he stood over six-foot three inches and weighed in at a solid and muscular two hundred and fifty-five pounds. He sported the signature long hair of the race that was twisted into a ponytail. Prior had known the twenty-six year old since he was born and his family worked several sections of land on Prior's property. His great-grandfather was believed to have struck the first blow in the slave revolt and was one of Kel's chief lieutenants. Through his own initiative, intelligence and unique capabilities, history had repeated itself. St.

Jacques was Prior's operations officer and third in command of the surveyors, and designated Chief Architect.

A fierce and relentless combatant, he was nicknamed the Mongoose and wherever he was you could be sure there would be action. He was highly disciplined and demanded the same of the Guardians under his command. Punishments for infractions of regulations, regardless of the size, were severe but those who served with him would not have had it any other way.

As Lupo scratched at the soft earth of the hill with his paw, Prior turned to St. Jacques. "Sit with me, Jack," she said lowering herself to the grass allowing Lupo to rest his head in her lap. St. Jacques joined her but remained rigid as if he were sitting at attention. "Relax, Jack. This may be the last time you get to do it for a while."

He looked at her, smiled and loosened up a bit. "Forgive me, Commander, but I have trouble relaxing in the field. I can't do it until we return to Tri-Rivers after completing a mission. It's a flaw in my character I haven't been able to overcome," he said in a strong Boroni accent.

The accent was nearly identical to that of those from the North Island Province and prevalent when a Boroni spoke the Kerguelen standard language. It was a comfort for her to hear the masculine tones and reminded her of home.

"It's nice to know you've gained a sense of humor," Prior said with a smile.

"I wasn't trying to be humorous," he replied blandly.

That was probably true Prior thought. St. Jacques had never told a joke or funny story in his life, and probably never would. He didn't know how. Still, the way he spoke sometimes caused others to find him very humorous.

"I hear you want to bring some privates up on charges," Prior said looking out over the hill.

"Yes, I do," he said settling into the ground.

"They're good Guardians, Jack."

"One of them is a undisciplined rogue and the other has a drinking problem," St. Jacques corrected.

"True, but they know what they're doing in the field. They're better than all of the second lieutenants we have… and some of the first lieutenants, for that matter," Prior countered.

"If they could transfer that discipline to their everyday lives they would be majors instead of privates."

"They got themselves into a twist, eh?" Prior asked with a grin well aware that the eccentricities of the privates had pushed him to his limit.

"While they were on patrol, they recovered two bottles of wine and captured two federal police officers," St. Jacques said.

"So what?" Prior said. "They should be commended."

"And they would have been, but then they screwed up when they got drunk on the wine and started to use excessive force to get information out of their prisoners," St. Jacques explained.

"So I guess there's no more wine," Prior quipped.

"No," St. Jacques said not realizing she was joking.

"Listen, Jack, I know they're a bit overzealous, but they're also exceptional Guardians, and they're only nineteen years old. Don't you remember having any youthful exuberance, Jack? Don't you remember being young?" she said with a smile.

"There's no such thing as a young Guardian. Untried, yes, untested… possibly, but not young," he said. "They didn't need to prove they were superior to those policemen. The fact they're Guardians makes that evident."

"Jack…"

"They're arrogant, Commander."

"Perhaps, but formal charges are excessive, I think. And confinement is too severe a punishment," Prior said.

"You may be right, Commander," he agreed reluctantly.

"Place them on three days of 'piss and ponk' and turn them over to Capt. Ernst for extra duty when you return to Tri-Rivers. That should be adequate," Prior said.

St. Jacques considered her punishment and agreed that it would suffice. There was always more to what she said anyway. Her words always had an underlying meaning, intent and purpose. In this case, her punishment would ripple through the ranks and have a definite effect. Being placed on bread and water was harsh while operating in the field. A Guardian went through calories in the field like an albino went through sunscreen at the beach. It was a hard punishment and St. Jacques was sure the privates would have rather been confined or lost pay instead. Prior used the Boroni term for the punishment to remind St. Jacques of what it meant to her and to remind him of how their ancestors had been treated in captivity. Bread and water was the staple given to slaves undergoing punishment and the meager food rations had been augmented by other more traditional means to keep the slaves in line. Beatings, chains and branding were more commonplace, but bread and water was more effective. An adult Boroni needed huge caloric intakes every few days to stay alive and healthy, without it, their bodies would shut down and they would die.

"Very well, Commander," nodded St. Jacques in agreement.

"I'll speak to them before I leave, Jack. They won't be a problem in the future," Prior said. "It's our responsibility to maintain discipline, isn't it, Major?"

"Yes it is, Commander," he said. He was positive all of his men would remember it. He turned to her. "Do you have something else more pressing to discuss with me, Commander?"

She remained silent for a moment, closing her eyes and lifting her head to the warm sunlight. She leaned in and kissed Lupo on the head and he growled softly in response. She scratched his head and spoke to St. Jacques in the Boroni language.

"<We're in perilous times, Jack. I don't know how bad, but I do know we need to be vigilant against deception, even from those we think we can trust>," she said in a strong accent.

"<Why do you use our native tongue, sister? We are not in danger of being overheard>," he replied.

"<No one can hear what you don't say, brother>," she responded.

The Boroni language was a derivative of the language spoken by the original natives of the Western Province. It was known only to the Boroni and was passed down from parents and elders to the children. No formal schooling had ever been established to teach it though the children were expected to be proficient in it by the time their training in the use of their enhanced senses was completed. The slave masters never condescended low enough to even bother to learn the rudiments of the guttural nonsense as they called it. Of the twenty-five dialects of Kerguelen, the Boroni language was the only one that remained unknown beyond its borders, and no Boroni would ever teach it to an outsider. To do so would mean death. It was the only thing that was truly their own and had never been taken away. Every Boroni was proud of that fact.

"<Quite profound, but why the subterfuge>?" he asked.

"<Danger, Jack, danger. There are subdued forces at work. We must take care>," she cautioned. "<I have prepared an order for you to take command of the surveyors until Col. Arcuri returns from her mission if something happens to me>."

"<Why would something happen to you>?"

"<I have to do some things that may get me killed, so I prepared a succession order>," Prior explained.

"<I have heard rumors of a dark beast>," St. Jacques said.

"<What rumors>?"

"<My sources tell me The Argent has returned>," he said with a look of terror on his face. It was something she had never seen before and it was obvious he was truly scared.

The tale of The Argent was one of the oldest in Kerguelen folklore. Its history could be traced back far beyond the time of Koenig, possibly in excess of ten thousand years. Most believed The Argent came from the time of the Holy Scriptures. When exactly was irrelevant. What mattered was that many people believed The Argent was real. They were powerful and unstoppable beings, sometimes mortal and sometimes immortal depending on who was telling the story, and created by The Second, and could be identified by the silver-colored tunics they wore. They were filled with all of The Second's hate and rage and more powerful than any single being or creature on Kerguelen and they only had one goal: To wreak unbridled havoc upon the planet in retribution for The Second being banished to the Netherworld. Scientific scholars rationalized that it was just another legend or spook story to tell around campfires, but even the most learned could not refute the reference to The Argent in the eighth chapter of the *Origin*, the first book of the *Old Covenant*, the Holy Scripture of Kerguelen. It read:

"And The Second summoned all of the hate and disdain he had for the Almighty into a massive swirl of darkness. From that manifestation he

created The Argenta, sending it out to the provinces to pillage and plague The Seed of Kerguelen."

The story continued by retelling the tale of the many lives lost in the fight to save Kerguelen from The Argenta. It cited the bravery of the grandchildren of Astral and Luna but despite their courage, they were losing the battle. Many years passed, how many are unknown, but after a time the Almighty awoke Katana. Katana had traveled to a far away corner of Kerguelen with her twin brother Kullen. It is believed that this region was the Western Province. Katana had been in a self-induced hibernation since she and Kullen finished delivering God's Laws to The Seed of Kerguelen. The Almighty spoke to Katana via dreams as she slept telling her she had much to do. Katana awoke from her slumber and once resurrected she gathered a thousand Kerguelen, each province equally represented, and defeated The Argenta. The story concludes with the Almighty appearing as a vision to the one thousand souls that fought with Katana. The Almighty commended them for their faith and told them that as long as they maintained their faith, She would never abandon them. Katana would come back whenever she was needed and when she did, this second coming would usher in a new age.

Throughout the history of Kerguelen, whenever an unexplained destructive force threatened the planet, The Argent, as it was now called, was blamed and whoever stopped it was considered to be the next Katana. Who could say that these believers were wrong? Even *The Book of Prophecy*, the last book in the *New Covenant* of the Holy Scriptures, foretells of a time when The Argenta will walk Kerguelen unchecked and during this time of planetary turmoil, the Almighty will invade Katana's dreams and awaken her once more. Some believe this resurrection happened during the reign of Koenig and that the Guardians were the embodiment of Katana. Others believe that The Argent was still waiting for their chance to fulfill the wishes of their creator. They would strike at a time when the people's faith was at its lowest and with a lack of faith in the Almighty, The Argent would strike their final blow and destroy Kerguelen.

"<Jack, my dear provincial brother>," Prior said placing a hand on his shoulder. "<We've both heard and read the stories of The Argent and Katana before. We've been saturated with them ever since we were children>."

"<They are not unfounded tall tales, sister>," he said grimly.

"<Jack>," she said in a reassuring tone. "<The Argent is an old wife's tale meant to scare children into behaving correctly. There are no groups of boogey men out there waiting to pounce on us. It's just a story>."

"<I've got evidence, sister. I beg you to listen to me. The Argent is a real entity>," St. Jacques said. "<The Argent murdered Commanders Jordan and Giles>."

Prior could tell that he was serious in his belief, but had to smile at his strong superstitious streak. He seemed child-like and in desperate need of comfort. She rose to her feet and took his hand and helped him up. She brought him close to her and despite his height she found his lips, kissed them softly and then took his hands in hers.

"<Dear Jack>," she said softly. He tried to speak but she put her fingers against his lips. "<The Argent *is not* real. Trust me. Have faith in the Almighty and believe in Katana if you have to, but forget about an army of demons from the Netherworld coming to get you. It's not going to happen>."

"<How can you be so sure? My sources say that The Argent is the *real* cause of the unrest. Anyone else involved is just a pawn>," St. Jacques said refusing to let go of his fear. "<How can you be positive that the story is just legend and not fact>?"

"<I have to confront Cardinal Gregor soon. I believe he is the pawn that you refer to. I have a source of my own that told me he is a Summoner, a priest that can conjure demons. I don't believe in such things, but if Exorcists and Summoners are fact, that means I'll have to face The Argent sooner or later. And that would be problematic>," Prior said.

"<Why is that>?" St. Jacques asked.

Prior looked into his eyes, saw her reflection in them and hoped her face didn't reveal the dread she now felt inside. "<I'm not Katana>."

8
The Technology Council Headquarters, Capitol City, Central Province, Planet Kerguelen

Prior's boots emitted a sharp cadence on the synthetic stone walkway leading to the entrance of the Technology Council Headquarters building. As she and her canine companion neared the doors, they received curious glances from people passing them and from others exiting the structure. The sight of a Guardian at the Technology Council was a rare occurrence despite their years of close coordination. Prior's gait was very brisk and Lupo moved at a slow jog to keep pace with her.

It wasn't her intention to come here but an urgent message from Lieutenant Addison had changed her plans and upon her return to Capitol City, Prior immediately made her way to the complex.

The building was constructed a little over fifty years ago but remained one of the most stunning architectural achievements on the planet. Only the Kerguelen Spire was more recognizable. The building was located on the western shore of the Cannon River, a tributary of the Tri-Rivers systems. The Cannon River curved and flowed eastward until it emptied into Province Bay and was a great attraction to tourists and locals. During the Season of Growth, the warm weather kept the shoreline filled with family picnics, children playing and others watching sailboats and crew teams working out on the placid waters. It was a beautiful and relaxing setting and many a person came to the shores of the Cannon just to rejuvenate after a long and stressful day before heading to their homes.

The Technology Council facilities stretched for nearly three miles along the banks of the river and the administrators constructed several public areas for the citizens to use. Bandstands for concerts, stages for children's performers and small sports pitches were mixed with picnic areas and garden paths. The designers of the complex felt there was no reason why man-made construction projects couldn't mesh with nature. Opponents to the facilities argued that such an immense project would cause an irreversible negative effect to the ecology of the area, but the architects and planners were confident that their civil engineering masterpiece would be nothing more than a backdrop to the environment. Ecologists continued their protests but the Technology Council mega-facility was just the first of many such works that would follow planet-wide in the decades after its completion.

When it was finished, those for and against the project marveled at its beauty. Though intricate in its design, the facility had managed to become part of the landscape. To look at it, one would think the complex was natural and had grown out from the soil of the planet. It had been such a seamless integration the news media had called the complex man-made nature.

Despite its breathtaking landscape, the Technology Council did not pick the Cannon River location solely for its esthetic qualities. The broad river provided the numerous laboratories in the complex the vast quantities of water needed for experiments and research. The discharged effluent from the labs was sent to a state-of-the-art water treatment facility costing twelve billion credits. The discharged water under went four stages of special processing before it returned to the river and then out into the bay. The tremendous effort and astronomical cost would be worth it in the end. The lessons learned from the treatment center provided an untold wealth of knowledge to aid in cleaning the planet's water sources. In two decades, ninety percent of Kerguelen's water resources were restored to healthy conditions.

Prior entered the administration section of the complex through a set of transparent automatic doors with Lupo trailing. The administrative section was a tremendous glass tower in the center of the complex and in spite of its size, did not obscure the view of the Cannon River from any part of Capitol City. She quickly made her way through the large foyer toward a bank of elevators. She pressed the call button and waited patiently as Lupo slowly traveled across the marble floors to her side.

She looked around the multi-colored lobby and it reminded her of one of the federal art museums. The walls were covered with various styles of oil paintings and frescos done by the scientists and engineers of the Technology Council. It seemed that many of them were throwbacks to the Renaissance Age of Kerguelen when scientists, engineers and architects were also accomplished artists and sculptors. Technically, the pieces were very well done, but they lacked true artistic freedom. They just didn't shock, awe or bring out any emotion in those who viewed them. The pieces were painted so they did not offend the sensibilities. Everyone would like them. But no true artist cared what others thought. He painted to convey an ideal or message. They were rebellious and tried to evoke an emotional response in whoever viewed their work, and these did not.

Prior shivered slightly from the building's cool temperature as Lupo looked up at her. She patted him on the head and smiled at him. As the doors to the elevator opened, she jerked her head.

"Come, Lupo. We've got to see some friends," she said.

He barked and followed her inside as his throaty response echoed throughout the cavernous entryway. Several startled people turned and were surprised at the sight of a canine in the building. They continued to watch Prior and Lupo until the doors shut.

Prior tilted her head upwards and spoke in a clear voice. "Sub-level twelve, please," she said.

"Would you like to listen to music or view the news, ma'am?" said an interactive male computer voice possessing a North Island Province accent.

"No, thank you," Prior said. "Just take me to the requested level, please."

"Very well. Please place your coin in front of the optical scanner," the voice said. Prior removed a platinum coin from her pocket and waved it in front of the scanner and the panel illuminated in green. "Thank you, Commander Prior. Stand-by."

Lupo looked around for the source of the voice that did not belong to his mistress and became agitated when he didn't find it. He barked loudly and Prior patted his head. He ceased barking and sat quietly on the floor.

"Is there a canine animal in the car with you, Commander?" the voice asked.

"Yes. Access my file for authorization, please," Prior said.

"Searching," the voice said. Three seconds later, the voice said, "Search complete. Canine authorized."

"Proceed to requested destination," Prior said.

"Proceeding," the voice said.

Five seconds later, the elevator proceeded downwards and Prior rubbed the coin in her hand. It had been six months since she had been in the subterranean section she was going to. It was the area known as Sigma 4 and was only accessible to a select group of engineers, technicians and scientists on Kerguelen. Sigma 4 was part fraternity and part think tank and a place where some of the brightest minds of the planet exchanged ideas. Prior had been admitted to Sigma 4 after she obtained her doctorate and accolades as a professional surveyor and as the elevator came to a stop, she wondered why Lieutenant Addison had requested a rendezvous here.

"Sub-level twelve, Commander," the voice said.

"Thank you," Prior answered and exited the elevator.

Prior walked through the carpeted hallway and waved her coin at a scanner when she came to a solid metal door. It opened and a young man greeted her. He was no more than twenty and looked as if he were from the Eastern Province. He was not very tall and seemed delicate to Prior, but he had bright intelligent eyes. Prior didn't know who he was but his eyes were familiar to her.

A thin hand emerged from underneath the purple robe he wore and he stuck it out sharply intending to shake her hand. He pulled it back as quickly as he offered it when Lupo let loose a fierce growl and stepped between the man and Prior. He raised his hands and backed away in defense. Prior shook her head and smiled in an attempt to calm the young man down. She tapped Lupo on the back and spoke to him in a commanding voice.

"Lupo... out!" she said. The canine ceased growling and walked around her once and stopped at her right ankle. She scratched behind his ears and then patted him once lightly. He sat down and seemed tamed but his eyes remained locked on the man. "I'm sorry. He's a little overprotective of his mistress."

"I-I understand... I think," the man said slowly removing a handkerchief. He wiped his forehead and introduced himself. "I'm Reyes, aide to the Chief Technologist."

"I'm…" Prior began.

"Cdr. Prior. Yes, I know," Reyes finished for her. She held out her hand and he tentatively extended his, looking at Lupo all the way. He shook her hand vigorously and he beamed with delight. He acted as if he was meeting his childhood hero. "This is an honor, Commander. I've been anxious to see you again. I could hardly contain myself when the chief technologist said you were coming."

"See me again?" Prior asked confused by his statement.

"Yes, I've wanted to see you again ever since… well, it was a long time ago," Reyes said with sadness and joy all wrapped together.

"I don't understand. What was a long time ago?" Prior asked tilting her head.

"The Guardians came to my village when I was a little boy," Reyes said.

"Which village?" she asked.

"Domtar, in the Eastern Province," he answered.

"Domtar," Prior said softly. Her brow furrowed for a moment as she recalled the name of the insignificant little community of fishermen and their families.

The village of Domtar was filled with one of the last groups of holdouts refusing to fully integrate the Federal Church into their lives. They accepted the Church, but still wanted to practice their own ancient and traditional religion, which was legal under the planetary constitution. They believed in a male deity who was murdered by food poisoning while in his mortal form. The followers of the sect worshipped jade statuettes in his likeness and would sit fresh food and water at the base of the idols to show their respect and faith, even when food was scarce, as it often was in Domtar. A few of the surrounding villages, afraid that Domtar's failure to convert to the Federal Church would reflect undesirably on them as well, pooled their meager resources together and hired a group of five hundred mercenaries to convince the people of Domtar to convert totally to the Federal Church or die. There would be no other options. The 8,500 residents of Domtar were passive, pious and defenseless… and would not convert. It would be a wonderful slaughter.

A detachment of 105 Guardians was rushed into the area to protect the villagers until a settlement could be brokered. The Guardians assigned were a mixture from every battalion and among their ranks was a green combat engineer second lieutenant on her first major deployment. Her name was Prior and she had graduated from the Academy six months earlier. She was full of training, discipline and regulations, but no experience. That would all change at Domtar. At the Battle of Domtar, the innocence of a young woman would die and the legend of a warrior would be born.

The Guardians arrived too late to initiate negotiations. By the time they reached Domtar, all but 400 of the villagers were dead. Guardian Elder Antoine, then a colonel, commanded the company of Guardians and devised a plan to rescue the remaining villagers and get out of the area.

On the 16th day of the second month of Harvest in the year 2819, one of the most horrifying and deadliest Guardian engagements in recent history ensued. During the two-day battle, forty-seven Guardians were killed and another thirty-eight sustained serious combat injuries. Only three of the twelve officers present weren't either wounded or dead and Antoine was too incapacitated to lead. He and the rest of the senior leadership had gone down early in the fray.

The officers still on their feet were unsure of what to do, all but young Second Lieutenant Prior. Though wounded herself and junior to the other officers, she took command of what was left of the beleaguered company and against recommendations to retreat, she ordered them to dig in. Outnumbered nearly five-to-one, the Guardians held their ground and repelled numerous assaults by the mercenaries. When their weapons charges were almost depleted, she ordered a counter-assault with combat knives and drove the mercenaries off during a savage hand-to-hand struggle and rescued 387 of the remaining 400 villagers.

After the battle, Prior was awarded the Humanitarian Medal, the Medal of Valor, and the Legion of Honor with palm leaves. She had been credited with fifty-six confirmed kills, single handedly, and twelve more probable kills. She was promoted to captain and given an education sabbatical during which she completed the first of her two master's degrees. During her studies she met and fell in love with Omega. After the sabbatical, she was assigned as the engineering officer of the First and Second Battalions, commanding 36 combat engineers and surveyors. It was during this posting that she first encountered Venture who was a company commander in the First Battalion.

Shortly after her new assignment, Prior was awarded the Star of Kerguelen for her actions at Domtar and her career skyrocketed. The Battle of Domtar elevated her to greatness within the Corps and everything in her tenure as a Guardian was a direct result of those two bloody days. Though many Kerguelens have never heard of Domtar or even recall the crisis, Prior would never forget that so many had to die for her inner warrior to be born. At the same time, she had forever lost her fragile youth and remaining innocence. Her battle scars would heal but the gashes cut deep in her soul and the pain she had from them would never go away.

But Reyes had survived. He could not have been more than five or six years old at the time of the battle. He had been a mere child amongst all that carnage and death. Prior smiled inwardly at that thought. She had been only eighteen years old herself.

"You saved me and my mother," Reyes said. "Without you… well… thank you."

"I was but one of many Guardians at Domtar," she said modestly.

"You carried me while my mother ran behind us. She fell and you picked her up as well and carried us to safety even after you got shot. You were so strong. I had never seen anyone so strong then… or since," he said.

"How do you know it was me?" she asked.

He reached under his robe. "You gave me this," he said handing her an object.

It was a Surveyor's patch. She took it and felt the rough material between her fingers and smiled remembering how proud she was when she received it. She recalled that she had given a small boy she carried the patch to distract and occupy his attention. Prior had all but forgotten about it. She gave the patch back to Reyes and he returned it to his pocket.

"I'm glad you've done well for yourself," Prior said returning to her emotionally detached demeanor. "Your mother must be very proud."

"Yes, well, you know how mothers are," Reyes said.

"Yes, I do," Prior nodded.

Actually she had no clue what Reyes meant. Boroni mothers were not like their Kerguelen counterparts. They did not fawn over their offspring. They were hard on them and for the most part derogatory in their dealings with their children, at least until they were old enough and strong enough to learn how to fight and hunt. Prior couldn't say that her mother had been proud of her. At best, her mother had been satisfied with Prior's accomplishments, and for a Boroni mother, that was as close to pride as you could get.

Reyes stepped closer to Prior and embraced her. He quickly let go and backed away and she seemed embarrassed by his gesture. He cleared his throat and pointed down the hallway.

"I know your time is vital," he said. "One of your officers and the chief technologist are waiting. Follow me."

They entered a lounge area and Prior walked to Mackenzie and the women interlocked arms. Mackenzie was a few inches taller than Prior but it wasn't from the high heels she wore. Even in bare feet Mackenzie was two inches taller and her statuesque build was something Prior had always admired about Mackenzie, one of many things. Mackenzie was intelligent, tough-minded and like Prior, didn't care what others thought about her. Prior turned to Addison and interlocked arms with her as well. Mackenzie poured all of them a drink and handed them out. Prior took the Anise whiskey and sat down on a couch. The three women silently took a drink and Addison sat her glass down and stood in front of Prior.

"Commander, forgive me for asking you here, but what I have to show you is volatile," Addison said.

"What have you got?" Prior asked. She cocked her head to one side. "But first of all, how do you have access to Sigma 4, Addison?"

"Later, Prior," Mackenzie said. "Listen to what she has."

"Very well. Go ahead," Prior said.

"I managed to get into Cathedral Prime and access Cardinal Gregor's databases. Your suspicions were right on. He has been working in secret to stir up trouble planet-wide. He also worked with someone else to have Archbishop Cornelia assassinated. I have it all here on this data stick," Addison said handing it Prior.

"Have you seen this?" Prior asked Mackenzie as she held the data stick.

"Yes, and I'm afraid we have a big problem," Mackenzie nodded. "But we have other things to talk about as well."

It had been some time since she had seen Mackenzie, but the chief technologist looked the same as she had when Prior first met her ten years earlier. She seemed ageless and unchanged and there was no cosmetic augmentation apparent. She either had the planet's best plastic surgeon or the best genetics a woman could ask for. She only looked a few years older than Prior and that was impossible. Only Boroni held onto their youthful look beyond the age of fifty.

"What other things?" Prior asked.

"We have to discuss the Celeron," Mackenzie said. "And Addison is here because she knows what she obtained is vital to the goals of the Celeron."

"They must be alerted of Gregor's dealings at once," Addison said.

"You know about the Celeron?" Prior asked.

"Everything… and nothing," Mackenzie said.

"Have you read the scripture?" Addison asked.

"No I haven't," Prior said.

"Do so, Prior, and be thorough. It may be the most important document you've ever read," Mackenzie said.

"I don't understand all this," Prior said. "How do you two know about these things?"

"The Celeron have many people who assist them in their work," Addison said.

"Like Howard," Prior said.

"Yes. He and young Addison here are brother and sister," Mackenzie said. "I also am an aide to the Celeron."

"Why do you help the Celeron?" Prior asked. "They don't even allow females to visit the chateau. Not many anyway. They're a bunch of throwbacks and Neanderthals."

Mackenzie smiled. "But a vital group of Neanderthals," Mackenzie said. "I understand how you feel, Prior, but what they do is important to the survival and prosperity of Kerguelen. You must understand that."

"How long have you been involved with them, Addison?" Prior asked.

"About six years I guess," Addison replied.

"And you?" Prior asked Mackenzie.

"I suppose I've always been involved with the Celeron," Mackenzie said with a shrug. "I've aided them in numerous ways since I was about ten years old."

"Ten? Why would you do that?" Prior asked.

"You've met The Seven, haven't you?" Mackenzie asked and Prior nodded. "Well, the leader of The Seven and chairman of the Celeron is my father."

9
The threshold of the Kerguelen Star System's Heliosphere

San Mariner slowly arced and banked and began its entry into the Kerguelen star system. The ship was functioning satisfactorily, but Omega was still a bit anxious. There had been a series of unfamiliar bangs and shudders coming from the after portions of the ship and Omega prayed his spacecraft would hold together. His eyes darted back and forth to the readouts in front of him, ready for one system or another indicated to drop out. He averted his glance for a moment to look at Dela. She had been on her feet for the past two days and insisted on resuming her duties. They both knew she still needed more rest but they also were aware that Omega couldn't make the transition from interstellar space to the Kerguelen star system alone. Though the ship uplinks had been re-established, the navigational computer was still not functioning at full capacity. If it crashed, piloting and navigating the ship solo would be impossible.

Omega switched his gaze to the forward window and stared in awe at the brilliant flashes sparking intermittently before him. Without looking at a navigational position reading, any deep space star sailor would know exactly where the ship was. The ship was at the edge of the heliosphere, the extreme edge of a star's influence. Potentially harmful radiation from deep space was repelled by a star's solar wind in this area. Those violent collisions of powerful electromagnetic forces manifested themselves in a form that appeared to be lightning in the darkness of space. It was awe-inspiring and essential. The strength of their star's solar wind and a healthy planetary biosphere made life possible on Kerguelen, and if life existed elsewhere in the galaxy, similar conditions would need to be present. The only other star system he had seen with parallel conditions was system 1-Sol-8, and that was primarily why he had been confident that life was possible there. The discovery of the alien spacecraft had confirmed his theory… and hopes.

"We're back in town, Dela," Omega said over his shoulder.

"How does the old neighborhood look?" she asked without looking away from her panel.

"Just like we left it," he replied.

"It's good to know that things didn't change," she said.

"Just because things look the same doesn't mean they didn't change," Omega said warily.

"I'll keep that in mind," Dela said.

Dela stepped away from the flight engineer's console and slipped gingerly into the navigator's couch and tapped on the control console. She scanned the readouts on the flight computer screen and nodded in approval at what she saw. They were ready for entry into their home star system.

"We've rolled into Program 412," Dela said. "We're ready for entry."

"Stand-by for a little bump," Omega said.

San Mariner shuddered slightly as it crossed the threshold and into the solar system. Dela tapped on her console and punched up a position status on her screen.

"We're right on the numbers according to the computer," Dela said. "We've moved into Program 457. Do you want me to verify our position?"

Omega nodded and she stepped to the star scope. She scanned the star field and quickly locked in on one of the distant pinpricks of light. After entering the coordinates into the navigation computer, Dela sat back down in the navigator's couch and sighed.

"How are the ribs?" Omega asked as she grimaced.

"Better," Dela lied. They were on fire. "They'll be alright."

Omega nodded and then pointed at her console. "What's your score?" he asked.

"Perfect. Antares is exactly where it's supposed to be," she answered squirming in the couch. She was unable to find a comfortable position in it. "And Space Command should have a clear telemetry on us now."

"Let's hope so," Omega said. "And let's hope those repairs you made hold up."

"You don't know what my area of expertise is, do you?" Dela asked.

"I've recently found that I know very little about you," Omega said.

"Well, my undergrad degree was applied engineering and I hold a master's in reverse engineering," she said. "There isn't much that I can't figure out or adapt for usage."

"I assumed you had a doctorate," Omega said joking.

"I'm waiting for approval of my doctoral thesis from the Technology Council. I had my oral exam before we left and I should have word on my written work by the time we return," she said tapping on her console.

"Have you been published?" he asked.

"I've had a few papers published in the *Kerguelen Scientific Gazette*," she said. "They received modest reviews."

"What subject?"

"My best reviews came from an article I wrote on the use of theoretical mathematics in practical applications," she said studying her panel intensely.

"Unbelievable," Omega said. "Is there anything you can't do?"

"I have trouble keeping the seams of my stockings straight," she said giving him a quick glance.

Omega smiled and the flight deck went silent as they continued to monitor the ship systems. The only audible sounds came from the internal workings of *San Mariner*. Air recirculation and cooling systems and the hum of electronics were the sole indicators that they were still among the living. After a few minutes, a low dull electronic beep mixed in with other mechanical noises and Omega and Dela both looked at the source of the sound simultaneously. It was closer to Dela and Omega nodded to her.

"Answer it," he said.

Dela flipped a toggle switch to its "ON" position and listened carefully. Only garbled and unintelligible noise could be heard and she turned a knob next to the toggle switch to dial in the proper setting. First static and then more garbled noise came across the circuit. Dela turned the knob in small increments and slowly the noise became more understandable. She pushed a button and turned the knob again and the background interference cleared, though a bit of static still remained. However, they could now hear the distinct sound of words. Dela turned the knob back a bit and the static disappeared.

"*San Mariner, San Mariner*, this is *Jackknife*, please respond, over," a voice said.

Omega thought he recognized the voice but was not sure. He did know the ship calling was a planetary research spacecraft that conducted missions to the outer planets in their solar system. The crew of *Jackknife* prospected on the moons of the gas giants in search of potential raw minerals, precious metals and sources of water in the form of ice. Water was vital if Space Command wanted to establish an outpost in the outer regions. Without surface ice or subterranean water, a base was not possible. But what was *Jackknife* doing out here? There were no planetary bodies in this area. The only reasonable explanation was that they were looking for them.

"Respond," Omega said to Dela.

Dela flicked another toggle switch. "*Jackknife, Jackknife*, this is *San Mariner*. Over?" she said.

"*San Mariner*, this is *Jackknife*. You're coming in loud but not entirely clear," the voice said over the din of shouts in the background.

"*Jackknife, San Mariner*, we read you five-by-five," Dela said trying to contain her own excitement.

"Where's that son of a bitch Omega?" the voice said.

"I'm here. Who's this?" Omega said hoping his voice would carry clearly.

"This is Tartis, you old bastard! Who'd you think it was?" the man said.

Omega smiled as he recognized the familiar grumble of his fellow spacecraft commander. Tartis was one of the original star sailors selected for deep space exploration and had been in line for a mission to explore other solar systems but turned down the opportunity. He had been a star sailor for twenty years and had flown in every type of spacecraft made. He had survived crash landings on moons, major ship malfunctions and never-ending strings of bad luck. But it was a young wife that ultimately caused Tartis to lose his desire to take long and extended space missions. Suddenly, he had something on Kerguelen worth staying close to home for and he wanted to nurture that relationship as best as he could.

Even though Tartis now had three young children at home, he still kept himself in the flight rotation for short duration missions and his seniority allowed him to pick and choose which ones he would take and who would be in his crew. At a party, Omega remembered his wife saying that it would take an act of the Almighty to keep Tartis from suiting up and strapping into a space ship and she was looking forward to the day when the flight surgeons finally grounded him.

"Omega, where the hell have you been? Space Command has been trying to raise you for days and the whole star system has been waiting to hear from you again," Tartis said with concern.

"It's been a bastard out here. We've had problems with every system on the ship. Our communications system, for one, is patched as you can tell. Plus, we've had crew casualties. My flight engineer is all that's left, and she's seriously injured," Omega said wearily. The strain he was under was evident in his voice. "What are you doing out here? Did you get lost?"

"We're out here looking for you, what else?" Tartis replied. "Space Command diverted us from our primary mission to find you."

"We need your help, Tartis," Omega said. "Contact Space Command and let them know we're alive and well and en route to Kerguelen. All mission objectives completed. The alien craft is intact."

"No problem," Tartis said. "Let me get my crew off of their ass and make that happen. Stand-by." Tartis spoke to his crew and established a link with Space Command. In a few minutes, the link was broken and he spoke to *San Mariner* again. "Omega, I just got off the horn with Space Command and I've got new instructions."

"What's up?" Omega asked.

"*Jackknife* will…" Tartis began and then his voice was lost in a sea of static.

Dela tried to re-establish contact but could not raise *Jackknife*. She continued to make adjustments for a few minutes without success and then looked at her navigation console and cursed.

"We've got a problem," she said slowly standing up. She walked over to her flight engineer's console and began tapping on the console's keypad.

"What's the problem?" Omega asked.

"We've shifted into Program 512," she said.

"Already?" Omega said looking at his console.

"Yeah," Dela nodded. "The primary fuel cells have been shut down and we're on the batteries. Damn. I was afraid of this."

"What's wrong with that? That's what the program is supposed to do, isn't it?" Omega asked turning towards her.

"Yes, but in case of low voltage, the system selectively strips loads not vital for crew survival. We've lost communications, waste disposal, and auxiliary electronics… and we're about to lose artificial gravity," she said.

"Take manual control and get *Jackknife* back," Omega said.

"It'll take me a minute to bypass the safeties and regain control," she said.

"Just take the other stuff offline and get me communications," Omega ordered.

"I can't," Dela said. "We need everything that hasn't been stripped."

"What's online?"

"Life support, air recirculating, water systems and the shield," Dela said. "And the shield is drawing the lion's share of the power."

"Take the shield down then," Omega demanded.

"Commander," Dela said turning to Omega. "The Kerguelen sun has a unique distinction. It is the source of life on our planet and the source of many of the power systems that sustain us, but in the dark void of space, it's also a killer. Without our electromagnetic shield protecting us, the high-powered cosmic radiation will penetrate the ship's skin and we'll be dead within hours."

"What can we do?" Omega asked.

"Renew your faith with the Almighty and pray I can manipulate the system without losing everything. You better hope I'm as good as I think I am," Dela said as objects began to float around her. "And you'd better strap yourself in, Commander. We just lost artificial gravity."

The artificial gravity system had just gone offline and Dela hovered beside her console as her long hair began to rise towards the overhead. She carefully began her modifications and in a few minutes, took a deep breath and pushed a button. The lights flickered and some of the readouts faded in and out, but the fluctuations were short-lived. Dela sighed and gently floated back to the deck as her hair and other objects fell into place as normal gravity was restored.

"I've brought the fuels cells back up, but we don't have much time like this," Dela said. "Make the call and make it fast."

"*Jackknife*, this is *San Mariner*, over?" Omega said.

"*San Mariner*, we read you. What happened to you?" Tartis said.

"A minor problem," Omega lied. "What did Space Command say?"

"We'll shepherd you back home in case you have any more problems. I think a good point to rendezvous will be Sector Seven. I'm sending over the coordinates," Tartis said.

"I think we can make that," Omega said looking to Dela. She had shifted to the science console and had downloaded the information. She nodded receipt of the data.

"It should take us about forty-one hours reach this point," Dela said.

"I heard that," Tartis said. "We'll meet you there."

"Cdr. Tartis, we need a portable power pack to make it all the way home. Can you contact an outpost and see if they can help us out with that?" Dela asked.

"We have one onboard. When we rendezvous, we'll transfer it over," Tartis said.

Dela shifted back to her station, looked at her console and waved at Omega, giving him the cut signal. He nodded and sighed.

"Tartis, we've got to handle a few things over here. We'll see you in two days," Omega said. "*San Mariner*, out."

As radio contact was broken, the crew of *Jackknife* was silent. They all heard the tension in Omega's voice and one of them shook his head as the others began to resume their tasks. The flight engineer of *Jackknife*, a tall Southwestern Province native named Arista, saw the crewman shaking his head and stared at him. She was a beauty in anyone's eyes and a veteran star sailor. She pushed blonde tresses from her eyes and spoke.

"What's the matter, Francisco?" she asked.

"I never thought I'd see the day when a spacecraft commander would be so freaked out," he said.

"What do you mean?" she asked.

"He was clearly panicked. I mean, *he's* supposed to be the best there is in this business and he acts like a student pilot on his first flight. I don't get it," he said turning to her.

"I suppose you would have more composure in the same situation," Arista said as the rest of the crew stopped what they were doing to hear the exchange.

"He's nearly home and we're on our way to help. What's the problem? It's almost over," Francisco said clearly unimpressed at the legendary Omega. "If that's how a commander acts, I'd rather stay a third level mission specialist."

"You have no idea what you're talking about," Arista said.

"I don't?"

"No," Arista said shaking her head. "You're totally clueless. Omega has taken his ship over forty light-years from home and back again. Only one other ship has returned from a mission of such distance and duration. All of the other Type V ships are presumed lost. It takes a special crew... and commander to survive deep space."

"Those other ships failed mechanically or had navigation or crew errors," Francisco countered. "He's overcome that. Why be so distraught now?"

"Distraught?" Arista laughed. "He's got more deep space time than any other star sailor. And he has more hours using a spacecraft fecal matter collection unit than you've got flight hours on Kerguelen. He knows what he's doing. Besides Tartis, there's no one else I'd rather fly with."

"Are you serious?" Francisco asked and he received a single nod from her in response.

Arista, like Tartis, was an old hand in space. She was part of the second group of star sailors selected for deep space missions. She had been on two expeditions that traveled beyond the boundaries of the Kerguelen star system. The objectives of both missions were to verify FTL communications and navigational computers. She knew the hazards involved with Omega's mission all too well. She was second-in-command of *Jackknife* and the crew was familiar with her record and abilities. On their current mission, she had successfully landed a crew excursion module on one of the moons of the gas giant planet Moribund without the aid of computers. Francisco had been onboard with her and in his mind there was no better star sailor than Arista.

"Who do you think taught me how to fly an excursion module? Get your head out of your ass, rookie. Omega may be a lot of things, but panicky isn't one of them. I'd like to see how you'd be if you'd lost your crew and your ship was falling apart around you," Arista said in defense of Omega. "No, Francisco, that wasn't panic you heard in his voice, it was relief. That break in communications was no minor problem. His ship is dying from a lack of power." She looked about the compartment and saw the crew circled around and sighed. "Okay, listen up. We've got a rendezvous and transfer to plan and prep for and we need a contingency if we lose communications again. Let's break up this coffee clutch and get back to work... one of our own is in trouble."

Arista eyed the crew and they moved to their consoles. As they did, a crewman named Javier leaned over to Francisco and whispered in the young star sailor's ear.

"Did you know that Arista had a umbilical snap during an EVA?" he asked.

"No, really?" Francisco said.

"Yep. She was working on the Auxiliary Space Platform Project at the time. You heard about how many star sailors died during its construction, didn't you?" Javier said. Francisco nodded and he continued. "Her line broke and she started drifting off. Her comm. unit had malfunctioned and it was ten minutes or so before anyone noticed. Omega did an EVA rescue... used one of the old manned maneuvering units to get her back. They had to share his air supply on the way back because she had run out of O2."

"Gutsy move," Francisco said recalling the event. It was one of the stories his instructor had told during basic EVA training.

"It was a very gutsy move," Javier said. "Omega gave himself a tri-ox injection because he had no time to pre-breathe. And then he suited up and went after her. It was doubly risky because tri-ox wasn't all that reliable back then and because of her position."

"What do you mean?" Francisco asked.

"The platform was in low orbit. We constructed things in low orbit back then to make it easier to get material to the job site. After construction, it was boosted to high orbit where it is now. Everyone on the platform was scared that the planet's gravity would grab whoever went after her. We didn't have small orbital sleds in those days," Javier explained. "I remember she told me after she was back on the platform that she could feel herself going to meet the Almighty as the planet's gravity pulled her down. It felt like the hand of God she said. She knew it was over. Gravity was pulling her down and she was out of O2. Then, out of nowhere, Omega grabbed her and brought her to safety. Both of them nearly died, but she said she was glad Omega was there. Arista believes dying alone, especially in space, is the most horrifying way to die there is."

"You were there?" Francisco asked.

"Yes," Javier said almost ashamed to admit it.

"And you didn't go after her?" Francisco asked.

"No," Javier said shaking his head. "The odds... the odds were totally against a successful rescue. Computer projections placed successful retrieval at less than three percent."

"So everyone just waited around to see if he made it?" Francisco asked.

"I guess it's true when they say all men can't be brave in the same way, I suppose," Javier said shrugging his shoulders.

"Why did he do it if the risk was so great?" Francisco asked.

"He said it was worth the risk," Javier answered.

"But why did he risk his life so recklessly when no one else would?"

"We asked him that," Javier said. "His reply was, *'I have to go... one of our own is in trouble'.*"

PART FIVE

1

Sigma 4, Technology Council Headquarters, Capitol City, Central Province, Planet Kerguelen

The revelation that Mackenzie's father was the head of the Celeron ruling body stunned Prior. As the chief technologist spoke, Prior recalled The Seven in her mind. She tried to imagine what type of life Mackenzie had led as the child of a Celeron. From all indications her childhood was brief.

"Which one is your father?" Prior asked completely floored by what she had heard so far.

"He is the leader of the Celeron," Mackenzie said leaning back in the couch.

"But who is the leader?" Prior asked.

"They didn't reveal that?" Mackenzie chuckled. "That doesn't surprise me, not in the least. They always like to keep people guessing."

"I'm not in the mood for games," Prior said tersely. Despite her curiosity, she was beginning to become angry. "Everyone wants me to do their bidding but no one wants to come clean. I'm tired of the bullshit, Mackenzie."

Mackenzie smiled and was unfazed by Prior's outburst. "Look at me and recall The Seven. Which one of them do you think is my father?" Mackenzie said. "Think about it."

Prior took a deep breath and calmed down. For a moment she was about to walk out, but that wouldn't have solved anything. In the short term, she would be satisfied. In the long run, she would still have a million questions and not one single answer. Prior looked down to the carpeted floor and then to Mackenzie and gazed at her face. After some consideration, she nodded.

"Your father is very handsome for a man of advanced age," Prior said. "And I'm surprised he is still alive. I believed he was dead."

"He is a handsome man," Mackenzie agreed. "And he'll be glad to know that you think so. And he is far from being dead. My father is very well preserved in many aspects...according to my mother."

Mackenzie gave Prior a wink and the Guardian understood the meaning. It was obvious that her mother inferred that good old dad still desired the company of his wife in the evenings and even at his age, could still perform adequately. Once again Prior was surprised and shocked.

"So, Marshal Gideon is your father," Prior said.

"Yes," Mackenzie replied.

Prior shook her head. "He should have been dead a long time ago," she said. "Unless..."

Mackenzie remained straight-faced and nodded her head. Prior's mouth formed the word "no" but no sound came from her. Mackenzie nodded and patted Prior on the hand. She turned to Addison and asked her leave them alone for a few minutes and when she left, Mackenzie refilled their glasses. Prior held the glass in her hand and continued to shake her head as Mackenzie sipped her whiskey.

"There's no way for him to be your father," Prior said softly.

"Gideon is my father, Prior," Mackenzie said calmly. "He is still alive and he is the leader of the Celeron. And his existence is not a miracle."

"He would be well over a hundred years old. Kerguelens don't live that long," Prior said trying to understand all of it. "Besides, the Gideon I met looked closer to ninety."

"Gideon is one hundred and eighteen years old," Mackenzie said.

"And how old are you?" Prior asked.

"I'm seventy-eight," said Mackenzie proudly brushing her thick hair from her eyes.

"You look incredible, Mackenzie," Prior complemented. "If what you say is true, that means you're both..."

"We're both Boroni. Yes," Mackenzie said. "In fact, you and I are related."

"Either you're lying or someone has lied to you," Prior said. "I know who all of my relatives are."

"It's true, Prior. We're cousins," Mackenzie said.

"How are we cousins?" Prior scoffed.

"You've heard the rumor that the Celeron aided the Boroni in our revolution, haven't you?" Mackenzie asked. Prior nodded. "Well, it's true. The Celeron gave the Boroni weapons, equipment and training. The Celeron believed the time had come for slavery to end. They waited for the ideal moment because timing was everything. Despite the drain on manpower during the last Provincial Wars, the Central Province was still formidable. When the last Provincial Wars was reaching its zenith, the Central Province had no troops to spare as a garrison force in the Western Province. With only slaveholders in the province, Kel and the others struck. The Celeron believed that the rebellion was in the best interest of the planet and it was. But everything worthwhile has a price."

"And what price did the Boroni pay?" Prior asked.

"A male and female Boroni were taken by the Celeron," Mackenzie said.

"Why?" Prior asked. It didn't make sense to her that the Celeron would want a Boroni in their midst. And why would they want two?

"They wanted to assimilate a Boroni into the population and see the effects," Mackenzie answered. "The Boroni refused at first but in the end they knew it was the right thing to do. A young female stepped forward and volunteered. Her name was Kazan."

"Kazan was my great aunt. She's Kel's sister," Prior said. "I was told she died in the rebellion."

"That would be an untruth. Kazan and a male named Gilbert were taken by the Celeron to a remote region of the North Island Province and taught the ways of Kerguelen. In due time, they gave birth to a man-child," Mackenzie said.

"Gideon," Prior surmised. "Then you and he are my cousins."

"Yes, and as he grew, Gideon was educated at the best schools in the North Island Province and learned to harness his Boroni abilities. In addition, he and his parents were taught to tap into greater, latent Boroni abilities unknown to those in the Western Province," Mackenzie said.

"What latent abilities?" Prior asked curiously. "We have endeavored to extract all that we can from our unique gifts."

"Almost all," Mackenzie corrected. "There are other abilities you have not used and with the help of Celeron researchers, we do. The

Celeron decided to put those new skills to use by arranging Gideon's appointment to the Guardian Academy. Some years later, he returned to the Western Province and brought my mother back with him. The rest of his past you're familiar with."

"But why are you named Mackenzie? Boroni children's names are based on the first letter of the sire's name," Prior asked intrigued by the story.

"Those of us who were reared and reside outside of the Western Province receive their names based on the first letter of the mother's name. After Gideon, it was decided there should be a distinction between our cousins and us. My mother's name is Marathi," Mackenzie explained.

"How many of you are there?"

"Fourteen. We've managed to remain undiscovered while attaining a measure of success socially. You on the other hand, have managed to do what none of us had ever thought possible, even in our wildest dreams. You've achieved great notoriety and acclaim as a Boroni. You've made all of us proud, cousin Prior," Mackenzie said with a wide and beaming smile.

"Is that why you sponsored me for my doctorate?" Prior asked.

"Partly," Mackenzie admitted. "But mostly because of your potential as an engineer. I never had any doubt that you would succeed. You're my cousin after all."

"But you have blue eyes," Prior said. "Boroni don't have blue eyes."

"It's not easy to shed the trappings of our genetic coding but with effort, it can be done," Mackenzie said.

"All Boroni are very much the same," Prior said. "As much as I hate the caricature, we all look very much alike and we don't resemble each other very much, cousin. And you only resemble Gideon slightly."

"Is that all that causes you doubt? My appearance? I may not look like my father, Prior, but that doesn't matter. He didn't make me with his face," Mackenzie said.

"True," Prior smiled. "But facts are facts, two hundred and eighty plus years of fact. You may have the height and physique of a Boroni, but anyone can be tall and strong. You just need the right peerage."

"That's true," Mackenzie said.

"That's basic Boroni genetics," Prior said.

"I can show you that genetics, as far as the Boroni are concerned, are far from basic," Mackenzie said.

"This I'd like to see," Prior scoffed.

Mackenzie stood up, smiled briefly at Prior and then turned straight-faced. She shut her eyes and breathed deep. When she opened them, her irises were a soft topaz identical to Prior's. As she looked at Mackenzie, Prior would have sworn Mackenzie resembled her mother. She wore the same stoic countenance that Prior had grown to dislike and fear as a child. Her mother had been more of a taskmaster than a mentor and a parent. Her father had been the one who consoled her and taught her about relationships and feelings. Her mother taught her how to hunt and how to leave her feelings behind when dealing with others. Always negotiate from a position of strength, and the rest falls into place, her mother had said. In the brief instant that Prior had seen her mother in Mackenzie, she realized that what disturbed her most was that she saw her own reflection.

"Amazing," Prior said. "You can control eye color."

"Yes," Mackenzie said. "Try and hit me, Prior."

"What?" Prior said standing up.

"Try and hit me," Mackenzie said. She saw Prior laugh and added, "Don't worry, cousin, you won't lay a hand on me. You're not skilled enough to do me any real harm."

"As you wish," Prior said.

Prior took a step closer to Mackenzie and swung at her several times with short jabs and the chief technologist deftly dodged the punches with ease. Prior was shocked at Mackenzie's reflex speed and was even more stunned when Mackenzie countered and connected with a three-punch combination of her own. The blows were not intended to cause any damage, however, they did get Prior's full attention.

"Retention of strength and reflexes and agility in advanced age is one of the things the Celeron have taught us. Voluntary control of involuntary body processes is another. In addition, we have learned to extend our lives without the aid of medicine," Mackenzie said.

She shut her eyes again and took another deep breath. When she reopened them, her eyes had returned to the blue color they had been.

"How long does it take to learn that?" Prior asked.

"It took me about... three months," Mackenzie said. "But I was only four years old when I first did it and it wasn't until I was seven that I had mastered it."

Boroni eye color changed from brown to blue in extreme emotional stress. Normally, the event took place when a loved one had died, during the birth of children, in extreme rage or most commonly, during sexual intercourse. The change was completely involuntary but the metamorphosis could be controlled and stopped. There were many urban legends associated with Boroni eye color change and no non-Boroni could have ever sworn to actually witnessing the transformation. Eye color change was called "Flashing Blue", and was only momentary, visible only at the peak of an emotional state. But Mackenzie and the others had managed to somehow acquire the ability to change and maintain eye color change at will and the thought of it would keep Prior up all night.

"I'd like to learn that," Prior said.

"I'm sure you would. And it's possible for you to achieve as long as you're willing to unlearn many of the things you have learned," Mackenzie said. "But for now, you must concentrate on what lays before you."

"The Argent," Prior said.

"Yes. The Celeron will approach you and ask for your help to defeat The Argent and end their quest for supremacy of Kerguelen," Mackenzie said taking a drink of her whiskey.

"What can I bring to the table?" Prior said.

"Your religious faith and your strong belief in freedom for all are imperative. Without you, all may be lost. Though you are a child in the grand scheme of things, you will be more than able to repel the dark force that walks Kerguelen."

"The prophecy again."

"Read the scrolls, Prior."

"I will, but I'm not buying into any half-baked musings of dead scribes and seers. Sorry," Prior said shaking her head.

"You have to open your mind. You have a part to play in the prophecy just like the Celeron and The Argent," Mackenzie said.

"What makes all of you so sure that I have a part to play?" Prior refuted. "Because of a few small and obscure coincidences, I'm being recruited into a scenario that a tiny group of people have concocted? Uh-uh. You'll have to find another woman."

"What about the scrolls?"

"What about them?"

"We are a gnostic people, Prior. We take the gospels at face value. Don't turn your back on the truth simply because it's hard to accept," Mackenzie insisted.

Prior could not respond immediately. The Boroni were truly gnostic and of all the people of Kerguelen, the Boroni were the only ones who took the scriptures literally. In their minds it was simple: Why record something that wasn't true? Eventually the truth would surface. No lie holds forever.

"I'm devout, Mackenzie, but even in extremes there are limits."

"Faith is limitless, cousin. You can't put a ceiling on your beliefs. If you did, you'd never be able to love or trust," Mackenzie said.

"Then perhaps I never will," Prior replied.

Mackenzie laughed and then spoke in the Boroni language. "<Do you have the dream>?" she asked.

Prior was caught off guard by the use of her native tongue. If there had been any lingering doubt that Mackenzie was Boroni, it no longer existed. It took a second for the words to register.

"<Why do you ask that>?"

"<The scroll of Katana mentions a dream, as do many other books in the Holy Scriptures. Do you dream>?" Mackenzie said.

"<Yes, I do and it's upsetting. I haven't slept much because I'm afraid of the dream. It comes to me every time I shut my eyes>," Prior said.

"<Since it's been proven scientifically that Boroni are in incapable of dreaming, I can understand your attitude. But what does that tell you>?" Mackenzie said almost clinically.

"<I'm broken in some way>," Prior chuckled.

Tests had proven that Boroni did not dream and entered into a dormant state when they slept. The only neural activity that took place controlled the involuntary bodily functions. The fact that Prior did have dreams was a scientific curiosity.

"<You're not broken, cousin. What happens in the dream>?"

"<I'm lying in a field of tall grass and a voice awakens me. It tells me I have much to do and many people are waiting for me and I must

get up. It continues saying I have much to do and repeats itself over and over again until I wake up. I don't remember anything else. The last dream I had was very intense and I haven't slept since. It's been days>," Prior said.

"<You must sleep. Not for the dream, but for yourself. Not even Boroni can function without adequate periods of rest. You have your health to consider>," Mackenzie cautioned.

"<I will after I read the scroll. Tomorrow I meet with Gregor to confront him about the information Addison retrieved>," Prior said.

"<Take care, cousin. As you have learned, Cardinal Gregor is not one to be trusted>."

"<I'll be on guard>," Prior nodded.

"<Don't be on guard, be ready to kill him>," Mackenzie warned.

Prior once again saw her mother's reflection in Mackenzie's face. Prior nodded and embraced the chief technologist. She stepped away and when she reached the door, Addison returned and Prior took her by the hand so they could discuss her recon work in depth. When the Guardians left, Mackenzie pulled out her TELCOM device and clicked it on. She requested a number and the device quickly beeped in response. Though the person she was calling couldn't see her, they would have been enamored with her sparkling azure eyes.

"Hello, daddy," she said.

"You sound happy, my daughter. Did you see our cousin?" Gideon asked.

"I did. She was not receptive at first but was willing to listen after a bit of convincing. She's not ready to join us, but will read the scrolls," Mackenzie said.

"I'm not going to ask how you convinced her, daughter," Gideon said with a slight laugh. "Where is she now?"

"She's on her way home I believe," Mackenzie speculated.

"Good, I'll speak with her there."

"You're in Capitol City?"

"Yes," Gideon said. "Things are advancing in a direction unfavorable to us and I need to be more involved. And I believe I know how to convince our young cousin to take a more active role in our operation as well."

2
Capitol City, Central Province, Planet Kerguelen

As Prior's air ship escaped gravity and slowly rose skyward, she took stock of her emotional state and realized she was annoyed and it upset her. Though she had a right to be upset about the recent conflict in the Middle Provinces and the death of her operative Lieutenant Singh and countless other reasons, it was her meeting with Mackenzie that had irked her. It wasn't because the Celeron were trying to maneuver her to join their fight against The Argent, and it wasn't because she learned about the existence of distant relatives, nor was it because she found that these off Province Boroni possessed abilities far beyond that of other Boroni. No, her annoyance found life because her feelings were hurt.

For fifteen years she believed that she had been the first Boroni to graduate from the Guardian Academy and now, that honor had been stripped away from her. Gideon had been the first and unlike Prior, he had spent his entire career in the limelight. He had been lauded and praised and lofted to the pinnacle of Guardian and planetary success. Yes, she had been successful and received many accolades that Gideon had not, but the most important thing in her life had been being the first Boroni academy graduate and officer... and it was gone. It wouldn't take away any of her accomplishments but sometimes one big thing could outstrip hundreds of smaller ones.

Prior smiled and remembered the old joke about star sailors. Everyone remembered who the first star sailor that landed on the Kerguelen moon was and what he said when he took his first steps on the surface but no one remembered what the second man said. Who cared, he was second. She now knew how St. Jacques must have felt. As the last Boroni to attend the academy, his presence at the institution was little more than a footnote in academy records.

However, she knew her graduation status was of little consequence in the grand scheme of her life at the moment. There were many other fish to fry. She had to deal with a delicate situation concerning the Western Province Grange. It had to be dealt with immediately and she needed to handle it before she met with Cardinal Gregor tomorrow morning. In addition, she had to finish investigations concerning Singh's death and see his wife. Lastly, she had to read that damn scroll. She hoped that it would not reveal anything too spectacular but was afraid that it would open up a new floodgate of trouble for her.

Prior's air ship gently glided through the Capitol City skyline mixing in and out with other vehicles in the sky traffic pattern. Her air ship was accompanied by another air transport and the gunship. There was still a threat of danger to her as a Guardian leader and the gunship ensured that if she were ambushed, she had a better than decent chance of survival. The second air transport carried another combat team and they would be necessary as an escort. Prior was going to detain someone and the individual was very dangerous.

At this time of day, the air was filled with commuters heading home from work or those getting an early start to their evenings. Her pilot used the East Side air conduit to reach their destination due to the congestion of air vehicles. Below them was East Side Park, a nice place for young couples to stroll and discuss their day in an atmosphere of ease. Most of the young professionals living in this area were just starting out in their careers and beginning families. They had given up the life of partying and settled down and despite his bachelor status and promiscuous behavior Captain Hiroki loved this part of Capitol City and maintained a residence here. Prior smiled as she turned to Addison and pointed to a residential building.

"Capt. Hiroki lives in that building," Prior said.

"I know," Addison said. "He's been trying to get me into that love trap for months."

"Me too," Pana said looking up from her PDA screen. "If he was as relentless on the battlefield as he is in a bar, he'd be a colonel by now."

Addison laughed. "That's probably true," she said. "I have to give him credit though, he isn't discouraged easily. In a way, it's flattering. Creepy but flattering."

"Tell me about it," Rex said from the rear of the craft. "He even asked *me* to his apartment."

The women all laughed and Rex turned his seat around and went back to what he was working on. His remark was more humorous than it actually was because most Boroni males were not known for their ability to make people laugh.

"We'll be down in a few minutes, Commander," Micah called from the pilot's compartment.

Prior nodded and Micah called to the other ships and they increased speed as they cleared the mass of air traffic. In less than three minutes, they dropped down and commenced a landing in an expensive upscale neighborhood. The residences in this area were all high-end and occupied by the families of business executives or politicians.

Prior's air ship was first to touch down followed by the others at the end of the neighborhood's block. A landing area was set aside so no air vehicles flew directly overhead of the homes disturbing the elite class occupants. As the engines came to an idle, Prior made her way to the hatch with Lupo close behind. Before she exited, she turned to the pilot's compartment.

"Tell them to keep the engines warm, Micah. We won't be long," she said.

"No problem, boss," Micah replied.

Pana and Rex accompanied Prior but Addison remained on board. As they cleared the air ships, the team from the other air transport followed behind. First Lieutenant Francis commanded the second team. He was from the Oceanic Province and still carried the handsome and boyish looks of his teenage years. Now twenty-one years old, Francis had a thick muscular frame to augment his good looks and was constantly pursued by a gaggle of beautiful but clueless ingénues. Prior stopped at the edge the landing area so she could speak to the Guardians without raising her voice.

"Listen up," she said eying the Guardians. "This is a simple apprehension. Our target is in the third house on the left." She pointed to the dwelling and continued. "It's a simple task. Maintain your focus. This shouldn't take more than fifteen minutes."

"Is this a snatch and grab?" Francis asked.

"No, not quite. It's a grab for sure, but we need to handle this with kid gloves," Prior explained.

"Should we expect any resistance, Commander?" Francis asked.

"Expect it but I doubt there will be any. Once he realizes why I'm here and his situation, he'll submit understanding that we're his best hope of survival. But make sure you're ready to restrain him if he decides to make a break for it. If he does, take him down... hard and with malice. He's stronger than anyone on your team, Lieutenant, and thoroughly versed in unarmed combat," Prior cautioned.

"Who are we engaging, Commander?" one of Francis' men asked.

"My twin brother, Senator Poul," Prior sighed. She turned to Francis and added, "Give them the Deadly Force Brief, Lieutenant."

Francis read the brief to his team and when he finished they readied their gear. Prior led them to her brother's house when they were set and pressed the doorbell when she reached the entrance. The long-winded door chime had not ended when the door opened. Prior and her Guardians were greeted by a smiling face. Francis and his team were slightly stunned by the jovial expression. The man that owned it looked exactly like their commander, though none of them could ever remember Prior smiling so widely or pleasantly.

Poul was quite a bit taller than Prior and his hair was dark brown and in traditional male Boroni styling. It was combed straight and tied in several places reaching the middle of his back. He wore an expensive suit, identical to that worn by every other politician on Kerguelen. The dark blue blazer, white shirt, striped tie and Planetary Senate pin on the left lapel was the typical attire of male senators and provincial representatives. It was their uniform and none of them would ever allow themselves to be photographed not wearing the trappings of office. They honestly believed people expected to see them dressed in such a manner. Somehow that was supposed to give them credibility. Female politicians wore conservative suits of their own, but were allowed the latitude to express their own sense of style. Prior often wondered what would happen if a male politician's wardrobe ever strayed from the status quo haute couture.

Poul looked at the group of Guardians on his doorstep and nodded to them. "Come in," he said gesturing them indoors. "Make yourselves at home."

Prior turned to Francis and instructed him to have his men remain outside and they entered the house. Poul led them to his spacious living room where his aide and his housekeeper were waiting. Prior stepped to Poul and the siblings embraced and kissed each other on the lips. They kissed each other a little longer and fuller than was comfortable for Francis and he turned away slightly to hide his embarrassment. Boroni were known to display such affection to family members but seeing it for the first time was unsettling. Francis couldn't remember even his parents kissing in such a fashion or displaying that kind of affection. Perhaps if they had, they wouldn't have broken their bond. Poul gently caressed Prior's face and stepped to Pana and kissed her as well. He tapped Lupo lightly on the head as he nodded to Rex. The canine licked his hand in response and softly growled. Poul pointed to the bar on the far side of the room and offered the Guardians refreshments.

"Thank you, Poul, but we can't indulge in spirits at the moment," Prior said. "But please feel free to have something yourself."

"You're on duty, eh?" Poul said. He nodded to his housekeeper and she brought him a tall drink. She and the aide departed after he took the glass and he sat down when they left. "It's always a pleasure to see you, sister, but what brings you by?"

"As I said on the TELCOM, I really need to speak with you about an urgent matter," Prior said.

"As do I," he said. He looked at the others and continued. "But I was hoping we could speak alone."

"Sorry, Poul, but a Guardian commander never goes anywhere without an escort," she explained. "Is there anyone else here besides your aide and housekeeper?"

"Yes," he nodded. "My air vehicle pilot and secretary, but they're on the other side of the house."

Prior nodded and gestured to Francis and he and Rex left the house. When they were gone Prior and Pana sat down and Lupo curled up at her feet. He gave Prior his glass and poured himself and Pana a drink. He gave Pana a glass and flopped down in a seat across from his sister. Prior let the whiskey breathe before she took a drink. She looked around the house and it was still as she remembered it. It was devoid of any Boroni-type furnishings or adornments. It was very conservative… and very Kerguelen.

"What's up, Poul?" Prior asked taking a sip of whiskey.

"I need a favor," he said leaning forward.

"What kind and how big?" she asked.

He smiled. "Just like when we were kids," he said. "You haven't changed, Prior. Always suspicious and cautious."

"You haven't changed either, Poul," Prior said returning the smile. "You're in a jam and need my help to get out of it."

"Here we go again," Poul said standing up. "Every time I ask something of you, you have to give a lecture along with it."

"That's right, Poul, I do lecture you, but only the Almighty knows why I bother. It always falls on deaf ears. You manage to get yourself into pickle after pickle and big sister has to bail you out," Prior scolded.

Ever since they were children, Prior had protected Poul from the rage of their mother, Boroni trying to kill him, gambling debts and many other predicaments. She had killed more than one Boroni defending him and their family's honor. The last time she helped him he had gotten himself in an ill-advised sexual encounter with a Kerguelen woman. He had been accused of criminal assault and it was all she could do to make the entire thing go away. She could only imagine what kind of trouble his latest escapade had landed him in.

"If I'm so much trouble, why do you always come when I call?" he asked.

"You're my brother, Poul. We were conceived together and that means a great deal to me. I can't put it into words, but suffice it to say, I must do everything in my power to help you," Prior said. She looked at him harder and her voice became sterner as she continued. "Most importantly, you're a member of my House. Everything you do reflects on it and maintaining the integrity of our House is paramount to me."

"Our House?" Poul scoffed. "It's your House, Prior. I was just born into it. Four minutes too late as it turns out. A fact I'm reminded of constantly when I'm in the Western Province."

"The fact I was born first didn't matter, Poul. You didn't do what was necessary to become leader of the House. You had your chance but you let it slip away," Prior corrected.

"I've always despised Boroni rites," he said taking another drink.

"All you had to do was kill a wolf and a deer and capture a falcon," Prior said. "I was at the Academy when we reached the Age of Ascension. You had plenty of time to accomplish those tasks before I returned home on my semester break and claim the title as primary heir."

For potential leaders of Boroni households, a simple set of tasks was given to them to complete. They had to finish the tasks in a five-day period and they could start anytime after reaching the Age of Ascension, or fourteen years of age. The tasks had to be completed before they reached the age of fifteen and each task had a specific purpose. Slaying a wolf meant one could defend their House and its livestock from danger and used the fur to clothe the members of the House. Killing a deer demonstrated one could feed the members of their House and capturing a falcon meant that they could tame the beasts of the land proving their dominance over animals.

Prior had been given a special leave from the Academy to perform the rite and the pressure was on because she would not receive another leave until after she was fifteen. She completed the tasks in three days and returned to the Academy. When she returned home again, she was formally installed as the heir apparent and future head of the House of Ahrens. Upon the death of her mother, she would take control of and own the entire wealth of her family. Poul had put off trying to complete the tasks sure that Prior would not finish the rite in the time allotted to her and he could complete them in his leisure. But he had been wrong and ever since, he had been a thorn in her side for one reason or another.

"Well, even though I didn't complete the tasks set forth in that outdated ritual, I should have been made head of the House by default," Poul argued. "You left. You abandoned the province to become an adventurer."

"Regardless of how you feel about Boroni customs and traditions, I was fairly selected as head of the House. Though there were many who shared your opinion about me and my selection, the success and growth of the House under my leadership has silenced the critics," Prior said. She had become annoyed again and was no longer empathetic to Poul. "And I don't have to do anything to help you, Poul. I could expel you from the House for your past deeds and leave you to your own devices and no one would shed a tear."

Poul studied her and saw that she had run out of patience. She was in her right to expel him and they both knew it. No one would raise a voice in dissent against her. The power the House of Ahrens wielded in the Western Province, and on Kerguelen, surpassed that of all but one other house.

"Now, what's your problem, Poul?" Prior asked.

"I've been working with a group of people that I think you should talk to," Poul said.

"I know that you've been dealing with all three major parties, Poul, but I have no compulsion to sit down with any politician, whether they be Fundamentalist, Centrist, or Egalitarian. I know you've left the Centrist party and joined the Egalitarians. Those liberals must be salivating over the fact you're one of them now. They need new blood in that morass of bleeding hearts," Prior said.

"You know I've switched parties?" he asked.

"Of course, Poul. As head of our House it's my job to stay on top of such things. Did you think my globetrotting would make me unaware of your activities?" Prior said.

"This isn't about political parties, but... you know what? Forget it," Poul said walking to the bar and refilling his glass. "I don't know why I bothered trying to bring you onboard with this."

"No, Poul, I can't forget it,' Prior said. "Let's get to the real reason I'm here. I know about your attempts to upset the balance of the Western Province Grange. Your plans to undermine the financial stability of the company were discovered. Your group has been uncovered and the leaders have been dealt with."

"What?" Poul gasped in the middle of taking a drink.

"And I've had the house and land mother left to you closed and sectioned off. Anyone who was on the property was evicted," Prior explained.

"You've taken my land?" Poul asked. He swallowed the contents of his glass and wiped his mouth when he was finished. "You can't do that. Mother left that land to me. You don't have the right to take it."

"Yes, I do. As head of the House that land is actually mine and your possession of it was merely a concession for being our mother's son," Prior said.

"I won't stand for this, Prior. If you want a fight, you've got it," Poul said.

"There won't be a fight, Poul," Prior said shaking her head. "But you can contact the governor general about it. I'm sure Aunt Paige would be glad to hear your side of this matter. She was very intrigued by my version."

"You told great aunt Paige about this? She knows?" Poul asked sitting down in a chair.

Paige was their father's aunt and possibly the most powerful and influential Boroni alive. She was governor general of the Western Province and head of Cabot House, arguably the most powerful family in the Western Province. Paige had also rejected an appointment to the planetary judiciary, the only person to ever do so. She was the toughest negotiator and fiercest Boroni who had ever lived. When the Central Province attempted to regain control of the Boroni and the Western Province after the last Provincial Wars ended, Paige had led the forces that kept the Western Province free. She was considered a grandmother to all and was worshipped amongst the Boroni.

"You see, Poul, our mother was an unfeeling bitch, devoid of even the slightest of emotions, but she had the unique vision and forward thinking to prepare me for something like this. She told me that the Western Province Grange was more than merely a company designed to make money. And for it to be truly effective, it had to stay solvent and intact. It had to stay whole and I had to be ready to defend it against hostile takeovers and attempts to split it into smaller pieces. That's why it remains a private company solely controlled by the House of Ahrens and in the hands of our family. She made me swear to take care of it and never let it be split up… no matter what the cost," Prior said.

Poul scoffed. He was uninterested in the wisdom their mother bequeathed Prior on her deathbed. "What does all that mean, Prior?"

"She told me to trust no one, not even a twin brother. So I don't. I have several shell companies that monitor the activities of every member of the family that has an interest in the Grange. It became easier to watch you once my bank was established. I've recovered all of the bearer bonds you've sold and put in safeguards against the inside information you've exchanged with others. Setting it up was expensive and time consuming but well worth it," Prior said.

"Then you know," Poul said. "You know about everything."

"I do. Your attempt to cause a collapse in the financial base of the company and force me to concentrate on saving the Grange so I would be distracted from other affairs is over," Prior said smiling. "It was a slick maneuver, Poul, I give you that. I would have had to go public with the Grange and possibly lost majority control if your plan was successful. A non-Boroni or a competitive House in the province might have taken control. Tsk. I guess I got lucky."

"What are you going to do?" Poul asked.

"Though you haven't actually broken any planetary laws, you have shattered Boroni ideals. But I have been judicial about what I've related to others. Only Paige knows the extent of your deception. I'm sure the Provincial Solicitor will go easy on you. It was the least I could do... after all, you are my brother," Prior said.

"Listen, Prior," Poul said shifting in his chair. "You don't know what I'm into. The group I'm dealing with will kill me if I don't continue with my work. They're extremely powerful."

"Who is this group, Poul?" Prior asked. "Give me a name."

"You don't want to know, sister. They're pure evil... in a biblical way. They'll stop at nothing to reach their goals. They'll be running the planet soon and you can't stop them. Retaining the Grange in your hands won't delay the inevitable," Poul said. Prior could see the fear in his eyes as he continued. "I've got to disappear. Give me some money and I'll take care of the rest."

"Spoken like a true liberal. Throwing money at a problem doesn't necessarily mean the problem will be fixed. It only means that money has been spent," Prior countered.

"If I don't get out of sight, I'm dead."

"Be thankful I don't kill you myself, Poul. With the shame and dishonor you've brought down on our House, I'd be justified," Prior scowled. "But don't worry, little brother, as usual, I'll protect you. I'm sending you to Guardian Central Command until Paige can send an air ship to bring you back to the Western Province."

"It's not safe at Central Command," he protested.

"Only a fool would come after you there. You'll live to see your day of reckoning, Poul," Prior said standing up. "And then you can tell us who you're in league with."

"I know I'm stupid for refusing to tell you, but I can't," he said.

Prior helped her brother to his feet and kissed him again. "Luckily for the world, stupidity isn't a crime. You'll have time to think about what you will tell Paige while you're in custody," Prior said. She led him to the door and opened it. She nodded to Francis and he took Poul by the arm. "I'm sorry it had to end like this, Poul, I truly am. But going against your own family is treacherous. It's a slippery slope and there are never any guarantees."

As the air ship carrying Francis, his team and Poul departed, Prior watched it disappear from sight and sighed when she could no longer see it. For some reason she didn't feel sadness or regret. She felt sorry for Poul. His life as he knew it was over and everything he had struggled to create was gone and she was responsible. He had caused it, but she had forced him to face the repercussions of his actions. He would never forgive her for it but she had responsibilities of her own and they precluded any feelings she had for her twin brother and though he would not like it, he would understand it.

"What's our next stop?" Pana asked.

"We have a courtesy call to make, Pana," Prior said.

"You should let a chaplain do that," Pana said understanding that they were going to see the spouse of a fallen Guardian.

"Normally I would, but this is a special case," Prior said.

"Too bad Capt. Hiroki isn't here," Pana said. "If it's a widow, we could let him handle it."

"It's Lt. Singh's wife and though she's young she has a child," Prior said.

They both smiled knowing that when it came to women, Hiroki had no morals. They walked to the air ship and Pana entered the craft as Prior looked back at Poul's house.

She sighed. "Well, mother, I did what you told me. The Grange is safe," she said to herself.

She climbed aboard the craft and Pana shut the hatch. After Prior was in her seat, Micah pushed the throttle forward and they climbed into the sky toward their next destination and Prior dreaded her next appointment more than she had disliked taking her brother into custody.

3

Gilford, the suburbs of Capitol City, Central Province, Planet Kerguelen

Ten minutes after they took off, Prior's air ship was orbiting a modest residential neighborhood. Children were playing in a courtyard below and Prior could see their wide smiles even aloft and at a distance. She turned to Pana who was huddle over the surveillance and tracking panel.

"Is she home?" Prior asked.

"Affirmative," Pana nodded. "Thermal scans show one female adult matching her description, early to mid-twenties, in the dwelling."

"Good. Take us down, Micah," Prior called to her pilot.

The air ship made a combat landing near the courtyard and the children scurried toward the ship abandoning the playground equipment and their toys. For children, the sight of air ships was awesome and filled their imaginations with wonder. As Prior, Addison and Pana stepped out of the craft the children were even more awestruck. The sight of Guardians in their own neighborhood was something they would never forget.

The children surrounded Prior, Pana and Addison and gave them the Guardian salute when they recognized their uniforms. Prior saluted back and smiled at them. The girls in the group gathered around Prior and started talking all at once. Prior raised her hand to cease the babbling and it finally ended. One of the girls spoke for the rest.

"Are you a Guardian?" the little girl asked. She was about six years old, fair-skinned and had a wonderful arrangement of golden curls framing her face.

"Yes I am," Prior said kneeling down to the girl's level. "We all are."

"I told you there were girl Guardians besides Commander Jordan," the girl said to one of the boys near Addison.

"Yes there are," Prior confirmed. "There are a lot of girls in the Guardian Corps." The little girl stuck out her tongue at the boy and he did the same. Prior smiled and continued. "But we all work together."

"Do you know Commander Jordan?" another girl asked. She was also fair and a little older than the first girl but her hair was styled in a fashion emulating Jordan.

"Yes I do," Prior nodded. "I've known her a long time. We used to work together."

"Are you going to shoot someone?" one of the boys asked looking at Pana.

"No," Pana said placing a hand on the boy's shoulder. "We're going to see a friend." She looked behind her. "There are other Guardians in our air ship. I'm sure they'd love to show you our stuff."

Prior smiled and tapped her TACCOM. "Micah, you're going to have several tiny visitors in a few seconds. Give them a tour of the ship," Prior said.

Another of the boys stepped closely to Lupo and stroked his fur. He looked at Prior curiously. "Is he a Guardian too?" the boy asked.

"Yes he is," Prior said. "His name is Lupo."

The boy continued to rub the dog's fur and the rest of the children giggled when Lupo licked the boy's face. Two of the children showed Prior holographic cards depicting Guardians. Apparently, they were collector's items and the children were proud of them. Another child had an action figure resembling Commander Jordan and showed Pana the various accessories that came with it.

Their attentions shifted when Rex stuck his head outside of the craft and waved. The eldest child looked at Prior and she nodded and told them to go to the ship. The kids scampered off leaving Prior, Lupo, Pana and Addison in their wake. Prior jerked her head and they walked to Lieutenant Singh's house. There was a small fence around the house and Pana opened the gate for Prior. Prior sighed as they reached the door and lowered her head as she pressed the doorbell. As it rang, Addison turned to Prior.

"You were good with those kids," Addison said.

"It's easy when you share the same mentality," Prior quipped. "Let's see how I do with the widow."

Addison and Pana nodded as the door opened. Singh's wife stared at Prior for a moment and then frowned when she realized who it was. She didn't say anything but opened the door wide enough for them to enter. Prior told Lupo to stay and the Guardians stepped in and followed her to the kitchen. They sat around a dinette table and Singh's wife opened the conversation before Prior could start.

"How dare you come here?" she said angrily.

"I wanted to express my sincere apologies for your loss," Prior said softly.

"You're here to stroke the widow," she scoffed. "Well, I don't want your platitudes, I want my mate."

She reached up to her neck and held the metal choker around it. Attached to the choker was an expensive and intricately engraved platinum ring symbolizing that she was bonded to another. She rubbed the ring between her fingers and scowled at the Guardians. Prior could feel the hatred flowing from the woman.

"I understand how you feel, Sunetra," Prior empathized. "I have lost several men close to me as well. I... I want them back too."

"Singh is dead because of you," Sunetra accused.

"I didn't kill him, Sunetra, but I have a good idea who did," Prior said.

"Someone else may have pulled the trigger, but you killed him," Sunetra said shaking her head. "You should have heard the way he talked about you. Almost everyday it was, Commander Prior this and Commander Prior that. He would have tried to move the planet for you even though he knew it was impossible. He would have done anything you asked."

"He was doing his duty," Prior said.

"I know what he was doing was beyond his duty as a Guardian. He did special things for you... far above what was necessary," Sunetra said.

"Listen, Sunetra, I won't deny that Singh conducted special missions, but it was entirely voluntary. He could have refused an assignment anytime. If I had suspected that he had any reservations about his assignments, I would have pulled him off of them," Prior said.

"He was killed because he was trying to prove himself to you," Sunetra said. "He told me as much."

"He had nothing to prove to me. He was a dedicated officer and died protecting lives," Prior said raising her voice slightly. "Not all of us get that chance, and fewer still die doing the thing that we have dedicated our lives to."

"That's easy for you to say. I loved him," Sunetra said as tears began to fill her soft brown eyes. Her lips quivered as she continued. "I loved him."

"So did I, Sunetra. He was one of my men," Prior said coldly and unfazed by the tears. "I know you loved him, but act accordingly. At his funeral, everyone will be looking at you. You need to represent not only your family but the Guardian Corps as well. You will not cry at the wake, the funeral, or in the presence of friends and family. You must be as proud and dignified as possible. If you must cry, do it in private."

"Guardian Corps spouses and children never cry," Sunetra said remembering the brief she had received from a Guardian Corps public affairs officer after she and Singh had bonded.

"That's right. Singh would have wanted you to be strong and that display of strength will bleed over to the rest. Give him an honorable burial," Prior said.

"I can't help crying," Sunetra said as more tears streaked down her light brown cheeks.

"Cry when you're alone," Prior instructed. "Get it out now. Wear a heavy veil if you think you'll lose it at the service. And always keep your head up."

"I understand," Sunetra said stifling her tears.

"Where is your son?" Pana asked.

"With his grandparents," Sunetra explained. "They will return tomorrow."

"Get your tears over with now," Prior said. "You may have lost a mate, but Singh's parents lost their only son. And your own son is now fatherless. Always remember there are others involved." Prior stood up and placed a hand on Sunetra's shoulder. "We must leave now. I just wanted to see you and extend my sympathies."

"I'm actually surprised you came," Sunetra said. "I was under the belief that commanders delegated such things to subordinates."

"Singh was special… as are all of my Guardians. He was more than just a junior officer to me. I relied on him greatly and I shall miss him dearly," Prior said.

"I thought you were stealing him from me," Sunetra said lowering her eyes in shame.

"I only wanted the best for him, Sunetra," Prior said. Sunetra began to rise but Prior held up her hand and shook her head. "We'll see ourselves out. If you need to talk, or you need money or anything, you call me directly. Understand?"

Sunetra took a plastic card from Prior and read it. It had Prior's TELCOM number and PIL address on it and she nodded. Prior patted Sunetra on the shoulder again and walked away. When the door shut, the widow wept long and loudly.

"That was impressive, Commander," Addison said as they walked back to the air ship. "I thought you were going to rip her head off when she accused you of Singh's death."

"I was prepared for her outburst. It's only natural. That's why clergymen are sent to make death notifications. People don't lash out at priests if they go wild when they hear the news," Prior said. "Singh was a special case though. And Sunetra needed to be told what to do and how to act. There will be enough sadness at the funeral."

"She thought you were stealing Singh from her," Addison said. "I can't believe that. If she knew anything about Guardians, she would know that was ridiculous."

"Addison, what most women fail to realize is that their mates or boyfriends are not stolen by another woman. They are relinquished. That's why men leave or stray. Once you get that in your head, it's easy to handle and control your intimate relationships," Prior said.

"If I die in battle, I hope you visit my parents," Addison said.

"If you die, Lieutenant, I won't visit your parents, I'll dance a jig on your grave," Prior said harshly. "You don't have permission to die."

Addison nodded and as they said goodbye to the children, Prior was once again friendly. The Guardians climbed aboard the air ship after giving the children souvenirs and as the ship rose into the late afternoon sky, the children waved and continued to watch the ship until it faded from sight.

As they soared back toward Capitol City, Addison was awed by Commander Prior's ability to turn her emotions on and off like a light switch. It was fine in battle, a necessity in fact, but what did she do when she wasn't fighting? Could someone with that skill set behave like a normal person? Addison chuckled to herself and knew what Prior's answer would have been: *"I'm not a normal person, Addison. I'm Boroni."*

4

The Spire, Capitol City,
Central Province, Planet Kerguelen

As Prior's air vehicle cruised into mid-town Capitol City, she called Pana and Rex to her side. They stopped the maintenance they were doing to one of the door guns and joined her.

"Pana, make sure the ships are fully loaded and outfitted for extended operations. We won't have the opportunity to re-supply for a while," Prior said.

"We'll see to it after we drop you off," Pana said pulling her PDA out and generating a work list.

"Hopefully it won't take you long," Prior said. "You should relax tonight."

"I plan on it," Pana said giving Prior a mischievous grin.

Pana and Rex stepped to the rear of the craft and continued with their work as Addison turned to Prior.

"You'll have no security this evening?" she asked.

"I always have some type of security, Lieutenant," Prior said looking at her PDA. "And I can take care of myself if push comes to shove."

"Of that I have no doubt, Commander," Addison said. "But regulations are clear. Guardian General Order Number Four is explicit: In the event a Guardian commander's escort has been killed or is otherwise absent, the senior Guardian present will have the privilege of assuming the duty as escort for the Commander until suitable replacements are provided."

Prior leaned back in her seat and looked at Addison. "I have other duties for you this evening, Lieutenant. I need you to follow up on the Singh investigation. Go to the commerce center and see what you can glean from the site. Contact me in the morning and let me know what you find out," Prior said.

"What am I looking for?" Addison asked.

"What the others have missed… or have omitted," Prior replied.

When the air ship reached the center of the city, Prior could feel the vehicle respond to Micah's gentle touch. As he caressed the controls, the craft rose out of the pack of congested air ships in the traffic pattern and ascended towards the upper landing platform of The Spire, located more than a quarter of a mile in the sky. The gunship accompanying them quickly acquired a position in orbit above them and held station.

"Commander," Micah called to Prior. "King 3 reports a problem with their port stabilizer."

"Have them break off and RTB. I need that ship fully functional tomorrow," Prior said.

"Very well," Micah said and conveyed the message to Lucas, the gunship pilot. He acknowledged the instructions and veered off to the south and headed for the Tri-Rivers complex. When King 3 was on its way, Micah contacted The Spire's landing control center. "Spire Control, this is WB-324 Alpha 1, requesting permission to initiate landing sequence."

"WB-324 Alpha 1, Spire Control. Permission granted to initiate landing sequence. Steer three two seven for immediate penetration and landing. You're alone in the pattern. Winds are ten knots and variable. The lights are on," the controller said in a monotone voice.

"Roger, steer three two seven. Winds are at ten knots and variable and the lights are on. Thank you, Spire Control," Micah said.

Prior was looking forward to getting back to The Spire for a bit of relaxation before she embarked on another mission. Her bouts of sleeplessness had begun to take its toll on her. Her team and support craft would benefit from a break as well. With everything that had been going on for the past weeks, an evening of lounging would go a long way.

The winds caused the landing to be a little rougher than Micah would have liked. He prided himself on gentle touchdowns. Though he set the craft down without bouncing it, he cursed himself for the jerky approach he made. Once they were down, Pana opened the hatch and extended the accommodation ladder. Prior grabbed her gear and clothing and made for the exit. She gestured for Lupo to exit and the canine gingerly stepped down the ladder.

"We'll be back on deck at the usual time, Commander. We'll be ready to go early if you want to saddle up sooner," Micah called.

"The usual time will be fine, Micah, and make sure that you all get some rest," Prior said.

"No problem," Pana said.

Prior stepped down from the craft and Pana retracted the ladder and spoke on her headset. As Prior walked away, the air ship's engines wound up and the craft leapt from the platform and into the air. Micah had the craft near full throttle by the time Prior turned to watch it vanish into the darkening sky. She turned and felt the breeze wash over her. She shut her eyes for a moment and then opened them abruptly. She dropped her bags as Lupo growled and drew her pistol. She lowered it when she saw why her dog had been alerted.

"Can we have a word, Commander?" a man said stepping out of the shadows so Prior could see him clearly.

It was the Van Dyke wearing Celeron, the former Guardian named Hamilton. As he stepped forward, Gideon and three others revealed themselves from the dark corner of the landing platform. The three men with Gideon were well built and around six feet tall. They had masks covering their faces and though no weapons were visible Prior knew they had something concealed.

She holstered her weapon and both she and her canine looked at them curiously. Lupo was still growling but the noise had grown softer. Prior tapped him on the back and he sat down beside her. She looked at the Celeron and was not surprised that they had shown up. She was curious to know how they ended up here and Spire Control had not alerted her to their presence. The Spire's landing platform was a highly restricted area. Obviously Gideon had used his considerable influence to overcome such inconveniences. Gideon smiled at Prior in his paternal manner and she smiled back as she kept a close eye on his companions.

"What's this all about?" she asked. "Why have you come to my home?"

"Straight to the point as usual," Hamilton chuckled. "You paid a visit to our home unannounced, so we decided to reciprocate."

"I was not exactly a party crasher," Prior smiled. "How long have you been here?"

"Not long," Hamilton said. "We arrived only a few minutes before you."

"I see," Prior said. "Forgive me for not being here when you arrived. Would you like to come inside?"

"Another time perhaps," Hamilton answered. "We have many appointments before our day is done and the night is now upon us. I'll be brief, Commander. The death of Venture has forced our hands. I need a decision from you about your intentions in regards to joining us."

"I haven't made up my mind yet… Colonel," Prior said.

"No need to use my former rank," he said. "Nor is it necessary to address me with any kind of… embellishment. Hamilton will suffice."

"Does that hold for you as well, Marshal?" Prior asked Gideon.

"Yes, Commander," Gideon said.

Prior saw his eyes dart back and forth and realized that he didn't want to discuss that fact they were related in present company. Obviously it would have been problematic.

"As you wish, Gideon," Prior nodded.

"We want you to lead a force against The Argent," Gideon said.

"At the moment I can't do that," Prior said shaking her head. "I already have a commission in the Guardian Corps. Any forces I lead would have to be part of that organization. Besides, I still have reservations and doubts about the entire situation."

"Yes, I was told that. Have you read the scroll?" he asked.

"No, I've been pretty busy lately," said Prior.

"Are you scared about involving yourself with us and our mission?" Hamilton asked.

"Naturally I have concerns about my safety," Prior said. "Do you think I'm reluctant in joining you because I'm happy?"

"I don't think you understand the seriousness of the situation, Commander," one of the masked Celeron said.

His voice was very familiar to her and her eyes narrowed. "I know you," she said pointing at the man. "Show your face."

The man slowly removed the solid black veiling that concealed the lower part of his face and Prior instantly knew who he was. His name was Marcellus. He was athletic, possessed a genius-level IQ, had an infectious laugh and was without a doubt the most beautiful Kerguelen man Prior had ever seen. He was perfect in every way… and she hated him with every fiber of her being.

Marcellus was an ex-Guardian and academy classmate of Prior. He had graduated with the only academic average in academy history higher than hers. He had breezed through the curriculum without even trying. All of the tasks required of cadets seemed to be second nature to him. Whether it was academics or military in scope, he was perfect. He never received a single demerit in six years and was the cadet brigade commander for an unprecedented two years. He had been number one at the academy and Prior number two, but despite his oneness with Guardian lifestyle, Prior had always felt he was not totally committed to being a Guardian and believed his true desires were focused elsewhere.

When others were shocked he left a promising career in the Corps after his minimum three-year obligation had expired, Prior had not been surprised that he resigned and took a teaching position as an associate professor at Hallbridge University. Located in the North Island Province, the famous private institute was without a doubt the greatest seat of higher learning on Kerguelen. He had done well there and in short order had earned a full professorship. Since leaving the Corps, he had earned three doctorates and several academic and scholastic professional awards, including the prestigious Kerguelen Prize. As in the Guardian Academy, civilian success had come easily for Marcellus and despite leaving the Corps twelve years ago, he was considered the most successful graduate of the Guardian Academy Class of 2819. And it was that unbridled respect for his achievements that gnawed at Prior.

Marcellus stepped forward and bowed. "Hello, Prior."

"Marcellus," Prior frowned. She replied to him in his native provincial tongue "Quelle surprise."

"Pour vous servee," he answered in his crib language. He smiled at her and continued in the Kerguelen standard language. His accent was strong and distinct. "You're looking well, Prior. I see success hasn't spoiled you yet."

"Nor you, Marcellus," she said trying hard not to admire his handsome features. "You're a long way from Hallbridge."

"I've taken a sabbatical," he said as his face turned intense. "You know how serious the conditions on Kerguelen are, Prior. Guardians and citizens are dying loud and painful deaths. We need you to lead us."

"Us?" Prior said surprised. "Why don't you lead them, Marcellus? You're more than able. Unless academia has softened you, I would have thought the Celeron would be honored to have you at the helm of a force determined to save the planet."

"You flatter me, but I'm merely a member of the force. My destiny is to serve in it not to lead it," he replied. He smiled as he continued. "Besides, no one kills people more loudly, swiftly or painfully than you, Prior. For you, it's an exact science."

"That's the sweetest thing anyone has ever said to me, Marcellus. You really know how to make a girl swoon. I'm getting all excited," Prior joked.

"This is serious. You must take the job," Marcellus insisted.

"And if I don't?"

"We'd be very disappointed," he said with a forced grin.

"I don't like to be coerced into anything and threatening me would be a grave mistake on your part," Prior said sternly. "But as I said, I will consider your proposition and let you know."

"Don't take too long. Time is short. The Argent may commence their attacks at any time," Marcellus said.

"You'll be hearing from me shortly, I guarantee it," Prior said. "The fact that we could possibly be working together is intriguing." She raised an eyebrow and turned to Gideon. "By the way, if I agree to lead this Celeron force, what's in it for me?"

"The honor of leading a thousand Kerguelen in the most important conflict in our history," Gideon said.

"A thousand? The prophecy again," Prior scoffed. "I'm supposed to be the anointed one who leads a thousand against the dreaded destructor of the race? You can't be serious, Gideon."

"What is written cannot be refuted," Marcellus offered.

"You too?" Prior said turning briefly to Marcellus. "I thought only The Argent took the ancient prophecies verbatim?"

"I said that The Argent took them literally, I never said that the Celeron didn't," Gideon said.

"That's what Venture and you truly disagreed about, wasn't it? Interpretation of prophecy," Prior speculated.

"I told you she was intuitive," Marcellus said to Gideon. He turned back to Prior and continued. "He refuted the prophecies and his place in them. But when you read the scroll, I hope you believe in their validity and your place in the prophecy."

"Marcellus, you are a distinguished scholar. It surprises me that a Kerguelen Prize winner is so enamored with a archaic parchment," Prior said. "I must tell you, that piques my curiosity to new levels. However, until I study them myself, I have to pass on your offer. I'm not quite ready to be Celeron."

"If you accept, you won't be Celeron. You will only lead the force," Gideon corrected. "I'm afraid you don't meet the… physical requirements for inclusion into our society."

Prior laughed. "So I can play with your toys but not inside your house. Don't you have a Celeron sorority or something?" she said.

Her statement caused Gideon to laugh as well. "No, I'm afraid not, Commander. But don't let that slight deter you from doing what is truly best for Kerguelen," he said.

"As I said, I'll consider it. Now if you'll excuse me, I must go. I have to reflect on this. Goodnight, gentlemen," Prior said as she canvassed the group of men. She tapped Lupo on his back and he stood, arching his back as he did. She turned slightly to Marcellus and added softly in his dialect, "Bon soir, Marcellus."

"A bientot, Prior," Marcellus replied in kind.

She walked away and when she reached the door leading inside, Prior turned back to them. To her amazement, the five Celeron were gone. They seemed to have vanished into the darkness of the coming night without a trace. There was no sign of a ship or any means of conveyance on the platform, but they were gone. Prior chuckled and chalked it up to the use of special adaptive camouflage. She listened intently for hints of their footsteps but heard nothing. She looked at Lupo and observed that he too was agitated at their disappearance. His nostrils flared in search of a trace scent. She shook her head and entered the building knowing that Marcellus' parting words to her were correct. She would see them again… and soon.

5
Cathedral Prime, Capitol City, Central Province, Planet Kerguelen

"Do you understand your responsibilities?" Gregor asked the leader of his Papal security force.

The native of the Northeastern Province nodded. His name was Hudson and he had been in the service of the Federal Church for sixteen years and was ruthless in meting out Church discipline throughout Kerguelen.

"Yes, Your Eminence," Hudson said. "The men chosen are ready for the tasking. They are my best."

"Good," Gregor nodded. "Remember, though she is a Guardian, Commander Prior is still only a female. Take her down swiftly and make sure you shoot to kill."

"Thy will be done, Your Eminence," Hudson said with a bow. As he turned to exit the cardinal's office he stopped and faced Gregor. "I've heard a lot about the commander. It will be a pleasure to be the one to kill the Helot responsible for so many Kerguelen deaths."

He continued out of the office and when the door closed, a large dark figure entered through a side entrance. He breathed heavily and snorted loudly as he approached Gregor's desk.

"You're making a mistake with the Helot female," the creature said. "Don't leave her disposition to anyone but me. Allow me the pleasure of the kill and honor her with a swift death."

"Why do you doubt me, Argent? Haven't I followed through with every one of my promises to you?" Gregor asked.

"You have, but the Helot female is dangerous. Why do you play games?" The Argent asked. "What if she comes in and shoots you without giving you a chance to work your plan?"

"She won't," Gregor said. "She'll want to know why I've done all of this and who else is involved. Her natural inquisitiveness will let the pieces fall into place in my favor. If I can't turn her to our side, my guards will kill her, simple as that. And that leaves you free to lead the force against our first target."

"When will they be ready to strike?" The Argent asked.

"They're moving into position as we speak," Gregor said.

6
Prior's Apartment, The Spire, Capitol City, Central Province, Planet Kerguelen

It had taken Prior about two hours to get settled after she got to her apartment. Quinn once again flooded her with dozens of business reports and messages from the Western Province and Prior quickly waded through them. And then there were her Guardian duties to attend to. She had to respond to e-mails from Central Command, write orders, and dig through intelligence and unit reports. Finally, she had a 115-pound canine to feed and tend to before she could see to her own needs. Luckily, she had help in the latter assignment. Quinn's eldest daughter, Pilar, had arrived the previous day and was all too eager to feed, wash and groom Lupo. Though the chore was completed, the disaster area Pilar left behind would cause Prior's housekeeper fits in the morning.

When Pilar had finished with Lupo, Quinn and Pilar left. Pilar was longing to get out and explore the big city. She had convinced her mother to take her to the latest big screen presentation offered by the entertainment industry. The Western Province did not have big screen cinemas and the chance to see a first run movie would be a treat for the young Boroni female.

After they had gone, Prior considered the Celeron offer. Her misgivings about it consumed her thoughts. She decided she needed a clear mind to come to a logical decision so she changed into exercise clothes and went to the room she had converted into a gym. As she stretched in preparation for her workout, she looked at herself in the mirror and was glad Captain Hiroki had never seen her in exercise clothes. The sight of her in a combat suit proved more than provocative for him and if Hiroki had viewed Prior wearing only a sports bra and tights, he might have had a coronary.

The mini-gym Prior built had reinforced floors, walls and ceiling and contained two treadmills, free weights and a multi-purpose exercise machine to work and isolate various individual muscle groups. She put on bio-med sensors and hopped on the treadmill after she finished stretching and began her cardio workout. The readouts from the sensors were displayed on a wall screen in front of her. After running a few minutes, she shifted the treadmill's incline to twelve degrees and continued with the pace she had used at zero degrees. Despite her exertions, her respiration and lactic acid levels were practically normal. After six minutes at the severe incline, the treadmill returned to zero degrees and she looked at the distance and elapsed time indicator. A total of ten minutes had passed and she had run an estimated distance of two and a half miles. She continued her run and after another ten minutes elapsed, she saw that she had completed an additional three miles.

A low beep emanated from the treadmill indicating her cardio session was over and the machine automatically shifted to the cool down cycle. As the treadmill slowed, Prior began to walk briskly and after three minutes of cool down, the bio-med readouts changed and gave her a complete breakdown of her cardiovascular results and calories expended. She gazed at the readout intensely and was satisfied with the results. She shifted the position of the bio-med sensors and walked over to the free weights.

She placed heavy plates on the barbell and pumped out twelve quick reps on the bench press. She replaced the bar shook out her arms and pumped out another two sets of twelve reps each. She shifted to the leg press and pumped another three sets of twelve reps. She then went to a resistance machine. She set the resistance at maximum and began curling a bar. Her biceps bulged as she exercised and after four reps, she lowered the bar and looked at the bio-med readout. According to the readout, she had a strength increase of two-point-three percent from the last time she conducted the resistance exercise. She sighed and wiped her face with a soft terrycloth towel.

She continued with her weightlifting regimen and after the torturous workout with free weights and her cardiac-inducing run, Prior felt she had done enough for the day and removed the bio-med sensors. She took a long and steamy shower and slipped on a pastel blue silk robe and padded into her kitchen in bare feet. She opened the refrigerator and removed a sixteen-ounce bottle and shook it several times very briskly and twisted off the cap. She drank the contents of the bottle completely and tossed the empty container in the recycling bin.

The supplement she drank was needed to replenish her nutrient level and replace used calories quickly. All Boroni used it after they exercised heavily or worked strenuously. She opened a food processor and saw the meal left for her by Quinn. She retrieved a plate containing two steaks; a large pile of asparagus and a tremendous baked potato and sat down. After a very brief prayer of thanks, she voraciously wolfed down the meal. She put her dishes and utensils in the sink and prepared a tray filled with a sliced apple, a small hunk of crusty bread and a quarter wheel of well-aged cheese. She placed a bottle of dark burgundy from the Northeastern Province wine country on the tray and carried it into her living room.

Prior told the computer that controlled the apartment's utilities to shut off the lights and she lit candles and turned on her radio. The smooth jazz tones that emanated from the surround speakers were soothing and the atmosphere she had created was quite relaxing and just what she needed. Lupo heard the music and stepped into the living room and walked around as Prior sat down and opened the Scroll of Katana.

The large living room was decorated in Boroni style with flecks of Kerguelen tradition thrown in. The carpeted floor was covered in comfortable cushions called floor couches. Floor couches were present in every Boroni home and Prior also added traditional couches and chairs for guests whose tastes were not quite so bohemian. At either end of the apartment's ground floor were glass windows with sliding doors leading to terraces. The drapes were pulled aside and the bright Capitol City skyline shown into the apartment and in the distance, air ships darted past. In the far corner of the ground floor was a dining room and near the entrance were the set of double doors leading to her study.

On the walls were paintings and though she could have afforded old masterpieces, Prior had opted for modern works of art. On a table, were her degree certificates and on another were two promotion declarations. One was her promotion to second lieutenant and the other was her promotion to commander. Her other promotion certificates and Guardian and civilian awards were in her study.

Many visitors often asked Prior why she didn't display all of her awards and medals and honoraries for all to see. She had answered she was not above having an "I Love Me' wall, but had opted to have it in her study. Most everyone who had ever received an award, no matter how slight or insignificant, usually placed them in their homes so visitors could see them when they entered. They could be a conversation starter or a way to brag without being vocally conceited. Sometimes they were just put up so a person could remember the times when they were the best. It didn't matter whether the achievements were as a youth, briefly as an adult or spread over a lifetime, it only mattered that they were placed about in good taste. Prior had asked her father why he didn't display any of his awards around their home in the Western Province and he had said achievement was its own reward and pride only obscured it. She had tried to live up to that ideal but it was difficult.

As she nibbled on a piece of cheese and studied the scroll, the call box to her apartment chimed. She walked to the viewer and clicked it on. In the view screen was Commander Mohab. Prior smiled and clicked on the speaker.

"Hi, Mohab," Prior said cheerfully. "Come on up."

She pressed a button on the security pad and sent her elevator to the ground floor. In a few minutes, Mohab arrived at the apartment. She greeted him with a smile and a hug and led him inside by the hand. He was surprised at her attentions and felt a little embarrassed. He stepped into the living room as Prior went to the kitchen and brought back a wine glass.

"Would you like some wine?" she asked. "It's a burgundy, Chateau Trilby 2741."

"2741? That's a fine vintage," he said. "I will have some of that."

"Good," Prior said stepping to her tray.

Mohab looked at the walls and saw that Prior had put up some new pictures and he assumed they were Prior's family. One was of Prior when she was a young adult, probably at the age of thirteen or fourteen. Surprisingly she looked no different now than she had then. She was a bit taller and more muscular now, but her face was the same. She had retained the same clear complexion of youth into her thirties and would keep it until she was well into her fifties.

Mohab's eyes drifted to another picture and found that he was looking at a family representation. A mother, father and a young girl smiled wide for the camera. They were a handsome family and the man resembled Prior greatly.

"Is this your brother Pierce?" he asked as Prior returned with the wine.

"Yes, and his wife Quinn and their eldest daughter Pilar. She was just three years old then," Prior said.

"She looks older than that," Mohab said. "She looks about eight or nine."

"Yes," Prior said proudly. "She was always well proportioned for her age. She's much bigger now and very swift afoot. She's training for the heptathlon."

"How old is she now?"

"She's ten," Prior said taking a sip of wine. She picked up another framed picture and gave it to Mohab. "This is a recent picture."

"And how tall is she now?"

"Five nine… nearly five ten and weighs about one hundred and thirty-five pounds," Prior said casually. "She's about average."

Mohab chuckled. A ten-year old girl nearly five feet ten inches tall and weighing one hundred and thirty-five pounds was about average. He looked at the picture again. Pilar's beauty was already blossoming. The Boroni were truly an amazing people.

"You'd better keep a close eye on her. She's going to be pursued by every knucklehead with a libido in a few years," Mohab cautioned.

"It's too late for that, Mohab," Prior smiled. "Pilar is engaged."

"Engaged? She's only ten. She doesn't start college for another two years," Mohab exclaimed.

"Calm down, Mohab," Prior said laughing. "The Boroni live accelerated lives. Getting engaged at ten years old is quite common and most of us belonging to influential Houses are married by the time we're twelve. Pana was married young, and so were Pierce and Quinn. It's tradition."

"I wouldn't like it if my sister was married at ten years old," Mohab said still unable to wrap the idea around his head.

"If she were Boroni, you'd be glad to get her out of the house," Prior joked. "But you didn't come here to talk about Boroni marriage rites. What on Kerguelen does bring you here?"

"I was in town and I'd thought I'd drop by," he said. He looked and gestured to what she was wearing and added, "I hope I'm not disturbing you?"

Prior shook her head. "No. I was just wearing something comfortable while I did some reading," she said. Her face turned serious as she continued. "But why don't you tell me the *real* reason why you're here?"

"What do you mean?" Mohab asked innocently.

"You forget the Boroni have enhanced senses. We can feel temperature changes in the body… and in some circumstances, hear heartbeats. In other words, we're walking lie detectors. So come clean. What's up?" Prior said.

Mohab sighed. "Okay, I'm here to make sure you don't do anything rash concerning the death of Lt. Singh. Central Command knows you're investigating the incident in depth," Mohab said.

"That's my right," Prior said. "Singh was one of my Guardians and if he died under mysterious circumstances, it's my responsibility to find out why." She saw that Mohab was still a bit nervous and probed to find out why. "But this isn't totally about Singh. What else have I done that concerns Central Command?"

"They're curious as to why you've ordered your Guardians from the Middle Provinces to a position around Central Command. They also want to know why your brother Senator Poul has been transferred to a detention cell there," Mohab answered. "I have to admit, I'm curious about those moves as well."

"I have my reasons, Mohab. That's all I need to say about that," Prior replied. "But why didn't Central Command ask me directly? Why the feint?"

"They thought our relationship might make the questioning less antagonistic," Mohab said.

"All they had to do was ask, Mohab. Boroni don't lie," Prior said. She waved her hand to him. "Come, sit with me."

Mohab followed her to the living room and loosened the buttons on his blazer and joined her on the floor. His civilian attire had caught

Prior off guard when she first saw him. It had been a long time since she had seen him out of uniform. He had always been a chic and fashionable dresser and the expensive cut of his clothes flattered his well-kept physique. He wore a black mock turtleneck pullover under a black blazer devoid of lapels. His trousers had sharp creases pressed into them and his shoes were handmade leather. As he lounged on the cushions he drank his wine and finished almost all of it before either offered any words. He was having a hard time keeping his eyes from peering at her ample bosom showing itself through an open fold in her robe and she made no attempts to close it.

"So, how long are you in town?" he asked clearing his throat.

"Until I clear up a few things requiring my attention," she said.

"Now you're the one being evasive," he said a little annoyed. "Just like before."

"What are you talking about?" she asked swallowing a slice of apple.

"You said nothing when you were going after Venture. I could have done something to help," he said.

"Is that still bothering you?" Prior asked dropping the piece of cheese she was holding and sighing loudly. "Mohab, you're a good officer and a better Guardian than most, but you're not a surveyor. We walk the point and scrounge around in the dirt and muck. We find the bad guys and take out threats. The job of finding Venture is something that I do. I was born to do it. If I told you I was going after Venture, you would have tried to help, but that kind of job is *not* your specialty."

"So, I'm not up for that type of job?" he asked feeling a bit slighted.

"It's wet work, Mohab. You don't do that," Prior said.

"And you do?" he scoffed.

"Yes, I do," she said coldly and nodding. "And often. Venture wasn't the first person I was ordered to kill, and as long as Marshal Garath has a list of targets, he won't be the last."

"I'm curious but I'm not sure I want to hear any more," he said.

"You don't, Mo," she said.

"I could find out more if I tried."

"Don't, Mohab. For your sake, leave it alone... please," she said.

"Okay," he said. "I won't turn over any stones." It was obvious she was doing things he was not privy to and in that case, it was better to let a sleeping dog lie. She had given him a subtle warning but it was loud and clear. If he found out any more about her business, she might be forced to silence him for security's sake. He took a drink and changed the subject. "What do you think about the state of our political leaders?"

"The Singh situation has reinforced them a bit, but they're still squirming," Prior said. "There is trouble in their hallowed halls and I don't trust them."

"I told you long ago that even the best political system is designed with flaws," Mohab said.

"And I have learned that all politicians are the same," Prior replied.

"But the next generation…"

"Will be just like the last," Prior interrupted. "Everyone has the same old dream that the next generation of politicians will usher in a change to the old standards. And you know, many of them start out that way, but it never lasts. They slowly revert back to the same old song and dance. And why? It's because they come to realize that the only way to make change is to stay in power, and the only way to stay in power is to adopt the same ways of the previous regime. In time, all the lofty ideals that they rode into power with become lost in the winds of what might have been. The only thing that keeps them in check is those of us outside of the political structure."

"I don't know, Prior. There are many young representatives trying to make a difference," Mohab offered. "It just takes time."

"No, Mohab, politicians are all the same. They have different faces and bodies, but they wear the same old suits. Time does not change what is at their core. No matter what province they hail from or political party or ideology they represent, they don't change. Those who maintain their convictions are assassinated. Assassinated with a bullet, like my father, or by scandal like others," she replied angrily.

"What about Senator Cul?" Mohab asked.

"Cul is no different," Prior said waving her hand. "He's so twisted he could hide behind a corkscrew. I wouldn't say he's dishonest but I would consider him ethically challenged."

"I'm sorry he burst your bubble," Mohab said seeing that the truth about Cul had hurt her deeply. "I know he is a family friend."

"He and my brother water their horses from the same troth. Whatever happens to them, they deserve," Prior said.

"Is he going to be charged with an impropriety in the Western Province?" Mohab asked.

"Let's just say there will be two freshmen senators representing the Boroni in the next session of the planetary legislature," Prior said.

"And what do you think of Shayesteh?" Mohab asked.

"The young vice president has a lot to prove. I know you think a lot of your cousin, Mohab, but she did almost nothing to stop the federal forces from entering Coastland. And that gives me reason to be suspicious of her," Prior said.

"How much could she possibly do? She has hardly had time to gain any political allies in the Senate," Mohab said.

"All I can say, Mohab, is that in a time of turmoil, real leadership reveals itself, it doesn't hide or act tentatively because of inexperience," Prior said. "One either is or is not great."

Mohab nodded in agreement. "Perhaps you're right. But I'm not ready to give up on her yet," he said.

"I hope your faith is justified," Prior said.

"I have to ask what you're planning to do next?" he said.

"I've had Thyssen's report about Singh's death reviewed. By tomorrow, I'll have all I need to go forward," Prior said.

And if you discover his report was false?"

"I'll have to kill him."

"I know you do certain things I shouldn't know about, but I know you don't like to kill fellow Guardians," Mohab said with empathy.

"I don't. I feel a kinship of sorts with all Guardians. Venture, Omega and I were close for a long time. However, Venture broke the code and needed to be dealt with. But I can tell you, if they had sent me after you, I would have resigned," Prior said softly.

She looked away from him and Mohab stared at her in silence, not sure of what to say. He had strong feelings for her as well; very-strong feelings, and they had been with him ever since they were in the academy together. He was sure she instinctively knew how much he cared for her and he knew that being a Guardian meant everything to her. To give it up because of him was a serious admission of friendship and revealed the deep connection between them. She had obviously given the concept considerable thought. When Prior turned back to Mohab, she flashed him a quick smile.

"Do you remember when we first met?" she asked.

He laughed. "Yes I do. It was orientation day of our plebe year, the first day on campus for new arrivals actually. I came to your room to say hello," he recalled.

"You came to my room because you thought I'd be naked," she corrected pointing a finger at him. "I know you believed the stories that Boroni females didn't wear clothes."

"That's not true," he denied.

"Oh yes it is. I know that's the reason you came to see me, Mo. I knew it even back then, but I wasn't mad at you. I understood that you were a twelve-year old Kerguelen boy, and no twelve-year old boy worth a damn is going to pass up the chance to see a genetically-enhanced twelve-year old girl naked," Prior said with a smile.

Prior was right on the money. That's exactly the reason he had shown up. She was five foot ten inches tall back then and fully matured. She was put together better and was bigger and curvier than any woman he had ever known. When he first saw her he thought she was some kind of goddess.

"You're right," he said nodding and chuckling. He raised his glass. "Well, here's to nudity and not having to kill each other."

She touched his glass with hers and drained it. He took the bottle and refilled her glass and then his own. They remained silent again for a long interval and then she broke the silence.

"Can you stay until morning, Mo?" she asked.

"I guess so. My crew isn't due to pick me up at my hotel until after eight," he said. "Why?"

"Don't be obtuse, Mohab," Prior said looking annoyed. "Can you stay *here* with *me* until morning?"

"Yes, I can," he said matching her seriousness.

"Good, wait here a sec," she said emotionlessly. She stood up and dashed up the spiral staircase to a bedroom retrieving Lupo. As the dog slowly lumbered down the stairs, outwardly incensed that he was ousted from his preferred place of slumber, Prior called to Mohab. "Come up."

Mohab stood up and as he walked toward the stairs, he petted Lupo. "Wish me luck, boy," he whispered to the canine. Lupo barked once and then settled on the floor with a loud grunt.

Though he appeared confident, Mohab was not exactly sure he was ready to spend the night with Prior. It was rare for Boroni females to consort sexually with Kerguelen males and those few males who had sex with Boroni related very little about the experience. Boroni mating rituals were something of a mystery. Mohab did know that Boroni females chose their partners based on the physical prowess of a male. The ability to provide for and protect the family was the determining factor in their sex drive. Strength was paramount to them and it was rumored that Boroni females had to be won, not courted, and once in a relationship, they were committed to it. However, it was also said that when a Boroni female wished to sever the ties of a relationship, it was over. Period. The separation was due to the female's belief the male had somehow become too weak to hold her.

Boroni females were sexually passionate, so intense that many accounts considered their love making animalistic in nature. All of these things traversed through Mohab's mind as he wound up the spiral staircase and made his way to the bedroom. He entered and saw that she was already naked. Prior shut the door behind him after he stepped into the room.

Her bedroom was huge and the bed was tremendous. It was at least twice as large as any king-sized bed he had ever seen. He speculated that it was Boroni in origin. The room was illuminated with several candles and their soft yellow glow pierced the darkness and gave the room a wonderful ambience. The aroma coming from the candles had a strange and heady effect on him and shook his head once and blinked his eyes in an effort to adjust to it. Prior walked to Mohab and stood in front of him. Even in her bare feet she was as tall as he was. She removed his blazer and began to undress him, staring directly into his eyes as she did. He stepped out his shoes and started to speak, but she silenced him.

"Shh," she said softly. "Don't do anything, not yet. Just relax, Mo. You're in my world now."

He breathed deeply and as she proceeded to disrobe him he felt his sexual urges beginning to rise so fast he could hardly control them. She must have noticed because she flashed her topaz-colored eyes provocatively and spoke even softer to him.

"It's the candles. They'll help you reach your... ultimate potential," she whispered.

She continued to look into his eyes as she lifted his turtleneck over his head and off. She kissed his chest and worked her way down his muscular torso until she reached the belt of his trousers. Prior unfastened his belt, unbuttoned his trousers and slipped them off of his legs. She stood up and rubbed her hands across his chest. As she did, she cooed softly and made other unrecognizable noises. The sounds were feline-like. Not domesticated cat types, but the sounds made by big game cats. She smiled as she pressed her hands on his chest and abdomen, obviously liking his physique.

Whether it was the candles or her attentions to his chest and abs, Mohab became excited again and he blushed as he moaned. Prior looked down and reached between his legs and took hold of what she found there and squeezed gently. His body reacted to her touch and he regained control of his body. He breathed deeply and looked at her quizzically, but she only smiled at him. She pulled off his undergarment and took his hand in hers and kissed his fingers tenderly.

She stepped backwards so he could see her completely. He had never seen her totally nude before and was awed at the spectacular symmetry of her physique. She saw his eyes roam over her and enjoyed that fact he was ogling her lecherously. Only one scar marred the near perfect female form. He touched it gently and his fingertips caused her to shudder.

"Why didn't you fix that?" Mohab asked.

Dermal regenerators could remove any scar and leave the skin unblemished. The procedure was quick and painless and anyone with even modest means could have it done. But for some reason she had not.

"I wanted to remember that if you're careless you can get killed," she said softly. "I wanted to prove I was a good hunter, as good as my mother, and trying to prove it I got gouged a bit by a stag."

She pressed her body against his and he felt her firm muscles embrace him. She moved backwards and led him to the bed and sat down. She slid to the head of the bed and when she got there she opened her arms wide.

"Come to me, Mohab," she said softly and enticingly.

He joined her and as he tried to embrace her, she took hold of his short hair and kissed him forcefully and deeply. He pulled away from the pain, but she pulled him back. He could feel the strength and power in her arms. He paused for a moment and grabbed the hand holding his hair. He pulled her hand away and she fought him back, grunting as his resistance increased. Prior rolled him over on his back and held him down. As he tried to move his arms, he found she was forcibly pinning him to the mattress. Mohab grunted and broke the hold she had on him and rolled her on her back.

She appeared to be angry and took hold of his throat and lifted him slightly off of the bed. He groped at her hand but she would not release him. He felt like he was choking but she would not let up. He made a fist and punched Prior in the mid-section. It did nothing and she bared her teeth as he gasped for air. He hit her again and she eased her grip and he broke the hold. She rolled him over on his back and they began to wrestle and not in a playful way.

Prior tried to pin him down again but he smacked her twice quickly. She appeared even angrier and put her hands in his armpits, lifted him into the air and threw him against the headboard. He rolled and grabbed her by the arm and threw her against the headboard. Before she could move he smacked her again and when he was about to hit her again, her face softened. He lowered his hand and she slid down onto her back submissively. The battle for dominance seemed to be over and she had given in.

She pulled him down to her and kissed him deeply but passionately this time, and when she pulled away he looked at her. He stroked her face where he hit her and kissed the area softly. She closed her eyes and when they opened, her topaz irises were cerulean and shining brightly. She could see he was startled, and maybe even a bit frightened, from the sight. She smiled and kissed him again.

"It's okay, Mo, I'm not possessed," she said with a laugh. "The rumors you've heard are true though. It's a natural occurrence in Boroni females. The deeper blue they appear, the greater the emotional experience we're having."

"What does it feel like when they change?" he asked.

"What does it feel like when you smile?" she replied.

"I-I thought I was hallucinating for a moment," he said. "But it's real."

"Oh, yes. It's real, Mo, you're not dreaming," she said sliding beneath him. "And if I do everything right it may feel like a dream, but believe me, you'll know it's real."

7

San Mariner, Planetary Sector Five, Kerguelen Star System, Eight days from Planet Kerguelen

After their rendezvous with *Jackknife*, *San Mariner's* power problems were eliminated. An emergency power pack unit was transferred over and was being used to supplement shortages in the battery system. Dela had squeezed every bit of energy out of the fuel cells and they were now totally exhausted. The batteries were slowly being recharged from the sun's rays and would soon be able to handle the entire load by themselves, until then, the power pack would suffice.

The rest of the ship was operating satisfactorily and Omega and Dela settled into a regular routine. Omega handled most of the requirements needed to maintain the ship while Dela rested as much as she could. Her ribs were still sore and every four or five hours, she took a brief catnap. Omega periodically turned on the cameras in the nose and portside of the ship to record a seldom seen sight. It was not often that Space Command ships traveled together and both ships photographed each other for posterity. They were currently slowly cruising in Planetary Sector Five of their star system and about to cross over into sector four, their home sector.

Space Command had divided the Kerguelen star system into eight sectors. Each planet in the system had its own sector and *San Mariner* and *Jackknife* were currently passing the planet of sector five. Named Cedilla, the planet was the third most populated celestial body in the star system. Only Kerguelen and its moon possessed more people than Cedilla.

At a distance of one hundred and thirty-six million miles from the Kerguelen sun, Cedilla was a world of contrasts. When viewing it from space, the planet appeared dark and foreboding. On the surface, it seemed more hospitable and familiar. On its surface were two vast deserts teeming with high dunes of pure silicon; in the equatorial region were numerous liquid methane rivers; and to the north and south tremendous polar ice caps dominated the landscape.

But Cedilla's esthetic qualities were not the reason for its large population. The planet was ideal for space operations. Cedilla possessed a gravity field 80% of that on Kerguelen and its thin atmosphere and position in the system made the viewing of celestial events and phenomena unsurpassed. The light gravity made traveling and working on Cedilla very easy, which meant less fuel and physical exertions had to be expended to work on Cedilla's surface. And for prospectors and speculators, that made Cedilla a true pot of gold. Fifteen years earlier, the first expedition to the planet found that it was a geologist's paradise. The star sailors discovered many variants of raw materials found in the mines of Kerguelen readily accessible on or very near the surface of Cedilla. These raw materials were now in short supply and becoming scarce on Kerguelen and the ability to find and mine them quickly had turned Cedilla from a scientific curiosity into a major economic concern.

More than three thousand miners, engineers, technicians, scientists and their families currently resided on Cedilla and were supported by a cadre of Space Command personnel. The support personnel operated and maintained the living and scientific facilities for the workforce and taught in the schools for their children. Another smaller contingent of executives managed the output of raw materials from Cedilla to their parent companies on Kerguelen. In all, around 4,500 people inhabited Cedilla and the planet was slowly becoming an entity all its own. A push for independent statehood had been circulated for the past two years but so far, no real strides had been made. Many believed the cry for independence was really an effort to make the public aware of the concerns of the colonists.

Regardless of the reasons, the companies involved on Cedilla would do whatever was necessary to keep the flow of material coming and had the backing of Space Command and the Technology Council. The colonists had to be kept happy at all costs.

Dela peered out of the flight deck window and looked at Cedilla. The ships were less than a hundred thousand miles from Cedilla and preparing to slingshot around it for the final push to Kerguelen. Dela saw the lights of the domiciles and work domes aglow on the ebon and gray landscape and wondered what everyday life was like for the people of Cedilla. The planet was eight days from Kerguelen using the highest standard speed and this far out it was understandable the people would develop their own set of philosophies and ideals. Perhaps she would take a trip to the planet one day and see for herself.

"I see the lights of Cedilla," she said to Omega.

Omega looked up and out of the window as well and nodded. "You're right," he agreed. "But there are a lot more lights on down there than usual." He clicked on the radio. "*Jackknife, San Mariner*, Cedilla is burning awfully bright out there."

"Affirmative, *San Mariner*, it's a greeting from the people of Cedilla," Arista answered. "If you look at the orbital station, you'll see it's flashing its lights as well."

"We see it," Omega replied.

"I just received a message from the station commander. It reads: '*Welcome home and good job. We are all proud of you.*' It's signed Escobar," Arista said.

"Sounds like we're celebrities," Dela said.

"Arista, pass on our thanks to the people of Cedilla and send my complements to Station Commander Escobar. I know the power they're expending is precious and dipping into their reserves for us was a great gesture," Omega said.

"Will do. Speaking of power, how are you guys doing?" Arista said.

"I think we'll be fine now. But we'll make it even if we have to pull out the sails," Omega said.

"I'll let you go so you can save as much power as possible," Arista said. She knew that even a short talk drew a lot of power. "See you soon, Omega."

Omega clicked off the radio and looked at Dela quizzically. She had a devilish expression on her face. "What?" he asked.

"*See you soon, Omega*," she said mocking Arista's voice perfectly. The tone Arista had used was overtly friendly and didn't go unnoticed by Dela. "She really likes you, Commander. Are you two, have you two ever…"

"No," Omega said tersely. "We are not now nor have we ever been involved that way. It wouldn't be fair to her anyway."

"Don't you think that's up to her?" Dela countered. "She's a big girl… and she's kind of hot." Dela's teasing was not appreciated by Omega but he let her go on. Dela's smile faded quickly and she turned serious. "If she's interested, she's smart enough to have fully considered the ramifications of getting involved with you. If she's willing, why not give it a try? What's the worse that could happen?"

"Getting involved with a excommunicated man could destroy her life," Omega said bluntly. "They made all kinds of threats to Prior at the end. It's not something I'd wish on anyone."

"Cdr. Prior is different. There is nothing the Church could have threatened her with that she couldn't handle. And she didn't end your relationship because of threats. She ended it because you chose space and your quest over her. She would have left the Corps and given up her company to live with you on the moon or Space Station *Condor*, but you pushed her away. So she let you go," Dela said.

"How do you know that?" Omega asked.

"She and I discussed you at length before we left," Dela confided. "She told me more than I wished she had. But you shouldn't have worried about Prior. She's Boroni. Kerguelen threats no longer have any meaning to them."

"You're a lot like Prior," he said. "Maybe if everyone was, things would be better on Kerguelen."

"No, I don't think so," Dela disagreed. "Prior is unique and only a Boroni could have her mentality or outlook on things. But she and I do share one thing. We both believe that Kerguelens are not as afraid of the Papal seat's power as the cardinals think. If you wanted to keep your life with Prior or start a new one with Arista, I think the people would disregard your excommunication, especially now. If I were you, I'd play it smart and take advantage of my new found popularity. Your stock will never be higher."

"You're probably right, Dela," Omega said nodding. "But that's the thing. You're not me… and I've never been that smart."

8

Cathedral Prime, Capitol City, Central Province, Planet Kerguelen

A member of The Argent leadership and Cardinal Gregor sat across from each other in a darkened room. They each sipped wine and Gregor was wearing the silver and black vestments of the Summoner and held his crosier in his left hand. In the corner of the room, The Argent himself sat erect in a special chair designed for his use but Gregor could see that it was not quite up to the job. The huge behemoth struggled to get comfortable without destroying the seat and finally settled on one position.

"Are you sure your men can handle this Guardian?" the creature asked, his voice echoed off of the walls as he spoke.

Gregor nodded. "Of course," he said.

"And after the Helot female there is only one other Guardian commander?" the member of The Argent leadership asked.

"Yes," Gregor said. "While my men are taking care of Prior, another of our associates will dispose of Cdr. Mohab."

"The last two commanders taken out with a single blow," the creature nodded in approval.

"And what of *San Mariner*?" The Argent leader asked.

"I've made arrangements for that as well," Gregor said. "At the same time the commanders die, our primary assault and secondary missions will take place. In a few days, Kerguelen will have a new leader and the planet will be ripe for the picking."

Gregor raised his glass to the creature. The creature nodded his head and knew that the cardinal was correct. The planet would be ripe for the picking, but what the good cardinal did not know was that there would only be one harvester. And that harvester would not be the cardinal or any of his friends or associates… nor anyone else dwelling on this world or in this dimension.

9

Prior's Apartment, The Spire, Capitol City, Central Province, Planet Kerguelen

"Prior, you have many things to do. You must fulfill your destiny. Do not be afraid. You have everything you need to succeed."

The voice was everywhere and nowhere. It brought Prior out of her brief slumber and she sat up and looked around. Immediately she realized she was in her bedroom. The dream had victimized her again. She looked at the chronometer on her night table and sighed. It was two-thirty in morning and she had only slept for a little over two hours and that wouldn't do. She needed to do something to induce sleep. Beside her, Mohab was in deep sleep, almost comatose and he would remain that way until first light, and she envied him that. The effects of the aphrodisiac candles would make him rest. She disliked using the now smoldering candles but Kerguelen men just didn't have the natural stamina to fully sate the sexual desires of Boroni females. If they continued having intimacies, she would have to use them until he learned how to manipulate his body to please her without external stimuli. But it would take time… and a lot of practice.

Prior waved her hand in front of a sensor strip and the lights slowly came up to minimal illumination and she slipped out of bed and walked down to the living room opting not to wrap herself in a robe or covering. Lupo raised his head as she entered and watched his nude mistress lie down on the floor couches and pick up the scroll given to her by Gideon. It took her a minute to get into the right mindset in order to read it. The ancient biblical language was not easy to comprehend and required tremendous concentration in order to understand it.

Before she knew it, she had nearly worked her way through the entire scroll. She looked at the living room's chronometer and it read four o'clock. She was impressed that she had gotten through so much so quickly. She carried the scroll to her study and she poured herself a tall glass of Anise whiskey and downed it all in one swallow. She hoped the reading and the whiskey would do the trick and help her sleep. She put the scroll down on her desk and exited the study.

"Lights… off," she said and the lower level lights of her apartment slowly dimmed until they were extinguished.

She tapped her thigh and Lupo joined her side and they went upstairs to her bedroom. Lupo stepped up on the mattress and curled up at the foot of the bed as Prior slipped underneath the blankets. She set her alarm for six-thirty and waved her hand across the sensor strip to shut off the lights. As the lights went out, she nestled closely to Mohab and rested her head on his chest and felt very safe next to him for some reason. She kissed his chest and closed her eyes and thought about the Scroll of Katana.

The scroll was filled with the usual things that most scriptures contained but primarily discussed Katana. The similarities between Prior and Katana were too many to be mere coincidence. Katana was female and a first-born twin just like Prior and she and her brother Kullen were the first twins born in the history of Kerguelen. Prior and her brother Poul were the first Boroni twins ever born and their birth was considered impossible and a good omen and as babies, they were visited by almost all of the Boroni in the Western Province and showered with gifts. Poul was a senator, a lawgiver, and Kullen was the deliverer of the Almighty's Laws. Prior was a Guardian and protector of the law just as Katana was. Seduced by The Second, Kullen was coerced by evil and had broken the Almighty's Law and Katana had been forced to deal with him. She didn't kill him but had him sent away for the Almighty to judge him. She ultimately banished his eternal soul to the Netherworld. And Prior had been forced to do the same to her brother Poul.

Katana was an outcast amongst her brothers and sisters and lived in a self-imposed exile in a remote section of Kerguelen. Prior was an enigma in the Guardian Corps and was never fully embraced by the Kerguelen society she had sworn to defend with her life. She lived high above the rest of the populace in an isolated penthouse. She and Katana both possessed great strength and they both had animal companions that were wolves. Though Lupo was only half-wolf, the fact remained that he was not behaviorally modified with an obedience chip. Compared to other domesticated animals, Lupo was as wild as any beast of the land.

There were other similarities but the most telling was the dreams. Boroni didn't dream and she was visited by dreams every time she tried to sleep. The words she heard in her dreams were exactly the same as those written in the scroll. Prior was led to believe the voice in the dream was the Almighty, but the scroll had called it The Incubus. If The Incubus was truly speaking to her that meant the prophecy was true, and it also meant something bad was going to happen soon. Katana was only awakened in the desperate hours of Kerguelen.

As Prior drifted off to sleep, she made her decision about the Celeron. She hoped it was the right choice because the fate of the planet may be in her hands. She snuggled closer to Mohab as sleep took hold of her and she breathed in his scent and processed it into her memory. For better or worse, she would always remember it. It seemed lately everything that involved her was tentative and required hard choices… and maybe that was what life was all about.

10
Prior's Apartment, The Spire, Capitol City, Central Province, Planet Kerguelen

Mohab slowly opened his eyes, rolled over on his back and stared at the ceiling. He looked around the room and saw that he was alone. He knew he was still at Prior's apartment, but she was gone. At the foot of the bed was Lupo. When Mohab stirred, the canine lifted his head and stared at him curiously. Mohab's head throbbed and his body ached. He felt worn out and drained but at the same time he felt a strange sensation of ease throughout him. He swung his feet over the edge of the bed but when he tried to stand, he fell back to the mattress. He was still feeling lightheaded and decided to take it slower. He stood again and managed to keep himself erect long enough to reach the bathroom and take a shower.

The water revived him and the fuzziness that clouded his mind eventually dissipated. After the shower, he wrapped a towel around him and stepped into the bedroom. Waiting for him was a woman holding a rectangular box.

"Good morning, Commander," the woman said with a smile. "I hope you slept well?"

The woman was an older but still youthful looking Boroni female. There were strands of gray and silver hairs mixed in with the dark brown ones. She was taller than Mohab and had intense sparking brown eyes.

"Good morning," Mohab said. "I did sleep well. Thank you."

"Good. My name is Breck and I'm the housemaid. I'm here to see if there is anything you require," she said.

"Just my clothes," Mohab said looking around the bedroom.

"These are for you," Breck said handing him the box.

"I have my own clothes," Mohab said taking the box.

"The Mistress insisted that you have fresh garments," Breck said with a smile.

Mohab looked at the box and read the script lettering on it. The box came from Marquandt's, an upscale men's clothier. He looked at the chronometer and saw that it was still too early for Breck to have gone to the store to buy them.

"These are new," he said. "I didn't realize Marquandt's was open at this hour."

"The Mistress had one of the tailors deliver these a few minutes ago. I hope they're to your liking," Breck said.

Mohab opened the box and examined the garments and nodded. "They'll do just fine. Thank you, Breck," he said.

"Then I'll leave you to get dressed. There are grooming materials and oral hygiene equipment at your disposal in the bathroom. Please come down for breakfast when you're finished," Breck said and walked out of the bedroom.

Mohab dressed, shaved and brushed his teeth and left the room with Lupo trailing close behind. He went to the railing of the landing overlooking the lower level of the apartment and saw Pana and Quinn sitting at the dining room table. They looked up and smiled. Pana waved to him and he waved back and carefully meandered down the stairs with Lupo at his heels. Pana stood as he approached.

"Good morning, Commander," Pana said. "Did you sleep well?"

"I don't know, the jury is still out," he said rubbing his temple. The early morning sun was shining strongly through the windows and the brightness hurt his eyes. He squinted as he continued. "Where's Cdr. Prior?"

"In her study," Pana said examining him. "Sit down and we'll get you squared away."

Mohab sat and Pana called Breck and the maid brought in a glass containing a green liquid. She handed it to Mohab and he looked at it warily unsure he wanted to consume the contents.

"Drink it," Quinn said with a smile. "In a few minutes you'll feel better."

"What is it?" he asked holding up the glass to the light. The liquid was so thick the light would not pass through it.

"It's a combination of herbs, roots and fruit pulp from the Western Province. It will counter the effects of the Tracki. Drink it," a youthful voice said from the far side of the room.

Mohab looked to the voice and saw a young Boroni female. She looked like a miniature version of Quinn, dressed in black leggings and a white oversized pullover. She plopped down in a chair next to Mohab and smiled. She looked closely at Mohab and seemed to be examining him.

"And what are Tracki?" he asked the girl.

"That's the name of the candles," Quinn said. "They're made from the essence of a rare flower found in our province. Young Boroni males give the flower to females as gifts when they are courting. It's a sexual innuendo or metaphor indicating their intentions. But the candles are most commonly used when experimenting with sex."

"They are seldom used by Boroni older than eight or nine though," the girl offered. "It helps remove inhibitions and fear."

"Eight or nine years old?" exclaimed Mohab.

"Yes," the girl nodded. "The age when we normally have our first encounters."

"Be silent, Pilar," Quinn said sternly. She saw that what her daughter said had troubled Mohab and tried to clear it up for him. "Boroni mature at an accelerated rate, Commander, in all aspects. The use of the candles would be an X-rated version of Kerguelen youths playing house or post office... without the stamps."

"I see," Mohab chuckled and drank down the thick opaque slurry. It took a bit to get it all down but he succeeded. He handed the empty glass to Breck and smiled. "Thank you."

"You're welcome, Commander," she said.

"He's cute... for a Kerguelen," Pilar said shamelessly. She continued to look at Mohab carefully and Breck tapped the girl on the shoulder.

"Come help me, Pilar," Breck said silently scolding the young Boroni girl with her eyes.

"But..." she began to protest.

"Now," the maid said firmly and the young girl and the maid walked into the kitchen. Breck and Pilar returned and the girl placed a plate of fruit and a glass of water in front of Mohab and smiled.

"Enjoy your breakfast… Commander," Pilar giggled. Breck tugged at her pullover and Pilar frowned as the maid led her back into the kitchen.

"I doubt if I can keep this down," he said pushing the plate away.

Pana pushed the plate back in front of him. "Trust me, you need to eat. Your body needs to intake vitamin C. If you don't, the effects of the candles can be unpredictable. You may become ill," she cautioned.

Mohab knew that Pana was some type of Boroni medical professional. What her qualifications were was a mystery to him but he accepted what she said as gospel. As he started to eat, his appetite returned to him. Pana smiled as he dug in and she and Quinn got up to leave.

"Sgt. Major Pana?" he called to her and she turned. "I need to contact my people."

"Cdr. Prior has already seen to that. She informed them to expect a call from you within an hour," Pana said. "By that time, you will have recovered fully."

"Thank you," he said.

"Just eat. Cdr. Prior will be with you shortly," Pana said and she and Quinn left him alone to finish his breakfast.

In the study, Prior knelt before a priest holding a religious amulet in her hands as she looked at him. Every member of the Federal Church of Kerguelen possessed a religious icon depicting their faith, but no two were exactly alike. Though most had an icon with the Great Prophet Virgil or one of his ten disciples on it attached to a chain and worn around the neck, Prior opted for a different type. She had an amulet that had Luna on it. The small platinum disk was attached to a bracelet, which made wearing it much easier. On the back of the disk was an inscription written in the biblical language which read, *'The Almighty does not dwell in a house made with the hands of Man'*. Prior had chosen to have Luna's image placed on her amulet so she would always remember that no matter how far you stray, you can always return back to the bosom of the Almighty.

"Forgive me, Almighty, as I confess my sins to you," Prior said.

"How long has it been since your last confession?" the priest asked.

"Two weeks, Father," she answered.

He nodded. "What are your sins?"

"I have killed Kerguelens," she said.

"How many?"

"Does it matter?"

"I suppose not," he said almost chuckling. "Do you have other sins?"

"I arrested my twin brother."

"How do you feel about that?"

"Not very good, Father," she said.

"I wouldn't think so. To denounce one's own brother, especially a twin can be..."

"I should have killed him, Father," Prior said interrupting him.

"Why?" he asked astonished by her admission.

"He betrayed our family. Tradition holds that as head of my House, I should have killed him. I guess I was either too weak to do my duty or I loved him too much... or both," she said.

"Interesting," he said rubbing his chin. "And what will become of him?"

"That's for a Boroni tribunal to decide. I will accept their judgment," she said.

"And if the tribunal decrees death for your brother, then what?"

"It's out of my hands. He will die," she said matter-of-factly.

"But if you could stop it, would you?"

"No."

"Why not?"

"The Almighty could save everyone on Kerguelen from death, but deems death necessary. Her power is absolute but allows things on Kerguelen to proceed without Her interference. Who am I to act differently?" Prior reasoned.

"As a Guardian you prevent death," the priest countered.

"As a Guardian I protect the people and ensure the inalienable rights of the people are maintained," she corrected the priest. "In doing so, I both prevent death and kill. Ironically, both acts preserve life."

"Your perspective is very intriguing," the priest said.

"Everyone forgets our true name," Prior said. "We are the Guardians of the Light, and not merely soldiers following orders. Our duty is to keep the Light burning."

"What Light do you speak of?"

"The Light of Truth; The Light of Faith; The Light of the Almighty. And we keep it burning for all men. What they do with it, is their own concern," she explained.

The priest touched her forehead, moved his forefinger in the shape of a triangle and said a prayer in the biblical language. When he finished he gave Prior instructions for her penance and then gestured for her to stand. She stood and shook his hand.

"Thank you for coming, Father," she said.

"It was my pleasure to hear your confession, child. I hope to see you at our services soon," he said gathering his things.

"If I can manage it, I will. But I have many things to do. When they are accomplished, I will have more time," she said leading him to the door.

They exited the study as Mohab was finishing his breakfast. Lupo walked over to them as Prior said her goodbyes to the priest. When he was gone, she turned and saw Mohab standing by the dining room table. She smiled at him and scratched behind Lupo's ears. She walked to the table and saw the remains of the fruit on his plate and popped an orange slice into her mouth. After she swallowed it, she took Mohab by the hand and gestured for him to sit.

"Well, you don't look too bad," she said scanning him. "How do you feel?"

"Okay. I feel better now that I have some food in me. Pana was right about that," he said.

"Pana is a good doctor," Prior nodded in agreement.

"I didn't know she was an actual medical doctor," he said. "I thought she was just a nurse or a medic of some kind."

"She's one of the better young Boroni doctors," Prior said. "She specializes in both internal medicine and holistic treatments. You couldn't have been in more capable hands."

"She sure fights with the precision of a surgeon, that's for sure," he said.

"Naturally, she's my cousin. Our peerage prides itself on their professional accomplishments but also the ability to fight," Prior said smiling. She tapped his hand and continued. "Your people are expecting to hear from you within the hour so they can pick you up. I told them you would call when you were ready. As much as I'd love to sit and talk, we've both got work to do."

"You're right," he said as he reached into his pocket for his TELCOM device. He put it in his ear but didn't make a call. He stared at Prior instead. Before he could speak, Pilar entered.

Prior smiled at her. She extended a hand and Pilar joined her side. Pilar nodded respectfully to Prior and remained silent.

"Have you met my niece?" she asked Mohab.

"I have," Mohab said.

"And what do you think of her?"

"I don't know. Impetuous and headstrong I would say. But most youths are when they come of age."

"Hmm," Prior said tilting her head to the side. "Pilar, what is the Sixth Principle of Self Determination?"

"Aunt Prior," Pilar said groaning. "I'm on vacation. Why do I have to do school work?"

"When we stop learning, Pilar, we might as well die," Prior said. "Now, answer me."

"The Sixth Principle? The Sixth Principle of Self Determination states: The highest doctrine is the principle of the individual conscience," Pilar said.

"What is the Second Principle?"

"Self-preservation takes precedence above all things," Pilar answered.

"And what is the Fourth Principle?"

"Self-sacrifice overrides self-preservation in the face of a staunch belief," Pilar said.

"Very good, Pilar," Prior said approvingly.

"Thank you, but Aunt Prior, how does one really know when to follow the Second Principle or the Fourth?" Pilar asked.

"When you can answer that, Pilar, it will no longer be a question," Prior said. "Now run along." Pilar bowed slightly and went away to the kitchen. When she was gone, Prior turned back to Mohab.

"What was that all about?" he asked.

"I made Pilar recite three of the Eight Principles of Self Determination. They are part of basic Boroni philosophy and govern much of the way we live our lives," Prior said. "They are designed to enlighten young

Boroni and force them to contemplate many things." She saw that he understood but could also see that something troubled him as well. "What's wrong?"

"You know, you're not very good on the ego, Prior," he said.

"What do you mean?"

"We spend the night together and when I wake up you're with a priest. You could give it some time before you regret sleeping with me. There's a protocol to these things, you know," he said smiling.

Prior laughed. "I was just in confession. It had been two weeks since my last one, so I asked the good Father to come up. That's all. I have no regrets, Mohab," she said. "Besides, it's nice to know that despite their influence, a Guardian commander can roust a bishop out of his bed for an early morning confession at a moments notice."

"A bishop? I'm impressed," Mohab said.

"I don't mess around, Mohab," Prior said standing up. "Like my liquor and cigarettes, I like my religion straight and unfiltered. And you might want to consider another reason I may have called a priest."

"And what might that be?"

"That's for you to decide," she said slyly. "Think about what else a priest could be used for."

Prior walked away and left Mohab alone to ponder about the other functions a priest could provide. It didn't take him longer than a second to figure out what she had eluded to. He smiled and clicked on his TELCOM and made arrangements for his crew to pick him up.

11
Commander Prior's air ship, Capitol City, Central Province, Planet Kerguelen

When Prior's air ship landed, Rex was surprised to see Prior, Pana and Lupo already standing by and waiting for them. They entered the craft and Prior greeted him and Micah with a nod. There was an eerie quiet in the cabin of the ship as Prior settled into her seat. Rex took note of her good mood and observed that she appeared well rested, invigorated and had an uncharacteristic smile on her face. He didn't know what had transpired the previous night but he wished Pana could have bottled it for future use. As Pana checked the ship, he sat down next to Prior and gave her a brief.

"My duty report, Commander," he said. She nodded and he commenced his report. "The ship is fully serviced and ready for extended field operations."

"What about the gunship?" she asked.

He sighed. "That's a problem, Commander."

"Explain."

"It seems there's a serious problem with one its stabilizers. They're going to be a little late in joining up with us," Rex answered.

"I don't like this," Prior frowned. "How long before another gunship can be readied for operation?"

"I'll find out," Rex said.

"See to it at once," Prior said.

"Commander," Micah said. "Finding another ship to join us may be impossible. There is a problem procuring fuel cells and power packs for the guns."

"What do you mean?"

"Supply tried to give me the runaround when I requisitioned extra supplies. The officer-in-charge said that all units would have to make due with what they had until further notice," Micah explained. "I managed to get what we needed, but if others are not as resourceful…"

"We could be looking at real trouble," Prior said nodding. "I know the supply officer personally. He was a year or two behind me at the Academy. He can be a immoveable force when he wants to be, but I'm sure his orders are coming from a higher plane."

"What do we do then? Without fuel cells or power packs we might as well stay home," Micah said.

"Micah, do you know where the name engineer came from?" Prior asked her pilot. He shook his head. "It comes from one of the ancient languages spoken by one of the great civilizations of Kerguelen. It means, 'Man of Ingenuity'."

"What does that mean to us?" Micah asked indifferent to the history lesson.

"It means we go around the obstruction," Prior said. "The supply depot isn't the only place where we can get what we need." She tapped on her TELCOM device and when it beeped, she spoke again. "Reyes? I need to speak with the chief technologist, please. Who's calling? Tell her it's her cousin."

12
Prior's apartment, The Spire, Capitol City, Central Province, Planet Kerguelen

As Mohab waited for his air ship to arrive, he looked at the pictures on the walls of Prior's apartment. Quinn walked up to him quietly and her sudden presence startled him. She could see he was surprised and smiled.

"Forgive my stealth," she said. "We learn at an early age to tread softly."

"I understand," Mohab nodded.

"May I ask you a question?" she said.

"Of course," he said turning to her.

"Why does Prior interest you?"

"I'm interested in any woman old enough to have had a little experience and young enough to want a little more," he said smiling. Seeing by Quinn's expression she didn't appreciate his joke, he continued on in a more serious tone. "But to answer your question, I'm not sure what the status of our relationship is. And not knowing where you stand in a relationship with a Boroni could be problematic, in many ways."

"That's logical. Boroni are considered unpredictable."

"What do you mean?"

"Kerguelens say we're too mysterious," Quinn said. "They may be right."

"Why is that?" Mohab asked with piqued curiosity.

"They say a Boroni may follow you into a revolving door, but they'll come out first," Quinn said.

Mohab smiled. He had heard that before. "Do you think Prior will ever want children?" he asked.

Quinn frowned. "That's a subject I suggest you don't bring up with her, Cdr. Mohab," Quinn said in a severe tone.

"Why?"

"Prior had a child."

"When?"

"When she was thirteen. She became pregnant and gave birth during the four-month vacation between terms at the academy. She and her mate conceived a beautiful male child," Quinn replied.

"Mate? She's married?"

"Not any longer. You'd call it getting divorced, but we call it unbinding or severing the bond. She terminated the bond of marriage when she was sixteen. It was a troubled pairing from the beginning, most of our matings are, but eventually most of them take after time. All first born Boroni mate early, and that's where most of the problems occur, but it's our way," Quinn explained.

"How old was she when she bonded?"

"Let me see, she was Pilar's age I believe. Yes, I think she was ten. Yes, she was ten because every six years, according to our law, either pair in a bond can petition for unbinding, or a severing and termination of the bond," Quinn said.

"Amazing."

"Not really. It's quite common actually. Prior petitioned, it was granted and then they fought," Quinn said.

"Who fought?"

"Prior and her mate. Prior had to beat him in hand-to-hand combat to be released from the bond. It was touch and go for a while but she eventually prevailed. She could be quite relentless when necessary as a youth. But her fiery temper has cooled over the years," Quinn said.

Mohab found it difficult to imagine an angrier version of Prior and wondered how dangerous that incarnation was. "What happened to her mate?" Mohab asked scratching his head trying to absorb everything he had heard.

"I'm sorry?" Quinn said.

"Did he bond again?"

"He's dead, Commander. Prior killed him. I thought you understood that. We bond for life, like an eagle. In order for Boroni to divorce and bond again, one mate must die. Either naturally or by the hand of their mate," Quinn said.

"She killed her husband?" Mohab said. "I-I… I can't believe it."

"Unfortunately, it is so," Quinn nodded.

"What about her son? What happened to him?"

"He died. It was very sad," Quinn said. Though she did not show it, Mohab could tell it was a somber episode in the history of the House of Ahrens. "He was only seven months old when he died, but we all knew it would happen. However, Prior was attending the academy, so we took a chance. What else could we do?"

"I don't understand."

"Boroni are quite resilient as I'm sure you are aware. We are resistant to disease and illness, but it's only because of our birth mothers. After a child is born, it must be suckled for three months at a minimum, in order for our unique anti-bodies to build up in our systems. Without the birth mother's milk, a Boroni child is highly susceptible to disease and infection. Our doctors thought that perhaps any milk Prior left behind along with milk provided by Prior's mother would sustain and strengthen the child, but it only prolonged the inevitable. The child contracted Lassa fever and died. Prior was devastated, as was her mate."

"Why didn't she try again?"

"Her mate wanted to, but she wanted to wait until she graduated. She had already broke academy rules by being bonded and having a child as it was. She didn't want to continue to violate regulations. He wanted her to leave the academy but she declined. They argued... violently and often. She filed for divorce and he's dead. End of story," Quinn said.

"Is Pana married?"

"Yes. She bonded when she was eleven. Like Prior, it was a match arranged by their parents. Sometimes solidifying bloodlines and strengthening family holdings are more important than individual concerns," Quinn said. "As I said, it's quite common."

"Does she have children?"

"A male and a female. They're with their sire... as they should be."

"Why do you say that?" Mohab asked.

"Children require a sire's guidance. It's his responsibility to provide their moral upbringing. The sires teach children about love and honor and have the patience to deal with a child's nonsense," Quinn said.

"Then why is your daughter with you now?"

"She has reached the age where she is no longer a burden to me and now that she will bond soon, there are things I need to teach her,"

Quinn said. "Though Pilar is mature and ready to assume her role as a female mate, her sire was a bit too indulgent with her. There are a few rough edges in her character that I have to smooth out. Boroni matings can be… difficult enough on the young without one of them being too playful and casual concerning marriage."

"You're concerned about her marriage not taking?"

"Yes, I am. As you can tell, Pilar is very curious. She, like all young Boroni, has a strong fascination about Kerguelens. Part of her reason for being here is to quench that curiosity. She knows Prior had sex with you and if Prior does something, young Boroni feel there must be something to it. I want to get that out of her system now so it doesn't become the source of a problem down the line," Quinn said.

"So among other things, Pilar is here to sow her wild oats," Mohab said.

"Yes," Quinn said.

"Have you ever considered divorce, Quinn?"

"Yes, there was a time when it crossed my mind," Quinn said. "But as much as I might have wanted to divorce Pierce, my children need a father for their development. When Boroni children are young, there are things we females cannot do for them. Ours wasn't a love match, but I've learn to love him and I guess I've grown fond of him over the eighteen years we've been married." She chuckled and continued. "He has a way of making me laugh when we're together. I don't think I could ever divorce him. He's not unpleasant enough to kill."

"I have the distinct feeling that you don't like me, Quinn. Why is that?" Mohab asked.

"You're a distraction. And I don't mind distractions as long as they are short-lived. Boroni females have needs that must be sated or problems can arise, problems with tremendous consequences. I don't begrudge her the desire to be with you but if Prior decides to become more seriously involved with you, you could become a problem to me. If she ever bonded with you, she would have to forfeit control of the House of Ahrens," Quinn said.

"Why would that be bad for you?"

"Actually, it wouldn't. It would be to my advantage. Pierce would assume control of the House and Pilar would be the heir apparent. But that would not be what's best for our family. In my position, I ensure the security of the House is maintained. Only Prior's presence maintains stability and keeps the wolves at bay. Her reputation alone is incalculable to the status of the House of Ahrens," Quinn explained.

"In other words…" Mohab began.

"In other words, I want your relationship to wither and die on its vines," Quinn finished for him. "I don't wish to get involved, but if I have to I will. And it won't be pleasant for you if I do. Forgive my bluntness."

"Not at all," Mohab said. "But be aware I'm also formidable, Quinn."

"Of that I'm sure. Prior wouldn't have chosen to sleep with you if she didn't feel you could protect her if she needed it. But I am a Boroni female, and the protection and security of my House is paramount. My associates and I would kill you if necessary. I just want you to know that. It's not personal, it's necessary," Quinn said. "I hope you understand."

"I do," Mohab said realizing that Quinn's words were not a threat but a promise.

Mohab's TELCOM beeped saving him from further disturbing words with Quinn. He excused himself and answered it. His air ship was waiting and he said his goodbyes and went to the landing platform.

After he climbed onboard his ship and it lifted off, he changed into his combat gear and reclined in his seat. The ship climbed into the morning sky and joined the other air commuters of Capitol City. His crew had been all smiles when they picked him up and his silence about his whereabouts the previous night only fueled their speculations about what he was doing and whom he was doing it with. Whatever happened, they could tell it had been one hell of a party.

Mohab clicked on his PDA and scanned it for new messages. He stopped when saw a text message from Prior. He smiled and opened the message.

'Mo,

Had a wonderful night. Hope we can talk soon, we have a lot to discuss. Take care of yourself.

Smiles and Hugs,
Prior'

Mohab closed the message and scanned the rest of his inbox but found no other new messages. He thought about calling Prior but changed his mind. He needed to focus on his current tasking. When it was over, he would have plenty of time for romance. He looked out of the window and saw that they must be close to their destination.

"How long, Emil?" he asked his pilot.

"I'm working our way down now," said Emil. "Less than a minute to landing."

"Right. Okay, let's get ready," Mohab said.

His crew stood up and less than a minute later, the door of the air ship opened. Mohab exited first and then was followed by the members of his team. One of his, Captain Leslie, was already on the scene and he ran up to Mohab. Leslie had been on the ground since sunrise and Mohab hoped he had uncovered some evidence to tell them what exactly took place when Lieutenant Singh was killed. Mohab was hoping he could find something that would prevent Prior and Thyssen from clashing over the incident.

"What have you found?" Mohab asked Leslie.

"Not much. My work has been made more difficult by the presence of Lt. Addison," Leslie said pointing at a female Guardian waving a portable scanning device over the tarmac.

"She's one of Cdr. Prior's surveyors," Mohab said.

"She has pointed out that these blasts are remains from a Guardian caliber energy weapon. The pattern is unmistakable," Leslie said gesturing to a light post.

"Are you sure?" Mohab said looking closely at the post.

"We both are," Leslie nodded. "Whoever made the initial report of this incident was either incompetent, blind, or never set foot here... or lied. There's no doubt about it. Col. Thyssen's team made a gross error or they're covering up something."

"Calling a Guardian colonel a liar without definitive proof is a courts-martial offense, Captain," Mohab said sternly.

"Excuse me, Commander, I forgot myself for a moment," Leslie apologized.

"That's better," Mohab said.

"May I offer that Col. Thyssen's team are speakers of untruths," Leslie said.

"Now that is more reasonable, Captain," Mohab said with a smile. "Have you acquired enough data to prepare a preliminary report to Central Command?"

"Yes, but I'm missing a vital piece of data," Leslie said.

"What?"

"Singh's surveillance gear. He should have had a recording device of some kind planted around here but I haven't found it yet," Leslie said.

"Have you asked Addison where it might be?"

"Not yet."

"You should ask her and then search that area of trees over there," Mohab said pointing to the trees surrounding the landing zone. "If I were scouting this area, that's where I'd set up. It gives you full coverage of the commerce center."

"I'll take a look," Leslie said.

"How long before you can wrap up here?"

"Ten or fifteen minutes, Commander," Leslie said.

"Make it ten," Mohab instructed. "This landing zone has been secured for too long, and rumors could soon blossom."

Leslie departed to finish up his work and Mohab joined Addison. She was kneeling and looking at the tarmac closely. She looked up and saw Mohab and came to attention when she recognized him.

"Good morning, Commander," she said saluting.

He saluted back. "At ease. What have you found?"

"Boot prints. This pattern in the blood belongs to a Guardian from the Second Battalion," she said.

"Thyssen's men were here investigating," Mohab said. "It's not a surprise that they may have walked through some of it by accident."

"The print has been here as long as the blood, Commander," Addison said. "They were here during the incident."

"Are you sure?" Mohab asked.

"Positive, Commander," Addison said.

"Gather up your evidence, Lieutenant," Mohab said. "I don't want to go into this out here. We handle this according to regulations."

"Very well, Commander," Addison said. "As the officer-in-charge, I just thought you should know what I've found."

"Have you found Singh's surveillance device?"

"It's in the tree line over there," Addison said pointing. "All of our gear have GPS chips in them. It wasn't hard to locate."

"Good. Once we review it…" Mohab began but stopped mid-sentence when he heard the sound of multiple air ships descending from above. "Jacob, your glasses."

Mohab took the field glasses from an officer of his team and focused on the three craft coming down toward them.

"They look like Guardian craft," Jacob said cupping his eyes.

"Which unit?" Addison asked looking up as well. "Can you tell?"

Mohab adjusted his view and instantly recognized the unit the ships belonged to. All of them were gray and had a black fleur-de-lis on the nose, the distinctive markings of the Guardian Second Battalion. Mohab knew their arrival here was no coincidence. He had to get his team moving.

"They're Second Battalion craft," Mohab said and then shouted to his men on the ground. "Take cover! Take cover!" He tapped his TACCOM unit and called to Emil. "Red Fox 1! Get airborne now! Everyone stay away from the air ship!"

Before Emil could get the ship off of the ground, the descending air vehicles fired a volley of plasma energy weapons into it. The upper engine housing of Mohab's ship took the full blast of the guns and the resulting explosions reduced the craft and its lone occupant to their lowest common denominators. Mohab led Addison and his team to cover and opened fire on the air ships. They managed to hit one but missed the other two. The slightly damaged air ship banked away and out of range of their small arms. The other ships renewed their attack on Mohab and the other Guardians.

"I hate to admit it, but I think we're going to need some help on this one," Jacob quipped as weapons fire peppered the meager protection he had crowded into.

"I think you're right, Lieutenant," Mohab said with a half smile. "As much as I hate to bother people in the morning, I think it would be wise. Get the Gray Wolves on the horn. Tell them we need an emergency egress from this location. And tell them to load for bear."

"I'm on it," Jacob said. He flipped open a pouch on his belt containing a portable field communications unit and adjusted his TACCOM frequency and made the call. "Any Gray Wolf unit, any Gray Wolf unit, emergency egress requirement for Red Fox Actual and support team. Location: Capitol City, Metro Section Commerce Center. Red Fox Actual under attack from three, I repeat, three air ships. Red Fox Actual indicates threat level as Warning Red, Weapons Free!"

13
Prior's air ship, Capitol City, Central Province, Planet Kerguelen

"Cousin Prior," Mackenzie said cheerfully. "What can I do for you?"

"I believe it's started, Mackenzie," Prior said.

"What has started?" Mackenzie asked totally confused.

"*It*. The thing you and Gideon warned me about. It's on," Prior said almost babbling.

"Take it easy, Prior," Mackenzie said sitting up in her chair. "What's going on?"

"Tactical supplies are being withheld and I can't operate without them. I need fuel cells for my air ships and power packs for their weapons. I was hoping you could help me out," Prior explained.

"I can't make your distribution center dole out supplies, but I can provide you the material you require. I can call it a temporary loan on the basis for field trials," Mackenzie said. "In fact, we've just developed some new fuel cells. I think this would be an opportune time to test them for their practical viability."

"There will be two gun ships coming to you for that material," Prior said.

"Good," Mackenzie said. "I may even be able to throw in a bonus surprise or two for you as well."

"Thanks a million, Mackenzie," Prior said as the weight of the world eased off of her. "Talk to you later."

"I'll keep a line open, cousin. Good hunting," Mackenzie said terminating the TELCOM connection.

Prior put her TACCOM device in her ear and asked Pana to open up a circuit with the gun ships. "King 3, this is Gray Wolf Actual. Proceed to the Technology Council Headquarters in Capitol City for fuel cells and power packs. Chief Technologist Mackenzie will be waiting," Prior said.

"Roger, Actual," the pilot said. "King 3 and 5 are en route."

"Gray Wolf Actual, Out," Prior said ending the call.

"Commander," Micah said. "We're about one minute out from Cathedral Prime."

"Thank you," Prior said. "Pana, take care of Lupo for me."

Pana nodded and Prior stood up and checked her gear. She was armed with her TKP-7 pistol, a radio frequency weapon, a single boot knife and two short blades. She would try and avoid a gunfight, but there was no telling what would happen. And if the cardinal wanted to create a scene of animosity, she would have her own props.

"Cathedral Prime has given us permission to land, Commander," Micah said. "And the cardinal's aide reports the Pontiff is ready to see you."

"Very good, Micah," Prior said. "Take us in."

14
Cardinal Gregor's office, Cathedral Prime, Capitol City, Central Province, Planet Kerguelen

As Prior strode up the wide, natural stone walkway that led to the entrance of Cathedral Prime, she tried to put her personal feelings aside. She knew that Gregor had been instrumental in the downfall of Venture and had sponsored Omega's excommunication, but she had to forget about that. She had to focus on what was current. She had evidence that Gregor had committed illegal activities and it was her duty to confront him about it. The fact that he was inviting her in with open arms made this encounter even more intriguing.

She tied the belt of her leather trench coat around her as she entered the main administration building to cover her body and stepped in. The combat suit she wore was not ideal attire for the cathedral. The skintight garment revealed too much of her virtues and would be offensive to the delicate sensibilities of the priests and nuns in the building, not to mention her array of weapons. But the coat would do the trick.

She quickly scaled the winding marble stairs in the foyer of the building and was met by Cardinal Gregor's assistant Monsignor Kellan at the top of the stairs. Kellan led her down the walkway about twenty feet and opened the door to the cardinal's outer office for her. She thanked him and he followed her into the inner office. She stood in front of the cardinal's desk and waited for Gregor to turn around. He was looking out of his window when she came in but didn't turn around until Kellan cleared his throat.

He turned around and smiled at Prior. "Good morning, Commander. It's a pleasure to see you again," he said holding out his left hand.

"Good morning to you, Your Eminence," Prior said taking his hand and kissing his ring. She didn't return his smile but greeted him in the biblical language. "Dominus vobiscum."

"Ah, you know the old language," he said impressed. He looked to Kellan. "You may go now, Kellan." Kellan bowed and departed. When the door closed, Gregor continued. "It's a pleasure to hear the old language spoken by non-Clerics. Especially from young people."

He sat down and since he didn't offer her a chair, Prior remained standing as she replied. "I was raised a child of the Church. Learning the biblical language was a requirement. And I'm not that young," she said.

"It's so difficult to tell with… people today," Gregor said tactfully. Prior knew he meant it was hard to tell how old a Boroni was. "I know I shouldn't ask a female this question, but how old are you?"

Prior smiled. "I'm not offended, Your Eminence, but to maintain my feminine mystique, I'll say I'm old enough to know how and young enough to prove it."

Gregor seemed to like her response and pointed to the chair in front of his desk. "Did you know Venture refused to speak the old language," he said. "Even while in the company of clerics."

"Venture was a priest. Perhaps he felt it was unnecessary to use a language that few speak and even fewer understand," she said loosening the belt of her coat and sitting down.

"Perhaps you're right, Commander," he said leaning forward. "You know, the more I'm exposed to you the more you intrigue me."

"If you weren't a Cleric, I would think you were flirting with me," Prior said allowing a smile to show.

"Not at all," Gregor said. "It's just that despite the fact you're Boroni, you're among the best and brightest of the planet. You should shed your Guardian trappings and look to the future."

"What does my being Boroni have to do with anything?"

"There will be a place for all when this current crisis is over. Everyone will be needed to rebuild once order has been restored," he replied. "But the Boroni choose to isolate themselves and that is counterproductive."

"You make it sound as if the Boroni are a blight on society," Prior said with a frown.

"There is a distinction between science and God's domain. Dr. Boroni crossed that line when he created your ancestors," he said.

"I disagree. There isn't a distinction at all. God gave up exclusive rights on that when She gave us the ability to reason, to think and to practice free will. Dr. Boroni only did what God empowered us to do. We're well past the time to postulate on whether it was right or wrong," Prior said.

"You're just trying to justify your own existence."

"Doesn't everyone?" Prior countered.

Prior's TACCOM beeped and she pulled it out. "Excuse me, Cardinal, I have to take this," she said. Gregor nodded and she stepped to the far side of the office. "This is Prior."

"Commander, we've just received an emergency egress requirement from Red Fox Actual. Situation critical. Warning Red, Weapons Free. We're en route to them now. I've ordered King 3 and 5 to rendezvous when they're clear. We're less than two minutes out," Micah said.

"Who's attacking them?" Prior asked.

"It's an air attack. Three air ships bearing Green Terrapin colors are strafing them," Micah said.

"Where?"

"The Metro Section Commerce Center, Commander," Micah said.

Prior paused for a moment and exhaled. "Do whatever it takes to get them out... even if you have to engage those Second Battalion units. Just get them out of there, Micah," she instructed.

"Understand. Will contact you when we are clear," Micah said breaking the circuit.

Prior tapped the side of her TACCOM and took a second before turning to Gregor. She had been right. It had started. When she turned to Gregor he had a concerned look on his face. She wondered if he knew anything about the attack. It was possible he was orchestrating the event. It was also possible he knew nothing about it. Which ever it was, she would have to tread lightly.

"Is there anything wrong, Commander?" he asked.

"Just a minor problem, Cardinal," she said returning to her seat.

"Good," he said. He looked at her curiously and continued. "Do you consider yourself Boroni or Kerguelen?"

"I describe myself as a Guardian who is Boroni," she said.

"You have unique distinctions. A Guardian, a Boroni and a PhD. A very rare combination," he said.

"At one time, all Boroni were PhDs," Prior said.

"Really?"

"Yes. Poor, hungry and desperate," Prior replied. "But in the modern Kerguelen way of life, we're all pretty much equal."

"You believe that all people are equal?"

"God intended for all people to be equal, but the Boroni were truly created equal. Male and female have equal strength and IQ. There is no weaker sex," Prior said. "But to answer your question, for the most part, everyone has the same chance. Choice and fate decide how you end up."

"And why are Boroni so devout?"

"I can only answer for myself," Prior said. "But I have a simple outlook. To think there is nothing beyond our own flesh would be an empty existence. It's not a unique perspective but it's mine. Just know I believe in the Almighty and why is my own affair."

"Do you believe in the power of prayer?"

"People pray because they're thankful to be alive, not because they particularly believe in a supreme deity," Prior said. "They'd believe in a rock if they had proof it created them or it could save their life."

"You believe that?"

"Yes. People are generally fickle I've discovered," Prior said. "They bend with the wind or the prevailing trend."

"Do you believe life exists beyond Kerguelen?"

"That question is pointless. Whether I do or don't is of no consequence. *San Mariner* is bringing proof that such a concept is true," Prior said.

"Taking the alien ship out of the question, what do you believe?"

"If I said I didn't believe in gravity, would that mean it didn't exist?" Prior answered. "What do my beliefs have to do with anything? Why all the questions, Cardinal?"

"I just wanted to know where your true loyalties lie," Gregor said. "Now I know."

"I'm happy for you," Prior said.

"I was intending to offer you the chance to help rule the planet. Everything could be laid out at your feet," Gregor said.

"You know The Second once offered The Great Prophet the same thing," Prior said with a hint of disrespect in her voice. "You, like The Second, fail to realize that Kerguelen is not a negotiable commodity. Many have tried to possess it all but everyone who has tried has failed, from despots to religious zealots. You need the support of people to succeed and no matter what you try, they will eventually see through the fog of deception and discover the truth."

"The strength of the planet is being sapped by its lowest elements: militants, agitators, protestors, anarchists; grisly people reducing a civilization to rubble. When the explosion comes, I'll pick up the pieces," Gregor said.

"After you've helped ignite the fuse that will cause the blow up," Prior replied.

"I was afraid you'd see it that way," Gregor said.

"I have a few questions of my own," Prior said. "Why is Col. Thyssen attacking Cdr. Mohab? Why did you frame Venture and who is behind the discord brewing all over the planet?"

"I have no idea what you're talking about, Commander," Gregor said innocently.

"How long has your conspiracy been going on?" Prior demanded.

"You're leveling serious charges, Commander. Perhaps you should take a moment to calm down," he said.

"I know what the charges are and I want answers. Now!" she said firmly.

"Venture accused me of crimes and he's dead. I'd be very careful if I were you. I hold the Papal seat and I'm Keeper of the Holy See. Don't presume you can walk in here and demand anything from me!" Gregor said.

"You can hold whatever you'd like," Prior said. "Your refusal to answer my questions has confirmed what I already believed to be true."

"What do you plan to do?"

"Bring you to justice. You're guilty of something. How far your corruption goes is a matter for the Judicial Branch, but you are far from innocent," Prior said.

"You're going to forcibly take me from Cathedral Prime? You're insane. All Guardians are insane and foolish. You think you can do what you want to do, without repercussions. But you're wrong. There is no individuality on Kerguelen. There can't be. Everyone exists to serve the establishment. The individual, the one, doesn't matter. Only the group, the whole, is of consequence. But you can't see that. Venture couldn't see that. Omega wouldn't see that. And your father... your father was completely blind and refused to see that," Gregor said glaring at her.

It took a second for what he said to register in Prior's brain. When it did sink in, she gripped the arms of her chair tightly to harness her anger.

"You had my father killed?" she asked barely able to get the words out. She took a breath and continued. "And I suppose you're responsible for making his son betray his family as well?"

Gregor nodded. "Yes, and before I did that, I had your mother killed. And now I have to kill the daughter," he said. "I thought I could use you, but like your mother, you're too dangerous to be left alive."

"My mother?" Prior gasped.

"She discovered I had your father assassinated and learned about other dealings I was conducting. When I told her why I was doing it, she promised to kill me. Before she could act, I had her taken out," Gregor said.

Prior suddenly felt a swirl of emotions concerning her mother. She didn't know that her mother had taken it upon herself to find out who killed her father. Prior believed her mother had not cared very deeply for her father, but realized now she had been wrong. And that love she had and the desire to seek retribution had killed her mother. Before she could reflect any more on the subject, the door to Gregor's office opened and a group of six Papal security guards entered the room. Prior stood and opened her coat as she faced them. The leader of the guards looked to Gregor as he placed his hand on his holstered weapon.

"I've learned my lesson in dealing with Guardians, Commander," Gregor said. "I believe there are enough men to handle the situation."

Prior answered Gregor by sweeping her coat aside revealing her sidearm. She drew her pistol from its quick release holster using her lightning fast reflexes and fired six times at the guards. They quickly fell over like ducks in a shooting gallery and hit the floor in succession. Prior walked over to them and scowled. When she reached the leader of the detail, she shot him in the head and did the same to the next guard lying there. She ejected the spent magazine and inserted a fresh one in the weapon and proceeded to shoot the next four guards in the head as well. She turned to Gregor and shook her head. Gregor raised his left arm and backed away from his desk. He had a pleading look on his face and Prior snorted as she approached his desk.

"Put your arm down, Cardinal," Prior said. "I'm a Guardian, and I'm Boroni. I was trained to kill Kerguelens as child. Your security guards never had a chance. You should have known that."

"I can't believe it," Gregor said. "You killed all six of them. It was so fast they never knew what happened."

"Yes," Prior said. "Boroni are vastly quicker than Kerguelens, Cardinal. Your security chief should have tried to shoot me in the back. Trying to attack me head on… face-to-face… gave me an unfair advantage."

A sliding door behind her and to the right opened suddenly and a darkly clad, imposing figure emerged. He had black scaly skin and was huge, close to seven feet tall by Prior's estimate. His eyes were red and looked like they were illuminated with searing hot coals. He bent down and picked up one of the Papal security guard's plasma energy pistols and pointed it at Prior. Prior was startled by what she saw before her but didn't hesitate longer than a split second. She pointed her pistol at the creature and fired twice, hitting him squarely in the chest. His body seemed to absorb the tungsten alloy bullets as if they were mosquito bites. She looked at him quizzically and then fired again until her weapon's magazine was empty.

The creature staggered a bit but was unfazed by Prior's weapon and she couldn't believe her eyes. She had put four .45 caliber tungsten alloy bullets into a target no more than ten feet away and they had no effect. And that was impossible. No mortal creature on Kerguelen could withstand the force of a kinetic energy weapon, but this thing had.

She backed away and the creature smiled, baring a set of shark-like teeth. He raised the weapon in his hand and fired. A single blast erupted from the weapon, striking Prior in the chest, lifting her body a foot into the air and backwards another fifteen. She was airborne until she hit the wall on the other side of the room and bounced off of it. She landed face first on the floor and didn't move. The creature looked at the weapon in his hand with disgust and tossed it to the floor.

"It is done," the creature said to Gregor.

Gregor nodded. He didn't know why the creature was here, but was glad he had showed. He was also pleased the sight of the creature had brought fear upon Commander Prior. The rest of the planet would feel the same way very soon. The sight and the threat of him would once again plague Kerguelen. He was fear and evil manifested in Kerguelen form. He was The Argent.

15
The Metro Section Commerce Center, Capitol City, Central Province, Planet Kerguelen

When Micah flew the air ship into the area, Pana took stock of what she was seeing in the air and on the ground and didn't like it. She quickly assessed the situation and made up her mind to which course of action they had to take. Considering they had no other options, there was nothing else to do. They could not effect an extraction of Commander Mohab and the Guardians on the ground until the Second Battalion air ships were gone and since they were not going to vacate voluntarily, they would have to be forced out. The result of such an action would be an air battle over a heavily populated metropolitan district, and that had not occurred since the last Provincial Wars. Once the engagement began, neither side could relent and civilian casualties could be high. But it was her own preservation, and that of Rex and Micah, which occupied Pana. They were outnumbered and the odds they would survive such a battle were low. As they proceeded, Pana hoped they would live up to the combat engineer's motto: Innovate, Adapt and Overcome.

Pana ordered Micah to bring their ship into an attack position and take on the other ships one-by-one until the ships retired, were destroyed or they themselves were knocked out of the sky. Their initial attack quickly dispatched the first target. A direct hit in the engine compartment caused the ship to burst into flames and it spiraled down into the ground a safe distance from the commerce center. The remaining craft were stubborn and Micah had trouble evading their assaults. To make matters worse, bystanders had begun to step out into the open and view the air spectacle. It would only take a few stray plasma energy blasts or loose masonry toppling from a building to turn this situation into a deadly catastrophe.

"Pana, we have to disengage soon or risk being destroyed," Micah said as he tried to aim the forward weapons array. "I don't know how long we can stay lucky."

Pana grasped a handle above her head as Micah banked. "Stay with it. If we leave, Cdr. Mohab and the others will certainly be killed… and you don't want to have to explain that to the boss," Pana said.

"Watch it, Micah!" Rex said. He was hanging from the lanyard attached to his back in the open right hand side hatch. "One of them is swinging around trying to get on our six. If he gets there, we'll be bracketed."

Pana turned her laser pulse door gun extending out of the left side hatch toward one of the ships and fired several shots. She missed but the action forced the ship to slow down a bit. Rex, manning a gun on the other side, also missed his target. Both of them had been firing continuously since the battle commenced but had not scored a hit since firing the opening salvos. Lupo was playing cheerleader, barking at every opportunity he could. He gnawed at the straps that secured him into the seat in an attempt to get loose but was not able to get free. He too wanted to get into the action.

"Where is he, Pana?" Micah shouted. "Which side is he on?"

"Port side. He's almost there!" Pana shouted back.

Rex pulled a spent power pack from his gun and reached for another. He grabbed the heavy power pack with one hand and placed it inside its slot. The gun powered up and he poked his head out of the hatch to see where the attacking ships were. As he suspected, they were too close.

"I can't lose them, they've got us. Hang on, be ready to fire," Micah said as he banked the air ship hard to the right.

As the craft veered, the trailing ship's nose became exposed and Rex let loose two bursts from his weapon. His first volley missed cleanly and the second only did superficial damage to the ship. It shuddered a bit but continued its pursuit of them.

"No joy, Micah, I missed," Rex said. "He's still coming."

"And we've got company on the left," Pana added.

Micah's maneuver was unsuccessful and instead of getting rid of one ship, had brought them into the line of fire of another. The pilot of the pursuing ship wasted no time in acting on that advantage. He swung his craft in behind and to the left. Micah jerked the controls and slid underneath him just in time. The shots fired barely missed as they maneuvered away.

Pana pointed her gun upwards and unleashed a torrent of laser fire on the attacking ship. The lower section of the craft's forward windscreen shattered and a huge section of the nose split off and flew into the open door passing within inches of Pana. The scrap of metallic hydrogen imbedded itself in the side of the ship just above Lupo. He looked at it and barked in protest of its presence.

"I know, Lupo," Pana said apologetically. "Sorry, boy."

Smoke began to billow out of the wounded ship as it spun downwards. They were only a few hundred feet in the air and the crippled craft quickly found the ground. Bystanders pointed to the sky, shrieked and ran for their lives as the ship slammed into the street below. The shockwave from the crater it created knocked the pedestrians off of their feet and broke out the windows of nearby buildings. Rex gave a triumphant yell but they all knew the battle was far from won. The last of the Second Battalion air ships was still airborne and closing fast.

"Damn it!" Micah said as an alarm sounded in the cockpit and the engine monitors on his instrument panel began flashing red. He knew immediately what was wrong.

"What's happened?" Pana asked.

"Air turbine over temperature alarm," Micah explained. "We've got to slow down."

"Forget it. Keep going," Pana demanded shaking her head.

"I can't, even if I wanted to. The flight computer will slow us down automatically even if I don't. It's out of my hands," Micah said pulling the throttle back.

Pana saw that the trailing ship was closing and in a few seconds would be in point blank firing range. At that range, no maneuvering would help them. The blast from the ship's guns would rip them to pieces.

"They're right on top of us, Micah! I can't get a shot off! Move it!" she said.

"Sorry, there's nothing I can do," Micah said.

Pana shut her eyes in preparation for the explosion she knew was about to send her into oblivion. As she whispered her final prayers, she heard an explosion... but it wasn't them. She opened her eyes and the air ship following them started to smoke and heel to the left. It dropped about eighty feet before the pilot regained control and accelerated out of the area. Pana scanned the sky and saw a gunship with three blue interlocking diamonds along the side of its fuselage come into view and she smiled.

"Gray Wolf 1, this is King 3, your play date is vacating the area," the pilot radioed Micah. "Shall we pursue?"

"Are you alone?" Micah asked.

"Affirmative, but King 5 is only three or four minutes behind," the pilot said.

"Have King 5 track the vehicle if he can. You stay and cover our extraction of ground personnel," Micah ordered.

"Copy that," the pilot said. "Public safety units and the fire brigades are en route."

King 3 climbed and began to orbit the landing area as Micah brought the ship in. He wasn't sure where Mohab and the others were located but assumed they sought cover in the nearby tree line.

"I don't see them," Pana said. "Call them, Micah."

"Hold on," he said switching frequencies on his radio set. "Red Fox Actual, this is Gray Wolf 1. The groundhog saw its shadow and went back inside its hole. We're waiting for you."

"We're in the tall grass," Mohab replied. "We're popping some smoke in your honor."

"Do you have any casualties?" Micah asked.

"Nothing terrible, but they'll need some attention," Mohab said.

"We'll be standing by," Micah said.

Micah informed Pana and Rex to ready the cabin for casualties and he brought the ship down near the blue smoke wafting up from the tree line on the edge of the landing area. The ship gently touched down and Mohab and his team slowly moved to it. Three of his men were badly burned from plasma energy weapon discharges but would survive. Pana and Rex helped them onboard and Addison and Mohab were the last to climb in. When the cabin hatches were shut, Pana told Micah they were ready to leave. As the ship slowly powered into the sky, Mohab went forward to the cockpit. Lupo barked and snapped at him as he passed, still struggling to free himself from the restraints that held him.

"Thanks for the lift," Mohab said to Micah as he sat down in the co-pilot's seat.

"Anytime, Commander," Micah said.

"Where's Commander Prior?" Mohab asked.

"At Cathedral Prime. She knows we came here to extract you. I've been trying to raise her and inform her that we have you, but she's not answering," Micah said as a concerned look crossed his face. "I'm surprised she's not burning up the air waves wanting an update."

"Today has been full of surprises," Mohab said looking equally troubled. "But Cdr. Prior not calling for an update is not a surprise, it's an impossibility. Let's get to Cathedral Prime on the double. I know you've got a heavy load, but do your best."

Micah nodded and pushed the craft to its limit. The turbines responded to his inputs and Micah was satisfied with the ship's performance as it danced in the sky. The turbines were squealing in protest to the speed asked of them but answered every request from Micah. As the air ship lurched forward, Micah looked at Mohab and saw deep worry lines on the commander's face.

"Don't worry, Commander," Micah said looking out of the window. "Prior can handle any situation. I feel sorry for the pitiful creature that would try and cause any animosity towards her."

"I hope you're right, Micah," Mohab said. "I hope you're right."

Unfortunately, Mohab knew that Prior was facing Cardinal Gregor at the moment. And the clergyman was many things and described using several different adjectives, but pitiful wasn't one of them.

16
Cardinal Gregor's office, Cathedral Prime,
Capitol City, Central Province, Planet Kerguelen

"I told you the Helot female was dangerous," The Argent said to Gregor. He looked at Prior's unmoving body and spat. "And I hate resorting to using mortal weapons."

"Perhaps, but this time they worked just fine. Take her body out of here and leave it in a conspicuous place so it can be easily found. The report of her death will send a shockwave rippling through the Guardian Corps shattering whatever confidence that still remains in their ranks," Gregor said.

"All of that because a Helot female is dead?"

"A very unique Helot female, Argent," Gregor said. "With both she and Mohab dead, our next attack will be unchallenged and glorious." The TELCOM on his desk beeped and he answered it. "Yes?"

"Forgive me, Your Eminence," the voice belonging to Colonel Thyssen said. "But we have a problem."

"What is it, Colonel?" Gregor asked.

"Mohab has escaped."

"Fools!" Gregor said. He rubbed his temple and exhaled. "Meet the others as scheduled. I'm coming now."

"What about the next phase? Should we delay?" Thyssen asked.

"No. We can't now even if we wanted to. The wheels are already in motion. Mohab won't make any difference. The most important half of the plan has succeeded. Prior is dead, and that was paramount. Mohab was only an added bonus. I'll be there in ten minutes," Gregor said slamming his hand against the TELCOM device to end the call. He turned to The Argent. "Finish up here and meet us at the rendezvous point. I've got to go and keep that incompetent idiot from damaging us any further."

"Do you want me to kill him?" The Argent asked hopefully.

"There'll be plenty of time for that," Gregor said. "Your next target is Mohab. He should be the easiest of all the commanders to kill."

The Argent nodded and Gregor departed through the side door. The Argent looked at Prior admiring her form as he sat on the edge of Gregor's desk. It creaked and strained against his oppressive weight but miraculously didn't collapse.

"They should have told me about you sooner, woman," The Argent said aloud. "I wouldn't have wasted my time with the others. There was something special about you. I could feel it. You look very much like the other one." He sighed and stood. "I must get started, there is much to do."

The last five words he spoke and sound of his reverberating voice caused Prior to open her eyes. The pain in her chest was excruciating and it hurt to breathe, but she was alive. Thank the Almighty for the ablative armor and mirrored glass filaments in her combat suit, she thought. And thank goodness she hadn't been shot in the head. The weapon she was shot with was not a Guardian weapon for sure but even it could kill a Boroni at close range.

Though she had been lucky on two accounts, her luck would run out once The Argent discovered she was not dead. And if she rose to face the monstrosity posing as a man she would need more than luck, she would have to be good. All of her luck had been used up. But the creature believed she was dead and she would use that for all it was worth. She needed to be quick and strike him with everything she had.

The sharp pain from the shot had subsided to a dull throbbing sensation and she was ready to make her move. She lifted her head just as the creature slid off of the desk and sprang to her feet sprinting towards him. As she was about to reach him she leapt at him with outstretched arms. He was startled but before she could get her hands on him, he shifted his body and took hold of her left arm. He spun on his toes in an attempt to throw her into the wall beyond them. He didn't have a firm grip though, and Prior slipped out of his grasp and took hold of his forearm. As they spun around she let go of him and to his surprise, The Argent found he was flying through the air. He hit the wall and the crash upset everything near to it. Pictures flew off of the wall and the frames broke into pieces.

Prior examined her handiwork. The Argent was not too stunned and smiled as he extricated himself from the concave indentation the impact created. He was more shocked and amazed than hurt or injured. Prior smiled back at him as she stripped her coat off and tossed it aside.

"Well, well, look at this," The Argent said showing Prior his teeth as he smiled. "It seems the little girl has grown up and I have a true opponent. I wasn't aware there were others impervious to the crude weapons of mortals." He rolled his shoulders and stepped closer to Prior.

"I'm full of surprises," she said kicking a chair out of her way.

"Even a blind squirrel occasionally finds a nut, woman. But not often enough," he said snapping a jab at Prior.

The punch was so quick it took Prior's brain nearly two full seconds to register that it had connected. When it did, she fell down and rolled away from him. She shook her head trying to regain her senses and bearings before he was on her again. He moved like lightning despite his tremendous size and was in front of her before she could react. Prior took three more blows to the chest and was knocked flat on her back. She clutched her bosom but had no time to reflect on the pain for he was on the move again. The Argent followed her to the floor, leaping through the air and coming down with his fist. Prior anticipated the move and shifted her head just in time. The fist dented the floor as he landed and his body straddled hers.

Before he could move again Prior thrust her leg upwards and lifted him up and over her. He landed on his back with a loud thud and he groaned. She rolled onto her feet and saw that she had finally affected him. Even though it was a minor score, she wasted no time pressing what little advantage she had. He had gotten to his feet but his reaction time had slowed.

She closed the distance between them and fired a rapid succession of punches to his torso and head. Prior could tell that the body shots caused him pain. The bullets from her weapon had obviously weakened him. She stopped her assault and shoved him into the wall behind him. He bounced off of the wall and stumbled towards her. She grabbed his arm and swung him in a circle. The Argent had nearly completed two full rotations before she released him. She managed to get the three hundred pound behemoth airborne and he flew in the air and into the door of the office. He crashed through it with great force and landed hard on the floor.

Prior surveyed The Argent and saw that he was lying in a crumpled ball in the outer office. She took a deep breath and paused for a moment. She flexed her fingers and as she was catching her breath, The Argent stood up and smiled at her.

"Well done, girl," he said rubbing his scaly jaw. "I've waited a long time for a duel like this."

The noise of the fight had brought Father Kellan back to his office and Prior saw part of his body peeking out from behind The Argent.

"Get the hell out of here!" Prior commanded and Kellan took her advice and darted away.

The Argent came closer to her and as he did, he flexed the muscles in his chest and arms in preparation for a renewed attack. Prior took a step back and readied for it. He ran at her and Prior pulled out the two short blades from her weapons harness and thrust them into his chest. He growled in pain as Prior pressed them into his body. She pushed him backwards and he fell to his knees. She punched him in the head and he fell the rest of way to the floor.

Prior looked him over as he groaned. He stood up and removed the blades from his body and they dropped to the floor with a tinny sound. As he slowly rose to his feet, Prior pulled her radio frequency weapon out its holster and clicked on the power button. As it powered up, she chose a setting and aimed it at The Argent's head. He glanced at the weapon and then smiled at her again.

"Your mortal weapons are useless against me, woman," he said. "You should have more faith in yourself than in those blasphemous instruments."

Prior ignored his words and saw that the power indicator had turned green. She tapped the trigger and the weapon hummed and released a powerful stream of invisible electromagnetic energy towards the creature. At first she thought the weapon hadn't worked, then she began to see the effects of her high-tech bombardment. The Argent took a step forward and then several steps backwards. He clutched both sides of his head with his hands and tilted his head upwards in agony.

"Arghhhh!" The Argent screamed in pain. The shrill banshee-like wail echoed and vibrated the walls of the office cracking the glass of the picture frames.

He doubled over, fell to his knees and lowered his head. Prior kept the weapon trained on the black-skinned creature until the weapon stopped humming. She punched him in the head again and The Argent hit the floor once more. She watched him and this time, he didn't move. Prior flexed her hand again. Hitting his hard scaly face hurt a bit but the pain was worth the result. She holstered the radio frequency weapon and picked up her knives and then grabbed her TKP-7 pistol.

She pressed a tab on the weapon's grip and the magazine fell out and bounced across the floor. She inserted a fresh magazine in the weapon and chambered a round. She turned to The Argent and saw he was on his feet again. He backed away from her but retained his smile.

"We shall meet again, woman," The Argent said. "I have no time to finish this now. When we do meet, you won't be so fortunate."

He turned and exited the office and Prior chased after him. When she reached the hallway, The Argent had disappeared and a burst of low-caliber plasma energy fire had replaced his presence. She ducked back into the office as the gunfire dotted the doorway. She had barely avoided being hit and cursed loudly.

Father Kellan must have called the Papal security force after he saw the fight. She was now boxed in and there was no way out of the building except past them. If she put up a fight, she would eventually have to surrender from a lack of ammunition. She had to think of a way out.

Her TACCOM beeped and she clicked on it. "This is Prior," she said.

"This is Micah. We're above Cathedral Prime. What's your status?" he asked.

"I created a bit of animosity," Prior said as a volley of plasma energy fire hit the wall.

"We'll set down in front of the building," Micah said.

"I can't make it out the front," Prior said looking behind her. She saw the large window behind Gregor's desk and smiled. "Stand-by, Micah." She slammed the door shut and went to the window. The courtyard was empty and contained only a few trees. It looked clear enough for Micah to land in. "Micah, come to the courtyard in the center of the buildings. There are a few trees but I think it's viable… and the only choice."

"I know where it is," Micah said. "Get ready. One minute, Commander."

Prior holstered her pistol and looked at the window. There was no way to open it and she cursed again. She looked around and went to the leader of the fallen Papal security guards. She picked him up and slung his body through the window. The corpse broke out most of the glass and framing and Prior used her boot knife to break out the remaining jagged pieces. She stepped onto the ledge and looked down. It was a hell of a drop and didn't know if she could jump to the ground without injuring herself. Even a minor fracture would be too much right now. She tapped her TACCOM and Rex answered.

"Go," he said.

"I can't get down to the ground," Prior said.

"Pana didn't think you could," Rex said. "She has another idea."

"Great," Prior said as she saw the air ship descend into the courtyard and come to a hover.

Pana was standing in the open hatch and called to Prior. "Prior, catch!" she said.

Pana tossed a shot line over to Prior. She caught it and pulled a penetrator assembly used for ground extraction to her. She took hold of the assembly and jumped from the window as the Papal security guards burst into the office. As Prior dangled from the penetrator, Pana and the guards exchanged fire. The air ship was taking heavy damage and Prior tapped her TACCOM.

"Micah, give them your rear end, then gun it. Full throttle!" Prior said.

Micah complied and spun the craft so the engine exhaust faced the guards. He slammed the throttle forward and the superheated air from the turbines filled the open window. The guards stopped firing and backed way. As the craft went forward, Micah pulled the control stick back and the ship climbed into the air. As they cleared the courtyard, Prior was slammed into the top branches of an old tree but held on.

Pana looked down and saw that Prior was still holding on and turned on the winch bringing her up to the hatch. When the winch stopped, Pana pulled Prior inside and she gave her cousin a hug and looked her over.

"Rex, my med-kit," Pana said.

"I'm alright, Pana," Prior said. She looked around the cabin and saw that it was jammed with people. She got to her feet and worked her way forward and found Lupo. He was still strapped into his seat and very agitated. She released him and he nearly knocked her down as he jumped into her arms. "There's my boy. Did you miss me?" She kissed his head as he barked repeatedly and licked her hands.

She looked to the cockpit and saw Mohab. He smiled at her and she smiled back. "Are you okay?" he asked.

She nodded. "My discussion with the good cardinal became heated, but I'm fine," she said. She saw his concerned looked and added, "Don't worry, he's still alive. How about you?"

"We're fine. Your people do good work," Mohab said.

"The attacks on us were planned, Mohab. Calculated and premeditated. But they're only the beginning of something bigger," Prior said. "You need to contact your battalion and put them on the alert."

"They are," Mohab said.

"Good," Prior said. She turned to Pana. "What does St. Jacques have at his disposal?"

"Full field gear for all of the men. Mines, heavy explosives… and tactical warfare equipment," Pana said.

"And who has the strategic packages?" Prior asked.

"Captain Hiroki," Pana said.

"Send a flash priority message on our coded frequency. Tell him to use the package if he has to. And send it at once, Pana," Prior instructed.

"I'm on it," Pana said setting up the messages and orders.

"Are you sure it's necessary to consider the use of strategic weapons at this stage?" Mohab asked Prior.

"It's always necessary to consider every option at your disposal, Mohab," Prior said.

"They haven't been used since the Provincial Wars," he said.

"And hopefully I won't have to use them, but I won't rule them out either. We're dealing with a dangerous situation," she said.

"I hope Providence and luck are on our side," he said.

"I hope we win the coming battle," Prior said. "Micah, where are we headed?"

"All Saints Memorial Hospital," he replied. "The wounded need attention."

"How long?" Prior asked.

"Two minutes," Micah said.

Mohab's aide, Lieutenant Jacob walked up to his commander and cleared his throat. Mohab and Prior turned to him and saw he looked confused.

"What is it, Jacob?" Mohab asked.

"Part of the TACCOM network is down. We only have three useable circuits for our battalion. The units are stepping all over each other and computer traffic has all but ceased," Jacob said.

"Why? Is there solar activity?" Mohab asked.

"Unknown, Commander," Jacob said.

Prior thought for a moment. "Rex, contact Space Command. The Atmospheric and Oceanographic Bureau. Ask them if we're experiencing a spatial phenomena," she said.

"I'm sure it's just a glitch, Prior," Mohab said.

"I don't think so, do you, Lt. Jacob?" Prior asked.

"I've never seen an anomaly like it before," Jacob said.

"What are you getting at, Prior?" Mohab asked.

"Lt. Addison, let's show the commander how intelligent my junior officers are," Prior said. Addison joined her side and nodded. "How would you commence an attack on the Guardian Corps?"

"You're talking about a combined tactical and strategic strike?" Addison asked. Prior nodded. "Well, if I were going to do it, I'd disrupt military operations. I'd use a five-point plan. First, I would split forces using a feint of some kind and then I'd take out as many senior officers as possible. Preferably by subtle means such as making them sick, if necessary by assassination. Then I'd cut vital supply lines and then sever communications."

"And then you'd attack the weakest point in the line," Mohab said finishing the plan for her. "Okay, Prior, she's brilliant. Assign her as a strategic planner. But what does it prove?"

"It's all happened, Mohab," Prior said. "Coincidence? I don't think so."

"But an attack on a main Guardian unit hasn't happened," Mohab said.

"Not yet," Addison said. "With communications disrupted, how would we know?"

"Cdr. Prior," Rex said. "There are no spatial disruptions expected for at least another month."

"Thank you, Rex," Prior said. He nodded and began to walk away but she called him back. "Rex, if you were attacking the Guardians, which unit would you consider the weakest link?"

"The weakest part of the Corps is the Academy, but there is no strategic or tactical advantage to be gained by attacking there," he said thoughtfully. "After the Academy, Central Command would be the next on the pecking order."

"Central Command," Prior nodded in agreement.

"You've gone off the deep end," Mohab said. "There's no way anyone would ever think of striking there. It's madness."

"That's exactly why it will be hit... and soon," Prior said.

"Commander, we're coming in for landing," Micah said.

She nodded and the craft set down on the hospital's landing platform. A large group of nurses and doctors and orderlies swarmed the air ship with medical equipment and gurneys. In a few minutes, the craft was unloaded and the Guardians were being attended to.

Prior stood outside her craft and looked up into the sky. A second gunship had joined King 3 in orbit above them. "Is that King 5?" she asked as Pana stepped out of the air ship.

Pana nodded. "Yes. They were unable to find the Second Battalion ship. But there is something you need to hear, Commander," she said.

Prior and Pana stepped into the ship and Prior slipped on a headset and listened carefully to the transmission. After a few seconds, she handed the headset to Mohab. He had a surprised look on his face and glanced to Prior. She nodded and he handed the headset to Pana.

"What is that?" Jacob said listening to his own TACCOM receiver. "I've never heard that transmission before. It keeps repeating itself and is jamming the air waves."

"Jacob, have every unit break off what they're doing, no matter what it is, and have them report to Central Command at best speed. If you can, get through to Centurion Beatty of the Third Battalion, tell her, 'Mohammed has climbed the mountaintop'," Mohab said.

"But, Commander..." Jacob began.

"Lieutenant, if you can't do what is ordered, I'll find another officer who can," Mohab said tersely.

"I'll see to it, Commander," Jacob said.

"Make sure you use my call sign... and be quick," Mohab said.

"Pana, where are our units?" Prior asked.

"From what I can figure out, they're engaging someone just outside of Central Command Headquarters," Pana said.

"Micah, how long will it take for us to get to Central Command?" Prior said.

"At least three hours," he said.

"Let's get ready to move out," Prior ordered.

"Commander, I've instructed our units to communicate using the TELCOM network. It'll leave us vulnerable to jamming and intercept, but it's the best we've got right now," Pana said. "St. Jacques says that they're facing overwhelming numbers and have taken significant casualties but are pushing forward. However, they'll need support." Prior nodded and Pana saw that she was deeply troubled, but knew her concerns were not caused by the status of her Guardians alone. "What was that message, cousin?"

"It was a message that has never been sent in the history of the Corps. I thought I would never hear it in my lifetime. It's an OP-REQ 3 Guardian Code Blue," Prior explained. "It's an emergency recall command for all commanders to sortie and bring their Guardians to Central Command because it's under attack and in danger of being overrun."

As her explanation sunk in, Prior wrestled with the problem. All of this was too well planned. If she and Mohab had been killed, there would have been no commanders alive to recognize the recall and send units. Only a commander knew what the message meant. To anyone else, it was gibberish.

Their forces were split, most of the senior leadership killed, communications disrupted, tactical supplies cut off and an attack on the weakest part of the force had commenced. It all added up to a siege spawned by The Argent. They were the only ones powerful enough to force the Guardian Elders to call for help and they had been acquiring Guardian weapons. Prior knew there was only one way to save Central Command and the forces St. Jacques was leading.

Prior placed her TELCOM in her ear and called the most recent number she had added to her address book. It didn't take long for the party to answer. After a brief conversation, lasting less than two minutes, she hung up. She sat down and stroked Lupo's soft fur. Mohab joined her and saw that she was shaking a bit.

"What's up?" he asked softly.

"We can't reach Central Command in time to save them, Mo. I had to call for some… special help. I hoped they would be wrong, but in the end I knew they were right. I knew they were right all along," she said.

Her face was a blank slate and Mohab had never seen Prior look so lost. It appeared as though all of her feelings and thoughts had abandoned her. Something had overtaken her.

"What is it, Pri? Who was right?" he asked confused by her expression and words. "Tell me, I want to help."

"You can't help, Mo," she said shaking her head. "I had to call the only people who truly understand what this madness is all about to help us. In return, I sold myself into their service."

"Sold yourself to whom?" Mohab asked unsure if even she knew what she was talking about.

"As much as I fought and resisted, somehow deep down inside I knew they were right," Prior continued as if she hadn't heard him. "I knew they were right all along."

"They were right about what, Pri? Who was right?" Mohab asked putting his hands on her shoulders and shaking her. She seemed to snap out of her trance-like state and stared directly into his eyes. "Who was right, Pri?"

"Gideon. Gideon was right," Prior answered. "I joined his group and they gave me an army to save the Corps."

"Who's Gideon? What army are you talking about?" Mohab asked not believing her. He was afraid that the stress she had been under had finally caused her to crack.

"The Seven," she said plainly. "The army belongs to The Seven."

PART SIX

1
Prior's air ship, en route to Guardian Central Command, Planet Kerguelen

Prior's air vehicle and the accompanying gun ships were a half hour into their flight across the Great Sea and Micah was pushing the craft for all it was worth. The air turbines whined loudly in protest to the work they were given. There was an unusual vibration throughout the fuselage and the noise in the interior of Prior's craft was almost deafening. Onboard with Prior were Lupo, Addison, Pana, Rex, Commander Mohab and his aide Lieutenant Jacob. The air ship seemed to be flying at a low rate of speed and Prior wondered why.

"What's wrong? Why are we moving so slow?" Prior called to Micah over the groaning of the engines.

"The air turbines were stressed during our battle with Col. Thyssen's ships," Micah explained. "They can't reach maximum output any longer."

"How long will it take us to get to Central Command?" Prior queried.

"Over four hours," Micah replied. "Besides the air turbine problem, we're bucking a strong head wind."

"The battle will be over by then," Prior said. She turned to Pana. "Do you still have St. Jacques on the TELCOM?"

"Yes," Pana said. "He reports they're engaged with a large airborne force that came from nowhere and without warning. They've repelled the first attack wave but took heavy losses and are losing ground."

"It's The Argent. How big is the force?" Prior asked.

"He estimates the odds are greater than five-to-one," Pana said.

"Prior, get your men out of there," Mohab said. "They can't possibly hold against a force that size."

Prior seemed to ignore Mohab. "How far are they from the main building?" she asked.

Pana asked the question and turned to Prior when she received the answer. "A little less than a mile," Pana said.

"Tell him to have Fukuani and Tanith placed the specials about a hundred and fifty yards from the main structure," Prior instructed. "If they have to fall back, have them go all the way inside and light off the specials when The Argent get in range. They need to try to take out as many as possible."

As Pana gave St. Jacques the orders, Prior turned to Mohab and saw he had a concerned look on his face.

"What's the matter, Mohab?" she asked.

"Obviously they want to break off," he said. "They wouldn't have told you the odds they were facing if they thought they had a chance of success."

Prior shook her head. "They'll hold," she said. "They're surveyors and The Mongoose is leading them."

"But the majority of the defenders are the contracted security guards. They don't have Guardian training," Mohab offered. "The smart thing to do is get them out of there and regroup."

"The Elders have not called for a retreat," Prior countered. "And my forces have never left the enemy with control of the battlefield. Even if I did order them out, honor would compel them to stay and fight."

"Honor?" Mohab scoffed not believing his ears. "There's nothing honorable about wasting lives, Prior. What will honor do for them when they're dead? There's nothing dishonorable about retreating against a force greater than five times your size. They'll get over a seeming lack of honor by continuing to live."

"*Honor compromised, is honor no longer,*" Prior said. "The president who said that wasn't a Guardian, but he understood that sometimes a leader has to make hard choices."

"Be sure to inscribe that quote on the tombstones of your men, Prior," Mohab said.

"Don't test my patience, Cdr. Mohab," Prior said tersely and with a scowl. "There are limits to it." She called to Micah. "Have King 3 and King 5 break off and continue on without us, Micah." She then turned to Pana. "Tell St. Jacques to hold for all he's worth. Help is on the way."

Pana nodded and spoke quietly into her TELCOM. Mohab stared hard at Prior. He didn't know why she was willing to so casually sacrifice her men needlessly.

"If you don't mind me asking, Prior, where is this help going to come from? The nearest units are still hours away," Mohab said.

"The Seven are sending reinforcements," Prior said clicking on her own TELCOM device. When the connection was made, she spoke. "Howard, this is Prior. How long?" She listened intently to the Celeron liaison as he spoke. When he was done, she nodded briefly. "Outstanding. My Guardians will be waiting. Contact me when you arrive on scene."

Prior clicked off her TELCOM and then turned to Mohab when she felt his eyes on her. She raised an eyebrow at him and he frowned as he spoke.

"Who or what are The Seven?" he asked.

"Friends," Prior said. "Pana, tell St. Jacques a large force will arrive by air in ten minutes from the southeast to reinforce him. They'll be flying my colors."

Pana nodded again and spoke into her TELCOM. Mohab was about to ask a dozen more questions when Prior's TELCOM beeped and saved her from his interrogations.

"This is Prior," she said answering the call.

"Capt. Chikiko here," a female voice said. "I've been tracking and monitoring some strange activity from up here. Do you need us?"

"As a matter-of-fact, I do, Captain," said Prior. "By the way, how are you contacting me?"

Captain Chikiko was in charge of Prior's space operations team. Located in orbit onboard Space Station *Condor*, Prior wondered how the captain was able to reach her via TELCOM.

"You've given me a lot of money to turn the impossible into something possible," Chikiko said. "Contacting you via TELCOM from space is a sample of how your money's been spent. And since the TACCOM network appears to be down, I figured there was a problem that needed our attention."

Daryl Edwards

"Well, I'm glad you called, Captain, because I need more of your wizardry... and I need it quick, fast and in a hurry," Prior said.

"I'm awaiting your orders, Commander," Chikiko said.

Prior quickly laid out her requirements to Chikiko and was pleased that the Eastern Province native and her team had developed contingencies for a possible communications breakdown. Chikiko's team would establish a set of emergency channels routing TACCOM communications through a seldom-used weather satellite and then task the satellite to perform surveillance over the Central Command area.

"How is your team able to do all this?" Mohab asked.

"A loss of global Guardian and non-Guardian communications and surveillance systems has always been a possibility, Mohab," Prior explained. "I have people tasked to keep an eye on things and develop contingencies for such an event."

"I don't understand," Mohab said.

"Basically, my people spy on other Guardians," Prior said plainly.

"Why?" he asked.

"Because the only way for our network to fail is by sabotage... internal sabotage. A corrupt Guardian in the right place can cripple the Corps. I've placed very intelligent personnel in the right place to counter it," Prior said.

"And how much does all that cost?" Mohab asked.

"A lot," Prior said with a chuckle and a smile.

It took Chikiko and her team less than thirty minutes to do their work. Once they were done, Prior's demeanor changed quite dramatically. With the ability to see what was happening on the ground and communicate directly with her forces, Prior began coordinating the activities of her Guardians with those of the Celeron that had arrived to reinforce them. Major St. Jacques didn't know who they were or why they carried Prior's battle banner, but he didn't care. All he knew was that they had turned certain defeat and death into a possible victory.

The Guardians and the Celeron force Prior called The Seven made a massive push. Under Prior's direction they were attempting to surround The Argent units attacking Central Command and crush them. They were beginning to fall back and the leaders of The Argent force were doing their best to prevent their men from scattering in disarray. Prior stared hard into the screen in front of her and shouted orders into the mouthpiece of the headset she wore.

"Keep pushing forward, Jack," Prior said. "I can see The Argent line breaking up to your left. Throw in all your reserves and take them down. You have support on both sides now from The Seven."

"We're on the move," St. Jacques replied and Prior could hear him giving orders to his men. "But, Commander, just so you know, we have no reserves. What you see is all that there is."

"It will be enough, Jack," Prior said. "The Seven will make sure you don't get cut off."

Prior muted the speaker on her headset and sighed. She leaned back and punched the armrest of her seat in response to what she saw on the satellite surveillance.

"We've got them!" she said aloud to no one in particular. "All they need to do is push!"

Mohab sat down next to her and tapped her shoulder. "Take a break for a minute, Prior. There's nothing else you can do until this plays itself out," he said.

"I won't rest until the battle has been decided," Prior said shrugging his hand off of her shoulder.

She glanced at the satellite imagery in front of her and could see The Argent force retreating very quickly now. The push was working. A call from The Seven came through the temporary communications circuit and Prior answered it quickly.

"This is Prior," she said.

"Mistress, we have broken The Argent force in the center and on the right. The Guardians have penetrated on the left. The Argent is in full retreat and heading for their air vehicles. Do we pursue?" a strong male voice said.

"Negative, Dillon. Do not follow in force. It may only be a feint. Surround and destroy as many as you can and establish a defensive perimeter. Send a recon unit to trail The Argent that have retreated," Prior ordered. "Instruct them not to engage. Just track them and let me know where they've gone."

"Affirmative," Dillon said.

"How are your losses?" Prior asked.

"Minimal," Dillon replied.

"See to the medical needs of the wounded and maintain a strong and alert picket line. I don't want any surprises if The Argent try to counter-attack," Prior said.

"It will be done, Mistress," Dillon said. "An air patrol will be established as well."

"Good," Prior said. She looked at her screen and tilted her head to one side unsure of what she was seeing. Something strange had appeared on the screen. "Dillon, what is that to the north?"

"What are you talking about, Mistress?" Dillon asked.

"That black swirl," Prior said. "You've got to be able to see it. It's getting larger."

Dillon looked to the north and saw the apparition Prior was referring to. It was jet black and looked like a dark whirlpool spinning in the air. It seemed to be growing larger and darker as each second passed. When it stopped swelling, a huge man-like creature stepped out of it. Prior and Dillon both realized what it was at the same time and gasped in unison.

"The Argent!" Dillon said. "He's come to rally his forces!"

"Dillon, you've got to fire on it!" Prior said. "Kill it! Kill it now!"

"We can't kill it, Mistress," Dillon said. "Not with these weapons."

"They'll slow it down so you can reach the fortress," Prior said. "Fire everything you've got and then get out of there!"

Dillon did as ordered and a tremendous volley of plasma energy fire bombarded The Argent entity. The ground shuddered, and the intense light emitted from the hundreds of weapons being fired at once blinded all persons on the field of battle. When their vision cleared, they viewed the results.

A giant crater, a hundred yards in diameter and twenty feet deep was created. Dillon and St. Jacques stepped a few paces forward, more out of curiosity than for any military consideration. As they looked through the smoke billowing out of the crater, they saw their target slowly crawl out of the hole.

"Get everyone into the fortress," St. Jacques ordered.

Dillon backed away and then turned and ran to his men and the remaining Guardians. He ordered them inside the main structure of the Central Command headquarters and they quickly complied. Prior saw them move and nodded in approval. She quickly became concerned when she saw a body closing in on The Argent entity.

"Dillon, who is that moving toward The Argent?" she asked.

"St. Jacques," Dillon replied.

"St. Jacques!" Prior exclaimed. "God Almighty, he'll be ripped apart." She adjusted the frequency on her communications unit and called to St. Jacques. "Jack, don't do it! Come back!"

"I'm just going to buy the others some time, Commander," he replied.

He closed in on The Argent and the creature walked slowly towards him. The Argent was visibly stunned from the plasma energy fire but was far from done. The creature brushed dirt from his body and looked at the wisps of smoke wafting from multiple points on his seared skin and smiled.

St. Jacques knelt and brought his plasma rifle to bear and fired three times at The Argent. Two shots hit the creature in the chest and the third connected with its head. The Argent's head snapped back and he was staggered by the blasts.

The Argent seemed to be hurt again and St. Jacques continued to fire. This time, the blasts seemed to have no effect and the dark creature continued to move forward unfazed by the weapon. The Argent gestured to the invading forces and they gave a loud yell and began to run toward the fortress. St. Jacques saw the ineffectiveness of his weapon and the encroaching force and decided it was a good idea to make a hasty retreat himself. He raced to the point where Fukuani and Tanith were standing by and snatched a device from Fukuani's hand.

"Get out of here," he said to the Guardians. "I'll be right behind you."

They followed the rest to the safety of the fortress and St. Jacques took a deep breath as he watched The Argent and his force approach. Around him the ground began to be peppered by weapons fire and he kneeled and primed the detonator he held. Via satellite, Prior and Mohab watched the events unfold on the screen and Mohab tilted his head to one side.

"What's he doing? They're almost on top of him," Mohab said.

"He's readying the specials Fukuani planted," Prior said.

"Doesn't the detonator have a remote firing capability?" Mohab asked.

"It does," Prior said.

"Then what is he doing?" Mohab asked.

"A sacrifice play," Prior said. "He's giving himself up for the others."

"Get him out of there, Prior!" Mohab said.

"He wouldn't leave even if I ordered it," Prior said.

"But…" Mohab began.

"The Fourth Rule of Battle, Mohab," Prior said sadly. "Guardians fight to the death."

Prior watched in horror as The Argent and his forces came within optimum firing range. St. Jacques was hit several times and he staggered backwards. The Argent's weapons pounded him with thunderous blows but his Boroni physiology allowed him to stay alive long enough for his plan to work.

St. Jacques fell to his knees and looked up at the force beginning to encircle him. He smiled and depressed the button on the detonator. A second later, a bright blue wave of light and a large and powerful shockwave erupted along a line in front of the fortress. A piercing shrill sound filled the air around the fallen Guardian. The bulk of The Argent forces were knocked off of their feet and squirmed and writhed in pain on the ground. The Argent forces closest to the blast died a slow and painful death, while those more distant merely collapsed to the ground and lost control of their limbs and faded in and out of consciousness.

Mohab saw the results of Prior's special weapon and spun her around in her chair. "What in the Netherworld was that?" he asked.

"You just witnessed the employment of an ultrasonic weapon," Prior said. "One of my specials. You can't see it clearly from this distance, but within the primary blast zone, the USW has liquefied the living tissue of everyone there and in the secondary zone, it causes ataxia."

Mohab looked at the screen and saw The Argent forces that were still standing retreat to their air vehicles and vacate the area. It seemed as though they had enough for the day.

"It's driven them off," Mohab said. "I hope you're happy."

"I am," Prior said. "A large majority of The Argent forces have been killed or incapacitated and Central Command has been saved."

"But you used an illegal weapon to do it," Mohab said. "We have a moral obligation to do right, regardless of the situation. You broke the faith, Prior."

"Perhaps, but I saved lives," Prior said.

"But it cost St. Jacques his life. If you would have retreated when you should have, none of this would have been necessary," Mohab said. "All of them could have been saved."

"Do you really believe that, Mohab?" Prior said. "If you do, then you're a fool. If we had retreated now, we would have had to fight The Argent in another place... one of their choosing. Now we have the opportunity to prepare our forces for a concentrated effort against them. If you think The Argent are a group of disgruntled citizens with guns, you're wrong. They are committed and well led. You saw how they rallied when the creature appeared. They worship that beast. This is a serious campaign and we have to stop it now."

"By any means necessary?" he asked.

"Yes," Prior nodded. She turned her chair and clicked on the communications circuit. "Dillon, is your recon unit following The Argent?"

"Yes, Mistress," he said.

"Good. I'll be on deck in about an hour to receive a report," Prior said.

"We await your arrival, Mistress," Dillon said ending the transmission.

Prior turned to Pana. "Contact Hiroki or Fukuani or whoever is senior and try and find out the status of the Elders," Prior said.

Pana nodded and Mohab sat down next to Prior. "What do we do now?" he asked.

"We take care of our casualties and bury our dead," Prior said. "And then we go after those who are responsible."

"But you're responsible, Prior," Mohab said.

"Mohab, don't be a child," she said harshly. "You sound as if I wanted those men and women to die. If I could have traded places with them, I would have. Remember, those were my Guardians down there, not yours. I had to sit here and watch them fight and die from fifteen hundred miles away. St. Jacques was a member of my House. I've got to tell his family he's dead, not you. But he was well aware of what he was doing and the risks involved. All of them did. And if you ask them, they'd do it again. It's what surveyors do."

"You always seem to have an answer, Prior," Mohab said.

"What are you trying to say, Mohab?" Prior said with a raised eyebrow. "It's easy to have an answer when you have truth on your side. And you never had a problem with my surveyors when they were on point for you. When they were injured protecting your Guardians you didn't seem to have a problem with what we do or how we did it."

"I never needlessly risked lives," Mohab said.

"You've never been in real heavy shit before either," Prior said. She took a deep breath and continued. "Listen, Mohab, I don't want to argue with you. I'm your friend. But don't accuse me of something subversive. It wouldn't be wise… or healthy."

"I have questions that need answers, Prior," he said.

"And you'll get them," Prior said. "But there are more pressing and important issues to deal with at the present." She paused for a moment and then added, "You think I'm evil and heartless, don't you? Don't bother responding I already know the answer. We're in a war now, Mohab, like it not. And when it comes to battle, I take on the demeanor of the situation. That attitude and my actions do not reflect who or what I really am. But while the conflict rages, it's who and what I have to be."

Mohab thought for a moment and nodded. "I'll let it go for now," Mohab agreed.

Her attitude was unacceptable and her actions inexcusable and it all made Mohab suspicious of Prior. He suddenly didn't know who she was and didn't trust her. It was the first time he had ever felt that way toward Prior and it concerned him greatly. But what troubled him more were the questions etched into his mind. Where did those troops called The Seven come from and why were they in a position to aid the Guardians just when all was lost? Where did she get those special weapons? And why was she so evasive about it all? For the good of the Corps and the safety and security of Kerguelen he had to know. And if he had to arrest her to find out those answers, he would.

2
The Sacred City of Shiloh,
The Middle Provinces, Planet Kerguelen

"Are these reports accurate?" Gregor said looking at a PDA screen. He was openly disturbed by the reports he had received from the ill-fated attack on Guardian Central Command.

The cardinal, Colonel Thyssen and two members of The Argent leadership were contemplating their next moves in a secret enclave in the Sacred City of Shiloh, the Place of Peace.

"Yes, I'm afraid those messages are correct," one of The Argent military leaders said.

"How? How could this have happened? Everything was so carefully planned. Where did all of those Guardians come from?" Gregor asked.

"They weren't Guardians," Thyssen offered. "They're private contractors or mercenaries. Whoever they are, they screwed this thing into a cocked hat."

"That's all you have to offer?" Gregor said. "You're supposed to be my military advisor. Don't you have any information on them?"

"All we know is that they came from the southeast and quickly turned the tide of battle. We do know that Prior was coordinating their movements," Thyssen said.

"Prior? That's impossible. I saw The Argent shoot her myself," Gregor said.

"Then she has a clone because her voice print was verified on the transmissions we intercepted," Thyssen said. "I told you she was a tactical genius and needed to be killed before we commenced operations. It was reported those mysterious troops were flying her battle banner. If that is true and she is still alive, we need to modify our plans."

"We can't change plans, Colonel. There are too many pieces on the board already moving. If she is in fact still alive, our final ace in the hole may be exactly what we need to counter the cunning Cdr. Prior," Gregor said.

"I hope you're right," Thyssen said. "We lost at least four hundred of our men attacking Central Command. We haven't got exact numbers yet, but regardless of how many, they were irreplaceable losses. That tactical weapon they fired off broke our back. With the Guardians from the Third and Fourth Battalions, Prior's surveyors and those other troops, the odds are evening up."

"Does a fair fight scare you, Colonel?" Gregor asked.

"Anyone engaging in a fair fight has failed to plan properly," Thyssen replied. "Those aren't my words, they're Prior's."

"What was that blasphemous weapon the Guardians used?" the second Argent leader asked.

"It was an experimental tactical weapon," Thyssen said. "It's called a USW, a powerful ultrasonic device. Its development was supposed to have been stopped and banned by the Technology Council. It's illegal to possess the technology, let alone experiment, test or employ it against others."

"What did it do to our men?" Gregor asked.

"At close range it liquefies living tissue. At longer range it causes a loss of full control of bodily movements," Thyssen explained. He shrugged his shoulders and continued. "That's the theory anyway. It was initially banned because its power and range was unpredictable. I don't think anyone knows for sure how the device would actually react or how much damage it can cause when employed."

"The men who died from the device do," the second Argent leader said.

Thyssen sighed and nodded. "You're right, but how could Prior have acquired such a device? As I said, it's an illegal weapon," he said.

"It seems as though we found someone who likes to play as rough as we do, Colonel. And since she chose to use such an unpredictable weapon against us without knowing if it would kill everyone, it tells me she knows exactly what's at stake. What do you think Prior will do next?" Gregor asked.

"Once she ensures Central Command is stabilized and the Elders are safe, she will gather up as many troops as she can muster and track down our forces. If she defeats them, she'll come after you... and me," Thyssen said. "And not necessarily in that order."

Gregor nodded. "Then let's hope her next encounter with The Argent will be her last."

3

Guardian Central Command, Northeastern Province, Planet Kerguelen

As they neared the end of their journey across the Great Sea, Micah was overjoyed at the sight of the Northeastern Province's Hinterlands. He was also elated that Commander Prior's complaining had come to an end. Everyone onboard knew how important it was to reach Central Command as soon as possible and Micah would have done anything he could to arrive sooner. Though the battle was over and the invaders had been routed, no one knew what to expect when they landed. They might be setting down in a graveyard of Guardians. Whatever the situation, all they could do was wait until they got there.

From above, they could see units on the ground reinforcing positions and policing what had been a battlefield. The once pristine and manicured lawns and greenery that surrounded the Central Command structures were littered with bodies and smoldering pyres and in the distance, was a tremendous crater hole. The castle that housed Central Command headquarters was smoking in sections and parts of the thick stonewalled parapets had been reduced to rubble.

Every minute, more and more air ships from the Third and Fourth Battalions arrived and waited for their turn to land. As they orbited above, Pana made contact with someone on the ground. She handed a headset to Prior and the commander snatched it from her hands impatiently and spoke to the senior officer on the scene.

"This is Commander Prior," she said. "Report status."

"This is Centurion Beatty, Commander. The enemy forces have totally withdrawn and we have reinforced our position," Beatty said. "Casualties are being tended to, but we could use any med techs you have with you."

"My personal physician is onboard and will assist, Centurion. I'll be down in two minutes. Meet me at the landing area," Prior instructed.

"I'm in our makeshift communications and command post bunker, Commander. It will take me a few minutes to wrap up what I'm doing," Beatty said.

"Very well, Centurion. I'll meet you at the C.P. Prior, out," she said taking off the headset and tossing it to Pana. "Take us down, Micah."

When they landed, Prior and Lupo stepped out of the air ship and the commander looked over the defensive positions that had been set up. They seemed adequate and looked as though they could withstand a siege. The majority of the Third and Fourth Battalions had arrived and when the remainder of those units finally made it, Central Command would be safe and able to repel any attack. A platoon from the Third Battalion had been sent to the Guardian Academy to protect those assets and the cadets and the Academy Superintendent was glad that someone had remembered that the young men and women there were vulnerable to attack.

As Prior surveyed the defensive works, a major from the Third Battalion came up to greet her. He saluted and led her to the command post. The air was foul and reeked of death and their path to the C.P. was littered with the bodies of fallen Guardians, Central Command security guards and others. Prior assumed, by the silver tunics they wore, the unfamiliar dead men, and there were a lot of them, were Argent warriors. It seemed these modern Argent warriors wore the traditional garb of their ancestors. Lupo stopped every few feet to sniff the corpses and lagged behind his mistress. Prior stopped abruptly and spun around to face the major. He could see that she was visibly angry.

"Major, I want these bodies cleared out of here," she said sternly.

"Centurion Beatty has given instructions for that, Commander. It's just taking some time to get it all coordinated," the major said.

"It doesn't take a whole lot to do that, Major," Prior said tapping on her TACCOM. "Rex, find some surveyors and form a burial detail. The vultures are already circling."

"Right away, Commander," Rex said.

Prior clicked off the TACCOM and continued on. By all indications it was a bloody affair. No one went down without a fight and the agony and anguish the troops on both sides experienced at the end of their lives was etched into their faces for all eternity. The scene changed her opinion of the security guards assigned to Central Command. She had thought because of their minimal training and experience they were ill prepared for a contested battle. How wrong she had been. Those men had fought heroically against a well-armed, well-trained and well-led force.

The Argent warriors taken down by the USW experienced an entirely different kind of death than those killed by plasma weapons and hand-to-hand combat. Those in the primary blast area had died slowly as their skin disintegrated before their eyes. Prior knew it had to be excruciating and the pain they experienced overwhelming.

"Do you know how many men were taken prisoner, Major?" Prior asked.

"No. They were taken by the time my unit arrived. Accounts vary depending on whom you ask. Centurion Beatty has the exact numbers," the major said. He pointed to a group of men wearing dark gray combat suits, trimmed with black and teal colored markings. Except for the color, the suits were identical to that worn by the Guardians. Prior recognized them as the Celeron. "Those men set up the defensive positions we now occupy. According to the Guardians who fought here, it was they who drove off the invaders. I don't know who they are, but thank the Almighty for them."

"They didn't identify themselves?" Prior asked.

The major shook his head. "They refused to and they won't take any orders. Centurion Beatty finally instructed us to relieve them and say nothing to them," he said. "Once we relieved them they began gathering up their casualties."

"Have the bodies been searched?" Prior asked.

"Not yet."

Prior scoffed. "What in the Netherworld have you been doing, Major, sightseeing? Oh, don't bother answering," Prior said becoming more agitated.

Prior shook her head and knelt down to examine one of The Argent warriors. She searched the uniform and looked at his weapon closely. It was a high-powered weapon equal in stopping force to a Guardian-style weapon. She reached into a pouch and pulled out an object. She looked at it closely and then put it in one of her belt pouches. She searched another body and found the same items but no identification. She stood up and they continued on to the command post. Prior glanced to her right and saw her battle banner on a standard waving defiantly in the breeze. Dark gray combat suit clad men stood around it and when they saw her they stopped what they were doing, came to attention and watched her pass in silent reverie.

"We asked them why they flew your banner, Commander," the major said. "But they refused to answer that question as well."

"Is that so?" Prior said. "Well, don't worry, Major. They had my permission to fly it."

There was a lot of activity in the command post when Prior and the major arrived. A diminutive female Guardian centurion was quietly giving orders to a group of officers surrounding her. Her light brown hair was loose and waved like a pennant in the stiff wind that was blowing. She dismissed the officers after giving them her final instructions and they saluted and departed. The centurion looked up and saw Prior, smiling when she recognized her. She saluted and approached.

"Commander Prior," the centurion said. "It's good to see you again."

"Centurion Beatty," Prior replied returning her salute. "It's a pleasure to see you as well."

"That will be all, Major," Beatty said to the officer escorting Prior. He saluted and turned to leave, but she called him back. "By the way, Major, I told you to take care of the casualties. It may take hours to accomplish the task but not hours to get started. I'm not pleased about that, Major."

"The Commander shares your concerns, Centurion. I informed the Commander we've had some coordination problems," the major said.

"Your excuses are your own, Major," Beatty said. "Hold their hands, sing them a song, do whatever it takes but have the troopers get it done. Give it your full attention. Dismissed."

The major saluted and quickly left before Beatty could remember anything else he had done wrong. When they were alone Prior and Beatty stepped closer together and interlocked arms. They smiled at each other and Beatty pointed to a camp chair. Prior sat and Beatty poured them some coffee.

Beatty graduated a few years after Prior and had recently been promoted to the rank of centurion and assigned as deputy commander of the Third Battalion. A field officer by training, Beatty had struggled with her grades at the Academy. She finished fifth from the bottom of her class and because of that, was not assigned as a battalion field officer initially. Though she lacked the requisite knowledge, she was assigned to Prior and trained as a combat engineer. Beatty proved to be a fairly good student and Prior wrote her solid evaluation reports. After two years, Prior managed to secure Beatty a posting as a platoon leader in the Third Battalion. She skyrocketed through the ranks and was now, due to the death of Commander Jordan, commander of the Third Battalion. Prior was proud of her protégé and they had stayed closed through the years. If her luck held out, Beatty would eventually join Central Command as an Elder. She was a spitfire and tenacious and was well thought of throughout the Corps.

"I'm sorry I had to undress my major in front of you," Beatty said handing Prior a cup of coffee. "But dead bodies lying around is bad for morale." She sighed and sipped her coffee.

"How is your battalion?" Prior asked.

"Fine, but only two-thirds of them are here. I've sent a platoon to the academy as you know and the rest are in Shiloh. They're all worried about this, but as soon as I get a handle on it, I'll soothe their souls. I'm sorry we missed the fight though. Luckily your friends were here to push the enemy out," she said giving Prior a sideways glance. "Who are they, Prior? What's their story?"

"They're special units," Prior said. "They are based in Canton-on-Heath."

"No wonder they got here so fast," Beatty said.

"They represent every province on Kerguelen though. I call them the Army of The Seven. They're... acquaintances of mine," Prior said.

"Acquaintances? You know all those men?" Beatty said with a sly smile. "My, my, Prior. You do get around, don't you?"

"It's complicated, Beatty," Prior said.

"A spokesman for them said they won't do anything until receiving orders from you," Beatty said. "When did you get your own private army?"

Prior exhaled. "Like I said, it's complicated. I can't explain it right now. They're basically on loan to me and they're here to help," Prior said trying not to be too evasive. "They warned me about the threat facing us and tried to prepare me for it."

"You can't give me any more than that?" Beatty asked. "They fly your colors and they've got weapons and equipment I've never seen before. And their air ships... well, you have to see them to believe them."

"Right now, besides standing by to aid the Guardians, they're doing some scouting work for me. I wish I could tell you more, but I can't," Prior said regretfully.

Beatty decided to change the subject since she wasn't going to get any information. "The medics believe almost everyone brought in will survive," she said. "Our makeshift field hospital isn't the best, but the med techs are doing great work." She paused and then added, "I'm sorry about St. Jacques, Prior. I know how you felt about him."

"His empty chair will haunt me... as will the loss of all the others," Prior said softly. She sighed and asked, "How are the Elders?"

"Not good," Beatty said sadly. "But I think seeing you will help. Come on."

Prior followed Beatty to the field hospital and stopped before she entered. She told Lupo to wait for her and then went inside. Prior had to dial down her enhanced senses as she walked around. The smell of blood and seared flesh filled the ramshackle enclosure and the med techs were working desperately to save limbs and lives. Pana was elbow deep in the chest of a Guardian and was cursing the treatment he had received so far.

"Be careful with him, Hancock! Are you trying to finish the job the plasma weapon didn't? What kind of medic are you?" Pana scowled at the tech beside her. "You have the touch of a blacksmith."

"I'm better as a scout than as a medic," the Guardian said.

"I've seen your abilities as a tracker," Pana scoffed. "You couldn't track a bear through a flour mill."

After she stabilized the Guardian she was working on, Pana moved to another awaiting treatment. The female Guardian lying on the cot was squirming and moaning from her wounds. Pana ran a medical scanner across the woman and handed it to the medic assisting her.

"Anesthetic," Pana said.

"We're out," the medic replied.

"She can't survive treatment while she's conscious," Pana said.

"We don't have anything to give her and we can't just make anesthetics from the dirt," the medic said.

"Maybe we can," Pana said thoughtfully. "In the meantime, this will have to suffice." Pana lifted the patient's head and pressed firmly on a bundle of nerves at the base of the neck and the woman passed out. Pana turned to the medic. "Okay, we can work on her now. But we have to be quick, she won't be out long."

"What did you do?" the medic asked taking out equipment.

"I temporarily cut off the signal to her brain that keeps her awake," Pana explained. "But it can't work in all cases. Your suggestion about getting anesthetics from the dirt was brilliant however."

"What do you mean?" the medic asked.

Pana grabbed an orderly standing near her and pulled him close. "Tell one of the Boroni pilots I need for him to go out in the woods and bring back as much snake root as he can find."

"Snake root? What the hell for?" the medic exclaimed.

"We can ground up snake root into a powder and add water to it. In that form, snake root is an alkaline tranquilizer," Pana explained. "We'll have the patients drink the solution and it will serve to sedate them until we can get proper anesthetics. Now go!"

The orderly departed and Pana carefully began cleaning the woman's wound. She looked up and saw Prior and shook her head. Prior stepped closer.

"Anything I can do?" Prior asked looking at the female Guardian.

"We need more medicine, we're running short on everything," Pana said looking to the cot beside her. The medic there was having trouble stopping the bleeding of a Guardian with a gash above his left eye. Pana took the medic's hand and placed his fingers firmly in front of the injured Guardian's left ear. "You should know there's a pressure point here. Press firmly and hold it and the bleeding will slow down."

Just then another medic joined them. Pana took the medical bag he had slung over his shoulder from him and emptied it on the table. She rifled through the contents until she found a bottle containing small white capsules. She added water to a glass and dropped four of the capsules into the water and used a swab to stir the mixture until the capsules had dissolved. When she was done, she took some gauze and wiped dirt and blood from the deep cut and then inserted the swab into it. The Guardian writhed from her attentions but she continued until the gash was clear of dirt and enough of the solution she had made was swabbed into it. She tossed the used swab away and then bandaged the gash.

The medic watched her work and nodded approvingly. "Nice work, doctor," he said. "I wouldn't have thought of using adrenaline capsules to stop the bleeding. I'll put some stitches in that after you're done here."

Pana nodded and returned to the cot where the unconscious woman lay and finished treating her.

"I'll see what I can do about getting more medicine," Prior said. She turned to an orderly. "Have one of the gray suited men come inside."

The orderly left and in a minute, returned with one of the Celeron. He bowed to Prior and she looked him over. She did not know who he was but he looked impressive.

"Do you know Howard, my liaison?" Prior asked.

The soldier thought for a moment and then nodded. "Yes, Mistress," he said.

"Good. Contact him and inform him I need a full complement of medical supplies delivered here at once," Prior said.

"We have two medical air ships fully loaded with supplies, Mistress," he said.

"Have Howard release those supplies to her," Prior ordered as she pointed to Pana.

"At once, Mistress," he said.

Prior thanked and dismissed him and turned to Pana. Pana grunted in response to the news and Prior continued on, confident that the patients were in good hands.

As she neared her destination, the sight of her surveyors on stretchers and operating tables sickened her. When she saw the Elders in that state she felt even worse. It was no way for a long time warrior to spend their last moments. She stopped when she reached the cot containing Marshal Pace. He was writhing in pain and the medics could barely hold him still for treatment. Beside Pace was Marshal Aca. She seemed to be resting comfortably. Beyond her was Garath. The Supreme Commander had more tubes protruding out of him than an octopus had tentacles. His breathing seemed labored and his blue eyes were cloudy and empty. He appeared as though he was waiting for the Angel of Death to come for him. Prior stepped to his cot and took his hand in hers. His eyes cleared responding to her touch and slowly turned his head to her. His eyes widened and Prior could see that he recognized her.

"How are you, Garath?" Prior said softly.

"Pri-or," he said weakly.

She could tell it hurt just to talk. "Don't try to speak, Marshal. Just rest. The young ones are here to take care of you," she said.

She had never seen a man so proud and full of vitality reduced to such a stricken state. His body was broken and his dark brown skin was covered with maroon colored burn marks from hits delivered by plasma energy weapons. The fact that he was still alive was a testament to his strength.

"W-Why save my… breath… The Almighty will be doing all of the talking soon," he said with a crooked smirk. "When I die… I become a private and She… becomes the Supreme Commander." He squeezed her hand and continued. "Y-You were right, Pri-or. We should have… listened to you."

"Don't worry about that now," she said. "You need to rest."

"Sure, sure," he chuckled as blood dripped from the corner of his mouth. Prior picked up a piece of gauze and wiped away the blood. He raised a twisted finger at Prior. "Unite… the Corps. Promise me you will lead them."

"I'll do what I can," Prior said.

"Ceca did this. My final order to you is to kill her," Garath said weakly.

Prior nodded and Garath's eyes fluttered. He had a full body spasm and his back arched in response to it. He growled loudly and a med tech ran a medical scanner over his body. She gave him a shot from a hypodermic and he settled down. His vitals stabilized and his grip loosened. Prior placed his hand on his chest and backed away.

"He needs to rest now, Commander," the med tech said.

Prior nodded and spun around to the cot containing Aca. She picked up her medical chart and frowned. Though the PDA told Prior that her wounds were not bad and she would be healed in a few days, she didn't like seeing one of her mentors in such a condition. When she put the PDA down she saw that Aca was looking at her.

"Late as usual, eh, Commander?" Aca asked quietly trying to make light of the situation.

"I'll summon a field courts-martial immediately, Marshal," Prior said playing along.

"Make sure you charge the Elders with neglect and stupidity. We should have listened to you. Look at us now. Antoine, Demos and Rina are dead. Garath, Pace and I are all busted up and half of the Corps has broken away from the fold," Aca said. She knew that her admission of guilt wouldn't solve anything but she had to say it. "All of the security guards are dead, but they fought like Guardians."

"I believe it," Prior said. "What's this about Ceca? What did she do? And who has broken away?"

"Ceca betrayed us. She was the one who ordered fuel cells and power packs to be withheld from the field units. She also shut down part of the computer and communications network. She even took our automated defense and early warning system offline. By the time we knew what she had done, it was too late," Aca explained. "Ceca and Thyssen have taken the First and Second Battalions as their own."

"You still held on here in spite of her deception," Prior said. "I know about the Second Battalion. Thyssen's air ships attack Mohab in Capitol City. We were barely able to rescue him. And Thyssen killed one of my men assigned to the protection of Father Joubert. I didn't know the First Battalion was also part of the conspiracy though."

"They are, but the troops are being lied to. It's the leadership that's behind it. We could have done better if Ceca had not given the enemy an opening. I tried to kill her but missed. However, the damage was already done. I was hit when I led the security force against the initial assault. They were so powerful. It's a miracle that any of us survived. If it weren't for those dark gray angels, I'd be dead," Aca said. She glanced hard at Prior. "Who are they? They carry your banner, Prior."

"Friends of mine, Aca. They used my banner so you would know they were here to help," Prior said. She patted Aca's hand. "You get some rest. We'll be back."

"Do you know who attacked us?" Aca asked.

"A group that are descendents of the ancient Argent faction," Prior answered.

"The Argent?" gasped Beatty in horror at the name.

"If it is The Argent, this is as dangerous as you said," Aca said. She raised her hand and pointed a finger at Prior. "You are senior now, you must take command of the Corps."

"I can't, Aca. Mohab is here though. You can appoint him as regimental commander," Prior said.

"Why?" Beatty asked.

"There are many reasons, but I can't assume that responsibility at the moment," Prior explained.

"You are senior to him by five years," Beatty said.

"And you have far more combat experience and leadership ability," Aca added. "This is no time to be magnanimous."

"I need to be in the field. I'm a surveyor, not an administrator. If a regimental commander is necessary, Mohab must be the one," Prior said.

"Why?" Aca asked.

"I have to find The Argent and kill their leader," Prior explained. "Once he is dead, The Argent threat will die with him."

"Why you?" asked Beatty.

"Only I can do it," Prior said. "And I need to be free to follow The Argent wherever they are or wherever they go. From here to the Netherworld if necessary."

Aca relented. "I won't make the mistake of not listening to your advice again," she said and turned to Beatty. "Centurion, send a Central Command aide to me... if there are any left... so I can send out the order appointing Mohab as regimental commander."

"And then spend some time with your aunt," Prior added.

Beatty turned a startled face to Prior and the Boroni commander smiled at her. Beatty had kept the fact that Aca was a relation a secret hoping to advance as a Guardian through her ability not because of favoritism. She thought she had been successful in keeping that knowledge hidden. As Prior walked away, Beatty wondered how Prior had obtained the knowledge.

"How did she know you were my aunt?" Beatty asked.

"I wouldn't worry about that," Aca said with a chuckle. "Prior has a knack for finding out things. She probably knows what the Almighty had for breakfast."

Prior walked out of the hospital and tapped her thigh. Lupo stood and joined her as she walked to the castle. She stopped and looked at a section of the eastward rampart. It had been blasted away by weapons fire and a demolitions charge. The hole led to a part of Central Command that she was not too familiar with. As she peered inside she heard movement and then saw Rex emerge from the darkness.

When he saw her, he stopped in his tracks, looked behind him and continued towards her. She climbed through the hole and gave Rex a quizzical look. Rex jerked his head and Prior followed him out of the structure. He stopped at a tree that had somehow avoided being hit by weapons fire and sat down leaning his broad back against the trunk. It's colorful leaves were in stark contrast to what was around it. Prior joined him and as she settled on the ground, Lupo nestled in between the two Boroni and rested his head on the grass. Rex was sullen and far too quiet.

"What were you doing in the castle?" Prior asked.

"There were a few casualties inside and I went to check them out. They were almost dead and beyond saving. All I could do was ease their journey into the next life," Rex said staring at the field in front of him.

"Who was inside?" Prior asked.

"Five Guardians and a civilian," Rex said.

"A civilian? What part of the castle is in there?" Prior asked pointing toward the hole.

"The detention cells," Rex said turning to her.

Prior's eyes opened wide. "No, it can't be," she said shaking her head.

Rex nodded and Prior's head fell on his shoulder. Rex placed his arms around her but Prior pushed away from him. She stood and walked to the castle and stared inside of the hole.

"There's no way you could have known this would happen," he said trying to console her.

Prior knew he was right but it didn't matter. She had forgotten that Lieutenant Francis and his team had brought her brother Poul here.

They were still present when the attack commenced. Following her orders, they tried to protect Poul and in doing so, died. Five Guardians and Poul were gone. Despite what he had done, Prior felt half of her had died with him. She wrapped her arms around herself tightly and closed her eyes. Prior started to weep and a trail of tears began to run down both of her cheeks. She wiped one side of her face and then the other and opened her eyes and looked up. The clouds parted and gave way to a bright and clear cerulean sky, a sky as deep and blue as her eyes were at that moment.

4

Guardian Central Command, Northeastern Province, Planet Kerguelen

Commander Mohab and Centurion Beatty were bent over a small table in the command post when Captain Hiroki entered. He had a pronounced limp and a large battle dressing bulged underneath his combat suit. He had refused to be placed on light duty while his wound healed and though it was a courageous gesture he was far from fit for full duty and the pain he endured showed. It took several 1,000-mg pain capsules to ease his discomfort and Hiroki required hour-long periods of rest during the day to keep him on his feet. He saluted and Mohab waved him over to the table. Mohab gestured for him to sit and Beatty gave him a cup of coffee.

"How's the leg, Captain?" Mohab asked.

"I'm getting along, Commander," Hiroki said sipping his coffee.

"I can see that," Mohab said eying him. "I'll get right to the point, Captain. You've been detailed with escorting Cdr. Prior home to the Western Province. The body of Senator Poul has been prepped and is ready for transport. Take her home and then report to the Guardian Academy for convalescence. Stay there until you receive further orders," Mohab said.

"As much as I, and the lovely ladies of the Palisades, appreciate the leave, I'm afraid that is an impossible tasking, Commander," Hiroki said. "Cdr. Prior is adamant about staying here."

"Is that so?" Mohab said folding his arms.

"I don't want to sound belligerent, but it wouldn't be in my best interest, health wise, to suggest such a trip to her," Hiroki said rubbing his thigh.

"Then I'll suggest it," Mohab said. "Just get ready to leave within the hour. Any questions?" Hiroki shook his head. "Good. Dismissed."

Hiroki sat his cup down and slowly stood. He was about to salute and leave but changed his mind and spoke instead.

"Begging the Commander's pardon, but why are you forcing this, sir?" Hiroki asked.

"She needs to go home," Mohab said bluntly.

"Forgive me, sir, but I've served with the commander for five years now, and I think I can read her very well. She doesn't need to go home. She needs action," Hiroki offered.

"I've known Cdr. Prior for over twenty years, Captain, and I think I know her better than you," Mohab said. "If I need any input, I'll be sure and ask you."

Hiroki came to attention, saluted and slowly limped out of the command post. When he was gone, Beatty sat down and leaned back in her chair. She knew it was the moral thing to do insisting that Prior go home and bury her brother, but she wasn't sure it was the right thing to do. She brought her coffee to her lips but didn't drink. She put the cup down and rubbed her forehead.

"I know what you're thinking," Mohab said looking at her. "But she needs to go home. She can't be in a good frame of mind right now. And we need her in her right mind."

"She's not just a grieving sister, she's also a Guardian… and Boroni," Beatty countered. "She's seen plenty of death before and just as close to her personally. She was at Sierra de Retan when her youngest brother was killed, vaporized by a tactical nuclear weapon. She dealt with that and she can deal with this."

"She dealt with Pike's death by killing thirty terrorists after they had surrendered," Mohab said.

"What happened then has always been speculative and no misdeeds by her concerning those events have ever been proven," Beatty replied.

"I can't take the chance of her going on another kill crazy rampage," Mohab said.

"You can't force her to go home, Mohab," Beatty said.

Mohab sighed and started to pace around the small command post. After a few seconds he turned to Beatty. "Where is she now?"

"She's talking to the leaders of her army," Beatty said. Mohab nodded and started to exit. "I wouldn't bother her right now if I were you."

"I've got to, Beatty. Come on," he said.

At the bivouac of the Army of The Seven, Prior was talking to several of the dark gray clad warriors and they listened intently to her. Circled around her were unit leaders and she wanted to familiarize herself with them. But that would be difficult. For the sake of security they wore masks covering their lower faces.

"Do you have any orders for us, Mistress?" the leader named Dillon asked.

"When we receive word of where The Argent went, we'll jump off. Be ready to move out at any time," Prior said. "When we do move, it will be you and my surveyors only."

"We will be ready, Mistress," Dillon said.

"Your ships are standing by to transport you whenever you give the word, Mistress," another said.

"My ships?" Prior asked.

"You command us, Mistress," Dillon said. "Our ships are your ships."

"Do I have a specific ship?" Prior asked.

"Yes," another said stepping forward. "My team is at your disposal, Mistress. We man your ship."

"What's your name?"

"Chandler," he said.

"Do I know you?" Prior asked eying him closely.

"You do, Mistress," he said removing his mask.

"You were senior to me at the academy. You were brigade XO if I'm not mistaken," Prior said recognizing him at once.

"I was in the Class of 2815, Mistress," Chandler said replacing the mask. "Many of us are Academy graduates or former NCOs. You know or have seen all of us before. In time, you will know us all but while we're here we will remain masked while in the presence of the Guardians. Our anonymity is paramount and our greatest asset."

"I agree," Prior said. "Be ready to saddle up any time, Chandler."

He nodded and they all came to attention as she walked away. On her way back to the Guardians, Mohab and Beatty caught up with her. She stopped and crossed her arms as they approached.

"Save your breath, Mohab. I already got wind of what you're planning. I'm not going home," Prior said. "My brother Pell is coming to pick up Poul's body."

"You should go with him," Mohab said.

"If I do, I'd bury Poul in a shallow grave," Prior said. "Don't let the disposition of Senator Poul trouble you any further, Mohab. It's all been taken care of."

"Prior, your brother is dead," Mohab said. "You need to go home and bury him and mourn your loss. The loss of a brother can be debilitating. You can't possibly be able to function at one hundred percent right now."

"Do you have any siblings, Mohab?" Prior asked.

"You know I don't," he said.

"Then how can you possibly know how I'm going to be affected by this," Prior said. "I'm Boroni, not Kerguelen. We mourn in our own unique way. There is nothing I can do about Poul. He's dead. I can't change that. But what I can do is kill everyone responsible. And that's what I'm going to do."

"Prior, that won't solve anything," Mohab said.

"That's the way Boroni mourn... and it'll make me feel better," Prior said with a smile. "And you do want me to feel better, don't you? That's what all of this concern is about, isn't it?"

"I can't let you go off like this," Mohab insisted ignoring her quip.

"You sound as if you have a choice," Prior said. "You don't. You can't stop me. I'm going to hunt down and kill everyone involved. If you get in my way, I'll kill you too."

"Prior, you don't mean that," Beatty said.

"Yes I do," Prior said turning to Beatty. "He thinks just because we slept together once, he has some sort of hold over me." She turned back to Mohab and continued. "But you don't. You're my best friend, Mohab. I love you dearly. And though the sex we had was pleasurable, it was designed to fulfill a need I had, not to bind us in any way. I don't want to be your mate and I have no plans for us to go to some secluded hideaway so you can 'roger me rigid' for two weeks. I was hoping you understood that."

"Why don't you let us help you at least," Beatty implored her friend.

"You can't help, Beatty," Prior said. "This is something I must do alone."

Mohab exhaled loudly and switched his tack. "Okay then, are you ready to tell me who those mystery men are over there?" he asked.

"They work for me and they'll follow my orders when the time comes for action," she said. "And that's all you need to know."

"Do they know who was behind this?" Beatty asked.

"Yes, and so do I. Besides Ceca and Thyssen, Cardinal Gregor and several influential businessmen are at the core of this terror we face. Unfortunately, they believe they control The Argent, and that will be their undoing. It is The Argent we must stop. And that's what that one thousand man army is for," Prior said.

"The legend of The Argent is just a story, Prior," Mohab said. "Their existence is only part of Holy Scripture. You don't believe in myths do you?"

"I believe in facts and the facts are the more I see the more I believe. And I believe the Elders were attacked by The Argent, you've seen the tunics they wore. It's straight out of Scripture," Prior said.

"But the scriptures were written long after the events in them even took place," Mohab argued. "How can you place so much faith in them?"

"A biography is no different, Mohab. It's a volume of the many recollections spoken around hearths and someone else's individual interpretations," Prior countered. "I believe the scriptures are the same thing. A biography... a history of what was. And they were written from the stories passed down through the years. They are interpretations and recollections. And I believe the old newspaper maxim fits in this case: When the legend becomes fact, print the legend. I believe that the legend of The Argent we're familiar with made for better copy, so that's what was written in the Scriptures. The true version was probably a lot more serious and a hell of a lot deadlier than any of us could imagine. And if we don't destroy them, we'll lose our world... and our souls to them."

Before Beatty or Mohab could argue, the sound of an air ship filled the sky. Prior was surprised that she hadn't heard it sooner. They gazed into the sky and saw a sleek and impressive looking ship drop down and land within a hundred feet of them. Beatty recognized the ship but neither Prior nor Mohab had ever seen anything like the craft before and they looked at each other briefly as the muffled engines became completely silent.

"That ship belongs to your troops, Prior," Beatty said.

The side hatch opened on the craft and a masked, dark gray combat suit clad form emerged from it. He hurried to Prior and came to attention when he reached her.

"Mistress, I'm here to make my report," the man said. Despite his muffled voice and the mask, Prior recognized him. It was Marcellus.

"Make your report," Prior said.

"The Argent went to Shiloh. They have reformed and are prepping for another assault," he said. "It is our belief that the Guardians Ceca and Thyssen are with them."

"That can only mean one thing," Prior said. She turned to Beatty. "Contact your Guardians in Shiloh. Put them on full alert. They may be attacked any minute."

"Not even The Argent would desecrate the Sacred City," Beatty said.

"Don't bet on it," Prior said. "If they can control Shiloh, the people will surrender to them and concede to their demands. And all will be lost."

"I agree, Mistress," Marcellus said.

"More superstitious nonsense," Mohab said.

"Commander, you forget your history," Marcellus said. "The power of Shiloh is engrained into the very fiber of every Kerguelen. It may be nonsense, but it's what the people believe. It worked for Koenig two and a half millennia ago, and it can work equally well today. The Argent is counting on that belief to fuel their campaign of total dominance and supremacy."

"And once it's started, it will be unstoppable," Prior said.

Another air ship appeared overhead, but this time, Prior heard it coming. She could see it was one of her own craft and it landed almost on top of them. The hatch opened quickly and out of it emerged Metis and Ernst. They quickly ran to her and saluted.

"What have you two got?" Prior asked.

"There's a defrocked priest you need to speak to at once, Commander," Metis said.

"It concerns the tasking you gave us," Ernst added.

"Who is this defrocked priest?" Prior asked.

"Her name is Vaughn," Metis said.

"Monsignor Vaughn? Monsignor Vaughn of the Northern Province?" Prior asked in disbelief.

"The same," Metis said.

A maverick amongst clergymen, Monsignor Vaughn was once a great and revered Cleric. It was said that she could lift her congregation so high they had to look down to see the Almighty. But radical idealism led to her defrocking. Though she had rekindled spiritualism in her parish and drew scores of young people back to the Church, her new age thinking met with great resistance from the leaders of the Federal Church. Despite their reservations, the Congress of Cardinals could not argue with the results. It was standing room only during Vaughn's sermons and no other priest on Kerguelen could match her attendance numbers. Vaughn's popularity had renewed the vigor and viability of the Federal Church.

Despite her success, there was one component of her new ideals that couldn't be overlooked by the Congress of Cardinals. Vaughn believed that it was not necessary for a priest or nun to practice celibacy and abstinence. There was no official rule or edict that required celibacy or abstinence to be practiced by clergy members, it was just something that had always been done. However, Vaughn believed that in order to truly serve their flocks the Clerics needed to live like the people to understand their problems. She also believed that a person could only advise another in affairs of marriage if they were married as well. In her opinion, the old ways were not the best option to spiritually lead the people in the modern age.

Vaughn opted to wed and was defrocked and excommunicated. She disappeared soon after and was never heard from again. The irony of her story was that two years after her fall from grace, the Federal Church formally approved marriage for priests and nuns.

It had been years since she had heard anything about Vaughn and Prior believed that she was dead. Obviously she had gone deep underground and made a new life for herself.

"Does she know how we can stop Gregor from conjuring The Argent?" Prior asked.

"No, but she does know how to kill it," Ernst said.

"That's very good news," Prior smiled. She turned to Marcellus. "Have Chandler ready my ship. We leave within the hour."

"Yes, Mistress," Marcellus said.

"Is Vaughn inside the ship?" Prior asked Metis.

"Yes and she's waiting for you," Metis replied. "She's a little rattled so take it easy on her."

Prior nodded and entered the air ship. She walked to a woman sitting in one of the eight seats in the cabin. Vaughn was in her mid-sixties and had short silver and black colored hair. She was still quite attractive for a Kerguelen woman her age and had a petite frame. She sat quietly with hands folded in her lap but turned abruptly when she heard Prior approaching her. Prior smiled and sat down beside her.

"Vaughn, I'm Cdr. Prior," she said.

Vaughn nodded to her and then turned away. "You need to know how to kill The Argent," Vaughn said.

"Yes," Prior nodded.

"The only way is to best him in one-on-one combat, a duel to the death. That means you have to fight him using ancient weapons. The creature is impervious to modern technology," Vaughn said looking at Prior. "It will be a difficult battle. The creature is strong."

"I know, I've encountered him before," Prior said.

"Have you? Then beware, Commander. I'm sure he is even more formidable now," Vaughn cautioned.

"I'll take care. And we will see to your safety," Prior said. "I understand how difficult it was for you to come out of seclusion."

"I don't think you do, Commander. If Gregor finds out I was responsible for revealing any information on The Argent to you, he will have me killed in a brutal and sadistic manner," Vaughn said.

"I will assign protection for you," Prior said.

"I'm not sure even Guardians can protect me. Gregor has been practicing black arts and summoning demons from the Netherworld for decades. I know that sounds childish but it's true. I've seen some of the manifestations he's conjured over the years," Vaughn said visibly frightened.

"I believe you, Vaughn. I know that Gregor is a Summoner," Prior said. "I can end his reign of terror, but I need your help. Do you know where in Shiloh Gregor might be?" Vaughn nodded. "I need to know everything you can tell me about it."

Vaughn looked down to the deck of the air ship and remained silent for over a minute. She lifted her head slowly, and told Prior all that she could. When she finished, Prior took her by the hand and led her out of the craft. They walked to where Captain Hiroki and his team were camped. Hiroki stood uneasily on his wounded leg and saluted. Prior saluted back and looked around.

"Where is Sgt. Elias?" she asked.

"In our air ship," Hiroki said pointing to an air vehicle.

Prior nodded and brought Vaughn to the craft. They stepped inside and found Elias tinkering with a door gun. He looked up and stopped his work when he saw them. He stood and nodded to Prior.

"Yes, Commander?" he said.

"Sergeant, this is Vaughn. She is a former priest and an asset and requires 'Class A' protection. You will see to her personal safety until further notice," Prior said.

"One man? I've seen what those people are capable of. One man isn't enough," Vaughn protested. "No offense to your capabilities, Sergeant, but I'd feel better with a larger security force."

"That's okay with me, lady," Elias said. "No one is trying to kill me."

"Quiet, Sergeant," Prior said scowling at him. "I'm afraid one man is all I can spare. And if I'm right, your fear of Gregor will end shortly."

Vaughn sighed and collapsed in a seat. "Well, if one Guardian is all you have, then so be it," she said. "I tell you, this whole situation is twisting my insides into knots. My nerves are shot and my stomach is so upset I've barely been able to keep even water down."

"Then how about a drink?" Elias said reaching into an overhead compartment and removing a bottle. He rubbed the label and read the writing on it. Satisfied with the vintage, he smiled and opened it offering the bottle to Vaughn.

She raised her hands. "I don't think I should," she said. "My stomach."

"*Drink no longer water, but use a little wine for thy stomach's sake,*" Elias said quoting scripture and forcing the bottle into Vaughn's tiny hands.

"That's from Scripture," Vaughn said amazed at the reference.

"The benefits of a classical education," Elias said and bowed with half-hearted modesty.

"I wouldn't have believed you were a spiritual man by looking at you, Sergeant," Vaughn said taking a small sip from the bottle.

"I just wanted you to know you're in good company," Elias said taking the bottle from Vaughn.

"Good and sober company," Prior said taking the bottle from Elias before he could get his lips on it. She replaced the cork and stowed the bottle back in the overhead compartment.

Elias frowned as Vaughn sighed. "I'm still not comfortable with this," she said.

"You believe in the Almighty, don't you?" Prior asked. Vaughn nodded. "For as long as I can remember, I was inundated with the assurances that if I did right by my fellow man, the Almighty would make sure that my place in Paradise was reserved." She placed a hand on Vaughn's shoulder and continued. "You did the right thing in giving up the information and the Almighty will ensure you will be safe. At the very least, you'll have confirmed your reservation in Paradise. The Almighty certainly knows you've done right. She is after all omniscient and omnipotent."

"Very amusing, Commander," Vaughn said slumping in the air ship seat. "Very amusing."

Prior left Vaughn with Elias and caught up with Mohab and Beatty. Neither Guardian looked very pleased with Prior.

"I must get to Shiloh at once," Prior said. "The Argent is there, as are Ceca and Thyssen most likely."

"Did that woman tell you this?" Beatty asked.

"No, but if The Argent are preparing to fight Guardians, Ceca and Thyssen will probably advise them on tactics," Prior said. "If I can catch them together, I can clean the slate with one swipe."

"It sounds too convenient," Mohab said.

"I have to follow up on anything that could lead me to them," Prior said.

"We are ready to depart, Mistress," Chandler said walking up to Prior.

Prior nodded. "I'll take the point in your ship. Micah will bring Pana and Rex to back me up. The rest of the surveyors and the Army of The Seven will follow and attack The Argent force," she said.

"You can't do this," Beatty protested.

"I promised Garath that I would kill Ceca," Prior said.

"This is no time for your lone wolf antics," Mohab said. "If Ceca and Thyssen are there they need to be brought in. We need to do this together."

"We will do it together, Mohab. I'm just taking the point. I'm a surveyor, that's where I belong," Prior said. She stepped away from them and put her TACCOM in her ear and tapped on it. "Rex, I need you to get some things for me. Go to the old weapon's display inside the castle and bring me a dory, the best that you can find. Bring it and my xiphos to me." He acknowledged her and she clicked the device off.

"I still don't like you going off alone," Mohab said.

"Whatever I do, I won't be alone. Lupo will be with me. For some strange reason I feel he will be very important during this fight," Prior said.

"What if this new intelligence is a trap?" Beatty said. "What if this is how they got Jordan and Giles? What then?"

"Then I'll have made a mistake," Prior said. "And Pana and Rex will have to save my ass. If this is a false lead, the Third and Fourth Battalions won't be committed and will be able to strike the true target. Stop worrying about me. You two have other Guardians to concern yourselves with. You need to look to their welfare. I'll be fine."

"We can leave as soon as you're ready, Mistress," Chandler reported. "Your escort is waiting onboard."

"Excellent," Prior said. She whistled loudly and Lupo bounded toward her. She scratched his head and knelt down. "We've got a mission, Lupo." He barked loudly and repeatedly as if he understood completely and Prior smiled.

Beatty and Mohab looked at each other and shrugged their shoulders in defeat. Unfortunately, there was no way to change Prior's mind. They could only hope her luck would hold out.

5
The Sacred City of Shiloh, The Middle Provinces, Planet Kerguelen

Located at the geographical center of the Middle Province's Cataract Desert, the Sacred City of Shiloh was built around a massive oasis known as Targus Spring. Like a rose on a cactus, Shiloh's beauty was unmatched in the region. Date and palm trees abounded on the city's perimeter and lush hanging gardens flourished in Shiloh's town square. But the signature feature, and most important part of Shiloh was the cool and placid waters flowing from Targus Spring.

Resembling a main artery, the largest and longest arm that emanated from the spring ran through the heart of Shiloh and out into the desert to Shiloh's sister city of Memphis. The long and twisting channel was the sole source of water for two hundred square miles; and also supplied Kerguelen with history, folklore, legends, myths and mysteries dating back countless millennia.

Since before recorded biblical times, Targus Spring provided the desert Bedouins of the area with life-sustaining water. It had never run dry, nor had its flow ever ebbed in the slightest. Because of this, the people considered the spring a gift from the Almighty. It was said that the spring was formed when the Almighty gazed upon the world She created and wept from its beauty. Her tears fell on Kerguelen and formed the spring. That was why the waters were considered sacred and blessed and believed to possess healing qualities.

The Great Prophet Virgil and his disciples taught the Almighty's Laws and preached brotherhood, charity, love and peace in Shiloh and used the waters of the spring to baptize their followers. The Kerguelens believed that Virgil was the son of the Almighty and believed the source of the amazing powers he displayed came from Shiloh and the waters of Targus Spring. The people also believed the region Shiloh and Memphis inhabited had been the site where Paradise once stood. There was no definitive proof or empirical evidence to support these claims, but belief in spiritual things did not require proof, only faith.

So strong was the Kerguelen's belief in the spiritual power of Shiloh and its waters, even Koenig set his sights on the region. Shiloh was the first major area he conquered, believing that possessing and controlling the waters would allow him to dominate the planet. After he was defeated, the citizens demanded the Sacred City be forever protected. They petitioned Central Command to permanently station a detachment of Guardians in Shiloh to prevent it from being violated again. So, for the better part of two millennia, Guardians had watched over Shiloh, the Place of Peace.

Over their many centuries of duty in Shiloh, the Guardians assigned to the region had repelled countless attempts of individuals and groups to gain control of the Sacred City and had developed numerous ways to protect Shiloh. They had a strong counter-intelligence network and had become one with the desert environment they worked in and a seamless part of the society in which they lived. The most unique aspect of how the Guardians protected Shiloh was the fact they did it without being seen. Everyone in Shiloh, and on the planet, knew the Guardians were there, but who they were and where they were located was unknown.

The Guardians didn't wear uniforms. They wore traditional Bedouin garb with their combat suits and weapons worn underneath. Central Command allowed grooming standards to become lax and some even took on regular jobs during the day to give them access to the people and move about freely in all parts of Shiloh.

The only one who knew the true identities and locations of the Guardians in Shiloh was a man named Deneb, the mayor of the city. Deneb was nearing the end of his active years and though his health was failing and his daily activities limited, he still felt he had more to give to his people. At seventy-four years old, he had accomplished much and had nothing more to prove, but he still believed he could add to his legacy. Despite having been lauded by the Federal Government and praised by his people for his past work, primarily his insistence that Shiloh maintain its old world flair, he felt he had more to do.

Modern transportation did not directly service Shiloh or its sister city of Memphis and the vast array of technology available to all Kerguelens everywhere on the planet was not visible. To enter Shiloh was like walking into a time machine and stepping back a thousand years. The people loved the pristine environment Deneb had helped maintain and went about their day as their ancestors had for centuries. Only in their homes did the people shed their austere old world trappings and embrace the modern conveniences of The Age of Advancements.

Deneb had hoped he could continue to be a positive influence on the people until he was forced to retire on his seventy-fifth birthday, but from where he sat at the moment, that dream was fading fast.

In the cellar of a secluded house, nestled beside a large grove of date trees just east of Shiloh, Mayor Deneb sat uncomfortably in a hard plastic chair. It wasn't the chair's lack of padding which caused him to squirm it was the interrogation he was enduring. Commander Ceca and a duo of Argent warriors had subjected Deneb to many Bedouin rites of punishment to extract the information they wanted, but so far, the elderly man had resisted. Ceca hoped he wouldn't die before he told her what she wanted to know. Ceca sighed as Deneb drifted in and out of consciousness and turned to The Argent warriors beside her.

"Watch him," Ceca said as Deneb opened his eyes briefly. She saw him staring at her and she smiled and continued. "When he is fully awake, we will continue. Perhaps we should start with the bisha'a."

The Argent warriors nodded and Deneb cringed with fear as Ceca left the cellar and joined Cardinal Gregor, Thyssen and The Argent entity in the sitting room of the house. The large dark beast of man grunted when he saw Ceca enter.

The cardinal was quietly listening to Thyssen's reports and recommendations on how to proceed. The Argent listened as well but was visibly annoyed. Gregor was not pleased either but was satisfied with most of their accomplishments.

Though The Argent had failed to kill Prior, the Guardian Corps had lost most of its senior leadership and the ones that remained were in no condition to lead them in a large-scale operation. Half of the Guardian's strength was being controlled by Thyssen and Ceca and would not be a factor in the upcoming battle. Though the strike force that had attacked Central Command suffered major losses, the assault was a necessary component to their overall plans. Soon the final push against the remaining Guardians would begin and they would crumble under the sheer force of numbers that confronted them. They soon would control Shiloh and without the Guardians to oppose them, Gregor and The Argent forces would conquer the planet. All that was left was a few details.

"We have to strike them now while they're still in a state of confusion and licking their wounds," Thyssen said adamantly. "There won't be a better time. We should not delay. The longer we wait, the better prepared they will be. I suggest a surprise attack."

"A surprise attack?" Ceca asked. "Like the one you planned against Mohab? Hmm, I wonder how that turned out?"

"How was I to know that Prior's Guardians would be able to mobilize in time to rescue him? It was totally unpredictable," Thyssen argued throwing his hands up in defeat and shaking his head in disgust.

"Anticipating those possibilities is the reason you were retained for this operation, Colonel," Ceca chastised. "You should never underestimate Prior."

"And what have you done to stop her?" Thyssen countered. "Where did the men come from that drove off the strike force at Central Command? Before you start berating me, you'd better check yourself."

"Silence," The Argent said in his low baritone. "I've heard enough of bickering and finger pointing between a weakling male and an aging woman." He saw that Ceca and Thyssen were insulted and his remarks had sufficiently bit into them and continued. "Neither of you know how to attack, you only know how to defend. And that will be the downfall of your pathetic Corps."

"Our men stand ready to attack. My troops can defeat the Third Battalion and the Fourth is no match for the First Battalion, in spite of its armor components," Thyssen offered. "All that remains are the Guardians here in Shiloh and the disposition of Prior's surveyors."

"Most of them will support and reinforce the Third and Fourth Battalions. Some of their strength was lost in the defense of Central Command," Ceca said. "Whatever is left can be handled by the strike forces."

Ceca had a gleam in her eyes at the thought of Prior's pride and joy being wiped off the face of Kerguelen. She leaned back in a chair and folded her arms.

"What the strike force does will not be governed by *you*, woman," The Argent growled. "Remember that. I foolishly allowed you to use them to kill your fellow geriatrics but that loan does not give you ownership."

Ceca would have responded but remembered The Argent didn't have a forgiving nature. Incurring his wrath could be deadly. She bowed her head submissively and remained silent. Gregor stood up and paced. After a few moments, he spoke.

"I hope you three can keep from killing each other long enough for us to complete our goals. I can't be around you continuously to break up fights," he said. "I have tasks of my own to accomplish. I must make arrangements for the transfer of power in the government to be smooth when the time comes."

"I thought that was a done deal?" Ceca asked.

"Not quite. The Technology Council will have to be gutted, if not totally eliminated, and the Judiciary will also have to be replaced. If Justice Thom manages to sway some of the senators to his side, we'll have problems. The loss of Senator Poul has weakened our position," explained Gregor. "If those senators opposing us fail to see the light, they will have to suddenly vanish."

"Tell me which ones and I'll send someone to… talk to them," Ceca said.

"Senators Reid, Albert and Connor, for a start," Gregor said.

"What about Bacor?" Ceca asked. "Can't he do something?"

"The Grand Senator is on our team. He's been involved with this from the inception," Gregor admitted with satisfaction. "He has been playing both sides of the fence very well. No one has a clue where his true loyalties lie, but he has to tread very lightly."

"What have you gotten from Deneb?" Thyssen asked.

"Nothing as yet," Ceca said. "The sheikh is a stubborn and foolish old man, but my next session with him will make him see the light… quite literally I imagine."

"I hope what you have planned will give us answers quickly," Gregor said. "We must know where the Guardians in Shiloh are at once."

"I tried your way, Cardinal, now I will expose Deneb to something he's more familiar with… the bisha'a," Ceca said.

"What is that?" Thyssen asked.

"Ordeal by fire," Ceca explained. "It's a well-known Bedouin practice of lie detection. He will be begging to tell me what I want to know. And once we have the names and locations of the Guardians, eliminating them will be an easy task."

"Bah!" The Argent said standing up. As he walked across the floor, his steps caused the house to shake. "All of this... subterfuge... is ridiculous. I say we simply blast them all into the Netherworld and let 'He who is Dark' sort them out."

"We need to be subtle. Too much overt activity can be detrimental to our cause. We want the people to come to us willingly, not kicking and dragging. It will be hard enough as it is," Gregor said.

"You sound as if the people will have a choice of what they want when this is over," The Argent said.

"That's exactly what I want them to believe," Gregor said with a smile. "It will be just like it was at the end of the last Provincial Wars. When the chaos begins, the people will look for help. They will be on their knees begging for forgiveness and praying for salvation but this time, no one will hear their cries. No Guardian battalions will form to defend them and preserve their so-called God-given rights. In fact, there won't be any Guardians at all."

6
The Sacred City of Shiloh,
The Middle Provinces, Planet Kerguelen

Prior was always surprised how cold the desert became at night. Though her combat suit kept her body at a constant sixty-eight degrees, she could feel the air temperature dropping rapidly. As she stood outside of the Celeron air ship that transported her, Prior readied for her upcoming battle.

The Celeron air ships were very swift, faster than any air ship of the same class and Prior was surprised at how quickly they arrived in Shiloh. She was glad the ships were fast. Prior had been forced to argue with Pana and Rex before she left. They were far from pleased about her going off without them. Mohab and Beatty had also continued to voice their displeasure over her intentions, but she assured them all that her army would be with her and she would be fine. As she shut the door of the air ship in preparation to leave, Prior was not completely sure of her choices either, and hoped her instructions for Pana and Rex to contact the Guardians protecting Shiloh when they arrived would not be the last orders she would ever issue.

The delay in departure had not upset her timetable and the flight barely gave her enough time to consider what she was going to do. As she adjusted Lupo's body armor, Prior could see that Chandler and his team were chomping at the bit, ready to jump into action.

They were unexpectedly shocked when Prior informed them that she would be going off alone. Lupo would join her but no one else. Despite the vehement protests of Chandler, she had remained firm and hoped her stubbornness would not be her undoing. Chances were high that one or even all of them could be killed, and every one of the Celeron would be needed when the heavy fighting she knew was coming commenced. As she was about to step off, Chandler attempted to persuade her to change her mind one last time.

"Mistress, I must insist," Chandler said. "You shouldn't do this alone."

"You're probably right, Chandler," Prior said looking up at him. She stuffed four magazines for the two TKP-7 pistols she wore into pouches and clipped small explosive charges to her weapons harness and smiled. "In fact, I'm positive that you are."

"Then why go without us? Who knows what lies out there? They could be waiting for you," Chandler said.

"I'm sure they are," Prior agreed. "During the flight here, I considered that possibility and decided instead of all of us stepping into a buzz saw, it'll just be me. If you don't hear from me within ninety minutes, assume that I'm dead and commence the assault on The Argent as planned. Instruct Marcellus to take command of the Celeron until a successor is chosen by Gideon."

"You said we would back you up. That's the only reason the Guardians allowed you to go. But you never had any intention of using us, did you?" Chandler surmised.

"No," Prior said.

"There are two things that I detest, Mistress," Chandler said.

"Only two? You're lucky, Chandler," Prior quipped.

Chandler ignored her levity. "First, I detest people who don't use a knife and fork when they eat," he said.

Prior smiled. "And the other?" she asked.

"I don't like being purposely misled and used as a pawn," he said.

"My plan freed me of my aides," Prior said. "You, above all others, know I must confront The Argent alone. The Celeron should be pleased that I have accepted my role in this madness."

"Regardless, I dislike working this way. You could have told me your plan at least. I wouldn't have approved, but I would have accepted it," Chandler said.

"Like the person who eats their meal without cutlery, my plan while not pleasant, got the job done. Let's not stand here and quarrel over successful maneuvers, Chandler, there are enough unsuccessful ones to stew over," Prior said. She placed a hand on his shoulder as he frowned. "I know what danger awaits me, and as a commander… and The Chosen One, it's my right to face it alone."

"Tradition is a poor reason to walk into your death, Mistress. I was told you thought beyond the old ways," Chandler said.

"I do," Prior nodded. "But this is an old style problem and it requires an old style solution. Not everything is black and white, Chandler. Be assured that I do know what I'm doing."

Though she appeared confident, Prior felt a deep loathing within her. She wasn't sure if what she was feeling was apprehension or something else. She wouldn't have been able to put it into words if she had to describe it, but her feelings and everything around her was somehow out of balance.

"I can't allow this," Chandler said grabbing her arm forcibly.

Prior grabbed his wrist, spun around and twisted Chandler's arm behind his back. She forced him to his knees and released him when he relaxed. He stood up and bowed his head slightly. He knew he had overstepped his limits and deserved the physical reprimand he received. As he massaged his sore shoulder, Prior knew her actions would go a long way in solidifying her position with the rest of the Celeron.

"Don't you ever touch me again," she sneered. "Not if you want to stay healthy."

"Forgive me, Mistress," Chandler apologized.

She looked at the Celeron in the craft, eying each one. "Listen up, no one is to follow me. I will call you when it's over. I must do this alone. Understand?"

They all nodded. Chandler stepped forward and added, "Good hunting, Mistress."

She nodded and grabbed the dory Rex had given her and her xiphos and slapped her thigh. Lupo stood up and followed her. They were several miles away from Shiloh, and the desert sand slowed their progress as they jogged toward the Sacred City. Thirty-five minutes after she and her canine left the air ship they reached their destination. Prior took out her canteen and took a long swallow. She put a tube on the canteen's opening and stuck it in Lupo's mouth. He lapped at the tube until the canteen was nearly empty. As Lupo drank, Prior scanned her surroundings. The thick grove of date and palm trees obscured almost everything. But she knew lost amid the trees she was looking at was a quaint cottage. And inside that house was her quarry.

She put the canteen away, and they continued on. As they weaved through the desert grove, she could feel they were not alone. She felt a pang in her stomach and ducked down. Lupo stopped next to her and held his head high in order to sniff the air. Prior scanned the trees ahead and saw four men moving towards her. She held Lupo with one hand and gripped the dory tightly in the other positioning it in the event she needed to use it.

A dory was a six-foot long spear that was two inches in diameter and once was the primary weapon of a Guardian. The three-pound weapon featured a deadly iron spearhead and on the back of the spear was an iron butt-plate, which provided balance and another means of attack. The Boroni were trained to use a similar weapon as children and Prior had favored it when she was young.

She neither saw nor smelled nor heard any others and knew these men were all that were in the vicinity. A patrol of some kind, no doubt, and it was unfortunate for them they were heading in her direction. They stopped at a thick tree and huddled together. They seemed to be taking a break and talking. She didn't care what they were doing or why. She did know she had to kill them.

The closest man to her fell into his friends when the dory entered his back. The man next to him crumpled to the ground a second later, the victim of a thrown knife. Stunned by the stealthy attack, the remaining members of the patrol were easy prey for Prior. She quickly pounced on them and snapped their necks before they could react. Prior held one of them in her arms and searched him. In a pouch she found an item just like that she had found on the fallen enemy back at the Central Command battlefield. It was a Pharisee Stone.

The Pharisee Stone was the ancient symbol of The Argent's religious sect. The gold coin with the sign of the cross etched into it, was the equivalent of membership cards, secret handshake or password used by exclusive men's clubs. The cross was a unique symbol and set The Argent apart from the rest of Kerguelen. The triangle, symbolizing the Almighty, Her son and the Almighty's spirit, had been the planet's designation for religion for over three millennia. And just the sight of a Pharisee Stone could cause widespread panic around the planet.

It was said that the stone could only be obtained after a long and arduous apprenticeship and many did not survive the training. The holder of a Pharisee Stone believed unconditionally in The Argent's cause and swore to die a thousand deaths to preserve their way of life.

Prior hoped all of them were as eager to die as was believed. Throughout Kerguelen history, religious zealotry had led to slavery, not in standard terms, but in a slow progression. As individual spirit and ideologies died, so did personal freedoms. The loss of those freedoms ultimately led to the enslavement and subjugation of the masses. Those who refused to submit and convert to the new ways of the land would suffer wholesale slaughter and extinction by torture and executions.

Prior let the body fall to the ground and clutched her stomach. She knew the discomfort she was feeling was a warning and more men were coming towards her. She retrieved the dory and her knife and continued toward the cottage with Lupo close behind. In a minute, she came upon another patrol and dropped the dory as she drew her pistols. The patrol saw her but it was too late for them. She unleashed a hail of tungsten bullets into them and they fell in their tracks.

Prior knelt down and examined the bodies. They all appeared to be dead, but Prior put a single bullet into each of their heads to be certain. She reloaded her pistols and continued on. In short order she saw the house. It was dimly lit and Prior could see the shadow of someone walking inside past the large window in the front of the house. Two guards were posted outside of the front door, obviously to prevent anyone from entering unannounced or without an invitation. It looked as though Prior was going to have to crash the party.

Inside the house, Gregor, Ceca and Thyssen sat in the living room discussing future plans. An explosion from outside abruptly ended their conversation. The house rocked from the blast and before they could speak, the front door imploded, blown off of its hinges and flung inside the house. Prior had used a petard to blow the door and the sound of the explosive's detonation briefly deafened the trio inside. They were still stunned when the bodies of the two guards stationed outside joined them in the living room. One was tossed through the opening created by the lack of a door and the other flew through the window.

Thyssen covered himself as shards of glass darted in his direction. Both guards were unconscious and the unnatural way their limbs appeared suggested that each had multiple broken bones. Prior stepped inside and smiled at the threesome when she saw them. She had a pistol in one hand and the dory in the other. She scanned the room and didn't sense any other guards and whistled. Lupo slowly bounded inside and sniffed the room.

"Sorry to interrupt, but I really needed to speak with you," Prior quipped.

"Prior," Ceca scowled. "I see you've met our sentries."

Prior nodded and stepped between the fallen men. One of them began to stir and she put a single bullet into his head and then one into the other's skull.

"And introduced yourself in your usual manner," Ceca said shaking her head and sitting down.

Prior chuckled and leaned the dory against the wall. "Watch 'em, Lupo," she said.

The canine turned to Gregor, Ceca and Thyssen and softly growled as she reloaded her pistol and holstered it. She retrieved the dory and looked the conspirators over.

"No need to be so antagonistic, Commander," Gregor said smiling. "Come in... join us. Sit and rest from your exertions."

"I'll pass on your hospitality, Cardinal. I'm not in a tolerable mood," Prior said.

Ceca looked at her closely. She saw the handle of the sword peeking out over her shoulder and the spear in her hand and pointed to them. "A dory and a xiphos? What is this, Prior? Are you going to give us a history lesson?" she asked.

"I wanted to make sure there was something in the room older than you, Ceca," Prior said. Ceca scoffed at her remark. Thyssen thought about making a move for his pistol but Prior shook her head at him. She could see the tension grow in his face. "Your weapon is strapped in, Colonel. Don't try it."

Thyssen heeded her warning and eased a bit. "What are you doing here, Prior?" he asked.

"I came for him," Prior said pointing to Gregor. "And I'm doing you a favor by arresting you, Cardinal. You have no idea what you're dealing with. And neither do these two idiots with you."

"To hell with you, Prior!" Thyssen said pointing a finger at her. "It's you who doesn't know what you're into!"

"Still trying to play the big man, aren't you, Thyssen?" Prior said with a smile.

"You're still an indignant little Boro bitch, Prior," Ceca said.

Gregor smiled as well and was thoroughly entertained at how simply Prior had pulled the chains of his companions, while she remained relaxed and unassuming. Her demeanor continued to intrigue him. It was too bad she had to die.

"And neither of you can help what you are," Prior said.

"And you are what you are as well," Ceca said.

"Yes, I am and you… you're nothing. The sight of you disgusts me. Just being in the same room with you makes my skin crawl," Prior said as she turned back to Gregor. "How long have these two been on your payroll?"

"For quite some time, but it's only recently that I've called in my markers. You'd be surprised who I have on retainer," Gregor said.

"It takes money to make one's way through life in comfort," Thyssen offered. "I have worked hard to keep the planet safe and what do I have to show for it? Nothing but debt."

"Did you sleep through ethics class or have you always been so base?" Prior asked.

Thyssen scoffed. "I'm sorry, I wanted more that just a medal and the people's admiration," he said.

"You've learned nothing in the fifteen years you've been a Guardian, Thyssen. All the transgressions and evil in the world can be summed up and linked together by just one sin from the Scriptures… jealousy," Prior said.

"Shut up, Prior. No one wants to hear your philosophical revelations," Ceca said with a dismissive wave.

"No, wait," said Gregor sitting forward in his chair. "Go on, Commander. This should be interesting."

"Thyssen, your hate, anger and all the lashing out you do, especially towards me, stems from the fact your family no longer has slaves or the property they once illegally possessed. That's what gave you and those like you, your feeling of superiority. Your ability to take, not give, was your yardstick of accomplishment. You're jealous of those who now have more material wealth than you. Without it, you don't think you're any different than any other commoner. If you were truly great and superior, money and possessions wouldn't matter. But in that lay the ultimate questions: Is your soul and personal worth only as deep as your pocketbook? And once your wallet is empty, is the very core of your being empty as well? Are you worthless? You must let your hatred go, Thyssen, or it will destroy you. It's already caused you to betray your fellow Guardians," Prior said.

"It's easy for you to be cavalier. When have you ever had to struggle?" Thyssen said.

"Everyday of my life, Thyssen. Neither my accomplishments nor all the platinum on Kerguelen could ever make me equal to you in your eyes. I'm a Boro. Remember? I'm 6/10ths of a Kerguelen and my value and worth is measured solely by how much crop I can pick or how much ore I can dig in a day. But still, here I am. I've survived your discrimination, insults, censure and abuse and I've become a Guardian commander. I'm better than you are or ever could be in two lifetimes. Your father probably berates you about it every time you go home… if you can muster the guts to face him, that is," Prior said.

"You think you're superior to me? You'll never be superior to me, Prior. Your ancestors were enslaved by mine for a thousand years," Thyssen said.

"But in those thousand years can you truly say they were defeated? People have managed to domesticate dogs, cats and horses. The great beasts of the land have been collected and placed in zoos. A falconer can stand upon a hill and call the mighty avian to his gauntlet. But in spite of this, we have to use obedience chips in them to ensure compliance. And why? Because a dog will always revert back to that ancient animal he was; a lion will always believe he is King of the Beasts and a falcon will always soar high above us in a state of grace and freedom. We can break the will of the collective with the chains of bondage, but you can never, *ever*, destroy the spirit and heart of the individual. The spirit remains unfettered and that's what your forbearers failed to understand and that's why they lost what they had," Prior said. "And for the record, I never thought I was superior to you. I only wanted to be your equal."

"Rubbish," Thyssen said. "What you say is total nonsense."

"You're a dreamer, Prior. Plain and simple," Ceca said.

Gregor laughed loudly. "Very good, very good indeed," he said.

"What's so funny?" Ceca asked.

"Prior is the only intelligent person on Kerguelen. And she's against me. Ha!" Gregor said. "You should have been the Cleric instead of Venture. You've missed your calling, Prior. You've grasped the simple concepts that have eluded almost everyone on the planet. You're right. The majority of the people don't want to share and that greed has caused them to turn away from and reject the 'Good for all' ideal. And the few who do understand this must be destroyed so those who want more than to just be happy can reach the goal of complete power and dominance over all others."

"That's why the Guardians exist," Prior said. "To stop those people."

"That's why the Guardians must be destroyed," Gregor corrected. "Your death will be tragic but the planet will persevere. Once The Argent has helped us establish order, we'll usher in a new era... a new age."

"Your alliance with The Argent is not an ad hoc partnership. They will kill you all if the Guardians lose, and without anyone to protect the people, they will become slaves to The Argent. You know their history, Cardinal. Their belief is not the same as ours," Prior said. She knew what she was saying was falling on deaf ears but she had to try.

"Whoever said I wasn't a member of The Argent?" Gregor said smiling.

"You'll pay for your betrayal of Kerguelen," Prior said shaking her head.

"Oh, I think not," said Gregor. He stood and bowed to her. "I must be going now. I believe Ceca and Thyssen can finish up for me. Our conversation has been enlightening, Commander. In case you're wondering, The Argent is in Shiloh and will attack the Guardians here within the hour. And by tomorrow, half of the planet will be ours. Good evening and good bye."

Gregor exited the room and Thyssen removed the strap securing his sidearm in its holster. He squared up on Prior and flexed his fingers.

"Thyssen, don't do this," Prior warned. "There's a difference between target practice and facing down a real person. Shooting to kill slows down most people's reaction time."

"Really? What percentage?" he asked.

"Ninety-seven point six percent of the population," Prior said dropping the dory to the floor.

Thyssen took a deep breath and reached for his pistol. Prior was much quicker though. She drew the pistol from her left holster and squeezed the trigger twice. The heavy metal bullets blew the top of his head away splattering brain matter and blood across the room. He fell back against the couch and slid to the carpet. Prior put another bullet into what remained of his head and spat.

"I don't happen to be part of that percentage," Prior said as she aimed her pistol at Ceca.

"How long before your team arrives?" Ceca asked standing up.

"I'm alone," Prior said holstering her weapon. "I promised Garath I'd do this personally. I want to kill you so bad, my nipples are hard, Ceca."

Ceca smiled. "You're adventurous. That's commendable, but your temerity will be your undoing," she said moving towards her. "I'm going to send you to Hell, Prior."

"There's only two things wrong with Hell, Ceca," Prior said preparing for her attack. "Not enough water and you can't choose your own company."

Ceca pulled a knife from its scabbard and waved it in Prior's direction. As she came forward with it, Prior moved in. She grabbed the wrist of Ceca's knife hand with her left and Ceca's throat with the other. She squeezed Ceca's wrist and forced her to drop the knife. Prior then lifted Ceca into the air and threw her against the wall. Ceca crumpled into a ball and Prior moved in again. She grabbed Ceca by the hair and snatched her off of the floor. Ceca squirmed and Prior tossed her across the room once more.

Stunned and tired of being tossed around like a rag doll, Ceca stood and reached for her pistol but Prior moved like a blur across the room and knocked the weapon out of her hand. Prior broke her nose with a single well-placed overhand punch and Ceca fell to her knees nearly blinded from the pain and instinctively held her nose. Prior grabbed her hair again and forced Ceca's head between her legs and squeezed. Lupo barked loudly as if he was cheering his mistress on.

Ceca looked ridiculous on her knees as her head poked out from in between Prior's muscular thighs. Ceca gasped for air and groped at Prior's legs in a futile attempt to get free.

"How does that feel, Ceca? Do you like it down there? I know how much you like the company of younger women," Prior said referring to Ceca's sexual proclivity.

"You're crazy, bitch," Ceca said in a raspy voice. It was getting harder for her to breathe. "Release... me..."

"As you wish," Prior said.

She flexed and squeezed her massive thighs locking Ceca's head in place. She then took a step backwards with one foot and quickly twisted her hips. The swift and violent motion instantly snapped Ceca's neck. After she heard the dried twig-like cracking sound, Prior relaxed her leg muscles and allowed Ceca's body to collapse to the floor.

"I hope that was as good for you as it was for me, Ceca," Prior said.

She stepped away from Ceca and picked up the dory as the pain in her stomach assaulted her again. She took a deep breath and saw Lupo looking at her with a tilted head. She smiled at him and tapped his head.

"Come on, boy. A friend is waiting for us."

They walked through the house and exited through the rear door. When she entered the backyard, it was empty. Then the ground beneath her began to tremble. The twinge in her stomach came back with a vengeance and she saw the reason appear and stand in the rear of the trim lawn.

"Good evening, woman," The Argent said. "Welcome to the last day of your life."

7
The Sacred City of Shiloh,
The Middle Provinces, Planet Kerguelen

Prior stood some distance from The Argent ready to pounce as Lupo barked and growled angrily. The canine rose up and down on his hind legs and snarled at the figure in front of him. The Argent seemed unwilling to begin their contest though and Prior looked around and scanned the entire yard. They were alone and the feeling in the pit of her stomach had faded but she felt the whole scenario playing out before her was somehow orchestrated. Prior eased a little and turned her head slightly to the side and listened for sounds. She sniffed the air for unfamiliar scents but all was tranquil and still. Not even the night's wildlife made a whisper.

"Easy, Lupo," Prior said and the canine calmed down and sat by her side.

"We are alone, woman. There is no one here but us," The Argent said in his deep voice.

He loomed larger in the garden than he had been in Gregor's office, now standing by Prior's estimate, seven and a half feet tall and weighing four hundred pounds. Prior assumed his bigger size had something to do with the cardinal's conjuring. His steps were delicate and graceful, and his movements were filled with power and purpose like a dancer's.

"But you know we are alone, don't you?" he continued. "Yes, I know you can sense the presence of my followers… or others that may threaten you. Yes, that extra sense is one of the many gifts and special talents you've received, isn't it?"

Prior looked at him curiously and wondered where he received his insight. He was right about her ability to sense danger and his knowledge unsettled her.

"Argent or no, you'll have no dominion over men as long as I breathe, monster," she said.

"And a child shall lead them," The Argent scoffed. "Where is your army, woman? Don't tell me they were afraid to face me."

"I need no army to fight a grotesque creature like you, I only need my hands," Prior said raising a fist.

"Calling me names won't vanquish me, woman. But you might as well. You haven't the power to stop me, and your preaching and feeble warnings to the Summoner will not be heeded. Soon a new world will emerge from the dust and debris I will create. In a matter of days, I will have total dominion over this world. And then it will be time to move on to the next," The Argent smiled.

"The people won't crumble as easily as you believe," Prior countered. "And after tonight, your brief reign will be over. I'm going to destroy you."

The Argent shook his massive head. "Though millennia have passed since we last met, you still cling to the old ideals, Katana. I was weaker in our past encounters, but your former victories against me have no meaning. I have a renewed vigor. I am stronger and more powerful than I ever was," The Argent said sitting on the ground. He leaned back against his elbow to get a better look at her. "You look well, Katana, much more pleasing to the eye than the last time we met. Besides strength and wisdom, you've been endowed with a great superficial surface quality as well. I'm sure it serves you as well if not better than your strength."

He ran a large scaly hand through his long black hair and smiled at her provocatively. His hair was silky and shone brightly in the night like highly polished onyx. It matched his obsidian colored skin perfectly. Prior was surprised his long talon-like fingernails didn't get snagged in it. She smiled but was not impressed or distracted by his attentions or comments concerning her physical appearance. But she did take note of the mouthful of sharp teeth and rippling muscles of his arms and legs. If he ever got a good hold of her, it could turn out to be a bad day for her.

What did fill her thoughts briefly was his belief that she was the reincarnation of Katana. She wondered if she resembled her in some way. She didn't believe she was, but the Celeron and this creature did.

If The Argent believed she was the mythical destroyer of evil, so be it. That would be to her advantage. In the end, she knew who and what she was.

"You can call me anything you like, monster, but name is Prior, not Katana," she said. "And this will be the last time we ever encounter each other."

"You refute who and what you are, eh? Perhaps The One of the Light has not chosen the Preserver as carefully as I thought," The Argent said sounding disappointed.

"The One of the Light?" Prior queried.

"Forgive me, you refer to Her as… the Almighty," The Argent said rolling his eyes. He was barely able to get the last words out of his mouth without spitting.

"The Almighty has not chosen me. I'm here on my own accord," she replied. "Why you think I'm here is none of my concern. No scriptures or prophecies lead me, I deal in the present and in reality, not in some mystical celestial plane."

"It is you who fails to embrace reality, Katana," he said. "But in the words of one of your famous planetary leaders to another: *'Neither of us should die before we really know each other'.*" He shifted a bit and then continued. "I am the child of the one you refer to as The Second. His real name you cannot say because it can never be spoken while She has dominion over this world. But I refer to him as He who is Dark. I am the culmination of all of the despair and doubt and greed and hate in this world. The greater the lack of faith there is, the more alive I become. It nurtures me, and there has never been a more glorious time for me. I do not age and I cannot die as long as there is one among you who refuses to believe in The One of the Light."

"You don't look like the description of The Argent written in scripture," Prior said.

"Everyone sees me differently, Katana. We all have an appearance that is unique to every individual. It's called perception. Not Her greatest gift to people, but one of my favorites," he said with a smile.

"And what am I to you?" Prior asked.

"You are Katana, the Preserver, the champion of The One of the Light. She empowers you and provides you with all that you need to defeat me and other so-called evil. She has seen to it that your path through life has given you the knowledge and strength to combat me when the time comes. Our meeting is not coincidental, it's preordained. Unfortunately, you do not possess the skill to win," The Argent explained.

"I turned you away before," Prior said.

"Your vile weapon was unfamiliar to me. I am impervious to it now. It will take more than sorcery to beat me this time," The Argent said.

"It was not sorcery but science that defeated you, creature," Prior boasted.

"And now you feel comfortable and at ease, confident in your ability to win because of your science," he said. He tilted his head slightly and pointed at her. "But you are not armed with implements of science. Your instincts have taken over your decision making process. Yes, you know what you need to fight me. You feel the strength and power flowing through you. You can hardly contain it. Your senses and intuition are at the height of efficiency. You can feel danger around you and know who has genuine goodness in their heart. You have animal-like senses and reflexes, but they're mated with human understanding, knowledge and compassion and the strength of The One of the Light. Yes, you truly are Katana."

"So I was created and programmed like a piece of machinery designed to perform a function and nothing more, is that it?" Prior offered.

"Weren't you? Are you not the creation of a man? Synthesized from both natural and man-made building blocks?" The Argent argued. "You are not Kerguelen, you are Boroni. No Kerguelen could have survived my earlier assault. The One of the Light ensured you would be created and traveled a road that strengthened you for me. You have always survived the most extreme of circumstances when others have died. Haven't you ever wondered why you were luckier than others? Haven't you ever wondered why you've walked a higher and more difficult path than your peers?"

"It is written that the Almighty does not interfere. Scripture says She will never manipulate us. Our choices are our own," Prior said.

"In my point of view, She picks the most inopportune times to interfere," The Argent said allowing himself to laugh. "Though subtle, She has Her hands in everything that happens on this world. Why She does I have no idea, especially since Kerguelen is but one of Her many concerns."

"What are you talking about?"

"She has many interests besides this fragile world," The Argent said.

"I only care about this world, creature," Prior said.

"Do you think the personal losses in your life were just fate? How sad a life She has made for you," he said with feigned sympathy.

"My choices are my own," Prior said shaking her head. "It was my decision to not bond with another, not because the Almighty willed it and wanted me to remain alone."

"A choice between a mate and The One of the Light is no choice at all," he said.

Prior said nothing but knew he was right. She could not have lived without God in her life. Though she had loved Omega deeply and desperately, she could not have faced excommunication. Even then, she knew her place was on Kerguelen, not in exile. There was much she had to do.

"The scriptures..." she began.

"The scriptures? Bah!" The Argent scoffed. "You are much more powerful than any man and have the appearance of a woman, but you have the eyes of a child, Katana. The scriptures, as you call them, are nothing more than inarticulate scratching created from the mad ramblings of supposed Holy men." He sighed loudly. "However, they often mar the surface of what is true."

"So they are factual accounts," Prior concluded.

"The perceptions of ancient events as told by a few do not make what they have related to others facts. The scriptures tell a story, nothing more. And only from one side of the argument," The Argent said. "But the core of what the writings say is truth."

"So She interfered in that too?" Prior asked.

"Only slightly. She interferes only enough to serve Her purposes, though Her influence is at a much lesser degree than I would pursue. She has an ethos and would never completely manipulate the planet as I would, or He who is Dark wants to. She is no different than any other mother. She loves Her children and thinks you're special. But even a crow thinks its babies are pretty. Ha, Ha, Ha," The Argent said sitting up. "She has Her own agenda… for all of us."

"I can sense there is truth in what you say but I don't completely believe you, creature. Like all liars you sprinkle irrefutable truths into your stories and tales," Prior said.

"Then let me give you some truths. You call the Almighty the Creator, don't you?" he asked and Prior nodded. "If She is so great, why did She need to create anything? Have you ever thought about that? It's simple. You have pets, friends, mates and children. Why? No one wants to be alone… not even Gods."

"People are different. They have flesh and blood. They need to be with others… all things do. Dogs run in packs, lions have prides and people have families," Prior argued.

"Yes, but then there is the lone wolf," he said.

"There are exceptions to every rule," Prior said.

"But why? How can there be so many absolutes and then an exception. It happens all of the time. People don't have the physiology to fly, but you overcome that with technology. Science says that nothing travels faster than light, but you have vehicles that have speeds far in excess of light's velocity," he replied.

"Are you saying that the Almighty is not omnipotent or omniscient? Are you saying that She is not perfect?" Prior asked.

"Omnipotence and omniscience are just measurements you've given to describe the scope and breadth of Her powers. You cannot fathom how far Her power and strength reaches or comprehend the depth of Her knowledge in mortal terms. You have no frame of reference for it, so you have created an arbitrary description for it. But Her power and knowledge is not infinite," he said condescendingly. "And She has made a mistake or two occasionally."

"Are you saying She is not a God?" Prior asked.

"No, but what constitutes a God? Is it a matter of worship? No, it's perception. As a small child you worshipped your parents because they seemed to be all knowing and all powerful. If you had a question, they answered it. If you were sick, they healed you, sometimes with just their touch. If you were scared, they protected you. And they punished you when you erred, not because they wanted to but because they wanted to teach you that there were repercussions for every action. As you got older and your own knowledge and experience increased, you realized that your parents were only human and just as mortal and fallible as you," he said.

"I did worship my parents," Prior admitted. "But I knew they weren't Gods. I knew they were people."

"But the Boroni worship their creator, don't they?" he asked.

"We hold Dr. Boroni in a certain regard, yes. He created us, not the Almighty. It's Her universe but he took the pieces and made us," Prior said. "We're as close to being perfect humans as you can get, but the doctor did make a few mistakes."

"As did the Almighty. You might call them typos. Why else would there be black holes in space or disease in man? Wouldn't She make it perfect? I would agree that She is omniscient but She is far from omnipotent. And that's what makes Her human," he said.

"The Almighty is not human," Prior refuted. "I refuse to believe that there is not a greater being than us. And if She is human, how are we here? Reproduction requires two."

"Not asexual reproduction. If a worm can reproduce in such a way then why can't a God? If man can excite light atoms and make lasers and if man can split or fuse atoms to produce tremendous power, don't you think a mega-intelligence could create a universe and seed it with life? Man makes improved strains of grain, breeds animals and purifies water, why couldn't a powerful entity create water?" The Argent said. He saw that Prior was now seriously contemplating his words. He tilted his head towards her. "Vengeance is Mine, She has said. Doesn't that mean She has emotion? You are not allowed to destroy but She can. The *Old Covenant* section of your Holy Scripture is rife with examples of that wrath. Do not kill is one of Her many commandments to you, but She is frequently guilty of the sin. Do as I say but not as I do. What God or Supreme Being allows themselves to be influenced by emotions? You also believe that you were created in Her image. Rationally, wouldn't that mean She looks like you?"

"No. It only means that Man resembles what She wanted us to look like," Prior said.

"If you want to believe that you can. But She does look like you," The Argent said. "I've seen Her."

"What you say won't change my beliefs," Prior said. "Like the master you serve, you feed on doubt and despair and strive to confuse people. But it is you who is in despair if you think you can manipulate me by skewing facts."

"For every action, there is an equal but opposite reaction. That's not science, my unenlightened foe. It's philosophy. Love and Hate; Life and Death; Joy and Sadness; and Health and Sickness. The scientific maxims came as a result of understanding that. What is true in man must exist in nature. You have a governing philosophy among your people. The Fifth Principle of Self Determination: Only by observing and understanding nature and the natural order of things can one truly find the meaning of their own existence. Is that not correct?" The Argent said.

Prior nodded and was upset that the creature knew so much about her people and their way of thinking.

"Everything was created out of the same building blocks. The same is true of our relationship, Katana. The One of the Light and The Second have a symbiotic existence," he said. "One cannot exist without the other."

"I don't believe you," she said.

"The real name of The Second is Lucifer and your God's name is Noor," The Argent said. He smiled when he saw her reaction to the names. "Those names have meaning for you, don't they, Katana?"

"Yes," she nodded. If what he had said was true, the reason for The Second was clear. The name Noor meant Light and Lucifer meant, 'One who brings Light'. The scriptures said that when The Second arrives, the Almighty, The One of the Light, emerges soon after. Light follows darkness, another proof of The Argent's equal and opposite theorem. She looked long and hard at The Argent and frowned. "If you're telling the truth, I understand why The Second exists."

"I have no reason to lie to you, Katana. There is nothing I want from you except your life," he said with a cackle. "I could go on for hours discussing all the concepts of Her Divinity, and of our being in this place, at this precise moment, but suffice it to say that I am the corporeal manifestation of The Second and you are the physical embodiment of The One of the Light. And tonight, we consummate our relationship."

His deep hearty laughter filled the quiet night echoing far out into the distance.

"That's a good choice of words, Argent," she said holding the dory in both hands and pointing it at him. "Because tonight, you're going to get fucked."

8
The Sacred City of Shiloh,
The Middle Provinces, Planet Kerguelen

"Don't worry, Katana, this won't take long," The Argent said.

He stood and grabbed an object lying next to him. Prior stared hard and saw that it was a pike of some type. It was at least eight feet long with a two-foot curved blade at the end. The sharp sickle-like blade glistened in the night. It looked familiar and she was sure she had seen it before. Then it came back to her like a shot to the heart. While touring Cathedral Prime as an academy cadet, she had seen the pike in a painting in the Cathedral's gallery.

The painting depicted Katana and The Argent in battle and the creature was holding a weapon identical to what she was looking at now. The pike was known as the Devil's Toothpick. But that was a layman's term for it. Its proper name was the Scythe of Destruction. And she prayed it wasn't the same weapon. Legends said the weapon was created in the Netherworld and the smiths that made the blade used forges fueled by the anger and hate of The Second, causing the blade to become sharper every time it was used to kill. If that was true, the blade should have been able to carve through a mountain by now. The shaft of the weapon was unbreakable and impervious to damage.

As Prior stared at the weapon, The Argent smiled at her and took long practice swings with the pike. He wielded it as if it were an extension of his own body. Though he was still some distance away, Prior could feel the breeze it created when he swung it in the air.

Prior cautiously moved closer to him and held the dory out in front of her. He seemed to move tentatively as well, keeping well away from her weapon. Lupo also moved nearer to The Argent and began to growl again as his hair stood on end. The canine slowly trotted back and forth in front of The Argent, occasionally snapping at him. Prior considered having Lupo attack him on one side while she came in from the opposite direction. Two against one was the way to go.

"Watch 'em, Lupo," she said and the half-wolf reared up on his hind legs.

"You're not the only one who commands lowly creatures, Katana," The Argent said.

He put two fingers in his mouth and blew through them. The sharp and shrill whistle he emitted echoed loudly in Prior's ears and caused Lupo to howl. Out of the inky darkness emerged two huge jackals. They were as black as The Argent and a little bigger than Lupo and they obediently sat on either side of The Argent. Prior thought they resembled the dogs depicted in the Scriptures guarding the gates of the Netherworld. They looked up at The Argent and he pointed at Prior. Both jackals turned and sat up and bounded towards her, leaping in the air. Before they could reach her, Lupo leapt to meet them and collided with both bedeviled creatures.

The animals rolled across the earth and when they got back on all fours, the jackals slowly circled Lupo. Lupo watched them both and a second later they were snapping and barking at each other. Lupo arched his back and sprang into the air. He quickly became entangled with one of the jackals and they disappeared from sight behind a group of tall and thick hedges. The second jackal followed them.

A loud yelp from the hedges caused Prior to be concerned for the safety of her pet but she had no time to worry about him. The Argent had moved in front of her and was prepping his attack. She turned her attentions to him as he swung his pike. It missed cleanly, passing within inches of her chest, and she moved forward. As the weapon passed by her, Prior thrust the dory forward and into his chest. The jab punctured his skin and knocked him backwards. She pulled the weapon back and ducked down to avoid the pike's blade as The Argent counter-attacked. He rubbed his chest and snorted when he saw that she had drawn first blood. The blow she landed seemed more powerful than he had been prepared for and the weapon she wielded stronger than he anticipated. The woman had learned to trust her instincts and he nodded his approval.

"You have truly become an instrument of the One of the Light, Katana," he said.

He twirled the pike in his hands and stepped closer to Prior. She raised the dory again and thrust it forward. Her act stopped the pike from spinning and she batted the weapon away and jabbed The Argent just below the sternum. He bent slightly and she swung the dory connecting against the side of his head. She flipped the dory and jabbed the butt-plate into his throat and The Argent gasped.

He dropped the pike and clutched his throat and gurgled several unintelligible words. Prior punched him as hard as she could and the blow staggered him. As he stumbled backwards, Prior pivoted and gave him a roundhouse kick knocking him into another set of bushes decorating the perimeter of the lawn and garden. Prior turned to look for Lupo and saw him and one of the jackals rolling through other bushes and out of sight again. When she turned back to The Argent, he was standing up. He rubbed his throat, swallowed and smiled at her. He coughed and then spat a glob of black liquid from his mouth and came towards her.

"Very good," he said in a raspy grumble. He cleared his throat and continued. "I'm going to enjoy this."

He moved quicker than she anticipated and was on top of her before she was ready. The Argent threw a quick jab and Prior's head snapped back sharply. He grabbed her face and palmed her head like a basketball. He lifted her up like she was a doll and flung her across the yard in a single motion. She landed hard and grunted loudly as she rolled to a stop. She got to her knees and shook her head. Her head was ringing and throbbing from pain. She had lost the dory and The Argent was now circling her like a shark. She knew she had to move and quickly or she was done for.

Prior rose to her feet and saw the dory just beyond him. She lunged forward in his direction and avoided his outstretched arms. She curled in a ball and rolled until she reached the dory. She went into a crouch and picked the weapon up. The Argent ran towards her and she thrust the weapon out. He grabbed the end of it before it could strike him and jerked his wrist. The dory snapped like a sun-dried bone in his powerful hand and he threw the two-foot section he held away.

Prior tossed the broken dory aside and attacked. He was unprepared for her speed and took the full brunt of her assault. She tackled him and they both grunted as The Argent fell on his back. Prior landed on top of him and let loose a furious set of punches. At first it seemed as though the blows were ineffective, then she saw blood trickle from his mouth and nose and continued pounding him with renewed energy. His head snapped to the left and to the right like a metronome with each combination she threw. When his eyes shut, Prior stopped hitting him.

She climbed off of him and slowly backed away. After a few steps, she turned around and moved to where Lupo and the jackals had been scuffling. As she neared the bushes, she heard the unmistakable sound of her dog crying in pain. The sound stopped her in her tracks.

"Lupo!" she screamed in horror.

As she was about to breech the hedgerow, The Argent leapt through the air and landed both feet squarely into her back. She fell face first into the ground and cried out her own screams of pain. She rolled onto her back and stared up at The Argent. He was smiling and glanced beyond them to the bushes. Another shrill cry came from the distance and he smiled even wider as he turned back to Prior.

"It seems my jackals have finished with your dog, Katana. I believe I will be feasting on wolf meat tonight," he gloated.

He stepped away and grabbed his pike as Prior struggled to stand. She was dazed but far from being down and out, though her back was on fire. He swung the pike in a downward motion and she barely avoided it. The blade buried itself in the soft earth as Prior stepped into him drawing her xiphos from its sheath. She stuck the sword's two-foot blade half way into The Argent's side and twisted it. As she pulled it out, a gusher of dark blood erupted from the wound covering her body.

The Argent howled and threw a wild punch that somehow landed against the side of her head, splitting the skin on the corner of her eye. Prior spun away and wiped the stream of blood that had started to run down her face from the gash. The blood stung and her vision was momentarily blurred. He hit her in the stomach and Prior felt the bones of her rib cage give. She doubled over as the air went out of her and she fell to her knees and gasped.

Though seriously wounded, The Argent seized the opportunity and pulled the pike from the dirt and brought it up. Once again he tried to take out Prior with a downward blow. She painfully raised the xiphos in time to block the pike. However, in her weakened condition the force of the pike's blow knocked the sword from her hand. She stood up, facing The Argent unarmed and waited for his next move. He grinned ear-to-ear and his blood stained, razor teeth told volumes of what he planned to do with her once she was dead.

The bushes near them rustled and Lupo limped out of them. Behind him, both jackals appeared. The jackals stumbled a few steps forward and then fell dead on the ground. Lupo was exhausted and lowered his head and opened his mouth to allow blood to drip from his tongue. The canine raised his head slowly and saw his mistress and the giant engaged in combat. The canine went from lethargic to dynamic in the blink of an eye and attacked The Argent. He moved in and chewed on the demonic creature's ankle. The Argent shifted his body and kicked the dog and Lupo was lifted in the air and landed several yards away. He slid to a stop and remained motionless.

The Argent was distracted long enough for Prior to grab the pike with both hands. She pulled the shaft down causing The Argent to bend and using the pike as a lever, flipped him onto his back. He still held on to the pike but let go after Prior kicked him in the face. She drew the blade across his body digging a furrow into his abdomen. He rolled to his side and somehow quickly stood before she could attack him again. He snorted and ran his hand across his stomach and lapped up the blood that had pooled in it.

Prior took the pike and swung it upwards between his legs. It connected solidly but he showed no indication that the weapon had struck anything vital. Prior cocked her head to the side in amazement.

The creature snorted again. "Perceptions, Katana. Not everything is what it seems. I am not a man... not completely," he said.

He struck her in the head and she backed up, nearly falling to the ground. She felt her eye begin to swell and tried to shake the pain away but it remained. The blow hurt as much as he thought it did and she had almost dropped the pike. But he was hurting as well, however, a standoff was not what she was hoping for.

"Perceptions will be the death of you, woman," The Argent said moving forward.

"Argent," Prior said straightening herself. "Perceive this!"

Using her enhanced reflexes, she moved like a blur and brought the pike upwards with all of her strength as he stepped forward. The blade dug deep into his torso, carving a channel from his waist towards his head. The blade traveled the length of his torso, slicing his neck and splitting The Argent's jawbone in two. Prior's face was covered in his blood and some of the dark maroon colored fluid flung off of her face as she spun and flattened the blade and swung it one final time.

When the pike's blade separated The Argent's head from his body, Prior was completely drenched in blood. She stepped back and slowly lowered herself to the ground with the aid of the pike. She closed her eyes and prayed silently and when she finished, staggered to her feet and stumbled to Lupo. She dropped the pike and hugged her pet. He whimpered in her arms and she let him go to examine him. He was covered with bite marks and large patches of fur were missing from his coat. His left front paw and a hind leg were also covered in blood and in bad shape. But he had killed the jackals and saved her life.

She reached for her TACCOM and placed it in her ear gingerly. She activated it and made a call.

"This is Chandler."

"This is Prior," she said breathing heavily. Suddenly her limbs went numb and her breathing became labored.

"Mistress, what's your status?" Chandler asked.

"I'm still here if that's what you mean," she chuckled painfully. "Ceca and Thyssen are dead. Gregor has escaped, but you can inform Gideon that The Argent has been defeated." She took a deep breath and continued. "Chandler, send forces into Shiloh... the forces of The Argent are going to attack the Guardians there any time now. They'll need to be fully reinforced."

"That battle is nearing its conclusion, Mistress," Chandler said.

"What's happened?" Prior asked.

"Our preemptive strike surprised The Argent forces and what's left of them are retreating," Chandler reported. "They may do well in a surprise attack or ambush but don't have much stomach for traditional confrontations."

Before Prior could respond, another voice came across the circuit. "We've got a lock on your signal, Prior. We're less than three minutes away," a voice said. It was Pana. "How are you? Do you need anything?"

"Pana?" Prior said gasping for air.

"Yes," she said. "What's wrong?"

"Lupo and I are going to need you ASAP," she said lowering her head. A jolt of pain ran through her and she felt her chest tighten. As she fell to her back she knew The Argent's attack had damaged her spine and lungs and her exertions had compounded the damage. She was heading toward paralysis. "Come and get me… please…"

Her head rolled to the side and then her world turned as black as the demon she had been fighting.

9
Technology Council Medical Center, Capitol City, Central Province, Planet Kerguelen

"Prior... you have much to do," a voice said. It was constant and repeated itself over and over again. *"Prior... you have much to do. Prior... you have much to do."*

It was the same voice that had been visiting Prior almost every time she closed her eyes over the past weeks. She now knew it was The Incubus. Like a shadow on a sunny day, it was always there, a constant companion. It was a friendly sounding voice and she was not afraid of it, but when it spoke, Prior found that she was transported to different places and placed in different scenes. No two scenarios were alike but the voice was identical each time she dreamt.

Because Boroni were incapable of dreaming, she had no knowledge of the phenomena. Every dream she experienced was a frightening ordeal. For many weeks now she had been haunted by the voice and the unique visions specially created for her. If she had known anything about dreams, Prior would have described them as nightmares.

To her senses, the visions were real. When she dreamt she was in the mountains, she could feel the cool air tingling her skin and had to adjust her breathing to account for the thin air. At other times her dreams took her to a city, or to the familiar landscapes of her home in the Western Province. She had even been transported to the beach and on the water, far out to sea. No matter where she found herself, the voice was the same... and so was the enemy she had to face. She was unable to resist the call of the voice and it pulled her deeper and deeper into the dream.

The current version of her dream was like all of the other chapters in the subconscious saga she had endured. It ended with Prior standing surrounded in a sheath of blinding white light screaming, not in pain or fear or anguish, but in victory.

Prior saw an orb above her, spinning and shining brightly. As its rotation slowed and finally came to a stop, she realized the orb was a light bulb. Her eyes were open and she was lying on her back. It took a few seconds for her to recognize the surroundings but she quickly surmised she was in a hospital room. She didn't know why she was in a hospital but she did know the starched antiseptic whiteness and brightness of the room hurt her eyes. She also knew she was safe again. The dream was over and the voice of The Incubus was gone.

She closed her eyes and then slowly opened them again. She adjusted her vision to compensate for the conditions of the room and the pain in her eyes dissipated. Prior attempted to raise her hands to rub her eyes but couldn't move them. She tried to move her head to find out why and realized her head was in some type of restraint. Prior tried to move different parts of her body and found that she was completely immobilized. There was also something on the side of her face. It was cold and foreign and vibrating against her skin. She figured it was some type of medical equipment, but why was she immobilized?

Prior shifted her eyes from the ceiling to the shadow that now crossed her body. Someone was here with her. Prior looked up again and saw Pana standing over her. Pana's face was expressionless as she examined Prior. She tapped on the PDA in her hand with a stylus and then put it in the pocket of the lab coat she wore.

"Welcome back," Pana said. "You gave us a little scare for a while." Prior tried to speak but Pana hushed her. "Don't try to speak yet, Prior. Just relax." Pana grabbed a small object that resembled an atomizer and placed the nozzle in Prior's mouth. She squeezed the trigger twice and removed it. "Swallow." Prior forced the liquid down and Pana smiled. "How do you feel?"

Prior cleared her throat. "I don't feel anything," she said in a raspy voice. "What is all this? Where am I?"

"You're in an immobilization rig and you're currently at the Technology Council Medical Center," Pana said.

"Am I paralyzed?" Prior asked surprisingly calm.

"No," Pana said shaking her head. "But you sustained a spinal column contusion and your natural healing properties shut your nervous system down to protect you. The bruising was severe but you're okay now."

"My ribs. I damaged my ribs too, didn't I?" Prior asked recalling The Argent's body shot.

"Just a slight fracture. They're good as platinum again," Pana said.

Pana nodded to a med tech and they began removing the immobilizing equipment and Prior slowly began to move and flex her limbs. Prior touched her face and felt the device on it.

"And what is this?" she asked.

"A dermal regenerator. You had a bad laceration but it wasn't too deep for the procedure. It should be fine now, but I would like to keep it on for a few more hours. You'll be good as new, no scars and no damage," Pana said.

"The marvels of modern science," Prior chuckled.

"That's right," Pana nodded.

The dermal regenerator was cosmetic surgery's greatest achievement. No longer did people have to live with unsightly scars, blemishes or disfigurement. Though the process was usually long, uncomfortable, and sometimes extremely painful, it was well worth the discomfort and cost of the procedure. During surgery it was indispensable. The device closed and sterilized wounds and basically gave surgeons an extra pair of hands.

"Let's sit you up slowly," Pana said.

The med tech and Pana helped Prior sit up and adjusted the bed. The med tech put a serving tray in front of Prior and handed her a glass filled with a thick, pink colored liquid. Prior took it and gave Pana a puzzled look.

"It's a new nutritional supplement they've been using in the Western Province. It will help restore your strength," Pana said.

"How long have I been out?" Prior asked drinking the supplement. It tasted surprisingly good.

"Five days," Pana said.

"Five days?" Prior said stunned. She had never been ill before and never been in a hospital longer than a day. "Where is Lupo?"

"In the veterinary ward," Pana said. "He was pretty battered. Broken ribs, bruises and he got a weird infection that took them three days to figure out. One of his hind legs was crushed beyond repair though. I had them replaced it with one of those new carbon fiber limbs. He's received a new coat of fur and recovering nicely and will be as good as a newly born pup. But doesn't like being in the pen."

"He's never been locked up," Prior said concerned.

"He's got plenty of room," Pana assured her. "I think he just misses you."

Prior nodded as a nurse entered the room rolling in a tray. Prior's olfactory came alive instantly. The aroma of the covered food leapt at her and she smiled at Pana.

"I was wondering when I could eat," Prior said.

"I've got a lot of food coming. Eat it all," Pana instructed.

"What's been happening?" Prior asked.

"I'll let Cdr. Mohab fill you in," Pana said stepping out of the room. When she returned, she was with visitors.

Prior began to dig into the food in front of her as Mohab and Lindsey entered. She smiled when she saw them. Lindsey nodded to her and Mohab squeezed her hand firmly. She held onto to it as he sat down next to her. She shoved a huge forkful of food into her mouth with her free hand and it was still partially full when she spoke.

"What's been happening, Mohab?" she asked wiping her mouth.

"The Corps has been very active," Mohab said.

"Cdr. Mohab has been officially installed as the regimental commander of the Corps," Lindsey said.

"Congratulations," Prior said smiling at Mohab. "Does that mean I have to salute you now?"

"No," a voice said. "The fact is, he has to salute you... Marshal Prior."

Prior looked up and saw Supreme Commander Garath being pushed into her room in an anti-gravity hover chair. Marshal Aca was pushing him and they both wore hospital scrubs and large smiles. The Elders still showed signs of their injuries but at least both were no longer on their backs and could move around now.

"Look at this. The walking wounded are carrying the stretcher cases," Prior said.

"An Elder's work is never done. As you will soon find out," Garath said handing her a PDA.

She wiped her hands on a napkin and took the device. She looked at the screen and her mouth opened as she read an official communiqué sent by Supreme Commander Garath to all units in the Corps. Prior had been promoted the rank of marshal and was now an Elder and full member of Central Command. It also noted that Colonel Arcuri was promoted to the rank of centurion and was now regimental officer in charge of construction.

"Is this for real?" Prior said giving the device back to Garath.

"It's real… and well deserved," Garath said. He turned to Aca and nodded as he handed her the PDA.

"Attention to orders," said Aca.

The Guardians in the room came to attention and Prior sat as erect as she could.

Aca cleared her throat and read the PDA. "Cdr. Prior, having shown fidelity, zeal and unswerving devotion to duty to your fellow Guardians and the population of Kerguelen, and displaying unequaled temerity in the face of the enemy, it is my pleasure to promote you to the rank of Marshal and confirm you as a Guardian Elder and member of Central Command. Signed, Marshal Garath, Supreme Commander."

The Guardians clapped and Garath handed Prior the insignia of her new office. Prior took the silver device and shook hands with Garath. She looked at the device and was speechless. The marshal's insignia was a silver falcon with spread wings superimposed on a shield and in its talons, were a xiphos and a dory. Prior looked up and nodded to both Garath and Aca.

"Thank you," Prior said.

"Thank you, Marshal Prior… for everything," Garath said patting her hand. "I know you need your rest… as do I. We will speak again soon. We have much to discuss."

Aca spun the chair around and she and Garath left the room. When they were gone, Prior lowered her body. Pana adjusted the bed so it was more comfortable and Mohab tapped her hand.

"We'll be going too," he said. Mohab tried to leave but Prior grabbed his hand.

"Give me an update, Mohab," Prior said. "I can tell a lot has happened."

"Issuing orders already, eh?" Mohab said. "Well, Beatty's Guardians, with the help of your surveyors and your private army, routed The Argent forces in Shiloh. The Sacred City is secure. Elements of your army tracked them to The Edge. The Guardians of the First and Second Battalions broke free from their mutinous leadership when they discovered what they had been pushed into and engaged the force of Argent troops just south of The Edge," he said.

"What happened?" Prior asked.

"The First and Second Battalions took heavy losses," Mohab said with a sigh. "But they took a lot of The Argent with them. They lived up to the spirit of the Corps. Considering they were extremely outnumbered and in an unfavorable position when the battle started, I would consider the engagement a victory by the Guardians. Historians will undoubtedly call it a draw at best. I guess it depends on your point of view."

"Perceptions," Prior said softly. "How much did the battle cost?"

"One hundred and seventy-eight were lost," Mohab said somberly. "Only twenty-six were lost from the Third Battalion in Shiloh."

Prior nodded. "How many surveyors?" she asked.

"Eight," Lindsey said stepping forward.

Prior saw a scar above the lieutenant's eye and pointed to it. "Were you at Shiloh, Lieutenant?" she asked.

"I was, Marshal," Lindsey nodded.

"Well, it looks like Hiroki will have his work cut out for him. As my new aide, he will have to wear a deep groove in the recruiting trail to find replacements," Prior said. She saw Lindsey look down and stared at him. "What's wrong, Lindsey?"

"Capt. Hiroki was one of the eight, Marshal," Lindsey said.

"Who else?" Prior said.

"Sgt. Arrix, and six others assigned to the Third Battalion," Lindsey said.

"Hiroki sacrificed himself and saved a dozen Guardians in the effort. I'm sorry, Marshal, I know he was special to you," Mohab said.

"Yes he was," Prior said. "It seems Centurion Arcuri will be extremely busy. With St. Jacques and Hiroki gone, she's going to need a lot of help when she assumes command."

"And so will Central Command," Mohab said.

"I know what you're getting at, Mohab, but I have no desire in fighting the Battle of the Paperclips," Prior said shaking her head. "Administration is more your style."

"I'm just as good a field commander as you are," Mohab said insulted by her remark.

"I meant no slight to your generalship, but you're better suited for dealing with politicians than I am. You've wanted to be a member of Central Command ever since we were at the academy. It's been your dream, but one I've never shared. I've never wanted that," Prior said.

Mohab knew she never wanted a position in Guardian Central Command. Her aspirations had been limited to one day commanding the surveyors. He on the other hand wanted desperately to be supreme commander one day. And as much as he refuted it, organization and administration were his strong suits, not strategy and combat.

"We'll need your assessment for restructuring the Corps," Mohab said.

"What are our numbers?" Prior asked.

"A little over six hundred. If we had to go into battle, we could put about five hundred and fifty or so on the line. We're thin," Mohab said.

"Very thin," Prior agreed. "But I think some of the dead weight we've been carrying for years is gone. In some ways, we have to thank The Argent forces."

"The empty chairs are numerous," Mohab said. "However, with The Argent forces all but decimated and on the run, we can allow ourselves a bit of a breather."

"I suggest you shift personnel and create three solid and fully equipped battalions," Prior offered. "It will make the Corps stronger despite the fact our numbers are smaller. It will also allow promotions to continue without watering down the qualifications."

"It seems as though you're already fighting the Battle of the Paperclips," Mohab said.

"It's my businesswoman side showing itself," Prior said with a chuckle. "Streamlining companies and being more productive with less is my strong suit." She paused for a moment and then added, "By the way, where is my army now?"

"They are continuing to track The Argent. It's allowed us to take a step back and regroup and make plans for future engagements," Mohab said. "How long will we have their services?"

"For a while longer. They were created as a contingency for our current situation," Prior said. "Speaking of which, the surveyors are obviously in need of new team leaders as well. I personally like captains for those posts. How would you assess Lindsey's aptitude for that, Cdr. Mohab?" Prior asked.

"Well, he has cut his teeth in battle now and availed himself quite admirably according to all reports," Mohab said. "WO Fukuani can't say enough good things about him. He's quite a warrior. I would say he is very well suited, Marshal Prior."

Prior could see Lindsey was not happy about filling the shoes of his friend and mentor, Captain Hiroki and tried to ease his mind.

"Lieutenant, we all lose friends in our business. The Almighty knows I've lost my share, but I need a captain. The empty spots in the ranks need to be filled. I know you can do it. Your job now is to find a lieutenant to replace you in the slot. Things have a way of coming around full circle. Hiroki replaced a lieutenant five years ago and took the place of my previous captain when he was killed. You will now replace Hiroki. It's your turn. You're up," Prior said.

"I'll give it my full attention, Marshal," Lindsey said. "I won't fail you."

"Arcuri is your boss now," Prior corrected. "And you'd better not fail her." Prior took a breath and close her eyes for a moment. When she opened them she smiled at Lindsey. "And if I were you, I wouldn't try going after her the way Hiroki pursued me. You might not like where it leads."

Lindsey smiled and nodded. "I'd like to have Elias on my team," he said.

Prior laughed loudly. "You've taken to the old war horse, eh? I'm sure that would be fine and he is an excellent first choice," she said.

"I guess you're interested to find out what happened in the elections?" Mohab asked.

"Are they over?" Prior asked. "What happened?"

"Almost a complete turnover of senators," Lindsey said.

"The people seemed pleased and the protests have ended," Mohab said. "Everything seems to be returning to normal. What The Argent was attempting has been hardly noticed. Gregor is still at large but Metis and Ernst are searching high and low for him. The Federal Church has been working overtime on the PR circuit. There's been damage to them but they will survive and won't face any severe scrutiny."

"When Gregor's found, I want him," Prior said. She saw Mohab's concerned look. "Yes, Mohab, my reasons are purely personal."

"What will you do when you have him?" Mohab asked.

"I'm going to torture him until he confesses to everything he has done and reveals the names of everyone that has conspired with him during this madness. Then, I'm going to kill him," Prior said.

Mohab and Lindsey could see that she meant what she said and let that part of their conversation end without further comment. Mohab asked Lindsey and Pana to leave them alone for a moment and when they were gone, Mohab took Prior's hand.

"Prior, I know that…" he began but Prior interrupted him.

"Leave the Gregor Situation alone, Mohab," Prior said softly. "Trying to change my mind on it will only cause animosity between us, and I wouldn't like that."

"As you wish," Mohab said. "But concerning Lindsey, I do have concerns."

"What concerns?" she asked.

"You can't just throw a young officer into a hard situation like that, Prior," he said.

"The only way to find out if something will grow is to plant it," Prior replied.

"A Guardian junior officer is not a like a new strain of wheat," he countered. "Farming isn't the same as what we do."

"My mother taught me more about being a leader than any military course I've had since I've been a Guardian. Farming and war, and life in general for that matter, are similar in one respect, Mohab. My mother said the only way to know how much work a mule or a man can do is to put him in the field," Prior said. "The barbarians are still at the gate and danger will continue to loom large on Kerguelen as long as there are those who have dreams of conquest. There is no time for coddling and slowly nurturing our officers. There is only time to act. For better or worse, he's got to go out there."

Mohab nodded and saw that Prior was tiring. As he said his goodbyes, Chief Technologist Mackenzie stepped into the room. She nodded to Mohab as he passed her and she turned and smiled at Prior. Prior smiled back and Mackenzie went to her bedside.

She gently squeezed Prior's hand. "Teima, cousin," she said using the Boroni word for hello.

"Teima, Mackenzie," Prior replied.

"Well, you seem to be recovering nicely," Mackenzie said.

"I'm okay," Prior said.

"You did an excellent job with The Argent. I'm happy you were able to vanquish him without having to die yourself," Mackenzie said.

"So am I," Prior chuckled. "But I tell you, Mackenzie, he disturbed me greatly."

"Religious creatures are supposed to be strong and dangerous," Mackenzie said. "That's why our folklore is replete with them."

"That's not what I mean. He caused me to question things for a brief time. It was… I don't know. It was as emotionally draining as it was physically dangerous," Prior said.

"I'm afraid there may be more of same ahead for you, cousin," Mackenzie said. "An unfortunate series of events that occurred two days ago will soon require your full attention."

"What's happened?"

"I'm afraid I let my personal feelings cloud my better judgment and the decisions I made years ago have placed the planet in jeopardy," Mackenzie said. "I…"

As Mackenzie was about to explain, the door to Prior's room opened. Pana and a petite woman with her hair tightly wrapped in a bun entered the room and the woman frowned when she saw that Prior had a visitor. She looked studious and very stern in her white lab coat. She was definitely an academic type and appeared very competent. She took a medical PDA from her pocket and reviewed Prior's medical chart and stuffed it back in the pocket when she had finished. She nodded to the Mackenzie and the chief technologist smiled in response.

"We will finish our discussion later… Marshal," Mackenzie said.

When Mackenzie departed, the woman stuck her hands in the pockets of her lab coat and smiled briefly at Prior.

"I'm Dr. Carney. How are you?" she asked holding out her hand.

"Ready to go home," Prior said shaking her hand. The doctor's grip felt cold and Prior quickly released her hand.

"You've recovered very quickly," Carney said. "Your... personal physician... has explained the remarkable recuperative powers of Boroni woman, but I didn't believe it until I saw it for myself."

"Yes, we're very resilient," said Prior.

The enhanced genetic coding of Boroni allowed the females to recover from pain and trauma extremely fast, faster than even their male counterparts. It was said that a Boroni female could give birth at eight in the morning and be in the fields by noon. This was an exaggeration of course, but not by much.

"I'm recommending that you be released in two days," Carney said.

"They're very precautionary here," Pana said.

"Yes, we are," said Carney.

"Two days is far too long," Pana argued.

"Less than a week in hospital for a spinal injury of this severity is unheard of," Carney countered.

"You don't understand Boroni physiology, Doctor. The longer we lie around the worse it is. The best medicine we can administer to Prior is allowing her to resume her lifestyle," Pana said.

"Perhaps, Dr. Pana, but for my piece of mind, I'm asking for two days," Carney said unwavering in her position.

Pana sighed. "Very well, but if she shows the marked improvement I know she will, *I'm* releasing her," she said firmly.

"Agreed," Carney nodded.

"I'm glad you two see eye-to-eye on something," Prior said. "Now if you don't mind, I'd like to close my eyes for a bit. You two can argue someplace else."

Carney nodded to her and Pana picked up the food tray and they both left Prior alone to rest. Prior nestled in the bed and pulled the small thin hospital blanket over her. She always wondered why hospital bed coverings were so inadequate. They were either too short or too thin and she didn't know anyone who was pleased with them. As her eyes closed, she thought about Hiroki and the five years they spent together. He had been a good and loyal officer and she would miss his smile and constant appeals to date her. Before she drifted off to sleep, her thoughts shifted to St. Jacques. He was like a brother to her, and she had no idea of what she would write to his family. His being a Guardian was her fault. She had endorsed his decision to apply for an appointment to the academy. She hoped they wouldn't blame her for his death. She already would have a heavy heart for the rest of her life. As her body went into sleep mode, she was once again captured by her dreams.

This time she was on an unfamiliar hill, but she knew it was near the city of Boleen, the former name of territory known as The Edge. She could see The Argent forces on a cold and desolate plain below her marching in a large formation. Their numbers were tremendous, stretching as far as she could see and the ground trembled under their advance. The phalanx of troops was advancing towards another party, but because of a dense fog blanketing the far end of the field, Prior could not identify the force they were going to engage. The Argent moved with mechanical precision and then suddenly made an oblique turn toward their opponents. With the forty-five degree movement, The Argent had doubled the amount of firepower they could bring to bear. A strong wind swept through the battlefield and cleared the fog that covered it, revealing a battalion of Guardians. The Guardians fired on The Argent and moved forward to press on their attack.

The first two rows of The Argent phalanx were riddled with plasma energy blasts. As the number of fallen bodies in front of them grew, the forward progress of the phalanx slowed. They began to spread out to avoid the casualties and maintain the speed of their advance. No matter how many of The Argent troops the Guardians shot, more bodies appeared to replace them, and once they were in optimum weapon's range, they commenced firing. The number of weapons used during each volley was too much for the relatively small Guardian unit to withstand and when the firing stopped, the remnants of the decimated battalion fell back in disarray.

Prior screamed in her dreams and made an attempt to help her comrades, but could not move. All she could do was watch as one-by-one the Guardians were struck down by The Argent. It was merciful in that the slaughter did not last long. When the battle was over, the wind kicked up again and The Argent continued their march, disappearing into another eerie fog bank that had formed at the far end of the field.

Prior could see the Guardians clearly and recognized many of them. They were members of the First, Second and Third Battalions. She turned abruptly and saw St. Jacques and Hiroki sprawled out on the cold ground and their lifeless eyes stared towards the heavens. Prior screamed in rage and dropped to her knees and hung her head in sorrow. When she lifted her head, she heard the familiar and haunting voice of The Incubus sweep over her.

"Prior... you have much to do."

She felt the wind crash against her body and the tempest-like force lifted her into the dark sky. As she spun upwards, the voice continued, but now the words had changed.

"Wake up, Prior... you have much to do. You cannot save those Guardians. It is too late for them. What has happened cannot be changed, but it is not too late to save others. Go and save the others in the sky. Wake up, Prior."

When Prior opened her eyes, she saw Dr. Carney staring at her. Her face looked concerned and she was speaking.

"Wake up, Prior," she said. Prior shook her head and sat up as Carney placed a hand on her shoulder to keep her still. "Stay still."

"What's going on?" Prior asked a bit bewildered.

"You had a bad dream. A *really* bad dream apparently. Your monitors were jumping off the scale. I was about to sedate you," Carney said holding Prior's arm with one hand and hypodermic in the other.

"I have no time for sedatives, Doctor," Prior said holding Carney's arm forcefully. She didn't realize how much force she was using and Carney's knees buckled slightly. "I need to get up."

"As you wish, but I would appreciate it if you let me go," Carney said grabbing Prior's hand.

"I'm sorry, Doctor," said Prior releasing her. "But I have an aversion to being handled when I don't want to be."

"I can see that," Carney said rubbing the soreness from her wrist. "But I really think you should take something."

"I'm fine, Doctor. What I really need is this dermal regenerator removed from my face," Prior said tapping the device. "And if you don't remove it, I will."

Carney sighed and took the device off. She gasped at what she saw or rather didn't see. Prior saw her astonishment and moved the doctor's hands away to feel her face. As she moved her fingers across her skin, she felt nothing.

"I-I don't understand this," Carney stammered. "There still should be some sign of your wound, but there's nothing. There's not even a hint of a scar or blemish of any kind."

Carney gently touched Prior's face and was stunned. It was impossible for anyone, or anything, to heal so fast.

"Your equipment is better than you thought, Doctor," Prior said swinging her legs out of the bed and standing up. She was a little stiff and stretched as she looked around the room. "What time is it?"

"It's mid-afternoon. You've been sleeping for a little over five hours," Carney said.

Prior looked out of the window and felt the sun on her face and body. The sky was clear and there was an unlimited ceiling. As she looked upward she knew that was the direction her path would lead her.

"I need clothes," Prior said walking around the room. She stripped off her hospital gown and searched the closets for something to wear.

"Why? Where do you think you're going?" Carney asked. "You still need more rest."

"What I need are clothes," Prior said. "Tell Pana I need a combat suit... and a weapon." Carney hesitated and Prior added, "I could look for her myself, but I don't think you want me roaming the halls naked."

Carney relented. "Where should I say you're planning to go?" she asked.

"Space Station *Condor*," Prior said.

"I realize *San Mariner* is returning this evening, but everyone wants to be there. Even if you could find a ship, you just can't fly up there. Access to the station has been restricted," Carney said.

"Perhaps, but someone without authorization *is* going to be on that station tonight, Doctor, and it's going to be a bad day for everyone concerned if I don't get up there," Prior said.

"How do you know that?" Carney asked.

"It came to me in a dream," Prior said tersely. She saw the doctor had a million questions but Prior neither had the time or inclination to answer them. "Don't ask me how I know, I just know. Now, if you wouldn't mind, please find Pana. There's little time and I have much to do."

Carney sighed and left the room as Prior turned back to the window and looked into the sky. She shut her eyes and prayed she would not be too late to stop what was about to happen on the space station.

10
Hanford, Southern Province, Planet Kerguelen

Cardinal Gregor had been on the run for the past five days and only managed to make it to his home province without being arrested by the skin of his teeth. The Congress of Cardinals had instructed all Papal security forces to make it their sole activity to find him. He had been lucky and avoided capture but he knew that his plan to rule Kerguelen had gone up in smoke. Even if he had not been a realist, the messages he received from the leaders of The Argent forces still at large would have convinced him his dream was over.

"Look at these reports," Gregor said holding up the PDA in his hand. The beautiful woman from the Middle Provinces with him only shrugged her shoulders and he continued. "The Argent forces are retreating on every front. What has gotten into them?"

"Belief in spiritual nonsense has been your undoing, Gregor," the woman said in a heavy accent. "I told you that aspect of their cult was unpredictable and teeming with the seeds of failure. As soon as they found out The Argent entity was defeated, they believed the ancient prophecy was fulfilled and they lost their resolve. You should have seen this coming and planned accordingly."

The woman leaned forward and poured herself a cup of tea and offered Gregor some. He declined and she added milk and sugar to the cup and slowly stirred the contents with a tiny silver spoon.

"I had no idea Prior would be resourceful enough to defeat the destructor. Perhaps she is the second coming of Katana and destined to save the planet from an age of darkness," Gregor said.

"There you go reciting the same rhetoric as those superstitious zealots," the woman said. "Prior is not a reincarnation of the greatest warrior in Kerguelen history. She is just a Guardian."

"She is *not* just a Guardian," Gregor countered. "I made the mistake of jumping to that conclusion and it's cost us almost everything."

"It's true she is a cut above her peers, but she still is only one Guardian and now she is not up to par according to my reports," the woman said sipping her tea. "She is in hospital and her condition is guarded. Though she is expected to recover quickly because of her Boroni physiology, the injuries she has sustained will slow her down and that fits into my plans perfectly."

"We can't operate as we did before," Gregor said. "We don't have the resources or the assets to mount a substantial offensive."

"Gregor," the woman began sitting her cup down. She stood up and walked closer to him. "You keep using the words 'us' and 'we'. You are no longer a partner in any endeavor I'm involved with."

"What do you mean?" Gregor asked.

"You have become a liability and my partners no longer require your services," the woman said. "We will continue to shelter you and protect you from prosecution, but you are no longer a part of the grand scheme of things."

"But I came to you with this idea," Gregor said. "Without me, none of this could have become reality."

"You're right, Gregor," the woman said. "The results of the past few days have been because of you. The loss of most of our political allies because the people refuted your foolish edicts; the loss of hundreds of mercenary forces in ill-conceived battle plans; and the loss of several Guardians that could have been of use to us in the future has all been your fault."

"You're blaming me for all of this?"

"Of course," the woman said. "You're the last man standing. In addition to your bungling of other affairs, your insistence that Camden destroy *San Mariner* in a martyr-type operation clearly shows your incompetence. Just be glad my partners decided not to drop you like a bad habit. Despite your short comings and crippling blunders, we all feel that you are owed something."

"Destroying the space ship should have worked. *Seventh Sojourn* suffered a mysterious demise at the hand of one of my operatives and if *San Mariner* came to a similar end in the void of space, who would question it?" Gregor said.

"The same person that put operatives onboard to prevent it," the woman said. "The same person that has thwarted your every move... Cdr. Prior."

"Are you sure she had something to do with it?" Gregor asked.

The woman shook her head. "I'm only sure that since *San Mariner* is due to arrive in the next few hours, someone obviously stopped Camden," she said. "And I'm sure Omega is no longer capable of such a feat."

"If that's true, you're not free and clear either," Gregor said. "It was you who had Cornelia assassinated. When the Guardians find that out, you'll be a public enemy as well."

"Me?" the woman said innocently. "I'm clear of any misdeeds, Gregor. My conversations with Cornelia's security were conducted via throwaway encrypted TELCOM devices. And my in-person dealings with you all took place after you were shot by Venture. Obviously I was visiting to console you during your convalescence. I was nowhere near any subversive or illegal activity. When things were at their worst, I was where every vice president should be at such times... in an undisclosed location for my personal safety. Everyone who knows about my involvement in your coup is dead or unable to give me away because they would compromise themselves. No, my dear former Pontiff, I have no worries."

"How can you be so sure?" Gregor asked.

"I'm not powerful enough to be threatening. I'm only the vice president," she said with a smile. "I am unobtrusive and beyond reproach. I have a stellar record in the Middle Provinces and am well respected by the business community...and I also look spectacular in pictures. The best part is my cousin, who loves me dearly, is now the new Guardian Corps Regimental Commander. And in a few hours I will be installed as the new planetary president after the unfortunate assassination of President Ward."

"You will still have to deal with Prior," Gregor said.

"Unlike you, I will deal with Prior by making her face something that all of the people of Kerguelen know is capable of destroying the very fabric of their civilization. I'm not talking about making pacts with devils and demons. I'm talking about something tangible. What she will face will not only threaten her, but everyone on Kerguelen," the woman said.

"And who or what is this force?" Gregor asked.

"The Onyx Group," the woman said.

EPILOG

Space Station *Condor*,
530 miles above Planet Kerguelen

Space Station *Condor* was the newest and largest of the manned space platforms currently orbiting Kerguelen. It was not only the primary operations center for Space Command missions, it was also one of the premier vacation spots for the population. Spanning three miles at its widest point, one section of the station was open to civilian visitors affording the people the chance to experience space and zero gravity. Because of the station's exorbitant cost, Space Command sold the public on the premise that a portion of the station would be always available to the people year-round. Construction workers and students, housewives and scout troops, grandmothers and the just plain curious came to *Condor* when it finally opened to the public. A constant flow of civilian space traffic traveled to and from the station everyday and new businesses were created to handle the needs of amateur space travelers. As long as a person had a valid travel permit, they could get a seat on the various space transports leaving daily from Kerguelen. Though one could stay indefinitely, the average duration of a visit was only a day or two.

Most days, travel to and from *Condor* filled a twenty-hour schedule, but since the arrival of *San Mariner* and *Jackknife* had been verified, operations were running round-the-clock and reservations for suites and rooms on the station were filled to capacity. The added arrivals and departures were taxing the resources and manpower of the station and the station manager was at his wits end on how to please everyone. Anyone of consequence had overpaid, bribed or lied to get onboard and the chaos created by the huge numbers of dignitaries, politicians, celebrities and sports figures would be unprecedented. Media coverage for the arrival of *San Mariner* would be provided by every major and minor news service on and off Kerguelen and the reporters scrambled to get to *Condor* to cover the greatest news event in Kerguelen's history.

The manic conditions on the station grew as *San Mariner* and *Jackknife* reported that they would be an hour early. The media representatives went into panic mode and a frenetic stream of messages flooded the communications center. The technicians could barely keep up with the traffic and the joyous occasion was turning into a nightmare for the station's personnel.

A few hours before *Condor* was to receive the massive influx of visitors that now crowded its decks, the station's safety department met with the station manager. The manager hoped they could come up with a plan of how to best deal with the multitude of guests. They not only had to see to the desires of their privileged guests, they also had to ensure that their presence would not endanger the station. They were in uncharted territory and were writing the book on the operation as they went along.

One of the safety department personnel suggested that they just give the visitors the run of the station for the duration of their stay. The rush on the station would last only a few hours and once they got enough face time in front of the cameras and the catering ran out, they would get bored and leave. All they had to do was make sure every craft was thoroughly checked as it docked. With the entire safety department at the docking ports, no undesirables or contraband could make its way onboard and the dignitaries would have two or three hours free from the scrutiny of security guards. Most importantly, the safety department would save themselves the migraines associated with dealing with the elite-class. The station's concierge services and public relations office were better suited for handling those kinds of problems. Harrison, the station manager, approved the proposal and left it to the chief of the safety department to iron out the details.

As Harrison left the meeting, he was glad Space Command had implemented a plan that was going to make his life somewhat easier. Except in an emergency, no ships returning to Kerguelen from the moon or deep space would dock at *Condor*. The other stations in orbit would handle that traffic so *Condor* could be free to deal with vessels inbound for the ceremony.

When the first ship due for the ceremony announced its arrival, the safety department went into action. The ship was the largest of the transports scheduled and would serve perfectly for a test of their plan.

Though it was thirty minutes early, the extra time would give the men of the safety department the time to really work out the procedures for the rest of the inbound vessels. Ten minutes after the ship docked, the passengers were cleared for entry into the station. Five minutes after that, unbeknownst to Harrison or any of the other station's personnel, the entire safety department had been killed and replaced.

The rest of the ships scheduled arrived on time and their passengers were quickly processed and allowed to proceed to the reception area. The last ship to arrive was *Kerguelen Prime*, President Ward's space transport. As alcohol flowed and hors d'oeuvres were consumed, the excitement over *San Mariner's* arrival became infectious and Harrison, dressed uncomfortably in his only formal attire, smiled as he saw *San Mariner* and *Jackknife* come into view. The jubilant throng of spectators crowded closer to the observation windows and pressed against each other to get a glimpse of what was now the most famous spacecraft in history returning home.

Omega was at the pilot's station and Dela was in the navigator's couch as *San Mariner* slowly approached the space station. Omega looked out of the window and saw one of the large construction space docks and pointed at the completed ship in it.

"That's one of the new two-hundred meter class deep space ships. It's the latest and greatest," he said.

"It was just a skeletal framework when we left. Now look at it," Dela said looking at the ship. "It's even been christened."

Omega looked at the hull and saw the ship's name. "It's called *Gjoa*. It's named after the sailing vessel used by the arctic explorer who found a route from one ocean to another using a polar passage," he said.

"And soon it will find another civilization," Dela said.

"Let's hope so," Omega said. "You must have seen them build the framework when you were doing all of that orbital stuff."

"Yes I did," Dela said. "I never thought it would turn out to be so massive... or impressive looking."

"What did your orbital work consist of?" Omega asked.

"That work is classified, Commander," Dela said tersely.

"Sorry I asked," Omega said. "I was only curious."

"Forgive me, Commander," Dela said. She tapped on her console briefly and then continued. "My work in orbit can never be talked about. I hope you understand."

"I do, Dela," Omega said. He looked at their position and adjusted in his couch. He took the attitude controls in his hand and took manual control of the ship. "Okay, Dela, let's dock the ship."

Dela nodded and was sure Omega would have a very different opinion of her if he knew the nature of her orbital work. Like other missions done by Prior's special operations teams, her work was illegal and if anyone outside of the loop had known the extent of the activity, everyone with knowledge of the mission and approved of it would have been placed in jail for life. But that was a concern for another day. Today, they were coming home and nothing could spoil that.

San Mariner docked with smooth precision and when the ship's systems were secured and a positive hatch seal was established and verified, Omega and Dela emerged and were greeted with an onslaught of applause and cheers. The lights from the many cameras blinded them momentarily and they raised their hands to shield their eyes. A trio of PR men led Omega and Dela to a platform where President Ward waited. Lost in the fanfare was the arrival and docking of *Jackknife* and the debarkation of its crew. The station support crews could barely do their job attaching external power cords, life-support conduits and docking cables due to the mass of guests crowding the area. Tartis and his crew mixed in with the audience and led their own round of applause for the crew of *San Mariner*.

The crowds and attention overwhelmed Omega and Dela. President Ward and several members of the planetary legislature shook their hands and gave them hearty congratulatory slaps on the backs. Sports figures and entertainers jockeyed for position in order to get a photo with them. Arista and Tartis managed to worm their way through the mob and reach the stage. They hugged their fellow star sailors and Arista draped her arms around Omega and kissed him deeply. Only one photographer got a picture and video of the embrace and kiss, and sent it out immediately with his handheld PIL device. The picture was instantly downloaded by millions of PIL users all over the planet.

Naturally, the tabloid representatives asked how long Omega and Arista had been dating. Faster than either could answer the rumor of an interstellar romance flooded the airwaves. Reporters from more reputable news services bombarded Omega and Dela with questions concerning the mission, the alien craft and the other crewmembers, but they received only short and brief answers as per regulations. Luckily, they were shielded from more pointed questions by the public relations personnel. Omega and Dela still needed to be debriefed by Space Command and were not allowed to answer mission related questions. Even if their mission had not suffered the tragedies it had, they would not have been able to address such questions.

President Ward made himself available for questions and statements as well, but found it difficult to find any reporter willing... or interested in talking to him. They only wanted the star sailors and after a few minutes of being snubbed, Ward grabbed a reporter from a secondary news outlet by the arm and led him to Omega. Much to the displeasure of a primetime Class-A reporter getting an exclusive, Ward used executive privilege and interrupted the interview.

"Well done, Commander," Ward said in the recording devices as he leaned in close to Omega to ensure he was in the photos. "On behalf of a grateful planet, may I say, congratulations on a superior and singular accomplishment and welcome home!" Ward beamed his best smile as another round of deafening applause filled the reception area and the cameras zoomed in.

Harrison worked his way to Omega and frowned when he saw the members of the safety department herding people further inside the already cramped reception area. He thought they had agreed that they would stay away from the ceremony. Maybe the plans they had made earlier had run into a snag of some kind. Before he could find the safety department chief and question him about it, the members of the safety department pulled weapons out and tossed sensory disruption grenades into the crowd.

The intense lights blinded all of them and the high-pitched ultra sonic sound emanating from the devices dropped some of the dignitaries to their knees. When their vision cleared and the ringing in their ears ended, the sight of the weapon-wielding men elicited fearful screams and shouts from the dazed and disoriented crowd. Harrison didn't know what was happening but he knew these men weren't members of his safety department, and the way they were brandishing their weapons he also knew they were professionals and meant business. As the initial shock subsided, the lone female in the group spoke. She was tall and muscular and looked vaguely familiar to Harrison.

"Everyone! Listen to me!" she said in a heavy North Island Province accent. The panicked mass of people turned to her and she continued. "We have control of this section of the station and will keep control only until our task is completed. We have no interest in you and do not wish to harm anyone. If you cooperate with my comrades and follow instructions, our stay will be brief and this will only be a bad memory. You will be treated kindly, but make no mistake, if you interfere, we will have to make adjustments to that policy. We are not thieves, terrorists or kidnappers. We only have one thing to accomplish, and when that is done, we will leave."

"How dare you come here and do this?" Ward said stepping forward showing uncharacteristic bravado. "By what right do you disturb this glorious day?"

"We dare do this and many other things that might disturb you, President Ward. But you are right, this is a glorious day," the female said stepping forward. Harrison could see she had deeply tanned skin and there was a strong determination in her violet-blue colored eyes. She smiled devilishly as she canvassed the crowd. "Today is the first day of a new era in the history of Kerguelen."

"Who are you?" Harrison asked.

"We are the true representatives of the Almighty," the female said. "We are the Onyx Group."

~ The End of Book One ~